Modern Classics of

Fantasy

Modern Classics of

Fantasy

EDITED BY GARDNER DOZOIS

ST. MARTIN'S PRESS

NEW YORK

For the editors, often forgotten now, who bought these stories, frequently against orders, because they loved good fantasy—and wanted to share it with the world.

Edited by Gordon Van Gelder

Designed by Nancy Resnick

Library of Congress Cataloging-in-Publication Data

Modern classics of fantasy / Gardner Dozois, editor. —1st ed.
    p.   cm.
  ISBN 0–312–15173–X
  1. Fantastic fiction, American. I. Dozois, Gardner R.
PS648.F3M64   1997
813'.0876608—dc20   96–32347

First edition: January 1997

10 9 8 7 6 5 4 3 2 1

SF
Mod

Acknowledgments

I would like to thank the following people for their help and support: Susan Casper, Jack Dann, Michael Swanwick, Ellen Datlow, Virginia Kidd, Vaughne Hanson, Darrell Schweitzer, George Scithers, Kirby McCauley, Ralph M. Vicinanza, Richard Curtis, Marilyn E. Marlow, Elizabeth Harding, Shawna McCarthy, Susan Ann Protter, Grania Davis, Joanna Rakoff, E. J. Gold, David Franko, Charles R. Chilton, Margaret Gaines Swann, Robert Sampson, David Pringle, David Langford, John Clute, L. Sprague de Camp, Peter S. Beagle, Tanith Lee, Howard Waldrop, Esther M. Friesner, Bruce Sterling, James Blaylock, Suzy McKee Charnas, Judith Tarr, George Alec Effinger, Poul Anderson, Lucius Shepard, Sheila Williams, Shara Thomas, Scott Towner, Corin See; and, of course, special thanks to my own editor on this project, Gordon Van Gelder.

CONTENTS

PREFACE

Fantasy has probably existed ever since the Cro-Magnons told stories around the fire in the deep caves of Lascaux and Altamira and Rouffignac—and perhaps even for considerably longer than that, for who knows what tales the Neanderthals told around *their* fires during the long Ice Age nights, thousands of years earlier? By the time that Homer was telling stories to fireside audiences in Bronze Age Greece, the tales he was telling contained recognizable fantasy elements—man-eating giants, spells and counterspells, enchantresses who turned men into swine—that were probably recognized *as* fantasy elements and responded to as such by at least the more sophisticated members of his audience.

Toward the end of the eighteenth century, something recognizably akin to modern literary fantasy was beginning to precipitate out from the millennia-old body of oral traditions—folktales, fairy tales, mythology, songs and ballads, wonder tales, travelers' tales, rural traditions about the Good Folk and haunted standing stones and the giants who slept under the countryside. First these came in the form of Gothic stories, ghost stories, and Arabesques, and later, by the middle of the next century, in a more self-conscious literary form in the work of writers such as William Morris and George MacDonald, who reworked the subject matter of the oral traditions to create *new* fantasy worlds for an audience sophisticated enough to respond to the fantasy elements as literary tropes rather than as fearfully regarded, half-remembered elements of folk beliefs, people who were more likely to be entertained by the idea of putting a saucer of milk out for the fairies than to actually *do* such a thing.

By the late nineteenth and early twentieth centuries, most respectable literary figures—Dickens, Twain, Kipling, Doyle, Saki, Chesterton, Wells—had written fantasy in one form or another, if only ghost stories or "Gothic" stories, and a few, like Thorne Smith, James Branch Cabell, and Lord Dunsany, had even made something of a specialty of it. But as World War II loomed ever closer over the horizon, fantasy somehow began to fall into disrepute, increasingly being considered as unhip, "anti-modern," non-progressive, socially irresponsible, even *déclassé*. By the sterile and unsmiling 1950s, very little fantasy was being published in any form, and fantasy as a genre, as a separate publishing category, did not exist.

Although hardly welcomed to the bosom of the literary establishment with open arms, a grudging, condescending, partial exception was made for a specialized form of fantasy called science fiction, mostly on the grounds that it was "rationalistic," "modern," "progressive," "predicted the future," and so forth. In other words, SF had a didactic function, a social *teaching* function, that partially excused its excursions away from the "normal world" as it was very rigidly defined in the 1950s. While a faint whiff of raffishness remained, science fiction could be justified as a specialized form of children's or Young Adult literature—as literature with training wheels on it, something that would teach the kids to be familiar with Science and Technology and to think progressively about The Future (much in the fashion of the famous "World of the Future" dioramas at the 1939 World's Fair) until they were ready to put aside childish things and turn to "real literature" about "the real world." SF, then, although it did somewhat distastefully deal with things that were "not real," could be tolerated grudgingly as a necessary evil for children and even some weak-minded adults. The idea that this "teaching function" *justified* the existence of SF was a note sounded over and over again, sometimes rather shrilly, in the genre magazines of the day. *The Magazine of Fantasy & Science Fiction,* for instance, used to run endorsements on the back cover from "real people," sober respectable adults like Clifton Fadiman and Steve Allen, assuring readers that it was okay, socially respectable (really!), to read SF—a strategy very similar to the current advertising campaign for Kellogg's Frosted Flakes that shows a succession of shamefaced adults, sometimes masked or in darkened rooms, admitting that they like to eat Frosted Flakes even though it's a "kid's cereal."

Fantasy had no such justification, and even many of those who admitted (usually somewhat defensively) that they read science fiction would often draw the line at admitting that they read fantasy—which not only dealt, by definition, with things that "weren't real," but which had no mitigating didactic function.

This justifying didactic purpose of SF was also strongly emphasized in ads for and the cover copy of the early SF novels and anthologies that slowly began to get published at about the same time . . . and it seems to have worked, since SF as a commercial genre, as a separate publishing category, *was* successfully established in the 1950s, largely through the efforts of pioneers such as Ian and Betty Ballantine and Don Wollheim. It grew and flourished throughout the rest of that decade and on through the 1960s, with one publisher after another launching genre SF lines. By the early 1970s, SF was not only an established genre but actually a rather large popular category.

Perhaps because it lacked the sanction of a "teaching function," fantasy remained largely despised and disreputable as science fiction proliferated. In the 1950s and throughout most of the 1960s, where it was possible to sell a science fiction novel, it was usually flat-out *im*possible to sell a fantasy novel, or at least to sell it as a genre product. (Occasionally a Real Writer, an accepted literary figure like John Steinbeck or Roald Dahl, could get away with selling a fantasy, but it would be published as high-end High Art, as literature, with the fact that it was a fantasy either not mentioned or explicitly denied in the cover copy). This led to an odd situation, described by Michael Swanwick and other commentators, where much fantasy was published by "disguising" it as science fiction. This strategy is clear in L. Sprague de Camp's "Krishna" series, as well as in much of the work of Leigh Brackett, Ray Bradbury, and other regular *Planet Stories* writers: get your characters to another "planet" as quickly and unobtrusively as possible, and then, once you're there, spend the bulk of your time telling a standard fantasy swashbuckler with lots of swordplay and evil wizardry, with the magic disguised as "alien technology" or, even better, as "PSI powers." ("Disguised fantasy" also shades nearly imperceptibly into "rationalized fantasy"–where you have, say, a dragon, but you explain its existence in rationalistic, science fictional terms: as a product of genetic engineering, perhaps, or as an alien creature from another planet–and also on into the kind of hybrid of fantasy and science fiction sometimes described as "fantasy with rivets," fantasy written from the aesthetic perspective of science fiction, where you have an overt fantasy trope, such as a dragon, but you think up clever rationalizations for its existence under the laws of physics that apply in the real world, or put a lot of thought into working out how those physical laws might *constrain* the possible actions of such a fantasy creature if it *did* actually exist; this last is the strategy of Poul Anderson's *Three Hearts and Three Lions* and Robert Heinlein's "The Devil Makes the Law" as well as much other work, almost all of it published as "science fiction" by established science fiction lines, as Roger Zelazny's first five Amber books were published throughout the 1970s.)

By the late 1950s, although I was an avid consumer of science fiction, I didn't know a lot about fantasy. Like most of the audience of the time, especially those of us still in high school or grade school, I didn't have a lot of money, and so of necessity limited my book buying to cheap mass-market paperbacks–which meant that the occasional "high-end" literary fantasy was beyond both my purview and my reach. If the work of past masters such as Lord Dunsany, E. R. Eddison, and Clark Ashton Smith, was available at all (often it wasn't), it was available only as expensive hardcover reprints; consequently, I knew nothing of them either, or of the books that J. R. R. Tolkien had already begun to issue in hardcover in Britain. Most of what I knew of fantasy at that point, as opposed to SF, came from fairy tales, Disney cartoon features, and from "children's books" such as Rudyard Kipling's *The Jungle Books* (which still remains perhaps my favorite "children's book"—today it is probably published as Young Adult—of all time, and which is perhaps even *more* rewarding to the adult reader).

By the early 1960s, this had begun to change. One of the first cracks in the armor, for me, anyway, happened in 1962, when an SF mass-market line named Pyramid Books published a paperback edition of L. Sprague de Camp and Fletcher Pratt's *The Incomplete Enchanter,* with a quote on it from Basil Davenport—one of *F&SF*'s back-cover adults— saying that "you never met anything *exactly like* it in your life." I agreed—I never *had* met anything exactly like it in my life, and it made a large impression on me. When Pyramid Books published the sequel, *The Castle of Iron,* a few months later, I pounced on that as well. In 1963, Pyramid brought out an anthology of stories, edited by D. R. Bensen, from the by-then long extinct fantasy magazine *Unknown,* where the de Camp and Pratt "Harold Shea" stories that had gone into making up *The Incomplete Enchanter* had originally appeared; sensitized by this connection, I bought the anthology, one of the first anthologies I can remember buying. In its pages, encountered for the first time Fritz Leiber's Fafhrd and the Gray Mouser, as well as discovering the work of Manly Wade Wellman and H. L. Gold. A few months later, I came across another Pyramid anthology, this one edited by L. Sprague de Camp and called *Swords & Sorcery,* a deliberate attempt by de Camp to preserve at least, and perhaps revive, a then-Endangered Literary Species called "sword & sorcery" or "heroic fantasy." Here was another Gray Mouser story, and here for the first time I also encountered Robert E. Howard's Conan and C. L. Moore's Jirel of Joiry, first read the work of Lord Dunsany and H. P. Lovecraft, and first read the fantasy work—I was already familiar with his science fiction—of Poul Anderson; a later de Camp anthology, *The Spell of Seven,* introduced me to Michael Moorcock's Elric stories. (D. R. Bensen, who was the editor of Pyramid Books during this period, and who therefore was responsible for bringing all this material back into print, can be seen, in fact, as one of the unsung and forgotten progenitors of the whole modern fantasy revival.)

Inspired by these books, I began to rummage through secondhand bookstores, and soon had come up with yellowing old back copies of *Unknown* and *Weird Tales* and *The Magazine of Fantasy & Science Fiction.* A bit later, I discovered that new copies, current copies, of *F&SF* were available on a few newsstands. And at about this time I discovered Cele Goldsmith's *Fantastic,* just as she succeeded in coaxing Fritz Leiber to contribute a *new* sequence of Fafhrd and Gray Mouser stories to the magazine—and I was hooked. In fact, although I occasionally picked up a copy of *Galaxy* or *F&SF, Fantastic* was the first genre magazine I bought regularly, and I would haunt the newsstands waiting for the new issue to appear with an intense impatience I hadn't known before and have rarely felt since.

More fantasy books began to squeeze through into print. At Ace, Don Wollheim began to re-issue almost the complete works of Edgar Rice Burroughs in affordable paperback editions with wonderfully evocative covers by Roy Krenkel and Frank Frazetta of sword-swinging heroes, beautiful princesses in diaphanous gowns, and huge glowering Tharks with a sword in each of their four hands, and somehow these books fit in perfectly to the fantasy *gestalt* that was growing, even though most of them had been published originally as science fiction. Similarly, Mary Renault's *The King Must Die* and *The Bull from the Sea,* although ostensibly historical novels, *felt* like fantasy, and helped to stoke the growing hunger of the reading audience for fantasy. Somewhere during this period, the success of the Broadway musical *Camelot* allowed the book which had inspired the play, T. H. White's *The Once and Future King,* to come out in an affordable (by my standards) mass-market paperback; it was seized instantly and gladly by me and by thousands of others like me. L. Sprague de Camp began writing new Conan stories and novels, building them from fragments and unfinished drafts by the late Robert E. Howard. The first of the Conan imitators, such as John Jakes's stories of "Brak the Barbarian," began to appear. And then we came to Tolkien.

J. R. R. Tolkien's *The Lord of the Rings* trilogy is often cited as having single-handedly created the modern fantasy genre, but, while it is certainly hard to *over*estimate Tolkien's influence—almost every subsequent fantasist was hugely influenced by Tolkien, even, haplessly, those who didn't like him and reacted *against* him—what is sometimes forgotten these days is that Don Wollheim published the infamous "pirated" edition of *The Fellowship of the Ring* (the opening book of the trilogy) in the *first* place because he was casting desperately around for something—*any*thing!—with which to feed the hunger of the swelling audience for "sword & sorcery." The cover art of the Ace edition of *The Fellowship of the Ring* makes it clear that Wollheim thought of it as a "sword & sorcery" book, and his signed interior copy makes that explicit by touting the Tolkien volume as "a book of sword-and-sorcery that anyone can read with delight and pleasure." In other words, in the United States at least, the genre audience for fantasy definitely *predated* Tolkien, rather than being created by him, as the modern myth would have it. Don Wollheim, one of the most canny editors who ever lived, knew very well that there was a genre fantasy audience already out there, a hungry audience waiting to be fed—although I doubt if even he had the remotest idea just how tremendous a response there would be to the tidbit of "sword & sorcery" that he was about to feed them.

After Tolkien, everything changed. The audience for genre fantasy may have existed already, but there can be no doubt that Tolkien *widened* it tremendously. The immense commercial success of Tolkien's work also opened the eyes of other publishers to the fact that there was an intense hunger for fantasy in the reading audience—and they, too, began looking around for something to feed to that hunger. On the strength of Tolkien's success, Lin Carter was able to create the first mass-market paperback fantasy line, the "Ballantine Adult Fantasy" line, which brought back into print long-forgotten and long-unavailable works by writers such as Clark Ashton Smith, E. R. Eddison, James Branch Cabell, Mervyn Peake, and Lord Dunsany, as well as somewhat more recent but equally unavailable and long out-of-print books such as de Camp and Pratt's *Land of Unreason* and Evangeline Walton's *The Island of the Mighty*. A few years later, Lester del Rey took over from Lin Carter, and, aided by the matchless marketing savvy of his wife, Judy-Lynn del Rey, began to search for more commercial, less high-toned stuff that would appeal more directly to an audience still hungry for something just like Tolkien. In 1977, he brought out Terry Brooks's *The Sword of Shannara,* and although it was dismissed by most critics as a clumsy retread of Tolkien, it proved hugely successful commercially, as did its many sequels. Del Rey also scored big that year with *Lord Foul's Bane,* the beginning of the somewhat quirkier and less derivative trilogy *The Chronicles of Thomas Covenant the Unbeliever,* by Stephen R. Donaldson, and *its* many sequels. At about this time, the Ballantine SF and fantasy lines would be renamed Del Rey Books in honor of the unprecedented success of both del Reys in finding and publishing best-sellers, books that were selling better than any SF or fantasy titles had ever sold before; Lester del Rey would remain editor of Del Rey Fantasy, and, for both better *and* worse, also remain one of the most influential fantasy editors in the business, until his retirement in 1991.

The floodgates had opened. No longer would fantasy books need to be "disguised" as science fiction in order to be sold. Fantasy was becoming a genre, and a separate commercial publishing category, of its own.

"Sword & Sorcery" or "Heroic Fantasy" was probably the most common form of genre fantasy book at first, but by the 1980s that form had faded (although it's showing signs of revival in the middle 1990s, with publishers such as White Wolf issuing retrospective collections of core "sword & sorcery" work by authors like Fritz Leiber and Michael Moorcock). It was largely replaced by "High Fantasy," a somewhat less swashbuckling and more mood-oriented form, closer to Tolkien and the pseudo-medieval romances of William Morris than it is to Conan. Ursula K. Le Guin was a pioneer of this form with her "Earthsea" books (originally published as Young Adult fiction, perhaps because at the time no one knew where else to put them), and other writers who have earned reputations in "High Fantasy" include (but are no means limited to) Patricia A. McKillip, Robin McKinley, Guy Gavriel Kay, Jane Yolen, Parke Godwin, Judith Tarr, Marion Zimmer Bradley, Lisa Goldstein, Susan Cooper, Joy Chant, and many others. In its most common form, sometimes referred to sneeringly by critics as "the standard Celtic Fantasy Trilogy," High Fantasy still dominates bookstore shelves. It fades off into Arthurnalia, fantasy books dealing with The Matter of Britain, into what has been called "Mannerism" (typified by the work of Ellen Kushner, Delia Sherman, Elizabeth Willey, and some of the non-comic work of Esther Friesner), and on into the historical fantasy—and thus also off, sometimes nearly imperceptibly, into both the historical novel and that subcategory of the mystery novel known as the "historical mystery" (sometimes making for works that are very difficult to categorize: to which genre, for instance, does a mystery novel set in ancient Rome which features historical characters tracking down a vampire belong? Are Mary Stewart's *Merlin* books such as *The Crystal Cave* historical novels with fantasy elements, or fantasy novels set in a strongly developed historic *milieu*?) On the other end, High Fantasy shades off into what has been called "Urban Fantasy" (similar to *Unknown*-style comic fantasy that deals with the interactions between the mundane world and the worlds of fantasy, but in a different key, more somber and lyrical) and which is represented by the work of authors such as Charles de Lint, Megan Lindholm, Emma Bull, Will Shetterly, Marina Fitch, and others. The work of eccentric, harder-to-classify authors such as Robert Holdstock, Keith Roberts, Mary Gentle, Gene Wolfe, Gwyneth Jones, M. John Harrison, and Tanith Lee is probably related to this central massif in some way, as is the flourishing subcategory of "updated fairy tales" recently popularized by a series of fantasy anthologies such as *Snow White, Blood Red* edited by Ellen Datlow and Terri Windling. The work of eccentrics such as Tim Powers, James P. Blaylock (Powers and Blaylock are sometimes considered to form a sub-category of their own, and are also identified with—see below— "steampunk"), John Crowley, Jonathan Carroll, Howard Waldrop, Terry Bisson, Rebecca Ore, and Neal Barrett, Jr. probably also fits in somewhere on the Urban Fantasy end of the High Fantasy spectrum . . . or fits in there as well as it fits in anywhere, at least. On the far end, Urban Fantasy also shades off into the literary territory known as "Magic Realism," although the distinctions between fantasy and Magic Realism are subjective enough and complex enough to daunt all but the most fearless of critics. (High Fantasy was also the major influence on most fantasy role-playing games such as Dungeons & Dragons, and, later, on fantasy-adventure computer games, and such mediums have diffused the influence of this type of fantasy throughout the culture far beyond the traditional boundaries of the print genre, but also out of our purview here.)

Sometime in the early 1980s, prompted by the unprecedented commercial success of Stephen King, horror began to separate out from fantasy and establish itself as an individual commercial publishing category of its own, with book lines specializing in horror being launched, and with separately labeled shelves set up for horror in most large bookstores. This trend accelerated throughout the 1980s and into the 1990s, and today, while fantasy titles are not always separated from science fiction titles in large bookstores (usually they are *not* separated, in fact), horror is almost always separated out from both fantasy and science fiction and racked as an individual category of its own. Horror had become a genre in its own right. (Later still, in the early 1990s, horror itself would begin to split, with a variety sometimes called "Dark Suspense" beginning to be differentiated from the more traditional supernatural horror; closer to the "true crime/suspense novel" subgenre of mystery than to the work of earlier horror writers such as Lovecraft, the rapidly growing "Dark Suspense" subcategory is mostly concerned with a seemingly endless parade of serial killers, murderous rapists, and child molesters—horror in the Hitchcockian sense rather than in the supernatural sense—and, since it usually contains no fantastic element, passes quickly beyond our purview here. "Erotic Horror"—sometimes featuring a supernatural element, sometimes not, but almost always blood-soaked, gore-splattered, and escalatingly grotesque, specializing in depictions of rape, murder, sexual violence, S&M, bondage, and mutilation, all described with relishing, hand-rubbing glee—also seems to be calving from the main body of horror as a subgenre of its own. Vampire stories, once to be encountered largely in fantasy, also show signs of becoming a separate subcategory of horror on their own—22 percent of the horror books published in 1995 were vampire books—but at least they usually retain a fantastic element, almost by definition. Most modern horror, though, has moved so far away from its fantasy roots that it need not be really considered further in this anthology.)

Although horror is increasingly perceived as a separate genre of its own (and mostly feels that way, too), some writers do continue to work both territories, and there is an ambiguous borderland between fantasy and horror, sometimes called "Dark Fantasy"—work that partakes of the qualities of both forms without being clearly distinguishable as either. Much of Tanith Lee's work fits into this border country, as do novels like James P. Blaylock's *All the Bells on Earth* and some of the work of Tim Powers, Elizabeth Hand, Jonathan Carroll, and others.

There are other subgenres, of course, in almost bewildering profusion. "Steampunk," for instance, can be considered a form of Urban Fantasy wherein the "modern world" depicted is that of the Victorian era, or a fun-house-mirror reflection of an alternative Victorian age, at least; depending on whom you ask, steampunk can be considered to be either science fiction or fantasy, and some of the authors who have been associated with it include Tim Powers, James Blaylock, K. W. Jeter, Bruce Sterling, William Gibson (for one novel in collaboration with Sterling, *The Difference Engine*), Kim Newman, Paul J. McAuley, Paul Di Filippo, and, perhaps the progenitor of this form, Michael Moorcock. "Outlaw Fantasy"—gonzo fantasy made up of an eclectic stew of various pop-culture icons—was briefly considered to be a subcategory in the 1980s; best typified by the work of Howard Waldrop, although writers such as Neal Barrett, Jr., Tom Reamy, Joe Landsdale, and Bruce Sterling in his fantasy-writing mode have been associated with it. Outlaw Fantasy later seemed to be evolving into "cowpunk," a cross between gonzo fantasy, horror, SF, and the classic Western story, and several "cowpunk" anthologies were published at the end of the decade. "Comic Fantasy," with roots that go all the way back to *Unknown,* is sometimes considered to be a subcategory of its own; among its most prominent practitioners are Terry Pratchett (one of the best-selling authors in Britain), Piers Anthony, Douglas Adams, Esther M. Friesner, Tom Holt, Christopher Stasheff, Craig Shaw Gardner, and others. Lately, a new subcategory called "Hard Fantasy" has been proposed, an as-yet only vaguely defined hybrid between Tolkienesque fantasy, technologically oriented "hard" science fiction, and steampunk, with perhaps a jigger of Outlaw Fantasy thrown in; the best examples of this nascent form to date are to be found in Michael Swanwick's *The Iron Dragon's Daughter,* Walter Jon Williams's *Metropolitan,* and in some of the short work—such as "The Giving Mouth"—of Ian R. MacLeod, although I suspect that Geoff Ryman's "The Unconquered Country" is also ancestral in some way.

Of course, all of these classification schemes are, to a large extent, arbitrary. Authors constantly complicate things by working in more than one form, or by creating not-easily-pigeonholeable works that blur the boundaries between several different categories, and some of the more eccentric and individual authors such as Gene Wolfe, Mary Gentle, and John Crowley don't really fit in comfortably *anywhere.* About the best you can do is to perceive vague taxonomic lines and lineages; you can tell that some writers are related *somehow,* that somewhere down their family trees they share common ancestors, but the species continue to radiate, filling new ecological niches, evolving, specializing, forming new species, and then combining to form new hybrids in bewildering profusion . . . so that in the end all you can really say is that they all share, say, a common bone in the foot, or the shape of a hip-joint. Making this all even more subjective is the fact that many of these subcategories are distinguishable mainly by Attitude. After all, Leiber's "Smoke Ghost," Gold's "Trouble with Water," Avram Davidson's "The Golem," Waldrop's "God's Hooks!," Robert Sampson's "A Gift of the People," Harlan Ellison's "Pretty Maggie Moneyeyes," Esther M. Friesner's "Blunderbore," Stephen King's "The Mangler," and Bernard Malamud's "The Jewbird" (among examples that could be multiplied almost endlessly) could all validly be described as stories wherein the supernatural intrudes into the modern world—but they are all very distinct in tone and mood and emotional color, in flavor, in Attitude. The whale, the bat, and the lemur may have shared a common ancestor, but they are still very different animals today, for all that.

However you try to flense and parse it, the reality is that today, more

than twenty years after fantasy initially became a separate marketing category, the fantasy genre has grown into an enormous, varied, and vital
industry, rivaling its longer-established cousin science fiction in numbers
of titles published and in the amount of bookstore rack space devoted to
the form.

By 1995, ironically, one prominent British SF writer was complaining
that he could only sell science fiction, in Britain at least, by "disguising"
it as fantasy.

When the last Ice Age started, and the glaciers ground down from the
north to cover most of the North American continent, thousands of
species of plants and trees, as well as the insects, birds, and animals associated with them, retreated to "cove forests" in the south, in what would
eventually come to be called the Great Smoky Mountains; in those cove
forests, they waited out the long domain of the Ice, eventually moving
north again to re-colonize the land as the climate warmed and the glaciers retreated. Similarly, the lowly genre fantasy and science fiction magazines—*Weird Tales* and *Unknown* in the 1930s and 1940s, *The Magazine of
Fantasy & Science Fiction, Fantastic,* and the British Science Fantasy in the
1950s and 1960s—were the "cove forests" that sheltered fantasy during
its long retreat from the glaciers of Social Realism, giving it a refuge in
which to endure until the climate warmed enough to allow it to spread
and repopulate again.

Oddly, those fantasy magazines have often been ignored by histories
of fantasy and retrospective fantasy anthologies to date, which often
choose to focus upon the more respectable high-end literary ancestors of
fantasy instead. Since that territory has recently been covered in two excellent retrospective anthologies, David G. Hartwell's *Masterpieces of Fantasy and Enchantment* and Tom Shippey's *The Oxford Book of Fantasy Stories*
(both of which *do* also acknowledge fantasy's debt to the genre magazines),
I've decided to concentrate in this anthology on modern fantasy as it developed and cross-fertilized and flourished in the hothouse atmosphere
of those "cove forests," the genre fantasy magazines of fantasy's "lost period," from the 1930s to the 1960s, taking a look as well at what happened
to the form *after* it was no longer necessary for it to hide in the magazines
in order to survive. After the Tolkien Explosion of the late 1960s, it became possible to make a reputation as a fantasist by writing novels alone;
in fact, many major modern fantasy writers from Tim Powers to Terry
Brooks to Guy Gavriel Kay to Terry Pratchett have established themselves
while writing few, if any, short stories. Nevertheless, evolutionarily important work continued to appear in short story form throughout the
1970s, 1980s, and 1990s, in genre magazines such as *The Magazine of Fantasy & Science Fiction* and *Asimov's Science Fiction* magazine, as well as in the
occasional original fantasy anthology, which functioned in much the same

way as the magazines . . . and it is from those fantasy magazines and anthologies that the majority of the stories in this anthology are drawn.

As was true of my other two retrospective anthologies, *Modern Classics of Science Fiction* and *Modern Classic Short Novels of Science Fiction,* none of the stories here were selected on ideological grounds, because they help buttress some polemic or aesthetic argument about the nature of fantasy, or because they express some critical theory, or because they grind some particular political axe. Nor were they selected because they are good examples of one type or another of fantasy—although, in retrospect, it can be seen that a few of them *are* good examples of one subcategory or another of fantasy. That is not why they are here, though.

No, as usual with my retrospective anthologies, the stories here were selected on the appallingly naive basis that I *liked* them.

These are the stories that stuck in my mind after more than thirty years of reading fantasy, ever since I first picked up that anthology of stories from *Unknown* in 1963. These are the stories that spoke to something in me, that moved me and shook me, that opened my eyes to new worlds of wonder and enchantment, that made me experience life inside someone else's—or some*thing* else's—skin. Stories that have been personal friends of mine, friends that have seen me through some of the darkest times and longest nights of my life. Stories that I enjoyed—uncritically, instinctively—as a reader. Stories that I would want to read again. I decided some years ago that this was the only valid way to put together a retrospective anthology—for me, anyway—and that's the way I've assembled this one as well.

Even collecting stories that fit only the above criteria, though, I found that I was still left with enough material to fill an anthology twice as long as this one, longer than was feasible. Some winnowing-screens were needed. After thinking about this, I decided that although stories such as Theodore Sturgeon's "It" and Fritz Leiber's "Smoke Ghost" were able to coexist comfortably along with stories such as H. L. Gold's "Trouble with Water" and L. Sprague de Camp's "The Hardwood Pile" in the 1930s in the pages of a fantasy magazine such as *Unknown,* it was clear in retrospect that "It" and "Smoke Ghost" were part of a different taxonomic line, one that lead not to modern fantasy, but instead, on through stories like Harlan Ellison's "Pretty Maggie Moneyeyes" and Joanna Russ's "My Dear Emily" and Robert Bloch's "Yours Truly, Jack the Ripper" to the modern horror genre—that, in fact, they would all be more appropriate to a book called *Modern Classics of Horror* than to a book called *Modern Classics of Fantasy.* So, arbitrarily, I omitted them, and other similar stories that I decided arbitrarily were better thought of as horror-ancestors rather than fantasy-ancestors. Deciding to concentrate on "modern" fantasy as it evolved in the genre magazines eliminated a whole range of other stories, including classics by Lord Dunsany, Kipling, Saki, and others. The constraints of a technically feasible book-length dictated the omission of other stories, although I did manage to squeeze in a few of my favorite fantasy novellas. And the practical difficulties involved in assembling an anthology necessitated the omission of still other stories, those, say, which had recently appeared in a competing anthology, or those for which the reprint rights were either encumbered or priced too high for me to be able to afford them on the limited budget I had to work with (which explains why there is no Ray Bradbury story here, so don't bother to write and ask).

Some critics will no doubt complain that some of the stories I have used here are not "really" fantasy, but, as I think this anthology demonstrates, the line between fantasy and science fiction is an ambiguous one, and always *has* been. De Camp's "The Gnarly Man" was published in the foremost fantasy magazine of its day, but makes a stab at a rationalistic "science-fictional" rationale for its fantastic element . . . although one that was rather weak even in 1939. Damon Knight's "Extempore" was published in a science fiction magazine, yet offers no rationalistic explanation for its fantastic element at all, which, stripped of some technobabble, comes down to "wishing will make it so," clearly a fantasy trope. Roger Zelazny's "Death and the Executioner," which was later built into one of the most famous science fiction novels of the 1960s, functions perfectly as a fantasy except for a few lines of back-story toward the end. Keith Roberts's "The Signaller" was later built into *Pavane,* which is usually thought of as a science fiction novel—and yet the story features a visitation by Elves. Fritz Leiber's "Scylla's Daughter" is a key story in one of the core fantasy series, a sword & sorcery series at that, and yet a time-traveller from the future comes blundering into the story in the middle of it—and, to complicate things, the time-traveller arrives riding on a dragon! Richard McKenna's "Casey Agonistes" and R. A. Lafferty's "Narrow Valley," which I used in my *Modern Classics of Science Fiction* without a single critical eyebrow being raised, would fit with equal ease into *this* anthology. And so on.

Much of both modern fantasy and modern horror, it seems to me, still deals with the relationship of the ordinary human world with Faërie, the Land Beyond the Hill, the World Beyond the Wood, that land of ghosts and shadows and unearthly Powers that still flickers just beyond the periphery of our bright, tidy, rational modern world—or so our ancient hindbrain assures us, anyway, no matter how much our skeptical forebrain scoffs. The major difference between the two, I think, is not so much subject matter as Attitude, the prevalent emotional weather or coloring of each. Michael Swanwick has pointed out that the Fafhrd and Gray Mouser stories by rights *ought* to read like horror, most of the stories bringing the two comrades into conflict with a shuddersome crew of hideous monsters and supernatural menaces in a fictional universe ruled by as cruel and remorseless a pantheon of dark gods as is to be found in anything by Lovecraft. That they do *not* read as horror, that they are instantly recognizable as fantasy instead, is due to Attitude—to the *élan,* the gusto, and the great, good-natured humor with which Fafhrd and the Mouser face even the most grisly and gruesome of adversaries. (Humor seems to be a particular dividing line; there's lots of funny fantasy, but almost no funny horror—in fact, that comes close to being a contradiction in terms.)

Much of modern horror has succumbed to—in fact, wholeheartedly embraced—a numbing sort of nihilism and fashionable designer despair, the message of which seems to be: you can't win, nothing matters, neither ethics nor morals nor religion are an effective guide to behavior, and none of them will save you; you can survive for a while by turning yourself into a savage predator, devoid of remorse or compassion or pity, but there's always a *bigger* predator in wait somewhere; in the end, the grave will get you, and sometimes you will continue to be flayed and tormented even beyond death. The house always wins, you always lose, and nothing you can do has any significance at all.

This perception of the universe may be closer to "reality" than that of fantasy, but my reaction to it is always, Yeah, well, so what? It's hardly news, after all, that everyone is bound for the grave; in fact, it's a rather obvious truism. So *what?* What can you *do* with a message that everything is hopeless nihilism and black despair, that nothing you can do matters at all, except to use it as another good reason to commit suicide as soon as possible?

Fantasy instead teaches us that there *is* something worthwhile you can do on the way to the grave: you can dream. And that maybe that dreaming is not only intrinsically valuable, for its own sake, but that sometimes the dream can take on a life of its own, a life that persists, and that shapes and sometimes even ennobles the lives of others that it touches, sometimes long after the original dreamer is gone from this earth.

So here are many such dreams, some of them pastel and fragile, and yet, in their own way, curiously tough. Such dreams persist, and cross the gulf of generations and even the awful gulf of the grave, cross all barriers of race or age or class or sex or nationality, transcend time itself. Here are dreams that, it is my fervent hope, will still be touching other people's minds and hearts and stirring *them* in their turn to dream long after everyone in this anthology or associated with it has gone to dust.

HORACE L. GOLD

Trouble with Water

Although the late Horace L. Gold published seven million words
of fiction in every field but sports and air war, he was perhaps
best known as the founder and first editor of *Galaxy* magazine.
He edited the magazine throughout its "Golden Age" in the
1950s, publishing dozens of classic stories by Alfred Bester,
Damon Knight, Theodore Sturgeon, William Tenn, C. M. Korn-
bluth, Frederik Pohl, and many others—in fact, Gold was one of
the most influential editors in the history of science fiction, rat-
ing right up there with editors such as John W. Campbell Jr. and
Anthony Boucher. His books include eleven *Galaxy* anthologies,
The Old Die Rich and Other Stories, What Will They Think of Last?,
and *Ultima Zero.* Gold died in 1995.

Long before he assumed the editorial chair at *Galaxy,* however,
Gold had secured his reputation within the field on the basis of
the classic story that follows, one of the best stories ever published in the renowned fantasy magazine *Unknown,* and, in fact,
one of the most famous modern fantasies ever written, as bittersweet and funny today as it was in 1939. In it, Gold shows us
the wisdom of a simple rule: Never pick a fight until you know
exactly *who* it is you're fighting *with* . . .

Greenberg did not deserve his surroundings. He was the first fisherman
of the season, which guaranteed him a fine catch; he sat in a dry boat—
one without a single leak—far out on a lake that was ruffled only enough
to agitate his artificial fly. The sun was warm, the air was cool; he sat comfortably on a cushion; he had brought a hearty lunch; and two bottles of
beer hung over the stern in the cold water.

Any other man would have been soaked with joy to be fishing on such
a splendid day. Normally, Greenberg himself would have been ecstatic,
but instead of relaxing and waiting for a nibble, he was plagued by worries.

This short, slightly gross, definitely bald, eminently respectable businessman lived a gypsy life. During the summer, he lived in a hotel with kitchen privileges in Rockaway; winters he lived in a hotel with kitchen privileges in Florida; and in both places he operated concessions. For years now, rain had fallen on schedule every week end, and there had been storms and floods on Decoration Day, July 4th and Labor Day. He did not love his life, but it was a way of making a living.

He closed his eyes and groaned. If he had only had a son instead of his Rosie! Then things would have been mighty different—

For one thing, a son could run the hot dog and hamburger griddle, Esther could draw beer, and he would make soft drinks. There would be small difference in the profits, Greenberg admitted to himself; but at least those profits could be put aside for old age, instead of toward a dowry for his miserably ugly, dumpy, pitifully eager Rosie.

"All right—so what do I care if she don't get married?" he had cried to his wife a thousand times. "I'll support her. Other men can set up boys in candy stores with soda fountains that have only two spigots. Why should I have to give a boy a regular International Casino?"

"May your tongue rot in your head, you no-good piker!" she would scream. "It ain't right for a girl to be an old maid. If we have to die in the poorhouse, I'll get my poor Rosie a husband. Every penny we don't need for living goes to her dowry!"

Greenberg did not hate his daughter, nor did he blame her for his misfortunes; yet, because of her, he was fishing with a broken rod that he had to tape together.

That morning, his wife opened her eyes and saw him packing his equipment. She instantly came awake. "Go ahead!" she shrilled—speaking in a conversational tone was not one of her accomplishments—"Go fishing, you loafer! Leave me here alone. I can connect the beer pipes and the gas for soda water. I can buy ice cream, frankfurters, rolls, syrup, and watch the gas and electric men at the same time. Go ahead—go fishing!"

"I ordered everything," he mumbled soothingly. "The gas and electric won't be turned on today. I only wanted to go fishing—it's my last chance. Tomorrow we open the concession. Tell the truth, Esther, can I go fishing after we open?"

"I don't care about that. Am I your wife or ain't I, that you should go ordering everything without asking me—"

He defended his actions. It was a tactical mistake. While she was still in bed, he should have picked up his equipment and left. By the time the argument got around to Rosie's dowry, she stood facing him.

"For myself I don't care," she yelled. "What kind of a monster are you that you can go fishing while your daughter eats her heart out? And on a day like this yet! You should only have to make supper and dress Rosie up. A lot you care that a nice boy is coming to supper tonight and maybe take Rosie out, you no-good father, you!"

From that point it was only one hot protest and a shrill curse to find himself clutching half a broken rod, with the other half being flung at his head.

Now he sat in his beautifully dry boat on an excellent game lake far out on Long Island, desperately aware that any average fish might collapse his taped rod.

What else could he expect? He had missed his train; he had had to wait for the boathouse proprietor; his favorite dry fly was missing; and, since morning, not a fish struck at the bait. Not a single fish!

And it was getting late. He had no more patience. He ripped the cap off a bottle of beer and drank it, in order to gain courage to change his fly for a less sporting bloodworm. It hurt him, but he wanted a fish.

The hook and the squirming worm sank. Before it came to rest, he felt a nibble. He sucked in his breath exultantly and snapped the hook deep into the fish's mouth. Sometimes, he thought philosophically, they just won't take artificial bait. He reeled in slowly.

"Oh, Lord," he prayed, "a dollar for charity—just don't let the rod bend in half where I taped it!"

It was sagging dangerously. He looked at it unhappily and raised his ante to five dollars; even at that price it looked impossible. He dipped his rod into the water, parallel with the line, to remove the strain. He was glad no one could see him do it. The line reeled in without a fight.

"Have I—God forbid!—got an eel or something not kosher?" he mumbled. "A plague on you—why don't you fight?"

He did not really care what it was—even an eel—anything at all.

He pulled in a long, pointed, brimless green hat.

For a moment he glared at it. His mouth hardened. Then, viciously, he yanked the hat off the hook, threw it on the floor and trampled on it. He rubbed his hands together in anguish.

"All day I fish," he wailed, "two dollars for train fare, a dollar for a boat, a quarter for bait, a new rod I got to buy—and a five-dollar mortgage charity has got on me. For what? For you, you hat, you!"

Out in the water an extremely civil voice asked politely: "May I have my hat, please?"

Greenberg glowered up. He saw a little man come swimming vigorously through the water toward him: small arms crossed with enormous dignity, vast ears on a pointed face propelling him quite rapidly and efficiently. With serious determination he drove through the water, and, at the starboard rail, his amazing ears kept him stationary while he looked gravely at Greenberg.

"You are stamping on my hat," he pointed out without anger.

To Greenberg this was highly unimportant. "With the ears you're swimming," he grinned in a superior way. "Do you look funny!"

"How else could I swim?" the little man asked politely.

"With the arms and legs, like a regular human being, of course."

"But I am not a human being. I am a water gnome, a relative of the more common mining gnome. I cannot swim with my arms, because they must be crossed to give an appearance of dignity suitable to a water gnome; and my feet are used for writing and holding things. On the other hand, my ears are perfectly adapted for propulsion in water. Consequently, I employ them for that purpose. But please, my hat—there are several matters requiring my immediate attention, and I must not waste time."

Greenberg's unpleasant attitude toward the remarkably civil gnome is easily understandable. He had found someone he could feel superior to, and, by insulting him, his depressed ego could expand. The water gnome certainly looked inoffensive enough, being only two feet tall.

"What you got that's so important to do, Big Ears?" he asked nastily.

Greenberg hoped the gnome would be offended. He was not, since his ears, to him, were perfectly normal, just as you would not be insulted if a member of a race of atrophied beings were to call you "Big Muscles." You might even feel flattered.

"I really must hurry," the gnome said, almost anxiously. "But if I have to answer your questions in order to get back my hat—we are engaged in restocking the Eastern waters with fish. Last year there was quite a drain. The bureau of fisheries is coöperating with us to some extent, but, of course, we cannot depend too much on them. Until the population rises to normal, every fish has instructions not to nibble."

Greenberg allowed himself a smile, an annoyingly skeptical smile.

"My main work," the gnome went on resignedly, "is control of the rainfall over the Eastern seaboard. Our fact-finding committee, which is scientifically situated in the meteorological center of the continent, coördinates the rainfall needs of the entire continent; and when they determine the amount of rain needed in particular spots of the East, I make it rain to that extent. Now may I have my hat, please?"

Greenberg laughed coarsely. "The first lie was big enough—about telling the fish not to bite. You make it rain like I'm President of the United States!" He bent toward the gnome slyly. "How's about proof?"

"Certainly, if you insist." The gnome raised his patient, triangular face toward a particularly clear blue spot in the sky, a trifle to one side of Greenberg. "Watch that bit of the sky."

Greenberg looked up humorously. Even when a small dark cloud rapidly formed in the previously clear spot, his grin remained broad. It could have been coincidental. But then large drops of undeniable rain fell over a twenty-foot circle; and Greenberg's mocking grin shrank and grew sour.

He glared hatred at the gnome, finally convinced. "So you're the dirty crook who makes it rain on week ends!"

"Usually on week ends during the summer," the gnome admitted. "Ninety-two percent of water consumption is on weekdays. Obviously we must replace that water. The week ends, of course, are the logical time."

"But, you thief!" Greenberg cried hysterically, "you murderer! What do you care what you do to my concession with your rain? It ain't bad enough business would be rotten even without rain, you got to make floods!"

"I'm sorry," the gnome replied, untouched by Greenberg's rhetoric. "We do not create rainfall for the benefit of men. We are here to protect the fish.

"Now please give me my hat. I have wasted enough time, when I should be preparing the extremely heavy rain needed for this coming week end."

Greenberg jumped to his feet in the unsteady boat. "Rain this week end—when I can maybe make a profit for a change! A lot you care if you ruin business. May you and your fish die a horrible, lingering death."

And he furiously ripped the green hat to pieces and hurled them at the gnome.

"I'm really sorry you did that," the little fellow said calmly, his huge ears treading water without the slightest increase of pace to indicate his anger. "We Little Folk have no tempers to lose. Nevertheless, occasionally we find it necessary to discipline certain of your people, in order to retain our dignity. I am not malignant; but, since you hate water and those who live in it, water and those who live in it will keep away from you."

With his arms still folded in great dignity, the tiny water gnome flipped his vast ears and disappeared in a neat surface dive.

Greenberg glowered at the spreading circles of waves. He did not grasp the gnome's final restraining order; he did not even attempt to interpret it. Instead he glared angrily out of the corner of his eye at the phenomenal circle of rain that fell from a perfectly clear sky. The gnome must have remembered it at length, for a moment later the rain stopped. Like shutting off a faucet, Greenberg unwillingly thought.

"Good-by, week end business," he growled. "If Esther finds out I got into an argument with the guy who makes it rain—"

He made an underhand cast, hoping for just one fish. The line flew out over the water; then the hook arched upward and came to rest several inches above the surface, hanging quite steadily and without support in the air.

"Well, go down in the water, damn you!" Greenberg said viciously, and he swished his rod back and forth to pull the hook down from its ridiculous levitation. It refused.

Muttering something incoherent about being hanged before he'd give in, Greenberg hurled his useless rod at the water. By this time he was not surprised when it hovered in the air above the lake. He merely glanced red-eyed at it, tossed out the remains of the gnome's hat, and snatched up the oars.

When he pulled back on them to row to land, they did not touch the water—naturally. Instead they flashed unimpeded through the air, and Greenberg tumbled into the bow.

"A-ha!" he grated. "Here's where the trouble begins." He bent over the side. As he had suspected, the keel floated a remarkable distance above the lake.

By rowing against the air, he moved with maddening slowness toward shore, like a medieval conception of a flying machine. His main concern was that no one should see him in his humiliating position.

At the hotel, he tried to sneak past the kitchen to the bathroom. He knew that Esther waited to curse him for fishing the day before opening, but more especially on the very day that a nice boy was coming to see her Rosie. If he could dress in a hurry, she might have less to say—

"Oh, there you are, you good-for-nothing!"

He froze to a halt.

"Look at you!" she screamed shrilly. "Filthy—you stink from fish!"

"I didn't catch anything, darling," he protested timidly.

"You stink anyhow. Go take a bath, may you drown in it! Get dressed in two minutes or less, and entertain the boy when he gets here. Hurry!"

He locked himself in, happy to escape her voice, started the water in the tub, and stripped from the waist up. A hot bath, he hoped, would rid him of his depressed feeling.

First, no fish; now, rain on week ends! What would Esther say—if she knew, of course. And, of course, he would not tell her.

"Let myself in for a lifetime of curses!" he sneered. "Ha!"

He clamped a new blade into his razor, opened the tube of shaving cream, and stared objectively at the mirror. The dominant feature of the soft, chubby face that stared back was its ugly black stubble; but he set his stubborn chin and glowered. He really looked quite fierce and in-domitable. Unfortunately, Esther never saw his face in that uncharacter-istic pose, otherwise she would speak more softly.

"Herman Greenberg never gives in!" he whispered between savagely hardened lips. "Rain on week ends, no fish—anything he wants; a lot I care! Believe me, he'll come crawling to me before I go to him."

He gradually became aware that his shaving brush was not getting wet. When he looked down and saw the water dividing into streams that flowed around it, his determined face slipped and grew desperately anx-ious. He tried to trap the water—by catching it in his cupped hands, by creeping up on it from behind, as if it were some shy animal, and shov-ing his brush at it—but it broke and ran away from his touch. Then he jammed his palm against the faucet. Defeated, he heard it gurgle back down the pipe, probably as far as the main.

"What do I do now?" he groaned. "Will Esther give it to me if I don't take a shave! But how! . . . I can't shave without water."

Glumly, he shut off the bath, undressed, and stepped into the tub. He lay down to soak. It took a moment of horrified stupor to realize that he was completely dry and that he lay in a waterless bathtub. The water, in one surge of revulsion, had swept out onto the floor.

"Herman, stop splashing!" his wife yelled. "I just washed that floor. If I find one little puddle I'll murder you!"

Greenberg surveyed the instep-deep pool over the bathroom floor. "Yes, my love," he croaked unhappily.

With an inadequate washrag he chased the elusive water, hoping to mop it all up before it could seep through to the apartment below. His washrag remained dry, however, and he knew that the ceiling underneath was dripping. The water was still on the floor.

In despair, he sat on the edge of the bathtub. For some time he sat in silence. Then his wife banged on the door, urging him to come out. He started and dressed moodily.

When he sneaked out and shut the bathroom door tightly on the floor inside, he was extremely dirty and his face *was* raw where he had experimentally attempted to shave with a dry razor.

"Rosie!" he called in a hoarse whisper. "Sh! Where's mamma?"

His daughter sat on the studio couch and applied nail-polish to her stubby fingers. "You look terrible," she said in a conversational tone. "Aren't you going to shave?"

He recoiled at the sound of her voice, which, to him, roared out like a siren. "Quiet, Rosie! Sh!" And for further emphasis, he shoved his lips out against a warning finger. He heard his wife striding heavily around the kitchen. "Rosie," he cooed, "I'll give you a dollar if you'll mop up the water I spilled in the bathroom."

"I can't papa," she stated firmly. "I'm all dressed."

"Two dollars, Rosie—all right, two and a half, you blackmailer."

He flinched when he heard her gasp in the bathroom; but, when she came out with soaked shoes, he fled downstairs. He wandered aimlessly toward the village.

Now he was in for it, he thought: screams from Esther, tears from Rosie—plus a new pair of shoes for Rosie and two and a half dollars. It would be worse, though, if he could not get rid of his whiskers—

Rubbing the tender spots where his dry razor had raked his face, he mused blankly at a drugstore window. He saw nothing to help him, but he went inside anyhow and stood hopefully at the drug counter. A face peered at him through a space scratched in the wall case mirror, and the druggist came out. A nice-looking, intelligent fellow, Greenberg saw at a glance.

"What you got for shaving that I can use without water?" he asked.

"Skin irritation, eh?" the pharmacist replied. "I got something very good for that."

"No. It's just—Well, I don't like to shave with water."

The druggist seemed disappointed. "Well, I got brushless shaving cream." Then he brightened. "But I got an electric razor—much better."

"How much?" Greenberg asked cautiously.

"Only fifteen dollars, and it lasts a lifetime."

"Give me the shaving cream," Greenberg said coldly.

With the tactical science of a military expert, he walked around until some time after dark. Only then did he go back to the hotel, to wait outside. It was after seven, he was getting hungry, and the people who entered the hotel he knew as permanent summer guests. At last a stranger passed him and ran up the stairs.

Greenberg hesitated for a moment. The stranger was scarcely a boy, as Esther had definitely termed him, but Greenberg reasoned that her term was merely wish-fulfillment, and he jauntily ran up behind him.

He allowed a few minutes to pass, for the man to introduce himself and let Esther and Rosie don their company manners. Then, secure in the knowledge that there would be no scene until the guest left, he entered.

He waded through a hostile atmosphere, urbanely shook hands with Sammie Katz, who was a doctor—probably, Greenberg thought shrewdly, in search of an office—and excused himself.

In the bathroom, he carefully read the directions for using brushless shaving cream. He felt less confident when he realized that he had to wash his face thoroughly with soap and water, but without benefit of either, he spread the cream on, patted it, and waited for his beard to soften. It did not, as he discovered while shaving. He wiped his face dry. The towel was sticky and black, with whiskers suspended in paste, and, for that, he knew, there would be more hell to pay. He shrugged resignedly. He would have to spend fifteen dollars for an electric razor after all; this foolishness was costing him a fortune!

That they were waiting for him before beginning supper, was, he knew, only a gesture for the sake of company. Without changing her hard, brilliant smile, Esther whispered: "Wait! I'll get you later—"

He smiled back, his tortured, slashed face creasing painfully. All that could be changed by his being enormously pleasant to Rosie's young man. If he could slip Sammie a few dollars—more expense, he groaned—to take Rosie out, Esther would forgive everything.

He was too engaged in beaming and putting Sammie at ease to think of what would happen after he ate caviar canapes. Under other circumstances Greenberg would have been repulsed by Sammie's ultra-professional waxed mustache—an offensively small, pointed thing—and his commercial attitude toward poor Rosie; but Greenberg regarded him as a potential savior.

"You open an office yet, Doctor Katz?"

"Not yet. You know how things are. Anyhow, call me Sammie."

Greenberg recognized the gambit with satisfaction, since it seemed to please Esther so much. At one stroke Sammie had ingratiated himself and begun bargaining negotiations.

Without another word, Greenberg lifted his spoon to attack the soup. It would be easy to snare this eager doctor. *A doctor!* No wonder Esther and Rosie were so puffed with joy.

In the proper company way, he pushed his spoon away from him. The soup spilled onto the tablecloth.

"Not so hard, you dope," Esther hissed.

He drew the spoon toward him. The soup leaped off it like a live thing and splashed over him—turning, just before contact, to fall on the floor. He gulped and pushed the bowl away. This time the soup poured over the side of the plate and lay in a huge puddle on the table.

"I didn't want any soup anyhow," he said in a horrible attempt at levity. Lucky for him, he thought wildly, that Sammy was there to pacify Esther with his smooth college talk—not a bad fellow, Sammie, in spite of his mustache; he'd come in handy at times.

Greenberg lapsed into a paralysis of fear. He was thirsty after having eaten the caviar, which beats herring any time as a thirst raiser. But the knowledge that he could not touch water without having it recoil and perhaps spill, made his thirst a monumental craving. He attacked the problem cunningly.

The others were talking rapidly and rather hysterically. He waited until his courage was equal to his thirst; then he leaned over the table with a glass in his hand. "Sammie, do you mind—a little water, huh?"

Sammie poured from a pitcher while Esther watched for more of his tricks. It was to be expected, but still he was shocked when the water exploded out of the glass directly at Sammie's only suit.

"If you'll excuse me," Sammie said angrily, "I don't like to eat with lunatics."

And he left, though Esther cried and begged him to stay. Rosie was too stunned to move. But when the door closed, Greenberg raised his agonized eyes to watch his wife stalk murderously toward him.

Greenberg stood on the boardwalk outside his concession and glared blearily at the peaceful, blue, highly unpleasant ocean. He wondered what would happen if he started at the edge of the water and strode out. He could probably walk right to Europe on dry land.

It was early—much too early for business—and he was tired. Neither he nor Esther had slept; and it was practically certain that the neighbors hadn't either. But above all he was incredibly thirsty.

In a spirit of experimentation, he mixed a soda. Of course, its high water content made it slop onto the floor. For breakfast he had surreptitiously tried fruit juice and coffee, without success.

With his tongue dry to the point of furriness, he sat weakly on a board-walk bench in front of his concession. It was Friday morning, which meant that the day was clear, with a promise of intense heat. Had it been Saturday, it naturally would have been raining.

"This year," he moaned, "I'll be wiped out. If I can't mix sodas, why should beer stay in a glass for me? I thought I could hire a boy for ten dollars a week to run the hot-dog griddle; I could make sodas, and Esther could draw beer. All I can do is make hot dogs, Esther can still draw beer; but twenty or maybe twenty-five a week I got to pay a sodaman. I won't even come out square—a fortune I'll lose!"

The situation really was desperate. Concessions depend on too many factors to be anything but capriciously profitable.

His throat was fiery and his soft brown eyes held a fierce glaze when the gas and electric were turned on, the beer pipes connected, the tank of carbon dioxide hitched to the pump, and the refrigerator started.

Gradually, the beach was filling with bathers. Greenberg writhed on his bench and envied them. They could swim and drink without having liquid draw away from them as if in horror. They were not thirsty—

And then he saw his first customer approach. His business experience was that morning customers buy only soft drinks. In a mad haste he put up the shutters and fled to the hotel.

"Esther!" he cried. "I got to tell you! I can't stand it—"

Threateningly, his wife held her broom like a baseball bat. "Go back to the concession, you crazy fool. Ain't you done enough already?"

He could not be hurt more than he had been. For once he did not cringe. "You got to help me, Esther."

"Why didn't you shave, you no-good bum? Is that any way—"

"That's what I got to tell you. Yesterday I got into an argument with a water gnome—"

"A what?" Esther looked at him suspiciously.

"A water gnome," he babbled in a rush of words. "A little man so high, with big ears that he swims with, and he makes it rain—"

"Herman!" she screamed. "Stop that nonsense. You're crazy!"

Greenberg pounded his forehead with his fist. "I *ain't* crazy. Look, Esther. Come with me into the kitchen."

She followed him readily enough, but her attitude made him feel more helpless and alone than ever. With her fists on her plump hips and her feet set wide, she cautiously watched him try to fill a glass of water.

"Don't you see?" he wailed. "It won't go in the glass. It spills over. It runs away from me."

She was puzzled. "What happened to you?"

Brokenly, Greenberg told of his encounter with the water gnome, leaving out no single degrading detail. "And now I can't touch water," he ended. "I can't drink it. I can't make sodas. On top of it all, I got such thirst, it's killing me."

Esther's reaction was instantaneous. She threw her arms around him, drew his head down to her shoulder, and patted him comfortingly as if he were a child. "Herman, my poor Herman!" she breathed tenderly. "What did we ever do to deserve such a curse?"

"What shall I do, Esther?" he cried helplessly.

She held him at arm's length. "You got to go to a doctor," she said firmly. "How long can you go without drinking? Without water you'll die. Maybe sometimes I am a little hard on you, but you know I love you—"

"I know, mamma," he sighed. "But how can a doctor help me?"

"Am I a doctor that I should know? Go anyhow. What can you lose?"

He hesitated. "I need fifteen dollars for an electric razor," he said in a low, weak voice.

"So?" she replied. "If you got to, you got to. Go, darling. I'll take care of the concession."

Greenberg no longer felt deserted and alone. He walked almost confidently to a doctor's office. Manfully, he explained his symptoms. The doctor listened with professional sympathy, until Greenberg reached his description of the water gnome.

Then his eyes glittered and narrowed. "I know just the thing for you, Mr. Greenberg," he interrupted. "Sit there until I come back."

Greenberg sat quietly. He even permitted himself a surge of hope. But it seemed only a moment later that he was vaguely conscious of a siren screaming toward him; and then he was overwhelmed by the doctor and two interns who pounced on him and tried to squeeze him into a bag.

He resisted, of course. He was terrified enough to punch wildly. "What are you doing to me?" he shrieked. "Don't put that thing on me!"

"Easy now," the doctor soothed. "Everything will be all right."

It was on that humiliating scene that the policeman, required by law to accompany public ambulances, appeared. "What's up?" he asked.

"Don't stand there, you fathead," an intern shouted. "This man's crazy. Help us get him into this strait jacket."

But the policeman approached indecisively. "Take it easy, Mr. Greenberg. They ain't gonna hurt you while I'm here. What's it all about?"

"Mike!" Greenberg cried, and clung to his protector's sleeve. "They think I'm crazy—"

"Of course he's crazy," the doctor stated. "He came in here with a fantastic yarn about a water gnome putting a curse on him."

"What kind of a curse, Mr. Greenberg?" Mike asked cautiously.

"I got into an argument with the water gnome who makes it rain and takes care of the fish," Greenberg blurted. "I tore up his hat. Now he won't let water touch me. I can't drink, or anything—"

The doctor nodded. "There you are. Absolutely insane."

"Shut up." For a long moment Mike stared curiously at Greenberg. Then: "Did any of you scientists think of testing him? Here, Mr. Greenberg." He poured water into a paper cup and held it out.

Greenberg moved to take it. The water backed up against the cup's far lip; when he took it in his hand, the water shot out into the air.

"Crazy, is he?" Mike asked with heavy irony. "I guess you don't know there's things like gnomes and elves. Come with me, Mr. Greenberg."

They went out together and walked toward the boardwalk. Greenberg told Mike the entire story and explained how, besides being so uncomfortable to him personally, it would ruin him financially.

"Well, doctors can't help you," Mike said at length. "What do they know about the Little Folk? And I can't say I blame you for sassing the gnome. You ain't Irish or you'd have spoke with more respect to him. Anyhow, you're thirsty. Can't you drink *anything?*"

"Not a thing," Greenberg said mournfully.

They entered the concession. A single glance told Greenberg that business was very quiet, but even that could not lower his feelings more than they already were. Esther clutched him as soon as she saw them.

"Well?" she asked anxiously.

Greenberg shrugged in despair. "Nothing. He thought I was crazy."

Mike stared at the bar. Memory seemed to struggle, behind his reflective eyes. "Sure," he said after a long pause. "Did you try beer, Mr. Greenberg? When I was a boy my old mother told me all about elves and gnomes and the rest of the Little Folk. She knew them, all right. They don't touch alcohol, you know. Try drawing a glass of beer—"

Greenberg trudged obediently behind the bar and held a glass under the spigot. Suddenly his despondent face brightened. Beer creamed into the glass—and stayed there! Mike and Esther grinned at each other as Greenberg threw back his head and furiously drank.

"Mike!" he crowed. "I'm saved. You got to drink with me!"

"Well—" Mike protested feebly.

By late afternoon, Esther had to close the concession and take her husband and Mike to the hotel.

The following day, being Saturday, brought a flood of rain. Greenberg nursed an imposing hangover that was constantly aggravated by his having to drink beer in order to satisfy his recurring thirst. He thought of forbidden ice bags and alkaline drinks in an agony of longing.

"I can't stand it!" he groaned. "Beer for breakfast—phooey!"

"It's better than nothing," Esther said fatalistically.

"So help me, I don't know if it is. But, darling, you ain't mad at me on account of Sammie, are you?"

She smiled gently. "Poo! Talk dowry and he'll come back quick."

"That's what I thought. But what am I going to do about my curse?"

Cheerfully Mike furled an umbrella and strode in with a little old woman, whom he introduced as his mother. Greenberg enviously saw evidence of the effectiveness of ice bags and alkaline drinks, for Mike had been just as high as he the day before.

"Mike told me about you and the gnome," the old lady said. "Now I know the Little Folk well, and I don't hold you to blame for insulting him, seeing you never met a gnome before. But I suppose you want to get rid of your curse. Are you repentant?"

Greenberg shuddered. "Beer for breakfast! Can you ask?"

"Well, just you go to this lake and give the gnome proof."

"What kind of proof?" Greenberg asked eagerly.

"Bring him sugar. The Little Folk love the stuff—"

Greenberg beamed. "Did you hear that, Esther? I'll get a barrel—"

"They love sugar, but they can't eat it," the old lady broke in. "It melts in water. You got to figure out a way so it won't. Then the little gentleman'll know you're repentant for real."

"A-ha!" Greenberg cried. "I knew there was a catch!"

There was a sympathetic silence while his agitated mind attacked the problem from all angles. Then the old lady said in awe: "The minute I saw your place I knew Mike had told the truth. I never seen a sight like it in my life—rain coming down, like the flood, everywhere else; but all around this place, in a big circle, it's dry as a bone!"

While Greenberg scarcely heard her, Mike nodded and Esther seemed peculiarly interested in the phenomenon. When he admitted defeat and came out of his reflected stupor, he was alone in the concession, with only a vague memory of Esther's saying she would not be back for several hours.

"What am I going to do?" he muttered. "Sugar that won't melt—" He drew a glass of beer and drank it thoughtfully. "Particular they got to be yet. Ain't it good enough if I bring simple syrup—that's sweet."

He pottered about the place, looking for something to do. He could not polish the fountain on the bar, and the few frankfurters broiling on the griddle probably would go to waste. The floor had already been swept. So he sat uneasily and worried his problem.

"Monday, no matter what," he resolved, "I'll go to the lake. It don't pay to go tomorrow. I'll only catch a cold because it'll rain."

At last Esther returned, smiling in a strange way. She was extremely gentle, tender and thoughtful; and for that he was appreciative. But that night and all day Sunday he understood the reason for her happiness.

She had spread word that, while it rained in every other place all over town, their concession was miraculously dry. So, besides a headache that made his body throb in rhythm to its vast pulse, Greenberg had to work like six men satisfying the crowd who mobbed the place to see the miracle and enjoy the dry warmth.

How much they took in will never be known. Greenberg made it a practice not to discuss such personal matters. But it is quite definite that not even in 1929 had he done so well over a single week end.

Very early Monday morning he was dressing quietly, not to disturb his wife. Esther, however, raised herself on her elbow and looked at him doubtfully.

"Herman," she called softly, "do you really have to go?"

He turned, puzzled. "What do you mean—do I have to go?"

"Well—" She hesitated. Then: "Couldn't you wait until the end of the season, Herman, darling?"

He staggered back a step, his face working in horror. "What kind of an idea is that for my own wife to have?" he croaked. "Beer I have to drink instead of water. How can I stand it? Do you think I *like* beer? I can't wash myself. Already people don't like to stand near me; and how will they act at the end of the season? I go around looking like a bum because my beard is too tough for an electric razor, and I'm all the time drunk—the first Greenberg to be a drunkard. I want to be respected—"

"I know, Herman, darling," she sighed. "But I thought for the sake of our Rosie—Such a business we've never done like we did this week end. If it rains every Saturday and Sunday, but not on our concession, we'll make a *fortune!*"

"Esther!" Herman cried, shocked. "Doesn't my health mean anything?"

"Of course, darling. Only I thought maybe you could stand it for—"

He snatched his hat, tie and jacket, and slammed the door. Outside, though, he stood indeterminedly. He could hear his wife crying, and he realized that, if he succeeded in getting the gnome to remove the curse, he would forfeit an opportunity to make a great deal of money.

He finished dressing more slowly. Esther was right, to a certain extent. If he could tolerate his waterless condition—

"No!" he gritted decisively. "Already my friends avoid me. It isn't right that a respectable man like me should always be drunk and not take a bath. So we'll make less money. Money isn't everything—"

And with great determination, he went to the lake.

But that evening, before going home, Mike walked out of his way to stop in at the concession. He found Greenberg sitting on a chair, his head in his hands, and his body rocking slowly in anguish.

"What is it, Mr. Greenberg?" he asked gently.

Greenberg looked up. His eyes were dazed. "Oh, you, Mike," he said blankly. Then his gaze cleared, grew more intelligent, and he stood up and led Mike to the bar. Silently, they drank beer. "I went to the lake today," he said hollowly. "I walked all around it hollering like mad. The gnome didn't stick his head out of the water once."

"I know," Mike nodded sadly. "They're busy all the time."

Greenberg spread his hands imploringly. "So what can I do? I can't write him a letter or send him a telegram; he ain't got a door to knock on or a bell for me to ring. How do I get him to come up and talk?"

His shoulders sagged. "Here, Mike. Have a cigar. You been a real good friend, but I guess we're licked."

They stood in an awkward silence. Finally Mike blurted: "Real hot, today. A regular scorcher."

"Yeah. Esther says business was pretty good, if it keeps up."

Mike fumbled at the cellophane wrapper. Greenberg said: "Anyhow, suppose I did talk to the gnome. What about the sugar?"

The silence dragged itself out, became tense and uncomfortable. Mike was distinctly embarrassed. His brusque nature was not adapted for comforting discouraged friends. With immense concentration he rolled the cigar between his fingers and listened for a rustle.

"Day like this's hell on cigars," he mumbled, for the sake of conversation. "Dries them like nobody's business. This one ain't, though."

"Yeah," Greenberg said abstractedly. "Cellophane keeps them—"

They looked suddenly at each other, their faces clean of expression.

"Holy smoke!" Mike yelled.

"Cellophane on sugar!" Greenberg choked out.

"Yeah," Mike whispered in awe. "I'll switch my day off with Joe, and I'll go to the lake with you tomorrow. I'll call for you early."

Greenberg pressed his hand, too strangled by emotion for speech. When Esther came to relieve him, he left her at the concession with only the inexperienced griddle boy to assist her, while he searched the village for cubes of sugar wrapped in cellophane.

The sun had scarcely risen when Mike reached the hotel, but Greenberg had long been dressed and stood on the porch waiting impatiently. Mike was genuinely anxious for his friend. Greenberg staggered along toward the station, his eyes almost crossed with the pain of a terrific hangover.

They stopped at a cafeteria for breakfast. Mike ordered orange juice, bacon and eggs, and coffee half-and-half. When he heard the order, Greenberg had to gag down a lump in his throat.

"What'll you have?" the counterman asked.

Greenberg flushed. "Beer," he said hoarsely.

"You kidding me?" Greenberg shook his head, unable to speak. "Want anything with it? Cereal, pie, toast—"

"Just beer." And he forced himself to swallow it. "So help me," he hissed at Mike, "another beer for breakfast will kill me!"

"I know how it is," Mike said around a mouthful of food.

On the train they attempted to make plans. But they were faced by a phenomenon that neither had encountered before, and so they got nowhere. They walked glumly to the lake, fully aware that they would have to employ the empirical method of discarding tactics that did not work.

"How about a boat?" Mike suggested.

"It won't stay in the water with me in it. And you can't row it."

"Well, what'll we do then?"

Greenberg bit his lip and stared at the beautiful blue lake. There the gnome lived, so near to them. "Go through the woods along the shore, and holler like hell. I'll go the opposite way. We'll pass each other and meet at the boathouse. If the gnome comes up, yell for me."

"O.K.," Mike said, not very confidently.

The lake was quite large and they walked slowly around it, pausing often to get the proper distance for particularly emphatic shouts. But two hours later, when they stood opposite each other with the full diameter of the lake between them, Greenberg heard Mike's hoarse voice: "Hey, gnome!"

"Hey, gnome!" Greenberg yelled. "Come on up!"

A hour later they crossed paths. They were tired, discouraged, and their throats burned; and only fishermen disturbed the lake's surface.

"The hell with this," Mike said. "It ain't doing any good. Let's go back to the boathouse."

"What'll we do?" Greenberg rasped. "I can't give up!"

They trudged back around the lake, shouting half-heartedly. At the boathouse, Greenberg had to admit that he was beaten. The boathouse owner marched threateningly toward him.

"Why don't you maniacs get away from here?" he barked. "What's the idea of hollering and scaring away the fish? The guys are sore—"

"We're not going to holler any more," Greenberg said. "It's no use."

When they bought beer and Mike, on an impulse, hired a boat, the owner cooled off with amazing rapidity, and went off to unpack bait.

"What did you get a boat for?" Greenberg asked. "I can't ride in it."

"You're not going to. You're gonna walk."

"Around the lake again?" Greenberg cried.

"Nope. Look, Mr. Greenberg. Maybe the gnome can't hear us through all that water. Gnomes ain't hardhearted. If he heard us and thought you were sorry, he'd take his curse off you in a jiffy."

"Maybe." Greenberg was not convinced. "So where do I come in?"

"The way I figure it, some way or other you push water away, but the water pushes you away just as hard. Anyhow, I hope so. If it does, you can walk on the lake." As he spoke, Mike had been lifting large stones and dumping them on the bottom of the boat. "Give me a hand with these."

Any activity, however useless, was better than none, Greenberg felt.

He helped Mike fill the boat until just the gunwales were above water. Then Mike got in and shoved off.

"Come on," Mike said. "Try to walk on the water."

Greenberg hesitated. "Suppose I can't?"

"Nothing'll happen to you. You can't get wet; so you won't drown."

The logic of Mike's statement reassured Greenberg. He stepped out boldly. He experienced a peculiar sense of accomplishment when the water hastily retreated under his feet into pressure bowls, and an unseen, powerful force buoyed him upright across the lake's surface. Though his footing was not too secure, with care he was able to walk quite swiftly.

"Now what?" he asked, almost happily.

Mike had kept pace with him in the boat. He shipped his oars and passed Greenberg a rock. "We'll drop them all over the lake—make it damned noisy down there and upset the place. That'll get him up."

They were more hopeful now, and their comments, "Here's one that'll wake him," and "I'll hit him right on the noodle with this one," served to cheer them still further. And less than half the rocks had been dropped when Greenberg halted, a boulder in his hands. Something inside him wrapped itself tightly around his heart and his jaw dropped.

Mike followed his awed, joyful gaze. To himself, Mike had to admit that the gnome, propelling himself through the water with his ears, arms folded in tremendous dignity, was a funny sight.

"Must you drop rocks and disturb us at our work?" the gnome asked.

Greenberg gulped. "I'm sorry, Mr. Gnome," he said nervously. "I couldn't get you to come up by yelling."

The gnome looked at him. "Oh. You are the mortal who was disciplined. Why did you return?"

"To tell you that I'm sorry, and I won't insult you again."

"Have you proof of your sincerity?" the gnome asked quietly.

Greenberg fished furiously in his pocket and brought out a handful of sugar wrapped in cellophane, which he tremblingly handed to the gnome.

"Ah, very clever, indeed," the little man said, unwrapping a cube and popping it eagerly into his mouth. "Long time since I've had some."

A moment later Greenberg spluttered and floundered under the surface. Even if Mike had not caught his jacket and helped him up, he could almost have enjoyed the sensation of being able to drown.

L. Sprague de Camp

The Gnarly Man

L. Sprague de Camp is a seminal figure, one whose career spans almost the entire development of modern fantasy and SF. Much of the luster of the "Golden Age" of *Astounding* during the late 1930s and the 1940s is due to the presence in those pages of de Camp (along with his great contemporaries Robert A. Heinlein, Theodore Sturgeon, and A. E. van Vogt). At the same time, for *Astounding*'s sister fantasy magazine, *Unknown,* de Camp helped to create a whole new modern style of fantasy writing—funny, whimsical, and irreverent—of which he is still the most prominent practitioner. De Camp's stories for *Unknown* are among the best short fantasies ever written, and include such classics as "The Wheels of If," "Nothing in the Rules," "The Hardwood Pile," and (written in collaboration with Fletcher Pratt), the famous "Harold Shea" stories that would later be collected as *The Complete Enchanter.* In science fiction, he is the author of *Lest Darkness Fall,* in my opinion one of the three or four best Alternate Worlds novels ever written, as well as the at-the-time highly controversial novel *Rogue Queen,* and a body of expertly crafted short fiction such as "Judgment Day," "Divide and Rule," "A Gun for Dinosaur," and "Aristotle and the Gun."

De Camp's other books include *The Glory That Was, The Search for Zei, The Tower of Zanid, The Hostage of Zir, The Great Fetish, The Reluctant King* and, with Fletcher Pratt, *The Carnelian Cube* and *The Land of Unreason,* and the collection *Tales from Gavagan's Bar.* He has also written a long sequence of critically acclaimed historical novels, including *The Bronze God of Rhodes, An Elephant for Aristotle,* and *The Dragon of the Ishtar Gate,* as well as a number of nonfiction books on scientific and technical topics, literary biographies such as his painstaking examination of the life of H. P. Lovecraft, *Lovecraft: A Biography,* and *Dark Valley Destiny: The Life of Robert E. Howard* (written in collaboration with Catherine Crook de Camp and Jane Whittington Griffin), and critical/biographical studies of fantasy and fantasy writers such as *Literary Swordsmen and Sorcerers*. As an anthologist, he edited the historically significant *Swords & Sorcery* in 1963, an attempt to preserve and revive an at-the-time Endangered Literary Species he called "Heroic Fantasy," and many a young reader was introduced to Robert E. Howard's "Conan the Barbarian" stories or C. L. Moore's "Jirel of Joiry" stories for the first time in the pages of that anthology; he followed it up with two other important anthologies, *The Spell of Seven, The Fantastic Swordsmen,* and *Warlocks and Warriors*. His short fiction has been collected in *The Best of L. Sprague de Camp, A Gun for Dinosaur, The Purple Pterodactyls,* and *Rivers in Time*. De Camp has won the Grand Master Nebula Award, and the Gandalf or Grand Master of Fantasy Award. He lives in Texas with his wife, writer Catherine Crook de Camp, in collaboration with whom he has produced his most recent books, *The Stones of Nomuru, The Incorporated Knight, The Pixilated Peeress,* and *The Swords of Zinjahan*.

De Camp was the quintessential *Unknown* writer. Nobody did a better job than de Camp of capturing that elusive tone and mood—bright, playful, deliberately anachronistic, smart, sassy, ironic—that characterized the best of the stories from that magazine . . . and de Camp himself has rarely done a better job of writing an *"Unknown*-style" story than he does in the sly tale that follows, one of the most acclaimed and popular from *Unknown*'s first year of publication.

Dr. Matilda Saddler first saw the gnarly man on the evening of June 14, 1946, at Coney Island.

The spring meeting of the Eastern Section of the American Anthropological Association had broken up, and Dr. Saddler had had dinner with two of her professional colleagues, Blue of Columbia and Jeffcott of Yale. She mentioned that she had never visited Coney, and meant to go there that evening. She urged Blue and Jeffcott to come along, but they begged off.

Watching Dr. Saddler's retreating back, Blue of Columbia cackled: "The Wild Woman from Wichita. Wonder if she's hunting another husband?" He was a thin man with a small gray beard and a who-the-hell-are-you-sir expression.

"How many has she had?" asked Jeffcott of Yale.

"Two to date. Don't know why anthropologists lead the most disorderly private lives of any scientists. Must be that they study the customs and morals of all these different peoples, and ask themselves, 'If the Eskimos can do it, why can't we?' I'm old enough to be safe, thank God."

"I'm not afraid of her," said Jeffcott. He was in his early forties and looked like a farmer uneasy in store clothes. "I'm so very thoroughly married."

"Yeah? Ought to have been at Stanford a few years ago, when she was there. Wasn't safe to walk across the campus, with Tuthill chasing all the females and Saddler all the males."

Dr. Saddler had to fight her way off the subway train, as the adolescents who infest the platform of the B.M.T.'s Stillwell Avenue station are probably the worst-mannered people on earth, possibly excepting the Dobu Islanders, of the western Pacific. She didn't much mind. She was a tall, strongly built woman in her late thirties, who had been kept in trim by the outdoor rigors of her profession. Besides, some of the inane remarks in Swift's paper on acculturation among the Arapaho Indians had gotten her fighting blood up.

Walking down Surf Avenue toward Brighton Beach, she looked at the concessions without trying them, preferring to watch the human types that did and the other human types that took their money. She did try a shooting gallery, but found knocking tin owls off their perch with a .22 too easy to be much fun. Long-range work with an army rifle was her idea of shooting.

The concession next to the shooting gallery would have been called a side show if there had been a main show for it to be a side show to. The usual lurid banner proclaimed the uniqueness of the two-headed calf, the bearded woman, Arachne the spider girl, and other marvels. The pièce de resistance was Ungo-Bungo, the ferocious ape-man, captured in the Congo at a cost of twenty-seven lives. The picture showed an enormous Ungo-Bungo squeezing a hapless Negro in each hand, while others sought to throw a net over him.

Dr. Saddler knew perfectly well that the ferocious ape-man would turn out to be an ordinary Caucasian with false hair on his chest. But a streak of whimsicality impelled her to go in. Perhaps, she thought, she could have some fun with her colleagues about it.

The spieler went through his leather-lunged harangue. Dr. Saddler guessed from his expression that his feet hurt. The tattooed lady didn't interest her, as her decorations obviously had no cultural significance, as they have among the Polynesians. As for the ancient Mayan, Dr. Saddler thought it in questionable taste to exhibit a poor microcephalic idiot that way. Professor Yoki's legerdemain and fire eating weren't bad.

There was a curtain in front of Ungo-Bungo's cage. At the appropriate moment there were growls and the sound of a length of chain being slapped against a metal plate. The spieler wound up on a high note: "—ladies and gentlemen, the one and only UNGO-BUNGO!" The curtain dropped.

The ape-man was squatting at the back of his cage. He dropped his chain, got up, and shuffled forward. He grasped two of the bars and shook them. They were appropriately loose and rattled alarmingly. Ungo-Bungo snarled at the patrons, showing his even, yellow teeth.

Dr. Saddler stared hard. This was something new in the ape-man line. Ungo-Bungo was about five feet three, but very massive, with enormous hunched shoulders. Above and below his blue swimming trunks thick, grizzled hair covered him from crown to ankle. His short, stout-muscled arms ended in big hands with thick, gnarled fingers. His neck projected slightly forward, so that from the front he seemed to have but little neck at all.

His face—well, thought Dr. Saddler, she knew all the living races of men, and all the types of freak brought about by glandular maladjustment, and none of them had a face like *that*. It was deeply lined. The forehead between the short scalp hair and the brows on the huge supraorbital ridges receded sharply. The nose, although wide, was not apelike; it was a shortened version of the thick, hooked Armenoid nose, so often miscalled Jewish. The face ended in a long upper lip and a retreating chin. And the yellowish skin apparently belonged to Ungo-Bungo.

The curtain was whisked up again.

Dr. Saddler went out with the others, but paid another dime, and soon was back inside. She paid no attention to the spieler, but got a good position in front of Ungo-Bungo's cage before the rest of the crowd arrived.

Ungo-Bungo repeated his performance with mechanical precision. Dr. Saddler noticed that he limped a little as he came forward to rattle the bars, and that the skin under his mat of hair bore several big whitish scars. The last joint of his left ring finger was missing. She noted certain things about the proportions of his shin and thigh, of his forearm and upper arm, and his big splay feet.

Dr. Saddler paid a third dime. An idea was knocking at her mind somewhere. If she let it in, either she was crazy or physical anthropology was haywire or—something. But she knew that if she did the sensible thing, which was to go home, the idea would plague her from now on.

After the third performance she spoke to the spieler. "I think your Mr. Ungo-Bungo used to be a friend of mine. Could you arrange for me to see him after he finishes?"

The spieler checked his sarcasm. His questioner was so obviously not a—not the sort of dame who asks to see guys after they finish.

"Oh, him," he said. "Calls himself Gaffney—Clarence Aloysius Gaffney. That the guy you want?"

"Why, yes."

"I guess you can." He looked at his watch. "He's got four more turns to do before we close. I'll have to ask the boss." He popped through a curtain and called, "Hey, Morrie!" Then he was back. "It's O. K. Morrie says you can wait in his office. Foist door to the right."

Morrie was stout, bald, and hospitable. "Sure, sure," he said, waving his cigar. "Glad to be of soivice, Miss Saddler. Chust a min while I talk to Gaffney's manager." He stuck his head out. "Hey, Pappas! Lady wants to talk to your ape-man later. I meant *lady*. O. K." He returned to orate on the difficulties besetting the freak business. "You take this Gaffney, now. He's the best damn ape-man in the business; all that hair rilly grows outa him. And the poor guy rilly has a face like that. But do people believe it? No! I hear 'em going out, saying about how the hair is pasted on, and the whole thing is a fake. It's mawtifying." He cocked his head, listening. "That rumble wasn't no rolly-coaster; it's gonna rain. Hope it's over by tomorrow. You wouldn't believe the way a rain can knock ya receipts off. If you drew a coive, it would be like this." He drew his finger horizontally through space, jerking it down sharply to indicate the effect of rain. "But as I said, people don't appreciate what you try to do for 'em. It's not just the money; I think of myself as an ottist. A creative ottist. A show like this got to have balance and propawtion, like any other ott—"

It must have been an hour later when a slow, deep voice at the door said: "Did somebody want to see me?"

The gnarly man was in the doorway. In street clothes, with the collar of his raincoat turned up and his hat brim pulled down, he looked more or less human, though the coat fitted his great, sloping shoulders badly. He had a thick, knobby walking stick with a leather loop near the top end. A small, dark man fidgeted behind him.

"Yeah," said Morrie, interrupting his lecture. "Clarence, this is Miss Saddler. Miss Saddler, this is Mr. Gaffney, one of our outstanding creative ottists."

"Pleased to meetcha," said the gnarly man. "This is my manager, Mr. Pappas."

Dr. Saddler explained, and said she'd like to talk to Mr. Gaffney if she might. She was tactful; you had to be to pry into the private affairs of Naga headhunters, for instance. The gnarly man said he'd be glad to have a cup of coffee with Miss Saddler; there was a place around the corner that they could reach without getting wet.

As they started out, Pappas followed, fidgeting more and more. The gnarly man said: "Oh, go home to bed, John. Don't worry about me." He grinned at Dr. Saddler. The effect would have been unnerving to anyone but an anthropologist. "Every time he sees me talking to anybody, he thinks it's some other manager trying to steal me." He spoke general American, with a suggestion of Irish brogue in the lowering of the vowels in words like "man" and "talk." "I made the lawyer who drew up our contract fix it so it can be ended on short notice."

Pappas departed, still looking suspicious. The rain had practically ceased. The gnarly man stepped along smartly despite his limp.

A woman passed with a fox terrier on a leash. The dog sniffed in the direction of the gnarly man, and then to all appearances went crazy, yelping and slavering. The gnarly man shifted his grip on the massive stick and said quietly, "Better hang onto him, ma'am." The woman departed hastily. "They just don't like me," commented Gaffney. "Dogs, that is."

They found a table and ordered their coffee. When the gnarly man took off his raincoat, Dr. Saddler became aware of a strong smell of cheap perfume. He got out a pipe with a big knobby bowl. It suited him, just as the walking stick did. Dr. Saddler noticed that the deep-sunk eyes under the beetling arches were light hazel.

"Well?" he said in his rumbling drawl.

She began her questions.

"My parents were Irish," he answered. "But I was born in South Boston . . . let's see . . . forty-six years ago. I can get you a copy of my birth certificate. Clarence Aloysius Gaffney, May 2, 1900." He seemed to get some secret amusement out of that statement.

"Were either of your parents of your somewhat unusual physical type?"

He paused before answering. He always did, it seemed. "Uh-huh. Both of 'em. Glands, I suppose."

"Were they both born in Ireland?"

"Yep. County Sligo." Again that mysterious twinkle.

She thought. "Mr. Gaffney, you wouldn't mind having some photographs and measurements made, would you? You could use the photographs in your business."

"Maybe." He took a sip. "Ouch! Gazooks, that's hot!"

"What?"

"I said the coffee's hot."

"I mean, before that."

The gnarly man looked a little embarrassed. "Oh, you mean the 'gazooks'? Well, I . . . uh . . . once knew a man who used to say that."

"Mr. Gaffney, I'm a scientist, and I'm not trying to get anything out of you for my own sake. You can be frank with me."

There was something remote and impersonal in his stare that gave her a slight spinal chill. "Meaning that I haven't been so far?"

"Yes. When I saw you I decided that there was something extraordinary in your background. I still think there is. Now, if you think I'm crazy, say so and we'll drop the subject. But I want to get to the bottom of this."

He took his time about answering. "That would depend." There was another pause. Then he said: "With your connections, do you know any really first-class surgeons?"

"But . . . yes, I know Dunbar."

"The guy who wears a purple gown when he operates? The guy who wrote a book on 'God, Man, and the Universe'?"

"Yes. He's a good man, in spite of his theatrical mannerisms. Why? What would you want of him?"

"Not what you're thinking. I'm satisfied with my . . . uh . . . unusual physical type. But I have some old injuries—broken bones that didn't knit properly—that I want fixed up. He'd have to be a good man, though. I have a couple of thousand dollars in the savings bank, but I know the sort of fees those guys charge. If you could make the necessary arrangements—"

"Why, yes, I'm sure I could. In fact, I could guarantee it. Then I *was* right? And you'll—" She hesitated.

"Come clean? Uh-huh. But remember, I can still prove I'm Clarence Aloysius if I have to."

"Who *are* you, then?"

Again there was a long pause. Then the gnarly man said: "Might as well tell you. As soon as you repeat any of it, you'll have put your professional reputation in my hands, remember.

"First off, I wasn't born in Massachusetts. I was born on the upper Rhine, near Mommenheim. And I was born, as nearly as I can figure out, about the year 50,000 B.C."

Matilda Saddler wondered whether she'd stumbled on the biggest thing in anthropology, or whether this bizarre personality was making Baron Munchausen look like a piker.

He seemed to guess her thoughts. "I can't prove that, of course. But so long as you arrange about that operation, I don't care whether you believe me or not."

"But . . . but . . . *how?*"

"I think the lightning did it. We were out trying to drive some bison into a pit. Well, this big thunderstorm came up, and the bison bolted in the wrong direction. So we gave up and tried to find shelter. And the next thing I knew I was lying on the ground with the rain running over me, and the rest of the clan standing around wailing about what had they done to get the storm god sore at them, so he made a bull's-eye on one of their best hunters. They'd never said *that* about me before. It's funny how you're never appreciated while you're alive.

"But I was alive, all right. My nerves were pretty well shot for a few weeks, but otherwise I was O. K., except for some burns on the soles of my feet. I don't know just what happened, except I was reading a couple of years ago that scientists had located the machinery that controls the replacement of tissue in the medulla oblongata. I think maybe the lightning did something to my medulla to speed it up. Anyway, I never got any older after that. Physically, that is. I was thirty-three at the time, more or less. We didn't keep track of ages. I look older now, because the lines in your face are bound to get sort of set after a few thousand years, and because our hair was always gray at the ends. But I can still tie an ordinary *Homo sapiens* in a knot if I want to."

"Then you're . . . you mean to say you're . . . you're trying to tell me you're—"

"A Neanderthal man? *Homo neanderthalensis?* That's right."

Matilda Saddler's hotel room was a bit crowded, with the gnarly man, the frosty Blue, the rustic Jeffcott, Dr. Saddler herself, and Harold McGannon, the historian. This McGannon was a small man, very neat and pink-skinned. He looked more like a New York Central director than a professor. Just now his expression was one of fascination. Dr. Saddler looked full of pride; Professor Jeffcott looked interested but puzzled; Dr. Blue looked bored—he hadn't wanted to come in the first place. The gnarly man, stretched out in the most comfortable chair and puffing his overgrown pipe, seemed to be enjoying himself.

McGannon was formulating a question. "Well, Mr.—Gaffney? I suppose that's your name as much as any."

"You might say so," said the gnarly man. "My original name meant something like Shining Hawk. But I've gone under hundreds of names since then. If you register in a hotel as 'Shining Hawk,' it's apt to attract attention. And I try to avoid that."

"Why?" asked McGannon.

The gnarly man looked at his audience as one might look at willfully stupid children. "I don't like trouble. The best way to keep out of trouble is not to attract attention. That's why I have to pull up stakes and move every ten or fifteen years. People might get curious as to why I never got any older."

"Pathological liar," murmured Blue. The words were barely audible, but the gnarly man heard them.

"You're entitled to your opinion, Dr. Blue," he said affably. "Dr. Saddler's doing me a favor, so in return I'm letting you all shoot questions at me. And I'm answering. I don't give a damn whether you believe me or not."

McGannon hastily threw in another question. "How is it that you have a birth certificate, as you say you have?"

"Oh, I knew a man named Clarence Gaffney once. He got killed by an automobile, and I took his name."

"Was there any reason for picking this Irish background?"

"Are you Irish, Dr. McGannon?"

"Not enough to matter."

"O. K. I didn't want to hurt any feelings. It's my best bet. There are real Irishmen with upper lips like mine."

Dr. Saddler broke in. "I meant to ask you, Clarence." She put a lot of warmth into his name. "There's an argument as to whether your people interbred with mine, when mine overran Europe at the end of the

Mousterian. Some scientists have thought that some modern Europeans, especially along the west coast of Ireland, might have a little Neanderthal blood."

He grinned slightly. "Well—yes and no. There never was any back in the Stone Age, as far as I know. But these long-lipped Irish are my fault."

"How?"

"Believe it or not, but in the last fifty centuries there have been some women of your species that didn't find me too repulsive. Usually there were no offspring. But in the sixteenth century I went to Ireland to live. They were burning too many people for witchcraft in the rest of Europe to suit me at that time. And there was a woman. The result this time was a flock of hybrids—cute little devils, they were. So the Irishmen who look like me are my descendants."

"What did happen to your people?" asked McGannon. "Were they killed off?"

The gnarly man shrugged. "Some of them. We weren't at all warlike. But then the tall ones, as we called them, weren't either. Some of the tribes of the tall ones looked on us as legitimate prey, but most of them let us severely alone. I guess they were almost as scared of us as we were of them. Savages as primitive as that are really pretty peaceable people. You have to work so hard to keep fed, and there are so few of you, that there's no object in fighting wars. That comes later, when you get agriculture and livestock, so you have something worth stealing.

"I remember that a hundred years after the tall ones had come, there were still Neanderthalers living in my part of the country. But they died out. I think it was that they lost their ambition. The tall ones were pretty crude, but they were so far ahead of us that our things and our customs seemed silly. Finally we just sat around and lived on the scraps we could beg from the tall ones' camps. You might say we died of an inferiority complex."

"What happened to you?" asked McGannon.

"Oh, I was a god among my own people by then, and naturally I represented them in their dealings with the tall ones. I got to know the tall ones pretty well, and they were willing to put up with me after all my own clan were dead. Then in a couple of hundred years they'd forgotten all about my people, and took me for a hunchback or something. I got to be pretty good at flint working, so I could earn my keep. When metal came in, I went into that, and finally into blacksmithing. If you'd put all the horseshoes I've made in a pile, they'd—well, you'd have a damn big pile of horseshoes, anyway."

"Did you . . . ah . . . limp at that time?" asked McGannon.

"Uh-huh. I busted my leg back in the Neolithic. Fell out of a tree, and had to set it myself, because there wasn't anybody around. Why?"

"Vulcan," said McGannon softly.

"Vulcan?" repeated the gnarly man. "Wasn't he a Greek god or something?"

"Yes. He was the lame blacksmith of the gods."

"You mean you think that maybe somebody got the idea from me? That's an interesting theory. Little late to check up on it, though."

Blue leaned forward and said crisply: "Mr. Gaffney, no real Neanderthal man could talk as fluently and entertainingly as you do. That's shown by the poor development of the frontal lobes of the brain and the attachments of the tongue muscles."

The gnarly man shrugged again. "You can believe what you like. My own clan considered me pretty smart, and then you're bound to learn something in fifty thousand years."

Dr. Saddler beamed. "Tell them about your teeth, Clarence."

The gnarly man grinned. "They're false, of course. My own lasted a long time, but they still wore out somewhere back in the Paleolithic. I grew a third set, and they wore out, too. So I had to invent soup."

"You *what?*" It was the usually taciturn Jeffcott.

"I had to invent soup, to keep alive. You know, the bark-dish-and-hot-stones method. My gums got pretty tough after a while, but they still weren't much good for chewing hard stuff. So after a few thousand years I got pretty sick of soup and mushy foods generally. And when metal came in I began experimenting with false teeth. Bone teeth in copper plates. You might say I invented them, too. I tried often to sell them, but they never really caught on until around 1750 A. D. I was living in Paris then, and I built up quite a little business before I moved on." He pulled the handkerchief out of his breast pocket to wipe his forehead; Blue made a face as the wave of perfume reached him.

"Well, Mr. Shining Hawk," snapped Blue with a trace of sarcasm, "how do you like our machine age?"

The gnarly man ignored the tone of the question. "It's not bad. Lots of interesting things happen. The main trouble is the shirts."

"Shirts?"

"Uh-huh. Just try to buy a shirt with a twenty neck and a twenty-nine sleeve. I have to order 'em special. It's almost as bad with hats and shoes. I wear an eight and one half hat and a thirteen shoe." He looked at his watch. "I've got to get back to Coney to work."

McGannon jumped up. "Where can I get in touch with you again, Mr. Gaffney? There's lots of things I'd like to ask you."

The gnarly man told him. "I'm free mornings. My working hours are two to midnight on weekdays, with a couple of hours off for dinner. Union rules, you know."

"You mean there's a union for you show people?"

"Sure. Only they call it a guild. They think they're artists, you know. Artists don't have unions; they have guilds. But it amounts to the same thing."

Blue and Jeffcott saw the gnarly man and the historian walking slowly toward the subway together. Blue said: "Poor old Mac! Always thought he had sense. Looks like he's swallowed this Gaffney's ravings, hook, line, and sinker."

"I'm not so sure," said Jeffcott, frowning. "There's something funny about the business."

"What?" barked Blue. "Don't tell me that *you* believe this story of being alive fifty thousand years? A caveman who uses perfume! Good God!"

"N-no," said Jeffcott. "Not the fifty thousand part. But I don't think it's a simple case of paranoia or plain lying, either. And the perfume's quite logical, if he were telling the truth."

"Huh?"

"Body odor. Saddler told us how dogs hate him. He'd have a smell different from ours. We're so used to ours that we don't even know we have one, unless somebody goes without a bath for a month. But we might notice his if he didn't disguise it."

Blue snorted. "You'll be believing him yourself in a minute. It's an obvious glandular case, and he's made up this story to fit. All that talk about not caring whether we believe him or not is just bluff. Come on, let's get some lunch. Say, see the way Saddler looked at him every time she said 'Clarence'? Like a hungry wolf. Wonder what she thinks she's going to do with him?"

Jeffcott thought. "I can guess. And if he *is* telling the truth, I think there's something in Deuteronomy against it."

The great surgeon made a point of looking like a great surgeon, to pince-nez and Vandyke. He waved the X-ray negatives at the gnarly man, pointing out this and that.

"We'd better take the leg first," he said. "Suppose we do that next Thursday. When you've recovered from that we can tackle the shoulder. It'll all take time, you know."

The gnarly man agreed, and shuffled out of the little private hospital to where McGannon awaited him in his car. The gnarly man described the tentative schedule of operations, and mentioned that he had made arrangements to quit his job. "Those two are the main thing," he said. "I'd like to try professional wrestling again some day, and I can't unless I get this shoulder fixed so I can raise my left arm over my head."

"What happened to it?" asked McGannon.

The gnarly man closed his eyes, thinking. "Let me see. I get things mixed up sometimes. People do when they're only fifty years old, so you can imagine what it's like for me.

"In 42 B. C. I was living with the Bituriges in Gaul. You remember that Cæsar shut up Werkinghetorich—Vercingetorix to you—in Alesia, and the confederacy raised an army of relief under Caswollon."

"Caswollon?"

The gnarly man laughed shortly. "I meant Wercaswollon. Caswollon was a Briton, wasn't he? I'm always getting those two mixed up.

"Anyhow, I got drafted. That's all you can call it; I didn't want to go. It wasn't exactly *my* war. But they wanted me because I could pull twice as heavy a bow as anybody else.

"When the final attack on Cæsar's ring of fortifications came, they sent me forward with some other archers to provide a covering fire for their infantry. At least, that was the plan. Actually, I never saw such a hopeless muddle in my life. And before I even got within bowshot, I fell into one of the Romans' covered pits. I didn't land on the point of the stake, but I fetched up against the side of it and busted my shoulder. There wasn't any help, because the Gauls were too busy running away from Cæsar's German cavalry to bother about wounded men."

The author of "God, Man, and the Universe" gazed after his departing patient. He spoke to his head assistant: "What do you think of him?"

"I think it's so," said the assistant. "I looked over those X rays pretty closely. That skeleton never belonged to a human being. And it has more healed fractures than you'd think possible."

"Hm-m-m," said Dunbar. "That's right, he wouldn't be human, would he? Hm-m-m. You know, if anything happened to him—"

The assistant grinned understandingly. "Of course, there's the S.P.C.A."

"We needn't worry about *them*. Hm-m-m." He thought, you've been slipping; nothing big in the papers for a year. But if you published a complete anatomical description of a Neanderthal man—or if you found out why his medulla functions the way it does—Hm-m-m. Of course, it would have to be managed properly—

"Let's have lunch at the Natural History Museum," said McGannon. "Some of the people there ought to know you."

"O. K.," drawled the gnarly man. "Only I've still got to get back to Coney afterward. This is my last day. Tomorrow, Pappas and I are going up to see our lawyer about ending our contract. Guy named Robinette. It's a dirty trick on poor old John, but I warned him at the start that this might happen."

"I suppose we can come up to interview you while you're . . . ah . . . convalescing? Fine. Have you ever been to the museum, by the way?"

"Sure," said the gnarly man. "I get around."

"What did you . . . ah . . . think of their stuff in the Hall of the Age of Man?"

"Pretty good. There's a little mistake in one of those big wall paintings. The second horn on the woolly rhinoceros ought to slant forward more. I thought of writing them a letter. But you know how it is. They'd say: 'Were you there?' and I'd say, 'Uh-huh,' and they'd say, 'Another nut.' "

"How about the pictures and busts of Paleolithic men?"

"Pretty good. But they have some funny ideas. They always show us with skins wrapped around our middles. In summer we didn't wear skins, and in winter we hung them around our shoulders, where they'd do some good.

"And then they show those tall ones that you call Cro-Magnon men clean-shaven. As I remember, they all had whiskers. What would they shave with?"

"I think," said McGannon, "that they leave the beards off the busts to . . . ah . . . show the shape of the chins. With the beards they'd all look too much alike."

"Is that the reason? They might say so on the labels." The gnarly man rubbed his own chin, such as it was. "I wish beards would come back into style. I look much more human with a beard. I got along fine in the sixteenth century when everybody had whiskers.

"That's one of the ways I remember when things happened, by the hair-cuts and whiskers that people had. I remember when a wagon I was dri-ving in Milan lost a wheel and spilled flour bags from hell to breakfast. That must have been in the sixteenth century, before I went to Ireland, because I remember that most of the men in the crowd that collected had beards. Now—wait a minute—maybe that was the fourteenth. There were a lot of beards then, too."

"Why, why didn't you keep a diary?" asked McGannon with a groan of exasperation.

The gnarly man shrugged characteristically. "And pack around six trunks full of paper every time I moved? No, thanks."

"I . . . ah . . . don't suppose you could give me the real story of Richard III and the princes in the tower?"

"Why should I? I was just a poor blacksmith, or farmer, or something most of the time. I didn't go around with the big shots. I gave up all my ideas of ambition a long time before that. I had to, being so different from other people. As far as I can remember, the only real king I ever got a good look at was Charlemagne, when he made a speech in Paris one day. He was just a big, tall man with Santa Claus whiskers and a squeaky voice."

Next morning McGannon and the gnarly man had a session with Sved-berg at the museum. Then McGannon drove Gaffney around to the lawyer's office, on the third floor of a seedy office building in the West Fifties. James Robinette looked something like a movie actor and something like a chipmunk. He looked at his watch and said to McGannon: "This won't take long. If you'd like to stick around, I'd be glad to have lunch with you." The fact was that he was feeling just a trifle queasy about being left with this damn queer client, this circus freak or whatever he was, with his barrel body and his funny slow drawl.

When the business had been completed, and the gnarly man had gone off with his manager to wind up his affairs at Coney, Robinette said: "Whew! I thought he was a half-wit, from his looks. But there was nothing half-witted about the way he went over those clauses. You'd have thought the damn contract was for building a subway system. What *is* he, anyhow?"

McGannon told him what he knew.

The lawyer's eyebrows went up. "Do you *believe* his yarn? Oh, I'll take tomato juice and filet of sole with tartar sauce—only without the tartar sauce—on the lunch, please."

"The same for me. Answering your question, Robinette, I do. So does Saddler. So does Svedberg up at the museum. They're both top-notchers in their respective fields. Saddler and I have interviewed him, and Svedberg's examined him physically. But it's just opinion. Fred Blue still swears it's a hoax or . . . ah . . . some sort of dementia. Neither of us can prove anything."

"Why not?"

"Well . . . ah . . . how are you going to prove that he was, or was not, alive a hundred years ago? Take one case: Clarence says he ran a sawmill in Fairbanks, Alaska, in 1906 and '07, under the name of Michael Shawn. How are you going to find out whether there was a sawmill operator in Fairbanks at that time? And if you did stumble on a record of a Michael Shawn, how would you know whether he and Clarence were the same? There's not a chance in a thousand that there'd be a photograph or a detailed description that you could check with. And you'd have an awful time trying to find anybody who remembered him at this late date.

"Then, Svedberg poked around Clarence's face, yesterday, and said that no *Homo sapiens* ever had a pair of zygomatic arches like that. But when I told Blue that, he offered to produce photographs of a human skull that did. I know what'll happen. Blue will say that the arches are practically the same, and Svedberg will say that they're obviously different. So there we'll be."

Robinette mused, "He does seem damned intelligent for an ape-man."

"He's not an ape-man, really. The Neanderthal race was a separate branch of the human stock; they were more primitive in some ways and more advanced in others than we are. Clarence may be slow, but he usually grinds out the right answer. I imagine that he was . . . ah . . . brilliant, for one of his kind, to begin with. And he's had the benefit of so much experience. He knows an incredible lot. He knows us; he sees through us and our motives."

The little pink man puckered up his forehead. "I do hope nothing happens to him. He's carrying around a lot of priceless information in that big head of his. Simply priceless. Not much about war and politics; he kept clear of those as a matter of self-preservation. But little things, about how people lived and how they thought thousands of years ago. He gets his periods mixed up sometimes, but he gets them straightened out if you give him time.

"I'll have to get hold of Pell, the linguist. Clarence knows dozens of ancient languages, such as Gothic and Gaulish. I was able to check him on some of them, like vulgar Latin; that was one of the things that convinced me. And there are archeologists and psychologists—

"If only something doesn't happen to scare him off. We'd never find him. I don't know. Between a man-crazy female scientist and a publicity-mad surgeon—I wonder how it'll work out—"

The gnarly man innocently entered the waiting room of Dunbar's hospital. He, as usual, spotted the most comfortable chair and settled luxuriously into it.

Dunbar stood before him. His keen eyes gleamed with anticipation behind their pince-nez. "There'll be a wait of about half an hour, Mr. Gaffney," he said. "We're all tied up now, you know. I'll send Mahler in; he'll see that you have anything you want." Dunbar's eyes ran lovingly over the gnarly man's stumpy frame. What fascinating secrets mightn't he discover once he got inside it?

Mahler appeared, a healthy-looking youngster. Was there anything Mr. Gaffney would like? The gnarly man paused as usual to let his massive mental machinery grind. A vagrant impulse moved him to ask to see the instruments that were to be used on him.

Mahler had his orders, but this seemed a harmless enough request. He went and returned with a tray full of gleaming steel. "You see," he said, "these are called scalpels."

Presently the gnarly man asked: "What's this?" He picked up a peculiar-looking instrument.

"Oh, that's the boss's own invention. For getting at the midbrain."

"Midbrain? What's that doing here?"

"Why, that's for getting at your— That must be there by mistake—"

Little lines tightened around the queer hazel eyes. "Yeah?" He remembered the look Dunbar had given him, and Dunbar's general reputation. "Say, could I use your phone a minute?"

"Why . . . I suppose . . . what do you want to phone for?"

"I want to call my lawyer. Any objections?"

"No, of course not. But there isn't any phone here."

"What do you call that?" The gnarly man got up and walked toward the instrument in plain sight on a table. But Mahler was there before him, standing in front of it.

"This one doesn't work. It's being fixed."

"Can't I try it?"

"No, not till it's fixed. It doesn't work, I tell you."

The gnarly man studied the young physician for a few seconds. "O. K., then I'll find one that does." He started for the door.

"Hey, you can't go out now!" cried Mahler.

"Can't I? Just watch me!"

"Hey!" It was a full-throated yell. Like magic more men in white coats appeared.

Behind them was the great surgeon. "Be reasonable, Mr. Gaffney," he said. "There's no reason why you should go out now, you know. We'll be ready for you in a little while."

"Any reason why I shouldn't?" The gnarly man's big face swung on his thick neck, and his hazel eyes swiveled. All the exits were blocked. "I'm going."

"Grab him!" said Dunbar.

The white coats moved. The gnarly man got his hands on the back of a chair. The chair whirled, and became a dissolving blur as the men closed on him. Pieces of chair flew about the room, to fall with the dry, sharp *ping* of short lengths of wood. When the gnarly man stopped swinging, having only a short piece of the chair back left in each fist, one assistant was out cold. Another leaned whitely against the wall and nursed a broken arm.

"Go on!" shouted Dunbar when he could make himself heard. The white wave closed over the gnarly man, then broke. The gnarly man was on his feet, and held young Mahler by the ankles. He spread his feet and swung the shrieking Mahler like a club, clearing the way to the door. He turned, whirled Mahler around his head like a hammer thrower, and let the now mercifully unconscious body fly. His assailants went down in a yammering tangle.

One was still up. Under Dunbar's urging he sprang after the gnarly man. The latter had gotten his stick out of the umbrella stand in the vestibule. The knobby upper end went *whoosh* past the assistant's nose. The assistant jumped back and fell over one of the casualties. The front door slammed, and there was a deep roar of "Taxi!"

"Come on!" shrieked Dunbar. "Get the ambulance out!"

James Robinette was sitting in his office, thinking the thoughts that lawyers do in moments of relaxation, when there was a pounding of large feet in the corridor, a startled protest from Miss Spevak in the outer office, and the strange client of the day before was at Robinette's desk, breathing hard.

"I'm Gaffney," he growled between gasps. "Remember me? I think they followed me down here. They'll be up any minute. I want your help."

"They? Who's they?" Robinette winced at the impact of that damn perfume.

The gnarly man launched into his misfortunes. He was going well when there were more protests from Miss Spevak, and Dr. Dunbar and four assistants burst into the office.

"He's ours," said Dunbar, his glasses agleam.

"He's an ape-man," said the assistant with the black eye.

"He's a dangerous lunatic," said the assistant with the cut lip.

"We've come to take him away," said the assistant with the torn coat.

The gnarly man spread his feet and gripped his stick like a baseball bat by the small end.

Robinette opened a desk drawer and got out a large pistol. "One move toward him and I'll use this. The use of extreme violence is justified to prevent commission of a felony, to wit: kidnaping."

The five men backed up a little. Dunbar said: "This isn't kidnaping. You can only kidnap a person, you know. He isn't a human being, and I can prove it."

The assistant with the black eye snickered. "If he wants protection, he better see a game warden instead of a lawyer."

"Maybe that's what *you* think," said Robinette. "You aren't a lawyer. According to the law, he's human. Even corporations, idiots, and unborn children are legally persons, and he's a damn sight more human than they are."

"Then he's a dangerous lunatic," said Dunbar.

"Yeah? Where's your commitment order? The only persons who can apply for one are: (a) close relatives and (b) public officials charged with the maintenance of order. You're neither."

Dunbar continued stubbornly: "He ran amuck in my hospital and nearly killed a couple of my men, you know. I guess that gives us some rights."

"Sure," said Robinette. "You can step down to the nearest station and swear out a warrant." He turned to the gnarly man. "Shall we throw the book at 'em, Gaffney?"

"I'm all right," said that individual, his speech returning to its normal slowness. "I just want to make sure these guys don't pester me anymore."

"O. K. Now listen, Dunbar. One hostile move out of you and we'll have a warrant out for you for false arrest, assault and battery, attempted kidnaping, criminal conspiracy, and disorderly conduct. *And* we'll slap on a civil suit for damages for sundry torts, to wit: assault, deprivation of civil rights, placing in jeopardy of life and limb, menace, and a few more I may think of later."

"You'll never make that stick," snarled Dunbar. "We have all the witnesses."

"Yeah? And wouldn't the great Evan Dunbar look sweet defending such actions? Some of the ladies who gush over your books might suspect that maybe you weren't such a damn knight in shining armor. We can make a prize monkey of you, and you know it."

"You're destroying the possibility of a great scientific discovery, you know, Robinette."

"To hell with that. My duty is to protect my client. Now beat it, all of you, before I call a cop." His left hand moved suggestively to the telephone.

Dunbar grasped at a last straw. "Hm-m-m. Have you got a permit for that gun?"

"Damn right. Want to see it?"

Dunbar sighed. "Never mind. You *would* have." His greatest opportunity for fame was slipping out of his fingers. He drooped toward the door.

The gnarly man spoke up. "If you don't mind, Dr. Dunbar, I left my hat at your place. I wish you'd send it to Mr. Robinette here. I have a hard time getting hats to fit me."

Dunbar looked at him silently and left with his cohorts.

The gnarly man was giving the lawyer further details when the telephone rang. Robinette answered: "Yes. . . . Saddler? Yes, he's here. . . . Your Dr. Dunbar was going to murder him so he could dissect him. . . . O. K." He turned to the gnarly man. "Your friend Dr. Saddler is looking for you. She's on her way up here."

"Zounds!" said Gaffney. "I'm going."

"Don't you want to see her? She was phoning from around the corner. If you go out now you'll run into her. How did she know where to call?"

"I gave her your number. I suppose she called the hospital and my boardinghouse, and tried you as a last resort. This door goes into the hall, doesn't it? Well, when she comes in the regular door I'm going out this one. And I don't want you saying where I've gone. It's nice to have known you, Mr. Robinette."

"Why? What's the matter? You're not going to run out now, are you? Dunbar's harmless, and you've got friends. I'm your friend."

"You're durn tootin' I'm going to run out. There's too much trouble. I've kept alive all these centuries by staying away from trouble. I let down my guard with Dr. Saddler, and went to the surgeon she recommended. First he plots to take me apart to see what makes me tick. If that brain instrument hadn't made me suspicious, I'd have been on my way to the alcohol jars by now. Then there's a fight, and it's just pure luck I didn't kill a couple of those internes, or whatever they are, and get sent up for manslaughter. Now Matilda's after me with a more-than-friendly interest. I know what it means when a woman looks at you that way and calls you 'dear.' I wouldn't mind if she weren't a prominent person of the kind that's always in some sort of garboil. That would mean more trouble, sooner or later. You don't suppose I *like* trouble, do you?"

"But look here, Gaffney, you're getting steamed up over a lot of damn—"

"Ssst!" The gnarly man took his stick and tiptoed over to the private entrance. As Dr. Saddler's clear voice sounded in the outer office, he sneaked out. He was closing the door behind him when the scientist entered the inner office.

Matilda Saddler was a quick thinker. Robinette hardly had time to open his mouth when she flung herself at and through the private door with a cry of "Clarence!"

Robinette heard the clatter of feet on the stairs. Neither the pursued nor the pursuer had waited for the creaky elevator. Looking out the window, he saw Gaffney leap into a taxi. Matilda Saddler sprinted after the cab, calling: "Clarence! Come back!" But the traffic was light and the chase correspondingly hopeless.

They did hear from the gnarly man once more. Three months later Robinette got a letter whose envelope contained, to his vast astonishment, ten ten-dollar bills. The single sheet was typed, even to the signature.

Dear Mr. Robinette:

I do not know what your regular fees are, but I hope that the inclosed will cover your services to me of last June.

Since leaving New York I have had several jobs. I pushed a hack—as we say—in Chicago, and I tried out as pitcher on a bush league baseball team. Once I made my living by knocking over rabbits and things with stones, and I can still throw fairly well. Nor am I bad at swinging a club, such as a baseball bat. But my lameness makes me too slow for a baseball career, and it will be some time before I try any remedial operations again.

I now have a job whose nature I cannot disclose because I do not wish to be traced. You need pay no attention to the postmark; I am not living in Kansas City, but had a friend post this letter there.

Ambition would be foolish for one in my peculiar position. I am satisfied with a job that furnishes me with the essentials, and allows me to go to an occasional movie, and a few friends with whom I can drink beer and talk.

I was sorry to leave New York without saying good-by to Dr. Harold McGannon, who treated me very nicely. I wish you would

explain to him why I had to leave as I did. You can get in touch
with him through Columbia University.

If Dunbar sent you my hat as I requested, please mail it to me:
General Delivery, Kansas City, Mo. My friend will pick it up. There
is not a hat store in this town where I live that can fit me. With best
wishes, I remain,

> Yours sincerely,
> Shining Hawk
> Alias Clarence Aloysius Gaffney.

The Golem

For many years, the late Avram Davidson was one of the most eloquent and individual voices in science fiction and fantasy, and there were few writers in any literary field who could match his wit, his erudition, or the stylish elegance of his prose. He deserves to be ranked, at the very least, with Collier and Saki and Thurber, and to be taught in the same kind of academic anthologies in which they are taught—and no doubt *would* be if he had not spent his entire forty-year career laboring in the obscurity of genre pulp magazines. The fact is that, at his finest, Davidson was simply one of the best short-story writers of modern times, in any genre.

Davidson was one of two authors (the other was Fritz Leiber) whose work spanned *such* a broad range of different kinds of fantasy, and was so deeply influential all the way across that range, that I was unable to limit myself to using just one story by them; even devoting two stories apiece to them only begins to hint at the variety and eclecticism of their work. Later in this anthology I'll bring you one of Davidson's Jack Limekiller stories, a work from near the end of his career, but, even though it's one of Davidson's most-reprinted stories, no book calling itself *Modern Classics of Fantasy* could afford to omit the story that follows, a tale from the very *beginning* of Davidson's career, a near-perfect little masterpiece called "The Golem."

During his long career, Davidson won the Hugo (for that other mad little classic, "Or All the Seas with Oysters," which detailed the sex cycles of coat hangers and safety pins), the Edgar, and the World Fantasy Award, including the prestigious Lifetime Achievement Award. Although all of his novels are erudite and entertaining, and a few are memorable (including one of the most influential of modern fantasy novels, *The Phoenix and the Mirror*—sometimes claimed as the first work of "Hard Fantasy," because although the technology in the book is as rigorously worked out and as self-consistently utilized as in any "hard science" story, that "technology" is the technology of the Middle Ages, namely alchemy . . . and so, to *us,* reads as Magic), Davidson's talents found their purest expression in his short fiction. He sold his first story in 1954, and by only the next year had written the classic story "The Golem," which appeared, as much of his output would over the following decades, in *The Magazine of Fantasy & Science Fiction* . . . a magazine that he edited for several years in the early 1960s. (In some ways, in fact, Davidson can be thought of as the ideal or archetypical *F&SF* author, much as critics discussing H. L. Gold's reign sometimes cite Damon Knight or Alfred Bester or Theodore Sturgeon as quintessential *Galaxy* writers, or as L. Sprague de Camp is sometimes cited as the quintessential *Unknown* writer.) After a silence of several years in the middle sixties, Davidson returned to writing toward the end of that decade, and by the mid-seventies he was engaged in turning out a long series of stories about the bizarre exploits of Doctor Engelbert Eszterhazy (later gathered in one of the best fantasy collections ever published, the marvelous *The Adventures of Doctor Eszterhazy*) and another series detailing the strange adventures of Jack Limekiller (inexplicably, as yet uncollected—alas) that are Davidson at the height of his considerable powers, and that must be counted as some of the very finest work produced in the final decades of the century.

Davidson's short work has been assembled in landmark collections such as *The Best of Avram Davidson, Or All the Seas with Oysters, The Redward Edward Papers, What Strange Stars and Shore, Collected Fantasies,* and *The Adventures of Doctor Eszterhazy*. His novels include *Masters of the Maze, Rogue Dragon, Peregrine: Primus, Rork!, Clash of Star-Kings,* and *Vergil In Averno.* His most recent books are a novel in collaboration with Grania Davis, *Marco Polo and the Sleeping Beauty,* and a posthumously released collection of his erudite and witty essays, *Adventures in Unhistory.* Coming up is a mammoth retrospective collection, a new version of *The Best of Avram Davidson.*

The grey-faced person came along the street where old Mr. and Mrs. Gumbeiner lived. It was afternoon, it was autumn, the sun was warm and soothing to their ancient bones. Anyone who attended the movies in the twenties or the early thirties has seen that street a thousand times. Past these bungalows with their half-double roofs Edmund Lowe walked arm-in-arm with Leatrice Joy and Harold Lloyd was chased by Chinamen waving hatchets. Under these squamous palm trees Laurel kicked Hardy and Woolsey beat Wheeler upon the head with codfish. Across these pocket-handkerchief-sized lawns the juveniles of the Our Gang Comedies pursued one another and were pursued by angry fat men in golf knickers. On this same street—or perhaps on some other one of five hundred streets exactly like it.

Mrs. Gumbeiner indicated the grey-faced person to her husband.

"You think maybe he's got something the matter?" she asked. "He walks kind of funny, to me."

"Walks like a *golem*," Mr. Gumbeiner said indifferently.

The old woman was nettled.

"Oh, I don't know," she said. *"I* think he walks like your cousin Mendel."

The old man pursed his mouth angrily and chewed on his pipestem. The grey-faced person turned up the concrete path, walked up the steps to the porch, sat down in a chair. Old Mr. Gumbeiner ignored him. His wife stared at the stranger.

"Man comes in without a hello, good-bye, or howareyou, sits himself down and right away he's at home. . . . The chair is comfortable?" she asked. "Would you like maybe a glass tea?"

She turned to her husband.

"Say something, Gumbeiner!" she demanded. "What are you, made of wood?"

The old man smiled a slow, wicked, triumphant smile.

"Why should *I* say anything?" he asked the air. "Who am I? Nothing, that's who."

The stranger spoke. His voice was harsh and monotonous.

"When you learn who—or, rather, what—I am, the flesh will melt from your bones in terror." He bared porcelain teeth.

"Never mind about my bones!" the old woman cried. "You've got a lot of nerve talking about my bones!"

"You will quake with fear," said the stranger. Old Mrs. Gumbeiner said that she hoped he would live so long. She turned to her husband once again.

"Gumbeiner, when are you going to mow the lawn?"

"All mankind—" the stranger began.

"Shah! I'm talking to my husband. . . . He talks *eppis* kind of funny, Gumbeiner, no?"

"Probably a foreigner," Mr. Gumbeiner said, complacently.

"You think so?" Mrs. Gumbeiner glanced fleetingly at the stranger. "He's got a very bad color in his face, *nebbich*. I suppose he came to California for his health."

"Disease, pain, sorrow, love, grief—all are naught to—"

Mr. Gumbeiner cut in on the stranger's statement.

"Gall bladder," the old man said. "Guinzburg down at the *shule* looked exactly the same before his operation. Two professors they had in for him, and a private nurse day and night."

"I am not a human being!" the stranger said loudly.

"Three thousand seven hundred fifty dollars it cost his son, Guinzburg told me. 'For you, Poppa, nothing is too expensive—only get well,' the son told him."

"I am not a human being!"

"Ai, is that a son for you!" the old woman said, rocking her head. "A heart of gold, pure gold." She looked at the stranger. "All right, all right. I heard you the first time. Gumbeiner! I asked you a question. When are you going to cut the lawn?"

"On Wednesday, *odder* maybe Thursday, comes the Japaneser to the neighborhood. To cut lawns is *his* profession. *My* profession is to be a glazier—retired."

"Between me and all mankind is an inevitable hatred," the stranger said. "When I tell you what I am, the flesh will melt—"

"You said, you said already," Mr. Gumbeiner interrupted.

"In Chicago where the winters were as cold and bitter as the Czar of Russia's heart," the old woman intoned, "you had strength to carry the frames with the glass together day in and day out. But in California with the golden sun to mow the lawn when your wife asks, for this you have no strength. Do I call in the Japaneser to cook for you supper?"

"Thirty years Professor Allardyce spent perfecting his theories. Electronics, neuronics—"

"Listen, how educated he talks," Mr. Gumbeiner said, admiringly. "Maybe he goes to the University here?"

"If he goes to the University, maybe he knows Bud?" his wife suggested.

"Probably they're in the same class and he came to see him about the homework, no?"

"Certainly he must be in the same class. How many classes are there? Five *in ganzen:* Bud showed me on his program card." She counted off on her fingers. "Television Appreciation and Criticism, Small Boat Building, Social Adjustment, The American Dance . . . The American Dance—*nu,* Gumbeiner—"

"Contemporary Ceramics," her husband said, relishing the syllables. "A fine boy, Bud. A pleasure to have him for a boardner."

"After thirty years spent in these studies," the stranger, who had continued to speak unnoticed, went on, "he turned from the theoretical to the pragmatic. In ten years' time he had made the most titanic discovery in history: he made mankind, *all* mankind, superfluous: he made *me.*"

"What did Tillie write in her last letter?" asked the old man.

The old woman shrugged.

"What should she write? The same thing. Sidney was home from the Army, Naomi has a new boyfriend—"

"He made ME*!"*

"Listen, Mr. Whatever-your-name-is," the old woman said; "maybe

where you came from is different, but in *this* country you don't interrupt
people the while they're talking. . . . Hey. Listen—what do you mean, he
made you? What kind of talk is that?"

The stranger bared all his teeth again, exposing the too-pink gums.

"In his library, to which I had a more complete access after his sudden
and as yet undiscovered death from entirely natural causes, I found a complete collection of stories about androids, from Shelley's *Frankenstein*
through Capek's *R.U.R.* to Asimov's—"

"Frankenstein?" said the old man, with interest. "There used to be
Frankenstein who had the soda*wasser* place on Halstead Street: a Litvack,
nebbich."

"What are you talking?" Mrs. Gumbeiner demanded. "His name was
Franken*thal,* and it wasn't on Halstead, it was on Roosevelt."

"—clearly shown that all mankind has an instinctive antipathy towards
androids and there will be an inevitable struggle between them—"

"Of course, of course!" Old Mr. Gumbeiner clicked his teeth against
his pipe. "I am always wrong, you are always right. How could you stand
to be married to such a stupid person all this time?"

"I don't know," the old woman said. "Sometimes I wonder, myself. I
think it must be his good looks." She began to laugh. Old Mr. Gumbeiner
blinked, then began to smile, then took his wife's hand.

"Foolish old woman," the stranger said; "why do you laugh? Do you
not know I have come to destroy you?"

"What!" old Mr. Gumbeiner shouted. "Close your mouth, you!" He
darted from his chair and struck the stranger with the flat of his hand.
The stranger's head struck against the porch pillar and bounced back.

"When you talk to my wife, talk respectable, you hear?"

Old Mrs. Gumbeiner, cheeks very pink, pushed her husband back in
his chair. Then she leaned forward and examined the stranger's head. She
clicked her tongue as she pulled aside a flap of grey, skin-like material.

"Gumbeiner, look! He's all springs and wires inside!"

"I *told* you he was a *golem,* but no, you wouldn't listen," the old man
said.

"You said he *walked* like a *golem.*"

"How could he walk like a *golem* unless he *was* one?"

"All right, all right. . . . You broke him, so now fix him."

"My grandfather, his light shines from Paradise, told me that when Mo-
HaRaL—Moreynu Ha-Rav Löw—his memory for a blessing, made the
golem in Prague, three hundred? four hundred years ago? he wrote on his
forehead the Holy Name."

Smiling reminiscently, the old woman continued, "And the *golem* cut the
rabbi's wood and brought his water and guarded the ghetto."

"And one time only he disobeyed the Rabbi Löw, and Rabbi Löw
erased the *Shem Ha-Mephorash* from the *golem's* forehead and the *golem* fell

down like a dead one. And they put him up in the attic of the *shule* and he's still there today if the Communisten haven't sent him to Moscow. . . . This is not just a story," he said.

"*Avadda* not!" said the old woman.

"I myself have seen both the *shule, and* the rabbi's grave," her husband said, conclusively.

"But I think this must be a different kind *golem,* Gumbeiner. See, on his forehead: nothing written."

"What's the matter, there's a law I can't write something there? Where is that lump clay Bud brought us from his class?"

The old man washed his hands, adjusted his little black skullcap, and slowly and carefully wrote four Hebrew letters on the grey forehead.

"Ezra the Scribe himself couldn't do better," the old woman said, admiringly. "Nothing happens," she observed, looking at the lifeless figure sprawled in the chair.

"Well, after all, am I Rabbi Löw?" her husband asked, deprecatingly. "No," he answered. He leaned over and examined the exposed mechanism. "This spring goes here . . . this wire comes with this one . . ." The figure moved. "But this one goes where? And this one?"

"Let be," said his wife. The figure sat up slowly and rolled its eyes loosely.

"Listen, Reb *Golem,*" the old man said, wagging his finger. "Pay attention to what I say—you understand?"

"Understand . . ."

"If you want to stay here, you got to do like Mr. Gumbeiner says."

"Do-like-Mr.-Gumbeiner-says . . ."

"*That's* the way I like to hear a *golem* talk. Malka, give here the mirror from the pocketbook. Look, you see your face? You see on the forehead, what's written? If you don't do like Mr. Gumbeiner says, he'll wipe out what's written and you'll be no more alive."

"No-more-alive."

"*That's* right. Now, listen. Under the porch you'll find a lawnmower. Take it. And cut the lawn. Then come back. Go."

"Go . . ." The figure shambled down the stairs. Presently the sound of the lawnmower whirred through the quiet air in the street just like the street where Jackie Cooper shed huge tears on Wallace Beery's shirt and Chester Conklin rolled his eyes at Marie Dressler.

"So what will you write to Tillie?" old Mr. Gumbeiner asked.

"What should I write?" old Mrs. Gumbeiner shrugged. "I'll write that the weather is lovely out here and that we are both, Blessed be the Name, in good health."

The old man nodded his head slowly, and they sat together on the front porch in the warm afternoon sun.

MANLY WADE WELLMAN

Walk Like a Mountain

The late Manly Wade Wellman was one of the finest modern practitioners of the "dark fantasy" tale. He was probably best known for his stories about John the Minstrel or "Silver John," scary and vividly evocative tales set against the background of a ghost-and-demon haunted rural Appalachia that, in Wellman's hands, is as bizarre and beautiful as many another writer's entirely imaginary fantasy world. The "Silver John" stories were originally collected in *Who Fears the Devil?*, generally perceived as Wellman's best book; more recently, the "Silver John" stories were gathered in an omnibus collection called *John the Balladeer*, which includes all the stories from *Who Fears the Devil?*, and adds a number of more recent uncollected "Silver John" stories as well. In recent years, there were also "Silver John" novels: *The Old Gods Waken, After Dark, The Lost and the Lurking, The Hanging Stones,* and *Voice of the Mountain.* Wellman's non-"Silver John" stories were assembled in the mammoth collection *Worse Things Waiting,* which won a World Fantasy Award as the Best Anthology/Collection of 1975. Wellman himself won the prestigious World Fantasy Award for Life Achievement. He died in 1986 at the age of eighty-two. His most recent book is the posthumously published collection *Mountain Valley Stories.*

Some of Wellman's stories are probably better classified as horror, but many of them, particularly the best of the "Silver John" stories, also function well as fantasy. In the one that follows, for instance, John encounters a creature right out of a fairy tale (or perhaps out of the Bible, which tells us that "there were giants in the earth in those days"), a genuine Giant, still abroad in the twentieth-century world—where he discovers that there's no man so big that he can't run up against a problem that's bigger still . . .

Once at Sky Notch, I never grudged the trouble getting there. It was so purely pretty, I was glad outlanders weren't apt to crowd in and spoil all.

The Notch cut through a tall peak that stood against a higher cliff. Steep brushy faces each side, and a falls at the back that made a trickly branch, with five pole cabins along the waterside. Corn patches, a few pigs in pens, chickens running round, a cow tied up one place. It wondered me how they ever got a cow up there. Laurels grew, and viney climbers, and mountain flowers in bunches and sprawls. The water made a happy noise. Nobody moved in the yards or at the doors, so I stopped by a tree and hollered the first house.

"Hello the house!" I called. "Hello to the man of the house and all inside!"

A plank door opened about an inch. "Hello to yourself," a gritty voice replied me. "Who's that out there with the guitar?"

I moved from under the tree. "My name's John. Does Mr. Lane Jarrett live up here? Got word for him, from his old place on Drowning Creek."

The door opened wider, and there stood a skimpy little man with gray whiskers. "That's funny," he said.

The funnyness I didn't see. I'd known Mr. Lane Jarrett years back, before he and his daughter Page moved to Sky Notch. When his uncle Jeb died and heired him some money, I'd agreed to carry it to Sky Notch, and, gentlemen, it was a long, weary way getting there.

First a bus, up and down and through mountains, stop at every pig trough for passengers. I got off at Charlie's Jump—who Charlie was, nor why or when he jumped, nobody there can rightly say. Climbed a high ridge, got down the far side, then a twenty-devil way along a deep valley river. Up another height, another beyond that. Then it was night, and nobody would want to climb the steep face above, because it was grown up with the kind of trees that the dark melts in around you. I made a fire and took my supper rations from my pocket. Woke at dawn and climbed up and up and up, and here I was.

"Funny, about Lane Jarrett," gritted the little man out. "Sure you ain't come about that business?"

I looked up the walls of the Notch. Their tops were toothy rocks, the way you'd think those walls were two jaws, near about to close on what they'd caught inside them. Right then the Notch didn't look so pretty.

"Can't say, sir," I told him, "till I know what business you mean."

"Rafe Enoch!" he boomed out the name, like firing two barrels of a gun. "That's what I mean!" Then he appeared to remember his manners, and came out, puny in his jeans and no shoes on his feet. "I'm Oakman Dillon," he named himself. "John—that's your name, huh? Why you got that guitar?"

"I pick it some," I replied him. "I sing." Tweaking the silver strings, I sang a few lines:

> *By the shore of Lonesome River*
> *Where the waters ebb and flow,*
> *Where the wild red rose is budding*
> *And the pleasant breezes blow,*
>
> *It was there I spied the lady*
> *That forever I adore,*
> *As she was a-lonesome walking*
> *By the Lonesome River shore. . . .*

"Rafe Enoch!" he grit-grated out again. "Carried off Miss Page Jarrett the way you'd think she was a banty chicken!"

Slap, I quieted the strings with my palm. "Mr. Lane's little daughter Page was stolen away?"

He sat down on the door-log. "She ain't suchy little daughter. She's six foot maybe three inches—taller'n you, even. Best-looking big woman I ever see, brown hair like a wagonful of home-cured tobacco, eyes green and bright as a fresh-squoze grape pulp."

"Fact?" I said, thinking Page must have changed a right much from the long-leggy little girl I'd known, must have grown tall like her daddy and her dead mammy, only taller. "Is this Rafe Enoch so big, a girl like that is right for him?"

"She's puny for him. He's near about eight foot tall, best I judge." Oakman Dillon's gray whiskers stuck out like a mad cat's. "He just grabbed her last evening, where she walked near the fall, and up them rocks he went like a possum up a jack oak."

I sat down on a stump. "Mr. Lane's a friend of mine. How can I help?"

"Nobody can't help, John. It's right hard to think you ain't knowing all this stuff. Don't many strangers come up here. Ain't room for many to live in the Notch."

"Five homes," I counted them with my eyes.

"Six. Rafe Enoch lives up at the top." He jerked his head toward the falls. "Been there a long spell—years, I reckon, since when he run off from somewhere. Heard tell he broke a circus man's neck for offering him a job with a show. He built up top the falls, and he used to get along with us. Thanked us kindly for a mess of beans or roasting ears. Lately, he's been mean-talking."

"Nobody mean-talked him back? Five houses in the Notch mean five grown men—couldn't they handle one giant?"

"Giant size ain't all Rafe Enoch's got." Again the whiskers bristled up. "Why! He's got powers, like he can make rain fall—"

"No," I put in quick. "Can't even science men do that for sure."

"I ain't studying science men. Rafe Enoch says for rain to fall, down it comes, any hour day or night he speaks. Could drown us out of this Notch if he had the mind."

"And he carried off Page Jarrett," I went back to what he'd said.

"That's the whole truth, John. Up he went with her in the evening, daring us to follow him."

I asked, "Where are the other Notch folks?"

"Up yonder by the falls. Since dawn we've been talking Lane Jarrett back from climbing up and getting himself neck-twisted. I came to feed my pigs, now I'm heading back."

"I'll go with you," I said, and since he didn't deny me I went.

The falls dropped down a height as straight up as a chimney, and a many times taller, and their water boiled off down the branch. Either side of the falls, the big boulder rocks piled on top of each other like stones in an almighty big wall. Looking up, I saw clouds boiling in the sky, dark and heavy and wet-looking, and I remembered what Oakman Dillon had said about big Rafe Enoch's rain-making.

A bunch of folks were there, and I made out Mr. Lane Jarrett, bald on top and bigger than the rest. I touched his arm, and he turned.

"John! Ain't seen you a way-back time. Let me make you known to these here folks."

He called them their first names—Yoot, Ollie, Bill, Duff, Miss Lulie, Miss Sara May and so on. I said I had a pocketful of money for him, but he just nodded and wanted to know did I know what was going on.

"Looky up against them clouds, John. That pointy rock. My girl Page is on it."

The rock stuck out like a spur on a rooster's leg. Somebody was scrouched down on it, with the clouds getting blacker above, and a long, long drop below.

"I see her blue dress," allowed Mr. Oakman, squinting up. "How long she been there, Lane?"

"I spotted her at sunup," said Mr. Lane. "She must have got away from Rafe Enoch and crope out there during the night. I'm going to climb."

He started to shinny up a rock, up clear of the brush around us. And, Lord, the laugh that came down on us! Like a big splash of water, it was clear and strong, and like water it made us shiver. Mr. Oakman caught onto Mr. Lane's ankle and dragged him down.

"Ain't a God's thing ary man or woman can do, with him waiting up there," Mr. Oakman argued.

"But he's got Page," said Mr. Lane busting loose again. I grabbed his elbow.

"Let me," I said.

"You, John? You're a stranger, you ain't got no pick in this."

"This big Rafe Enoch would know if it was you or Mr. Oakman or one of these others climbing, he might fling down a rock or the like. But I'm strange to him. I might wonder him, and he might let me climb all the way up."

"Then?" Mr. Lane said, frowning.

"Once up, I might could do something."

"Leave him try it," said Mr. Oakman to that.

"Yes," said one of the lady-folks.

I slung my guitar behind my shoulder and took to the rocks. No peep of noise from anywhere for maybe a minute of climbing. I got on about the third or fourth rock from the bottom, and that clear, sky-ripping laugh came from over my head.

"Name yourself!" roared down the voice that had laughed.

I looked up. How high was the top I can't say, but I made out a head and shoulders looking down, and knew they were another sight bigger head and shoulders than ever I'd seen on ary mortal man.

"Name yourself!" he yelled again, and in the black clouds a lightning flash wiggled, like a snake caught fire.

"John!" I bawled back.

"What you aiming to do, John?"

Another crack of lightning, that for a second seemed to peel off the clouds right and left. I looked this way and that. Nowhere to get out of the way should lightning strike, or a rock or anything. On notion, I pulled by guitar to me and picked and sang:

> *Went to the rock to hide my face,*
> *The rock cried out, "No hiding place!".* . . .

Gentlemen, the laugh was like thunder after the lightning.

"Better climb quick, John!" he hollered me. "I'm a-waiting on you up here!"

I swarmed and swarved and scrabbled my way up, not looking down. Over my head that rock-spur got bigger, I figured it for maybe twelve-fifteen feet long, and on it I made out Page Jarrett in her blue dress. Mr. Oakman was right, she was purely big and she was purely good-looking. She hung to the pointy rock with both her long hands.

"Page," I said to her, with what breath I had left, and she stared with her green eyes and gave me an inch of smile. She looked to have a right much of her daddy's natural sand in her craw.

"John," boomed the thunder-voice, close over me now. "I asked you a while back, why you coming up?"

"Just to see how you make the rain fall," I said, under the overhang of the ledge. "Help me up."

Down came a bare brown honey-hairy arm, and a hand the size of a scoop shovel. It got my wrist and snatched me away like a turnip coming out of a patch, and I landed my feet on broad flat stones.

Below me yawned up those rock-toothed tops of the Notch's jaws. Inside them the brush and trees looked mossy and puny. The cabins were like baskets, the pigs and the cow like play-toys, and the branch looked to run so narrow you might bridge it with your shoe. Shadow fell on the Notch from the fattening dark clouds.

Then I looked at Rafe Enoch. He stood over me like a sycamore tree over a wood shed. He was the almightiest big thing I'd ever seen on two legs.

Eight foot high, Oakman Dillon had said truly, and he was thick-made in keeping. Shoulders wide enough to fill a barn door, and legs like tree trunks with fringe-sided buckskin pants on them, and his big feet wore moccasin shoes of bear's hide with the fur still on. His shirt, sewed together of pelts—fox, coon, the like of that—hadn't any sleeves, and hung open from that big chest of his that was like a cotton bale. Topping all, his face put you in mind of the full moon with a yellow beard, but healthy-looking brown, not pale like the moon. Big and dark eyes, and through the yellow beard his teeth grinned like big white sugar lumps.

"Maybe I ought to charge you to look at me," he said.

I remembered how he'd struck a man dead for wanting him in a show, and I looked elsewhere. First, naturally, at Page Jarrett on the rock spur. The wind from the clouds waved her brown hair like a flag, and fluttered her blue skirt around her drawn-up feet. Then I turned and looked at the broad space above the falls.

From there I could see there was a right much of higher country, and just where I stood with Rafe Enoch was a big shelf, like a lap, with slopes behind it. In the middle of the flat space showed a pond of water, running out past us to make the falls. On its edge stood Rafe Enoch's house, built wigwam-style of big old logs leaned together and chinked between with clay over twigs. No trees to amount to anything on the shelf—just one behind the wigwam-house, and to its branches hung joints that looked like smoke meat.

"You hadn't played that guitar so clever, maybe I mightn't have saved you," said Rafe Enoch's thunder voice.

"Saved?" I repeated him.

"Look." His big club of a finger pointed to the falls, then to those down-hugged clouds. "When they get together, what happens?"

Just at the ledge lip, where the falls went over, stones looked halfway washed out. A big shove of water would take them out the other half, and the whole thing pour down on the Notch.

"Why you doing this to the folks?" I asked.

He shook his head. "John, this is one rain I never called for." He put one big pumpkin-sized fist into the palm of his other hand. "I can call for rain, sure, but some of it comes without me. I can't start it or either stop it, I just know it's coming. I've known about this for days. It'll drown out Sky Notch like a rat nest."

"Why didn't you try to tell them?"

"I tried to tell her." His eyes cut around to where Page Jarrett hung to the pointy rock, and his stool-leg fingers raked his yellow beard. "She was walking off by herself, alone. I know how it feels to be alone. But when I told her, she called me a liar. I brought her up here to save her, and she cried and fought me." A grin. "She fought me better than any living human I know. But she can't fight me hard enough."

"Can't you do anything about the storm?" I asked him to tell.

"Can do this." He snapped his big fingers, and lightning crawled through the clouds over us. It made me turtle my neck inside my shirt collar. Rafe Enoch never twitched his eyebrow.

"Rafe," I said, "you might could persuade the folks. They're not your size, but they're human like you."

"Them?" He roared his laugh. "They're not like me, nor you aren't like me, either, though you're longer-made than common. Page yonder, she looks to have some of the old Genesis giant blood in her. That's why I saved her alive."

"Genesis giant blood," I repeated him, remembering the Book, sixth chapter of Genesis. " 'There were giants in the earth in those days.' "

"That's the whole truth," said Rafe. "When the sons of God took wives of the daughters of men—their children were the mighty men of old, the men of renown. That's not exact quote, but it's near enough."

He sat down on a rock, near about as tall sitting as I was standing. "Ary giant knows he was born from the sons of the gods," he said. "My name tells it, John."

I nodded, figuring it. "Rafe—Raphah, the giant whose son was Goliath, Enoch—"

"Or Anak," he put in. "Remember the sons of Anak, and them scared-out spies sent into Canaan? They was grasshoppers in the sight of the sons of Anak, in more ways than just size, John." He sniffed. "They got scared back into the wilderness for forty years. And Goliath!"

"David killed him," I dared remind Rafe.

"By a trick. A slingshot stone. Else he'd not lasted any longer than that."

A finger-snap, and lightning winged over us like a hawk over a chicken run. I tried not to scrouch down.

"What use to fight little old human men," he said, "when you got the sons of the gods in your blood?"

I allowed he minded me of Strap Buckner with that talk.

"Who's Strap Buckner? Why do I mind you of him?"

I picked the guitar, I sang the song:

Strap Buckner he was called, he was more than eight foot tall,
And he walked like a mountain among men.
He was good and he was great, and the glorious Lone Star State
Will never look upon his like again.

"Strap Buckner had the strength of ten lions," I said, "and he used it as ten lions. Scorned to fight ordinary folks, so he challenged old Satan himself, skin for skin, on the banks of the Brazos, and if Satan hadn't fought foul—"

"Another dirty fighter!" Rafe got up from where he sat, quick as quick for all his size. "Foul or not, Satan couldn't whup me!"

"Might be he couldn't," I judged, looking at Rafe. "But anyway, the Notch folks never hurt you. Used to give you stuff to eat."

"Don't need their stuff to eat," he said, the way you'd think that was the only argument. He waved his hand past his wigwam-house. "Down yonder is a bunch of hollows, where ain't no human man been, except maybe once the Indians. I hoe some corn there, some potatoes. I pick wild salad greens here and yonder. I kill me a deer, a bear, a wild hog—ain't no human man got nerve to face them big wild hogs, but I chunk them with a rock or I fling a sharp ash sapling, and what I fling at I bring down. In the pond here I spear me fish. Don't need their stuff to eat, I tell you."

"Need it or not, why let them drown out?"

His face turned dark, the way you'd think smoke drifted over it.

"I can't abide little folks' little eyes looking at me, wondering themselves about me, thinking I'm not rightly natural."

He waited for what I had to say, and it took nerve to say it.

"But you're not a natural man, Rafe. You've allowed that yourself, you say you come from different blood. Paul Bunyan thought the same thing."

He grinned his big sugar-lump teeth at me. Then: "Page Jarrett," he called, "better come off that rock before the rain makes it slippy and you fall off. I'll help you—"

"You stay where you are," she called back. "Let John help."

I went to the edge of that long drop down. The wind blew from some place—maybe below, maybe above or behind or before. I reached out my guitar, and Page Jarrett crawled to where she could lay hold, and that way I helped her to the solid standing. She stood beside me, inches taller, and she put a burning mean look on Rafe Enoch. He made out he didn't notice.

"Paul Bunyan," he said, after what I'd been saying. "I've heard tell his name—champion logger in the northern states, wasn't he?"

"Champion logger," I said. "Bigger than you, I reckon—"

"Not bigger!" thundered Rafe Enoch.

"Well, as big."

"Know ary song about him?"

"Can't say there's been one made. Rafe, you say you despise to be looked on by folks."

"Just by little folks, John. Page Jarrett can look on me if she relishes to."

Quick she looked off, and drew herself up proud. Right then she appeared to be taller than what Mr. Oakman Dillon had reckoned her, and a beauty-looking thing she was, you hear what I say, gentlemen. I cut my eyes up to the clouds; they hung down over us, loose and close, like the roof of a tent. I could feel the closeness around me, the way you feel water when you've waded up to the line of your mouth.

"How soon does the rain start falling?" I asked Rafe.

"Can fall ary time now," said Rafe, pulling a grass-stalk to bite in his big teeth. "Page's safe off that rock point, it don't differ me a shuck when that rain falls."

"But when?" I asked again. "You know."

"Sure I know." He walked toward the pond, and me with him. I felt Page Jarrett's grape-green eyes digging our backs. The pond water was shiny tarry black from reflecting the clouds. "Sure," he said, "I know a right much. You natural human folks, you know so pitiful little I'm sorry for you."

"Why not teach us?" I wondered him, and he snorted like a big mean horse.

"Ain't the way it's reckoned to be, John. Giants are figured stupid. Remember the tales? Your name's John—do you call to mind a tale about a man named Jack, long back in time?"

"Jack the Giant Killer," I nodded. "He trapped a giant in a hole—"

"Cormoran," said Rafe. "Jack dug a pit in front of his door. And Blunderbore he tricked into stabbing himself open with a knife. But how did them things happen? He blew a trumpet to tole Cormoran out, and he sat and ate at Blunderbore's table like a friend before tricking him to death." A louder snort. "More foul fighting, John. Did you come up here to be Jack the Giant Killer? Got some dirty tricks? If that's how it is, you done drove your ducks to the wrong puddle."

"More than a puddle here," I said, looking at the clouds and then across the pond. "See yonder, Rafe, where the water edge comes above that little slanty slope. If it was open, enough water could run off to keep the Notch from flooding."

"Could be done," he nodded his big head, "if you had machinery to pull the rocks out. But they're bigger than them fall rocks, they ain't half washed away to begin with. And there ain't no machinery, so just forget it. The Notch washes out, with most of the folks living in it—all of them, if the devil bids high enough. Sing me a song."

I swept the strings with my thumb. "Thinking about John Henry," I said, half to myself. "He wouldn't need a machine to open up a drain-off place yonder."

"How'd he do it?" asked Rafe.

"He had a hammer twice the size ary other man swung," I said. "He drove steel when they cut the Big Bend Tunnel through Cruze Mountain. Out-drove the steam drill they brought to compete him out of his job."

"Steam drill," Rafe repeated me, the way you'd think he was faintly recollecting the tale. "They'd do that—ordinary size folks, trying to work against a giant. How big was John Henry?"

"Heard tell he was the biggest man ever in Virginia."

"Big as me?"

"Maybe not quite. Maybe just stronger."

"Stronger!"

I had my work cut out not to run from the anger in Rafe Enoch's face. "Well," I said, "he beat the steam drill. . . ."

> *John Henry said to his captain,*
> *"A man ain't nothing but a man,*
> *But before I let that steam drill run me down,*
> *I'll die with this hammer in my hand. . . ."*

"He'd die trying," said Rafe, and his ears were sort of cocked forward, the way you hear elephants do to listen.

"He'd die winning," I said, and sang the next verse:

> *John Henry drove steel that long day through,*
> *The steam drill failed by his side.*
> *The mountain was high, the sun was low,*
> *John he laid down his hammer and he died. . . .*

"Killed himself beating the drill!" and Rafe's pumpkin fist banged into his other palm. "Reckon I could have beat it and lived!"

I was looking at the place where the pond could have a drain-off.

"No," said Rafe. "Even if I wanted to, I don't have no hammer twice the size of other folks' hammers."

A drop of rain fell on me. I started around the pond.

"Where you going?" Rafe called, but I didn't look back. Stopped beside the wigwam-house and put my guitar inside. It was gloomy in there, but I saw his homemade stool as high as a table, his table almost chin high to a natural man, a bed woven of hickory splits and spread with bear and deer skins to be the right bed for Og, King of Bashan, in the Book of Joshua. Next to the door I grabbed up a big pole of hickory, off some stacked firewood.

"Where you going?" he called again.

I went to where the slope started. I poked my hickory between two rocks and started to pry. He laughed, and rain sprinkled down.

"Go on, John," he granted me. "Grub out a sluiceway there. I like to watch little scrabbly men work. Come in the house, Page, we'll watch him from in there."

I couldn't budge the rocks from each other. They were big—like trunks or grain sacks, and must have weighed in the half-tons. They were set in there, one next to the other, four-five of them holding the water back from pouring down that slope. I heaved on my hickory till it bent like a bow.

"Come on," said Rafe again, and I looked around in time to see him put out his shovel hand and take her by the wrist. Gentlemen, the way she slapped him with her other hand it made me jump with the crack.

I watched, knee-deep in water. He put his hand to his gold-bearded cheek and his eye-whites glittered in the rain.

"If you was a man," he boomed down at Page, "I'd slap you dead."

"Do it!" she blazed him back. "I'm a woman, and I don't fear you or ary overgrown, sorry-for-himself giant ever drew breath!"

With me standing far enough off to forget how little I was by them, they didn't seem too far apart in size. Page was like a small-made woman facing up to a sizeable man, that was all.

"If you was a man—" he began again.

"I'm no man, nor neither ain't you a man!" she cut off. "Don't know if you're an ape or a bull-brute or what, but you're no man! John's the only man here, and I'm helping him! Stop me if you dare!"

She ran to where I was. Rain battered her hair into a brown tumble and soaked her dress snug against her fine proud strong body. Into the water she splashed.

"Let me pry," and she grabbed the hickory pole. "I'll pry up and you tug up, and maybe—"

I bent to grab the rock with my hands. Together we tried. Seemed to me the rock stirred a little, like the drowsy sleeper in the old song. Dragging at it, I felt the muscles strain and crackle in my shoulders and arms.

"Look out!" squealed Page. "Here he comes!"

Up on the bank she jumped again, with the hickory ready to club at him. He paid her no mind, she stopped down toward where I was.

"Get on out of there!" he bellowed, the way I've always reckoned a buffalo bull might do. "Get out!"

"But—but—" I was wheezing. "Somebody's got to move this rock—"

"You ain't budging it ary mite!" he almost deafened me in the ear. "Get out and let somebody there can do something!"

He grabbed my arm and snatched me out of the water, so sudden I almost sprained my fingers letting go the rock. Next second he jumped in, with a splash like a jolt-wagon going off a bridge. His big shovelly hands clamped the sides of the rock, and through the falling rain I saw him heave.

He swole up like a mad toad-frog. His patchy fur shirt split down the middle of his back while those muscles humped under his skin. His teeth flashed out in his beard, set hard together.

Then, just when I thought he'd bust open, that rock came out of its bed, came up in the air, landing on the bank away from where it'd been.

"I swear, Rafe—" I began to say.

"Help him," Page put in. "Let's both help."

We scrabbled for a hold on the rock, but Rafe hollered us away, so loud and sharp we jumped back like scared dogs. I saw that rock quiver, and cracks ran through the rain-soaked dirt around it. Then it came up on end, the way you'd think it had hinges, and Rafe got both arms around it and heaved it clear. He laughed, with the rain wet in his beard.

Standing clear where he'd told her to stand, Page pointed to the falls' end.

Looked as if the rain hadn't had to put down but just a little bit. Those loose rocks trembled and shifted in their places. They were ready to go. Then Rafe saw what we saw.

"Run, you two!" he howled about that racketty storm. "Run, run— quick!"

I didn't tarry to ask the reason. I grabbed Page's arm and we ran toward the falls. Running, I looked back past my elbow.

Rafe had straightened up, straddling among the rocks by the slope. He looked into the clouds, that were almost resting on his shaggy head, and both his big arms lifted and his hands spread and then their fingers snapped. I could hear the snaps—*Whop! Whop!* like two pistol shots.

He got what he called for, a forked stroke of lightning, straight and hard down on him like a fish-gig in the hands of the Lord's top angel. It slammed down on Rafe and over and around him, and it shook itself all the way from rock to clouds. Rafe Enoch in its grip lit up and glowed, the way you'd think he'd been forge-hammered out of iron and heated red in a furnace to temper him.

I heard the almightiest tearing noise I ever could call for. I felt the rock shelf quiver all the way to where we'd stopped dead to watch. My thought was, the falls had torn open and the Notch was drowning.

But the lightning yanked back to where it had come from. It had opened the sluiceway, and water flooded through and down slope, and Rafe had fallen down while it poured and puddled over him.

"He's struck dead!" I heard Page say over the rain.

"No," I said back.

For Rafe Enoch was on his knees, on his feet, and out of that drain-off rush, somehow staggering up from the flat sprawl where the lightning had flung him. His knees wobbled and bucked, but he drew them up straight and mopped a big muddy hand across his big muddy face.

He came walking toward us, slow and dreamy-moving, and by now the rain rushed down instead of fell down. It was like what my old folks used to call raining tomcats and hoe handles. I bowed my head to it, and made to pull Page toward Rafe's wigwam; but she wouldn't pull, she held where she was, till Rafe came up with us. Then, all three, we went together and got into the tight, dark shelter of the wigwam-house, with the rain and wind battering the outside of it.

Rafe and I sat on the big bed, and Page on a stool, looking small there. She wrung the water out of her hair.

"You all right?" she inquired Rafe.

I looked at him. Between the drain-off and the wigwam, rain had washed off that mud that gaumed all over him. He was wet and clean, with his patch-pelt shirt hanging away from his big chest and shoulders in soggy rags.

The lightning had singed off part of his beard. He lifted big finters to wipe off the wet fluffy ash, and I saw the stripe on his naked arm, on the broad back of his hand, and I made out another stripe just like it on the other. Lightning had slammed down both hands and arms, and clear down his flanks and legs—I saw the burnt lines on his fringed leggings. It was like a double lash of God's whip.

Page got off the stool and came close to him. Just then he didn't look so out-and-out much bigger than she was. She put a long gentle finger on that lightning lash where it ran along his shoulder.

"Does it hurt?" she asked. "You got some grease I could put on it?"

He lifted his head, heavy, but didn't look at her. He looked at me. "I lied to you all," he said.

"Lied to us?" I asked him.

"I did call for the rain. Called for the biggest rain I ever thought of. Didn't pure down want to kill off the folks in the Notch, but to my reckoning, if I made it rain, and saved Page up here—"

At last he looked at her, with a shamed face.

"The others would be gone and forgotten. There'd be Page and me." His dark eyes grabbed her green ones. "But I didn't rightly know how she disgusts the sight of me." His head dropped again. "I feel the nearest to nothing I ever did."

"You opened the drain-off and saved the Notch from your rain," put in Page, her voice so gentle you'd never think it. "Called down the lightning to help you."

"Called down the lightning to kill me," said Rafe. "I never reckoned it wouldn't. I wanted to die. I want to die now."

"Live," she bade him.

He got up at that, standing tall over her.

"Don't worry when folks look on you," she said, her voice still ever so gentle. "They're just wondered at you, Rafe. Folks were wondered that same way at Saint Christopher, the giant who carried Lord Jesus across the river."

"I was too proud," he mumbled in his big bull throat. "Proud of my Genesis giant blood, of being one of the sons of God—"

"Shoo, Rafe," and her voice was gentler still, "the least man in size you'd call for, when he speaks to God, he says, 'Our Father.' "

Rafe turned from her.

"You said I could look on you if I wanted," said Page Jarrett. "And I want."

Back he turned, and bent down, and she rose on her toetips so their faces came together.

The rain stopped, the way you'd think that stopped it. But they never seemed to know it, and I picked up my guitar and went out toward the lip of the cliff.

The falls were going strong, but the drain-off handled enough water so there'd be no washout to drown the folks below. I reckoned the rocks would be the outdoingist slippery rocks ever climbed down by mortal man, and it would take me a long time. Long enough, maybe so, for me to think out the right way to tell Mr. Lane Jarrett he was just before having himself a son-in-law of the Genesis giant blood, and pretty soon after while, grandchildren of the same strain.

The sun came stabbing through the clouds and flung them away in chunks to right and left, across the bright blue sky.

Damon Knight

Extempore

A multitalented professional whose career as writer, editor, critic, and anthologist spans more than fifty years, Damon Knight has long been a major shaping force in the development of modern science fiction. He wrote the first important book of SF criticism, *In Search of Wonder,* and won a Hugo Award for it. He was the founder of the Science Fiction Writers of America, co-founder of the prestigious Milford Writer's Conference, and, with his wife, writer Kate Wilhelm, was deeply involved for many years in the operation of the Clarion workshop for new writers, which was modeled after the Milford Conference. He was the editor of *Orbit,* the longest running original anthology series in the history of American science fiction, and has also produced important works of genre history such as *The Futurians* and *Turning Points,* as well as dozens of influential reprint anthologies. Knight has also been highly influential as a writer, and may well be one of the finest short story writers ever to work in the genre. His books include the novels *A for Anything, The Other Foot, Hell's Pavement, The Man in the Tree, CV,* and *A Reasonable World,* and the collections *Rule Golden and Other Stories, Turning On, Far Out,* and *The Best of Damon Knight.* His most recent books are the collection *One Side Laughing* and the novel *Why Do Birds. Humpty Dumpty: An Oval* was published in September of 1996. Knight lives with his family in Eugene, Oregon.

Knight hasn't written much overt fantasy, but several of his stories blur the borderlines between fantasy and SF. As does the mordant and elegant story that follows, which shows that you *can* make Magic work, even in the most mundane of circumstances, if you just *want* it to work badly enough. Once it does work, though, you'd better be prepared to accept the consequences . . .

Everybody knew; everybody wanted to help Rossi the time-traveler. They came running up the scarlet beach, naked and golden as children, laughing happily.

"Legend is true," they shouted. "He is here, just like great-grandfathers say!"

"What year is this?" Rossi asked, standing incongruously shirt-sleeved and alone in the sunlight—no great machines bulking around him, no devices, nothing but his own spindling body.

"Thairty-five twainty-seex, Mista Rossi!" they chorused.

"Thank you. Good-bye."

"Good-byee!"

Flick. Flick. Flick. Those were days. *Flicketaflicketaflick*—weeks, months, years. WHIRRR . . . Centuries, millennia streaming past like sleet in a gale!

Now the beach was cold, and the people were buttoned up to their throats in stiff black cloth. Moving stiffly, like jointed stick people, they unfurled a huge banner: "SORI WI DO NOT SPIC YOUR SPICH. THIS IS YIR 5199 OF YOUR CALINDAR. HELO MR ROSI."

They all bowed, like marionettes, and Mr. Rossi bowed back. *Flick. Flick. Flicketaflicketa*WHIRRR . . .

The beach was gone. He was inside an enormous building, a sky-high vault, like the Empire State turned into one room. Two floating eggs swooped at him and hovered alertly, staring with poached eyes. Behind them reared a tilted neon slab blazing with diagrams and symbols, none of which he could recognize before *flicketa*WHIRRR . . .

This time it was a wet stony plain, with salt marshes beyond it. Rossi was not interested and spent the time looking at the figures he had scrawled in his notebook. 1956, 1958, 1965 and so on, the intervals getting longer and longer, the curve rising until it was going almost straight up. If only he'd paid more attention to mathematics in school . . . *flick*RRR . . .

Now a white desert at night, bitter cold, where the towers of Manhattan should have been. Something mournfully thin flapped by over *flk*RRRR . . .

Blackness and fog was all he could *fk*RRRR . . .

Now the light and dark blinks in the grayness melted and ran together, flickering faster and faster until Rossi was looking at a bare leaping landscape as if through soap-smeared glasses—continents expanding and contracting, icecaps slithering down and back again, the planet charging toward its cold death while only Rossi stood there to watch, gaunt and stiff, with a disapproving, wistful glint in his eye.

His name was Albert Eustace Rossi. He was from Seattle, a wild bony young man with a poetic forelock and the stare-you-down eyes of an animal. He had learned nothing in twelve years of school except how to get passing marks, and he had a large wistfulness but no talents at all.

He had come to New York because he thought something wonderful might happen.

He averaged two months on a job. He worked as a short-order cook (his eggs were greasy and his hamburgers burned), a platemaker's helper in an offset shop, a shill in an auction gallery. He spent three weeks as a literary agent's critic, writing letters over his employer's signature to tell hapless reading-fee clients that their stories stank. He wrote bad verse for a while and sent it hopefully to all the best magazines, but concluded he was being held down by a clique.

He made no friends. The people he met seemed to be interested in nothing but baseball, or their incredibly boring jobs, or in making money. He tried hanging around the Village, wearing dungarees and a flowered shirt, but discovered that nobody noticed him.

It was the wrong century. What he wanted was a villa in Athens; or an island where the natives were childlike and friendly, and no masts ever lifted above the blue horizon; or a vast hygienic apartment in some future underground Utopia.

He bought certain science-fiction magazines and read them defiantly with the covers showing in cafeterias. Afterward, he took them home and marked them up with large exclamatory blue and red and green pencil and filed them away under his bed.

The idea of building a time machine had been growing a long while in his mind. Sometimes in the morning on his way to work, looking up at the blue cloud-dotted endlessness of the sky, or staring at the tracery of lines and whorls on his unique fingertips, or trying to see into the cavernous unexplored depths of a brick in a wall, or lying on his narrow bed at night, conscious of all the bewildering sights and sounds and odors that had swirled past him in twenty-odd years, he would say to himself, Why not?

Why not? He found a secondhand copy of J. W. Dunne's *An Experiment with Time* and lost sleep for a week. He copied off the charts from it, Scotch-taped them to his wall; he wrote down his startling dreams every morning as soon as he awoke. There was a time outside time, Dunne said, in which to measure time; and a time outside that, in which to measure the time that measured time and a time outside that. . . . Why not?

An article in a barbershop about Einstein excited him, and he went to the library and read the encyclopedia articles on relativity and space-time, frowning fiercely, going back again and again over the paragraphs he never did understand, but filling up all the same with a threshold feeling, an expectancy.

What looked like time to him might look like space to somebody else, said Einstein. A clock ran slower the faster it went. Good, fine. Why not? But it wasn't Einstein, or Minkowski or Wehl who gave him the clue; it was an astronomer named Milne.

There were two ways of looking at time, Milne said. If you measured it by things that moved, like clock hands and the earth turning and going around the sun, that was one kind; Milne called it dynamical time and his symbol for it was τ. But if you measured it by things happening in the atom, like radioactivity and light being emitted, that was another kind; Milne called it kinematic time, or *t*. And the formula that connected the two showed that it depended on which you used whether the universe had ever had a beginning or would ever have an end—yes in τ time, no in *t*.

Then it all added together: Dunne saying you didn't really have to travel along the timetrack like a train, you just thought you did, but when you were asleep you forgot, and that was why you could have prophetic dreams. And Eddington: that all the great laws of physics we had been able to discover were just a sort of spidery framework, and that there was room between the strands for an unimaginable complexity of things.

He believed it instantly; he had known it all his life but had never had any words to think it in—that this reality wasn't all there was. Paychecks, grimy windowsills, rancid grease, nails in the shoe—how could it be?

It was all in the way you looked at it. That was what the *scientists* were saying—Einstein, Eddington, Milne, Dunne, all in a chorus. So it was a thing anybody could do, if he wanted it badly enough and was lucky. Rossi had always felt obscurely resentful that the day was past when you could discover something by looking at a teakettle or dropping gunk on a hot stove; but here, incredibly, was one more easy road to fame that everybody had missed.

Between the tip of his finger and the edge of the soiled plastic cover that hideously draped the hideous table, the shortest distance was a straight line containing an infinite number of points. His own body, he knew, was mostly empty space. Down there in the shadowy regions of the atom, in *t* time, you could describe how fast an electron was moving or where it was, but never both; you could never decide whether it was a wave or a particle; you couldn't even prove it existed at all, except as the ghost of its reflection appeared to you.

Why not?

It was summer, and the whole city was gasping for breath. Rossi had two weeks off and nowhere to go; the streets were empty of the Colorado vacationers, the renters of cabins in the mountains, the tailored flyers to Ireland, the Canadian Rockies, Denmark, Nova Scotia. All day long the sweaty subways had inched their loads of suffering out to Coney Island and Far Rockaway and back again, well salted, flayed with heat, shocked into a fishy torpor.

Now the island was still; flat and steaming, like a flounder on a griddle; every window open for an unimagined breath of air; silent as if the city were under glass. In dark rooms the bodies lay sprawled like a cannibal feast, all wakeful, all moveless, waiting for Time's tick.

Rossi had fasted all day, having in mind the impressive results claimed by Yogis, early Christian saints and Amerinds; he had drunk nothing but a glass of water in the morning and another at blazing noon. Standing now in the close darkness of his room, he felt that ocean of Time, heavy and stagnant, stretching away forever. The galaxies hung in it like seaweed, and down at the bottom it was silted unfathomably deep with dead men. (Seashell murmur: I am.)

There it all was, temporal and eternal, t and tau, everything that was and would be. The electron dancing in its imaginary orbit, the mayfly's moment, the long drowse of the sequoias, the stretching of continents, the lonely drifting of stars; it canceled them all against each other, and the result was stillness.

The sequoia's truth did not make the mayfly false. If a man could only see some other aspect of that totality, feel it, believe it—another relation of tau time to t . . .

He had chalked a diagram on the floor—not a pentacle but the nearest thing he could find, the quadrisected circle of the Michelson apparatus. Around it he had scrawled, "$e = mc^2$," "Z^2/n^2," "$M = M_O + 3K + 2V$." Pinned up shielding the single bulb was a scrap of paper with some doggerel on it:

$$\frac{t, \tau, t, \tau, t \, \tau \, t}{c}$$
$$R \sqrt{3}$$

Cartesian co-ordinates x, y, z
$- c^2 t^2 = me$

It was in his head, hypnotically repeating: *t, tau, t, tau, t tau t* . . .

As he stood there, the outlines of the paper swelled and blurred, rhythmically. He felt as if the whole universe were breathing, slowly and gigantically, all one, the smallest atom and the farthest star.

c over R times the square root of three . . .

He had a curious drunken sense that he was standing *outside,* that he could reach in and give himself a push, or a twist—no, that wasn't the word, either. . . . But something was happening; he felt it, half in terror and half in delight.

less c squared, t squared, equals . . .

An intolerable tension squeezed Rossi tight. Across the room the paper, too near the bulb, crisped and burned. And (as the tension twisted him somehow, finding a new direction for release) that was the last thing Rossi saw before *flick,* it was daylight, and the room was clotted with moist char, *flick,* someone was moving across it, too swift to *flick. Flick. Flick. Flick, flick, flicketaflicketa* . . .

And here he was. Most incredibly, what had seemed so true *was* true: by that effort of tranced will, he had transferred himself to another time rate, another relationship to *t* to τ—a variable relationship, like a huge merry-go-round that whirled, and paused, and whirled again.

He had got on; how was he going to get off?

And—most terrifying question—where was the merry-go-round going? Whirling headlong to extinction and cold death, where the universe ended—or around the wheel again, to give him a second chance?

The blur exploded into white light. Stunned but safe inside his portable anomaly, Rossi watched the flaming earth cool, saw the emerging continents furred over with green, saw a kaleidoscope whirl of rainstorm and volcanic fury, pelting ice, earthquake, tsunami, fire!

Then he was in a forest, watching the branches sway as some great shape passed.

He was in a clearing, watching as a man in leather breeches killed a copper-skinned man with an ax.

He was in a log-walled room, watching a man in a wide collar stand up, toppling table and crockery, his eyes like onions.

He was in a church, and an old man behind the pulpit flung a book at him.

The church again, at evening, and two lonely women saw him and screamed.

He was in a bare, narrow room reeking of pitch. Somewhere outside, a dog set up a frenzied barking. A door opened and a wild, whiskery face popped in; a hand flung a blazing stick and flame leaped up. . . .

He was on a broad green lawn, alone with a small boy and a frantic white duck. "Good morrow, sir. Will you help me catch this pesky . . ."

He was in a little pavilion. A gray-bearded man at a desk turned, snatching up a silver cross, whispering fiercely to the young man at his side, *"Didn't I tell you!"* He pointed the cross, quivering. "Quick, then! Will New York continue to grow?"

Rossi was off guard. "Sure. This is going to be the biggest city . . ."

The pavilion was gone; he was in a little perfumed nook, facing a long room across a railing. A red-haired youth, dozing in front of the fire, sat up with a guilty start. He gulped. "Who . . . who's going to win the election?"

"What election?" said Rossi. "I don't—"

"Who's going to win?" The youth came forward, pale-faced. "Hoover or Roosevelt? Who?"

"Oh, that election. Roosevelt."

"Uh, will the country . . ."

The same room. A bell was ringing; white lights dazzled his eyes. The bell stopped. An amplified voice said, "When will Germany surrender?"

"Uh, 1945," said Rossi, squinting. "May, 1945. Look—whoever you are—"

"When will Japan surrender?"

"Same year. September. Look, whoever you are . . ."

A tousle-headed man emerged from the glare, blinking, wrapping a robe around his bulging middle. He stared at Rossi while the mechanical voice spoke behind him.

"Please name the largest new industry in the next ten years."

"Uh, television, I guess. Listen, you right there, can't you . . ."

The same room, the same bell ringing. This was all wrong, Rossi realized irritably. Nineteen thirty-two, 1944 (?)—the next ought to be at least close to where he had started. There was supposed to be a row of cheap rooming houses—his room, *here*.

". . . election, Stevenson or Eisenhower?"

"Stevenson. I mean, Eisenhower. Now look, doesn't *anybody*—"

"When will there be an armistice in Korea?"

"Last year. *Next* year. You're mixing me up. Will you turn off that—"

"When and where will atomic bombs next be used in—"

"Listen!" Rossi shouted. "I'm getting mad! If you want me to answer questions, let me ask some! Get me some help! Get me—"

"What place in the United States will be safest when—"

"Einstein!" shouted Rossi.

But the little gray man with the bloodhound eyes couldn't help him, nor the bald mustachioed one who was there the next time. The walls were inlaid now with intricate tracings of white metal. The voice began asking him questions he couldn't answer.

The second time it happened, there was a *puff* and a massive rotten stench rolled into his nostrils. Rossi choked. "Stop that!"

"Answer!" blared the voice. "What's the meaning of those signals from space?"

"I don't know!" *Puff.* Furiously: "But there isn't any New York past here! It's all gone—nothing left but . . ."

Puff!

Then he was standing on the lake of glassy obsidian, just like the first time.

And then the jungle, and he said automatically, "My name is Rossi. What year . . ." But it wasn't the jungle, really. It had been cleared back, and there were neat rows of concrete houses, like an enormous tank trap, instead of grass-topped verandas showing through the trees.

Then came the savanna, and that was all different, too—there was a looming piled ugliness of a city rising half a mile away. Where were the nomads, the horsemen?

And next . . .

The beach: but it was dirty gray, not scarlet. One lone dark figure was hunched against the sun glare, staring out to sea; the golden people were gone.

Rossi felt lost. Whatever had happened to New York, back there—to the whole world, probably—something he had said or done had made it come out differently. Somehow they had saved out some of the old grimy, rushing civilization, and it had lasted just long enough to blight all the fresh new things that ought to have come after it.

The stick men were not waiting on their cold beach.

He caught his breath. He was in the enormous building again, the same tilted slab blazing with light, the same floating eggs bulging their eyes at him. That hadn't changed, and perhaps nothing he could do would ever change it; for he knew well enough that that wasn't a human building.

But then came the white desert, and after it the fog, and his glimpses of the night began to blur together, faster and faster. . . .

That was all. There was nothing left now but the swift vertiginous spin to the end-and-beginning, and then the wheel slowing as he came around again.

Rossi began to seethe. This was worse than dishwashing—his nightmare, the worst job he knew. Standing here, like a second hand ticking around the face of Time, while men who flickered and vanished threaded him with questions: a thing, a tool, a gyrating information booth!

Stop, he thought, and pushed—a costive pressure inside his brain—but nothing happened. He was a small boy forgotten on a carousel, a bug trapped between window and screen, a moth circling a lamp. . . .

It came to him what the trouble was. There had to be the yearning, that single candle-cone focus of the spirit: that was the moving force, and all the rest—the fasting, the quiet, the rhymes—was only to channel and guide.

He would have to get off at the one place in the whole endless sweep of time where he wanted to be. And that place, he knew now without surprise, was the scarlet beach.

Which no longer existed, anywhere in the universe.

While he hung suspended on that thought, the flickering stopped at the prehistoric jungle; and the clearing with its copper dead man; and the log room, empty; the church, empty, too.

And the fiery room, now so fiercely ablaze that the hair of his forearms puffed and curled.

And his cool lawn, where the small boy stood agape.

And the pavilion: the graybeard and the young man leaning together like blasted trees, livid-lipped.

There was the trouble: they had believed him, the first time around, and acting on what he told them, they had changed the world.

Only one thing to be done—destroy that belief, fuddle them, talk nonsense, like a ghost called up at a séance!

"Then you tell me to put all I have in land," says graybeard, clutching the crucifix, "and wait for the increase!"

"Of course!" replied Rossi with instant cunning. "New York's to be the biggest city—in the whole state of Maine!"

The pavilion vanished. Rossi saw with pleasure that the room that took its place was high-ceilinged and shabby, the obvious forerunner of his own roach-haunted cubbyhole in 1955. The long paneled room with its fireplace and the youth dozing before it were gone, snuffed out, a might-have-been.

When a motherly looking woman lurched up out of a rocker, staring, he knew what to do.

He put his finger to his lips. "The lost candlestick is under the cellar stairs!" he hissed, and vanished.

The room was a little older, a little shabbier. A new partition had been added, bringing its dimensions down to those of the room Rossi knew, and there was a bed, and an old tin washbasin in the corner. A young woman was sprawled open-mouthed, fleshy and snoring, in the bed; Rossi looked away with faint prim disgust and waited.

The same room: *his* room, almost: a beefy stubbled man smoking in the armchair with his feet in a pan of water. The pipe dropped from his sprung jaw.

"I'm the family banshee," Rossi remarked. "Beware, for a short man with a long knife is dogging your footsteps." He squinted and bared his fangs; the man, standing up hurriedly, tipped the basin and stumbled half across the room before he recovered and whirled to the door, bellowing, leaving fat wet tracks and silence.

Now; *now* . . . It was night, and the sweaty unstirred heat of the city poured in around him. He was standing in the midst of the chalk marks he had scrawled a hundred billion years ago. The bare bulb was still lighted; around it flames were licking tentatively at the edges of the table, cooking the plastic cover up into lumpy hissing puffs.

Rossi the shipping clerk; Rossi the elevator man; Rossi the *dishwasher!*

He let it pass. The room kaleidoscope-flicked from brown to green; a young man at the washbasin was pouring something amber into a glass, gurgling and clinking.

"Boo!" said Rossi, flapping his arms.

The young man whirled in a spasm of limbs, a long arc of brown droplets hanging. The door banged him out, and Rossi was alone, watching the drinking glass roll, counting the seconds until . . .

The walls were brown again; a calendar across the room said 1965 MAY 1965. An old man, spidery on the edge of the bed, was fumbling spectacles over the rank crests of his ears. "You're real," he said.

"I'm not," said Rossi indignantly. He added, "Radishes. Lemons. Grapes. Blahhh!"

"Don't put me off," said the old man. He was ragged and hollow-templed, like a bird skull, colored like earth and milkweed floss, and his mouth was a drum over porcelain, but his oystery eyes were burning bright. "I knew the minute I saw you—you're Rossi, the one that disappeared. If you can do that—" his teeth clacked—"you must know, you've got to tell me. Those ships that have landed on the moon—what are they building there? What do they want?"

"I don't know. Nothing."

"Please," said the old man humbly. "You can't be so cruel. I tried to warn people, but they've forgotten who I am. If you know: if you could just tell me . . ."

Rossi had a qualm, thinking of heat flashing down in that one intolerable blow that would leave the city squashed, glistening, as flat as the thin film of a bug. But remembering that, after all, the old man was not real, he said, "There isn't anything. You made it up. You're dreaming."

And then, while the pure tension gathered and strained inside him, came the lake to obsidian.

And the jungle, just as it ought to be—the brown people caroling, "Hello, Mister Rossi, hello again, hello!"

And the savanna, the tall black-haired people reining in, breeze-blown, flash of teeth: "Hillo, Misser Rossi!"

And the *beach*.

The scarlet beach with its golden, laughing people: "Mista Rossi, Mista Rossi!" Heraldic glory under the clear sky, and out past the breakers the clear heart-stirring glint of sun on the sea: and the tension of the longing breaking free (stop), no need for symbols now (stop), a lifetime's distillation of *I wish* . . . spurting, channeled, done.

There he stands where he longed to be, wearing the same pleased expression, forever caught at the beginning of a hello—Rossi, the first man to travel in Time, and Rossi, the first man to Stop.

He's not to be mocked or mourned. Rossi was born a stranger; there are thousands of him, unconsidered gritty particles in the gears of history: the ne'er-do-wells, the superfluous people, shaped for some world that has never yet been invented. The air-conditioned utopias have no place for them; they would have been bad slaves and worse masters in Athens. As

for the tropic isles—the Marquesas of 1800, or the Manhattan of 3526—
could Rossi swim a mile, dive six fathoms, climb a fifty-foot palm? If he
had stepped alive onto that scarlet shore, would the young men have had
him in their canoes, or the maidens in their bowers? But see him now,
stonily immortal, the symbol of a wonderful thing that happened. The
childlike golden people visit him every day, except when they forget. They
drape his rock-hard flesh with garlands and lay little offerings at his feet;
and when he lets it rain, they thump him.

FRITZ LEIBER

Space-Time for Springers

With a fifty-year career that stretched from the "Golden Age" *Astounding* of the 1940s to the beginning of the 1990s, the late Fritz Leiber was an indispensable figure in the development of modern science fiction, fantasy, and horror. It is impossible to imagine what those genres would be like today without him, except to say that they would be the poorer for it. No other figure of his generation (with the possible exception of L. Sprague de Camp) wrote in as many different genres as Leiber, or was as important as he was to the development of each. Leiber can be considered one of the fathers of modern "heroic fantasy," and his long sequence of stories about Fafhrd and the Gray Mouser remains one of the most complex and intelligent bodies of work in the entire subgenre of "Sword & Sorcery" (which term Leiber himself is usually credited with coining). He may also be one of the best—if not *the* best—writers of the supernatural horror tale since Lovecraft and Poe, and was writing updated "modern" or "urban" horror stories like "Smoke Ghost" and the classic *Conjure Wife* long before the work of Stephen King engendered the Big Horror Boom of the middle 1970s and brought that form to wide popular attention.

Leiber was also a towering Ancestral Figure in science fiction as well, having been one of the major writers of both John W. Campbell's "Golden Age" *Astounding* of the 1940s—with works like *Gather, Darkness*—and H. L. Gold's *Galaxy* in the 1950s—with works like the classic "Coming Attraction" and the superb novel *The Big Time,* which still holds up as one of the best SF novels ever written. Leiber *then* went on to contribute a steady stream of superior fiction to the magazines and anthologies of the 1960s, the 1970s, and the 1980s, as well as powerful novels such as *The Wanderer* and *Our Lady of Darkness. The Big Time* won a well-deserved Hugo in 1959, and Leiber also won a slew of other awards: all told, six Hugos and four Nebulas, plus three World

Fantasy Awards—one of them the prestigious Life Achievement Award—and a Grand Master of Fantasy Award.

As with Avram Davidson, I found it impossible to capture even a hint of the breadth of Leiber's range with just one story. One of the best of the Fafhrd and Gray Mouser stories follows, sword and sorcery at its absolute finest, but first here is Leiber in quite a different mood. Just as Leiber's "Smoke Ghost" might fairly be said to have invented the "urban horror" story, so the sly and sprightly story that follows invented a whole new subgenre as well, one that has spawned dozens if not hundreds of stories, novels, and anthologies in subsequent decades. "Space-Time for Springers," however, is still probably the best story of its type, unrivaled even after more than a quarter of a century. As you will see, it's no *ordinary* cat story, and it's about no ordinary *cat* . . .

Fritz Leiber's other books include *The Green Millennium, A Specter Is Haunting Texas, The Big Time,* and *The Silver Eggheads,* the collections *The Best of Fritz Leiber, The Book of Fritz Leiber, The Changewar, Night's Black Agents, Heroes and Horrors, The Mind Spider,* and *The Ghost Light,* and the seven volumes of Fafhrd–Gray Mouser stories.

Gummitch was a superkitten, as he knew very well, with an I. Q. of about 160. Of course, he didn't talk. But everybody knows that I. Q. tests based on language ability are very one-sided. Besides, he would talk as soon as they started setting a place for him at table and pouring him coffee. Ashurbanipal and Cleopatra ate horsemeat from pans on the floor and they didn't talk. Baby dined in his crib on milk from a bottle and he didn't talk. Sissy sat at table but they didn't pour her coffee and she didn't talk—not one word. Father and Mother (whom Gummitch had nicknamed Old Horsemeat and Kitty-Come-Here) sat at table and poured each other coffee and they *did* talk. Q. E. D.

Meanwhile, he would get by very well on thought projection and intuitive understanding of all human speech—not even to mention cat patois, which almost any civilized animal could play by ear. The dramatic monologues and Socratic dialogues, the quiz and panel show appearances, the felidological expedition to darkest Africa (where he would uncover the real truth behind lions and tigers), the exploration of the outer planets—all these could wait. The same went for the books for which he was ceaselessly accumulating material: *The Encyclopedia of Odors, Anthropofeline Psychology, Invisible Signs and Secret Wonders, Space-Time for Springers, Slit Eyes Look at Life,* et cetera. For the present it was enough to live existence to the hilt and soak up knowledge, missing no experience proper to his age level—to rush about with tail aflame.

So to all outward appearances Gummitch was just a vividly normal kitten, as shown by the succession of nicknames he bore along the magic path that led from blue-eyed infancy toward puberty: Little One, Squawker, Portly, Bumble (for purring not clumsiness), Old Starved-to-Death, Fierso, Loverboy (affection not sex), Spook and Catnik. Of these only the last perhaps requires further explanation: the Russians had just sent Muttnik up after Sputnik, so that when one evening Gummitch streaked three times across the firmament of the living room floor in the same direction, past the fixed stars of the humans and the comparatively slow-moving heavenly bodies of the two older cats, and Kitty-Come-Here quoted the line from Keats:

> *Then felt I like some watcher of the skies*
> *When a new planet swims into his ken;*

it was inevitable that Old Horsemeat would say, "Ah—Catnik!"

The new name lasted all of three days, to be replaced by Gummitch, which showed signs of becoming permanent.

The little cat was on the verge of truly growing up, at least so Gummitch overheard Old Horsemeat comment to Kitty-Come-Here. A few short weeks, Old Horsemeat said, and Gummitch's fiery flesh would harden, his slim neck thicken, the electricity vanish from everything but his fur, and all his delightful kittenish qualities rapidly give way to the earthbound single-mindedness of a tom. They'd be lucky, Old Horsemeat concluded, if he didn't turn completely surly like Ashurbanipal.

Gummitch listened to these predictions with gay unconcern and with secret amusement from his vantage point of superior knowledge, in the same spirit that he accepted so many phases of his outwardly conventional existence: the murderous sidelong looks he got from Ashurbanipal and Cleopatra as he devoured his own horsemeat from his own little tin pan, because they sometimes were given canned cat food but he never; the stark idiocy of Baby, who didn't know the difference between a live cat and a stuffed teddy bear and who tried to cover up his ignorance by making goo-goo noises and poking indiscriminately at all eyes; the far more serious—because cleverly hidden—maliciousness of Sissy, who had to be watched out for warily—especially when you were alone—and whose retarded—even warped—development, Gummitch knew, was Old Horsemeat and Kitty-Come-Here's deepest, most secret, worry (more of Sissy and her evil ways soon); the limited intellect of Kitty-Come-Here, who despite the amounts of coffee she drank was quite as featherbrained as kittens are supposed to be and who firmly believed, for example, that kittens operated in the same space-time as other beings—that to get from *here* to *there* they had to cross the space *between*—and similar fallacies; the mental stodginess of even Old Horsemeat, who although he understood quite a bit of the secret doctrine and talked intelligently to Gummitch when they were alone, nevertheless suffered from the limitations of his status—a rather nice old god but a maddeningly slow-witted one.

But Gummitch could easily forgive all this massed inadequacy and downright brutishness in his felino-human household, because he was aware that he alone knew the real truth about himself and about other kittens and babies as well, the truth which was hidden from weaker minds, the truth that was as intrinsically incredible as the germ theory of disease or the origin of the whole great universe in the explosion of a single atom.

As a baby kitten Gummitch had believed that Old Horsemeat's two hands were hairless kittens permanently attatched to the ends of Old Horsemeat's arms but having an independent life of their own. How he had hated and loved those two five-legged sallow monsters, his first play-mates, comforters and battle-opponents!

Well, even that fantastic discarded notion was but a trifling fancy compared to the real truth about himself!

The forehead of Zeus split open to give birth to Minerva. Gummitch had been born from the waist-fold of a dirty old terry-cloth bathrobe, Old Horsemeat's basic garment. The kitten was intuitively certain of it and had proved it to himself as well as any Descartes or Aristotle. In a kitten-size tuck of that ancient bathrobe the atoms of his body had gathered and quickened into life. His earliest memories were of snoozing wrapped in terrycloth, warmed by Old Horsemeat's heat. Old Horsemeat and Kitty-Come-Here were his true parents. The other theory of his origin, the one he heard Old Horsemeat and Kitty-Come-Here recount from time to time—that he had been the only surviving kitten of a litter abandoned next door, that he had had the shakes from vitamin deficiency and lost the tip of his tail and the hair on his paws and had to be nursed back to life and health with warm yellowish milk-and-vitamins fed from an eyedropper—that other theory was just one of those rationalizations with which mysterious nature cloaks the birth of heroes, perhaps wisely veiling the truth from minds unable to bear it, a rationalization as false as Kitty-Come-Here and Old Horsemeat's touching belief that Sissy and Baby were their children rather than the cubs of Ashurbanipal and Cleopatra.

The day that Gummitch had discovered by pure intuition the secret of his birth he had been filled with a wild instant excitement. He had only kept it from tearing him to pieces by rushing out to the kitchen and striking and devouring a fried scallop, torturing it fiendishly first for twenty minutes.

And the secret of his birth was only the beginning. His intellectual faculties aroused, Gummitch had two days later intuited a further and greater secret: since he was the child of humans he would, upon reaching this maturation date of which Old Horsemeat had spoken, turn not into a sullen tom but into a godlike human youth with reddish golden hair the color of his present fur. He would be poured coffee; and he would instantly be able to talk, probably in all languages. While Sissy (how clear it was now!) would at approximately the same time shrink and fur out into a sharp-clawed and vicious she-cat dark as her hair, sex and self-love her only concerns, fit harem-mate for Cleopatra, concubine to Ashurbanipal.

Exactly the same was true, Gummitch realized at once, for all kittens and babies, all humans and cats, wherever they might dwell. Metamorphosis was as much a part of the fabric of their lives as it was of the insects'. It was also the basic fact underlying all legends of werewolves, vampires and witches' familiars.

If you just rid your mind of preconceived notions, Gummitch told himself, it was all very logical. Babies were stupid, fumbling, vindictive creatures without reason or speech. What could be more natural than that they should grow up into mute sullen selfish beasts bent only on rapine and reproduction? While kittens were quick, sensitive, subtle, supremely alive. What other destiny were they possibly fitted for except to become the deft, word-speaking, book-writing, music-making, meat-getting-and-dispensing masters of the world? To dwell on the physical differences, to point out that kittens and men, babies and cats, are rather unlike in appearance and size, would be to miss the forest for the trees—very much as if an entomologist should proclaim metamorphosis a myth because his microscope failed to discover the wings of a butterfly in a caterpillar's slime or a golden beetle in a grub.

Nevertheless it was such a mind-staggering truth, Gummitch realized at the same time, that it was easy to understand why humans, cats, babies and perhaps most kittens were quite unaware of it. How to safely explain to a butterfly that he was once a hairy crawler, or to a dull larva that he will one day be a walking jewel? No, in such situations the delicate minds of man- and feline-kind are guarded by a merciful mass amnesia, such as Velikovsky has explained prevents us from recalling that in historical times the Earth was catastrophically bumped by the planet Venus operating in the manner of a comet before settling down (with a cosmic sigh of relief, surely!) into its present orbit.

This conclusion was confirmed when Gummitch in the first fever of illumination tried to communicate his great insight to others. He told it in cat patois, as well as that limited jargon permitted, to Ashurbanipal and Cleopatra and even, on the off chance, to Sissy and Baby. They showed no interest whatever, except that Sissy took advantage of his unguarded preoccupation to stab him with a fork.

Later, alone with Old Horsemeat, he projected the great new thoughts, staring with solemn yellow eyes at the old god, but the latter grew markedly nervous and even showed signs of real fear, so Gummitch desisted. ("You'd have sworn he was trying to put across something as deep as the Einstein theory or the doctrine of original sin," Old Horsemeat later told Kitty-Come-Here.)

But Gummitch was a man now in all but form, the kitten reminded himself after these failures, and it was part of his destiny to shoulder secrets alone when necessary. He wondered if the general amnesia would affect him when he metamorphosed. There was no sure answer to this question, but he hoped not—and sometimes felt that there was reason for his hopes. Perhaps he would be the first true kitten-man, speaking from a wisdom that had no locked doors in it.

Once he was tempted to speed up the process by the use of drugs. Left alone in the kitchen, he sprang onto the table and started to lap up the black puddle in the bottom of Old Horsemeat's coffee cup. It tasted foul and poisonous and he withdrew with a little snarl, frightened as well as revolted. The dark beverage would not work its tongue-loosening magic, he realized, except at the proper time and with the proper ceremonies. Incantations might be necessary as well. Certainly unlawful tasting was highly dangerous.

The futility of expecting coffee to work any wonders by itself was further demonstrated to Gummitch when Kitty-Come-Here, wordlessly badgered by Sissy, gave a few spoonfuls to the little girl, liberally lacing it first with milk and sugar. Of course Gummitch knew by now that Sissy was destined shortly to turn into a cat and that no amount of coffee would ever make her talk, but it was nevertheless instructive to see how she spat out the first mouthful, drooling a lot of saliva after it, and dashed the cup and its contents at the chest of Kitty-Come-Here.

Gummitch continued to feel a great deal of sympathy for his parents in their worries about Sissy and he longed for the day when he would metamorphose and be able as an acknowledged man-child truly to console them. It was heartbreaking to see how they each tried to coax the little girl to talk, always attempting it while the other was absent, how they seized on each accidentally wordlike note in the few sounds she uttered and repeated it back to her hopefully, how they were more and more possessed by fears not so much of her retarded (they thought) development as of her increasingly obvious maliciousness, which was directed chiefly at Baby . . . though the two cats and Gummitch bore their share. Once she had caught Baby alone in his crib and used the sharp corner of a block to dot Baby's large-domed lightly downed head with triangular red marks. Kitty-Come-Here had discovered her doing it, but the woman's first action had been to rub Baby's head to obliterate the marks so that Old Horsemeat wouldn't see them. That was the night Kitty-Come-Here hid the abnormal psychology books.

Gummitch understood very well that Kitty-Come-Here and Old Horse-meat, honestly believing themselves to be Sissy's parents, felt just as deeply about her as if they actually were and he did what little he could under the present circumstances to help them. He had recently come to feel a quite independent affection for Baby--the miserable little proto-cat was so completely stupid and defenseless--and so he unofficially constituted himself the creature's guardian, taking his naps behind the door of the nursery and dashing about noisily whenever Sissy showed up. In any case he realized that as a potentially adult member of a felino-human household he had his natural responsibilities.

Accepting responsibilities was as much a part of a kitten's life, Gummitch told himself, as shouldering unsharable intuitions and secrets, the number of which continued to grow from day to day.

There was, for instance, the Affair of the Squirrel Mirror.

Gummitch had early solved the mystery of ordinary mirrors and of the creatures that appeared in them. A little observation and sniffing and one attempt to get behind the heavy wall-job in the living room had convinced him that mirror beings were insubstantial or at least hermetically sealed into their other world, probably creatures of pure spirit, harmless imitative ghosts--including the silent Gummitch Double who touched paws with him so softly yet so coldly.

Just the same, Gummitch had let his imagination play with what would happen if one day, while looking into the mirror world, he should let loose his grip on his spirit and let it slip into the Gummitch Double while the other's spirit slipped into his body--if, in short, he should change places with the scentless ghost kitten. Being doomed to a life consisting wholly of imitation and completely lacking in opportunities to show initiative--except for behind-the-scenes judgment and speed needed in rushing from one mirror to another to keep up with the real Gummitch--would be sickeningly dull, Gummitch decided, and he resolved to keep a tight hold on his spirit at all times in the vicinity of mirrors.

But that isn't telling about the Squirrel Mirror. One morning Gummitch was peering out the front bedroom window that overlooked the roof of the porch. Gummitch had already classified windows as semi-mirrors having two kinds of space on the other side: the mirror world and that harsh region filled with mysterious and dangerously organized-sounding noises called the outer world, into which grown-up humans reluctantly ventured at intervals, donning special garments for the purpose and shouting loud farewells that were meant to be reassuring but achieved just the opposite effect. The coexistence of two kinds of space presented no paradox to the kitten who carried in his mind the 27-chapter outline of *Space-Time for Springers*--indeed, it constituted one of the minor themes of the book.

This morning the bedroom was dark and the outer world was dull and sunless, so the mirror world was unusually difficult to see. Gummitch was just lifting his face toward it, nose twitching, his front paws on the sill, when what should rear up on the other side, exactly in the space that the Gummitch Double normally occupied, but a dirty brown, narrow-visaged image with savagely low forehead, dark evil walleyes, and a huge jaw filled with shovel-like teeth.

Gummitch was enormously startled and hideously frightened. He felt his grip on his spirit go limp, and without volition he teleported himself three yards to the rear, making use of that faculty for cutting corners in space-time, traveling by space-warp in fact, which was one of his powers that Kitty-Come-Here refused to believe in and that even Old Horsemeat accepted only on faith.

Then, not losing a moment, he picked himself up by his furry seat, swung himself around, dashed downstairs at top speed, sprang to the top of the sofa, and stared for several seconds at the Gummitch Double in the wall-mirror—not relaxing a muscle strand until he was completely convinced that he was still himself and had not been transformed into the nasty brown apparition that had confronted him in the bedroom window.

"Now what do you suppose brought that on?" Old Horsemeat asked Kitty-Come-Here.

Later Gummitch learned that what he had seen had been a squirrel, a savage, nut-hunting being belonging wholly to the outer world (except for forays into attics) and not at all to the mirror one. Nevertheless he kept a vivid memory of his profound momentary conviction that the squirrel had taken the Gummitch Double's place and been about to take his own. He shuddered to think what would have happened if the squirrel had been actively interested in trading spirits with him. Apparently mirrors and mirror-situations, just as he had always feared, were highly conducive to spirit transfers. He filed the information away in the memory cabinet reserved for dangerous, exciting and possibly useful information, such as plans for climbing straight up glass (diamond-tipped claws!) and flying higher than the trees.

These days his thought cabinets were beginning to feel filled to bursting and he could hardly wait for the moment when the true rich taste of coffee, lawfully drunk, would permit him to speak.

He pictured the scene in detail: the family gathered in conclave at the kitchen table, Ashurbanipal and Cleopatra respectfully watching from floor level, himself sitting erect on chair with paws (or would they be hands?) lightly touching his cup of thin china, while Old Horsemeat poured the thin black steaming stream. He knew the Great Transformation must be close at hand.

At the same time he knew that the other critical situation in the household was worsening swiftly. Sissy, he realized now, was far older than Baby and should long ago have undergone her own somewhat less glamorous though equally necessary transformation (the first tin of raw horsemeat could hardly be as exciting as the first cup of coffee). Her time was long overdue. Gummitch found increasing horror in this mute vampirish being inhabiting the body of a rapidly growing girl, though inwardly equipped to be nothing but a most bloodthirsty she-cat. How dreadful to think of Old Horsemeat and Kitty-Come-Here having to care all their lives for such a monster! Gummitch told himself that if any opportunity for alleviating his parents' misery should ever present itself to him, he would not hesitate for an instant.

Then one night, when the sense of Change was so burstingly strong in him that he knew tomorrow must be the Day, but when the house was also exceptionally unquiet with boards creaking and snapping, taps adrip, and curtains mysteriously rustling at closed windows (so that it was clear that the many spirit worlds including the mirror one must be pressing very close), the opportunity came to Gummitch.

Kitty-Come-Here and Old Horsemeat had fallen into especially sound, drugged sleeps, the former with a bad cold, the latter with one unhappy highball too many (Gummitch knew he had been brooding about Sissy). Baby slept too, though with uneasy whimperings and joggings—moonlight shone full on his crib past a window shade which had whirringly rolled itself up without human or feline agency. Gummitch kept vigil under the crib, with eyes closed but with wildly excited mind pressing outward to every boundary of the house and even stretching here and there into the outer world. On this night of all nights sleep was unthinkable.

Then suddenly he became aware of footsteps, footsteps so soft they must, he thought, be Cleopatra's.

No, softer than that, so soft they might be those of the Gummitch Double escaped from the mirror world at last and padding up toward him through the darkened halls. A ribbon of fur rose along his spine.

Then into the nursery Sissy came prowling. She looked slim as an Egyptian princess in her long thin yellow nightgown and as sure of herself, but the cat was very strong in her tonight, from the flat intent eyes to the dainty canine teeth slightly bared—one look at her now would have sent Kitty-Come-Here running for the telephone number she kept hidden, the telephone number of the special doctor—and Gummitch realized he was witnessing a monstrous suspension of natural law in that this being should be able to exist for a moment without growing fur and changing round pupils for slit eyes.

He retreated to the darkest corner of the room, suppressing a snarl.

Sissy approached the crib and leaned over Baby in the moonlight, keeping her shadow off him. For a while she gloated. Then she began softly to scratch his cheek with a long hatpin she carried, keeping away from his eye, but just barely. Baby awoke and saw her and Baby didn't cry. Sissy continued to scratch, always a little more deeply. The moonlight glittered on the jeweled end of the pin.

Gummitch knew he faced a horror that could not be countered by running about or even spitting and screeching. Only magic could fight so obviously supernatural a manifestation. And this was also no time to think of consequences, no matter how clearly and bitterly etched they might appear to a mind intensely awake.

He sprang up onto the other side of the crib, not uttering a sound, and fixed his golden eyes on Sissy's in the moonlight. Then he moved forward straight at her evil face, stepping slowly, not swiftly, using his extraordinary knowledge of the properties of space *to walk straight through her hand and arm as they flailed the hatpin at him*. When his nose-tip finally paused a fraction of an inch from hers his eyes had not blinked once, and she could not look away. Then he unhesitatingly flung his spirit into her like a fistful of flaming arrows and he worked the Mirror Magic.

Sissy's moonlit face, feline and terrified, was in a sense the last thing that Gummitch, the real Gummitch-kitten, ever saw in this world. For the next instant he felt himself enfolded by the foul black blinding cloud of Sissy's spirit, which his own had displaced. At the same time he heard the little girl scream, very loudly but even more distinctly, *"Mommy!"*

That cry might have brought Kitty-Come-Here out of her grave, let alone from sleep merely deep or drugged. Within seconds she was in the nursery, closely followed by Old Horsemeat, and she had caught up Sissy in her arms and the little girl was articulating the wonderful word again and again, and miraculously following it with the command—there could be no doubt, Old Horsemeat heard it too—"Hold me tight!"

Then Baby finally dared to cry. The scratches on his cheek came to attention and Gummitch, as he had known must happen, was banished to the basement amid cries of horror and loathing chiefly from Kitty-Come-Here.

The little cat did not mind. No basement would be one-tenth as dark as Sissy's spirit that now enshrouded him for always, hiding all the file drawers and the labels on all the folders, blotting out forever even the imagining of the scene of first coffee-drinking and first speech.

In a last intuition, before the animal blackness closed in utterly, Gummitch realized that the spirit, alas, is not the same thing as the consciousness and that one may lose—sacrifice—the first and still be burdened with the second.

Old Horsemeat had seen the hatpin (and hid it quickly from Kitty-Come-Here) and so he knew that the situation was not what it seemed and that Gummitch was at the very least being made into a sort of scapegoat. He was quite apologetic when he brought the tin pans of food to the basement during the period of the little cat's exile. It was a comfort to Gummitch, albeit a small one. Gummitch told himself, in his new black halting manner of thinking, that after all a cat's best friend is his man.

From that night Sissy never turned back in her development. Within two months she had made three years' progress in speaking. She became an outstandingly bright, light-footed, high-spirited little girl. Although she never told anyone this, the moonlit nursery and Gummitch's magnified face were her first memories. Everything before that was inky blackness. She was always very nice to Gummitch in a careful sort of way. She could never stand to play the game "Owl Eyes."

After a few weeks Kitty-Come-Here forgot her fears and Gummitch once again had the run of the house. But by then the transformation Old Horsemeat had always warned about had fully taken place. Gummitch was a kitten no longer but an almost burly tom. In him it took the psychological form not of sullenness or surliness but an extreme dignity. He seemed at times rather like an old pirate brooding on treasures he would never live to dig up, shores of adventure he would never reach. And sometimes when you looked into his yellow eyes you felt that he had in him all the materials for the book *Slit Eyes Look at Life*—three or four volumes at least—although he would never write it. And that was natural when you come to think of it, for as Gummitch knew very well, bitterly well indeed, his fate was to be the only kitten in the world that did not grow up to be a man.

FRITZ LEIBER

Scylla's Daughter

There are only a few real giants in the "heroic fantasy" field; once you have made the obligatory bow to past masters like Robert E. Howard, Clark Ashton Smith, E. R. Eddison, C. L. Moore, and Lord Dunsany, you come very quickly to Fritz Leiber.

Even among contemporary heroic fantasy writers, Leiber is seriously rivaled for excellence only by Jack Vance (and, to a somewhat lesser degree, by Michael Moorcock and Poul Anderson). Leiber's roots, however, go all the way back to 1939, when he began publishing (in *Unknown*—for which magazine the stories were untypical, with editor John Campbell frequently complaining that they *ought* to be published in *Weird Tales* instead) the first of a long series of stories and novels about that swashbuckling pair of rogues, Fafhrd and the Gray Mouser, which ran throughout the late 1930s and early 1940s in *Unknown* until wartime paper shortages killed the magazine.

After a long gap in the 1950s following the death of *Unknown,* editor Cele Goldsmith coaxed Leiber to revive Fafhrd and the Gray Mouser for the pages of *Fantastic* in the early 1960s, and thereafter Leiber continued to produce new stories in the sequence from time to time right up until his death in 1992, the series finding a refuge in *The Magazine of Fantasy & Science Fiction* and in various other magazines and fantasy anthologies after the death of *Fantastic.* By the end of his life, Leiber had built the Fafhrd and Gray Mouser stories into the most complex, stylish, and intelligent body of work in the entire subgenre of "Sword & Sorcery;" not surprisingly, the only such story ever to win a Nebula and Hugo Award was Leiber's own "Ill Met in Lankhmar." The series is an essential foundation stone for a great deal of subsequent fantasy work, being, for instance (among many less obvious examples), the inspiration for Joanna Russ's later series of stories about the adventures of Alyx, and even a (somewhat more oblique) influence on Samuel R. Delany's *Nevèrÿon* series, which in some ways can be read, in part, as a postmodern comment on Leiber's Fafhrd and Gray Mouser stories. All told, there were eight volumes of stories about Fafhrd and the Gray Mouser, including *Swords against Death, Swords in the Mist, Swords and Deviltry, The Swords of Lankhmar, Swords against Wizardry, Swords and Ice Magic,* and *The Knight and Knave of Swords.* The entire series is being reissued in omnibus volumes by White Wolf, the first such volume being *Ill Met in Lankhmar.*

Here's one of the best of the Fafhrd and Gray Mouser stories: sleek, intelligent, sophisticated, and engrossing, as full of sly wit and understated humor as it is furnished with suspense, swashbuckling physical action, and dark supernatural menace, charged (as Leiber's work often was) with an undercurrent of eroticism and sensual tension—and even a stylishly decadent hint of fetishistic sex—and peopled with complex and fascinating characters, both human and decidedly *not* human . . .

With the motherly-generous west wind filling their brown triangular sails, the slim war galley and the five broad-beamed grain ships, two nights out of Lankhmar, coursed north in line ahead across the Inner Sea of the ancient world of Nehwon.

It was late afternoon of one of those mild blue days when sea and sky are the same hue, providing irrefutable evidence for the hypothesis currently favored by Lankhmar philosophers: that Nehwon is a giant bubble rising through the waters of eternity with continents, islands, and the great jewels that at night are the stars all orderly afloat on the bubble's inner surface.

On the afterdeck of the last grain ship, which was also the largest, the Gray Mouser spat a plum skin to leeward and boasted luxuriously, "Fat times in Lankhmar! Not one day returned to the City of the Black Toga after months away adventuring and I procure us this cushy job from the Overlord himself."

"I have an old distrust of cushy jobs," Fafhrd replied, yawning and pulling his fur-trimmed jerkin open wider so that the mild wind might trickle more fully through the tangled hair-field of his chest. "And you got us out of Lankhmar so quickly that we had not even time to pay our respects to the ladies. Nevertheless I must confess that you might have done worse. A full purse is the best ballast for any man-ship, especially one bearing letters of marque against ladies."

Ship's Master Slinoor looked back with hooded appraising eyes at the small lithe gray-clad man and his tall, more gaudily accoutered barbarian comrade. The master of the *Squid* was a sleek black-robed man of middle years. He stood beside the two stocky black-tunicked bare-legged sailors who held steady the great high-arching tiller that guided the *Squid*.

"How much do you two rogues really know of your cushy job?" Slinoor asked softly. "Or rather, how much did the arch-noble Glipkerio
choose to tell you of the purpose and dark antecedents of this voyaging?"
Two days of fortunate sailing seemed at last to have put the closed-
mouthed ship's master in a mood to exchange confidences, or at least
trade queries and lies.

From a bag of netted cord that hung by the taffrail, the Mouser speared
a night-purple plum with the hook-bladed dirk he called Cat's Claw.
Then he answered lightly, "This fleet bears a gift of grain from Overlord
Glipkerio to Movarl of the Eight Cities in gratitude for Movarl's sweeping the Mingol pirates from the Inner Sea and mayhap diverting the
steppe-dwelling Mingols from assaulting Lankhmar across the Sinking
Land. Movarl needs grain for his hunter-farmers turned cityman-soldiers
and especially to supply his army relieving his border city of Klelg Nar,
which the Mingols besiege. Fafhrd and I are, you might say, a small but
mighty rear guard for the grain and for certain more delicate items of Glipkerio's gift."

"You mean those?" Slinoor bent a thumb toward the larboard rail.

Those were twelve large white rats distributed among four silver-barred
cages. With their silky coats, pale-rimmed blue eyes and especially their
short, arched upper lips and two huge upper incisors, they looked like a
clique of haughty, bored inbred aristocrats, and it was in a bored aristocratic fashion that they were staring at a scrawny black kitten which was
perched with dug-in claws on the starboard rail, as if to get as far away
from the rats as possible, and staring back at them most worriedly.

Fafhrd reached out and ran a finger down the black kitten's back. The
kitten arched its spine, losing itself for a moment in sensuous delight, but
then edged away and resumed its worried rat-peering—an activity shared
by the two black-tunicked helmsmen, who seemed both resentful and fearful of the silver-caged afterdeck passengers.

The Mouser sucked plum juice from his fingers and flicked out his
tongue-tip to neatly capture a drop that threatened to run down his chin.
Then, "No, I mean not chiefly those high-bred gift rats," he replied to Slinoor and kneeling lightly and unexpectedly and touching two fingers sig-
nificantly to the scrubbed oak deck, he said, "I mean chiefly *she* who is
below, who ousts you from your master's cabin, and who now insists that
the gift-rats require sunlight and fresh air—which strikes me as a strange
way of cosseting burrow and shadow-dwelling vermin."

Slinoor's cropped eyebrows rose. He came close and whispered, "You
think the Demoiselle Hisvet may not be merely the conductress of the
rat-gift, but also herself part of Glipkerio's gift to Movarl? Why, she's the
daughter of the greatest grain merchant in Lankhmar, who's grown rich
selling tawny corn to Glipkerio."

The Mouser smiled cryptically but said nothing.

Slinoor frowned, then whispered even lower, "True, I've heard the story that Hisvet has already been her father Hisven's gift to Glipkerio to buy his patronage."

Fafhrd, who'd been trying to stroke the kitten again with no more success than to chase it up the aftermast, turned around at that. "Why, Hisvet's but a child," he said almost reprovingly. "A most prim and proper miss, I know not of Glipkerio, he seems decadent—" (The word was not an insult in Lankhmar) "—but surely Movarl, a northerner albeit a forest man, likes only strong-beamed, ripe, complete women."

"Your own tastes, no doubt?" the Mouser remarked, gazing at Fafhrd with half-closed eyes. "No traffic with childlike women?"

Fafhrd blinked as if the Mouser had dug fingers in his side. Then he shrugged and said loudly, "What's so special about these rats? Do they do tricks?"

"Aye," Slinoor said distastefully. "They play at being men. They've been trained by Hisvet to dance to music, to drink from cups, hold tiny spears and swords, even fence. I've not seen it—nor would care to."

The picture struck the Mouser's fancy. He visioned himself small as a rat, dueling with rats who wore lace at their throats and wrists, slipping through the mazy tunnels of their underground cities, becoming a great connoisseur of cheese and smoked meats, perchance wooing a slim rat queen and being surprised by her rat-king husband and having to dagger-fight him in the dark. Then he noted one of the white rats looking at him intently through the silver bars with a cold inhuman blue eye and suddenly his idea didn't seem amusing at all. He shivered in the sunlight.

Slinoor was saying, "It is not good for animals to try to be men." The *Squid's* skipper gazed somberly at the silent white aristos. "Have you ever heard tell of the legend of—" he began, hesitated, then broke off, shaking his head as if deciding he had been about to say too much.

"A sail!" The call winged down thinly from the crow's nest. "A black sail to windward!"

"What manner of ship?" Slinoor shouted up.

"I know not, master. I see only sail top."

"Keep her under view, boy," Slinoor commanded.

"Under view it is, master."

Slinoor paced to the starboard rail and back.

"Movarl's sails are green," Fafhrd said thoughtfully.

Slinoor nodded. "Ilthmar's are white. The pirates' were red, mostly, Lankhmar's sails once were black, but now that color's only for funeral barges and they never venture out of sight of land. At least I've never known . . ."

The Mouser broke in with, "You spoke of dark antecedents of this voyaging. Why dark?"

*   *   *

Slinoor drew them back against the taffrail, away from the stocky helmsmen. Fafhrd ducked a little, passing under the arching tiller. They looked
all three into the twisting wake, their heads bent together.

Slinoor said, "You've been out of Lankhmar. Did you know this is not
the first gift-fleet of grain to Movarl?"

The Mouser nodded. "We'd been told there was another. Somehow
lost. In a storm, I think. Glipkerio glossed over it."

"There were two," Slinoor said tersely. "Both lost. Without a living
trace. There was no storm."

"What then?" Fafhrd asked, looking around as the rats chittered a little. "Pirates?"

"Movarl had already whipped the pirates east. Each of the two fleets was
galley-guarded like ours. And each sailed off into fair weather with a good
west wind." Slinoor smiled thinly. "Doubtless Glipkerio did not tell you of
these matters for fear you might beg off. We sailors and the Lankhmarines
obey for duty and the honor of the City, but of late Glipkerio's had trouble hiring the sort of special agents he likes to use for second bow-strings.
He has brains of a sort, our overlord has, though he employs them mostly
to dream of visiting other world bubbles in a great diving-bell or sealed
brass diving-ship, while he sits with trained girls watching trained rats and
buys off Lankhmar's enemies with gold and repays Lankhmar's ever-
more-impatient friends with grain not soldiers." Slinoor grunted. "Movarl
grows most impatient, you know, He threatens, if the grain comes not, to
recall his pirate patrol, league with the land-Mingols and set them at
Lankhmar."

"Northerners, even though not snow-dwelling, league with Mingols?"
Fafhrd objected. "Impossible!"

Slinoor looked at him. "I'll say just this, ice-eating northerner. If I did
not believe such a leaguer both possible and likely—and Lankhmar
thereby in dire danger—I would never have sailed with this fleet, honor
and duty or no. Same's true of Lukeen who commands the galley. Nor
do I think Glipkerio would otherwise be sending to Movarl at Kvarch Nar
his noblest performing rats and dainty Hisvet."

Fafhrd growled a little. "You say both fleets were lost without a trace?"
he asked incredulously.

Slinoor shook his head. "The first was. Of the second, some wreckage
was sighted by an Ilthmar trader Lankhmar-bound. The deck of only one
grain ship. It had been ripped off its hull, splinteringly—how or by that,
the Ilthmart dared not guess. Tied to a fractured stretch of railing was the
ship's-master, only hours dead. His face had been nibbled, his body
gnawed."

"Fish?" the Mouser asked.

"Seabirds?" Fafhrd inquired.

"Dragons?" a third voice suggested, high, breathless, and as merry as a schoolgirl's. The three men turned around, Slinoor with guilty swiftness.

The Demoiselle Hisvet stood as tall as the Mouser, but judging by her face, wrists, and ankles was considerably slenderer. Her face was delicate and taper-chinned with small mouth and pouty upper lip that lifted just enough to show a double dash of pearly tooth. Her complexion was creamy pale except for two spots of color high on her cheeks. Her straight fine hair, which grew low on her forehead, was pure white touched with silver and all drawn back through a silver ring behind her neck, whence it hung unbraided like a unicorn's tail. Her eyes had china whites but darkly pink irises around the large black pupils. Her body was enveloped and hidden by a loose robe of violet silk except when the wind briefly molded a flat curve of her girlish anatomy. There was a violet hood, half thrown back. The sleeves were puffed but snug at the wrists. She was barefoot, her skin showing as creamy there as on her face, except for a tinge of pink about the toes.

She looked them all three one after another quickly in the eye. "You were whispering of the fleets that failed," she said accusingly. "Fie, Master Slinoor. We must all have courage."

"Aye," Fafhrd agreed, finding that a cue to his liking. "Even dragons need not daunt a brave man. I've often watched the sea monsters, crested, horned, and some two-headed, playing in the waves of outer ocean as they broke around the rocks sailors call the Claws. They were not to be feared, if a man remembered always to fix them with a commanding eye. They sported lustily together, the man dragons pursuing the woman dragons and going–" Here Fafhrd took a tremendous breath and then roared out so loudly and wailingly that the two helmsmen jumped–*"Hoongk! Hoongk!"*

"Fie, Swordsman Fafhrd," Hisvet said primly, a blush mantling her cheeks and forehead. "You are most indelicate. The sex of dragons–"

But Slinoor had whirled on Fafhrd, gripping his wrist and now crying, "Quiet, you monster-fool! Know you not we sail tonight by moonlight past the Dragon Rocks? You'll call them down on us!"

"There are no dragons in the Inner Sea," Fafhrd laughingly assured him.

"There's something that tears ships," Slinoor asserted stubbornly.

The Mouser took advantage of this brief interchange to move in on Hisvet, rapidly bowing thrice as he approached.

"We have missed the great pleasure of your company on deck, Demoiselle," he said suavely.

"Alas, sir, the sun mislikes me," she answered prettily. "Now his rays are mellowed as he prepared to submerge. Then too," she added with an equally pretty shudder, "these rough sailors–" She broke off as she saw that Fafhrd and the master of the *Squid* had stopped their argument and returned to her. "Oh, I meant not you, dear Master Slinoor," she assured him, reaching out and almost touching his black robe.

"Would the Demoiselle fancy a sun-warmed, wind-cooled black plum of Sarheenmar?" the Mouser suggested, delicately sketching in the air with Cat's Claw.

"I know not." Hisvet said, eyeing the dirk's needlelike point. "I must be thinking of getting the White Shadows below before the evening's chill is upon us."

"True," Fafhrd agreed with a flattering laugh, realizing she must mean the white rats. "But 'twas most wise of you, little mistress, to let them spend the day on deck, where they surely cannot hanker so much to sport with the Black Shadows—I mean, of course, their black free commoner brothers, and slim delightful sisters, to be sure, hiding here and there in the hold."

"There are no rats on my ship, sportive or otherwise," Slinoor asserted instantly, his voice loud and angry. "Think you I run a rat-brothel? Your pardon, Demoiselle," he added quickly to Hisvet. "I mean, there are no common rats aboard *Squid.*"

"Then yours is surely the first grain ship so blessed," Fafhrd told him with indulgent reasonableness.

The sun's vermillion disk touched the sea to the west and flattened like a tangerine. Hisvet leaned back against the taffrail under the arching tiller. Fafhrd was to her right, the Mouser to her left with the plums hanging just beyond him, near the silver cages. Slinoor had moved haughtily forward to speak to the helmsmen, or pretend to.

"I'll take that plum now, Dirksman Mouser," Hisvet said softly.

As the Mouser turned away in happy obedience and with many a graceful gesture, delicately palpating the net bag to find the most tender fruit, Hisvet stretched her right arm out sideways and without looking once at Fafhrd slowly ran her spread-fingered hand through the hair on his chest, paused when she reached the other side to grasp a fistful and tweak it sharply, then trailed her fingers lightly back across the hair she had ruffled.

Her hand came back to her just as the Mouser turned around. She kissed the palm lingeringly, then reached it across her body to take the black fruit from the point of the Mouser's dirk. She sucked delicately at the prick Cat's Claw had made and shivered.

"Fie, sir," she pouted. "You told me 'twould be sun-warmed and 'tis not. Already all things grow chilly with evening." She looked around her thoughtfully. "Why, Swordsman Fafhrd is all goose-flesh," she announced, then blushed and tapped her lips reprovingly. "Close your jerkin, sir. 'Twill save you from catarrh and perchance from further embarrassment a girl who is unused to any sight of man-flesh save in slaves."

"Here is a toastier plum," the Mouser called from beside the bag. Hisvet smiled at him and lightly tossed him backhanded the plum she'd sampled. He dropped that overboard and tossed her the second plum. She caught it deftly, lightly squeezed it, touched it to her lips, shook her head sadly though still smiling, and tossed back the plum. The Mouser, smiling gently too, caught it, dropped it overboard and tossed her a third. They played that way for some time. A shark following in the wake of the *Squid* got a stomachache.

The black kitten came single-footing back along the starboard rail with a sharp eye to larboard. Fafhrd seized it instantly as any good general does opportunity in the heat of battle.

"Have you seen the ship's catling, little mistress?" he called, crossing to Hisvet, the kitten almost hidden in his big hands. "Or perhaps we should call the *Squid* the catling's ship, for she adopted it, skipping by herself aboard just as we sailed. Here, little mistress. It feels sun-tested now, warmer than any plum," and he reached the kitten out sitting on the palm of his right hand.

But Fafhrd had been forgetting the kitten's point of view. Its fur stood on end as it saw itself being carried toward the rats and now, as Hisvet stretched out her hand toward it, showing her upper teeth in a tiny smile and saying, "Poor little waif," the kitten hissed fiercely and raked out stiff armed with spread claws.

Hisvet drew back her hand with a gasp. Before Fafhrd could drop the kitten or bat it aside, it sprang to the top of his head and from there onto the highest point of the tiller.

The Mouser darted to Hisvet, crying meanwhile at Fafhrd, "Dolt! Lout! You knew the beast was half wild!" Then, to Hisvet, "Demoiselle! Are you hurt?"

Fafhrd struck angrily at the kitten and one of the helmsmen came back to bat at it too, perhaps because he thought it improper for kittens to walk on the tiller. The kitten made a long leap to the starboard rail, slipped over it, and dangled by two claws above the curving water.

Hisvet was holding her hand away from the Mouser and he was saying, "Better let me examine it, Demoiselle. Even the slightest scratch from a filthy ship's cat can be dangerous," and she was saying, almost playfully, "No, Dirksman, I tell you it's nothing."

Fafhrd strode to the starboard rail, fully intending to flick the kitten overboard, but somehow when he came to do it he found he had instead cupped the kitten's rear in his hand and lifted it back on the rail. The kitten instantly sank its teeth deeply in the root of his thumb and fled up the aftermast. Fafhrd with difficulty suppressed a great yowl. Slinoor laughed.

"Nevertheless, I will examine it," the Mouser said masterfully and took Hisvet's hand by force. She let him hold it for a moment, then snatched it back and drawing herself up said frostily, "Dirksman, you forget your-self. Not even her own physician touches a demoiselle of Lankhmar, he touches only the body of her maid, on which the demoiselle points out her pains and symptoms. Leave me, Dirksman."

The Mouser stood huffily back against the taffrail. Fafhrd sucked the root of his thumb. Hisvet went and stood beside the Mouser. Without look-ing at him, she said softly, "You should have asked me to call my maid. She's quite pretty."

Only a fingernail clipping of red sun was left on the horizon. Slinoor addressed the crow's nest: "What of the black sail, boy?"

"She holds her distance, master," the cry came back. "She courses on abreast of us."

The sun went under with a faint green flash. Hisvet bent her head side-ways and kissed the Mouser on the neck, just under the ear. Her tongue tickled.

"Now I lose her, master," the crow's nest called. "There's mist to the northwest. And to the northeast . . . a small black cloud . . . like a black ship specked with light . . . that moves through the air. And now that fades too. All gone, master."

Hisvet straightened her head. Slinoor came toward them muttering, "The crow's nest sees too much." Hisvet shivered and said, "The White Shadows will take a chill. They're delicate, Dirksman." The Mouser breathed, "You are Ecstacy's White Shadow, Demoiselle," then strolled toward the silver cages, saying loudly for Slinoor's benefit, "Might we not be privileged to have a show of them, Demoiselle, tomorrow here on the afterdeck? 'Twould be wondrous instructive to watch you control them." He caressed the air over the cages and said, lying mightily, "My, they're fine handsome fellows." Actually he was peering apprehensively for any of the little spears and swords Slinoor had mentioned. The twelve rats looked up at him incuriously. One even seemed to yawn.

Slinoor said curtly, "I would advise against it, Demoiselle. The sailors have a mad fear and hatred of all rats. 'Twere best not to arouse it."

"But these are aristos," the Mouser objected, while Hisvet only re-peated, "They'll take a chill."

Fafhrd, hearing this, took his hand out of his mouth and came hurry-ing to Hisvet, saying, "Little Mistress, may I carry them below? I'll be gen-tle as a Kleshite nurse." He lifted between thumb and third finger a cage with two rats in it. Hisvet rewarded him with a smile, saying, "I wish you would, gallant Swordsman. The common sailors handle them too roughly. But two cages are all you may safely carry. You'll need proper help." She gazed at the Mouser and Slinoor.

So Slinoor and the Mouser, the latter much to his distaste and appre-hension, must each gingerly take up a silver cage, and Fafhrd two, and follow Hisvet to her cabin below the afterdeck. The Mouser could not forbear whispering privily to Fafhrd, "Oaf! To make rat-grooms of us! May you get rat-bites to match your cat-bite!" At the cabin door Hisvet's dark maid Frix received the cages, Hisvet thanked her three gallants most briefly and distantly and Frix closed the door against them. There was the muffled thud of a bar dropping across it and the jangle of a chain locking down the bar.

Darkness grew on the waters. A yellow lantern was lit and hoisted to the crow's nest. The black war galley *Shark*, its brown sail temporarily furled, came rowing back to fuss at *Clam*, next ahead of *Squid* in line, for being slow in getting up its masthead light, then dropped back by *Squid* while Lukeen and Slinoor exchanged shouts about a black sail and mist and ship-shaped small black clouds and the Dragon Rocks. Finally the galley went bustling ahead again with its Lankhmarines in browned-iron chain mail to take up its sailing station at the head of the column. The first stars twinkled, proof that the sun had not deserted through the waters of eternity to some other world bubble, but was swimming as he should back to the east under the ocean of the sky, errant rays from him lighting the floating star-jewels in his passage.

After moonrise that night Fafhrd and the Mouser each found private occasion to go rapping at Hisvet's door, but neither profited greatly thereby. At Fafhrd's knock Hisvet herself opened the small grille set in the larger door, said swiftly, "Fie, for shame, Swordsman! Can't you see I'm undressing?" and closed it instantly. While when the Mouser asked softly for a moment with "Ecstacy's White Shadow," the merry face of the dark maid Frix appeared at the grille, saying, "My mistress bid me kiss my hand good night to you." Which she did and closed the grille.

Fafhrd, who had been spying, greeted the crestfallen Mouser with a sardonic, "Ecstacy's White Shadow!"

"Little Mistress!" the Mouser retorted scathingly.

"Black Plum of Sarheenmar!"

"Kleshite Nurse!"

Neither hero slept restfully that night and two-thirds through it the *Squid's* gong began to sound at intervals, with the other ships' gongs replying or calling faintly. When at dawn's first blink the two came on deck, *Squid* was creeping through fog that hid the sail top. The two helmsmen were peering about jumpily, as if they expected to see ghosts. The sails hung slackly. Slinoor, his eyes dark-circled by fatigue and big with anxiety, explained tersely that the fog had not only slowed but disordered the grain fleet.

"That's *Tunny* next ahead of us, I can tell by her gong note. And beyond *Tunny*, *Carp*. Where's *Clam*? What's *Shark* about? And still not certainly past the Dragon Rocks! Not that I want to see 'em!"

"Do not some captains call them the Rat Rocks?" Fafhrd interposed. "From a rat colony started there from a wreck?"

"Aye," Slinoor allowed and then grinning sourly at the Mouser, observed, "Not the best day for a rat show on the afterdeck, is it? Which is some good from this fog. I can't abide the lolling white brutes. Though but a dozen in number they remind me too much of the Thirteen. Have you ever heard tell of the legend of the Thirteen?"

"I have," Fafhrd said somberly. "A wise woman of the Cold Waste once told me that for each animal kind—wolves, bats, whales, it holds for all and each—there are always thirteen individuals having almost manlike (or demonlike!) wisdom and skill. Can you but find and master this inner circle, the Wise Woman said, then through them you can control all animals of that kind."

Slinoor looked narrowly at Fafhrd and said, "She was not an altogether stupid woman."

The Mouser wondered if for men also there was an inner circle of Thirteen.

The black kitten came ghosting along the deck out of the fog forward. It made toward Fafhrd with an eager mew, then hesitated, studying him dubiously.

"Take for example, cats," Fafhrd said with a grin. "Somewhere in Nehwon today, mayhap scattered but more likely banded together, are thirteen cats of superfeline sagacity, somehow sensing and controlling the destiny of all catkind."

"What's this one sensing now?" Slinoor demanded softly.

The black kitten was staring to larboard, sniffing. Suddenly its scrawny body stiffened, the hair rising along its back and its skimpy tail a-bush.

"HOONGK!"

Slinoor turned to Fafhrd with a curse, only to see the Northerner staring about shut-mouthed and startled.

Out of the fog to larboard came a green serpent's head big as a horse's, with white dagger teeth fencing red mouth horrendously agape. With dreadful swiftness it lunged low past Fafhrd on its endless yellow neck, its lower jaw loudly scraping the deck, and the white daggers clashed on the black kitten.

Or rather, on where the kitten had just been. For the latter seemed not so much to leap as to lift itself, by its tail perhaps, onto the starboard rail and thence vanished into the fog at the top of the aftermast in at most three more bounds.

The helmsmen raced each other forward. Slinoor and the Mouser threw themselves against the starboard taffrail, the unmanned tiller swinging slowly above them affording some sense of protection against the monster, which now lifted its nightmare head and swayed it this way and that, each time avoiding Fafhrd by inches. Apparently it was searching for the black kitten or more like it.

Fafhrd stood frozen, at first by sheer shock, then by the thought that whatever part of him moved first would get snapped off.

Nevertheless he was about to jump for it—besides all else the monster's mere stench was horrible—when a second green dragon's head, four times as big as the first with teeth like scimitars, came looming out of the fog. Sitting commandingly atop this second head was a man dressed in orange and purple, like a herald of the Eastern Lands, with red boots, cape and helmet, the last with a blue window in it, seemingly of opaque glass.

There is a point of grotesquerie beyond which horror cannot go, but slips into delirium. Fafhrd had reached that point. He began to feel as if he were in an opium dream. Everything was unquestionably real, yet it had lost its power to horrify him acutely.

He noticed as the merest of quaint details that the two greenish yellow necks forked from a common trunk.

Besides, the gaudily garbed man or demon riding the larger head seemed very sure of himself, which might or might not be a good thing. Just now he was belaboring the smaller head, seemingly in rebuke, with a blunt-pointed, blunt-hooked pike he carried, and roaring out, either under or through his blue red helmet, a gibberish that might be rendered as:

*"Gottverdammter Ungeheuer!"**

The smaller head cringed away, whimpering like seventeen puppies. The man-demon whipped out a small book of pages and after consulting it twice (apparently he could see *out* through his blue window) called down in broken, outlandishly accented Lankhmarese, "What world is this, friend?"

Fafhrd had never before in his life heard that question asked, even by an awakening brandy guzzler. Nevertheless in his opium-dream mood he answered easily enough, "The world of Nehwon, oh sorcerer!"

"Gott sei dank!"‡ the man-demon gibbered.

Fafhrd asked, "What world do *you* hail from?"

This question seemed to confound the man-demon. Hurriedly consulting his book, he replied, "Do you know about other worlds? Don't you believe the stars are only huge jewels?"

Fafhrd responded, "Any fool can see that the lights in the sky are jewels, but we are not simpletons, we know of other worlds. The Lankhmarts think they're bubbles in infinite waters. *I* believe we live in the jewel-ceilinged skull of a dead god. But doubtless there are other such skulls, the universe of universes being a great frosty battlefield."

*"Goddamn monster!" German is a language completely unknown in Nehwon.
‡"Thank God!".

The tiller, swinging as *Squid* wallowed with sail a-flap, bumped the lesser head, which twisted around and snapped at it, then shook splinters from its teeth.

"Tell the sorcerer to keep it off!" Slinoor shouted, cringing.

After more hurried page-flipping the man-demon called down, "Don't worry, the monster seems to eat only rats. I captured it by a small rocky island where many rats live. It mistook your small black ship's cat for a rat."

Still in his mood of opium-lucidity, Fafhrd called up, "Oh sorcerer, do you plan to conjure the monster to your own skull-world, or world-bubble?"

This question seemed doubly to confound and excite the man-demon. He appeared to think Fafhrd must be a mind-reader. With much frantic book-consulting, he explained that he came from a world called simply Tomorrow and that he was visiting many worlds to collect monsters for some sort of museum or zoo, which he called in his gibberish *Hagenbeck's Zeitgarten.** On this particular expedition he had been seeking a monster that would be a reasonable facsimile of a wholly mythical six-headed sea-monster that devoured men off the decks of ships and was called Scylla by an ancient fantasy writer named Homer.

"There never was a Lankhmar poet named Homer," muttered Slinoor, who seemed to have none too clear an idea of what was going on.

"Doubtless he was a scribe of Quarmall or the Eastern Lands," the Mouser told Slinoor reassuringly. Then, grown less fearful of the two heads and somewhat jealous of Fafhrd holding the center of the stage, the Mouser leapt atop the taffrail and cried, "Oh sorcerer, with what spells will you conjure your Little Scylla back to, or perhaps I should say ahead to your Tomorrow bubble? I myself know somewhat of witchcraft. Desist, vermin!" (This last remark was directed with a gesture of lordly contempt toward the lesser head, which came questing curiously toward the Mouser. Slinoor gripped the Mouser's ankle.)

The man-demon reacted to the Mouser's question by slapping himself on the side of his red helmet, as though he'd forgotten something most important. He hurriedly began to explain that he traveled between worlds in a ship (or space-time engine, whatever that might mean) that tended to float just above the water—"a black ship with little lights and masts"—and that the ship had floated away from him in another fog a day ago while he'd been absorbed in taming the newly captured sea-monster. Since then the man-demon, mounted on his now-docile monster, had been fruitlessly searching for his lost vehicle.

---

*Literally, in German, "Hagenbeck's Timegarden," apparently derived from *Tiergarten,* which means animal-garden, or zoo.

The description awakened a memory in Slinoor, who managed to nerve himself to explain audibly that last sunset *Squid*'s crow's nest had sighted just such a ship floating or flying to the northeast.

The man-demon was voluble in his thanks and after questioning Slinoor closely announced (rather to everyone's relief) that he was now ready to turn his search eastward with new hope.

"Probably I will never have the opportunity to repay your courtesies," he said in parting. "But as you drift through the waters of eternity at least carry with you my name: Karl Treuherz of Hagenbeck's."

Hisvet, who had been listening from the middeck, chose that moment to climb the short ladder that led up to the afterdeck. She was wearing an ermine smock and hood against the chilly fog.

As her silvery hair and pale lovely features rose above the level of the afterdeck, the smaller dragon's head, which had been withdrawing decorously, darted at her with the speed of a serpent striking. Hisvet dropped. Woodwork rended loudly.

Backing off into the fog atop the larger and rather benign-eyed head, Karl Treuherz gibbered as never before and belabored the lesser head mercilessly as it withdrew.

Then the two-headed monster with its orange-and-purple mahout could be dimly seen moving around *Squid*'s stern eastward into thicker fog, the man-demon gibbering gentlier what might have been an excuse and farewell: *"Es tut mir sehr leid! Aber dankeschoen, dankeschoen!"** With a last gentle "Hoongk!" the man-demon dragon-dragon assemblage faded into the fog.

Fafhrd and the Mouser raced a tie to Hisvet's side, vaulting down over the splintered rail, only to have her scornfully reject their solicitude as she lifted herself from the oaken middeck, delicately rubbing her hip and limping for a step or two.

"Come not near me, Spoonmen," she said bitterly. "Shame it is when a demoiselle must save herself from toothy perdition only by falling helter-skelter on that part of her which I would almost shame to show you on Frix. You are no gentle knights, else dragons' heads had littered the afterdeck. Fie, fie!"

Meanwhile patches of clear sky and water began to show to the west and the wind to freshen from the same quarter. Slinoor dashed forward, bawling for his bosun to chase the monster-scared sailors up from the forecastle before *Squid* did herself an injury.

Although there was yet little real danger of that, the Mouser stood by the tiller, Fafhrd looked to the mainsheet. Then Slinoor, hurrying back aft followed by a few pale sailors, sprang to the taffrail with a cry.

The fogbank was slowly rolling eastward. Clear water stretched to the

---

*It was! "I am so very sorry! But thank you, thank you so nicely!"

western horizon. Two bowshots north of *Squid,* four other ships were emerging in a disordered cluster from the white wall: the war galley *Shark* and the grain ships *Tunny, Carp* and *Grouper.* The galley, moving rapidly under oars, was headed toward *Squid.*

But Slinoor was staring south. There, a scant bowshot away, were two ships, the one standing clear of the fogbank, the other half hid in it.

The one in the clear was *Clam,* about to sink by the head, its gunwales awash. Its mainsail, somehow carried away, trailed brownly in the water. The empty deck was weirdly arched upward.

The fog-shrouded ship appeared to be a black cutter with a black sail.

Between the two ships, from *Clam* toward the cutter, moved a multitude of tiny, dark-headed ripples.

Fafhrd joined Slinoor. Without looking away, the latter said simply, "Rats!" Fafhrd's eyebrows rose.

The Mouser joined them, saying, *"Clam's* holed. The water swells the grain, which mightily forces up the deck."

Slinoor nodded and pointed toward the cutter. It was possible dimly to see tiny dark forms—rats surely!—climbing over its side from out of the water. "There's what gnawed holes in *Clam,"* Slinoor said.

Then Slinoor pointed between the ships, near the cutter. Among the last of the ripple-army was a white-headed one. A little later a small white form could be seen swiftly mounting the cutter's side. Slinoor said, "There's what commanded the hole-gnawers."

With a dull splintering rumble the arched deck of *Clam* burst upward, spewing brown.

"The grain!" Slinoor cried hollowly.

"Now you know what tears ships," the Mouser said.

The black cutter grew ghostlier, moving west now into the retreating fog.

The galley *Shark* went boiling past *Squid's* stern, its oars moving like the legs of a leaping centipede. Lukeen shouted up, "Here's foul trickery! *Clam* was lured off in the night!"

The black cutter, winning its race with the eastward-rolling fog, vanished in whiteness.

The split-decked *Clam* nosed under with hardly a ripple and angled down into the black and salty depths, dragged by its leaden keel.

With war trumpet skirling, *Shark* drove into the white wall after the cutter.

Clam's masthead, cutting a little furrow in the swell, went under. All that was to be seen now on the waters south of *Squid* was a great spreading stain of tawny grain.

Slinoor turned brim-faced to his mate. "Enter the Demoiselle Hisvet's cabin, by force if need be," he commanded. "Count her white rats!"

Fafhrd and the Mouser looked at each other.

* * *

Three hours later the same four persons were assembled in Hisvet's cabin with the Demoiselle, Frix, and Lukeen.

The cabin, low-ceilinged enough so that Fafhrd, Lukeen and the mate must move bent and tended to sit hunch-shouldered, was spacious for a grain ship, yet crowded by this company together with the caged rats and Hisvet's perfumed, silver-bound baggage piled on Slinoor's dark furniture and locked sea chests.

Three horn windows to the stern and louver slits to starboard and larboard let in a muted light.

Slinoor and Lukeen sat against the horn windows, behind a narrow table. Fafhrd occupied a cleared sea chest, the Mouser an upended cask. Between them were racked the four rat cages, whose white-furred occupants seemed as quietly intent on the proceedings as any of the men. The Mouser amused himself by imagining what it would be like if the white rats were trying the men instead of the other way round. A row of blue-eyed white rats would make most formidable judges, already robed in ermine. He pictured them staring down mercilessly from very high seats at a tiny cringing Lukeen and Slinoor, round whom scuttled mouse pages and mouse clerks and behind whom stood rat pikemen in half armor holding fantastically barbed and curvy-bladed weapons.

The mate stood stooping by the open grille of the closed door, in part to see that no other sailors eavesdropped.

The Demoiselle Hisvet sat cross-legged on the swung-down sea-bed, her ermine smock decorously tucked under her knees, managing to look most distant and courtly even in this attitude. Now and again her right hand played with the dark wavy hair of Frix, who crouched on the deck at her knees.

Timbers creaked as *Squid* bowled north. Now and then the bare feet of the helmsmen could be heard faintly slithering on the afterdeck overhead. Around the small trapdoor-like hatches leading below and through the very crevices of the planking came the astringent, toastlike, all-pervasive odor of the grain.

Lukeen spoke. He was a lean, slant-shouldered, cordily muscled man almost as big as Fafhrd. His short coat of browned-iron mail over his simple black tunic was of the finest links. A golden band confined his dark hair and bound to his forehead the browned-iron five-pointed curvy-edged starfish emblem of Lankhmar.

"How do I know *Clam* was lured away? Two hours before dawn I twice thought I heard *Shark*'s own gong-note in the distance, although I stood then beside *Shark*'s muffled gong. Three of my crew heard it too. 'Twas most eerie. Gentlemen, I know the gong-notes of Lankhmar war galleys and merchantmen better than I know my children's voices. This that we heard was so like *Shark*'s I never dreamed it might be that of another ship—

I deemed it some ominous ghost-echo or trick of our minds and I thought no more about it as a matter for action. If I had only had the faintest suspicion . . ."

Lukeen scowled bitterly, shaking his head, and continued, "Now I know the black cutter must carry a gong shaped to duplicate *Shark*'s note precisely. They used it, likely with someone mimicking my voice, to draw *Clam* out of line in the fog and get her far enough off so that the rat horde, officered by the white one, could work its will on her without the crew's screams being heard. They must have gnawed twenty holes in her bottom for *Clam* to take on water so fast and the grain to swell so. Oh, they're far shrewder and more persevering than men, the little spade toothed fiends!"

"Midsea madness!" Fafhrd snorted in interruption. "Rats make men scream? And do away with them? Rats seize a ship and sink it? Rats officered and accepting discipline? Why this is the rankest superstition!"

"You're a fine one to talk of superstition and the impossible, Fafhrd," Slinoor shot at him, "when only this morning you talked with a masked and gibbering demon who rode a two-headed dragon."

Lukeen lifted his eyebrows at Slinoor. This was the first he'd heard of the Hagenbeck episode.

Fafhrd said, "That was travel between worlds. Another matter altogether. No superstition in it."

Slinoor responded skeptically. "I suppose there was no superstition in it either when you told me what you'd heard from the Wise Woman about the Thirteen?"

Fafhrd laughed. "Why, I never believed one word the Wise Woman ever told me. She was a witchery old fool. I recounted her nonsense merely as a curiosity."

Slinoor eyed Fafhrd with slit-eyed incredulity, then said to Lukeen, "Continue."

"There's little more to tell," the latter said. "I saw the rat-battalions swimming from *Clam* to the black cutter. I saw, as you did, their white officer." This with a glare at Fafhrd. "Thereafter I fruitlessly hunted the black cutter two hours in the fog until cramp took my rowers. If I'd found her, I'd not boarded her but thrown fire into her! Aye, and stood off the rats with burning oil on the waters if they tried again to change ships! Aye, and laughed as the furred murderers fried!"

"Just so," Slinoor said with finality. "And what, in your judgment, Commander Lukeen, should we do now?"

"Sink the white arch-fiends in their cages," Lukeen answered instantly, "before they officer the rape of more ships, or our sailors go mad with fear."

This brought an instant icy retort from Hisvet. "You'll have to sink me first, silver-weighted, oh Commander!"

Lukeen's gaze moved past her to a scatter of big-eared silver unguent jars and several looped heavy silver chains on a shelf by the bed. "That too is not impossible, Demoiselle," he said, smiling hardly.

"There's not one shred of proof against her!" Fafhrd exploded. "Little mistress, the man is mad."

"No proof?" Lukeen roared. "There were twelve white rats yesterday. Now there are eleven." He waved a hand at the stacked cages and their blue-eyed haughty occupants. "You've all counted them. Who else but this devilish demoiselle sent the white officer to direct the sharp-toothed gnawers and killers that destroyed *Clam*? What more proof do you want?"

"Yes, indeed!" the Mouser interjected in a high vibrant voice that commanded attention. "There is proof aplenty . . . *if* there were twelve rats in the four cages yesterday." Then he added casually but very clearly, "It is my recollection that there were eleven."

Slinoor stared at the Mouser as though he couldn't believe his ears. "You lie!" he said. "What's more, you lie senselessly. Why, you and Fafhrd and I all spoke of there being twelve white rats!"

The Mouser shook his head. "Fafhrd and I said no word about the exact number of rats. *You* said there were a dozen," he informed Slinoor. "Not twelve, but . . . a dozen. I assumed you were using the expression as a round number, an approximation." The Mouser snapped his fingers. "Now I remember that when you said a dozen I became idly curious and counted the rats. And got eleven. But it seemed to me too trifling a matter to dispute."

"No, there were twelve rats yesterday," Slinoor asserted solemnly and with great conviction. "You're mistaken, Gray Mouser."

"I'll believe my friend Slinoor before a dozen of you," Lukeen put in.

"True, friends should stick together," the Mouser said with an approving smile. "Yesterday I counted Glipkerio's gift-rats and got eleven. Ship's Master Slinoor, any man may be mistaken in his recollections from time to time. Let's analyze this. Twelve white rats divided by four silver cages equals three to a cage. Now let me see . . . I have it! There was a time yesterday when between us, we surely counted the rats—when we carried them down to this cabin. How many were in the cage you carried, Slinoor?"

"Three," the latter said instantly.

"And three in mine," the Mouser said.

"And three in each of the other two," Lukeen put in impatiently. "We waste time!"

"We certainly do," Slinoor agreed strongly, nodding.

"Wait!" said the Mouser, lifting a point-fingered hand. "There was a moment when all of us must have noticed how many rats there were in one of the cages Fafhrd carried—when he first lifted it up, speaking the while to Hisvet. Visualize it. He lifted it like this." The Mouser touched his thumb to his third finger. "How many rats were in that cage, Slinoor?"

Slinoor frowned deeply. "Two," he said, adding instantly, "and four in the other."

"You said three in each just now," the Mouser reminded him.

"I did not!" Slinoor denied. "Lukeen said that, not I."

"Yes, but you nodded, agreeing with him," the Mouser said, his raised eyebrows the very emblem of innocent truth-seeking.

"I agreed with him only that we wasted time," Slinoor said. "And we do." Just the same a little of the frown lingered between his eyes and his voice had lost its edge of utter certainty.

"I see," the Mouser said doubtfully. By stages he had begun to play the part of an attorney elucidating a case in court, striding about and frowning most professionally. Now he shot a sudden question: "Fafhrd, how many rats did you carry?"

"Five," boldly answered the Northerner, whose mathematics were not of the sharpest, but who'd had plenty of time to count surreptitiously on his fingers and to think about what the Mouser was up to. "Two in one cage, three in the other."

"A feeble falsehood!" Lukeen scoffed. "The base barbarian would swear to anything to win a smile from the Demoiselle, who has him fawning."

"That's a foul lie!" Fafhrd roared, springing up and fetching his head such a great hollow thump on a deck beam that he clapped both hands to it and crouched in dizzy agony.

"Sit down, Fafhrd, before I ask you to apologize to the roof!" the Mouser commanded with heartless harshness. "This is solemn civilized court, no barbarous brawling session! Let's see—three and three and five make . . . eleven. Demoiselle Hisvet!" He pointed an accusing finger straight between her red-irised eyes and demanded most sternly, "How many white rats did you bring aboard *Squid*? The truth now and nothing but the truth!"

"Eleven," she answered demurely. "La, but I'm joyed someone at last had the wit to ask me."

"That I know's not true!" Slinoor said abruptly, his brow once more clear. "Why didn't I think of it before?—'twould have saved us all this bother of questions and counting. I have in this very cabin Glipkerio's letter of commission to me. In it he speaks verbatim of entrusting to me the Demoiselle Hisvet, daughter of Hisvin, and twelve witty white rats. Wait, I'll get it out and prove it to your faces!"

"No need, Ship's-Master," Hisvet interposed. "I saw the letter writ and can testify to the perfect truth of your quotation. But most sadly, between the sending of the letter and my boarding of *Squid,* poor Tchy was gobbled up by Glippy's giant boarhound Bimbat." She touched a slim finger to the corner of her eye and sniffed. "Poor Tchy, he was the most winsome of the twelve. 'Twas why I kept to my cabin the first two days." Each time she spoke the name Tchy, the eleven caged rats chittered mournfully.

"Is it Glippy you call our overlord?" Slinoor ejaculated, genuinely shocked. "Oh shameless one!"

"Aye, watch your language, Demoiselle," the Mouser warned severely, maintaining to the hilt his new role of austere inquisitor. "The familiar relationship between you and our overlord the arch-noble Glipkerio Kistomerces does not come within the province of this court."

"She lies like a shrewd subtle witch!" Lukeen asserted angrily. "Thumbscrew or rack, or perchance just a pale arm twisted high behind her back would get the truth from her fast enough!"

Hisvet turned and looked at him proudly. "I accept your challenge, Commander," she said evenly, laying her right hand on her maid's dark head. "Frix, reach out your naked hand, or whatever other part of you the brave gentleman wishes to torture." The dark maid straightened her back. Her face was impassive, lips firmly pressed together, though her eyes searched around wildly. Hisvet continued to Slinoor and Lukeen, "If you know any Lankhmar law at all, you know that a virgin of the rank of demoiselle is tortured only in the person of her maid, who proves by her steadfastness under extreme pain the innocence of her mistress."

"What did I tell you about her?" Lukeen demanded of them all. "Subtle is too gross a term for her spiderwebby sleights!" He glared at Hisvet and said scornfully, his mouth a-twist, "Virgin!"

Hisvet smiled with cold long-suffering. Fafhrd flushed and although still holding his battered head, barely refrained from leaping up again. Lukeen looked at him with amusement, secure in his knowledge that he could bait Fafhrd at will and that the barbarian lacked the civilized wit to insult him deeply in return.

Fafhrd stared thoughtfully at Lukeen from under his capping hands. Then he said, "Yes, you're brave enough in armor, with your threats against girls and your hot imaginings of torture, but if you were without armor and had to prove your manhood with just one brave girl alone, you'd fail like a worm!"

Lukeen shot up enraged and got himself such a clout from a deck beam that he squeaked shudderingly and swayed. Nevertheless he gripped blindly for his sword at his side. Slinoor grasped that wrist and pulled him down into his seat.

"Govern yourself, Commander," Slinoor implored sternly, seeming to grow in resolution as the rest quarreled and quibbled. "Fafhrd, no more dagger words. Gray Mouser, this is not your court but mine and we are not met to split the hairs of high law but to meet a present peril. Here and now this grain fleet is in grave danger. Our very lives are risked. Much more than that, Lankhmar's in danger if Movarl gets not his gift-grain at this third sending. Last night *Clam* was foully murdered. Tonight it may be *Grouper* or *Squid, Shark* even, or no less than all our ships. The first two fleets went warned and well guarded, yet suffered only total perdition."

He paused to let that sink in. Then, "Mouser, you've roused some small doubts in my mind by your eleven-twelving. But small doubts are nothing where home lives and home cities are in peril. For the safety of the fleet and of Lankhmar we'll sink the white rats forthwith and keep close watch on the Demoiselle Hisvet to the very docks of Kvarch Nar."

"Right!" the Mouser cried approvingly, getting in ahead of Hisvet. But then he instantly added, with the air of sudden brilliant inspiration, *"Or* . . . better yet . . . appoint Fafhrd and myself to keep unending watch not only on Hisvet but also on the eleven white rats. That way we don't spoil Glipkerio's gift and risk offending Movarl."

"I'd trust no one's mere watching of the rats. They're too tricksy," Slinoor informed him. "The Demoiselle I intend to put on *Shark,* where she'll be more closely guarded. The grain is what Movarl wants, not the rats. He doesn't know about them, so can't be angered at not getting them."

"But he does know about them," Hisvet interjected. "Glipkerio and Movarl exchange weekly letters by albatross-post. La, but Nehwon grows smaller each year, Ship's Master—ships are snails compared to the great winging mail-birds. Glipkerio wrote of the rats to Movarl, who expressed great delight at the prospective gift and intense anticipation of watching the White Shadows perform. Along with myself," she added, demurely bending her head.

"Also," the Mouser put in rapidly, "I must firmly oppose—most regretfully, Slinoor—the transfer of Hisvet to another ship. Fafhrd's and my commission from Glipkerio, which I can produce at any time, states in clearest words that we are to attend the Demoiselle at all times outside her private quarters. He makes us wholly responsible for her safety—and also for that of the White Shadows, which creatures our overlord states, again in clearest writing, that he prizes beyond their weight in jewels."

"You can attend her in *Shark,*" Slinoor told the Mouser curtly.

"I'll not have the barbarian on my ship!" Lukeen rasped, still squinting from the pain of his clout.

"I'd scorn to board such a tricked-out rowboat or oar-worm," Fafhrd shot back at him, voicing the common barbarian contempt for galleys.

"Also," the Mouser cut in again, loudly, with an admonitory gesture at Fafhrd, "It is my duty as a friend to warn you, Slinoor, that in your reckless threats against the White Shadows and the Demoiselle herself, you

risk incurring the heaviest displeasure not only of our overlord but also of the most powerful grain merchant in Lankhmar."

Slinoor answered most simply, "I think only of the City and the grain fleet. You know that," but Lukeen, fuming, spat out a "Hah!" and said scornfully, "the Gray Fool has not grasped that it is Hisvet's very father Hisvin who is behind the rat-sinkings, since he thereby grows rich with the extra nation's-ransoms of grain he sells Glipkerio!"

"Quiet, Lukeen!" Slinoor commanded apprehensively. "This dubious guesswork of yours has no place here."

"Guesswork? Mine?" Lukeen exploded. "It was *your* suggestion, Slinoor—Yes, and that Hisvin plots Glipkerio's overthrow—Aye, and even that he's in league with the Mingols! Let's speak truth for once!"

"Then speak it for yourself alone, Commander," Slinoor said most sober-sharply. "I fear the blow's disordered your brain. Gray Mouser, you're a man of sense," he appealed. "Can you not understand my one overriding concern? We're alone with mass murder on the high seas. We must take measures against it. Oh, will none of you show some simple wit?"

"La, and I will, Ship's-Master, since you ask it," Hisvet said brightly, rising to her knees on the sea-bed as she turned toward Slinoor. Sunlight striking through a louver shimmered on her silver hair and gleamed from the silver ring confining it. "I'm but a girl, unused to problems of war and rapine, yet I have an all-explaining simple thought that I have waited in vain to hear voiced by one of you gentlemen, wise in the ways of violence.

"Last night a ship was slain. You hang the crime on rats—small beasties which would leave a sinking ship in any case, which often have a few whites among them, and which only by the wildest stretch of imagination are picturable as killing an entire crew and vanishing their bodies. To fill the great gaps in this weird theory you make me a sinister rat-queen, who can work black miracles, and now even, it seems, create my poor doting daddy an all-powerful rat-emperor.

"Yet this morning you met a ship's murderer if there ever was one and let him go honking off unchallenged. La, but the man-demon even confessed he'd been seeking a multi-headed monster that would snatch living men from a ship's deck and devour them. Surely he lied when he said his this-world foundling ate small fry only, for it struck at me to devour me—and might earlier have snapped up any of you, except it was sated!

"For what is more likely than that the two-head long-neck dragon ate all *Clam's* sailors off her deck, snaking them out of the forecastle and hold, if they fled there, like sweetmeats from a compartmented comfit-box, and then scratched holes in *Clam's* planking? Or perhaps more likely still, that *Clam* tore out her bottom on the Dragon Rocks in the fog and at the same time met the sea-dragon? These are sober possibilities, gentlemen, apparent even to a soft girl and asking no mind-stretch at all."

This startling speech brought forth an excited medly of reactions. Simultaneously the Mouser applauded, "A gem of princesswit, Demoiselle, oh you'd make a rare strategist;" Fafhrd said stoutly, "Most lucid, Little Mistress, yet Karl Treuherz seemed to me an honest demon;" Frix told them proudly, "My mistress outthinks you all;" the mate at the door goggled at Hisvet and made the sign of the starfish; Lukeen snarled, "She conveniently forgets the black cutter;" while Slinoor cried them all down with, "Rat-queen you say jestingly? Rat-queen you are!"

As the others grew silent at that dire accusation, Slinoor, gazing grimly fearful at Hisvet, continued rapidly, "The Demoiselle has recalled to me by her speech the worst point against her. Karl Treuherz said his dragon, living by the Rat Rocks, ate only rats. It made no move to gobble us several men, though it had every chance, yet when Hisvet appeared it struck at her at once. It knew her true race."

Slinoor's voice went shuddering low. "Thirteen rats with the minds of men rule the whole rat race. That's ancient wisdom from Lankhmar's wisest seers. Eleven are these silver-furred silent sharpies, hearing our every word. The twelfth celebrates in the black cutter his conquest of *Clam*. The thirteenth—" and he pointed finger "—is the silver-haired, red-eyed Demoiselle herself!"

Lukeen slithered to his feet at that, crying, "Oh most shrewdly reasoned, Slinoor! And why does she wear such modest shrouding garb except to hide further evidence of the dread kinship? Let me but strip off that cloaking ermine smock and I'll show you a white furred body and ten small black dugs instead of proper maiden breasts!"

As he came snaking around the table toward Hisvet, Fafhrd sprang up, also cautiously, and pinned Lukeen's arms to his sides in a bear-hug, calling, "Nay, and you touch her, you die!"

Meantime Frix cried, "The dragon was sated with *Clam*'s crew, as my mistress told you. It wanted no more coarse-fibered men, but eagerly seized at my dainty-fleshed darling for a dessert mouthful!"

Lukeen wrenched around until his black eyes glared into Fafhrd's green ones inches away. "Oh most foul barbarian!" he grated. "I forego rank and dignity and challenge you this instant to a bout of quarterstaves on middeck. I'll prove Hisvet's taint on you by trial of battle. That is, if you dare face civilized combat, you great stinking ape!" And he spat full in Fafhrd's taunting face.

Fafhrd's only reaction was to smile a great smile through the spittle running gummily down his cheek, while maintaining his grip of Lukeen and wary lookout for a bite at his own nose.

Thereafter, challenge having been given and accepted, there was naught for even the head-shaking, heaven-glancing Slinoor to do but hurry preparation for the combat or duel, so that it might be fought before sunset and leave some daylight for taking sober measures for the fleet's safety in the approaching dark of night.

As Slinoor, the Mouser and mate came around them, Fafhrd released Lukeen, who scornfully averting his gaze instantly went on deck to summon a squad of his marines from *Shark* to second him and see fair play. Slinoor conferred with his mate and other officers. The Mouser, after a word with Fafhrd, slipped forward and could be seen gossiping industriously with *Squid*'s bosun and the common members of her crew down to cook and cabin boy. Occasionally something might have passed rapidly from the Mouser's hand to that of the sailor with whom he spoke.

Despite Slinoor's urging, the sun was dropping down the western sky before *Squid*'s gongsman beat the rapid brassy tattoo that signalized the imminence of combat. The sky was clear to the west and overhead, but the sinister fogbank still rested a Lankhmar league (twenty bowshots) to the east, paralleling the northward course of the fleet and looking almost as solid and dazzling as a glacier wall in the sun's crosswise rays. Most mysteriously neither hot sun nor west wind dissipated it.

Black-suited, brown-mailed and brown-helmeted marines facing aft made a wall across *Squid* to either side of the mainmast. They held their spears horizontal and crosswise at arm's-length down, making an additional low fence. Black-tunicked sailors peered between their shoulders and boots, or sat with their own brown legs a-dangle on the larboard side of the foredeck, where the great sail did not cut off their view. A few perched in the rigging.

The damaged rail had been stripped away from the break in the afterdeck and there around the bare aftermast sat the three judges: Slinoor, the Mouser, and Lukeen's sergeant. Around them, mostly to larboard of the two helmsmen, were grouped *Squid*'s officers and certain officers of the other ship on whose presence the Mouser had stubbornly insisted, though it had meant time-consuming ferrying by ship's boat.

Hisvet and Frix were in the cabin with the door shut. The Demoiselle had wanted to watch the duel through the open door or even from the afterdeck, but Lukeen had protested that this would make it easier for her to work an evil spell on him, and the judges had ruled for Lukeen. However the grille was open and now and again the sun's rays twinkled on a peering eye or silvered fingernail.

Between the dark spear-wall of marines and the afterdeck stretched a great square of white oaken deck, empty save for the crane-fittings and like fixed gear and level except for the main hatch, which made a central square of deck a hand's span above the rest. Each corner of the larger square was marked off by a black-chalked quarter circle. Either constant stepping inside a quarter circle after the duel began (or springing on the rail or grasping the rigging or falling over the side) would at once forfeit the match.

In the foreward larboard quarter circle stood Lukeen in black shirt and hose, still wearing his gold-banded starfish emblem. By him was his second, his own hawk-faced lieutenant. With his right hand Lukeen gripped his quarterstaff, a heavy wand of close-grained oak as tall as himself and thick as Hisvet's wrist. Raising it above his head he twirled it till it hummed, smiling fiendishly.

In the after starboard quarter circle, next the cabin door, were Fafhrd and his second, the mate of *Carp,* a grossly fat man with a touch of the Mingol in his sallow features. The Mouser could not be judge and second both, and he and Fafhrd had diced more than once with *Carp*'s mate in the old days at Lankmar—losing money to him, too, which at least indicated that he might be resourceful.

Fafhrd took from him now his own quarterstaff, gripping it cross-handed near one end. He made a few slow practice passes with it through the air, then handed it back to *Carp*'s mate and stripped off his jerkin.

Lukeen's marines sniggered to each other at the Northerner handling a quarterstaff as if it were a two-handed broadsword, but when Fafhrd bared his hairy chest *Squid*'s sailors set up a rousing cheer and when Lukeen commented loudly to his second, "What did I tell you? A great hairy-pelted ape, beyond question," and spun his staff again, the sailors booed him lustily.

"Strange," Slinoor commented in a low voice. "I had thought Lukeen to be popular among the sailors."

Lukeen's sergeant looked around incredulously at that remark. The Mouser only shrugged. Slinoor continued to him, "If the sailors knew your comrade fought on the side of rats, they'd not cheer him." The Mouser only smiled.

The gong sounded again.

Slinoor rose and spoke loudly: "A bout at quarterstaves with no breathing spells! Commander Lukeen seeks to prove on the Overlord's mercenary Fafhrd certain allegations against a demoiselle of Lankhmar. First man struck senseless or at mercy of his foe loses. Prepare!"

Two ship's boys went skipping across the middeck, scattering handfuls of white sand.

Sitting, Slinoor remarked to the Mouser, "A pox of this footling duel! It delays our action against Hisvet and the rats. Lukeen was a fool to bridle at the barbarian. Still, when he's drubbed him, there'll be time enough."

The Mouser lifted an eyebrow. Slinoor said lightly, "Oh didn't you know? Lukeen will win, that's certain," while the sergeant, nodding soberly, confirmed, "The Commander's a master of staves. 'Tis no game for barbarians."

The gong sounded a third time.

Lukeen sprang nimbly across the chalk and onto the hatch, crying, "Ho, hairy ape! Art ready to double-kiss the oak?—first my staff, then the deck?"

Fafhrd came shambling out, gripping his wand most awkwardly and responding, "Your spit has poisoned my left eye, Lukeen, but I see some civilized target with my right."

Lukeen dashed at him joyously then, feinting at elbow and head, then rapidly striking with the other end of his staff at Fafhrd's knee to tumble or lame him.

Fafhrd, abruptly switching to conventional stance and grip, parried the blow and swung a lightning riposte at Lukeen's jaw.

Lukeen got his staff up in time so that the blow hit only his cheek glancingly, but he was unsettled by it and thereafter Fafhrd was upon him, driving him back in a hail of barely-parried blows while the sailors cheered.

Slinoor and the sergeant gaped wide-eyed, but the Mouser only knotted his fingers, muttering, "Not so fast, Fafhrd."

Then, as Fafhrd prepared to end it all, he stumbled stepping off the hatch, which changed his swift blow to the head into a slow blow at the ankles. Lukeen leaped up so that Fafhrd's staff passed under his feet, and while he was still in the air rapped Fafhrd on the head.

The sailors groaned. The marines cheered once, growlingly.

The unfooted blow was not of the heaviest, nonetheless it three-quarters stunned Fafhrd and now it was his turn to be driven back under a pelting shower of swipes. For several moments there was no sound but the rutch of soft-soled boots on sanded oak and the rapid dry musical *bong* of staff meeting staff.

When Fafhrd came suddenly to his full senses he was falling away from a wicked swing. A glimpse of black by his heel told him that his next inevitable backward step would carry him inside his own quarter circle.

Swift as thought he thrust far *behind* him with his staff. Its end struck deck, then stopped against the cabin wall, and Fafhrd heaved himself forward with it, away from the chalk line, ducking and lunging to the side to escape Lukeen's blows while his staff could not protect him.

The sailors screamed with excitement. The judges and officers on the afterdeck kneeled like dice-players, peering over the edge.

Fafhrd had to lift his left arm to guard his head. He took a blow on the elbow and his left arm dropped limp to his side. Thereafter he had to handle his staff like a broadsword indeed, swinging it one-handed in whistling parries and strokes.

Lukeen hung back, playing more cautiously now, knowing Fafhrd's one wrist must tire sooner than his two. He'd aim a few rapid blows at Fafhrd, then prance back.

Barely parrying the third of these attacks, Fafhrd riposted recklessly, not with a proper swinging blow, but simply gripping the end of his staff and lunging. The combined length of Fafhrd and his staff overtook Lukeen's retreat and the tip of Fafhrd's staff poked him low in the chest, just on the nerve spot.

Lukeen's jaw dropped, his mouth stayed open wide, and he wavered. Fafhrd smartly rapped his staff out of his fingers and as it clattered down, toppled Lukeen to the deck with a second almost casual prod.

The sailors cheered themselves hoarse. The marines growled surlily and one cried, "Foul!" Lukeen's second knelt by him, glaring at Fafhrd. *Carp*'s mate danced a ponderous jig up to Fafhrd and wafted the wand out of his hands. On the afterdeck *Squid*'s officers were glum, though those of the other grain ships seemed strangely jubilant. The Mouser gripped Slinoor's elbow, urging, "Cry Fafhrd victor," while the sergeant frowned prodigiously, hand to temple, saying, "Well, there's nothing I know of in the *rules* . . ."

At that moment the cabin door opened and Hisvet stepped out, wearing a long scarlet, scarlet-hooded silk robe.

The Mouser, sensing climax, sprang to starboard, where *Squid*'s gong hung, snatched the striker from the gongsman and clanged it wildly.

Squid grew silent. Then there were pointings and questioning cries as Hisvet was seen. She put a silver recorder to her lips and began to dance dreamily toward Fafhrd, softly whistling with her recorder a high haunting tune of seven notes in a minor key. From somewhere tiny tuned bells accompanied it tinklingly. Then Hisvet swung to one side, facing Fafhrd as she moved around him, and the questioning cries changed to ones of wonder and astonishment and the sailors came crowding as far aft as they could and swinging through the rigging, as the procession became visible that Hisvet headed.

It consisted of eleven white rats walking in single file on their hind legs and wearing little scarlet robes and caps. The first four carried in each forepaw clusters of tiny silver bells which they shook rhythmically. The next five bore on their shoulders, hanging down between them a little, a double length of looped gleaming silver chain—they were very like five sailors lugging an anchor chain. The last two each bore slantwise a slim silver wand as tall as himself as he walked erect, tail curving high.

The first four halted side by side in rank facing Fafhrd and tinkling their bells to Hisvet's piping.

The next five marched on steadily to Fafhrd's right foot. There their leader paused, looked up at Fafhrd's face with upraised paw, and squeaked three times. Then, gripping his end of the chain in one paw, he used his other three to climb Fafhrd's boot. Imitated by his four fellows, he then carefully climbed Fafhrd's trousers and hairy chest.

Fafhrd stared down at the mounting chain and scarlet-robed rats without moving a muscle, except to frown faintly as tiny paws unavoidably tweaked clumps of his chest hair.

The first rat mounted to Fafhrd's right shoulder and moved behind his back to his left shoulder, the four other rats following in order and never letting slip the chain.

When all five rats were standing on Fafhrd's shoulders, they lifted one strand of the silver chain and brought it forward over his head, most dexterously. Meanwhile he was looking straight ahead at Hisvet, who had completely circled him and now stood piping behind the bell-tinklers.

The five rats dropped the strand, so that the chain hung in a gleaming oval down Fafhrd's chest. At the same instant each rat lifted his scarlet cap as high above his head as his foreleg would reach.

Someone cried, "Victor!"

The five rats swung down their caps and again lifted them high, and as if from one throat all the sailors and most of the marines and officers cried in a great shout: "VICTOR!"

The five rats led two more cheers for Fafhrd, the men aboard *Squid* obeying as if hypnotized—though whether by some magic power or simply by the wonder and appropriateness of the rats' behavior, it was hard to tell.

Hisvet finished her piping with a merry flourish and the two rats with silver wands scurried up onto the afterdeck and standing at the foot of the aftermast where all might see, began to drub away at each other in most authentic quarterstaff style, their wands flashing in the sunlight and chiming sweetly when they clashed. The silence broke in rounds of exclamation and laughter. The five rats scampered down Fafhrd and returned with the bell-tinklers to cluster around the hem of Hisvet's skirt. Mouser and several officers were leaping down from the afterdeck to wring Fafhrd's good hand or clap his back. The marines had much ado to hold back the sailors, who were offering each other bets on which rat would be the winner in this new bout.

Fafhrd, fingering his chain, remarked to the Mouser, "Strange that the sailors were with me from the start," and under cover of the hubbub the Mouser smiling explained, "I gave them money to bet on you against the marines. Likewise I dropped some hints and made some loans for the same purpose to the officer of the other ships—a fighter can't have too big a claque. Also I started the story going round that the whiteys are anti-rat rats, trained exterminators of their own kind, sample of Glipkerio's latest device for the safety of the grain fleets—sailors eat up such tosh."

"Did you first cry victor?" Fafhrd asked.

The Mouser grinned. "A judge take sides? In *civilized* combat? Oh, I was prepared to, but 'twasn't needful."

At that moment Fafhrd felt a small tug at his trousers and looking down saw that the black kitten had bravely approached through the forest of legs and was now climbing him purposefully. Touched at this further display of animal homage, Fafhrd rumbled gently as the kitten reached his belt, "Decided to heal our quarrel, eh, small black one?" At that the kitten sprang up his chest, sunk his little claws in Fafhrd's bare shoulder and, glaring like a black hangman, raked Fafhrd bloodily across the jaw, then sprang by way of a couple of startled heads to the mainsail and rapidly climbed its concave taut brown curve. Someone threw a belaying pin at the small black blot, but it was negligently aimed and the kitten safely reached the mast-top.

"I forswear all cats!" Fafhrd cried angrily, dabbling at his chin. "Henceforth rats are my favored beasties."

"Most properly spoken, Swordsman!" Hisvet called gayly from her own circle of admirers, continuing, "I will be pleased by your company and the Dirksman's at dinner in my cabin an hour past sunset. We'll conform to the very letter of Slinoor's stricture that I be closely watched and the White Shadows too." She whistled a little call on her silver recorder and swept back into her cabin with the nine rats close at her heels. The quarterstaving scarlet-robed pair on the afterdeck broke off their drubbing with neither victorious and scampered after her, the crowd parting to make way for them admiringly.

Slinoor, hurrying forward, paused to watch. The *Squid*'s skipper was a man deeply bemused. Somewhere in the last half hour the white rats had been transformed from eerie poison-toothed monsters threatening the fleet into popular, clever, harmless animal-mountebanks, whom *Squid*'s sailors appeared to regard as a band of white mascots. Slinoor seemed to be seeking unsuccessfully but unceasingly to decipher how and why.

Lukeen, still looking very pale, followed the last of his disgruntled marines (their purses lighter by many a silver smerduk, for they had been coaxed into offering odds) over the side into *Shark*'s long dinghy, brushing off Slinoor when *Squid*'s skipper would have conferred with him.

Slinoor vented his chagrin by harshly commanding his sailors to leave off their disorderly milling and frisking, but they obeyed him right cheerily, skipping to their proper stations with the happiest of sailor smirks. Those passing the Mouser winked at him and surreptitiously touched their forelocks. The *Squid* bowled smartly northward a half bowshot astern of *Tunny,* as she'd been doing throughout the duel, only now she began to cleave the blue water a little more swiftly yet as the west wind freshened and her after sail was broken out. In fact, the fleet began to sail so swiftly now that *Shark*'s dinghy couldn't make the head of the line, although Lukeen could be noted bullying his marine-oarsmen into back-cracking efforts, and the dinghy had finally to signal *Shark* herself to come back and pick her up—which the war galley achieved only with difficulty, rolling dangerously in the mounting seas and taking until sunset, oars helping sails, to return to the head of the line.

"*He*'ll not be eager to come to *Squid*'s help tonight, or much able to either," Fafhrd commented to the Mouser where they stood by the larboard mid-deck rail. There had been no open break between them and Slinoor, but they were inclined to leave him the afterdeck, where he stood beyond the helmsmen in bent-head converse with his three officers, who had all lost money on Lukeen and had been sticking close to their skipper ever since.

"Not still expecting *that* sort of peril tonight, are you, Fafhrd?" the Mouser asked with a soft laugh. "We're far past the Rat Rocks."

Fafhrd shrugged and said frowningly, "Perhaps we've gone just a shade too far in endorsing the rats."

"Perhaps," the Mouser agreed. "But then their charming mistress is worth a fib and false stamp or two, aye and more than that, eh, Fafhrd?"

"She's a brave sweet lass," Fafhrd said carefully.

"Aye, and her maid too," the Mouser said brightly. "I noted Frix peering at you adoringly from the cabin entryway after your victory. A most voluptuous wench. Some men might well prefer the maid to the mistress in this instance. Fafhrd?"

Without looking around at the Mouser, the Northerner shook his head.

The Mouser studied Fafhrd, wondering if it were politic to make a certain proposal he had in mind. He was not quite certain of the full nature of Fafhrd's feelings toward Hisvet. He knew the Northerner was a goatish man enough and had yesterday seemed quite obsessed with the lovemaking they'd missed in Lankhmar, yet he also knew that his comrade had a variable romantic streak that was sometimes thin as a thread yet sometimes grew into a silken ribbon leagues wide in which armies might stumble and be lost.

On the afterdeck Slinoor was now conferring most earnestly with the cook, presumably (the Mouser decided) about Hisvet's (and his own and Fafhrd's) dinner. The thought of Slinoor having to go to so much trouble about the pleasures of three persons who today had thoroughly thwarted him made the Mouser grin and somehow also nerved him to take the uncertain step he'd been contemplating.

"Fafhrd," he whispered, "I'll dice you for Hisvet's favors."

"Why, Hisvet's but a gir—" Fafhrd began in accents of rebuke, then cut off abruptly and closed his eyes in thought. When he opened them, they were regarding the Mouser with a large smile.

"No," Fafhrd said softly, "for truly I think this Hisvet is so balky and fantastic a miss it will take both our most heartfelt and cunning efforts to persuade her to aught. And, after that, who knows? Dicing for such a girl's favors were like betting when a Lankhman night-lily will open and whether to north or south."

The Mouser chuckled and lovingly dug Fafhrd in the ribs, saying, "There's my shrewd true comrade!"

Fafhrd looked at the Mouser with sudden dark suspicions. "Now don't go trying to get me drunk tonight," he warned, "or sifting opium in my drink."

"Hah, you know me better than that, Fafhrd," the Mouser said with laughing reproach.

"I certainly do," Fafhrd agreed sardonically.

Again the sun went under with a green flash, indicating crystal clear air to the west, though the strange fogbank, now an ominous dark wall, still paralleled their course a league or so to the east.

The cook, crying, "My mutton!" went racing forward past them toward the galley, whence a deliciously spicy aroma was wafting.

"We've an hour to kill," the Mouser said. "Come on, Fafhrd. On our way to board *Squid* I bought a little jar of wine of Quarmall at the Silver Eel. It's still sealed."

From just overhead in the rat-lines, the black kitten hissed down at them in angry menace or perhaps warning.

Two hours later the Demoiselle Hisvet offered to the Mouser, "A golden rilk for your thoughts, Dirksman."

She was on the swung-down sea-bed once more, half reclining. The long table, now laden with tempting viands and tall silver wine cups, had been placed against the bed. Fafhrd sat across from Hisvet, the empty silver cages behind him, while the Mouser was at the stern end of the table. Frix served them all from the door forward, where she took the trays from the cook's boys without giving them so much as a peep inside. She had a small brazier there for keeping hot such items as required it and she tasted each dish and set it aside for a while before serving it. Thick dark pink candles in silver sconces shed a pale light.

The white rats crouched in rather disorderly fashion around a little table of their own set on the floor near the wall between the sea-bed and the door, just aft of one of the trapdoors opening down into the grain-redolent hold. They wore little black jackets open at the front and little black belts around their middles. They seemed more to play with than eat the bits of food Frix set before them on their three or four little silver plates and they did not lift their small bowls to drink their wine-tinted water but rather lapped at them and that not very industriously. One or two would always be scampering up onto the bed to be with Hisvet, which made them most difficult to count, even for Fafhrd, who had the best view. Sometimes he got eleven, sometimes ten. At intervals one of them would stand up on the pink coverlet by Hisvet's knees and chitter at her in cadences so like those of human speech that Fafhrd and the Mouser would have to chuckle.

"Dreamy Dirksman, two rilks for your thoughts!" Hisvet repeated, upping her offer. "And most immodestly I'll wager a third rilk they are of me."

The Mouser smiled and lifted his eyebrows. He was feeling very lightheaded and a bit uneasy, chiefly because contrary to his intentions he had been drinking much more than Fafhrd. Frix had just served them the main dish, a masterly yellow curry heavy with dark-tasting spices and originally appearing with "Victor" pricked on it with black capers. Fafhrd was devouring it manfully though not voraciously, the Mouser was going at it more slowly, while Hisvet all evening had merely toyed with her food.

"I'll take your two rilks, White Princess," the Mouser replied airily, "for I'll need one to pay the wager you've just won and the other to fee you for telling me *what* I was thinking of you."

"You'll not keep my second rilk long, Dirksman," Hisvet said merrily, "for as you thought of me you were looking not at my face, but most impudently somewhat lower. You were thinking of those somewhat nasty suspicions Lukeen voiced this day about my secretest person. Confess it now, you were!"

The Mouser could only hang his head a little and shrug helplessly, for she had most truly divined his thoughts. Hisvet laughed and frowned at him in mock anger, saying, "Oh, you are most indelicate minded, Dirksman. Yet at least you can see that Frix, though indubitably mammalian, is not fronted like a she-rat."

This statement was undeniably true, for Hisvet's maid was all dark smooth skin except where black silk scarves narrowly circled her slim body at breasts and hips. Silver net tightly confined her black hair and there were many plain silver bracelets on each wrist. Yet although garbed like a slave, Frix did not seem one tonight, but rather a lady-companion who expertly played at being slave, serving them all with perfect yet laughing, wholly unservile obedience.

Hisvet, by contrast, was wearing another of her long smocks, this of black silk edged with black lace, with a lace-edged hood half thrown back. Her silvery white hair was dressed high on her head in great smooth swelling sweeps. Regarding her across the table, Fafhrd said, "I am certain that the Demoiselle would be no less than completely beautiful to us in whatever shape she chose to present herself to the world—wholly human or somewhat otherwise."

"Now that was most gallantly spoken, Swordsman," Hisvet said with a somewhat breathless laugh. "I must reward you for it. Come to me, Frix." As the slim maid bent close to her, Hisvet twined her white hands round the dark waist and imprinted a sweet slow kiss on Frix's lips. Then she looked up and gave a little tap on the shoulder to Frix, who moved smiling around the table and, half kneeling by Fafhrd, kissed him as she had been kissed. He received the token graciously, without unmannerly excitement, yet when Frix would have drawn back, prolonged the kiss, explaining a bit thickly when he released her: "Somewhat extra to return to the sender, perchance." She grinned at him saucily and went to her serving table by the door, saying, "I must first chop the rats their meat, naughty barbarian." While Hisvet discoursed, "Don't seek too much, Bold Swordsman. That was in any case but a small proxy reward for a small gallant speech. A reward with the mouth for words spoken with the mouth. To reward you for drubbing Lukeen and vindicating my honor were a more serious matter altogether, not to be entered on lightly if at all. I'll think of it."

At this point the Mouser, who just had to be saying something but whose fuddled brain was momentarily empty of suitably venturesome yet courteous wit, called out to Frix, "Why chop you the rats their mutton, dusky minx? 'Twould be rare sport to see them slice it for themselves." Frix only wrinkled her nose at him, but Hisvet expounded gravely, "Only Skwee carves with any great skill. The others might hurt themselves, particularly with the meat shifting about in the slippery curry. Frix, reserve a single chunk for Skwee to display us his ability. Chop the rest fine. Skwee!" she called, setting her voice high. "Skwee-skwee-skwee!"

A tall rat sprang onto the bed and stood dutifully before her with forelegs folded across his chest. Hisvet instructed him, then took from a silver box behind her a most tiny carving set of knife, steel and fork in joined treble scabbard and tied it carefully to his belt. Then Skwee bowed low to her and sprang nimbly down to the rats' table.

The Mouser watched the little scene with clouded and heavy-lidded wonder, feeling that he was falling under some sort of spell. At times thick shadows crossed the cabin, at times Skwee grew tall as Hisvet or perhaps it was Hisvet tiny as Skwee. And then the Mouser grew small as Skwee too and ran under the bed and fell into a chute that darkly swiftly slid him, not into a dark hold of sacked or loose delicious grain, but into the dark spacious low-ceilinged pleasance of a subterranean rat metropolis, lit by phosphorus, where robed and long-skirted rats whose hoods hid their long faces moved about mysteriously, where rat swords clashed behind the next pillar and rat money chinked, where lewd female rats danced in their fur for a fee, where rat spies and rat informers lurked, where everyone—every-*furry*-one—was cringingly conscious of the omniscient overlordship of a supernally powerful Council of Thirteen, and where a rat Mouser sought everywhere a slim rat princess named Hisvet-sur-Hisvin.

The Mouser woke from his dinnerdream with a jerk. Somehow he'd surely drunk even more cups than he'd counted, he told himself haltingly. Skwee, he saw, had returned to the rats' table and was standing before the yellow chunk Frix had set on the silver platter at Skwee's end. With the other rats watching him, Skwee drew forth knife and steel with a flourish. The Mouser roused himself more fully with another jerk and shake and was inspired to say, "Ah, were I but a rat, White Princess, so that I might come as close to you, serving you!"

The Demoiselle Hisvet cried, "A tribute indeed!" and laughed with delight, showing—it appeared to the Mouser—a tongue half splotched with bluish black and an inner mouth similarly pied. Then she said rather soberly, "Have a care what you wish, for some wishes have been granted," but at once continued gayly, "Nevertheless, 'twas most gallantly said, Dirksman. I must reward you. Frix, sit at my right side here."

The Mouser could not see what passed between them, for Hisvet's loosely smocked form hid Frix from him, but the merry eyes of the maid peered steadily at him over Hisvet's shoulder, twinkling like the black silk. Hisvet seemed to be whispering into Frix's ear while nuzzling it playfully.

Meanwhile there commenced the faintest of high *skirrings* as Skwee rapidly clashed steel and knife together, sharpening the latter. The Mouser could barely see the rat's head and shoulders and the tiny glimmer of flashing metal over the larger table intervening. He felt the urge to stand and move closer to observe the prodigy—and perchance glimpse something of the interesting activities of Hisvet and Frix—but he was held fast by a great lethargy, whether of wine or sensuous anticipation or pure magic he could not tell.

He had one great worry—that Fafhrd would out with a cleverer compliment than his own, one so much cleverer that it might even divert Frix's mission to him. But then he noted that Fafhrd's chin had fallen to his chest, and there came to his ears along with the silvery *klirring* the barbarian's gently rumbling snores.

The Mouser's first reaction was pure wicked relief. He remembered gloatingly past times he'd gamboled while his comrade snored sodden. Fafhrd must after all have been sneaking many extra swigs or whole drinks!

Frix jerked and giggled immoderately. Hisvet continued to whisper in her ear while Frix giggled and cooed again from time to time, continuing to watch the Mouser impishly.

Skwee scabbarded the steel with a tiny *clash,* drew the fork with a flour-ish, plunged it into the yellow-coated meat-chunk, big as a roast for him, and began to carve most dexterously.

Frix rose at last, received her tap from Hisvet, and headed around the table, smiling the while at the Mouser.

Skwee up with a paper-thin tiny slice of mutton on his fork and flapped it this way and that for all to see, then brought it close to his muzzle for a sniff and a taste.

The Mouser in his dreamy slump felt a sudden twinge of apprehen-sion. It had occurred to him that Fafhrd simply couldn't have sneaked *that* much extra wine. Why, the Northerner hadn't been out of his sight the past two hours. Of course blows on the head sometimes had a de-layed effect.

All the same his first reaction was pure angry jealousy when Frix paused beside Fafhrd and leaned over his shoulder and looked in his forward-tipped face.

Just then there came a great squeak of outrage and alarm from Skwee and the white rat sprang up onto the bed, still holding carving knife and fork with the mutton slice dangling from it.

From under eyelids that persisted in drooping lower and lower, the Mouser watched Skwee gesticulate with his tiny implements, as he chit-tered dramatically to Hisvet in most manlike cadences, and finally lift the petal of mutton to her lips with an accusing squeak.

Then, coming faintly through the chittering, the Mouser heard a host of stealthy footsteps crossing the middeck, converging on the cabin. He tried to call Hisvet's attention to it, but found his lips and tongue numb and unobedient to his will.

Frix suddenly grasped the hair of Fafhrd's forehead and jerked his head up and back. The Northerner's jaw hung slackly, his eyes fell open, show-ing only whites.

There was a gentle rapping at the door, exactly the same as the cook's boys had made delivering the earlier courses.

A look passed between Hisvet and Frix. The latter dropped Fafhrd's head, darted to the door, slammed the bar across it and locked the bar with the chain (the grille already being shut) just as something (a man's shoulder, it sounded) thudded heavily against the thick panels.

That thudding continued and a few heartbeats later became much more sharply ponderous, as if a spare mast-section were being swung like a battering ram against the door, which yielded visibly at each blow.

The Mouser realized at last, much against his will, that something was happening that he ought to do something about. He made a great effort to shake off his lethargy and spring up.

He found he could not even twitch a finger. In fact it was all he could do to keep his eyes from closing altogether and watch through lash-blurred slits as Hisvet, Frix and the rats spun into a whirlwind of silent activity.

Frix jammed her serving table against the jolting door and began to pile other furniture against it.

Hisvet dragged out from behind the sea-bed various dark long boxes and began to unlock them. As fast as she threw them open the white rats helped themselves to the small blue-iron weapons they contained: swords, spears, even most wicked-looking blue-iron crossbows with belted cannisters of darts. They took more weapons than they could effectively use themselves. Skwee hurriedly put on a black-plumed helmet that fitted down over his furry cheeks. The number of rats busy around the boxes was ten—that much the Mouser noted clearly.

A split appeared in the middle of the piled door. Nevertheless Frix sprang away from there to the starboard trapdoor leading to the hold and heaved it up. Hisvet threw herself on the floor toward it and thrust her head down into the dark square hole.

There was something terribly animal-like about the movements of the two women. It may have been only the cramped quarters and the low ceiling, but it seemed to the Mouser that they moved by preference on all fours.

All the while Fafhrd's chest-sunk head kept lifting very slowly and then falling with a jerk as he went on snoring.

Hisvet sprang up and waved on the ten white rats. Led by Skwee, they trooped down through the hatch, their blue-iron weapons flashing and once or twice clashing, and were gone in a twinkling. Frix grabbed dark garments out of a curtained niche. Hisvet caught her by the wrist and thrust the maid ahead of her down the trap and then descended herself. Before pulling the hatch down above her, she took a last look around the cabin. As her red eyes gazed briefly at the Mouser, it seemed to him that her forehead and cheeks were grown over with silky white hair, but that may well have been a combination of eyelash-blue and her own disordered hair streaming and streaking down across her face.

The cabin door split and a man's length of thick mast boomed through, overturning the bolstering table and scattering the furniture set on and against it. After the mast end came piling in three apprehensive sailors followed by Slinoor holding a cutlass low and Slinoor's starsman (navigation officer) with a crossbow at the cock.

Slinoor pressed ahead a little and surveyed the scene swiftly yet intently, then said, "Our poppy-dust curry has taken Glipkerio's two lust-besotted rogues, but Hisvet's hid with her nymphy slave girl. The rats are out of their cages. Search, sailors! Starsman, cover us!"

Gingerly at first, but soon in a rush, the sailors searched the cabin, tumbling the empty boxes and jerking the quilts and mattress off the sea-bed and swinging it up to see beneath, heaving chests away from walls and flinging open the unlocked ones, sweeping Hisvet's wardrobe in great silken armfuls out of the curtained niches in which it had been hanging.

The Mouser again made a mighty effort to speak or move, with no more success than to widen his blurred eye-slits a little. A sailor louted into him and he helplessly collapsed sideways against an arm of his chair without quite falling out of it. Fafhrd got a shove behind and slumped face-down on the table in a dish of stewed plums, his great arms outsweeping unconsciously upsetting cups and scattering plates.

The starsman kept crossbow trained on each new space uncovered. Slinoor watched with eagle eye, flipping aside silken fripperies with his cutlass point and using it to overset the rats' table, peering the while narrowly.

"There's where the vermin feasted like men," he observed disgustedly. "The curry was set before them. Would they had gorged themselves senseless on it."

"Likely they were the ones to note the drug even through the masking spices of the curry, and warn the women," the starsman put in. "Rats are prodigiously wise to poisons."

As it became apparent neither girls nor rats were in the cabin, Slinoor cried with angry anxiety, "They can't have escaped to the deck—here's the sky-trap locked below besides our guard above. The mate's party bars the after hold. Perchance the sternlights—"

But just then the Mouser heard one of the horn windows behind him being opened and the *Squid*'s arms-master call from there, "Naught came this way. Where are they, captain?"

"Ask someone wittier than I," Slinoor tossed him sourly. "Certain they're not here."

"Would that these two could speak," the starsman wished, indicating the Mouser and Fafhrd.

"No," Slinoor said dourly. "They'd just lie. Cover the larboard trap to the hold. I'll have it up and speak to the mate."

Just then footsteps came hurrying across the middeck and the *Squid*'s mate with blood-streaked face entered by the broken door, half dragging and half supporting a sailor who seemed to be holding a thin stick to his own bloody cheek.

"Why have you left the hold?" Slinoor demanded of the first. "You should be with your party below."

"Rats ambushed us on our way to the after hold," the mate gasped. "There were dozens of blacks led by a white, some armed like men. The sword of a beam-hanger almost cut my eye across. Two foamy-mouthed springers dashed out our lamp. 'Twere pure folly to have gone on in the dark. There's scarce a man of my party not bitten, slashed or jabbed. I left them guarding the foreway to the hold. They say their wounds are poisoned and talk of nailing down the hatch."

"Oh monstrous cowardice!" Slinoor cried. "You've spoiled my trap that would have scotched them at the start. Now all's to do and difficult. Oh scarelings! Daunted by rats!"

"I tell you they were armed!" the mate protested and then, swinging the sailor forward, "Here's my proof with a spearlet in his cheek."

"Don't drag her out, captain, sir," the sailor begged as Slinoor moved to examine his face. " 'Tis barbed for certain and poisoned too, I wot."

"Hold still, boy," Slinoor commanded. "And take your hands away— I've got it firm. The point's near the skin. I'll drive it out forward so the barbs don't catch. Pinion his arms, mate. Don't move your face, boy, or you'll be hurt worse. If it's poisoned, it must come out the faster. There!"

The sailor squeaked. Fresh blood rilled down his cheek.

" 'Tis a nasty needle indeed," Slinoor commended, inspecting the bloody point. "Doesn't look poisoned. Mate, gently cut off the shaft aft of the wound, draw out the rest forward."

"Here's further proof, most wicked," said the starsman, who'd been picking about in the litter. He handed Slinoor a tiny crossbow.

Slinoor held it up before him. In the pale candlelight it gleamed bluely, while the skipper's dark-circled eyes were like agates.

"Here's evil's soul," he cried. "Perchance 'twas well you were ambushed in the hold. 'Twill teach each mariner to hate and fear all rats again, like a good grain-sailor should. And now by a swift certain killing of all rats on *Squid* wipe out today's traitrous folery, when you clapped for rats and let rats lead your cheers, seduced by a scarlet girl and bribed by that most misnamed Mouser."

The Mouser, still paralyzed and perforce watching Slinoor aslant as Slinoor pointed at him, had to admit it was a well-turned reference to himself.

"First off," Slinoor said, "drag those two rogues on deck. Truss them to mast or rail. I'll not have them waking to botch my victory."

"Shall I up with a trap and loose a dart in the after hold?" the starsman asked eagerly.

"You should know better," was all Slinoor answered.

"Shall I gong for the galley and run up a red lamp?" the mate suggested.

Slinoor was silent two heartbeats, then said, "No. This is *Squid*'s fight to wipe out today's shame. Besides, Lukeen's a hothead botcher. Forget I said that, gentlemen, but it is so."

"Yet we'd be safer with the galley standing by," the mate ventured to continue. "Even now the rats may be gnawing holes in us."

"That's unlikely with the Rat Queen below," Slinoor retorted. "Speed's what will save us and not stand-by ships. Now hearken close. Guard well all ways to the hold. Keep traps and hatches shut. Rouse the off watch. Arm every man. Gather on middeck all we can spare from sailing. Move!"

The Mouser wished Slinoor hadn't said "Move!" quite so vehemently, for the two sailors instantly grabbed his ankles and dragged him most enthusiastically out of the littered cabin and across the middeck, his head bumping a bit. True, he couldn't feel the bumps, only hear them.

To the west the sky was a quarter globe of stars, to the east a mass of fog below and thinner mist above, with the gibbous moon shining through the latter like a pale misshapen silver ghost-lamp. The wind had slackened. *Squid* sailed smoothly.

One sailor held the Mouser against the mainmast, facing aft, while the other looped rope around him. As the sailors bound him with his arms flat to his sides, the Mouser felt a tickle in his throat and life returning to his tongue, but he decided not to try to speak just yet. Slinoor in his present mood might order him gagged.

The Mouser's next divertisement was watching Fafhrd dragged out by four sailors and bound lengthwise, facing inboard with head aft and higher than feet, to the larboard rail. It was quite a comic performance, but the Northerner snored through it.

Sailors began to gather then on middeck, some palely silent but most quipping in low voices. Pikes and cutlasses gave them courage. Some carried nets and long sharp-tined forks. Even the cook came with a great cleaver, which he hefted playfully at the Mouser.

"Struck dumb with admiration of my sleepy curry eh?"

Meanwhile the Mouser found he could move his fingers. No one had bothered to disarm him, but Cat's Claw was unfortunately fixed far too high on his left side for either hand to touch, let alone get out of its scabbard. He felt the hem of his tunic until he touched, through the cloth, a rather small flat round object thinner along one edge than the other. Gripping it by the thick edge through the cloth, he began to scrape with the thin edge at the fabric confining it.

The sailors crowded aft as Slinoor emerged from the cabin with his officers and began to issue low-voiced orders. The Mouser caught "Slay Hisvet or her maid on sight. They're not women but were-rats or worse," and then the last of Slinoor's orders: "Poise your parties below the hatch or trap by which you enter. When you hear the bosun's whistle, move!"

The effect of this "Move!" was rather spoiled by a tiny *twing* and the arms-master clapping his hand to his eye and screaming. There was a flurry of movement among the sailors. Cutlasses struck at a pale form that scurried along the deck. For an instant a rat with a crossbow in his hands was silhouetted on the starboard rail against the moon-pale mist. Then the starsman's crossbow twanged and the dart winging with exceptional accuracy or luck knocked the rat off the rail into the sea.

"That was a whitey, lads!" Slinoor cried. "A good omen!"

Thereafter there was some confusion, but it was quickly settled, especially when it was discovered that the starsman had not been struck in the eye but only near it, and the beweaponed parties moved off, one into the cabin, two forward past the mainmast, leaving on deck a skeleton crew of four.

The fabric the Mouser had been scraping parted and he most carefully eased out of the shredded hem an iron tik (the Lankhmar coin of least value) with half its edge honed to razor sharpness and began to slice with it in tiny strokes at the nearest loop of the line binding him. He looked hopefully toward Fafhrd, but the latter's head still hung at a senseless angle.

A whistle sounded faintly, followed some ten breaths later by a louder one from another part of the hold, it seemed. Then muffled shouts began to come in flurries there were two screams, something thumped the deck from below, and a sailor swinging a rat squeaking in a net dashed past the Mouser.

The Mouser's fingers told him he was almost through the first loop. Leaving it joined by a few threads, he began to slice at the next loop, bending his wrist acutely to do it.

An explosion shook the deck, stinging the Mouser's feet. He could not conjecture its nature and sawed furiously with his sharpened coin. The skeleton crew cried out and one of the helmsmen fled forward but the other stuck by the tiller. Somehow the gong clanged once, though no one was by it.

Then *Squid*'s sailors began to pour up out of the hold, half of them without weapons and frantic with fear. They milled about. The Mouser could hear sailors dragging *Squid*'s boats, which were forward of the mainmast, to the ship's side. The Mouser gathered that the sailors had fared most evilly below, assaulted by batallions of black rats, confused by false whistles, slashed and jabbed from dark corners, stung by darts, two struck in the eye and blinded. What had completed their rout was that, coming to a hold of unsacked grain, they'd found the air above it choked with grain dust from the recent churnings and scatterings of a horde of rats, and Frix had thrown in fire from beyond, exploding the stuff and knocking them off their feet though not setting fire to the ship.

At the same time as the panic-stricken sailors, there also came on deck another group, noted only by the Mouser—a most quiet and orderly file of black rats that went climbing around him up the mainmast. The Mouser weighed crying an alarm, although he wouldn't have wagered a tik on his chances of survival with hysterical be-cutlassed sailors rat-slashing all around him.

In any case his decision was made for him in the negative by Skwee, who climbed on his left shoulder just then. Holding on by a lock of the Mouser's hair, Skwee leaned out in front of him, staring into the Mouser's left eye with his own two wally blue ones under his black-plumed silver helmet. Skwee touched pale paw to his buck-toothed lips, enjoining silence, then patted the little sword at his side and jerked his rat-thumb across his rat-throat to indicate the penalty for silence broken. Thereafter he retired into the shadows by the Mouser's ear, presumably to watch the routed sailors and wave on and command his own company—and keep close to the Mouser's jugular vein. The Mouser kept sawing with his coin.

The starsman came aft followed by three sailors with two white lanterns apiece. Skwee crowded back closer between the Mouser and the mast, but touched the cold flat of his sword to the Mouser's neck, just under the ear, as a reminder. The Mouser remembered Hisvet's kiss. With a frown at the Mouser the starsman avoided the mainmast and had the sailors hang their lanterns to the aftermast and the crane fittings and the forward range of the afterdeck, fussing about the exact positions. He asserted in a high babble that light was the perfect military defense and counterweapon, and talked wildly of light-entrenchments and light palisades, and was just about to set the sailors hunting more lamps, when Slinoor limped out of the cabin bloody-foreheaded and looked around.

"Courage, lads," Slinoor shouted hoarsely. "On deck we're still masters. Let down the boats orderly, lads, we'll need 'em to fetch the marines. Run up the red lamp! You there, gong the alarm!"

Someone responded, "The gong's gone overboard. The ropes that hung it—gnawed!"

At the same time thickening waves of fog came out of the east, shrouding *Squid* in deadly moonlit silver. A sailor moaned. It was a strange fog that seemed to increase rather than diminish the amount of light cast by the moon and the starsman's lantern. Colors stood out, yet soon there was only white wall beyond the *Squid*'s rails.

Slinoor ordered, "Get up the spare gong! Cook, let's have your biggest kettles, lids and pots—anything to beat an alarm!"

There were two splashing thumps as *Squid*'s boats hit the water.

Someone screamed agonizingly in the cabin.

Then two things happened together. The mainsail parted from the mast, falling to starboard like a cathedral ceiling in a gale, its lines and ties to the mast gnawed loose or sawed by tiny swords. It floated darkly on the water, dragging the boom wide. *Squid* lurched to starboard.

At the same time a horde of black rats spewed out of the cabin door and came pouring over the taffrail, the latter presumably by way of the stern lights. They rushed at the humans in waves, springing with equal force and resolution whether they landed on pike points or tooth-clinging to noses and throats.

* * *

The sailors broke and made for the boats, rats landing on their backs and nipping at their heels. The officers fled too. Slinoor was carried along, crying for a last stand. Skwee out with his sword on the Mouser's shoulder and bravely waved on his suicidal soldiery, chittering high, then leaped down to follow in their rear. Four white rats armed with crossbows knelt on the crane fittings and began to crank, load and fire with great efficiency.

Splashings began, first two and three, then what sounded like a half dozen together, mixed with screams. The Mouser twisted his head around and from the corner of his eye saw the last two of *Squid's* sailors leap over the side. Straining a little further around yet, he saw Slinoor clutch to his chest two rats that worried him and follow the sailors. The four white-furred arbalasters leaped down from the crane fittings and raced toward a new firing position on the prow. Hoarse human cries came up from the water and faded off. Silence fell on *Squid* like the fog, broken only by the inevitable chitterings and those few now.

When the Mouser turned his head aft again, Hisvet was standing before him. She was dressed in close-fitting black leather from neck to elbows and knees, looking most like a slim boy, and she wore a black leather helmet fitting down over her temples and cheeks like Skwee's silver one, her white hair streaming down in a tail behind making her plume. A slim dagger was scabbarded on her left hip.

"Dear, dear Dirksman," she said softly, smiling with her little mouth, "You at least do not desert me," and she reached out and almost brushed his cheek with her fingers. Then, "Bound!" she said, seeming to see the rope for the first time and drawing back her hand. "We must remedy that, Dirksman."

"I would be most grateful, White Princess," the Mouser said humbly. Nevertheless, he did not let go his sharpened coin, which although somewhat dulled had now sliced almost halfway through a third loop.

"We must remedy that," Hisvet repeated a little absently, her gaze straying beyond the Mouser. "But my fingers are too soft and unskilled to deal with such mighty knots as I see. Frix will release you. Now I must hear Skwee's report on the afterdeck. Skwee-skwee-skwee!"

As she turned and walked aft the Mouser saw that her hair all went through a silver-ringed hole in the back top of her black helmet. Skwee came running past the Mouser and when he had almost caught up with Hisvet he took position to her right and three rat-paces behind her, strutting with forepaw on sword-hilt and head held high, like a captain-general behind his empress.

As the Mouser resumed his weary sawing of the third loop, he looked at Fafhrd bound to the rail and saw that the black kitten was crouched fur-on-end on Fafhrd's neck and slowly raking his cheek with the spread claws of a forepaw while the Northerner still snored garglingly. Then the kitten dipped its head and bit Fafhrd's ear. Fafhrd groaned piteously, but then came another of the gargling snores. The kitten resumed its cheek-raking. Two rats, one white, one black, walked by and the kitten wauled at them softly yet direly. The rats stopped and stared, then scurried straight toward the afterdeck, presumably to report the unwholesome condition to Skwee or Hisvet.

The Mouser decided to burst loose without more ado, but just then the four white arbalasters came back dragging a brass cage of frightenedly cheeping wrens the Mouser remembered seeing hanging by a sailor's bunk in the forecastle. They stopped by the crane fittings again and started a wren-shoot. They'd release one of the tiny terrified flutterers, then as it winged off bring it down with a well-aimed dart—at distances up to five and six yards, never missing. Once or twice one of them would glance at the Mouser narrowly and touch the dart's point.

Frix stepped down the ladder from the afterdeck. She was now dressed like her mistress, except she had no helmet, only the tight silver hairnet, though the silver rings were gone from her wrists.

"Lady Frix!" the Mouser called in a light voice, almost gayly. It was hard to say how one should speak on a ship manned by rats, but a high voice seemed indicated.

She came towards him smiling, but "Frix will do better," she said. "Lady is such a corset title."

"Frix then," the Mouser called, "on your way would you scare that black witch cat from our poppy-sodden friend? He'll rake out my comrade's eye."

Frix looked sideways to see what the Mouser meant, but still kept stepping toward him.

"I never interfere with another person's pleasures or pains, since it's hard to be certain which are which," she informed him, coming close. "I only carry out my mistress's directives. Now she bids me tell you be patient and of good cheer. Your trials will soon be over. And this withal she sends you as a remembrancer." Lifting her mouth, she kissed the Mouser softly on each upper eyelid.

The Mouser said, "That's the kiss with which the green priestess of Djil seals the eyes of those departing this world."

"Is it?" Frix asked softly.

"Aye, 'tis," the Mouser said with a little shudder, continuing briskly, "so now undo me these knots, Frix, which is something your mistress has directed. And then perchance give me a livelier smack—after I've looked to Fafhrd."

"I only carry out the directives of my mistress's own mouth," Frix said, shaking her head a little sadly. "She said nothing to me about untying knots. But doubtless she will direct me to loose you shortly."

"Doubtless," the Mouser agreed, a little glumly, forbearing to saw with his coin at the third loop while Frix watched him. If he could but sever at once three loops, he told himself, he might be able to shake off the remaining ones in a not impossibly large number of heartbeats.

As if on cue, Hisvet stepped lightly down from the afterdeck and hastened to them.

"Dear mistress, do you bid me undo the Dirksman his knots?" Frix asked at once, almost as if she wanted to be told to.

"I will attend to matters here," Hisvet replied hurriedly. "Go you to the afterdeck, Frix, and harken and watch for my father. He delays overlong this night." She also ordered the white crossbow-rats, who'd winged their last wren, to retire to the afterdeck.

After Frix and the rats had gone, Hisvet gazed at the Mouser for the space of a score of heartbeats, frowning just a little, studying him deeply with her red-irised eyes.

Finally she said with a sigh, "I wish I could be certain."

"Certain of what, White Princessship?" the Mouser asked.

"Certain that you love me truly," she answered softly yet downrightly, as if he surely knew. "Many men—aye and women too and demons and beasts—have told me they loved me truly, but truly I think none of them loved me for myself (save Frix, whose happiness is in being a shadow) but only because I was young or beautiful or a demoiselle of Lankhmar or dreadfully clever or had a rich father or was dowered with power, being blood-related to the rats, which is a certain sign of power in more worlds than Nehwon. Do you truly love me for myself, Gray Mouser?"

"I love you most truly indeed, Shadow Princess," the Mouser said with hardly an instant's hesitation. "Truly I love you for yourself alone, Hisvet. I love you more dearly than aught else in Nehwon—aye, and in all other worlds too and heaven and hell besides."

Just then Fafhrd, cruelly clawed or bit by the kitten, let off a most piteous groan indeed with a dreadful high note in it, and the Mouser said impulsively, "Dear Princess, first chase me that were-cat from my large friend, for I fear it will be his blinding and death's bane, and then we shall discourse of our great loves to the end of eternity."

"That is what I mean," Hisvet said softly and reproachfully. "If you loved me truly for myself, Gray Mouser, you would not care a feather if your closest friend or your wife or mother or child were tortured and done to death before your eyes, so long as my eyes were upon you and I touched you with my fingertips. With my kisses on your lips and my slim hands playing about you, my whole person accepting and welcoming you, you

could watch your large friend there scratched to blindness and death by a cat—or mayhap eaten alive by rats—and be utterly content. I have touched few things in this world, Gray Mouser. I have touched no man, or male demon or larger male beast, save by the proxy of Frix. Remember that, Gray Mouser."

"To be sure, Dear Light of my Life!" the Mouser replied most spiritedly, certain now of the sort of self-adoring madness with which he had to deal, since he had a touch of the same mania and so was well-acquainted with it. "Let the barbarian bleed to death by pinpricks! Let the cat have his eyes! Let the rats banquet on him to his bones! What skills it while we trade sweet words and caresses, discoursing to each other with our entire bodies and our whole souls!"

Meanwhile, however, he had started to saw again most fiercely with his now-dulled coin, unmindful of Hisvet's eyes upon him. It enjoyed him to feel Cat's Claw lying against his ribs.

"That's spoken like my own true Mouser," Hisvet said with most melting tenderness, brushing her fingers so close to his cheek that he could feel the tiny chill zephyr of their passage. Then, turning, she called, "Holla, Frix! Send to me Skwee and the White Company. Each may bring with him two black comrades of his own choice. I have somewhat of a reward for them, somewhat of a special treat. Skwee! Skwee-skwee-skwee!"

What would have happened then, both instantly and ultimately, is impossible to say, for at that moment Frix hailed, "Ahoy!" into the fog and called happily down, "A black sail! Oh Blessed Demoiselle, it is your father!"

Out of the pearly fog to starboard came the shark's-fin triangle of the upper portion of a black sail, running alongside *Squid* aft of the dragging brown mainsail. Two boathooks a small ship's length apart came up and clamped down on the starboard middeck rail while the black sail flapped. Frix came running lightly forward and secured to the rail midway between the boathooks the top of a rope ladder next heaved up from the black cutter (for surely this must be that dire craft, the Mouser thought).

Then up the ladder and over the rail came nimbly an old man of Lankhmar dressed all in black leather and on his left shoulder a white rat clinging with right forepaw to a cheek-flap of his black leather cap. He was followed swiftly by two lean bald Mingols with faces yellow-brown as old lemons, each shoulder-bearing a large black rat that steadied itself by a yellow ear.

At that moment, most coincidentally, Fafhrd groaned again, more loudly, and opened his eyes and cried out in the faraway moan of an opium-dreamer, "Millions of black monkeys! Take him off, I say! 'Tis a black fiend of hell torments me! Take him off!"

At that the black kitten raised up, stretched out its small evil face, and bit Fafhrd on the nose. Disregarding this interruption, Hisvet threw up her hand at the newcomers and cried clearly, "Greetings, oh Cocommander my Father! Greetings, peerless rat captain Grig! *Clam* is conquered by you, now *Squid* by me, and this very night, after small business of my own attended to, shall see the perdition of all this final fleet. Then it's Movarl estranged, the Mingols across the Sinking Land, Glipkerio hurled down, and the rats ruling Lankhmar under my overlordship and yours!"

The Mouser, sawing ceaselessly at the third loop, chanced to note Skwee's muzzle at that moment. The small white captain had come down from the afterdeck at Hisvet's summoning along with eight white comrades, two bandaged, and now he shot Hisvet a silent look that seemed to say there might be doubts about the last item of her boast, once the rats ruled Lankhmar.

Hisvet's father Hisvin had a long-nosed, much wrinkled face patched by a week of white, old-man's beard, and he seemed permanently stooped far over, yet he moved most briskly for all that, taking very rapid little shuffling steps.

Now he answered his daughter's bragging speech with a petulant sideways flirt of his black glove close to his chest and a little impatient "Tsk-tsk!" of disapproval, then went circling the deck at his odd scuttling gait while the Mingols waited by the ladder-top. Hisvin circled by Fafhrd and his black tormenter ("Tsk-tsk!") and by the Mouser (another "Tsk!") and stopping in front of Hisvet said rapid and fumingly, still crouched over, jogging a bit from foot to foot, "Here's confusion indeed tonight! You catsing and romancing with bound men!—I know, I know! The moon coming through too much! (I'll have my astrologer's liver!) *Shark* oaring like a mad cuttlefish through the foggy white! A black balloon with little lights scudding above the waves! And but now ere we found you, a vast sea monster swimming about in circles with a gibbering demon on his head—it came sniffing at us as if we were dinner, but we evaded it!

"Daughter, you and your maid and your little people must into the cutter at once with us, pausing only to slay these two and leave a suicide squad of gnawers to sink *Squid!*"

"Sink *Squid*?" Hisvet questioned. "The plan was to slip her to Ilthmar with a Mingol skeleton crew and there sell her cargo."

"Plans change!" Hisvin snapped. "Daughter, if we're not off this ship in forty breaths, *Shark* will ram us by pure excess of blundering energy or the monster with the clown-clad mad mahout will eat us up as we drift here helpless. Give orders to Skwee! Then out with your knife and cut me these two fools' throats! Quick, quick!"

"But Daddy," Hisvet objected, "I had something quite different in mind for them. Not death, at least not altogether. Something far more artistic, even loving—"

"I give you thirty breaths each to torture ere you slay them!" Hisvin conceded. "Thirty breaths and not one more, mind you! I know your somethings!"

"Dad, don't be crude! Among new friends! *Why* must you always give people a wrong impression of me? I won't endure it longer!"

"Chat-chat-chat! You pother and pose more than your rat-mother."

"But I tell you I won't endure it. This time we're going to do things *my* way for a change!"

"Hist-hist!" her father commanded, stooping still lower and cupping hand to left ear, while his white rat Grig imitated his gesture on the other side.

Faintly through the fog came a gibbering. *"Gottverdammter Nebel! Freunde, wo sind Sie?"**

" 'Tiz the gibberer!" Hisvin cried under his breath. "The monster will be upon us! Quick, daughter, out with your knife and slay, or I'll have my Mingols dispatch them!"

Hisvet lifted her hand against that villainous possibility. Her proudly plumed head literally bent to the inevitable.

"I'll do it," she said. "Skwee, give me your crossbow. Load with silver."

The white rat captain folded his forelegs across his chest and chittered at her with a note of demand.

"No, you can't have him," she said sharply. "You can't have either of them. They're mine now."

Another curt chitter from Skwee.

"Very well, your people may have the small black one. Now quick with your crossbow or I'll curse you! Remember, only a smooth silver dart."

Hisvin had scuttled to his Mingols and now he went around in a little circle, almost spitting. Frix glided smiling to him and touched his arm but he shook away from her with an angry flirt.

Skwee was fumbling into his cannister rat-frantically. His eight comrades were fanning out across the deck toward Fafhrd and the black kitten, which leaped down now in front of Fafhrd, snarling defiance.

Fafhrd himself was looking about bloody-faced but at last lucid-eyed, drinking in the desperate situation, poppy-langour banished by nose-bite.

Just then there came another gibber through the fog. *"Gottverdammter Nirgendswelt!"‡*

Fafhrd's blood-shot eyes widened and brightened with a great inspiration. Bracing himself against his bonds, he inflated his mighty chest.

---

*"Goddamn fog! Friends, where are you?" Evidently Karl Treuherz' Lankhmarese dictionary was unavailable to him at the moment.
‡"Goddamn Nowhere-World!"

"HOONGK!" he bellowed. "HOONGK!"

Out of the fog came eager answer, growing each time louder: "Hoongk! *Hoongk!* HOONGK!"

Seven of the eight white rats that had crossed the deck now returned carrying stretched between them the still-snarling black kitten spread-eagled on its back, one to each paw and ear while the seventh tried to master but was shaken from side to side by the whipping tail. The eighth came hobbling behind on three legs, shoulder paralyzed by a deep-stabbing cat-bite.

From cabin and forecastle and all corners of the deck, the black rats scurried in to watch gloatingly their traditional enemy mastered and delivered to torment, until the mid-deck was thick with their bloaty dark forms.

Hisvin cracked a command at his Mingols. Each drew a wavy-edged knife. One headed for Fafhrd, the other for the Mouser. Black rats hid their feet.

Skwee dumped his tiny darts on the deck. His paw closed on a palely gleaming one and he slapped it in his crossbow, which he hurriedly handed up toward his mistress. She lifted it in her right hand toward Fafhrd, but just then the Mingol moving toward the Mouser crossed in front of her, his kreese point-first before him. She shifted crossbow to left hand, whipped out her dagger and darted ahead of the Mingol.

Meanwhile the Mouser had snapped the three cut loops with one surge. The others still confined him loosely at ankles and throat, but he reached across his body, drew Cat's Claw and slashed out at the Mingol as Hisvet shouldered the yellow man aside.

The dirk sliced her pale cheek from jaw to nose.

The other Mingol, advancing his kreese toward Fafhrd's throat, abruptly dropped to the deck and began to roll back across it, the black rats squeaking and snapping at him in surprise.

"HOONK!"

A great green dragon's head had loomed from the moon-mist over the larboard rail just at the spot where Fafhrd was tied. Strings of slaver trailed on the Northerner from the dagger-toothed jaws.

Like a ponderous jack-in-the-box, the red-mawed head dipped and drove forward, lower jaw rasping the oaken deck and sweeping up from it a swathe of black rats three rats wide. The jaws crunched together on their great squealing mouthful inches from the rolling Mingol's head. Then the green head swayed aloft and a horrid swelling traveled down the greenish yellow neck.

But even as it poised there for a second strike, it shrank in size by comparison with what now appeared out of the mist after it—a second green dragon's head fourfold larger and fantastically crested in red, orange and purple (for at first sight the rider seemed to be part of the monster). This head now drove forward as if it were that of the father of all dragons, sweeping up a black-rat swathe twice as wide as had the first and topping off its monster gobble with the two white rats behind the rat-carried black kitten.

It ended its first strike so suddenly (perhaps to avoid eating the kitten) that its parti-colored rider, who'd been waving his pike futilely, was hurled forward off its green head. The rider sailed low past the mainmast, knocking aside the Mingol striking at the Mouser, and skidded across the deck into the starboard rail.

The white rats let go of the kitten, which raced for the mainmast.

Then the two green heads, famished by their two days of small fishy pickings since their last real meal at the Rat Rocks, began methodically to sweep *Squid*'s deck clean of rats, avoiding humans for the most part, though not very carefully. And the rats, huddled in their mobs, did little to evade this dreadful mowing. Perhaps in their straining toward world-dominion they had grown just human and civilized enough to experience imaginative, unhelpful, freezing panic and to have acquired something of humanity's talent for inviting and enduring destruction. Perhaps they looked on the dragons' heads as the twin red maws of war and hell, into which they must throw themselves willy-nilly. At all events they were swept up by dozens and scores. All but three of the white rats were among those engulfed.

Meanwhile the larger people aboard *Squid* faced up variously to the drastically altered situation.

Old Hisvin shook his fist and spat in the larger dragon's face when after its first gargantuan swallow it came questing toward him, as if trying to decide whether this bent black thing were (ugh!) a very queer man or (yum!) a very large rat. But when the stinking apparition kept coming on, Hisvin rolled deftly over the rail as if into bed and swiftly climbed down the rope ladder, fairly chittering in consternation, while Grig clung for dear life to the back of the black leather collar.

Hisvin's two Mingols picked themselves up and followed him, vowing to get back to their cozy cold steppes as soon as Mingolly possible.

Fafhrd and Karl Treuherz watched the melee from opposite sides of the middeck, the one bound by ropes, the other by out-wearied astonishment.

Skwee and a white rat named Siss ran over the heads of their packed apathetic black fellows and hopped on the starboard rail. There they looked back. Siss blinked in horror. But Skwee, his black-plumed helmet pushed down over his left eye, menaced with his little sword and chittered defiance.

Frix ran to Hisvet and urged her to the starboard rail. As they neared the head of the rope ladder, Skwee went down it to make way for his empress, dragging Siss with him. Just then Hisvet turned like someone in a dream. The smaller dragon's head drove toward her viciously. Frix sprang in the way, arms wide, smiling, a little like a ballet dancer taking a curtain call. Perhaps it was the suddenness or seeming aggressiveness of her move that made the dragon sheer off, fangs clashing. The two girls climbed the rail.

Hisvet turned again. Cat's Claw's cut a bold red line across her face, and sighted her crossbow at the Mouser. There was the faintest silvery flash. Hisvet tossed the crossbow in the black sea and followed Frix down the ladder. The boathooks let go, the flapping black sail filled, and the black cutter faded into the mist.

The Mouser felt a little sting in his left temple, but he forgot it while whirling the last loops from his shoulders and ankles. Then he ran across the deck, disregarding the green heads lazily searching for last rat morsels, and cut Fafhrd's bonds.

All the rest of that night the two adventurers conversed with Karl Treuherz, telling each other fabulous things about each other's worlds, while Scylla's sated daughter slowly circled *Squid,* first one head sleeping and then the other. Talking was slow and uncertain work, even with the aid of the little Lankhmarese-German Dictionary for Space-Time Travelers, and neither party really believed a great deal of the other's tales, yet pretended to for friendship's sake.

"Do all men dress as grandly as you do in Tomorrow?" Fafhrd once asked, admiring the German's purple and orange garb.

"No, Hagenbeck just has his employees do it, to spread his monster zoo's fame," Karl Treuherz explained.

The last of the mist vanished just before dawn and they saw, silhouetted against the sea silvered by the sinking gibbous moon, the black ship of Karl Treuherz hovering not a bowshot west of *Squid,* its little lights twinkling softly.

The German shouted for joy, summoned his sleepy monster by thwacking his pike against the rail, swung astride the larger head, and swam off calling after him, "*Auf Wiedersehen!*"

Fafhrd had learned just enough Gibberish-German, during the night to know this meant, "Until we meet again."

When the monster and the German had swum below it, the space-time engine descended, somehow engulfing them. Then a little later the black ship vanished.

"It dove into the infinite waters toward Karl's Tomorrow bubble," the Gray Mouser affirmed confidently. "By Ning and by Sheel, the German's a master magician!"

Fafhrd blinked, frowned, and then simply shrugged . . .

The black kitten rubbed his ankle. Fafhrd lifted it gently to eye level, saying, "I wonder, kitten, if you're one of the Cats' Thirteen or else their small agent, sent to wake me when waking was needful?" The kitten smiled solemnly into Fafhrd's cruelly scratched and bitten face and purred.

Clear gray dawn spread across the waters of the Inner Sea, showing them first *Squid's* two boats crowded with men and Slinoor sitting dejected in the stern of the nearer but standing up with uplifted hand as he recognized the figures of the Mouser and Fafhrd; next Lukeen's war galley *Shark* and the three other grain ships *Tunny, Carp* and *Grouper;* lastly, small on the northern horizon, the green sails of two dragon-ships of Movarl.

The Mouser, running his left hand back through his hair, felt a short, straight, rounded ridge in his temple under the skin. He knew it was Hisvet's smooth silver dart, there to stay.

JACK VANCE

The Overworld

Although Jack Vance is perhaps best known as a science-fiction writer—author of such famous novels as *The Dragon Masters, Emphyrio, The Last Castle, The Blue World,* and the five-volume "Demon Princes" series, among many others—he has also been a seminal figure in the development of modern fantasy as well. Born in San Francisco in 1920, Vance served throughout World War II in the U.S. Merchant Navy. Most of the individual stories that would later be melded into his first novel, *The Dying Earth,* were written while Vance was at sea—he was unable to sell them, a problem he would also have with the book itself, the market for fantasy being almost non-existent at the time. *The Dying Earth* was eventually published in an obscure edition in 1950 by a small semi-professional press, went out of print almost immediately, and remained out of print for more than a decade thereafter. Nevertheless, it became an underground cult classic, and its effect on future generations of writers is incalculable: for one example, out of many, *The Dying Earth*—along with Clark Ashton Smith's *Zothique,* which probably influenced *it*—is one of the most recognizable influences on Gene Wolfe's *The Book of the New Sun* tetralogy (Wolfe has said, for instance, that *The Book of Gold* which is mentioned by Severian is supposed to be *The Dying Earth*). Vance returned to this *milieu* in 1965, with a series of stories introducing the sly and immoral trickster Cugel the Clever; collected in 1966 as *The Eyes of the Overworld,* the Cugel stories too had a profound effect on the state of the art of modern fantasy. In the early 1980s, Vance returned yet again with two collections of Cugel stories, *Cugel's Saga* and *Rhialto the Marvellous.* Taken together, *The Dying Earth* and the three volumes of Cugel stories represent one of the most impressive achievements in fantasy today.

Although almost quintessential "sense of wonder" stuff, marvelously evocative and effortlessly inventive, the Cugel stories are also elegant and intelligent, full of sly wit and subtle touches, all laced with Vance's typical dour irony and bleak deadpan humor. In "The Overworld"—one of the stories from *The Eyes of the Overworld*—Cugel earns the enmity of Iucounu the Laughing Magician, and reluctantly sets forth on an arduous and very dangerous mission, in the course of which he learns, to his sorrow, that beauty is most definitely in the eye of the beholder . . .

Vance has won two Hugo Awards, a Nebula Award, two World Fantasy Awards (one the prestigious Life Achievement Award), and the Edgar Award for best mystery novel. In addition to the Dying Earth/Cugel series, he has written another well-received fantasy series that includes *Lyonesse, The Green Pearl,* and *Madouc.* His other books, most of them science fiction, include *The Anome, The Star King, The Killing Machine, The Languages of Pao, The Palace of Love, The Face, The Book of Dreams, City of the Chasch, The Dirdir, The Pnume, The Gray Prince, The Brave Free Men, Trullion: Alastor 2262, Marune: Alastor 933,* and *Wyst: Alastor 1716,* among many others. His short fiction has been collected in *Eight Fantasms and Magics, The Best of Jack Vance, Green Magic, Lost Moons, The Complete Magnus Ridolph, The World Between and Other Stories, The Dark Side of the Moon,* and *The Narrow Land.* His most recent books are the novels *Araminta Station, Ecce and Olde Earth,* and *Throy,* plus an omnibus volume collecting three of his "Alastor" novels, *Alastor.*

On the heights above the river Xzan, at the site of certain ancient ruins, Iucounu the Laughing Magician had built a manse to his private taste: an eccentric structure of steep gables, balconies, sky-walks, cupolas, together with three spiral green glass towers through which the red sunlight shone in twisted glints and peculiar colors.

Behind the manse and across the valley, low hills rolled away like dunes to the limit of vision. The sun projected shifting crescents of black shadow; otherwise the hills were unmarked, empty, solitary. The Xzan, rising in the Old Forest to the east of Almery, passed below, then three leagues to the west made junction with the Scaum. Here was Azenomei, a town old beyond memory, notable now only for its fair, which attracted folk from all the region. At Azenomei Fair Cugel had established a booth for the sale of talismans.

Cugel was a man of many capabilities, with a disposition at once flexible and pertinacious. He was long of leg, deft of hand, light of finger, soft of tongue. His hair was the blackest of black fur, growing low down his forehead, coving sharply back above his eyebrows. His darting eye, long inquisitive nose and droll mouth gave his somewhat lean and bony face an expression of vivacity, candor, and affability. He had known many vicissitudes, gaining therefrom a suppleness, a fine discretion, a mastery of both bravado and stealth. Coming into the possession of an ancient lead coffin—after discarding the contents—he had formed a number of leaden lozenges. These, stamped with appropriate seals and runes, he offered for sale at the Azenomei Fair.

Unfortunately for Cugel, not twenty paces from his booth a certain Fianosther had established a larger booth with articles of greater variety and more obvious efficacy, so that whenever Cugel halted a passerby to enlarge upon the merits of his merchandise, the passerby would like as not display an article purchased from Fianosther and go his way.

On the third day of the fair Cugel had disposed of only four periapts, at prices barely above the cost of the lead itself, while Fianosther was hard put to serve all his customers. Hoarse from bawling futile inducements, Cugel closed down his booth and approached Fianosther's place of trade, in order to inspect the mode of construction and the fastenings at the door.

Fianosther, observing, beckoned him to approach. "Enter, my friend, enter. How goes your trade?"

"In all candor, not too well," said Cugel. "I am both perplexed and disappointed, for my talismans are not obviously useless."

"I can resolve your perplexity," said Fianosther. "Your booth occupies the site of the old gibbet, and has absorbed unlucky essences. But I thought to notice you examining the manner in which the timbers of my booth are joined. You will obtain a better view from within, but first I must shorten the chain of the captive erb which roams the premises during the night."

"No need," said Cugel. "My interest was cursory."

"As to the disappointment you suffer," Fianosther went on, "it need not persist. Observe these shelves. You will note that my stock is seriously depleted."

Cugel acknowledged as much. "How does this concern me?"

Fianosther pointed across the way to a man wearing garments of black. This man was small, yellow of skin, bald as a stone. His eyes resembled knots in a plank; his mouth was wide and curved in a grin of chronic mirth. "There stand Iucounu the Laughing Magician," said Fianosther. "In a short time he will come into my booth and attempt to buy a particular red libram, the casebook of Dibarcas Major, who studied under Great Phandaal. My price is higher than he will pay, but he is a patient man, and will remonstrate for at least three hours. During this time his manse stands untenanted. It contains a vast collection of thaumaturgical artifacts, instruments, and activans, as well as curiosa, talismans, amulets and librams. I'm anxious to purchase such items. Need I say more?"

"This is all very well," said Cugel, "but would Iucounu leave his manse without guard or attendant?"

Fianosther held wide his hands. "Why not? Who would dare steal from Iucounu the Laughing Magician?"

"Precisely this thought deters me," Cugel replied. "I am a man of resource, but not insensate recklessness."

"There is wealth to be gained," stated Fianosther. "Dazzles and displays, marvels beyond worth, as well as charms, puissances, and elixirs. But remember, I urge nothing, I counsel nothing; if you are apprehended, you have only heard me exclaiming at the wealth of Iucounu the Laughing Magician! But here he comes. Quick: turn your back so that he may not see your face. Three hours he will be here, so much I guarantee!"

Iucounu entered the booth, and Cugel bent to examine a bottle containing a pickled homunculus.

"Greetings, Iucounu!" called Fianosther. "Why have you delayed? I have refused munificent offers for a certain red libram, all on your account! And here—note this casket! It was found in a crypt near the site of old Karkod. It is yet sealed and who knows what wonder it may contain? My price is a modest twelve thousand terces."

"Interesting," murmured Iucounu. "The inscription—let me see . . . Hmm. Yes, it is authentic. The casket contains calcined fish-bone, which was used throughout Grand Motholam as a purgative. It is worth perhaps ten or twelve terces as a curio. I own caskets eons older, dating back to the Age of Glow."

Cugel sauntered to the door, gained the street, where he paced back and forth, considering every detail of the proposal as explicated by Fianosther. Superficially the matter seemed reasonable: here was Iucounu; there was the manse, bulging with encompassed wealth. Certainly no harm could result from simple reconnaissance. Cugel set off eastward along the banks of the Xzan.

The twisted turrets of green glass rose against the dark blue sky, scarlet sunlight engaging itself in the volutes. Cugel paused, made a careful appraisal of the countryside. The Xzan flowed past without a sound. Nearby, half-concealed among black poplars, pale green larch, drooping pall-willow, was a village—a dozen stone huts inhabited by bargemen and tillers of the river terraces: folk engrossed in their own concerns.

Cugel studied the approach to the manse; a winding way paved with dark brown tile. Finally he decided that the more frank his approach the less complex need be his explanations, if such were demanded. He began the climb up the hillside, and Iucounu's manse reared above him. Gaining the courtyard, he paused to search the landscape. Across the river hills rolled away into the dimness, as far as the eye could reach.

Cugel marched briskly to the door, rapped, but evoked no response. He considered. If Iucounu, like Fianosther, maintained a guardian beast, it might be tempted to utter a sound if provoked. Cugel called out in various tones; growling, mewing, yammering.

Silence within.

He walked gingerly to a window and peered into a hall draped in pale grey, containing only a tabouret on which, under a glass bell jar, lay a dead rodent. Cugel circled the manse. Investigating each window as he came to it, and finally reached the great hall of the ancient castle. Nimbly he climbed the rough stones, leapt across to one of Iucounu's fanciful parapets and in a trice had gained access to the manse.

He stood in a bedchamber. On a dais six gargoyles supporting a couch turned heads to glare at the intrusion. With two stealthy strides Cugel gained the arch which opened into an outer chamber. Here the walls were green and the furnishings black and pink. He left the room for a balcony circling a central chamber, light streaming through oriels high in the walls. Below were cases, chests, shelves and racks containing all manner of objects: Iucounu's marvelous collection.

Cugel stood poised, tense as a bird, but the quality of the silence reassured him: the silence of an empty place. Still, he trespassed upon the property of Iucounu the Laughing Magician, and vigilance was appropriate.

Cugel strode down a sweep of circular stairs into a great hall. He stood enthralled, paying Iucounu the tribute of unstinted wonder. But his time was limited; he must rob swiftly, and be on his way. Out came his sack; he roved the hall, fastidiously selecting those objects of small bulk and great value; a small pot with antlers, which emitted clouds of remarkable gasses when the prongs were tweaked; an ivory horn through which sounded voices from the past; a small stage where costumed imps stood ready to perform comic antics; an object like a cluster of crystal grapes, each affording a blurred view into one of the demon-worlds; a baton sprouting sweetmeats of assorted flavor; an ancient ring engraved with runes; a black stone surrounded by nine zones of impalpable color. He passed by hundreds of jars of powders and liquids, likewise forebore from the vessels containing preserved heads. Now he came to shelves stacked with volumes, folios and librams, where he selected with care, taking for preference those bound in purple velvet, Phandaal's characteristic color. He likewise selected folios of drawings and ancient maps, and the disturbed leather exuded a musty odor.

He circled back to the front of the hall past a case displaying a score of small metal chests, sealed with corroded bands of great age. Cugel selected three at random; they were unwontedly heavy. He passed by several massive engines whose purpose he would have liked to explore, but time was advancing, and best he should be on his way, back to Azenomei and the booth of Fianosther . . .

Cugel frowned. In many respects the prospect seemed impractical. Fianosther would hardly choose to pay full value for his goods, or, more accurately, Iucounu's goods. It might be well to bury a certain proportion of the loot in an isolated place . . . Here was an alcove Cugel had not previously noted. A soft light welled like water against the crystal pane, which separated alcove from hall. A niche to the rear displayed a complicated object of great charm. As best Cugel could distinguish, it seemed a minia-ture carousel on which rode a dozen beautiful dolls of seeming vitality. The object was clearly of great value, and Cugel was pleased to find an aperture in the crystal pane.

He stepped through, but two feet before him a second pane blocked his way, establishing an avenue which evidently led to the magic whirligig. Cugel proceeded confidently, only to be stopped by another pane which he had not seen until he bumped into it. Cugel retraced his steps and to his gratification found the doubtlessly correct entrance a few feet back. But this new avenue led him by several right angles to another blank pane. Cugel decided to forego acquisition of the carousel and depart the castle. He turned, but discovered himself to be a trifle confused. He had come from his left—or was it his right?

. . . Cugel was still seeking egress when in due course Iucounu returned to his manse.

Pausing by the alcove, Iucounu gave Cugel a stare of humorous as-tonishment. "What have we here? A visitor? And I have been so remiss as to keep you waiting! Still, I see you have amused yourself, and I need feel no mortification." Iucounu permitted a chuckle to escape his lips. He then pretended to notice Cugel's bag. "What is this? You have brought objects for my examination? Excellent! I am always anxious to enhance my collection, in order to keep pace with the attrition of the years. You would be astounded to learn of the rogues who seek to despoil me! That merchant of claptrap in his tawdry little booth, for instance—you could not conceive his frantic efforts in this regard! I tolerate him because to date he has not been bold enough in venture himself into my manse. But come, step out here into the hall, and we will examine the contents of your bag."

Cugel bowed graciously. "Gladly. As you assume, I have indeed been waiting for your return. If I recall correctly, the exit is by this passage . . ." He stepped forward, but again was halted. He made a gesture of rueful amusement. "I seem to have taken a wrong turning."

"Apparently so," said Iucounu. "Glancing upward, you will notice a dec-orative motif upon the ceiling. If you heed the flexion of the lunules you will be guided to the hall."

"Of course!" And Cugel briskly stepped forward in accordance with the directions.

"One moment!" called Iucounu. "You have forgotten your sack!"

Cugel reluctantly returned for the sack, once more set forth, and presently emerged into the hall.

Iucounu made a suave gesture. "If you will step this way I will be glad to examine your merchandise."

Cugel glanced reflectively along the corridor toward the front entrance.

"It would be a presumption upon your patience. My little knickknacks are below notice. With your permission I will take my leave."

"By no means!" declared Iucounu heartily. "I have a few visitors, most of whom are rogues and thieves. I handle them severely, I assure you! I insist that you at least take some refreshment. Place your bag on the floor."

Cugel carefully set down the bag. "Recently I was instructed in a small competence by a sea-hag of White Alster. I believe you will be interested. I require several ells of stout cord."

"You excite my curiosity!" Iucounu extended his arm; a panel in the wainscoting slid back; a coil of rope was tossed to his hand. Rubbing his face as if to conceal a smile, Iucounu handed the rope to Cugel, who shook it out with great care.

"I will ask your cooperation," said Cugel. "A small matter of extending one arm and one leg."

"Yes, of course," Iucounu held out his hand, pointed a finger. The rope coiled around Cugel's arms and legs, pinning him so that he was unable to move. Iucounu's grin nearly split his great soft head. "This is a surprising development! By error I called forth Thief-taker! For your own comfort, do not strain, as Thief-taker is woven of wasp-legs. Now then, I will examine the contents of your bag." He peered into Cugel's sack and emitted a soft cry of dismay. "You have rifled my collection! I note certain of my most treasured valuables!"

Cugel grimaced. "Naturally! But I am no thief; Fianosther sent me here to collect certain objects, and therefore—"

Iucounu held up his hand. "The offense is far too serious for flippant disclaimers. I have stated my abhorrence for plunderers and thieves, and now I must visit upon you justice in its most unmitigated rigor—unless, of course, you can suggest an adequate requital."

"Some such requital surely exists," Cugel averred. "This cord however rasps upon my skin, so that I find cogitation impossible."

"No matter. I have decided to apply the Charm of Forlorn Encystment, which constricts the subject in a pore some forty-five miles below the surface of the earth."

Cugel blinked in dismay. "Under these conditions, requital could never be made."

"True," mused Iucounu. "I wonder if after all there is some small service which you can perform for me."

"The villain is as good as dead!" declared Cugel. "Now remove these abominable bonds!"

"I had no specific assassination in mind," said Iucounu. "Come."

The rope relaxed, allowing Cugel to hobble after Iucounu into a side chamber hung with intricately embroidered tapestry. From a cabinet Iucounu brought a small case and laid it on a floating disk of glass. He opened the case and gestured to Cugel, who perceived that the box showed two indentations lined with scarlet fur, where reposed a single small hemisphere of filmed violet glass.

"As a knowledgeable and traveled man," suggested Iucounu, "you doubtless recognize this object. No? You are familiar, of course, with the Cutz Wars of the Eighteenth Aeon? No?" Iucounu hunched up his shoulders in astonishment. "During these ferocious events the demon Unda-Hrada—he listed as 16-04 Green in Thrump's Almanac—thought to assist his principals, and to this end thrust certain agencies up from the subworld La-Er. In order that they might perceive, they were tipped with cusps similar to the one you see before you. When events went amiss, the demon snatched himself back to La-Er. The hemispheres were dislodged and broadcast across Cutz. One of these, as you see, I own. You must procure its mate and bring it to me, whereupon your trespass shall be overlooked."

Cugel reflected. "The choice, if it lies between a sortie into the demon-world La-Er and the Spell of Forlorn Encystment, is moot. Frankly, I am at a loss for decision."

Iucounu's laugh almost split the big yellow bladder of his head. "A visit to La-Er perhaps will prove unnecessary. You may secure the article in that land once known as Cutz."

"If I must, I must," growled Cugel, thoroughly displeased by the manner in which the day's work had ended. "Who guards this violet hemisphere? What is its function? How do I go and how return? What necessary weapons, talismans and other magical adjuncts do you undertake to fit me out with?"

"All in good time," said Iucounu. "First I must ensure that, once at liberty, you conduct yourself with unremitting loyalty, zeal and singleness of purpose."

"Have no fear," declared Cugel. "My word is my bond."

"Excellent!" cried Iucounu. "This knowledge represents a basic security which I do not in the least take lightly. The act now to be performed is doubtless supererogatory."

He departed the chamber and after a moment returned with a covered glass bowl containing a small white creature, all claws, prongs, barbs and hooks, now squirming angrily. "This," said Iucounu, "is my friend Firx, from the star Achernar, who is far wiser than he seems. Firx is annoyed at being separated from his comrade with whom he shares a vat in my workroom. He will assist you in the expeditious discharge of your duties," Iucounu stepped close, deftly thrust the creature against Cugel's abdomen. It merged into his viscera, and took up a vigilant post clasped around Cugel's liver.

Iucounu stood back, laughing in that immoderate glee which had earned him his cognomen. Cugel's eyes bulged from his head. He opened his mouth to utter an objurgation, but instead clenched his jaw and rolled up his eyes.

The rope uncoiled itself. Cugel stood quivering, every muscle knotted.

Iucounu's mirth dwindled to a thoughtful grin. "You spoke of magical adjuncts. What of those talismans whose efficacy you proclaimed from your booth in Azenomei? Will they not immobilize enemies, dissolve iron, impassion virgins, confer immortality?"

"These talismans are not uniformly dependable," said Cugel. "I will require further competences."

"You have them," said Iucounu, "in your sword, your crafty persuasiveness and the agility of your feet. Still, you have aroused my concern and I will help you to this extent." He hung a small square tablet about Cugel's neck. "You now may put aside all fear of starvation. A touch of this potent object will induce nutriment into wood, bark, grass, even discarded clothing. It will also sound a chime in the presence of poison. So now—there is nothing to delay us! Come, we will go. Rope? Where is Rope?"

Obediently the rope looped around Cugel's neck, and Cugel was forced to march along behind Iucounu.

They came out upon the roof of the antique castle. Darkness had long since fallen over the land. Up and down the valley of the Xzan faint lights glimmered, while the Xzan itself was an irregular width darker than dark.

Iucounu pointed to a cage. "This will be your conveyance. Inside."

Cugel hesitated. "It might be preferable to dine well, to sleep and rest, to set forth tomorrow refreshed."

"What?" spoke Iucounu in a voice like a horn. "You dare stand before me and state preferences? You, who came skulking into my house, pillaged my valuables and left all in disarray? Do you understand your luck? Perhaps you prefer the Forlorn Encystment?"

"By no means!" protested Cugel nervously. "I am anxious only for the success of the venture!"

"Into the cage, then."

Cugel turned despairing eyes around the castle roof, then slowly went to the cage and stepped within.

"I trust you suffer no deficiency of memory," said Iucounu. "But even if this becomes the case, and if you neglect your prime responsibility, which is to say, the procuring of the violet cusp, Firx is on hand to remind you."

Cugel said, "Since I am now committed to this enterprise, and unlikely to return, you may care to learn my appraisal of yourself and your character. In the first place—"

But Iucounu held up his hand. "I do not care to listen; obloquy injures my self-esteem and I am skeptical of praise. So now—be off!" He drew back, stared up into the darkness, then shouted that invocation known as Thasdrubal's Laganetic Transfer. From high came a thud and a buffet, a muffled bellow of rage.

Iucounu retreated a few steps, shouting up words in an archaic language; and the cage with Cugel crouching within was snatched aloft and hurled through the air.

Cold wind bit Cugel's face. From above came a flapping and creaking of vast wings and dismal lamentation; the cage swung back and forth. Below all was dark, a blackness like a pit. By the disposition of the stars Cugel perceived that the course was to the north, and presently he sensed the thrust of the Maurenron Mountains below; and then they flew over that wilderness known as the Land of the Falling Wall. Once or twice Cugel glimpsed the lights of an isolated castle, and once he noted a great bonfire. For a period a winged sprite came to fly alongside the cage and peer within. It seemed to find Cugel's plight amusing and when Cugel sought information as to the land below; it merely uttered raucous cries of mirth. It became fatigued and sought to cling to the cage, but Cugel kicked it away, and it fell off into the wind with a scream of envy.

The east flushed the red of old blood, and presently the sun appeared, trembling like an old man with a chill. The ground was shrouded by mist; Cugel was barely able to see that they crossed a land of black mountains and dark chasms. Presently the mist parted once more to reveal a leaden sea. Once or twice he peered up, but the roof of the cage concealed the demon except for the tips of the leathern wings.

At last the demon reached the north shore of the ocean. Swooping to the beach, it vented a vindictive croak, and allowed the cage to fall from a height of fifteen feet.

Cugel crawled from the broken cage. Nursing his bruises, he called a curse after the departing demon, then plodded back through sand and dank yellow spinifex, and climbed the slope of the foreshore. To the north were marshy barrens and a far huddle of low hills, to east and west ocean and dreary beach. Cugel shook his fist to the south. Somehow, at some time, in some manner, he would visit revenge upon the Laughing Magician! So much he vowed.

A few hundred yards to the west was the trace of an ancient seawall. Cugel thought to inspect it, but hardly moved three steps before Firx clamped prongs into his liver. Cugel, rolling up his eyes in agony, reversed his direction and set out along the shore to the east.

Presently he hungered, and bethought himself of the charm furnished by Iucounu. He picked up a piece of driftwood and rubbed it with the tablet, hoping to see a transformation into a tray of sweetmeats or a roast fowl. But the driftwood merely softened to the texture of cheese, retaining the flavor of driftwood. Cugel ate with snaps and gulps. Another score against Iucounu! How the Laughing Magician would pay!

The scarlet globe of the sun slid across the southern sky. Night approached, and at last Cugel came upon human habitation: a rude village beside a small river. The huts were like birds'-nests of mud and sticks, and smelled vilely of ordure and filth. Among them wandered a people as unlovely and graceless as the huts. They were squat, brutish and obese; their hair was a coarse yellow tangle; their features were lumps. Their single noteworthy attribute—one in which Cugel took an instant and keen interest—was their eyes; blind-seeming violet hemispheres, similar in every respect to that object required by Iucounu.

Cugel approached the village cautiously but the inhabitants took small interest in him. If the hemisphere coveted by Iucounu were identical to the violet eyes of these folk, then a basic uncertainty of the mission was resolved, and procuring the violet cusp became merely a matter of tactics.

Cugel paused to observe the villagers, and found much to puzzle him. In the first place, they carried themselves not as the ill-smelling loons they were, but with a remarkable loftiness and a dignity which verged at times upon hauteur. Cugel watched in puzzlement: were they a tribe of dotards? In any event, they seemed to pose no threat, and he advanced into the main avenue of the village, walking gingerly to avoid the more noxious heaps of refuse. One of the villagers now deigned to notice him, and addressed him in grunting guttural voice. "Well, sirrah: what is your wish? Why do you prowl the outskirts of our city Smolod?"

"I am a wayfarer," said Cugel. "I ask only to be directed to the inn, where I may find food and lodging."

"We have no inn; travelers and wayfarers are unknown to us. Still, you are welcome to share our plenty. Yonder is a manse with appointments sufficient for your comfort." The man pointed to a dilapidated hut. "You may eat as you will; merely enter the refectory yonder and select what you wish; there is no stinting at Smolod."

"I thank you gratefully," said Cugel, and would have spoken further except that his host had strolled away.

Cugel gingerly looked into the shed, and after some exertion cleaned out the most inconvenient debris, and arranged a trestle on which to sleep. The sun was now at the horizon and Cugel went to that storeroom which had been identified as the refectory. The villager's description of the bounty available, as Cugel had suspected, was in the nature of hyperbole. To one side of the storeroom was a heap of smoked fish, to the other a bin containing lentils mingled with various seeds and cereals. Cugel took a portion to his hut, where he made a glum supper.

The sun had set; Cugel went forth to see what the village offered in the way of entertainment, but found the streets deserted. In certain of the huts lamps burned, and Cugel peering through the cracks saw the residents dining upon smoked fish or engaged in discourse. He returned to his shed, built a small fire against the chill and composed himself for sleep.

The following day Cugel renewed his observation of the village Smolod and its violet-eyed folk. None, he noticed, went forth to work, nor did there seem to be fields near at hand. The discovery caused Cugel dissatisfaction. In order to secure one of the violet eyes, he would be obliged to kill its owner, and for this purpose freedom from officious interference was essential.

He made tentative attempts at conversation among the villagers, but they looked at him in a manner which presently began to jar at Cugel's equanimity: it was almost as if they were gracious lords and he the ill-smelling lout!

During the afternoon he strolled south, and about a mile along the shore came upon another village. The people were much like the inhabitants of Smolod, but with ordinary-seeming eyes. They were likewise industrious; Cugel watched them till fields and fish the ocean.

He approached a pair of fishermen on their way back to the village, their catch slung over their shoulders. They stopped, eyeing Cugel with no great friendliness. Cugel introduced himself as a wayfarer and asked concerning the lands to the east, but the fishermen professed ignorance other than the fact that the land was barren, dreary and dangerous.

"I am currently guest at the village Smolod," said Cugel. "I find the folk pleasant enough, but somewhat odd. For instance, why are their eyes as they are? What is the nature of their affliction? Why do they conduct themselves with such aristocratic self-assurance and suavity of manner?"

"The eyes are magic cusps," stated the older of the fishermen in a grudging voice. "They afford a view of the Overworld; why should not the owners behave as lords? So will I when Radkuth Vomin dies, for I inherit his eyes."

"Indeed!" exclaimed Cugel, marveling. "Can these magic cusps be detached at will and transferred as the owner sees fit?"

"They can, but who would exchange the Overworld for this?" The fisherman swung his arm around the dreary landscape. "I have toiled long and at last it is my turn to taste the delights of the Overworld. After this there is nothing, and the only peril is death through a surfeit of bliss."

"Vastly interesting!" remarked Cugel. "How might I qualify for a pair of these magic cusps?"

"Strive as do all the others of Grodz: place your name on the list, then toil to supply the lords of Smolod with sustenance. Thirty-one years have I sown and reaped lentils and emmer and netted fish and dried them over slow fires, and now the name of Bubach Angh is at the head of the list, and you must do the same."

"Thirty-one years," mused Cugel. "A period of not negligible duration." And Firx squirmed restlessly, causing Cugel's liver no small discomfort.

The fishermen proceeded to their village Grodz; Cugel returned to

Smolod. Here he sought out that man to whom he had spoken upon his arrival at the village. "My lord," said Cugel, "as you know, I am a traveler from a far land, attracted here by the magnificence of the city Smolod."

"Understandable," grunted the other. "Our splendor cannot help but inspire emulation."

"What then is the source of the magic cusps?"

The elder turned the violet hemispheres upon Cugel as if seeing him for the first time. He spoke in a surly voice. "It is a matter we do not care to dwell upon, but there is no harm in it, now that the subject has been broached. At a remote time the demon Underherd sent up tentacles to look across Earth, each tipped with a cusp. Simbilis the Sixteenth pained the monster, which jerked back to his sub-world and the cusps became dislodged. Four hundred and twelve of the cusps were gathered and brought to Smolod, then as splendid as now it appears to me. Yes, I realize that I see but a semblance, but so do you, and who is to say which is real?"

"I do not look through magic cusps," said Cugel.

"True." The elder shrugged. "It is a matter I prefer to overlook. I dimly recall that I inhabit a sty and devour the coarsest of food—but the subjective reality is that I inhabit a glorious palace and dine on splendid viands among the princes and princesses who are my peers. It is explained thus: the demon Underherd looked from the sub-world to this one; we look from this to the Overworld, which is the quintessence of human hope, visionary longing, and beatific dream. We who inhabit this world—how can we think of ourselves as other than splendid lords? This is how we are."

"It is inspiring!" exclaimed Cugel. "How may I obtain a pair of these magic cusps?"

"There are two methods. Underherd lost four hundred and fourteen cusps; we control four hundred and twelve. Two were never found, and evidently lie on the floor of the ocean's deep. You are at liberty to secure these. The second means is to become a citizen of Grodz, and furnish the lords of Smolod with sustenance till one of us dies, as we do infrequently."

"I understand that a certain Lord Radkuth Vomin is ailing."

"Yes, that is he." The elder indicated a potbellied old man with a slack, drooling mouth, sitting in filth before his hut. "You see him at his ease in the pleasance of his palace. Lord Radkuth strained himself with a surfeit of lust, for our princesses are the most ravishing creations of human inspiration, just as I am the noblest of princes. But Lord Radkuth indulged himself too copiously, and thereby suffered a mortification. It is a lesson for us all."

"Perhaps I might make special arrangements to secure his cusps?" ventured Cugel.

"I fear not. You must go to Grodz and toil as do the others. As did I, in a former existence which now seems dim and inchoate. . . . To think I suffered so long! But you are young; thirty or forty or fifty years is not too long a time to wait."

Cugel put his hand to his abdomen to quiet the fretful stirrings of Firx. "In the space of so much time, the sun may well have waned. Look!" He pointed as a black flicker crossed the face of the sun and seemed to leave a momentary crust. "Even now it ebbs!"

"You are over-apprehensive," stated the elder. "To us who are lords of Smolod, the sun puts forth a radiance of exquisite colors."

"This may well be true at the moment," said Cugel, "but when the sun goes dark, what then? Will you take an equal delight in the gloom and the chill?"

But the elder no longer attended him. Radkuth Vomin had fallen sideways into the mud, and appeared to be dead.

Toying indecisively with his knife, Cugel went to look down at the corpse. A deft cut or two—no more than the work of a moment—and he would have achieved his goal. He swayed forward, but already the fugitive moment had passed. Other lords of the village had approached to jostle Cugel aside; Radkuth Vomin was lifted and carried with the most solemn nicety into the ill-smelling precincts of his hut.

Cugel stared wistfully through the doorway, calculating the chances of this ruse and that.

"Let lamps be brought!" intoned the elder. "Let a final effulgence surround Lord Radkuth on his gem-encrusted bier! Let the golden clarion sound from the towers; let the princesses don robes of samite; let their tresses obscure the faces of delight Lord Radkuth loved so well! And now we must keep vigil! Who will guard the bier?"

Cugel stepped forward. "I would deem it honor indeed."

The elder shook his head. "This is a privilege reserved for his peers. Lord Maulfag, Lord Glus: perhaps you will act in this capacity." Two of the villagers approached the bench on which Lord Radkuth Vomin lay.

"Next," declared the elder, "the obsequies must be proclaimed, and the magic cusps transferred to Bubach Angh, that most deserving squire of Grodz. Who, again, will go to notify this squire?"

"Again," said Cugel. "I offer my services, if only to requite in some small manner the hospitality I have enjoyed at Smolod."

"Well spoken!" intoned the elder. "So, then, at speed to Grodz: return with that squire who by his faith and dutiful toil deserves advancement."

Cugel bowed, and ran off across the barrens toward Grodz. As he approached the outermost fields he moved cautiously, skulking from tussock to copse, and presently found that which he sought: a peasant turning the dank soil with a mattock.

Cugel crept quietly forward and struck down the loon with a gnarled root. He stripped off the bast garments, the leather hat, the leggings and footgear; with his knife he hacked off the stiff straw-colored beard. Taking all and leaving the peasant lying dazed and naked in the mud, he fled on long strides back toward Smolod. In a secluded spot he dressed himself in the stolen garments. He examined the hacked-off beard with some perplexity, and finally, by tying up tufts of the coarse yellow hair and tying tuft to tuft, contrived to bind enough together to make a straggling false beard for himself. That hair which remained he tucked up under the brim of the flapping leather hat.

Now the sun had set; plum-colored gloom obscured the land. Cugel returned to Smolod. Oil lamps flickered before the hut of Radkuth Vomin, where the obese and misshapen village women wailed and groaned.

Cugel stepped cautiously forward, wondering what might be expected of him. As for his disguise: it would either prove effective or it would not. To what extent the violet cusps befuddled perception was a matter of doubt; he could only hazard a trial.

Cugel marched boldly up to the door of the hut. Pitching his voice as low as possible, he called, "I am here, revered princes of Smolod: Squire Bubach Angh of Grodz, who for thirty-one years has heaped the choicest of delicacies into the Smolod larders. Now I appear, beseeching elevation to the estate of nobility."

"As is your right," said the Chief Elder. "But you seem a man different from that Bubach Angh who so long has served the princes of Smolod."

"I have been transfigured—through grief at the passing of Prince Radkuth Vomin and through rapture at the prospect of elevation."

"This is clear and understandable. Come, then—prepare yourself for the rites."

"I am ready as of this instant," said Cugel. "Indeed, if you will but tender me the magic cusps I will take them quietly aside and rejoice."

The Chief Elder shook his head indulgently. "This is not in accord with the rites. To begin with you must stand naked here on the pavilion of this mighty castle, and the fairest of the fair will anoint you in aromatics. Then comes the invocation to Eddith Bran Maur. And then—"

"Revered," stated Cugel, "allow me one boon. Before the ceremonies begin, fit me with the magic cusps so that I may understand the full portent of the ceremony."

The Chief Elder considered. "The request is unorthodox, but reasonable. Bring forth the cusps!"

There was a wait, during which Cugel stood first on one foot then the other. The minutes dragged; the garments and the false beard itched intolerably. And now at the outskirts of the village he saw the approach of several new figures, coming from the direction of Grodz. One was almost certainly Bubach Angh, while another seemed to have been shorn of his beard.

The Chief Elder appeared, holding in each hand a violet cusp. "Step forward!"

Cugel called loudly. "I am here, sir."

"I now apply the potion which santifies the junction of magic cusp to right eye."

At the back of the crowd Bubach Angh raised his voice. "Hold! What transpires?"

Cugel turned, pointed. "What jackal is this that interrupts solemnities? Remove him: hence!"

"Indeed!" called the Chief Elder peremptorily. "You demean yourself and the dignity of the ceremony."

Bubach Angh crouched back, momentarily cowed.

"In view of the interruption," said Cugel, "I had as lief merely take custody of the magic cusps until these louts can properly be chastened."

"No," said the Chief Elder. "Such a procedure is impossible." He shook drops of rancid fat in Cugel's right eye. But now the peasant of the shorn beard set up an outcry: "My hat! My blouse! My beard! Is there no justice?"

"Silence!" hissed the crowd. "This is a solemn occasion!"

"But I am Bu—"

Cugel called, "Insert the magic cusp, lord; let us ignore these louts."

"A lout, you call me?" roared Bubach Angh. "I recognize you now, you rogue. Hold up proceedings!"

The Chief Elder said inexorably, "I now invest you with the right cusp. You must temporarily hold this eye closed to prevent a discord which would strain the brain, and cause stupor. Now the left eye." He stepped forward with the ointment, but Bubach Angh and the beardless peasant no longer would be denied.

"Hold up proceedings! You ennoble an imposter! I am Bubach Angh, the worthy squire! He who stands before you is a vagabond!"

The Chief Elder inspected Bubach Angh with puzzlement. "For a fact you resemble that peasant who for thirty-one years has carted supplies to Smolod. But if you are Bubach Angh, who is this?"

The beardless peasant lumbered forward. "It is the soulless wretch who stole the clothes from my back and the beard from my face."

"He is a criminal, a bandit, a vagabond—"

"Hold!" called the Chief Elder. "The words are ill-chosen. Remember that he has been exalted to the rank of prince of Smolod."

"Not altogether!" cried Bubach Angh. "He has one of my eyes. I demand the other!"

"An awkward situation," muttered the Chief Elder. He spoke to Cugel. "Though formerly a vagabond and cutthroat, you are now a prince, and a man of responsibility. What is your opinion?"

"I suggest a hiding for these obstreperous louts. Then—"

Bubach Angh and the beardless peasant, uttering shouts of rage, sprang forward. Cugel, leaping away, could not control his right eye. The lid flew open; into his brain crashed such a wonder of exaltation that his breath caught in his throat and his heart almost stopped from astonishment. But concurrently his left eye showed the reality of Smolod. The dissonance was too wild to be tolerated; he stumbled and fell against a hut. Bubach Angh stood over him with mattock raised high, but now the Chief Elder stepped between.

"Do you take leave of your senses? This man is a prince of Smolod!"

"A man I will kill, for he has my eye! Do I toil thirty-one years for the benefit of a vagabond?"

"Calm yourself, Bubach Angh, if that be your name, and remember the issue is not yet entirely clear. Possibly an error has been made—undoubtedly an honest error, for this man is now a prince of Smolod, which is to say, justice and sagacity personified."

"He was not that before he received the cusp," argued Bubach Angh, "which is when the offense was committed."

"I cannot occupy myself with casuistic distinctions," replied the elder. "In any event, your name heads the list and on the next fatality—"

"Ten or twelve years hence?" cried Bubach Angh. "Must I toil yet longer, and receive my reward just as the sun goes dark? No, no, this cannot be!"

The beardless peasant made a suggestion: "Take the other cusp. In this way you will have at least half of your rights, and so prevent the interloper from cheating you totally."

Bubach Angh agreed. "I will start with my one magic cusp; I will then kill that knave and take the other, and all will be well."

"Now then," said the Chief Elder haughtily, "this is hardly the tone to take in reference to a prince of Smolod!"

"Bah!" snorted Bubach Angh. "Remember the source of your viands! We of Grodz will not toil to no avail."

"Very well," said the Chief Elder. "I deplore your uncouth bluster, but I cannot deny that you have a measure of reason on your side. Here is the left cusp of Radkuth Vomin. I will dispense with the invocation, anointment and the congratulatory paean. If you will be good enough to step forward and open your left eye—so."

As Cugel had done, Bubach Angh looked through both eyes together and staggered back in a daze. But clapping his hand to his left eye he recovered himself, and advanced upon Cugel. "You now must see the futility of your trick. Extend me that cusp and go your way, for you will never have the use of the two."

"It matters very little," said Cugel. "Thanks to my friend Firx I am well content with the one."

Bubach Angh ground his teeth. "Do you think to trick me again? Your life has approached its end: not just I but all Grodz goes warrant for this!"

"Not in the precincts of Smolod!" warned the Chief Elder. "There must be no quarrels among the princes: I decree amity! You who have shared the cusps of Radkuth Vomin must also share his palace, his robes, appurtenances, jewels and retinue, until that hopefully remote occasion when one or the other dies, whereupon the survivor shall take all. This is my judgment; there is no more to be said."

"The moment of the interloper's death is hopefully near at hand," rumbled Bubach Angh. "The instant he sets foot from Smolod will be his last! The citizens of Grodz will maintain a vigil of a hundred years, if necessary!"

Firx squirmed at this news and Cugel winced at the discomfort. In a conciliatory voice he addressed Bubach Angh. "A compromise might be arranged: to you shall go the entirety of Radkuth Vomin's estate: his palace, appurtenances, retinue. To me shall devolve only the magic cusps."

But Bubach Angh would have none of it. "If you value your life, deliver that cusp to me this moment."

"This cannot be done," said Cugel.

Bubach Angh turned away and spoke to the beardless peasant, who nodded and departed. Bubach Angh glowered at Cugel, then went to Radkuth Vomin's hut and sat on the heap of rubble before the door. Here he experimented with his new cusp, cautiously closing his right eye, opening the left to stare in wonder at the Overworld. Cugel thought to take advantage of his absorption and sauntered off toward the edge of town. Bubach Angh appeared not to notice. Ha! thought Cugel. It was to be so easy, then! Two more strides and he would be lost into the darkness!

Jauntily he stretched his long legs to take those two strides. A slight sound—a grunt, a scrape, a rustle of clothes—caused him to jerk aside; down swung a mattock blade, cutting the air where his head had been. In the faint glow cast by the Smolod lamps Cugel glimpsed the beardless peasant's vindictive countenance. Behind him Bubach Angh came loping, heavy head thrust forward like a bull. Cugel dodged, and ran with agility back into the heart of Smolod.

Slowly and in vast disappointment Bubach Angh returned, to seat himself once more. "You will never escape," he told Cugel. "Give over the cusp and preserve your life!"

"By no means," replied Cugel with spirit. "Rather fear for your own sodden vitality, which goes in even greater peril!"

From the hut of the Chief Elder came an admonitory call. "Cease the bickering! I am indulging the exotic whims of a beautiful princess and must not be distracted."

Cugel, recalling the oleaginous wads of flesh, the leering slab-sided visages, the matted verminous hair, the wattles and wens and evil odors which characterized the women of Smolod, marveled anew at the power of the cusps. Babach Angh was once more testing the vision of his left eye. Cugel composed himself on a bench and attempted the use of his right eye, first holding his hand before his left. . . .

Cugel wore a shirt of supple silver scales, tight scarlet trousers, a dark blue cloak. He sat on a marble bench before a row of spiral marble columns overgrown with dark foliage and white flowers. To either side the palaces of Smolod towered into the night, one behind the other, with soft lights accenting the arches and windows. The sky was a soft dark blue, hung with great glowing stars; among the palaces were gardens of cypress, myrtle, jasmine, sphade, thyssam; the air was pervaded with the perfume of flowers and flowing water. From somewhere came a wisp of music; a murmur of soft chords, a sigh of melody. Cugel took a deep breath and rose to his feet. He stepped forward, moving across the terrace. Palaces and gardens shifted perspective; on a dim lawn three girls in gowns of white gauze watched him over their shoulders.

Cugel took an involuntary step forward, then, recalling the malice of Bubach Angh, paused to check on his whereabouts. Across the plaza rose a palace of seven stories, each level with its terrace garden, with vines and flowers trailing down the walls. Through the windows Cugel glimpsed rich furnishings, lustrous chandeliers, the soft movement of liveried chamberlains. On the pavilion before the palace stood a hawk-featured man with a cropped golden beard in robes of ocher and black, with gold epaulettes and black buskins. He stood one foot on a stone griffin, arms on bent knee, gazing toward Cugel with an expression of brooding dislike. Cugel marveled: could this be the pig-faced Bubach Angh? Could the magnificent seven-tiered palace be the hovel of Radkuth Vomin?

Cugel moved slowly off across the plaza, and now came upon a pavilion lit by candelabra. Tables supported meats, jellies and pastries of every description; and Cugel's belly, nourished only by driftwood and smoked fish, urged him forward. He passed from table to table, sampling morsels from every dish, and found all to be of the highest quality.

"Smoked fish and lentils I may still be devouring," Cugel told himself, "but there is much to be said for the enchantment by which they become such exquisite delicacies. Indeed, a man might do far worse than spend the rest of his life here in Smolod."

Almost as if Firx had been anticipating the thought, he instantly inflicted upon Cugel's liver a series of agonizing pangs, and Cugel bitterly reviled Iucounu the Laughing Magician and repeated his vows of vengeance.

Recovering his composure, he sauntered to that area where the formal gardens surrounding the palaces gave way to parkland. He looked over his shoulder, to find the hawk-faced prince in ocher and black approaching, with manifestly hostile intent. In the dimness of the park Cugel noted other movement and thought to spy a number of armored warriors.

Cugel returned to the plaza and Bubach Angh followed, once more to stand glowering at Cugel in front of Radkuth Vomin's palace.

"Clearly," said Cugel aloud for the benefit of Firx, "there will be no departure from Smolod tonight. Naturally I am anxious to convey the cusp to Iucounu, but if I am killed then neither the cusp nor the admirable Firx will ever return to Almery."

Firx made no further demonstration. Now, thought Cugel, where to pass the night? The seven-tiered palace of Radkuth Vomin manifestly offered ample and spacious accommodation for both himself and Bubach Angh. In essence, however, the two would be crammed together in a one-roomed hut, with a single heap of damp reeds for a couch. Thoughtfully, regretfully, Cugel closed his right eye, opened his left.

Smolod was as before. The surly Bubach Angh crouched before the door to Radkuth Vomin's hut. Cugel stepped forward and kicked Bubach Angh smartly. In surprise and shock, both Bubach Angh's eyes opened, and the rival impulses colliding in his brain induced paralysis. Back in the darkness the beardless peasant roared and came charging forward, mattock on high, and Cugel relinquished his plan to cut Bubach Angh's throat. He skipped inside the hut, closed and barred the door.

He now closed his left eye and opened his right. He found himself in the magnificent entry hall of Radkuth Vomin's palace, the portico of which was secured by a portcullis of forged iron. Without, the golden-haired prince in ocher and black, holding his hand over one eye, was lifting himself in cold dignity from the pavement of the plaza. Raising one arm in noble defiance, Bubach Angh swung his cloak over his shoulder and marched off to join his warriors.

Cugel sauntered through the palace, inspecting the appointments with pleasure. If it had not been for the importunities of Firx, there would have been no haste in trying the perilous journey back to the Valley of the Xzan.

Cugel selected a luxurious chamber facing to the south, doffed his rich garments for satin nightwear, settled upon a couch with sheets of pale blue silk, and instantly fell asleep.

In the morning there was a degree of difficulty remembering which eye to open, and Cugel thought it might be well to fashion a patch to wear over that eye not currently in use.

By day the palaces of Smolod were more grand than ever, and now the plaza was thronged with princes and princesses, all of utmost beauty.

Cugel dressed himself in handsome garments of black, with a jaunty green cap and green sandals. He descended to the entry hall, raised the portcullis with a gesture of command, and went forth into the plaza.

There was no sign of Bubach Angh. The other inhabitants of Smolod greeted him with courtesy and the princesses displayed noticeable warmth, as if they found him good address. Cugel responded politely, but without fervor: not even the magic cusp could persuade him against the sour wads of fat, flesh, grime and hair which were the Smolod women.

He breakfasted on delightful viands at the pavilion, then returned to the plaza to consider his next course of action. A cursory inspection of the parklands revealed Grodz warriors on guard. There was no immediate prospect of escape.

The nobility of Smolod applied themselves to their diversions. Some wandered the meadows; others went boating upon the delightful waterways to the north. The Chief Elder, a prince of sagacious and noble visage, sat alone on an onyx bench, deep in reverie.

Cugel approached; the Chief Elder aroused himself and gave Cugel a salute of measured cordiality. "I am not easy in my mind," he declared. "In spite of all judiciousness, and allowing for your unavoidable ignorance of our customs, I feel a certain inequity has been done, and I am at a loss as how to repair it."

"It seems to me," said Cugel, "that Squire Bubach Angh, though doubtless a worthy man, exhibits a lack of discipline unfitting the dignity of Smolod. In my opinion he would be all the better for a few years more seasoning at Grodz."

"There is something in what you say," replied the elder. "Small personal sacrifices are sometimes essential to the welfare of the group. I feel certain that you, if the issue arose, would gladly offer up your cusp and enroll anew at Grodz. What are a few years? They flutter past like butterflies."

Cugel made a suave gesture. "Or a trial by lot might be arranged, in which all who see with two cusps participate, the loser of the trial donating one of his cusps to Bubach Angh. I myself will make do with one."

The elder frowned. "Well—the contingency is remote. Meanwhile you must participate in our merrymaking. If I may say so, you cut a personable figure and certain of the princesses have been casting sheep's eyes in your direction. There, for instance, the lovely Udela Narshag—and there, Zokoxa of the Rose-Petals, and beyond the vivacious Ilviu Lasmal. You must not be backward here in Smolod; we live an uncircumscribed life."

"The charm of these ladies has not escaped me," said Cugel. "Unluckily I am bound by a vow of continence."

"Unfortunate man!" exclaimed the Chief Elder. "The princesses of Smolod are nonpareil! And notice—yet another soliciting your attention!"

"Surely it is you she summons," said Cugel, and the elder went to confer with the young woman in question who had come riding into the plaza in a magnificent boat-shaped car which walked on six swan-feet. The princess reclined on a couch of pink down and was beautiful enough to make Cugel rue the fastidiousness of his recollection, which projected every matted hair, mole, dangling underlip, sweating seam and wrinkle of the Smolod women to the front of his memory. This princess was indeed the essence of a daydream: slender and supple, with skin like still cream, a delicate nose, lucent brooding eyes, a mouth of delightful flexibility. Her expression intrigued Cugel, for it was more complex than that of the other princesses: pensive, yet willful; ardent yet dissatisfied.

Into the plaza came Bubach Angh, accoutered in military wise, with corselet, morion and sword. The Chief Elder went to speak to him; and now to Cugel's irritation the princess in the walking boat signaled to him.

He went forward. "Yes, princess; you saluted me, I believe?"

The princess nodded. "I speculate on your presence up here in these northern lands." She spoke in a soft clear voice like music.

Cugel said, "I am here on a mission; I stay but a short while at Smolod, and then must continue east and south."

"Indeed!" said the princess. "What is the nature of your mission?"

"To be candid, I was brought here by the malice of a magician. It was by no means a yearning of my own."

The princess laughed softly. "I see few strangers. I long for new faces and new talk. Perhaps you will come to my palace and we will talk of magic, and the strange circumstances which throng the dying earth."

Cugel bowed stiffly. "Your offer is kind. But you must seek elsewhere; I am bound by a vow of continence. Control your displeasure, for it applies not only to you but to Udela Narshag yonder, to Zokoxa, and to Ilviu Lasmal."

The princess raised her eyebrows, sank back in her down-covered couch. She smiled faintly. "Indeed, indeed. You are a harsh man, a stern relentless man, thus to refuse yourself to so many imploring women."

"This is the case, and so it must be." Cugel turned away to face the Chief Elder, who approached with Bubach Angh at his back.

"Sorry circumstances," announced the Chief Elder in a troubled voice. "Bubach Angh speaks for the village of Grodz. He declares that no more victuals will be furnished until justice is done, and this they define as the surrender of your cusp to Bubach Angh, and your person to a punitive committee who waits in the parkland yonder."

Cugel laughed uneasily. "What a distorted view! You assured them of course that we of Smolod would eat grass and destroy the cusps before agreeing to such detestable provisions?"

"I fear that I temporized," stated the Chief Elder. "I feel that the others of Smolod favor a more flexible course of action."

The implication was clear, and Firx began to stir in exasperation. In order to appraise circumstances in the most forthright manner possible, Cugel shifted the patch to look from his left eye.

Certain citizens of Grodz, armed with scythes, mattocks and clubs, waited at a distance of fifty yards: evidently the punitive committee to which Bubach Angh had referred. To one side were the huts of Smolod; to the other the walking boat and the princess of such—Cugel stared in astonishment. The boat was as before, walking on six bird-legs, and sitting in the pink down was the princess—if possible, more beautiful than ever. But now her expression, rather than faintly smiling, was cool and still.

Cugel drew a deep breath and took to his heels. Bubach Angh shouted an order to halt, but Cugel paid no heed. Across the barrens he raced, with the punitive committee in pursuit.

Cugel laughed gleefully. He was long of limb, sound of wind; the peasants were stumpy, knot-muscled, phlegmatic. He could easily run two miles to their one. He paused, and turned to wave farewell. To his dismay two legs from the walking boat detached themselves and leapt after him. Cugel ran for his life. In vain. The legs came bounding past, one on either side. They swung around and kicked him to a halt.

Cugel sullenly walked back, the legs hopping behind. Just before he reached the outskirts of Smolod he reached under the patch and pulled loose the magic cusp. As the punitive committee bore down on him, he held it aloft. "Stand back—or I break the cusp to fragments!"

"Hold! Hold!" called Bubach Angh. "This must not be! Come, give me the cusp and accept your just deserts."

"Nothing has yet been decided," Cugel reminded him. "The Chief Elder has ruled for no one."

The girl rose from her seat in the boat. "I will rule; I am Derwe Coreme, of the House of Domber. Give me the violet glass, whatever it is."

"By no means," said Cugel. "Take the cusp from Bubach Augh."

"Never!" exclaimed the squire from Grodz.

"What? You both have a cusp and both want two? What are those precious objects? You wear them as eyes? Give them to me."

Cugel drew his sword. "I prefer to run, but I will fight if I must."

"I cannot run," said Bubach Angh. "I prefer to fight." He pulled the cusp from his own eye. "Now then, vagabond, prepare to die."

"A moment," said Derwe Coreme. From one of the legs of the boat thin arms reached to seize the wrists of both Cugel and Bubach Angh. The cusps fell to earth; that of Bubach Angh struck a stone and shivered to fragments. He howled in anguish and leapt upon Cugel, who gave ground before the attack.

Bubach Angh knew nothing of swordplay; he hacked and slashed as if he were cleaning fish. The fury of his attack, however, was unsettling and Cugel was hard put to defend himself. In addition to Bubach Angh's sallies and slashes, Firx was deploring the loss of the cusp.

Derwe Coreme had lost interest in the affair. The boat started off across the barrens, moving faster and ever faster. Cugel slashed out with his sword, leapt back, leapt back once more, and for the second time fled across the barrens.

The boat-car jogged along at a leisurely rate. Lungs throbbing, Cugel gained upon it, and with a great bound leapt up, caught the downy gunwale and pulled himself astride.

It was as he expected. Derwe Coreme had looked through the cusp and lay back in a daze. The violet cusp reposed in her lap.

Cugel seized it, then for a moment stared down into the exquisite face and wondered if he dared more. Firx thought not. Already Derwe Coreme was sighing and moving her head.

Cugel leapt from the boat, and only just in time. Had she seen him? He ran to a clump of reeds which grew by a pond, and flung himself into the water. From here he saw the walking-boat halt while Derwe Coreme rose to her feet. She felt through the pink down for the cusp, then she looked all around the countryside. But the blood-red light of the low sun was in her eyes when she looked toward Cugel, and she saw only the reeds and the reflection of sun on water.

Angry and sullen as never before, she set the boat into motion. It walked, then cantered, then loped to the south.

Cugel emerged from the water, inspected the magic cusp, tucked it into his pouch, and looked back toward Smolod. He started to walk south, then paused. He took the cusp from his pocket, closed his left eye, and held the cusp to his right. There rose the palaces, tier on tier, tower above tower, the gardens hanging down the terraces. . . . Cugel would have stared a long time, but Firx became restive.

Cugel returned the cusp to his pouch, and once again set his face to the south, for the long journey back to Almery.

KEITH ROBERTS

The Signaller

One of the most powerful talents to enter the field in the last thirty years, Keith Roberts secured an important place in genre history in 1968 with the publication of his classic novel *Pavane,* one of the best books of the 1960s, and certainly one of the best Alternate History novels ever written (rivaled only by books such as L. Sprague de Camp's *Lest Darkness Fall,* Ward Moore's *Bring the Jubilee,* and Philip K. Dick's *The Man in the High Castle*). Trained as an illustrator—he did work extensively as an illustrator and cover artist in the British SF world of the 1960s—Roberts made his first sale to *Science Fantasy* in 1964. Later, he would take over the editorship of *Science Fantasy,* by then called *SF Impulse,* as well as providing many of the magazine's striking covers. But his career as an editor was short-lived, and most of his subsequent impact on the field would be as a writer, including the production of some of the very best short stories of the last three decades. Roberts's other books include the novels *The Chalk Giants, The Furies, The Inner Wheel, Molly Zero, Gráinne, Kiteworld,* and *The Boat of Fate,* one of the finest historical novels of the 1970s. His short work can be found in the collections *Machines and Men, The Grain Kings, The Passing of the Dragons, Ladies from Hell, The Lordly Ones,* and *Winterwood and Other Hauntings.* His most recent book is a new collection, *Kaeti On Tour.*

In "The Signaller"—one of the stories that was later melded into *Pavane*—he takes us sideways in time to an alternate England where Queen Elizabeth was cut down by an assassin's bullet, and England itself fell to the Spanish Armada—a twentieth-century England where the deep shadow of the Church Militant stretches across a still-medieval land of forests and castles and little huddled towns; an England where travelers in the bleak winter forests or on the desolate, windswept expanses of the heath must fear wolves and brigands and routiers; and, since the Old Things don't change even in an Alternate World, an England where it

is yet possible to encounter specters of a darker and more elemental kind . . .

On either side of the knoll the land stretched in long, speckled sweeps,
paling in the frost smoke until the outlines of distant hills blended with
the curdled milk of the sky. Across the waste a bitter wind moaned,
steady and chill, driving before it quick flurries of snow. The snow squalls
flickered and vanished like ghosts, the only moving things in a vista of
emptiness.

What trees there were grew in clusters, little coppices that leaned with
the wind, their twigs meshed together as if for protection, their outlines
sculpted into the smooth, blunt shapes of ploughshares. One such copse
crowned the summit of the knoll; under the first of its branches, and sheltered by them from the wind, a boy lay facedown in the snow. He was
motionless but not wholly unconscious; from time to time his body quivered with spasms of shock. He was maybe sixteen or seventeen, blond-
haired, and dressed from head to feet in a uniform of dark green leather.
The uniform was slit in many places; from the shoulders down the back
to the waist, across the hips and thighs. Through the rents could be seen
the cream-brown of his skin and the brilliant slow twinkling of blood. The
leather was soaked with it, and the long hair matted. Beside the boy lay
the case of a pair of binoculars, the Zeiss lenses without which no man
or apprentice of the Guild of Signallers ever moved, and a dagger. The
blade of the weapon was red-stained; its pommel rested a few inches beyond his outflung right hand. The hand itself was injured, slashed across
the backs of the fingers and deeply through the base of the thumb. Round
it blood had diffused in a thin pink halo into the snow.

A heavier gust rattled the branches overhead, raised from somewhere
a long creak of protest. The boy shivered again and began, with infinite
slowness, to move. The outstretched hand crept forward, an inch at a time,
to take his weight beneath his chest. The fingers traced an arc in the snow,
its ridges red-tipped. He made a noise halfway between a grunt and a
moan, levered himself onto his elbows, waited gathering strength.
Threshed, half turned over, leaned on the undamaged left hand. He hung
his head, eyes closed; his heavy breathing sounded through the copse.
Another heave, a convulsive effort, and he was sitting upright, propped
against the trunk of a tree. Snow stung his face, bringing back a little more
awareness.

He opened his eyes. They were terrified and wild, glazed with pain.
He looked up into the tree, swallowed, tried to lick his mouth, turned his
head to stare at the empty snow round him. His left hand clutched his
stomach; his right was crossed over it, wrist pressing, injured palm held
clear of contact. He shut his eyes again briefly; then he made his hand
go down, grip, lift the wet leather away from his thigh. He fell back, started

to sob harshly at what he had seen. His hand, dropping slack, brushed tree bark. A snag probed the open wound below the thumb; the disgusting surge of pain brought him round again.

From where he lay the knife was out of reach. He leaned forward ponderously, wanting not to move, just stay quiet and be dead, quickly. His fingers touched the blade; he worked his way back to the tree, made himself sit up again. He rested, gasping; then he slipped his left hand under his knee, drew upward till the half-paralysed leg was crooked. Concentrating, steering the knife with both hands, he placed the tip of its blade against his trews, forced down slowly to the ankle cutting the garment apart. Then round behind his thigh till the piece of leather came clear.

He was very weak now; it seemed he could feel the strength ebbing out of him, faintness flickered in front of his eyes like the movements of a black wing. He pulled the leather toward him, got its edge between his teeth, gripped, and began to cut the material into strips. It was slow, clumsy work; he gashed himself twice, not feeling the extra pain. He finished at last and began to knot the strips round his leg, trying to tighten them enough to close the long wounds in the thigh. The wind howled steadily; there was no other sound but the quick panting of his breath. His face, beaded with sweat, was nearly as white as the sky.

He did all he could for himself, finally. His back was a bright torment, and behind him the bark of the tree was streaked with red, but he couldn't reach the lacerations there. He made his fingers tie the last of the knots, shuddered at the blood still weeping through the strappings. He dropped the knife and tried to get up.

After minutes of heaving and grunting his legs still refused to take his weight. He reached up painfully, fingers exploring the rough bole of the tree. Two feet above his head they touched the low, snapped-off stump of a branch. The hand was soapy with blood; it slipped, skidded off, groped back. He pulled, feeling the tingling as the gashes in the palm closed and opened. His arms and shoulders were strong, ribboned with muscle from hours spent at the semaphores: he hung tensed for a moment, head thrust back against the trunk, body arced and quivering; then his heel found a purchase in the snow, pushed him upright.

He stood swaying, not noticing the wind, seeing the blackness surge round him and ebb back. His head was pounding now, in time with the pulsing of his blood. He felt fresh warmth trickling on stomach and thighs, and the rise of a deadly sickness. He turned away, head bent, and started to walk, moving with the slow ponderousness of a diver. Six paces off he stopped, still swaying, edged round clumsily. The binocular case lay on the snow where it had fallen. He went back awkwardly, each step requiring now a separate effort of his brain, a bunching of the will to force the body to obey. He knew foggily that he daren't stoop for the case; if he tried he would fall headlong, and likely never move again. He worked his foot into the loop of the shoulder strap. It was the best he could do; the leather tightened as he moved, riding up round his instep. The case bumped along behind him as he headed down the hill away from the trees.

He could no longer lift his eyes. He saw a circle of snow, six feet or so across, black-fringed at its edges from his impaired vision. The snow moved as he walked, jerking toward him, falling away behind. Across it ran a line of faint impressions, footprints he himself had made. The boy followed them blindly. Some spark buried at the back of his brain kept him moving; the rest of his consciousness was gone now, numbed with shock. He moved draggingly, the leather case jerking and slithering behind his heel. With his left hand he held himself, low down over the groin; his right waved slowly, keeping his precarious balance. He left behind him a thin trail of blood spots; each drop splashed pimpernel-bright against the snow, faded and spread to a wider pink stain before freezing itself into the crystals. The blood marks and the footprints reached back in a ragged line to the copse. In front of him the wind skirled across the land; the snow whipped at his face, clung thinly to his jerkin.

Slowly, with endless pain, the moving speck separated itself from the trees. They loomed behind it, seeming through some trick of the fading light to increase in height as they receded. As the wind chilled the boy the pain ebbed fractionally; he raised his head, saw before him the tower of a semaphore station topping its low cabin. The station stood on a slight eminence of rising ground; his body felt the drag of the slope, reacted with a gale of breathing. He trudged slower. He was crying again now with little whimperings, meaningless animal noises, and a sheen of saliva showed on his chin. When he reached the cabin the copse was still visible behind him, grey against the sky. He leaned against the plank door gulping, seeing faintly the texture of the wood. His hand fumbled for the lanyard of the catch, pulled; the door opened, plunging him forward onto his knees.

After the snow light outside, the interior of the hut was dark. The boy worked his way on all fours across the board floor. There was a cupboard; he searched it blindly, sweeping glasses and cups aside, dimly hearing them shatter. He found what he needed, drew the cork from the bottle with his teeth, slumped against the wall and attempted to drink. The spirit ran down his chin, spilled across chest and belly. Enough went down his throat to wake him momentarily. He coughed and tried to vomit. He pulled himself to his feet, found a knife to replace the one he'd dropped. A wooden chest by the wall held blankets and bed linen; he pulled a sheet free and haggled it into strips, longer and broader this time, to wrap round his thigh. He couldn't bring himself to touch the leather tourniquets. The white cloth marked through instantly with blood; the patches elongated, joined and began to glisten. The rest of the sheet he made into a pad to hold against his groin.

The nausea came again; he retched, lost his balance and sprawled on the floor. Above his eye level, his bunk loomed like a haven. If he could just reach it, lie quiet till the sickness went away. . . . He crossed the cabin somehow, lay across the edge of the bunk, rolled into it. A wave of blackness lifted to meet him, deep as a sea.

He lay a long time; then the fragment of remaining will reasserted itself. Reluctantly, he forced open gummy eyelids. It was nearly dark now; the far window of the hut showed in the gloom, a vague rectangle of greyness. In front of it the handles of the semaphore seemed to swim, glinting where the light caught the polished smoothness of wood. He stared, realizing his foolishness; then he tried to roll off the bunk. The blankets, glued to his back, prevented him. He tried again, shivering now with the cold. The stove was unlit; the cabin door stood ajar, white crystals fanning in across the planking of the floor. Outside, the howling of the wind was relentless. The boy struggled; the efforts woke pain again and the sickness, the thudding and roaring. Images of the semaphore handles doubled, sextupled, rolled apart to make a glistening silver sheaf. He panted, tears running into his mouth; then his eyes slid closed. He fell into a noisy void shot with colours, sparks, and gleams and washes of light. He lay watching the lights, teeth bared, feeling the throb in his back where fresh blood pumped into the bed. After a while, the roaring went away.

The child lay couched in long grass, feeling the heat of the sun strike through his jerkin to burn his shoulders. In front of him, at the conical crest of the hill, the magic thing flapped slowly, its wings proud and lazy as those of a bird. Very high it was, on its pole on top of its hill; the faint wooden clattering it made fell remote from the blueness of the summer sky. The movements of the arms had half hypnotized him; he lay nodding and blinking, chin propped on his hands, absorbed in his watching. Up and down, up and down, *clap* . . . then down again and round, up and back, pausing, gesticulating, never staying wholly still. The semaphore seemed alive, an animate thing perched there talking strange words nobody could understand. Yet words they were, replete with meanings and mysteries like the words in his *Modern English Primer*. The child's brain spun. Words made stories; what stories was the tower telling, all alone there on its hill? Tales of kings and shipwrecks, fights and pursuits, Fairies, buried gold. . . . It was talking, he knew that without a doubt; whispering and clacking, giving messages and taking them from the others in the lines, the great lines that stretched across England everywhere you could think, every direction you could see.

He watched the control rods sliding like bright muscles in their oiled guides. From Avebury, where he lived, many other towers were visible; they marched southwards across the Great Plain, climbed the westward heights of the Marlborough Downs. Though those were bigger, huge things staffed by teams of men whose signals might be visible on a clear day for ten miles or more. When they moved it was majestically and slowly, with a thundering from their jointed arms; these others, the little local towers, were friendlier somehow, chatting and pecking away from dawn to sunset.

There were many games the child played by himself in the long hours of summer; stolen hours usually, for there was always work to be found for him. School lessons, home study, chores about the house or down at his brothers' small-holding on the other side of the village; he must sneak off evenings or in the early dawn, if he wanted to be alone to dream. The stones beckoned him sometimes, the great gambolling diamond-shapes of them circling the little town. The boy would scud along the ditches of what had been an ancient temple, climb the terraced scarps to where the stones danced against the morning sun; or walk the long processional avenue that stretched eastward across the fields, imagine himself a priest or a god come to do old sacrifice to rain and sun. No one knew who first placed the stones. Some said the Fairies, in the days of their strength; others the old gods, they whose names it was a sin to whisper. Others said the Devil.

Mother Church winked at the destruction of Satanic relics, and that the villagers knew full well. Father Donovan disapproved, but he could do very little; the people went to it with a will. Their ploughs gnawed the bases of the markers, they broke the megaliths with water and fire and used the bits for patching dry stone walls; they'd been doing it for centuries now, and the rings were depleted and showing gaps. But there were many stones; the circles remained, and barrows crowning the windy tops of hills, *hows* where the old dead lay patient with their broken bones. The child would climb the mounds, and dream of kings in fur and jewels; but always, when he tired, he was drawn back to the semaphores and their mysterious life. He lay quiet, chin sunk on his hands, eyes sleepy, while above him Silbury 973 chipped and clattered on its hill.

The hand, falling on his shoulder, startled him from dreams. He tensed, whipped round and wanted to bolt; but there was nowhere to run. He was caught; he stared up gulping, a chubby little boy, long hair falling across his forehead.

The man was tall, enormously tall it seemed to the child. His face was brown, tanned by sun and wind, and at the corners of his eyes were networks of wrinkles. The eyes were deep-set and very blue, startling against the colour of the skin; to the boy they seemed to be of exactly the hue one sees at the very top of the sky. His father's eyes had long since bolted into hiding behind pebble-thick glasses; these eyes were different. They had about them an appearance of power, as if they were used to looking very long distances and seeing clearly things that other men might miss. Their owner was dressed all in green, with the faded shoulder lacings and lanyard of a Serjeant of Signals. At his hip he carried the Zeiss glasses that

were the badge of any Signaller; the flap of the case was only half secured
and beneath it the boy could see the big eyepieces, the worn brassy sheen
of the barrels.

The Guildsman was smiling; his voice when he spoke was drawling
and slow. It was the voice of a man who knows about Time, that Time
is forever and scurry and bustle can wait. Someone who might know
about the old stones in the way the child's father did not.

"Well," he said, "I do believe we've caught a little spy. Who be you,
lad?"

The boy licked his mouth and squeaked, looking hunted. "R-Rafe
Bigland, sir. . . ."

"And what be 'ee doin'?"

Rafe wetted his lips again, looked at the tower, pouted miserably, stared
at the grass beside him, looked back to the Signaller and quickly away.
"I . . . I . . ."

He stopped, unable to explain. On top of the hill the tower creaked and
flapped. The Serjeant squatted down, waiting patiently, still with the little half-smile, eyes twinkling at the boy. The satchel he'd been carrying
he'd set on the grass. Rafe knew he'd been to the village to pick up the
afternoon meal; one of the old ladies of Avebury was contracted to supply food to the Signallers on duty. There was little he didn't know about
the working of the Silbury station.

The seconds became a minute, and an answer had to be made. Rafe
drew himself up a trifle desperately; he heard his own voice speaking as
if it was the voice of a stranger, and wondered with a part of his mind at
the words that found themselves on his tongue without it seemed the conscious intervention of thought. "If you please, sir," he said pipingly, "I was
watching the t-tower. . . ."

"Why?"

"I . . ."

Again the difficulty. How explain? The mysteries of the Guild were not
to be revealed to any casual stranger. The codes of the Signallers and other
deeper secrets were handed down, jealously, through the families privileged to wear the Green. The Serjeant's accusation of spying had had some
truth to it; it had sounded ominous.

The Guildsman helped him. "Canst thou read the signals, Rafe?"

Rafe shook his head, violently. No commoner could read the towers.
No commoner ever would. He felt a trembling start in the pit of his stomach, but again his voice used itself without his will. "No, sir," it said in a
firm treble. "But I would fain learn. . . ."

The Serjeant's eyebrows rose. He sat back on his heels, hands lying
easy across his knees, and started to laugh. When he had finished he
shook his head. "So you would learn. . . . Aye, and a dozen kings, and
many a high-placed gentleman, would lie easier abed for the reading of

the towers." His face changed itself abruptly into a scowl. "Boy," he said, "you mock us. . . ."

Rafe could only shake his head again, silently. The Serjeant stared over him into space, still sitting on his heels. Rafe wanted to explain how he had never, in his most secret dreams, ever imagined himself a Signaller; how his tongue had moved of its own, blurting out the impossible and absurd. But he couldn't speak anymore; before the Green, he was dumb. The pause lengthened while he watched inattentively the lurching progress of a rain beetle through the stems of grass. Then, "Who's thy father, boy?"

Rafe gulped. There would be a beating, he was sure of that now; and he would be forbidden ever to go near the towers or watch them again. He felt the stinging behind his eyes that meant tears were very close, ready to well and trickle. "Thomas Bigland of Avebury, sir," he said. "A clerk to Sir William M-Marshall."

The Serjeant nodded. "And thou wouldst learn the towers? Thou wouldst be a Signaller?"

"Aye, sir. . . ." The tongue was Modern English of course, the language of artisans and tradesmen, not the guttural clacking of the landless churls; Rafe slipped easily into the old-fashioned usage of it the Signallers employed sometimes among themselves.

The Serjeant said abruptly, "Canst thou read in books, Rafe?"

"Aye, sir. . . ." Then falteringly, "If the words be not too long. . . ."

The Guildsman laughed again, and clapped the boy on the back. "Well, Master Rafe Bigland, thou who would be a Signaller, and can read books if the words be but short, my book learning is slim enough as God He knows; but it may be I can help thee, if thou hast given me no lies. Come." And he rose and began to walk away toward the tower. Rafe hesitated, blinked, then roused himself and trotted along behind, head whirling with wonders.

They climbed the path that ran slantingly round the hill. As they moved, the Serjeant talked. Silbury 973 was part of the C class chain that ran from near Londinium, from the great relay station at Pontes, along the line of the road to Aquae Sulis. Its complement . . . but Rafe knew the complement well enough. Five men including the Serjeant; their cottages stood apart from the main village, on a little rise of ground that gave them seclusion. Signallers' homes were always situated like that, it helped preserve the Guild mysteries. Guildsmen paid no tithes to local demesnes, obeyed none but their own hierarchy; and though in theory they were answerable under common law, in practice they were immune. They governed themselves according to their own high code; and it was a brave man, or a fool, who squared with the richest Guild in England. There had been deadly accuracy in what the Serjeant said; when kings waited on their messages as eagerly as commoners they had little need to fear.

The Popes might cavil, jealous of their independence, but Rome herself leaned too heavily on the continent-wide networks of the semaphore towers to do more than adjure and complain. Insofar as such a thing was possible in a hemisphere dominated by the Church Militant, the Guildsmen were free.

Although Rafe had seen the inside of a signal station often enough in dreams he had never physically set foot in one. He stopped short at the wooden step, feeling awe rise in him like a tangible barrier. He caught his breath. He had never been this close to a semaphore tower before; the rush and thudding of the arms, the clatter of dozens of tiny joints, sounded in his eyes like music. From here only the tip of the signal was in sight, looming over the roof of the hut. The varnished wooden spars shone orange like the masts of a boat; the semaphore arms rose and dipped, black against the sky. He could see the bolts and loops near their tips where in bad weather or at night when some message of vital importance had to be passed, cressets could be attached to them. He'd seen such fires once, miles out over the Plain, the night the old King died.

The Serjeant opened the door and urged him through it. He stood rooted just beyond the sill. The place had a clean smell that was somehow also masculine, a compound of polishes and oils and the fumes of tobacco; and inside too it had something of the appearance of a ship. The cabin was airy and low, roomier than it had looked from the front of the hill. There was a stove, empty now and gleaming with blacking, its brasswork brightly polished. Inside its mouth a sheet of red crepe paper had been stretched tightly; the doors were parted a little to show the smartness. The plank walls were painted a light grey; on the breast that enclosed the chimney of the stove rosters were pinned neatly. In one corner of the room was a group of diplomas, framed and richly coloured; below them an old daguerreotype, badly faded, showing a group of men standing in front of a very tall signal tower. In one corner of the cabin was a bunk, blankets folded into a neat cube at its foot; above it a hand-coloured pinup of a smiling girl wearing a cap of Guild green and very little else. Rafe's eyes passed over it with the faintly embarrassed indifference of childhood.

In the centre of the room, white-painted and square, was the base of the signal mast; round it a little podium of smooth, scrubbed wood, on which stood two Guildsmen. In their hands were the long levers that worked the semaphore arms overhead; the control rods reached up from them, encased where they passed through the ceiling in white canvas grommets. Skylights, opened to either side, let in the warm July air. The third duty Signaller stood at the eastern window of the cabin, glasses to his eyes, speaking quietly and continuously. "Five . . . eleven . . . thirteen . . . nine . . ." The operators repeated the combinations, working the big handles, leaning the weight of their bodies against the pull of the signal arms overhead, letting each downward rush of the semaphores help them into position for their next cypher. There was an air of concentration but not of strain; it all seemed very easy and practised. In front of the men, supported by struts from the roof, a telltale repeated the positions of the arms, but the Signallers rarely glanced at it. Years of training had given a fluidness to their movements that made them seem almost like the steps and posturings of a ballet. The bodies swung, checked, moved through their arabesques; the creaking of wood and the faint rumbling of the signals filled the place, as steady and lulling as the drone of bees.

No one paid any attention to Rafe or the Serjeant. The Guildsman began talking again quietly, explaining what was happening. The long message that had been going through now for nearly an hour was a list of current grain and fatstock prices from Londinium. The Guild system was invaluable for regulating the complex economy of the country; farmers and merchants, taking the Londinium prices as a yardstick, knew exactly what to pay when buying and selling for themselves. Rafe forgot to be disappointed; his mind heard the words, recording them and storing them away, while his eyes watched the changing patterns made by the Guildsmen, so much a part of the squeaking, clacking machine they controlled.

The actual transmitted information, what the Serjeant called the payspeech, occupied only a part of the signalling; a message was often almost swamped by the codings necessary to secure its distribution. The current figures for instance had to reach certain centres, Aquae Sulis among them, by nightfall. How they arrived, their routing on the way, was very much the concern of the branch Signallers through whose stations the cyphers passed. It took years of experience coupled with a certain degree of intuition to route signals in such a way as to avoid lines already congested with information; and of course while a line was in use in one direction, as in the present case with a complex message being moved from east to west, it was very difficult to employ it in reverse. It was in fact possible to pass two messages in different directions at the same time, and it was often done on the A Class towers. When that happened every third cypher of a northbound might be part of another signal moving south; the stations transmitted in bursts, swapping the messages forward and back. But coaxial signalling was detested even by the Guildsmen. The line had to be cleared first, and a suitable code agreed on; two lookouts were employed, chanting their directions alternately to the Signallers, and even in the best-run station total confusion could result from the smallest slip, necessitating reclearing of the route and a fresh start.

With his hands, the Serjeant described the washout signal a fouled-up tower would use; the three horizontal extensions of the semaphores from the sides of their mast. If that happened, he said, chuckling grimly, a head would roll somewhere; for a Class A would be under the command of a Major of Signals at least, a man of twenty or more years experience. He would be expected not to make mistakes, and to see in turn that none were made by his subordinates. Rafe's head began to whirl again; he looked with fresh respect at the worn green leather of the Serjeant's uniform. He was beginning to see now, dimly, just what sort of thing it was to be a Signaller.

The message ended at last, with a great clapping of the semaphore arms. The lookout remained at his post but the operators got down, showing an interest in Rafe for the first time. Away from the semaphore levers they seemed far more normal and unfrightening. Rafe knew them well; Robin Wheeler, who often spoke to him on his way to and from the station, and Bob Camus, who's split a good many heads in his time at the feastday cudgel playing in the village. They showed him the code books, all the scores of cyphers printed in red on numbered black squares. He stayed to share their meal; his mother would be concerned and his father annoyed, but home was almost forgotten. Toward evening another message came from the west; they told him it was police business, and sent it winging and clapping on its way. It was dusk when Rafe finally left the station, head in the clouds, two unbelievable pennies jinking in his pocket. It was only later, in bed and trying to sleep, he realized a long-submerged dream had come true. He did sleep finally, only to dream again of signal towers at night, the cressets on their arms roaring against the blueness of the sky. He never spent the coins.

Once it had become a real possibility, his ambition to be a Signaller grew steadily; he spent all the time he could at the Silbury Station, perched high on its weird prehistoric hill. His absences met with his father's keenest disapproval. Mr. Bigland's wage as an estate clerk barely brought in enough to support his brood of seven boys; the family had of necessity to grow most of its own food, and for that every pair of hands that could be mustered was valuable. But nobody guessed the reason for Rafe's frequent disappearances; and for his part he didn't say a word.

He learned, in illicit hours, the thirty-odd basic positions of the signal arms, and something of the commonest sequences of grouping; after that he could lie out near Silbury Hill and mouth off most of the numbers to himself, though without the codes that informed them he was still dumb. Once Serjeant Gray let him take the observer's place for a glorious half hour while a message was coming in over the Marlborough Downs. Rafe stood stiffly, hands sweating on the big barrels of the Zeiss glasses, and read off the cyphers as high and clear as he could for the Signallers at his back. The Serjeant checked his reporting unobtrusively from the other end of the hut, but he made no mistakes.

By the time he was ten Rafe had received as much formal education as a child of his class could expect. The great question of a career was raised. The family sat in conclave; father, mother, and the three eldest sons. Rafe was unimpressed; he knew, and had known for weeks, the fate they had selected for him. He was to be apprenticed to one of the four tailors of the village, little bent old men who sat like cross-legged hermits behind bulwarks of cloth bales and stitched their lives away by the light of penny dips. He hardly expected to be consulted on the matter; however he was sent for, formally, and asked what he wished to do. That was the time for the bombshell. "I know exactly what I want to be," said Rafe firmly. "A Signaller."

There was a moment of shocked silence; then the laughing started and swelled. The Guilds were closely guarded; Rafe's father would pay dearly even for his entry into the tailoring trade. As for the Signallers . . . no Bigland had ever been a Signaller, no Bigland ever would. Why, that . . . it would raise the family status! The whole village would have to look up to them, with a son wearing the Green. Preposterous . . .

Rafe sat quietly until they were finished, lips compressed, cheekbones glowing. He'd known it would be like this, he knew just what he had to do. His composure discomfited the family; they quietened down enough to ask him, with mock seriousness, how he intended to set about achieving his ambition. It was time for the second bomb. "By approaching the Guild with regard to a Common Entrance Examination," he said, mouthing words that had been learned by rote. "Serjeant Gray, of the Silbury Station, will speak for me."

Into the fresh silence came his father's embarrassed coughing. Mr. Bigland looked like an old sheep, sitting blinking through his glasses, nibbling at his thin moustache. "Well," he said. "Well, I don't know. . . . *Well. . . ."* But Rafe had already seen the glint in his eyes at the dizzying prospect of prestige. That a son of his should wear the Green. . . .

Before their minds could change Rafe wrote a formal letter which he delivered in person to the Silbury Station: it asked Serjeant Gray, very correctly, if he would be kind enough to call on Mr. Bigland with a view of discussing his son's entry to the College of Signals in Londinium.

The Serjeant was as good as his word. He was a widower, and childless; maybe Rafe made up in part for the son he'd never had, maybe he saw the reflection of his own youthful enthusiasm in the boy. He came the next evening, strolling quietly down the village street to rap at the Biglands' door; Rafe, watching from his shared bedroom over the porch, grinned at the gaping and craning of the neighbours. The family was all a-flutter; the household budget had been scraped for wine and candles, silverware and fresh linen were laid out in the parlour, everybody was anxious to make the best possible impression. Mr. Bigland of course was only too agreeable; when the Serjeant left, an hour later, he had his signed permission in his belt. Rafe himself saw the signal originated asking Londinium for the necessary entrance papers for the College's annual examination.

The Guild gave just twelve places per year, and they were keenly contested. In the few weeks at his disposal Rafe was crammed mercilessly; the Serjeant coached him in all aspects of Signalling he might reasonably be expected to know while the village dominie, impressed in spite of himself, brushed up Rafe's bookwork, even trying to instill into his aching head the rudiments of Norman French. Rafe won admittance; he had never considered the possibility of failure, mainly because such a thought was unbearable. He sat the examination in Sorviodunum, the nearest regional centre to his home; a week later a message came through offering him his place, listing the clothes and books he would need and instructing him to be ready to present himself at the College of Signals in just under a month's time. When he left for Londinium, well muffled in a new cloak, riding a horse provided by the Guild and with two russet-coated Guild servants in attendance, he was followed by the envy of a whole village. The arms of the Silbury tower were quiet; but as he passed they flipped quickly to Attention, followed at once by the cyphers for Origination and Immediate Locality. Rafe turned in the saddle, tears stinging his eyes, and watched the letters quickly spelled out in plaintalk. "Good luck. . . ."

After Avebury, Londinium seemed dingy, noisy, and old. The College was housed in an ancient, ramshackle building just inside the City walls; though Londinium had long since overspilled its former limits, sprawling south across the river and north nearly as far as Tyburn Tree. The Guild children were the usual crowd of brawling, snotty-nosed brats that comprised the apprentices of any trade. Hereditary sons of the Green, they looked down on the Common Entrants from the heights of an unbearable and imaginary eminence; Rafe had a bad time till a series of dormitory fights, all more or less bloody; proved to his fellows once and for all that young Bigland at least was better left alone. He settled down as an accepted member of the community.

The Guild, particularly of recent years, had been tending to place more and more value on theoretical knowledge, and the two-year course was intensive. The apprentices had to become adept in Norman French, for their further training would take them inevitably into the houses of the rich. A working knowledge of the other tongues of the land, the Cornish, Gaelic, and Middle English, was also a requisite; no Guildsman ever knew where he would finally be posted. Guild history was taught too, and the elements of mechanics and coding, though most of the practical work in those directions would be done in the field, at the training stations scattered along the south and west coasts of England and through the Welsh Marches. The students were even required to have a nodding acquaintance with thaumaturgy; though Rafe for one was unable to see how the attraction of scraps of paper to a polished stick of amber could ever have an application to Signalling.

He worked well nonetheless, and passed out with a mark high enough to satisfy even his professors. He was posted directly to his training station, the A Class complex atop Saint Adhelm's Head in Dorset. To his intense pleasure he was accompanied by the one real friend he had made at College; Josh Cope, a wild, black-haired boy, a Common Entrant and the son of a Durham mining family.

They arrived at Saint Adhelm's in the time-honored way, thumbing a lift from a road train drawn by a labouring Fowler compound. Rafe never forgot his first sight of the station. It was far bigger than he'd imagined, sprawling across the top of the great blunt promontory. For convenience, stations were rated in accordance with the heaviest towers they carried; but Saint Adhelm's was a clearing centre for B, C, and D lines as well, and round the huge paired structures of the A-Class towers ranged a circle of smaller semaphores, all twirling and clacking in the sun. Beside them, establishing rigs displayed the codes the towers spoke in a series of bright-coloured circles and rectangles; Rafe, staring, saw one of them rotate, displaying to the west a yellow Bend Sinister as the semaphore above it switched in midmessage from plaintalk to the complex Code Twenty-Three. He glanced sidelong at Josh, got from the other lad a jaunty thumbs-up; they swung their satchels onto their shoulders and headed up toward the main gate to report themselves for duty.

For the first few weeks both boys were glad enough of each other's company. They found the atmosphere of a major field station very different from that of the College; by comparison the latter, noisy and brawling as it had been, came to seem positively monastic. A training in the Guild of Signallers was like a continuous game of ladders and snakes; and Rave and Josh had slid back once more to the bottom of the stack. Their life was a near-endless round of canteen fatigues, of polishing and burnishing, scrubbing and holystoning. There were the cabins to clean, gravel paths to weed, what seemed like miles of brass rail to scour till it gleamed. Saint Adhelm's was a show station, always prone to inspection. Once it suffered a visit from the Grand Master of Signallers himself, and his Lord Lieutenant; the spitting and polishing before that went on for weeks. And there was the maintenance of the towers themselves; the canvas grommets on the great control rods to renew and pipe-clay, the semaphore arms to be painted, their bearings cleaned and packed with grease, spars to be sent down and re-rigged, always in darkness when the day's signalling was done and generally in the foullest of weathers. The semi-military nature of the Guild made necessary sidearms practice and shooting with the longbow and crossbow, obsolescent weapons now but still occasionally employed in the European wars.

The station itself surpassed Rafe's wildest dreams. Its standing complement, including the dozen or so apprentices always in training, was well over a hundred, of whom some sixty or eighty were always on duty or on call. The big semaphores, the Class A's, were each worked by teams of a dozen men, six to each great lever, with a Signal Master to control coordination and pass on the cyphers from the observers. With the station running at near capacity the scene was impressive; the lines of men at the controls, as synchronised as troupes of dancers; the shouts of the Signal Masters, scuffle of feet on the white planking, rumble and creak of the control rods, the high thunder of the signals a hundred feet above the roofs. Though that, according to the embittered Officer in Charge, was not Signalling but "unscientific bloody timber-hauling." Major Stone had spent most of his working life on the little Class C's of the Pennine Chain before an unlooked-for promotion had given him his present position of trust.

The A messages short-hopped from Saint Adhelm's to Swyre Head and from thence to Gad Cliff, built on the high land overlooking Warbarrow Bay. From there along the coast to Golden Cap, the station poised six hundred sheer feet above the fishing village of Lymes, to fling themselves in giant strides into the west, to Somerset and Devon and far-off Cornwall, or northwards again over the heights of the Great Plain en route for Wales. Up there Rafe knew they passed in sight of the old stone rings of Avebury. He often thought with affection of his parents and Serjeant Gray; but he was long past homesickness. His days were too full for that.

Twelve months after their arrival at Saint Adhelm's, and three years after their induction into the Guild, the apprentices were first allowed to lay hands on the semaphore bars. Josh in fact had found it impossible to wait and had salved his ego some months before by spelling out a frisky message on one of the little local towers in what he hoped was the dead of night. For that fall from grace he had made intimate and painful contact with the buckle on the end of a green leather belt, wielded by none other than Major Stone himself. Two burly Corporals of Signals held the miners' lad down while he threshed and howled; the end result had convinced even Josh that on certain points of discipline the Guild stood adamant.

To learn to signal was like yet another beginning. Rafe found rapidly that a semaphore lever was no passive thing to be pulled and hauled at pleasure; with the wind under the great black sails of the arms an operator stood a good chance of being bowled completely off the rostrum by the back-whip of even a thirty-foot unit, while to the teams on the A-Class towers lack of coordination could prove, and had proved in the past, fatal. There was a trick to the thing, only learned after bruising hours of practice; to lean the weight of the body against the levers rather than just using the muscles of back and arms, employ the jounce and swing of the semaphores to position them automatically for their next cypher. Trying to fight them instead of working with the recoil would reduce a strong man to a sweat-soaked rag within minutes; but a trained Signaller could work half the day and feel very little strain. Rafe approached the task assiduously;

six months and one broken collarbone later he felt able to pride himself on mastery of his craft. It was then he first encountered the murderous intricacies of coaxial signalling. . . .

After two years on the station the apprentices were finally deemed ready to graduate as full Signallers. Then came the hardest test of all. The site of it, the arena, was a bare hillock of ground some half mile from Saint Adhelm's Head. Built onto it, and facing each other about forty yards apart, were two Class D towers with their cabins. Josh was to be Rafe's partner in the test. They were taken to the place in the early morning, and given their problem; to transmit to each other in plaintalk the entire of the Book of Nehemiah in alternate verses, with appropriate Attention, Acknowledgement, and End-of-Message cyphers at the head and tail of each. Several ten-minute breaks were allowed, though they had been warned privately it would be better not to take them; once they left the rostrums they might be unable to force their tired bodies back to the bars.

Round the little hill would be placed observers who would check the work minute by minute for inaccuracies and sloppiness. When the messages were finished to their satisfaction the apprentices might leave, and call themselves Signallers; but not before. Nothing would prevent them deserting their task if they desired before it was done. Nobody would speak a word of blame, and there would be no punishment; but they would leave the Guild the same day, and never return. Some boys, a few, did leave. Others collapsed; for them, there would be another chance.

Rafe neither collapsed nor left, though there were times when he longed to do both. When he started, the sun had barely risen; when he left it was sinking toward the western rim of the horizon. The first two hours, the first three, were nothing; then the pain began. In the shoulders, in the back, in the buttocks and calves. His world narrowed; he saw neither the sun nor the distant sea. There was only the semaphore, the handles of it, the text in front of his eyes, the window. Across the space separating the huts he could see Josh staring as he engaged in his endless, useless task. Rafe came by degrees to hate the towers, the Guild, himself, all he had done, the memory of Silbury and old Serjeant Gray; and to hate Josh most of all, with his stupid white blob of a face, the signals clacking above him like some absurd extension of himself. With fatigue came a trance-like state in which logic was suspended, the reasons for actions lost. There was nothing to do in life, had never been anything to do but stand on the rostrum, work the levers, feel the jounce of the signals, check with the body, feel the jounce. . . . His vision doubled and trebled till the lines of copy in front of him shimmered unreadably; and still the test ground on.

At any time in the afternoon Rafe would have killed his friend had he been able to reach him. But he couldn't get to him; his feet were rooted to the podium, his hands glued to the levers of the semaphore. The signals grumbled and creaked; his breath sounded in his ears harshly, like an engine. His sight blackened; the text and the opposing semaphore swam in a void. He felt disembodied; he could sense his limbs only as a dim and confused burning. And somehow, agonizingly, the transmission came to an end. He clattered off the last verse of the book, signed End of Message, leaned on the handles while the part of him that could still think realized dully that he could stop. And then, in black rage, he did the thing only one other apprentice had done in the history of the station; flipped the handles to Attention again, spelled out with terrible exactness and letter by letter the message *"God Save the Queen."* Signed End of Message, got no acknowledgement, swung the levers up and locked them into position for Emergency-Contact Broken. In a signalling chain the alarm would be flashed back to the originating station, further information rerouted and a squad sent to investigate the breakdown.

Rafe stared blankly at the levers. He saw now the puzzling bright streaks on them were his own blood. He forced his raw hands to unclamp themselves, elbowed his way through the door, shoved past the men who had come for him and collapsed twenty yards away on the grass. He was taken back to Saint Adhelm's in a cart and put to bed. He slept the clock round; when he woke it was with the knowledge that Josh and he now had the right to put aside the cowled russet jerkins of apprentices for the full green of the Guild of Signallers. They drank beer that night, awkwardly, gripping the tankards in both bandaged paws; and for the second and last time, the station cart had to be called into service to get them home.

The next part of training was a sheer pleasure. Rafe made his farewells to Josh and went home on a two month leave; at the end of his furlough he was posted to the household of the Fitzgibbons, one of the old families of the Southwest, to serve twelve months as Signaller-Page. The job was mainly ceremonial, though in times of national crisis it could obviously carry its share of responsibility. Most well-bred families, if they could afford to do so, bought rights from the Guild and erected their own tiny stations somewhere in the grounds of their estate; the little Class-E towers were even smaller than the Class D's on which Rafe had graduated.

In places where no signal line ran within easy sighting distance, one or more stations might be erected across the surrounding country and staffed by Journeyman-Signallers without access to coding; but the Fitzgibbons' great aitch-shaped house lay almost below Swyre Head, in a sloping coombe open to the sea. Rafe, looking down on the roofs of the place the morning he arrived, started to grin. He could see his semaphore perched up among the chimney stacks; above it a bare mile away was the A repeater, the short-hop tower for his old station of Saint Adhelm's just over the hill. He touched heels to his horse, pushing it into a canter. He would be signalling direct to the A Class, there was no other outroute; he couldn't help chuckling at the thought of its Major's face when asked to hurl to Saint Adhelm's or Golden Cap requests for butter, six dozen eggs, or the services of a cobbler. He paid his formal respects to the station and rode down into the valley to take up his new duties.

They proved if anything easier than he had anticipated. Fitzgibbon himself moved in high circles at Court and was rarely home, the running of the house being left to his wife and two teenage daughters. As Rafe had expected, most of the messages he was required to pass were of an intensely domestic nature. And he enjoyed the privileges of any young Guildsman in his position; he could always be sure of a warm place in the kitchen at nights, the first cut off the roast, the prettiest serving wenches to mend his clothes and trim his hair. There was sea bathing within a stone's throw, and feast day trips to Durnovaria and Bourne Mouth. Once a little fair established itself in the grounds, an annual occurrence apparently; and Rafe spent a delicious half hour signalling the A Class for oil for its steam engines, and meat for a dancing bear.

The year passed quickly; in late autumn the boy, promoted now to Signaller-Corporal, was reposted, and another took his place. Rafe rode west, into the hills that crowd the southern corner of Dorset, to take up what would be his first real command.

The station was part of a D-Class chain that wound west over the high ground into Somerset. In winter, with the short days and bad seeing conditions, the towers would be unused; Rafe knew that well enough. He would be totally isolated; winters in the hills could be severe, with snow making travel next to impossible and frosts for weeks on end. He would have little to fear from the *routiers,* the footpads who legend claimed haunted the West in the cold months; the station lay far from any road and there was nothing in the cabins, save perhaps the Zeiss glasses carried by the Signaller, to tempt a desperate man. He would be in more danger from wolves and Fairies, though the former were virtually extinct in the south and he was young enough to laugh at the latter. He took over from the bored Corporal just finishing his term, signalled his arrival back through the chain, and settled down to take stock of things.

By all reports this first winter on a one-man station was a worse trial than the endurance test. For a trial it was, certainly. At some time through the dark months ahead, some hour of the day, a message would come along the dead line, from the west or from the east; and Rafe would have to be there to take it and pass it on. A minute late with his acknowledgement and a formal reprimand would be issued from Londinium; that might peg his promotion for years, maybe for good. The standards of the Guild were high, and they were never relaxed; if it was easy for a Major in charge of an A-Class station to fall from grace, how much easier for an unknown and untried Corporal! The duty period of each day was short, a bare six hours, five through the darkest months of December and

January; but during that time, except for one short break, Rafe would have to be continually on the alert.

One of his first acts on being left alone was to climb to the diminutive operating gantry. The construction of the station was unusual. To compensate for its lack of elevation a catwalk had been built across under the roof; the operating rostrum was located centrally on it, while at each end double-glazed windows commanded views to west and east. Between them, past the handles of the semaphore, a track had been worn half an inch deep in the wooden boards. In the next few months Rafe would wear it deeper, moving from one window to the other checking the arms of the next towers in line. The matchsticks of the semaphores were barely visible; he judged them to be a good two miles distant. He would need all his eyesight, plus the keenness of the Zeiss lenses, to make them out at all on a dull day; but they would have to be watched minute by minute through every duty period because sooner or later one of them would move. He grinned and touched the handles of his own machine. When that happened, his acknowledgement would be clattering before the tower had stopped calling for Attention.

He examined the stations critically through his glasses. In the spring, riding out to take up a new tour, he might meet one of their operators; but not before. In the hours of daylight they as well as he would be tied to their gantries, and on foot in the dark it might be dangerous to try to reach them. Anyway it would not be expected of him; that was an unwritten law. In case of need, desperate need, he could call help through the semaphores; but for no other reason. This was the true life of the Guildsman; the bustle of Londinium, the warmth and comfort of the Fitzgibbons' home, had been episodes only. Here was the end result of it all; the silence, the desolation, the ancient, endless communion of the hills. He had come full circle.

His life settled into a pattern of sleeping and waking and watching. As the days grew shorter the weather worsened; freezing mists swirled round the station, and the first snow fell. For hours on end the towers to east and west were lost in the haze; if a message was to come now, the Signallers would have to light their cressets. Rafe prepared the bundles of faggots anxiously, wiring them into their iron cages, setting them beside the door with the paraffin that would soak them, make them blaze. He became obsessed by the idea that the message had in fact come, and he had missed it in the gloom. In time the fear ebbed. The Guild was hard, but it was fair; no Signaller, in winter of all times, was expected to be a superman. If a Captain rode suddenly to the station demanding why he had not answered this or that he would see the torches and the oil laid and ready and know at least that Rafe had done his best. Nobody came; and when the weather cleared the towers were still stationary.

Each night after the light had gone Rafe tested his signals, swinging the arms to free them from their wind-driven coating of ice; it was good to feel the pull and flap of the thin wings up in the dark. The messages he sent into blackness were fanciful in the extreme; notes to his parents and old Serjeant Gray, lurid suggestions to a little girl in the household of the Fitzgibbons to whom he had taken more than a passing fancy. Twice a week he used the lunchtime break to climb the tower, check the spindles in their packings of grease. On one such inspection he was appalled to see a hairline crack in one of the control rods, the first sign that the metal had become fatigued. He replaced the entire section that night, breaking out fresh parts from store, hauling them up and fitting them by the improvised light of a hand lamp. It was an awkward, dangerous job with his fingers freezing and the wind plucking at his back, trying to tug him from his perch onto the roof below. He could have pulled the station out of line in daytime, signalled Repairs and given himself the benefit of light, but pride forbade him. He finished the job two hours before dawn, tested the tower, made his entry in the log and went to sleep, trusting in his Signaller's sense to wake him at first light. It didn't let him down.

The long hours of darkness began to pall. Mending and laundering only filled a small proportion of his off-duty time; he read through his stock of books, reread them, put them aside and began devising tasks for himself, checking and rechecking his inventories of food and fuel. In the blackness, with the long crying of the wind over the roof, the stories of Fairies and were-things on the heath didn't seem quite so fanciful. Difficult now even to imagine summer, the slow clicking of the towers against skies bright blue and burning with light. There were two pistols in the hut; Rafe saw to it their mechanisms were in order, loaded and primed them both. Twice after that he woke to crashings on the roof, as if some dark thing was scrabbling to get in; but each time it was only the wind in the skylights. He padded them with strips of canvas; then the frost came back, icing them shut, and he wasn't disturbed again.

He moved a portable stove up onto the observation gallery and discovered the remarkable number of operations that could be carried out with one eye on the windows. The brewing of coffee and tea were easy enough; in time he could even manage the production of hot snacks. His lunch hours he preferred to use for things other than cooking. Above all else he was afraid of inaction making him fat; there was no sign of it happening but he still preferred to take no chances. When snow conditions permitted he would make quick expeditions from the shack into the surrounding country. On one of these the hillock with its smoothly shaped crown of trees attracted his eye. He walked toward it jauntily, breath steaming in the air, the glasses as ever bumping his hip. In the copse, his Fate was waiting.

The catamount clung to the bole of a fir, watching the advance of the boy with eyes that were slits of hate in the vicious mask of its face. No one could have read its thoughts. Perhaps it imagined itself about to be attacked; perhaps it was true what they said about such creatures, that the cold of winter sent them mad. There were few of them now in the west; mostly they had retreated to the hills of Wales, the rocky peaks of the far north. The survival of this one was in itself a freak, an anachronism.

The tree in which it crouched leaned over the path Rafe must take. He ploughed forward, head bent a little, intent only on picking his way. As he approached the catamount drew back its lips in a huge and silent snarl, showing the wide pink vee of its mouth, the long needle-sharp teeth. The eyes blazed; the ears flattened, making the skull a round, furry ball. Rafe never saw the wildcat, its stripes blending perfectly with the harshness of branches and snow. As he stepped beneath the tree it launched itself onto him, landed across his shoulders like a spitting shawl; his neck and back were flayed before the pain had travelled to his brain.

The shock and the impact sent him staggering. He reeled, yelling; the reaction dislodged the cat but it spun in a flash, tearing upward at his stomach. He felt the hot spurting of blood, and the world became a red haze of horror. The air was full of the creature's screaming. He reached his knife but teeth met in his hand and he dropped it. He grovelled blindly, found the weapon again, slashed out, felt the blade strike home. The cat screeched, writhing on the snow. He forced himself to push his streaming knee into the creature's back, pinning the animal while the knife flailed down, biting into its mad life; until the thing with a final convulsion burst free, fled limping and splashing blood, died maybe somewhere off in the trees. Then there was the time of blackness, the hideous crawl back to the signal station; and now he lay dying too, unable to reach the semaphore, knowing that finally he had failed. He wheezed hopelessly, settled back farther into the crowding dark.

In the blackness were sounds. Homely sounds. A regular *scrape-clink, scrape-clink;* the morning noise of a rake being drawn across the bars of a grate. Rafe tossed muttering, relaxed in the spreading warmth. There was light now, orange and flickering; he kept his eyes closed, seeing the glow of it against the insides of the lids. Soon his mother would call. It would be time to get up and go to school, or out into the fields.

A tinkling, pleasantly musical, made him turn his head. His body still ached, right down the length of it, but somehow the pain was not quite so intense. He blinked. He'd expected to see his old room in the cottage at Avebury; the curtains stirring in the breeze perhaps, sunshine coming through open windows. It took him a moment to readjust to the signal hut; then memory came back with a rush. He stared; he saw the gantry under the semaphore handles, the rods reaching out through the roof; the whiteness of their grommets, pipe-clayed by himself the day before. The tarpaulin squares had been hooked across the windows, shutting out the night. The door was barred, both lamps were burning; the stove was alight, its doors open and spreading warmth. Above it, pots and pans simmered; and bending over them was a girl.

She turned when he moved his head and he looked into deep eyes, black-fringed, with a quick nervousness about them that was somehow like an animal. Her long hair was restrained from falling round her face by a band or ribbon drawn behind the little pointed ears; she wore a rustling dress of an odd light blue, and she was brown. Brown as a nut, though God knew there had been no sun for weeks to tan her like that. Rafe recoiled when she looked at him, and something deep in him twisted and needed to scream. He knew she shouldn't be here in this wilderness, amber-skinned and with her strange summery dress; that she was one of the Old Ones, the half-believed, the Haunters of the Heath, the possessors of men's souls if Mother Church spoke truth. His lips tried to form the word "Fairy" and could not. Blood-smeared, they barely moved.

His vision was failing again. She walked toward him lightly, swaying, seeming to his dazed mind to shimmer like a flame; some unnatural flame that a breath might extinguish. But there was nothing ethereal about her touch. Her hands were firm and hard; they wiped his mouth, stroked his hot face. Coolness remained after she had gone away and he realized she had laid a damp cloth across his forehead. He tried to cry out to her again; she turned to smile at him, or he thought she smiled, and he realized she was singing. There were no words; the sound made itself in her throat, goldenly, like the song a spinning wheel might hum in the ears of a sleepy child, the words always nearly there ready to well up through the surface of the colour and never coming. He wanted badly to talk now, tell her about the cat and his fear of it and its paws full of glass, but it seemed she knew already the things that were in his mind. When she came back it was with a steaming pan of water that she set on a chair beside the bunk. She stopped the humming, or the singing, then and spoke to him; but the words made no sense, they banged and splattered like water falling over rocks. He was afraid again, for that was the talk of the Old Ones; but the defect must have been in his ears because the syllables changed of themselves into the Modern English of the Guild. They were sweet and rushing, filled with a meaning that was not a meaning, hinting at deeper things beneath themselves that his tired mind couldn't grasp. They talked about the Fate that had waited for him in the wood, fallen on him so suddenly from the tree. *"The Norns spin the Fate of a man or of a cat,"* sang the voice. *"Sitting beneath Yggdrasil, great World Ash, they work; one Sister to make the yarn, the next to measure, the third to cut it at its end. . . ."* and all the time the hands were busy, touching and soothing.

Rafe knew the girl was mad, or possessed. She spoke of Old things, the things banished by Mother Church, pushed out forever into the dark and cold. With a great effort he lifted his hand, held it before her to make the sign of the Cross; but she gripped the wrist, giggling, and forced it down, started to work delicately on the ragged palm, cleaning the blood from round the base of the fingers. She unfastened the belt across his stomach, eased the trews apart; cutting the leather, soaking it, pulling it away in little twitches from the deep tears in groin and thighs. *"Ah . . . ,"* he said, *"ah . . ."* She stopped at that, frowning, brought something from the stove, lifted his head gently to let him drink. The liquid soothed, seeming to run from his throat down into body and limbs like a trickling anaesthesia. He relapsed into a warmness shot through with little coloured stabs of pain, heard her crooning again as she dressed his legs. Slid deeper, into sleep.

Day came slowly, faded slower into night that turned to day again, and darkness. He seemed to be apart from Time, lying dozing and waking, feeling the comfort of bandages on his body and fresh linen tucked round him, seeing the handles of the semaphores gleam a hundred miles away, wanting to go to them, not able to move. Sometimes he thought when the girl came to him he pulled her close, pressed his face into the mother-warmth of her thighs while she stroked his hair, and talked, and sang. All the time it seemed, through the sleeping and the waking, the voice went on. Sometimes he knew he heard it with his ears, sometimes in fever dreams the words rang in his mind. They made a mighty saga; such a story as had never been told, never imagined in all the lives of men.

It was the tale of Earth; Earth and a land, the place her folk called Angle-Land. Only once there had been no Angle-Land because there had been no planets, no sun. Nothing had existed but Time; Time, and a void. Only Time was the void, and the void was Time itself. Through it moved colours, twinklings, sudden shafts of light. There were hummings, shoutings, perhaps, musical tones like the notes of organs that thrummed in his body until it shook with them and became a melting part. Sometimes in the dream he wanted to cry out; but still he couldn't speak, and the beautiful blasphemy ground on. He saw the brown mists lift back waving and whispering, and through them the shine of water; a harsh sea, cold and limitless, ocean of a new world. But the dream itself was fluid; the images shone and altered, melding each smoothly into each, yielding place majestically, fading into dark. The hills came, rolling, tentative, squirming, pushing up dripping flanks that shuddered, sank back, returned to silt. The silt, the sea bed, enriched itself with a million-year snowstorm of little dying creatures. The piping of the tiny snails as they fell was a part of the chorus and the song, a thin, sweet harmonic.

And already there were Gods; the Old Gods, powerful and vast, looking down, watching, stirring with their fingers at the silt, waving the swirling brownness back across the sea. It was all done in a dim light, the cold glow of dawn. The hills shuddered, drew back, thrust up again like golden, humped animals, shaking the water from their sides. The sun stood over them, warming, adding steam to the fogs, making multiple and shimmering reflections dance from the sea. The Gods laughed; and over and again, uncertainly, unsurely, springing from the silt, sinking back to silt again, the hills writhed, shaping the shapeless land. The voice sang, whirring like a wheel; there was no "forward," no "back"; only a sense of continuity, of massive development, of the huge Everness of Time. The hills fell and rose; leaves brushed away the sun, their reflections waved in water, the trees themselves sank, rolled and heaved, were thrust down to rise once more dripping, grow afresh. The rocks formed, broke, re-formed, became solid, melted again until from the formlessness somehow the land was made; Angle-Land, nameless still, with its long pastures, its fields, and silent hills of grass. Rafe saw the endless herds of animals that crossed it, wheeling under the wheeling sun; and the first shadowy Men. Rage possessed them; they hacked and hewed, rearing their stone circles in the wind and emptiness, finding again the bodies of the Gods in the chalky flanks of downs. Until all ended, the Gods grew tired; and the ice came flailing and crying from the north, the sun sank dying in its blood and there was coldness and blackness and nothingness and winter.

Into the void, He came; only He was not the Christos, the God of Mother Church. He was Balder, Balder the Lovely, Balder the Young. He strode across the land, face burning as the sun, and the Old Ones grov-elled and adored. The wind touched the stone circles, burning them with frost; in the darkness men cried for spring. So he came to the Tree Ygg-drasil—*What Tree,* Rafe's mind cried despairingly, and the voice checked and laughed and said without anger, *"Yggdrasil, great World Ash, whose branches pierce the layers of heaven, whose roots wind through all Hells. . . ."* Balder came to the Tree, on which he must die for the sins of Gods and Men; and to the Tree they nailed him, hung him by the palms. And there they came to adore while His blood ran and trickled and gouted bright, while he hung above the Hells of the Trolls and of the Giants of Frost and Fire and Mountain, below the Seven Heavens where Tiw and Thunor and old Wo-Tan trembled in Valhalla at the mightiness of what was done.

And from His blood sprang warmth again and grass and sunlight, the meadow flowers and the calling, mating birds. And the Church came at last, stamping and jingling, out of the east, lifting the brass wedding cakes of her altars while men fought and roiled and made the ground black with their blood, while they raised their cities and their signal towers and their glaring castles. The Old Ones moved back, the Fairies, the Haunters of the Heath, the People of the Stones, taking with them their lovely bleed-ing Lord; and the priests called despairingly to Him, calling Him the Christos, saying he did die on a tree, at the Place Golgotha, the Place of the Skull. Rome's navies sailed the world; and England woke up, steam jetted in every tiny hamlet, and clattering and noise; while Balder's blood, still raining down, made afresh each spring. And so after days in the telling, after weeks, the huge legend paused, and turned in on itself, and ended.

The stove was out, the hut smelled fresh and cool. Rafe lay quiet, knowing he had been very ill. The cabin was a place of browns and clean bright blues. Deep brown of woodwork, orange brown of the control handles, creamy brown of planking. The blue came from the sky, shafting in through windows and door, reflecting from the long-dead semaphore in pale spindles of light. And the girl herself was brown and blue; brown of skin, frosted blue of ribbon and dress. She leaned over him smiling, all nervousness gone. *"Better,"* sang the voice. *"You're better now. You're well."*

He sat up. He was very weak. She eased the blankets aside, letting the air tingle like cool water on his skin. He swung his legs down over the edge of the bunk and she helped him stand. He sagged, laughed, stood again swaying, feeling the texture of the hut floor under his feet, looking down at his body, seeing the pink crisscrossing of scars on stomach and thighs, the jaunty penis thrusting from its nest of hair. She found him a tunic, helped him into it laughing at him, twitching and pulling. She fetched him a cloak, fastened it round his neck, knelt to push sandals on his feet. He leaned against the bunk panting a little, feeling stronger. His eye caught the semaphore; she shook her head and teased him, urging him toward the door. *"Come,"* said the voice. *"Just for a little while."*

She knelt again outside, touched the snow while the wind blustered wetly from the west. Round about, the warming hills were brilliant and still. *"Balder is dead,"* she sang. *"Balder is dead. . . ."* And instantly it seemed Rafe could hear the million chuckling voices of the thaw, see the very flowers pushing coloured points against the translucency of snow. He looked up at the signals on the tower. They seemed strange to him now, like the winter a thing of the past. Surely they too would melt and run, and leave no trace. They were part of the old life and the old way; for the first time he could turn his back on them without distress. The girl moved from him, low shoes showing her ankles against the snow; and Rafe followed, hesitant at first then more surely, gaining strength with every step. Behind him, the signal hut stood forlorn.

The two horsemen moved steadily, letting their mounts pick their way. The younger rode a few paces ahead, muffled in his cloak, eyes beneath the brim of his hat watching the horizon. His companion sat his horse quietly, with an easy slouch; he was grizzled and brown-faced, skin tanned by the wind. In front of him, over the pommel of the saddle, was hooked the case of a pair of Zeiss binoculars. On the other side was the holster of a musket; the barrel lay along the neck of the horse, the butt thrust into the air just below the rider's hand.

Away on the left a little knoll of land lifted its crown of trees into the
sky. Ahead, in the swooping bowl of the valley, was the black speck of a
signal hut, its tower showing thinly above it. The officer reined in quietly, took the glasses from their case and studied the place. Nothing
moved, and no smoke came from the chimney. Through the lenses the
shuttered windows stared back at him; he saw the black vee of the Semaphore arms folded down like the wings of a dead bird. The Corporal
waited impatiently, his horse fretting and blowing steam, but the Captain
of Signals was not to be hurried. He lowered the glasses finally, and
clicked to his mount. The animal moved forward again at a walk, picking its hooves up and setting them down with care.

The snow here was thicker; the valley had trapped it, and the day's
thaw had left the drifts filmed with a brittle skin of ice. The horses floundered as they climbed the slope to the hut. At its door the Captain dismounted, leaving the reins hanging slack. He walked forward, eyes on
the lintel and the boards.

The mark. It was everywhere, over the door, on its frame, stamped
along the walls. The circle, with the crab pattern inside it; rebus or pic-
tograph, the only thing the People of the Heath knew, the only message
it seemed they had for men. The Captain had seen it before, many times;
it had no power left to surprise him. The Corporal had not. The older
man heard the sharp intake of breath, the click as a pistol was cocked;
saw the quick, instinctive movement of the hand, the gesture that wards
off the Evil Eye. He smiled faintly, almost absentmindedly, and pushed
at the door. He knew what he would find, and that there was no danger.

The inside of the hut was cool and dark. The Guildsman looked round
slowly, hands at his sides, feet apart on the boards. Outside a horse
champed, jangling its bit, and snorted into the cold. He saw the glasses
on their hook, the swept floor, the polished stove, the fire laid neat and
ready on the bars; everywhere, the Fairy mark danced across the wood.

He walked forward and looked down at the thing on the bunk. The
blood it had shed had blackened with the frost; the wounds on its stomach showed like leafshaped mouths, the eyes were sunken now and dull;
one hand was still extended to the signal levers eight feet above.

Behind him the Corporal spoke harshly, using anger as a bulwark
against fear. "The . . . People that were here. They done this. . . ."

The Captain shook his head. "No," he said slowly. " 'Twas a wildcat."

The Corporal said thickly, "They were here though. . . ." The anger
surged again as he remembered the unmarked snow. "There weren't no
tracks, sir. *How could they come? . . .*"

"How comes the wind?" asked the Captain, half to himself. He looked
down again at the corpse in the bunk. He knew a little of the history of
this boy, and of his record. The Guild had lost a good man.

How did they come? The People of the Heath. . . . His mind twitched away from using the names the commoners had for them. What did they look like, when they came? What did they talk of, in locked cabins to dying men? Why did they leave their mark. . . .

It seemed the answers shaped themselves in his brain. It was as if they crystallized from the cold, faintly sweet air of the place, blew in with the soughing of the wind. *All this would pass,* came the thoughts, *and vanish like a dream. No more hands would bleed on the signal bars, no more children freeze in their lonely watchings. The Signals would leap continents and seas, winged as thought. All this would pass, for better or for ill. . . .*

He shook his head, bearlike, as if to free it from the clinging spell of the place. He knew, with a flash of inner sight, that he would know no more. The People of the Heath, the Old Ones; they moved back, with their magic and their lore. Always back, into the yet remaining dark. Until one day they themselves would vanish away. They who were, and yet were not. . . .

He took the pad from his belt, scribbled, tore off the top sheet. "Corporal," he said quietly. "If you please. . . . Route through Golden Cap."

He walked to the door, stood looking out across the hills at the matchstick of the eastern tower just visible against the sky. In his mind's eye a map unrolled; he saw the message flashing down the chain, each station picking it up, routing it, clattering it on its way. Down to Golden Cap, where the great signals stood gaunt against the cold crawl of the sea; north up the A line to Aquae Sulis, back again along the Great West Road. Within the hour it would reach its destination at Silbury Hill; and a grave-faced man in green would walk down the village street of Avebury, knock at a door. . . .

The Corporal climbed to the gantry, clipped the message in the rack, eased the handles forward lightly testing against the casing ice. He flexed his shoulders, pulled sharply. The dead tower woke up, arms clacking in the quiet. *Attention, Attention. . . .* Then the signal for Origination, the cypher for the eastern line. The movements dislodged a little cloud of ice crystals; they fell quietly, sparkling against the greyness of the sky.

THOMAS BURNETT SWANN

The Manor of Roses

The late Thomas Burnett Swann, a poet and academic who once taught English literature at Florida Atlantic University, was also a popular fantasist who composed a rich body of pastoral novels and stories about the fabulous creatures who inhabited the Old Worlds of Rome ("Where is the Bird of Fire?"), Egypt *(The Minikins of Yam)*, Minoan Crete *(Day of the Minotaur)*, Persia ("Vashi"), the Aegean of Ancient Greece ("The Dolphin and the Deep"), and elsewhere. His other books included *The Goat without Horns, Cry Silver Bells, Green Phoenix, The Forest of Forever, Lady of the Bees, Wolfwinter, The Gods Abide, The Tournament of Thorns, Will-o'-the-Wisp, The Not-World*, and *Queens Walk in the Dust*. His short fiction, which included some of his best work, was collected in *The Dolphin and the Deep* and *Where Is the Bird of Fire?* Swann died in 1976.

Swann was sometimes attacked for being saccharine and overly sentimental, and it is true that some of his stories will probably be too coy or cloying for modern tastes, and that others probably work better for children or for young adults than they do for an adult audience. The best of Swann's work, however, was evocative and powerful, compassionate and warmly sympathetic rather than falsely sentimental . . . and Swann never wrote any better than he did in the marvelous novella that follows, "The Manor of Roses," his masterpiece, in my opinion, and one of the best fantasy stories of the last thirty years.

I

I am thirty-five, a woman of middle years, and yet in this time of pox and plague, of early death and the dying of beauty before the body dies, it is said that I am still as beautiful as a Byzantine Madonna, poised in the heaven of a gold mosaic and wearing sorrow like a robe of white petals.

But sorrow is not a gown. It is a nakedness to the searching eye of the curious, to the magpie-tongued who love to pry out grief: She grieves too long. . . . The Manor demands an heir. . . . Who will defend us from the encroaching forest, the thieves and the Mandrake People?

It was eleven years ago, in the year 1202 of Our Lord, that my husband's comrade-in-arms, Edmund-the-Wolf, rode to me with the news of my husband's death and, as if for compensation, the riches captured before he had died in battle. Captured? Pillaged, I should say, in the sack of Constantinople. You see, it is a time when men are boys, rapacious and cruel, as ready to kill a Jew, a Hungarian, a Greek as an Infidel; happy so long as they wield a sword and claim to serve God. A time when boys who have not yet grown to their fathers' pride—Crusading, it is called—are the only true men.

And yet I loved my husband, a red-haired Norman, gay as the men of the South, and not like most of our stern northern people. I loved him for his gaiety, his hair the color of Roman bricks, and because he left me a son.

But the Crusader's code, like an evil demon of pox, also possesses children. Only last year in France and Germany, Stephen proclaimed his message from Christ, Nicholas piped his irresistible flute, and the children yearned to them as tides to the moon and flowed in a sea of immaculate white robes toward the shores of that greater sea, the Mediterranean.

Little of the madness crossed to England. Perhaps our children are not inclined to visions; perhaps they prefer the hunt to the drafty halls of a church and talks with God. But the madness, missing the thousands, somehow touched my son. He rode to London, astride his roan palfrey and dressed in a jerkin of sheepskin dyed to the yellow of gorse, with a leather belt at his waist and a fawn-colored pouch a-jingle with new-minted pennies. Ready to board a ship for Marseilles and join Stephen! But Stephen and most of his army were sold as slaves to the Infidel; Nicholas died of the plague before he reached the sea; and my son of fifteen summers, reaching London, stood on the banks of the Thames to choose what twin-castled ship would bear him across the channel, and fell to the blade of a common cutpurse. The Devil, I think, possessed the children, a jest to fling like a gauntlet in the teeth of God.

God is not blind, however. In less than a year, he sent me those other children, struck with the same madness: John, a dark-haired Norman; Stephen, a Saxon but named like the boy of France; and Ruth, whom they called their guardian angel (but no one knew if she came from Heaven or Hell). God, I felt, had made me His instrument to preserve them from my own son's ruin. Was He wrong to trust me with so precious and difficult a task? I tried, Mother of God how I tried! I sheltered them from the Mandrakes of the forest. Loved them, hurt them, and then at the last— But you shall judge me. . . .

*   *   *

He ran blinded by tears across the heath, startling birds into flight, pheasants and grouse enough to feast a king. Conies peered from their nests and submerged like frogs in a pond with a dull, simultaneous plop. Didn't they know that he, timorous John, who had lost his bow in the woods and scattered the arrows out of his quiver, was not a creature to fear? He had come from the hunt with his father, lord of Goshawk Castle, and the knights Robert, Arthur, Edgar, and the rest. The names of the knights were different, their features almost identical. Rough hands, calloused from wielding swords against the Infidel—and their fellow Englishmen. Cheeks ruddy with mead and not with the English climate. Odorous bodies enveloped by fur-lined surcoats which they pridefully wore even in the flush of summer, instead of imitating the villeins with their simple breechclouts or their trousers without tunics. Lank, sweat-dampened hair, long in the back, and cut in a fringe across their foreheads.

John, the Baron's son, had been allowed the first shot at a stag beleaguered by hounds. He was not a good bowman, but the stag had been much too close to miss except by design. He had missed by design. Once, gathering chestnuts with his friend Stephen, the shepherd, he had seen the same animal, a splendid beast with horns like wind-beaten trees along the North Sea.

"He isn't afraid of us," Stephen had whispered.

"Nor has he reason to be," said John. "We would never harm him. He's much too beautiful."

Now, the animal had turned and looked at him with recognition, it seemed, and resignation; harried by hounds, bemused in a clump of bracken. John had fired his arrow above the antlers. The stag had escaped, bursting out of the bracken as if the coarse ferns were blades of grass and leveling three dogs with his adamantine hooves.

"Girl!" his father had shouted, hoarse with rage at losing a feast and a pair of antlers to grace his barren hall. "I should get you a distaff instead of a bow!"

For punishment John was bladed. After the knights had downed a smaller animal, a young doe, they had stretched him across the warm, bloody carcass and each man had struck him with the flat of his sword. Most of the knights had softened their blows. After all, he was their liege-lord's son. But his father's blow had left him bleeding and biting his tongue to hold back shameful tears.

Then they had left him.

"Go to the kennels and get your friend Stephen to dry your tears," his father had sneered. A coarse guffaw greeted the taunt. Stephen was said to have lain with every villein's daughter between twelve and twenty, and men without daughters like to jest: "Girls weep till Stephen dries their tears."

Alone in the woods, John forgot his shame; he was too frightened. Just turned twelve, he knew of desperate thieves, sentenced to die by the rope, who had taken refuge among the sycamores which remembered the Romans, and the oaks which had drunk the blood of Druid sacrifices. As for animals, there were wolves and bears and long-tusked boars, and amphisbaenas too, the twin-headed serpents, and griffins with scaly wings. Worst of all, there were the Mandrake People who, grown like roots, clambered out of the ground to join their kin in acts of cannibalism.

Where could he go? Not to the castle, certainly, where the hunters had doubtless climbed in a broad wooden tub to scrape the grime of weeks from each other's backs, while kitchen wenches doused them with buckets of steaming water and ogled their naked brawn. Once, the castle had held his mother. Its darkness had shone with the whiteness of her samite; its odors were masked with the cloves and the cinnamon, the mace and the musk of her kitchen; its bailey had bloomed with a damson tree whose seeds had come from the Holy Land, and delicate shallots, the "Onions of Ascalon," had reared their tender shoots around the tree, like little guardian gnomes.

"If there must be fruits of war," she had said, "we must see that they are living things, not dead; sweet things, not bitter; soft things, not hard. The verdure of earth and not the gold from dead men's coffers."

Six years ago she had died of the pox. Now, when he knelt on the stone floor of the chapel, he prayed to Father, Son, and Mary, but Mary was Mother.

No, he could not go to the castle. He could but he did not wish to visit the abbot's cottage and face another lesson in logic and astrology, Lucan and Aristotle. He was a willing, indeed a brilliant scholar. But there were times to study and times to look for Stephen. In spite of his father's taunt, it was time to look for Stephen. It was not that his friend was soft or womanish like a sister. He was, in fact, as rough-swearing, ready-to-fight a boy as ever tumbled a girl in the hay. But he curbed his roughness with John, respected his learning, and ignored his weaknesses.

Stephen was a Saxon villein three years older than John. His forebears, he rightly claimed, had once been powerful earls. But the conquering Normans had reduced them to the status of serfs and attached them to their own former lands, which had once held a wooden hall surrounded by a palisade; now it was a castle built by John's grandfather, a square stone keep encircled by curtain walls whose gatehouse was toothed with a rusty portcullis and guarded by archers in hidden embrasures. Stephen's parents were dead, killed by the Mandrake People in one of their swift forays out of the forest to steal sheep and hogs. It was on that very day, two years ago, that he and Stephen had become inseparable friends. John had found him crouching above his mother's body. John, who did not even know his name, had laid a tentative arm around his shoulders—an act of extraordinary boldness for one so shy—and half expected a snarled rebuff or even a blow. But Stephen had buried his head in the arms of his master's son and sobbed convulsively without tears. It was not long before they agreed to adopt each other as brothers and, cutting their forearms with a hunting knife, mingled their blood to cement the bond.

From that time till now, Stephen had lived in a loft above the kennels, dog-boy, shepherd, farmer, fighter with fists and cudgel second to none. He could not read English, much less French and Latin, but the wolves feared his cudgel and grown men his fists. How could you best describe him? Angry, sometimes, but angry *for* things and not against them: for the serfs and the squalor in which they lived, the dogs which were run too hard in the hunt and gored by wild boars, the animals killed for sport and not for food. Sometimes, too, he was glad: loudly, radiantly, exuberantly keen on things—drawing a bow, feeding his dogs, swinging a scythe.

At other times he was neither angry nor glad, but beyond anger and gladness, enraptured by dreams: of meeting an angel or finding Excalibur or, best of all, buying his freedom and becoming a Knight Hospitaler to succor pilgrims and slaughter Infidels. ("But you would have to take an oath of chastity," John reminded him. "I'll think about that when the time comes," said Stephen.) Furthermore, he was one of those rarest of rarities, a dreamer who acts on his dreams, and lately he had talked about the ill-fated Children's Crusade, and how it was time for other Stephens, other Nicholases, to follow the first children and, armed with swords instead of crosses, succeed where they had failed.

It was John's unspeakable fear that Stephen would leave for Jerusalem without him, and yet he did not know if he had the courage for such a journey, through the dark Weald to London and then by ship to Marseilles and the ports of Outre-Mer, the Outer Land, the Saracen Land. Now, he quickened his pace and thought of arguments with which to dissuade his friend. He met old Edward scything in the Common Meadow, a tattered breechclout around his loins, his face and shoulders as coarse and brown as a saddle ridden from London to Edinburgh. Edward did not look up from his task, nor miss a stroke of the scythe. "Why look at the sky?" he liked to mutter. "It belongs to angels, not to serfs like me."

"Have you seen Stephen?" John asked.

Swish, swish, swish went the scythe, and the weeds collapsed as if they had caught the plague.

"HAVE YOU SEEN STEPHEN?"

"I'm not deaf," the old man growled. "Your father's taken my youth, my pigs, and my corn, but not my ears. Not yet, anyway. Your friend'll be losing his, though, 'less he does his work. He oughta be here in the Meadow right now."

"But where *is* he?" cried John in desperation.

"Making for the Roman Place with that look in his eyes. That's where he hides, you know. Daydreams. Didn't even speak to me."

The Roman Place. The ruin where the Romans had worshiped their adopted sun-god, Mithras, in an underground vault. Later, by way of apology to the Christian God, the Saxons had built a timber church to conceal the spot and turned the vault into a crypt for their dead. During the Norman conquest, women and children had hidden in the church, and the Normans had set a torch to the roof and burned the building with all of its occupants. The charred and misshapen remnants were almost concealed—healed, as it were—by flowering gorse, and a few blackened timbers, which thrust like seeking hands from the yellow flowers, summoned no worshippers to the buried gods.

A stranger would not suspect a vault beneath the gorse, but John parted the spiny branches and climbed through a narrow hole to a flight of stairs. A sacredness clung to the place, a sense of time, like that of a Druid stone which lichen had aged to a muted, mottled orange and which thrust at the stars as if to commune with them in cosmic loneliness. Here, the worshipers of Mithras had bathed themselves in the blood of the sacrificial bull and climbed through the seven stages of initiation to commune with the sun instead of the stars. A nasty pagan rite, said the abbot, and John had asked him why Jehovah had ordered Abraham to sacrifice Isaac. "It was only a test," snapped the abbot.

"But what about Jephthah's daughter? *She* wasn't a test." The abbot had changed the subject.

Already, at twelve, John had begun to ask questions about the Bible, God, Christ, and the Holy Ghost. To Stephen, religion was feeling and not thought. God was a patriarch with a flowing beard, and angels were almost as real as the dogs in his kennel. With John it was different. Only the Virgin Mary was not a subject for doubts, questions, arguments, but a beautiful, ageless woman robed in samite, dwelling in the high places of the air or almost at hand, outshining the sun and yet as simple as bread, grass, birds, and Stephen's love; invisible but never unreachable.

At the foot of the stairs he faced a long, narrow cave with earthen walls which contained the loculi of Christians buried in their cerements and which converged to the semicircle of an apse. Now the apse was empty of Mithras slaying the sacred bull and Mary holding the infant Christ. Stephen knelt in their place. He held a waxen candle which lit the frescoed roof: Jesus walking on water, multiplying loaves and fish, bidding the blind to see and the lame to walk.

"John," he gasped, "I have found—"

"A Madonna!"

She lay in a nest of bindweed shaped to a simple pallet. Her face was an ivory mask in the light of the candle. A carved Madonna, thought John, from the transept of a French cathedral, but flushed with the unmistakable ardors of life. No, he saw with a disappointment which approached dismay, she was much too young for the Virgin; a mere girl.

"An angel," said Stephen.

"An angel," sighed John, resenting her youthfulness. What did he need with a second angel, a girl at that? God (or the Virgin Mary) had sent him Stephen, angelic but not female and certainly not effeminate, his hair a riot instead of an aureole, his face more ruddy than pink: a Michael or Gabriel fit for sounding a trumpet instead of strumming a lyre.

The angel stirred and opened her eyes with a pretty fluttering; not with surprise or fright, but almost, thought John, with artful calculation, like some of the rustic lasses who flocked to Stephen's loft. Her teeth were as white as her linen robe, which was bound at the waist by a cord of cerulean silk. Her pointed slippers, unicorn leather trimmed with blue velvet, were such as might be worn in the soft pastures of heaven. She lacked only wings. Or had she concealed them under her robe? John was tempted to ask.

Stephen forestalled him. "Greet her," he whispered. "Welcome her!"

"In what language?" asked John sensibly. "I don't know the tongues of angels."

"Latin, I should think. She must know that, with all the priests muttering their Benedicites."

Stephen had a point. Rude English was out of the question, and also the French of the Normans, who, after all, had descended from barbarous Vikings.

"Quo Vadis?" asked John none too politely.

Her smile, though delectable, no doubt, to Stephen, did not answer the question.

"What are you doing here?" he repeated in Norman French.

Stephen, who understood some French, frantically nudged him. "You shouldn't question an angel. Welcome her! Worship her! Quote her a psalm or a proverb."

"We aren't sure she's an angel. She hasn't told us, has she?"

At last she spoke. "I do not know how I came here," she said in flawless Latin and, seeing the blankness on Stephen's face, repeated the words in English, but with a grave dignity which softened the rough tongue. At the same time, John noticed the crucifix which she held or rather clutched in her hands: a small Greek cross with arms of equal length, wrought of gold and encrusted with stones which he knew from his studies, though not from his father's castle, were the fabulous pearls of the east. "I remember only a darkness, and a falling, and a great forest. I wandered until I found the passage to this cave, and took shelter against the night. I must have been very tired. I feel as if I have slept for a long time." She lifted the cross and then, as if its weight had exhausted her slender hands, allowed it to sink becomingly against her breast.

"I suppose," said John with annoyance, "you're hungry."

Stephen sprang to his feet. "But angels don't eat! Can't you see, John? God has sent her to us as a sign! To lead us to the Holy Land! Stephen of France had his message from Christ. We have our angel."

"But look what happened to Stephen of France. Sold as a slave or drowned in the sea. Only the sharks know which."

"I don't think he's dead. And if he is, then he listened to the Devil's voice and not to God's. But we can *see* our angel."

"Indeed, you can see me," she said, "and you ought to see that I am famished. Angels do eat, I assure you–at least when they travel–and something more substantial than nectar and dew. Have you venison perhaps? Mead?"

"You must take her to the castle," said Stephen, clearly reluctant to part with his newfound angel. "I've nothing so fine in the kennels."

"No," said John. "I'm not taking anyone to the castle. I've decided to stay with you in the kennels."

"Because of your father?"

"Yes. He bladed me before all of his men, and then he called me a–" He could not bring himself to repeat the taunt, especially to Stephen. "He called me a churl. Because I missed a stag. *Our* stag. The one we promised never to harm."

Stephen nodded with understanding. "I'm glad you missed him. They say he's the oldest stag in the forest. They say"–and here he lowered his voice–"that he isn't a stag at all, but Merlin turned to a beast by Vivian. But John, how can you live with me in the kennels? It would wound your father's pride. A baron's son sharing a loft with a dog-boy! He'd give you more than a blading, and as for me! You mayn't remember he cut off my father's ears because he broke a scythe. And now with an angel on our hands, the only thing to do is–"

"Get the angel off our hands?"

"Leave at once for the Holy Land. I have a little food in the kennels, a change of wear. You needn't go back to the castle at all. We've only to follow the Roman road through the Weald to London, and take ship to Marseilles, and from thence to Outre-Mer."

"But Marseilles was where the French Stephen fell in the hands of slavers."

"But we have a guide!"

"If she isn't really an angel–"

"At least we'll have made our escape from the castle."

"You mean we should leave the castle *forever?*" The prospect of leaving his father exhilarated him; he would feel like a falcon with its hood removed. But the castle held all of his possessions, his codex, *The Kings of Britain,* written on the finest vellum and bound between ivory covers; and the parchment containing his favorite poem, "The Owl and the Nightingale," copied laboriously by his own precise hand. Much more important, it held his mother's ghost, his sum of remembering: stairs she had climbed, tapestries woven, garments mended; his mother living in song what she could not live in life and singing of noble warriors and deathless loves:

> *See, he who carved this wood commands me to ask*
> *You to remember, oh treasure-adorned one,*
> *The pledge of old. . . .*

"Leave my father's castle," he repeated, "and not come back? Ever?"

Stephen's face turned as red as the Oriflamme, the fiery banner of the French kings. *"Your father's castle?"* This land belonged to my ancestors when yours were scurvy Vikings! You think I'll stay here forever as dog-boy and shepherd? Serving a man who blades his own son? Giving him what I grow and what I hunt, and asking his leave to take a wife? John, John, there's nothing for either of us here. Ahead of us lies Jerusalem!"

To Stephen, the name was trumpet blast; to John, a death knell. "But a forest stands in the way, and then a channel, and a rough sea swarming with Infidels. They have ships too, you know, swifter than ours and armed with Greek fire."

But Stephen had gripped his shoulders and fixed him with his blue, relentless gaze. "You know I can't leave you."

"You know you won't have to," said John, sighing.

The angel interrupted them, looking a little peeved that in their exchange of pleas and protestations, of male endearments, they were neglecting their quest and their inspiration. "As for leading you to the Holy Land, I don't even know this forest through which you say we must pass. But here in the ground it is damp, and before I came here, I did not like the look of the castle. It seemed to me dark and fierce, with a dry ditch and a gloomy keep, and narrow windows without a pane of glass. A fortress and not a home. If indeed I am an angel, I hope to find dwellings more pleasant here on Earth. Or else I shall quickly return to the sky. In the meantime, let us set off for London, and you shall lead *me* until I begin to remember."

The angel between them, they climbed the stairs to the sun and, skirting old Edward, who was still busily scything in the Common Meadow, came at last to the kennels. It was midday. The Baron and his knights had remained in the castle since the hunt. His villeins, trudging out of the fields, had gathered in the shade of the water mill to enjoy their gruel and bread. Had anyone noticed the quick, furtive passage of the would-be Crusaders, he would have thought them engaged in childish sports, or supposed that Stephen had found a young wench to share with his master's son and probably muttered, "It's high time."

While Stephen's greyhounds lapped at their heels, they climbed to his loft above the kennels to get his few belongings: two clover-green tunics with hoods for wintry days; wooden clogs and a pair of blue stockings which reached to the calf of the leg; a leather pouch bulging with wheaten bread and rounds of cheese; a flask of beer; and a knotted shepherd's crook.

"For wolves," said Stephen, pointing to the crook. "I've used it often."

"And Mandrakes," added John wickedly, hoping to frighten the angel.

"But we have no change of clothes for a girl," said Stephen.

"Never mind." She smiled, guzzling Stephen's beer and munching his bread till she threatened to exhaust the supply before they began their journey. "When my robe grows soiled, I shall wash it in a stream and," she added archly, "the two of you may see if I am truly an angel."

The remark struck John as unangelic if not indelicate. As if they would spy on her while she bathed!

But Stephen reassured her. "We never doubted you were. And now—" A catch entered his voice. Quickly he turned his head and seemed to be setting the loft in order.

"We must leave him alone with his hounds," whispered John to the angel, leading her down the ladder.

A silent Stephen rejoined them in the Heath. His tunic was damp from friendly tongues, and his face was wet, but whether from tongues or tears, it was hard to say.

"You don't suppose," he said, "we could take one or two of them with us? The little greyhound without any tail?"

"No," said John. "My father will stomp and shout when he finds us gone, but then he'll shrug and say, 'Worthless boys, both of them, and no loss to the castle.' But steal one of his hounds, and he'll have his knights on our trail."

"But our angel has no name," cried Stephen suddenly and angrily, as if to say, "As long as she's come to take me from my hounds, she might at least have brought a name."

"I *had* a name, I'm sure. It seems to have slipped my mind. What would you like to call me?"

"Why not Ruth?" said Stephen. "She was always going on journeys in the Bible, leading cousins and such, wasn't she?"

"A mother-in-law," corrected John, who felt that, what with a Crusade ahead of them, Stephen should know the Scriptures.

"Leading and *being* led," observed the angel, whose memory, it seemed, had begun to return. "By two strapping husbands. Though," she hurried to explain, "not at the same time. Yes, I think you should call me Ruth."

She is much too young for Ruth, thought John, who guessed her to be about fifteen (though of course as an angel she might be fifteen thousand). The same age as Stephen, whose thoughts were attuned to angelic visions but whose bodily urges were not in the least celestial. Unlike a Knight

Templar, he had made no vow of chastity. The situation was not propi-
tious for a Crusade in the name of God.

But once they had entered the Weald, the largest forest in southern England, he thought of Mandrakes and griffins instead of Ruth. It was true
that the Stane, an old Roman highway, crossed the Weald to join London and Chichester—they would meet it within the hour—but even the
Stane was not immune to the forest.

II

At Ruth's suggestion, they carefully skirted the grounds of a neighboring
castle, the Boar's Lair.

"Someone might recognize John," she said. "Send word to his father."

"Yes," John agreed, staring at the Norman tower, one of the black
wooden keeps built by William the Conqueror to enforce his conquest.
"My father and Philip the Boar were once friends. Philip used to dine with
us on Michaelmas and other feast days, and I played the kettledrums for
him. Since then, he and my father have fallen out about their boundaries.
They both claim a certain grove of beechnut trees—pannage for their
swine. Philip wouldn't be hospitable, I'm sure."

Deviously, circuitously, by way of a placid stream and an old waterwheel
whose power no longer turned millstones and ground wheat into flour,
they reached the Roman Stane. Once a proud thoroughfare for uncon-
querable legions, it had since resounded to Saxon, Viking, and Norman,
who had used it for commerce and war but, unlike the conscientious Romans, never repaired the ravages of wheels and weather. Now it had
shrunk in places to the width of a peasant's cart, but the smooth Roman
blocks, set in concrete, still provided a path for riders and walkers and
great ladies in litters between two horses.

"I feel like the Stane," sighed Ruth, "much-trodden and a trifle weedy."
She had torn the edge of her robe on prickly sedges and muddied the
white linen. She had lost the circlet which haloed her head, and her silken
tresses, gold as the throats of convolvulus flowers, had spilled like their
trailing leafage over her shoulders. As for John, he was hot, breathless,
and moist with sweat, and wishing that, like a serf, he dared to remove
his long-sleeved tunic and revel in his breechclout.

"Stephen," Ruth called, "now that we've found the road, can't we rest
a little?" Her speech, though still melodious, had relaxed into easy, in-
formal English.

"We've just begun!" He laughed. "London lies days away. We want to
be leagues down the road before night."

"But it's mid-afternoon. Why not rest till it gets a little cooler?"

"Very well." He smiled, reaching out to touch her in good-humored acquiescence. Stephen, who found difficulty with words, spoke with his hands, which were nests to warm a bird, balms to heal a dog, bows to extract the music from swinging a scythe, wielding an ax, gathering branches for firewood. He could gesture or point or touch with the exquisite eloquence of a man who was deaf, dumb, and blind. When you said good morning to him, he clapped you on the shoulder. When you walked with him, he brushed against you or caught you by the arm. He liked to climb trees for the rough feel of the bark or swim in a winter stream and slap the icy currents until he warmed his body. But he saved his touch for the things or the people he loved. Neither ugly things nor unkind people.

"We'll rest as long as you like," he said.

Ruth smiled. "I think I should borrow one of your tunics. You see how my robe keeps dragging the ground."

With a flutter of modesty she withdrew to a clump of bracken and changed to a tunic.

"Watch out for basilisks," John called after her. "Their bite is fatal, you know." He muttered under his breath to Stephen, "First she ate your food, and now she wears your clothes."

"*Our* food and clothes," reproved Stephen. "Remember, we're Crusaders together."

John was shamed into silence. He had to listen to Ruth as she bent branches, snapped twigs, and rustled cloth, almost as if she wished to advertise the various stages of her change. He thought of the wenches—ten? twenty?—who had disrobed for Stephen. The subject of sexual love confused him. The Aristotelian processes of his brain refused to sift, clarify, and evaluate the problem; in fact, they crumpled like windmills caught in a forest fire. He had loved his mother—what was the word?—filially; Stephen he loved fraternally. But as for the other thing, well, he had not been able to reconcile the courtly code as sung by the troubadours—roses and guerdons and troths of deathless fidelity—and the sight of Stephen, surprised last year in his loft with a naked wench and not in the least embarrassed. Stephen had grinned and said, "In a year or so, John, we can wench together!" The girl, snickering and making no effort to hide her nakedness, had seemed to him one of those Biblical harlots who ought to be shorn, or stoned. Who could blame poor Stephen for yielding to such allurements? As for himself, however, he had sworn the chivalric oath to practice poverty, chastity, and obedience to God. He had thought of a monastery but rather than part with Stephen, who was not in the least monastic, he was willing to try a life of action.

"Has a crow got your tongue?" asked Stephen with a smile. "I didn't mean to scold." He encircled John's shoulder with his arm. "You smell like cloves."

John stiffened, not at the touch but at what appeared to be an insinuation. He had not forgotten his father's taunt: "Girl!" According to custom, it was girls and women who packed their gowns in clove-scented chests, while the men of a castle hung their robes in the room called the *garderobe,* another name for the lavatory cut in the wall beside the stairs, with a round shaft dropping to the moat. The stench of the shaft protected the room—and the robes—from moths.

"They belonged to my mother," he stammered. "The cloves, I mean. I still use her chest."

"My mother put flowering mint with her clothes," said Stephen. "All two gowns! I like the cloves better, though. Maybe the scent will rub off on me. I haven't bathed for a week." He gave John's shoulder a squeeze, and John knew that his manhood had not been belittled. But then, Stephen had never belittled him, had he? Teased him, yes, hurt him in play, and once knocked him down for stepping on the tail of a dog; but never had he made light of John's manliness.

"It's not a dangerous road," Stephen continued, talkative for once, perhaps because John was silent. "The abbots of Chichester patrol it for brigands. They don't carry swords, but Gabriel help the thief who falls afoul of their staves!"

"But the forest," John said. "It's all around us like a pride of griffins. With green, scaly wings. They look as if they're going to eat up the road. They've already nibbled away the edges, and"—he lowered his voice—*"she* came out of the forest, didn't she?"

Stephen laughed. "She came out of the sky, simpleton! What does it take to convince you? Didn't you hear her say she don't know nothing about the forest?"

Before John could lecture Stephen on his lapse in grammar, Ruth exploded between them as green as a down in the tenderness of spring. She blazed in Stephen's tunic, its hood drawn over her head. She had bound her waist with the gold sash from her robe and, discarding her velvet slippers, donned his wooden clogs, whose very ugliness emphasized the delicacy of her bare feet. She had bundled her linen robe around her slippers and crucifix.

"No one would ever guess that I'm an angel," she said, smiling. "Or even a girl."

"Not an angel," said Stephen appreciatively. "But a girl, yes. You'd have to roughen your hands and hide your curls to pass for a boy."

She made a pretense of hiding her hair, but furtively shook additional curls from her hood the moment they resumed their journey, and began to sing a familiar song of the day:

> *In a valley of this restless mind,*
> *I sought in mountain and in mead. . . .*

Though she sang about a man searching for Christ, the words rippled from her tongue as merrily as if she were singing a carol. John wished for his kettledrums and Stephen began to whistle. Thus, they forgot the desolation of the road, largely untraveled at such an hour and looking as if the griffin-scaly forest would soon complete its meal.

Then, swinging around a bend and almost trampling them, cantered a knight with a red cross painted on his shield—a Knight Templar, it seemed—and after him, on a large piebald palfrey, a lady riding pillion behind a servant who never raised his eyes from the road. The knight frowned at them; in spite of the vows demanded of his order, he looked more dedicated to war than to God. But the lady smiled and asked their destination.

"I live in a castle up the road," said John quickly in Norman French. Unlike his friends, he was dressed in the mode of a young gentleman, with a tunic of plum-colored linen instead of cheap muslin, and a samite belt brocaded with silver threads. Thus, he must be their spokesman. "I have come with my friends to search for chestnuts in the woods, and now we are going home."

The knight darkened his frown to a baleful glare and reined his steed, as if he suspected John of stealing a fine tunic to masquerade as the son of a gentlemen. Boys of noble birth, even of twelve, did not as a rule go nutting with villeins whom they called their friends, and not at such an hour.

"We have passed no castle for many miles," he growled, laying a thick-veined hand on the hilt of his sword.

"My father's is well off the road, and the keep is low," answered John without hesitation. "In fact, it is called the Tortoise, and it is *very* hard to break, like a tortoiseshell. Many a baron has tried!"

"Mind you get back to the Tortoise before dark," the lady admonished. "You haven't a shell yourself, and the Stane is dangerous after nightfall. My protector and I are bound for the castle of our friend, Philip the Boar. Is it far, do you know?"

"About two leagues," said John, and he gave her explicit directions in French so assured and polished that no one, not even the glowering knight, could doubt his Norman blood and his noble birth. It was always true of him that he was only frightened in anticipation. Now, with a wave and a courtly bow, he bade them Godspeed to the castle of the Boar, received a smile from the lady, and led his friends toward the mythical Tortoise.

"Such a handsome lad," he heard the lady exclaim, "and manly as well."

"If I hadn't been so scared," said Stephen, once a comfortable distance separated them from the knight, his lady, and the unresponsive servant, "I'd have split my tunic when you said your castle was named the Tortoise.

There isn't a castle for the next ten miles! It's the first fib I ever heard you tell."

"You were scared too?" asked John, surprised at such an admission.

"You can bet your belt I was! They were lovers, you know. Bound for a tryst at the castle of the Boar. He winks at such things, I hear. Runs a regular brothel for the gentry, including himself. That lady has a husband somewhere, and the Knight Templar might just have run us through to keep us from carrying tales."

With the fall of darkness, they selected a broad and voluminous oak tree, rather like a thicket set on the mast of a ship, and between them the boys helped Ruth to climb the trunk. With nimble hands, she prepared a nest of leaves and moss in the crook of the tree and, having removed her clogs and hidden them, along with her crucifix, settled herself with the comfort of perfect familiarity. She seemed to have a talent for nests, above or below the ground. After she had eaten some bread and cheese and drunk some beer, she returned to the ground, stubbornly refusing assistance from either boy, and showed herself a more than adept climber.

"Is she angry with us?" asked John.

"She drank all that beer," explained Stephen, "and while she's gone—"

They scrambled to the edge of the nest and, bracing themselves against a limb, aimed at the next oak. Gleefully, John pretended that Ruth was crouching under the branches.

He was sorry to see her emerge from an elm instead of the inundated oak and rejoin them in the nest.

"I was looking for rushes to keep us warm," she said. "But I didn't find a single one. We'll have to lie close together." She chose the middle of the nest, anticipating, no doubt, a boy to warm her on either side, and Stephen stretched on her left.

With the speed and deftness of Lucifer disguised as a serpent, John wriggled between them, forcing Ruth to the far side of the nest. Much to his disappointment, she accepted the arrangement without protest and leaned against him with a fragrance of galangal, the aromatic plant imported from Outre-Mer and used as base for perfume by the ladies of England.

"The stars are bright tonight," she said. "See, John, there's Arcturus peeping through the leaves, and there's Sirius, the North Star. The Vikings called it the Lamp of the Wanderer."

Stephen nudged him as if to say, "You see! Only an angel knows such things."

"Stephen," he whispered.

"Yes?"

"I'm not afraid anymore. Of leaving the castle. Not even of the forest!"

"Aren't you, John?"

"Because I'm not alone."

"I told you we were safe with our angel."

"I don't mean the angel." He made a pillow of Stephen's shoulder, and the scent of dogs and haylofts effaced Ruth's galangal.

"Go to sleep, little brother. Dream about London—and the Holy Land."

But fear returned to John before he could dream. At an hour with the feel of midnight, chill and misty and hushed of owls, he was roused by the blast of a horn and a simultaneous shriek like that of a hundred otters caught in a mill wheel. The sounds seemed to come from a distance and yet were harsh enough to make him throw up his hands to his ears.

"Hunters have found a Mandrake!" cried Stephen, sitting up in the nest. "It's a moonless night, and it must be just after twelve. That's when they hunt, you know. They blow on a horn to muffle the shriek. Let's see what they've caught."

But John was not eager to leave the tree. "If they've killed a Mandrake, they won't want to share it. Besides, they might be brigands."

Ruth had also been roused by the shriek. "John is right," she said. "You shouldn't want to see such a horrible sight. A baby torn from the earth!"

"I'll stay and keep Ruth company," said John, but Stephen hauled him out of the nest and sent him slipping and scraping down the trunk.

"But we can't leave Ruth alone!" he groaned, picking himself up from a bed of acorns.

"Angels don't need protection. Hurry now, or we'll miss the hunters."

They found the Mandrake hunters across the road and deep among the trees, a pair of rough woodsmen, father and son to judge from their height, build, and flaxen hair, though the elder was as bent and brown as a much-used sickle, and his son wore a patch over one of his eyes. The woodsmen were contemplating a dead Mandrake the size and shape of a newborn baby, except for the dirt-trailing tendrils, the outsized genitals, and the greenish tangle of hair which had grown above ground with purple, bell-shaped flowers. The pathetic body twitched like a hatcheted chicken. Dead at its side and bound to it by a rope lay a dog with bloody ears.

Though the night was moonless and the great stars, Arcturus and Sirius, were veiled by the mist of the forest, one of the hunters carried a lantern, and John saw the Mandrake, the dog, the blood in an eerie, flickering light which made him remember Lucifer's fall to Hell and wonder if he and Stephen had fallen after him.

One of the woodsmen saw them. "Might have gotten yourselves killed, both of you," he scolded, digging beeswax out of his ears with his little finger. "Laid out like that old hound with busted eardrums." He removed a long-bladed knife from his tunic and under his father's direction—"No, no, clean and quick. Cut it, don't bruise it"—sliced the Mandrake into little rootlike portions, resinous rather than bloody, which he wrapped in strips of muslin and placed carefully in a sharkskin pouch.

"One less of the devils," muttered the father, unbending himself to a rake instead of a sickle. "Another week and it'd have climbed right out of the ground. Joined its folk in the warrens."

"A Richard's ransom in aphro-aphro*disiacs!*" stuttered the son, completing the word with a flourish of triumph. The market for Mandrake roots was lucrative and inexhaustible: aging barons deserted by sexual powers, lovers whose love was unrequited. From Biblical times, the times of Jacob and Leah, the root had been recognized as the one infallible aphrodisiac. Yes, a Richard's ransom was hardly an overstatement. A man would pay gold and silver, land and livestock, to win his love or resurrect his lust.

When the woodsmen had finished their grisly dissection, the son smiled at the boys and offered them a fragment the size of a small pea. "You fellows put this in a girl's gruel, and she'll climb all over you."

"He doesn't need it," said John, intercepting the gift. "Girls climb over him as it is. Like ants on a crock of sugar!"

"But you need it, eh?" The son laughed, winking his single eye at John. One-eyed serfs were common in France and England, and most of them had lost their eyes to angry masters and not in fights. Perhaps the young woodsman had not been prompt to deliver firewood for the hearth in a great hall. "Now you'll be the crock. But where's the sugar?"

"He'll have it," said Stephen, noticing John's embarrassment. "Sugar enough for a nest! Give him a year or two. He's only twelve." Then he pointed to the carcass of the dog. "Did you have to use a greyhound? Couldn't you have done it yourselves? After all, you had the wax in your ears."

"Everyone knows a dog gives a sharper jerk. Gets the whole Mandrake at once. Like pulling a tooth, root and all. Besides, he was an old dog. Not many more years in his bones. We can buy a whole kennel with what we make from the root."

When the men had departed, talking volubly about the sale of their treasure at the next fair, and how they would spend their money in secret and keep their lord from his customary third, the boys buried the dog.

"I wish they had put beeswax in his ears too," said Stephen bitterly. "And see where they whipped him to make him jump!"

"Beeswax doesn't help a dog," said John. "At least I read that in a bestiary. His ears are so keen that the shriek penetrates the wax and kills him anyway."

"It's no wonder the Mandrakes eat us. The way we drag their babies from the ground and cut them up! If it weren't for my parents, I could pity the poor little brutes. Now, a lot of dirty old men will strut like cox-combs and chase after kitchen wenches."

"I suppose," said John, who had furtively buried the fragment of Man-drake with the dog, "the question is, who started eating whom first." Then he clutched Stephen's hand and said, "I think I'm going to be sick."

"No, you're not," said Stephen, steadying John with his arm. "We're going back to the tree and get some sleep."

But Stephen was trembling too; John could feel the tremors in his arm. *He's sad for the dog,* he thought. *I won't be sick. It would only make him sadder.*

Ruth was waiting for them with a look which they could not read in the misted light of the stars.

"We're sorry we left you so long," said Stephen, "but the hunters had just killed a Mandrake, and . . ."

"I don't want to hear about it."

"Mandrakes can't climb trees, can they?" asked John. "The parents might be about, you know."

"Of course they can climb trees," said Stephen, who was very knowl-edgeable about the woods and improvised what he did not know. "They *are* trees, in a way. Roots at least."

"Do you think they suspect we're up here? From the ground, they can't see us, but can they sniff us out?"

"I wish you two would stop talking about Mandrakes," snapped Ruth. "You would think they surrounded us, when everyone knows the poor creatures are almost extinct."

"Stephen's parents were killed by Mandrakes," said John sharply. He would have liked to slap the girl. She had a genius for interruptions or improprieties. It was proper and generous for Stephen to express com-passion for a Mandrake baby, but unforgivable for this ignorant girl to sympathize with the whole murderous race. Her ethereal origins now seemed about as likely to him as an angel dancing on the head of a pin, a possibility which, to John's secret amusement, his abbot had often de-bated with utmost seriousness.

Ruth gave a cry. "I didn't know."

"How could you?" said Stephen. "At least the ones who killed my par-ents fought like men. They didn't sneak up in the dark. They stormed out of the forest before dusk, waving their filthy arms and swinging clubs. We had a chance against them—except my mother, who was bringing us beer in the fields. We were haying at the time and we had our scythes for weapons. They only got one of us besides my parents, and we got four of them. It's the females who're really dangerous—the young ones who pass for human and come to live in the towns. The males can't do it, they're much too hairy right from the start, and—well, *you* know. Too well endowed. But the little girls look human, at least on the outside. Inside, it's a different matter—resin instead of blood, brown skeletons which're—what would you call them, John?"

"Fibrous."

Ruth listened in silence and shrank herself into a little ball. *Like a diadem spider,* thought John, *with brilliant gold patterns, drawing in her legs and looking half her size.*

"Tell her about them, John," said Stephen, who was getting breathless from such a long speech. "You know the whole story." And then to Ruth: "He knows everything. French, English, Latin. All our kings and queens from Arthur down to bad old King John. Even those naughty pagan goddesses who went about naked and married their brothers."

John was delighted to continue the history. He liked to deliver lectures, but nobody except Stephen ever listened to him.

"In the old days, before the Crusades," said John, who warmed to his tale like a traveling storyteller, "in the old days the Mandrakes lived in the forest, and they were so dirty and hairy that you could never mistake them for human. They weren't particular about their diet. They liked any meat—animal or human—and they trapped hunters in nets and roasted them over hot coals and then strewed their bones on the ground as we do with drumsticks at Michaelmas." Here, like a skilled jongleur, he paused and looked at Ruth to gauge the effect of his tale. The sight of her reassured him. If she pressed any harder against the edge of the nest, she would roll from the tree. "But one day a little Mandrake girl wandered out of the forest, and a simple blacksmith mistook her for a lost human child, naked and dirty from the woods, and took her into his family. The child grew plump and beautiful, the man and his wife grew peaked, and everyone said how generous it was for a poor blacksmith to give his choicest food—and there wasn't much food that winter for anyone—to a foundling. But in the summer the girl was run down and killed by a wagon loaded with hay. The townspeople were all ready to garrot the driver—until they noticed that the girl's blood was a mixture of normal red fluid and thick, viscous resin."

"What does 'viscous' mean?" interrupted Stephen.

"Gluey. Like that stuff that comes out of a spider when she's spinning her web. Thus, it was learned that Mandrakes are vampires as well as cannibals, and that the more they feed on humans, the less resinous their blood becomes, until the resin is almost replaced, though their bones never do turn white. But they have to keep on feeding or else their blood will revert.

"Well, the Mandrakes heard about the girl—from a runaway thief, no doubt, before they ate him—and how she had 'passed' until the accident. They decided to send some more of their girls into the villages, where life was easier than in the forest. Some of the Mandrakes slipped into houses at night and left their babies, well-scrubbed of course, in exchange for humans, which they carried off into the woods for you can imagine what foul purposes. The next morning the family would think that the fairies had brought them a changeling, and everyone knows that if you disown a fairy's child, you'll have bad luck for the rest of your life. It was a long time before the plan of the Mandrakes became generally known around the forest. Now, whenever a mother finds a strange baby in her crib, or a new child wanders into town, it's usually stuck with a knife. If resin flows out, the child is suffocated and burned. Still, an occasional Mandrake does manage to pass.

"You see, they aren't at all like the Crusaders in the last century who became vampires when they marched through Hungary—the Hungarian camp followers, remember, gave them the sickness, and then the Crusaders brought it back to England. They had to break the skin to get at your blood, and they had a cadaverous look about them before they fed, and then they grew pink and bloated. It was no problem to recognize and burn them. But the Mandrake girls, by simply pressing their lips against your skin, can draw blood right through the pores, and the horrible thing is that they don't look like vampires and sometimes they don't even know what they are or how they were born from a seed in the ground. They feed in a kind of dream and forget everything the next morning."

"I think it's monstrous," said Ruth.

"They are, aren't they?" agreed John happily, satisfied that his story had been a success.

"Not *them*. I mean sticking babies with knives."

"But how else can you tell them from roots? It's because a few people are sentimental like you that Mandrakes still manage to pass."

"Frankly," said Ruth, "I don't think Mandrakes pass at all. I think they keep to themselves in the forest and eat venison and berries and *not* hunters. Now go to sleep. From what you've told me, it's a long way to London. We all need some rest."

"Good night," said Stephen.

"Sweet dreams," said Ruth.

III

The next morning, the sun was a Saracen shield in the sky—Saladin's Shield, a Crusader would have said—and the forest twinkled with paths of sunlight and small white birds which spun in the air or perched on limbs and constantly flickered their tails. Ruth and Stephen stood in the crook of the tree and smiled down at John as he opened his eyes.

"We decided to let you sleep," said Stephen. "You grunted like a boar when I first shook you. So we followed a wagtail to find some breakfast."

"And found you some wild strawberries," said Ruth, her lips becomingly red from the fruit. She gave him a deep, brimming bowl. "I wove it from sedges." For one who professed an ignorance of the forest, she possessed some remarkable skills.

Once on the ground, they finished their breakfast with three-cornered, burry beechnuts, which required some skillful pounding and deft fingers to extract the kernels; and Ruth, appropriating Stephen's beer, took such a generous swallow that she drained the flask.

"To wash down the beechnuts," she explained.

"I don't know why the pigs like them so much," said Stephen. "They're not worth the trouble of shelling."

"The pigs don't shell them," reminded the practical John.

"Anyway," continued Stephen, "we hadn't much choice in this part of the forest. We found a stream, though." Hoisting the pouch which held their remnants of food and their few extra garments, he said, "Ruth, get your bundle and let's take a swim."

"I hid it," she reminded him, almost snappishly. "There may be thieves about. I'll get it after we swim."

All that mystery about a crucifix, thought John. *As if she suspected Stephen and me of being brigands. And after she drank our beer!*

The stream idled instead of gushed, and pepperwort, shaped like four-leafed clovers, grew in the quiet waters along the banks. Stephen, who took a monthly bath in a tub with the stable hands while the daughters of villeins doused him with water, hurried to pull his tunic over his head. He was justly proud of his body and had once remarked to John, "The less I wear, the better I look. In a gentleman's clothes like yours, I'd still be a yokel. But naked—! Even gentlewomen seem to stare."

But John was quick to restore the proprieties. In the presence of Ruth, he had no intention of showing his thin, white body, or allowing Stephen to show his radiant nakedness.

"You can swim first," he said to her. "Stephen and I will wait in the woods."

"No," she laughed. "You go first. Stephen is already down to his breech-clout, and *that* is about to fall. But I won't be far away."

"You won't peep, will you?" John called after her, but Ruth, striding into the forest as if she had a destination, did not answer him.

The stream was chilly in spite of the Saracen sun. John huddled among the pepperwort, the water as high as his knees, till Stephen drenched him with a monumental splash, and then they frolicked among the plants and into the current and scraped each other's backs with sand scooped from the bottom and, as far as John was concerned, Ruth and the road to London could wait till the Second Coming!

When they climbed at last on the bank, they rolled in the grass to dry their bodies. Stephen, an expert wrestler, surprised John with what he called his amphisbaena grip; his arms snaked around John's body like the ends of the two-headed serpent and flattened him on the ground.

"I'm holding you for ransom," he cried, perched on John's chest like the sasprite Dylan astride a dolphin. "Six flagons of beer with roasted malt!"

"I promise–" John began, and freed himself with such a burst of strength that Stephen sprawled in the grass beneath the lesser but hardly less insistent weight of John. "I promise you sixteen licks with an abbot's rod!"

Stephen was not disgruntled. "By Robin's bow," he cried, "you've learned all my tricks!"

"I guess we had better dress," said John, releasing his friend to avoid another reversal. "Ruth will want to swim too. I hope she didn't peep," he added, looking askance at some furiously agitated ferns beyond the grassy bank. To his great relief, they disgorged a white wagtail and not a girl. Still, something had frightened the bird.

"What do you think she would see?" laughed Stephen.

"You," said John, eyeing his friend with an admiration which was more wistful than envious. Stephen was a boy with a man's body, "roseate-brown from toe to crown," to quote a popular song, and comely enough to tempt an angel. When he shook his wet hair, a great armful of daffodils seemed to bestrew his head. A marriage of beauty and strength, thought John. For the hundredth time he marveled that such a boy could have chosen him for a brother; actually chosen, when they had no bond of blood, nor even of race. He peered down at himself and wished for his clothes. At the castle he never bathed in the tub with his father's friends: only with Stephen, sometimes, in the stream of the old millwheel, or alone in the heath from his own little bucket (even in the castle, he had no private room, but slept with the rancid sons of his father's knights).

But Stephen said, "You know, John, you're not so skinny now. You've started to fill out. The bones are there. The strength too, as you just proved. All you need is a little more meat. You'll be a man before you know it."

"Next year?" asked John, though such a prospect seemed as far from his grasp as a fiery-plummaged phoenix. "You were a man at thirteen."

"Eleven. But I'm different. I'm a villein. We grow fast. With you, I'd say two or possibly three more years. Then we can wench together for sure."

"Who would want me when she could have you?"

Stephen led him to the bank of the stream. "Look," he said, and pointed to their reflections in a space of clear water between the pepperworts: the bright and the dark, side by side, the two faces of the moon. "I have muscles, yes. But you have brains. They show in your face."

"I don't like my face. I won't even look in those glass mirrors they bring back from the Holy Land. I always look startled."

"Not as much as you did. Why, just since we left the castle, I've seen a change. Yesterday, when you faced down the Knight Templar, I was ready to wet my breechclout! But you never batted an eye. And you looked so *wise*. One day you'll have my muscles, but you can bet a brace of pheasants I'll never have your brains. Come on now, let's give Ruth a chance."

At Stephen's insistence—and he had to insist vigorously—they bundled their tunics and wore only their breechclouts, the shapeless strips of cloth which every man, whether priest, baron, or peasant, twisted around his loins. Now they would look like field hands stripped for a hot day's work, and John's fine tunic would not arouse suspicion or tempt thieves.

"But my shoulders," John began. "They're so white."

"They'll brown in the sun on the way to London," Stephen said, and then, "Ruth, you can take your swim!"

He had to repeat her name before she answered in a thin, distant voice: "Yes, Stephen?"

"You can swim now. You'll have the stream to yourself." To John he smiled. "She took you seriously about not peeping. But you know, John, *we* didn't promise."

"You'd spy on an angel?"

Stephen slapped his back. "Now who's calling her an angel? No, I wouldn't spy. I'd just *think* about it. I've always wondered if angels are built like girls. Let's do a bit of exploring while she bathes. I could eat another breakfast after that swim. But we mustn't stray too far from the stream."

Beyond a coppice of young beeches, Stephen discovered a cluster of slender stalks with fragrant, wispy leaves. "Fennels. Good for the fever you catch in London. We might just pick a few, roots and all."

But John, thinking of Mandrakes, had no use for roots and followed his nose to a bed of mint. "This is what your mother used to sweeten her gowns, isn't it?"

"Yes, and it's also good to eat." They knelt in the moist soil to pluck and chew the leaves, whose sweetly burning juices left them hoarse and breathless, as if they had gulped a heady muscatel.

But where was the stream, the road, the oak in which they had slept?

"The trees all look the same," said Stephen, "but there, that old beech. Haven't we seen it before? And there, the torn ground—"

They had wandered, it seemed, to the place of the Mandrake hunt. The hole remained in the earth, disturbingly human-shaped, with branching clefts from which the limbs had been wrenched by the hapless dog.

"Let's get away from here," said John, as nausea slapped him like the foul air of a *garderobe*.

"Wait," said Stephen. "There's a second hole. It's—it's where we buried the dog. *God's bowels!*" It was his crudest oath. "The dirty Infidels have dug him up and—"

Around the hole they saw a litter of bones . . . skull . . . femur . . . pelvis . . . stripped of their meat and scattered carelessly through the grass.

"Stephen," said John, seizing his friend's hand. "I know how you feel. It was cruel of them to eat the dog. But we've got to get away from here. They'll take us for the hunters!"

Something had waited for them.

At first it looked like a tree. No, a corpse exhumed from a grave with roots entwining its limbs. It wheezed, lurched, moved, swaying toward them. It was bleached to the color of a beechnut trunk—at least, those parts of the skin (or was it bark?) that showed through the greenish forest of hair (or rootlets?). Red eyes burned in black hollows. (*Tiny fire-dragon peering from caves,* thought John.) The mouth seemed a single harelip until it split into a grin which revealed triangular teeth like those of a shark: to crush, tear, shred.

"Run!" screamed John, tugging at his friend, but proud Stephen had chosen to fight.

"Dog-eater!" He charged the Mandrake and used his head for a ram.

The creature buckled like a rotten door but flung out its limbs and enveloped Stephen into its fall; fallen, it seemed a vegetable octopus, lashing viny tentacles around its prey.

Unlike Stephen, John grew cold with anger instead of hot; blue instead of flushed, as if he had plunged in a river through broken ice. First he was stunned. Then the frostcaves of his brain functioned with crystalline clarity. He knew that he was young and relatively weak; against that bark-tough skin, his naked fists would beat in vain. A blind, weaponless charge would not avail his friend. He fell to his knees and mole-like clawed the ground. Pebbles. Pinecones. Beechnuts. Pretty, petty, useless. Then, a stone, large and jagged. With raw, bleeding hands, he wrestled the earth for his desperately needed weapon and, without regaining his feet, lunged at the fallen Mandrake. The fibrous skull cracked and splintered sickeningly beneath the stone and spewed him with resin and green vegetable matter, like a cabbage crushed by a millstone.

"Stephen!" he cried, but the answer hissed above him, shrill with loathing.

"Human!"

Multitudinous fingers caught and bound him with coils of wild grapevine and dragged him, together with Stephen, over the bruising earth.

The Mandrake warrens were not so much habitations as lightless catacombs for avoiding men and animals. No one knew if the creatures had

built them or had found, enlarged, and connected natural caves and covered the floors with straw. John was painfully conscious as his thin body,
little protected by the shreds of his breechclout, lurched and scraped
down a tortuous passage like the throat of a dragon. His captors, he
guessed, could see in the dark, but only the scraping of Stephen's body
told him that he had not been separated from his friend.

"Mother of God," he breathed, "let him stay unconscious!"

For a long time he had to judge their passage from room to room by
the sudden absence of straw which marked a doorway. Finally, a capri-
cious light announced their approach to a fire, a council chamber perhaps—the end of the brutal journey.

The room of the fire was a round, spacious chamber where Mandrake
females were silently engaged in piling chunks of peat on a bed of coals.
Neither roots nor branches were used as fuel, John saw, since that which
began as a root did not use wood for any purpose. Wryly he wondered
how the Mandrakes would feel if they knew that the fuel they burned
had once been vegetation.

Their captors dumped them as men might deposit logs beside a hearth,
and joined the women in feeding the fire. John was tightly trussed, his
feet crossed, his hands behind his back, but he rolled his body to lie on
his side and look at Stephen's face. His friend's cheeks were scratched;
his forehead was blue with a large bruise; and the daffodils of his hair
were wilted with blood and cobwebs.

"Stephen, Stephen, what have they done to you?" he whispered, biting his lip to stifle the threat of tears. His hero, fallen, moved him to tenderness transcending worship. For once he had to be strong for Stephen.
He had to think of escape.

He examined the room. There were neither beds nor pallets. Apparently the Mandrakes slept in the smaller rooms and used their council
chamber as a baron used his hall. It was here that they met to talk and
feast. The earthen walls were blackened from many fires. Bones littered
the straw, together with teeth, fur, and hair: inedible items. The stench of
the refuse was overpowering and, coupled with that of excrement and
urine, almost turned John's stomach. He fought nausea by wondering how
his fastidious abbot would have faced the situation: identified himself, no
doubt, with Hercules in the Augean stables or Christ amid the corrup-
tions of the Temple.

Then, across the room, he saw the crucifix. Yes, it was unmistakable,
a huge stone cross. Latin, with arms of unequal length, and set in an alcove shaped like an apse. Turtle-backed stones served as seats. Between
the seats the ground had been packed and brushed by the knees of sup-
pliants. The place was clearly a chapel, and John remembered the tale—
a myth, he had always supposed—that after the Christians had come to
England with Augustine, a priest had visited the Mandrakes in their war-

rens. Once they had eaten him, they had reconsidered his words and adopted Christianity.

"Bantling-killer!"

A Mandrake slouched above him, exuding a smell of tarns stagnant with scum. His voice was guttural and at first unintelligible. Bantling-killer. Of course. *Baby*-killer. The creature was speaking an early form of English. He went on to curse all athelings in their byrnies—knights in their mail—and to wish that the whale-road would swallow the last of them as they sailed to their wars in ring-prowed ships of wood. Then, having blasted John's people, he became specific and accused John and Stephen of having killed the bantling with their dog. *His* bantling, he growled, grown from his own seed. Though the Mandrakes copulated like men and animals, John gathered that their females gave birth to objects resembling acorns, which they planted in the ground and nurtured into roots. If allowed by hunters to reach maturity, the roots burst from the ground like a turtle out of an egg, and their mothers bundled them into the warrens to join the tribe—hence, the word "bantling," from "bantle" or "bundle."

"No." John shook his head. "No. We did not kill your baby. Your bantling. It was hunters who killed him!"

The creature grinned. A grin, it seemed, was a Mandrake's one expression; anger or pleasure provoked the same bared teeth. Otherwise, he looked as vacant as a cabbage.

"Hunters," he said. "You."

The crowded room had grown as hot as the kitchen before a feast in a castle, but the figures tending the fire, hunched as if with the weight of dirt, toil, and time, seemed impervious to the heat. They had obviously built the fire to cook their dinner, and now they began to sharpen stakes on weathered stones. Even the stakes were tin instead of wood.

The whir of the flames must have alerted the young Mandrakes in the adjacent chambers. They trooped into the room and gathered, gesticulating, around the two captives. They had not yet lapsed into the tired shuffle of their elders; they looked both energetic and intelligent. Life in the forest, it seemed, slowly stultified quick minds and supple bodies. It was not surprising that the weary elders, however they hated men, should try to pass their daughters into the villages.

The girls John saw, except for one, appeared to be adolescents, but hair had already forested their arms and thickened their lips. The one exception, a child of perhaps four, twinkled a wistful prettiness through her grime. Her eyes had not yet reddened and sunken into their sockets; her mouth was the color of wild raspberries. She could still have passed.

The children seemed to have come from the midst of a game. Dice, it appeared, from the small white objects they rattled, a little like the whale-bone cubes which delighted the knights in John's castle. But the dice of the Mandrake children were not so much cubes as irregular, bony lumps scratched with figures. The Greeks, John recalled from the abbot's lectures, had used the knucklebones of sheep and other animals in place of cubes.

But the Mandrake children had found a livelier game. They stripped John and Stephen of their breechclouts and began to prod their flesh with fingers like sharp carrots and taunt them for the inadequacy of human loins. The Mandrake boys, naked like their parents, possessed enormous genitals; hence, the potency of the murdered, fragmented roots as aphrodisiacs. Stephen stirred fitfully but to John's relief did not awake to find himself the object of ridicule. With excellent reason, he had always taken pride in the badge of his manhood, and to find himself surpassed and taunted by boys of eight and nine would have hurt him more than blows. Only the girl of four, staring reproachfully at her friends, took no part in the game.

A church bell chimed, eerily, impossibly it seemed to John in such a place, and a hush enthralled the room. An aged Mandrake, rather like a tree smothered by moss, hobbled among the silenced children and paused between John and Stephen. Examining. Deliberating. Choosing. He chose Stephen. When he tried to stoop, however, his back creaked like a rusty drawbridge. *He will break,* thought John. *He will never reach the ground.* But he reached the ground and gathered Stephen in his mossy arms.

"Bloody Saracen!" shouted John. "Take your hands off my friend!" Stretching prodigiously, he managed to burst the bonds which held his ankles and drive his knee into the Mandrake's groin. The creature gave such a yelp that red-hot pokers seemed to have gouged John's ears. He writhed on the ground and raised his hands to shut out the shriek and the pain. Shadows cobwebbed his brain. When he struggled back to clarity, Stephen lay in the chapel before the crucifix. Looming above him, the aged Mandrake stood like Abraham above Isaac. The other adults, perhaps twenty of them, sat on the turtle-shaped stones, while the children sat near the fire to watch the proceedings from which their elders had barred them. The impression John caught of their faces—brief, fleeting, hazy with smoke and the dim light of the room—was not one of malice or even curiosity, but respect and fear, and the pretty child had turned her back and buried her face in the arms of an older girl.

The officiating Mandrake intoned what seemed to be a prayer and a dedication. John caught words resembling "Father" and "Son" and realized with horror if not surprise that just as the Christian humans burned a Yule log and decked their castles with hawthorn, holly, and mistletoe in honor of Christ, so the Christian Mandrakes were dedicating Stephen to a different conception of the same Christ. First, the offering, then the feast. The same victim would serve both purposes.

He had already burst the grapevines which held his ankles. In spite of his bound hands, he struggled to his feet and reeled toward the chapel. Once, he had killed a Mandrake with cold implacability. Now he had turned to fire: the Greek fire of the East, hurled at ships and flung from walls; asphalt and crude petroleum, sulphur and lime, leaping and licking to the incandescence of Hell. He felt as if stones and Mandrakes must yield before his advance; as if Mary, the Mother of Christ, must descend from the castles of heaven or climb from the sanctuary of his heart and deliver his friend.

But the Mandrakes rose in a solid palisade, and, shrunk to a boy of twelve, he hammered his impotent fists against their wood.

"No," he sobbed, falling to his knees. "Me. Not Stephen."

"JOHN."

His name tolled through the room like the clash of a mace against an iron helmet. "John, he will be all right." Her flaxen hair, coarsened with dirt and leaves, rioted over her shoulders like tarnished gold coins. She wore her linen robe, but the white cloth had lost its purity to stains and tears. She might have been a fallen angel, and her eyes seemed to smolder with memories of Heaven or visions of Hell.

She had entered the room accompanied by several Mandrakes; accompanied, not compelled. She was not their captive. *She has gained their favor,* he thought, *by yielding to their lust. But God will forgive her if she saves my friend, and I, John, will serve her until I die. If she saves my friend—*

He saw that she held her crucifix; gripped it as if you would have to sever the hand before you could pry her fingers from its gold arms.

One of her companions called to the priest, who stood impassively between his cross of stone and his congregation, and above Stephen. He neither spoke nor gestured, but disapproval boomed in his silence.

Ruth advanced to the fire and held her crucifix in the glow of the flames, which ignited the golden arms to a sun-washed sea, milkily glinting with pearls like Saracen ships, and the Mandrakes gazed on such a rarity as they had never seen with their poor sunken eyes or fancied in their dim vegetable brains. In some pathetic, childlike way, they must have resembled the men of the First Crusade who took Jerusalem from the Seljuk Turks and gazed, for the first time, at the Holy Sepulcher; whatever ignoble motives had led them to Outre-Mer, they were purged for that one transcendent moment of pride and avarice and poised between reverence and exaltation. It was the same with the Mandrakes.

The priest nodded in grudging acquiescence. Ruth approached him through the ranks of the Mandrakes, which parted murmurously like rushes before the advancing slippers of the wind, and placed the crucifix in his hands. His fingers stroked the gold with slow, loving caresses and paused delicately on the little mounds of the pearls. She did not wait to receive his dismissal. Without hesitation and without visible fear, she walked to John and unbound his hands.

"Help me with Stephen," she said. "I have traded the cross for your lives."

Once they had stooped from the shadows of the last cave and risen to face the late morning sun, the Mandrake left them without a look or a gesture, avid, it seemed, to return to the council chamber and the bartered crucifix. In the dark corridors, Stephen had regained consciousness but leaned on Ruth and John and allowed them to guide his steps, their own steps guided by the slow, creaking shuffle of the Mandrake.

"Stephen, are you all right?" John asked.

"Tired," he gasped, stretching his battered limbs in the grass and closing his eyes.

"And you, Ruth?" John looked at her with awe and wonderment and not a little fear. He had witnessed a miracle.

She did not look miraculous as she lay beside Stephen. Once she had seemed to shrink into a spider; now she reminded him of a wet linen tunic, flung to the ground, torn, trampled, forsaken.

"What happened, Ruth?"

"They found me by the bank after my swim. I reached for a stocking and looked up to see–them."

"And–?"

"They laid hands on me. Dragged me toward their warrens. I fought them, but the one who held me was very strong."

"And you thought of the crucifix? How they were Christians and might value it?"

"Yes. You remember, I had hidden it in our tree. I tried to make them understand that I would give them a treasure if they let me go. You know how they talk. Like little children just learning to speak. Words and phrases all run together. But strange, old-fashioned words. I kept shouting, 'Treasure, treasure!' but they didn't understand. Finally, I remembered an old word used by our ancestors. 'Folk-hoarding,' I cried, and 'Crucifix!' and they understood. They're very devout in their way. They grinned, argued, waved their snaky arms. Then they let me go. I led them to the tree. We passed the place where you and Stephen had fought. I saw bits of your breechclouts and knew their friends had captured you. I stopped in my tracks and said I wanted your freedom as well as mine. Otherwise, no exchange. One of them said, 'If crucifix ring-bright. If time–'

"They climbed right after me up the trunk of the tree. The sight of the crucifix as I unwrapped it made them hold their breath. I held it out to them, but they shook their heads. No, they wouldn't touch it. It was for their priest. They seemed to feel their own filth and ugliness might tarnish the gold or lessen the magic. They didn't grin or look vacant anymore. They looked as if they wanted to cry. They turned their backs and let me dress in the robe—and brought me here."

"And they kept their promise."

"Of course. They're Christians, aren't they?"

Her story troubled John. He had heard of many Christians who failed to keep promises; Crusaders, for example, with Greeks or Saracens. "But why—" he began, meaning to ask why the Mandrakes would feel themselves bound by a promise to a hated human girl.

"We can't sit here all day," she interrupted. "They might change their minds, Christian or not. Where is the road?"

Shakily they climbed to their feet, Stephen without help at his own request ("I must get my balance back"), and saw the trees which encircled and encaged them, great sycamores and greater oaks, looking as if they were sentient old kings in an old country, Celt, Roman, and Saxon, watchfully standing guard until the usurping Normans had felt the slow fingers of the land shape them to the lineaments of Britannia, Britain, England, as the paws and tongue of a bear sculpture her cub into her own small likeness.

"I think," said Stephen, "that the road lies *that* way."

But Stephen was still befuddled by the blows to his head. They walked for a long time and did not come to the road . . . but came to the Manor of Roses.

IV

I watched them as they struggled out of the forest, the stalwart boy supported by his friends, the slighter, dark-haired boy and the girl with angel hair. On a sunny morning, you see, I leave the Manor with the first twittering of sparrows and gather the white roses from the hedge which surrounds my estate, or visit the windmill, the first, I believe, in southern England, and watch the millstones, powered no longer by water, grinding grain for the bread of my kitchen. Now, it was afternoon. I had lunched in the shade of a mulberry tree (apricots, bread, and mead), returned to the hedge of roses, and seen the children. I must have gasped at the sight. They stopped and stared at me over the hedge. The girl stiffened and whispered to the boys. It was not a time when children called at strange manor houses. Startled sparrows, they seemed. Not in littleness or frailty, you understand. The girl and the older boy were more than children. It was rather their vulnerability. Something had almost broken them, and they did not know if I were hunter or friend. I had to prove my friendliness as if I were coaxing sparrows to eat from my hand.

"Follow the hedge to the right," I said, and smiled. "You will see the gate. If you've come from the forest, you must be tired and hungry. I can give you food and a place to sleep." I had made a basket of roses out of my arms. I had no fear of thorns, with my gloves of antelope leather; my long, tight sleeves buttoned at the wrist; my wimple and cap; and my blue, ankle-length skirt, brocaded with star-colored fleurs-de-lis and hanging in heavy folds from my low-belted waist. I watched the boys, clad in breech-clouts clumsily fashioned from leaves, and envied them a man's freedom to dress and ride where he will (unless he dresses in armor and rides to war).

The youngest, the dark-haired boy, still supporting his friend, addressed me with the courteous French of a gentleman.

"We are not attired for the company of a lady. You see, we have come from the forest." His face confirmed the impression of his speech. It is said that Saladin, England's noblest enemy, had such a face as a boy: ascetic, scholar, poet. But first and last, I saw his need and that of his friend, the Saxon lad with the build of wandering Aengus, the Great Youth, whose kisses were called his birds. Even the breechclout seemed an affront to his body. Still, he needed me. His mouth, though forked to a smile, was tight with fatigue and hunger, and a wound had raked his forehead. Both of the boys were spiderwebbed with scratches.

The girl, though her white gown was stained and torn, resembled an angel sculptured from ivory and set in the tympanum of a London cathedral: beautiful, aloof, expressionless. She was tired, I thought. Weariness had drained her face. Later I would read her heart.

I met them at the wicket in the hedge, a gate so small and low that my son had jumped it in a single bound when he rode for the Stane and London.

I held out my arms to greet them, my armful of roses.

They kept their ground, the dark boy straining toward me, the girl away from me, the Saxon drawn between them.

"I can offer you more than flowers," I said, spilling the roses.

The Norman said, "My Lady, whom have we the honor of addressing?"

"I am called the Lady Mary. You have come to the Manor of Roses."

"I thought," he said, "you might be another Mary. Will you help my friend? He has suffered a blow to his head." But it was the Norman and not his friend I helped. He swayed on his feet, leaned to my strength, and caught my outstretched hand.

"I will soil your gown. The fleurs-de-lis."

"With the good brown earth? It is the purest of all substances. The mother of roses."

"But you scattered your flowers on the ground."

"I have others." Supporting him with my arm and followed by his friends, I drew him toward the house.

Once, a moat had surrounded the Manor, but after my husband's death I had filled the water with earth and planted mulberry trees, aflutter now with linnets and silvery filamented with the webs of silkworms; the trees formed a smaller ring within the ring of the rose hedge to island but not to isolate my house, which was built of bricks instead of the cold gray stones preferred by the neighboring barons. My husband had offered to build me a manor for my wedding gift.

"Build it of bricks," I had said. "The color of your hair."

"And stoutly," he said. But the high curtain wall with its oaken door, its rows of weathered bricks from a ruined Roman villa, and its narrow embrasures for bowmen to fire their arrows, had somehow a look of having lost its threat, like armor hung on the wall. Gabriel knows, I could not stand a siege with my poor, bedraggled retainers: gardeners, gatemen, cooks, seneschal, stable-boy—thirty in all, without a knight among them. The wasting fever had not been kind to the Manor of Roses.

The gatekeeper moved to help me with the boy. "He will tire you, my Lady."

I shook my head. No burden can equal the ache of emptiness.

Once we had entered the bailey, Sarah the cook, who had slipped out of the kitchen and thrown back her hood to catch some sun, tossed up her ponderous hands—I suspect it required some effort—and squealed, "My Lady, what have you found?"

"Children, what else? Sarah, hurry to the kitchen and prepare a meal such as young boys—young men—like. Pheasant and—"

"I know, I know," she said. "You forget I've sons of my own, who serve you every night!" Sarah, her three sons and her two daughters, were new to the Manor, but she acted as if she had been my nurse since childhood. "I know what young boys like. The beast of the chase and the fowl of the warren. All that flies and all that goes on hooves, and two of everything unless it's as big as a boar!" She waddled ahead of us up the stairs to the door and, laboriously genuflecting, vanished under the lintel with its wooden Madonna cradling the Holy Infant.

"It's a lovely house," said the Saxon boy in English. "It looks like an abbot's grange."

"A very rich abbot," explained the Norman, fearful no doubt that I had misunderstood his friend's compliment, since poor abbots lived in squalid cottages.

"I meant," stammered the Saxon, "it looks so bright and peaceful, with its Mother and Child, and its—" He waited for his friend to complete his sentence.

"Its two pointed roofs instead of battlements, and real windows instead of slits for archers, with *glass* in the windows! And Stephen, see the herb garden. Parsley, thyme, bay leaf, marjoram, mace, tarragon—"

"You know a lot about herbs," I said.

"I've read an herbal."

Once in the Manor, I took them to the bath. In all of the Weald, I think, in all of England, no other house can claim a fountain for bathing enclosed under the roof. The mouth of a dolphin, hammered from bronze by the artisans of Constantinople, spewed a vigorous streamlet into a basin where tritons gamboled on varicolored tiles. For baths in the cold of winter, I stuffed the dolphin's mouth and filled the basin with kettles hot from the kitchen.

"Your friend shall bathe first," I said to the boys. All of us now were speaking English. And to her: "Your name is—?"

When the girl was slow to answer, the Saxon said, "Ruth. She is our guardian angel. She rescued us."

"From wild beasts?"

"From Mandrakes."

I shuddered. "They are much in the woods, poor misshapen brutes. They have never harmed me, though. You must tell me later about your escape. Now then, Ruth. You shall have the bath to yourself. After you have bathed, I shall send you clothes, and a perfume made from musk, and . . ."

She looked at me with cool, veiled eyes. "You are very kind." I wanted to say to her, "I am more than twice your age, and far less beautiful. Trust me, my dear. Trust me!"

I turned to the boys. The Norman, I learned, was John; the Saxon, Stephen. "When Ruth has finished, it will be your turn."

"Thank you, my Lady," said John. "We would like to bathe with a dolphin. But—"

"You would rather eat! What about bread and cheese and pennyroyal tea to hold you till time for supper? Or," I added quickly, "beer instead of tea." Pennyroyal indeed! I had been too much with women.

"Beer," they said in one breath. "But," said John, "my brother has a wound."

"Brother?" I asked, surprised. A Norman gentleman and a Saxon peasant!

"We adopted each other. Have you something for his head?"

"For my stomach," said Stephen, grinning. "That's where I hurt the most."

"For both," I said.

The hall of my manor house is hot and damp in the summer, the haunt of spiders and rats, and cold in the winter even with pine logs, as big around as a keg of beer, crackling on the hearth. It has always been a room for men: shouting, roistering, warming themselves with mead. For myself, I prefer the solar, the room of many purposes in which I sleep and dine and weave, and entertain the friends who come infrequently now to visit me. I left the boys in the solar with three loaves of bread, two enormous cheeses, and a flagon of beer, and told them to eat and afterward to bathe themselves with cloths dipped in camphor and wrap fresh linen around their waists.

"Call me after you've finished."

I had scarcely had time to find a gown for Ruth when I heard John's voice: "Lady Mary, we've finished."

I found them so fragrant with camphor that I overlooked the patches of dirt they had left on their knees and elbows. The bread, cheese, and wine had vanished as if there had been a raid by kitchen elves, denied their nightly tribute of crumbs. I tended the boys' wounds with a paste of fennel and dittany and they yielded themselves to my fingers without embarrassment, sons to a mother, and made me feel as if my hands had rediscovered their purpose.

"It doesn't burn at all," said Stephen. "My father used a poultice of adder's flesh pounded with wood-lice and spiders. But it burned like the devil, and stank too."

"Lady Mary's hands are like silk," said John. "That's why it doesn't burn."

The boys began to dress in tunics which had belonged to my son: John in green, with a fawn-colored cape drawn through a ring-brooch and knotted at his shoulder, and *chausses* or stockings to match the cape, and black leather shoes with straps; Stephen in blue, with a pale rose cape and silver *chausses,* but looking with each additional garment as if another chain had shackled him to the wall.

"I wouldn't show myself in the forest like this," he muttered. "I'd be taken for a pheasant and shot on sight."

"It's only for tonight," I said. "Don't you want to look the gallant for Ruth?"

"She's used to me naked. She'll take me for a jester."

"My lady."

Ruth had entered the room. She was dressed in a crimson gown or *cotte,* caught at the waist by a belt of gilded doeskin but falling around her feet in billows through which the toes of her slippers peeped like small green lizards. She had bound her hair in a moss-green net, and her yellow tresses twinkled like caged fireflies. (Strange, I always thought of her in terms of forest creatures: wild, unknowable, untamable.)

"My lady, the boys may have their bath. I thank you for sending me so lovely a gown."

"We've had our bath," said Stephen with indignation. "Can't you see we're dressed as gallants?"

"Lady Mary put fennel and dittany on our wounds," said John, "and now they don't hurt anymore."

"And we're going to eat," said Stephen.

"Again," said John.

Ruth examined the solar and almost relaxed from her self-containment. "Why, it's lovely," she said, extending her arm to include the whole of the room. "It's all made of sunlight."

"Not entirely." I smiled, pointing to the high, raftered ceiling with its tie-beam and king-post. "Cobwebs collect unless I keep after Sarah's sons. They have to bring a ladder, you see, and they don't like dusting among the dark crevices. They're afraid of elves."

"But the rest," Ruth said. "There's no darkness anywhere."

The room was kindled with afternoon light from the windows: the fireplace, heaped with logs; a tall-backed chair with square sides and embroidered cushions or bankers; a huge recessed window shaped like an arch and filled with roseate panes of glass from Constantinople; and, hiding the wooden timbers of the floor, a Saracen carpet of polygons, red, yellow, and white, with a border of stylized Persian letters. My wainscoted walls, however, were purely English, their oaken panels painted the green of leaves and bordered with roses to match the carpet.

Ruth explored the room with the air of a girl familiar with beauty, its shapes and its colors, but not without wonder. She touched my loom with loving recognition and paused at my canopied bed to exclaim, "It's like a silken tent!"

"But the linnets," she said, pointing to the wicker cage which hung beside the bed. "Don't they miss the forest?"

"They are quite content. I feed them sunflower seeds and protect them from stoats and weasels. In return, they sing for me."

"Is it true that a caged linnet changes his song?"

"Yes. His voice softens."

"That's what I mean. The wildness goes."

"Shouldn't it, my dear?"

"I don't know, Lady Mary."

We sat on benches drawn to a wooden table with trestles, John and I across from Ruth and Stephen. My husband and I had been served in the great hall by nimble, soft-toed squires who received the dishes from kitchen menials. After his death, however, I began to dine in the solar instead of the hall. For the last year I had been served by Shadrach, Meshach, and Abednego, the three illegitimate sons of my cook, Sarah. As a rule, I liked to dine without ceremony, chatting with the sons—identical triplets with fiery red hair on their heads and arms, and thus their name: they seemed to have stepped out of a furnace. But tonight, for the sake of my guests, I had ordered Sarah and her two illegitimate daughters, Rahab and Magdalena, to prepare, and her sons to serve, a banquet instead of a supper. The daughters had laid the table with a rich brocade of Saracen knights astride their swift little ponies, and they had placed among the knights, as if it were under siege, a molded castle of sugar, rice-flour, and almond-paste.

After I had said the grace, the sons appeared with lavers, ewers, and napkins and passed them among my guests. Stephen lifted a laver to his mouth and started to drink, but John whispered frantically, "It isn't soup, it's to wash your hands."

"There'll be other things to drink," I promised.

"I haven't felt this clean since I was baptized!" Stephen laughed, splattering the table with water from his laver.

Both Ruth and John, though neither had eaten from dishes of beaten silver, were fully at ease with knives and spoons; they cut the pheasant and duck before they used their fingers and scooped the fish-and-crabapple pie with the spoons. But Stephen watched his friends with wry perplexity.

"I never used a knife except to hunt or fish," he said. "I'll probably cut off a finger. Then you can see if I'm a Mandrake!"

"We'd know that already," said John. "You'd look like a hedgehog and somebody would have chopped you up a long time ago for aphrodisiacs. You'd have brought a fortune." His gruesome remarks, I gathered, were meant to divert me from the fact that he had furtively dropped his knife, seized a pheasant, and wrestled off a wing. His motive was as obvious as it was generous. He did not wish to shame his friend by his own polished manners.

I laughed heartily for the first time since the death of my son. "Knives were always a nuisance. Spoons too. What are fingers for if not to eat with? So long as you don't bite yourself!" I wrenched a drumstick and thigh from the parent bird and felt the grease, warm and mouth-watering, ooze between my fingers. "Here," I said to Stephen. "Take hold of the thigh and we'll divide the piece." The bone parted, the meat split into decidedly unequal portions. Half of my drumstick accompanied John's thigh.

"It means you're destined for love," I said.

"He's already had it," said John. "Haylofts full of it."

"She doesn't mean that kind," said Stephen, suddenly serious. "She means caring—taking care of—don't you, Lady Mary? I've had that too, of course." He looked at John.

"Then it means you'll always have it."

"I know," he said.

John smiled at Stephen and then at me, happy because the three of us were friends, but silent Ruth continued to cut her meat into small-sized portions and lift them to her mouth with the fastidiousness of a nun. (Her fingers, however, made frequent trips.)

Shadrach, Meshach, and Abednago scurried between the solar and the kitchen, removing and replenishing, but it looked as if John and Stephen would never satisfy their hunger. With discreet if considerable assistance from Ruth, they downed three pheasants, two ducks, two fish-and-crabapple pies, and four tumblers of mead.

"Leave some for us," hissed Shadrach in Stephen's ear. "This is the *last* bird." Stephen looked surprised, then penitent, and announced himself as full as a tick on the ear of a hound. Shadrach hurried the last bird back to the kitchen.

After the feast the boys told me about their adventures, encouraging rather than interrupting each other with such comments as, "You tell her about the stream with the pepperwort, John," or "Stephen, you're better about the fighting." John talked more because he was more at ease with words: Stephen gestured as much as he talked and sometimes asked John to finish a sentence for him; and Ruth said nothing until the end of the story, when she recounted, quietly, without once meeting my gaze, the episode of her capture and bargain with the Mandrakes. I studied her while she spoke. Shy? Aloof, I would say. Mistrustful. Of me, at least. Simple jealousy was not the explanation. I was hardly a rival for the kind of love she seemed to want from Stephen. No, it was not my beauty which troubled her, but the wisdom which youth supposes to come with age; in a word, my mature perceptions. There was something about her which she did not wish perceived.

"And now for the gifts," I said.

"Gifts?" cried John.

"Yes. The dessert of a feast is the gifts and not the pies."

"But we have nothing to give you."

"You have told me a wondrous and frightening story. No jongleur could have kept me more enthralled. And for you—I have—" I clapped my hands and Shadrach, Meshach, and Abednego appeared with my gifts, some musical instruments which had once belonged to my son. For Ruth, a rebec, a pear-shaped instrument from the East, three-stringed and played with a bow; for the boys twin nakers, or kettledrums, which Stephen strapped to his back and John began to pound with soft-headed wooden drumsticks.

Ruth hesitated with her rebec till Stephen turned and said, "Play for us, Ruth! What are you waiting for, a harp?"

Then Ruth joined them, the boys marching round and round the solar, Stephen first, John behind him pounding on the drums and thumping the carpet with his feet, and finally Ruth, playing with evident skill and forgetting to look remote and enigmatic. Shadrach, Meshach, and Abednego had lingered in the doorway, and behind them Sarah appeared with her plump, swarthy daughters. I was not surprised when they started to sing; I was only surprised to find myself joining them in the latest popular song:

Summer is a-comin' in,
Loud sing cuckoo.
Groweth seed and bloweth mead,
And springs the wood anew.
Sing, cuckoo!

In an hour the three musicians, their audience departed to the kitchen, had exhausted the energies which the meal had revived. Ruth sank in the chair beside the hearth. The boys, thanking me profusely for their gifts, climbed into the window seats. Stephen yawned and began to nod his head. John, in the opposite seat, gave him a warning kick.

"Come," I said to them. "There's a little room over the kitchen which used to belong to my son. The hall was too big, the solar too warm, he felt. I'll show you his room while Ruth prepares for bed. Ruth, we'll fix you a place in the window. You see how the boys are sitting opposite each other: I've only to join the seats with a wooden stool and add a few cushions to make a couch. Or"—and I made the offer, I fear, with visible reluctance—"you may share my own bed under the canopy."

"The window seats will be fine."

I pointed to the aumbry, a wooden cupboard aswirl with wrought iron scrollwork, almost like the illuminated page of a psalter. "There's no lock. Open the doors and find yourself a nightdress while I show the boys their room."

My son's room was as small as a chapel in a keep, with one little square of a window, but the bed was wide as well as canopied, and irresistible to the tired boys.

"It's just like yours!" John cried.

"Smaller. But just as soft."

"At home I slept on a bench against the wall, in a room with eight other boys—sons of my father's knights. I got the wall bench because my father owned the castle."

"I slept on straw," said Stephen, touching the mattress, sitting, stretching himself at length, and uttering a huge, grateful sigh. "It's like a nest of puppies. What makes it so soft?"

"Goose-feathers."

"The geese we ate tonight—their feathers will stuff a mattress, won't they?"

"Two, I suspect." I fetched them a silk-covered bearskin from a small, crooked cupboard which my son had built at the age of thirteen. "And now I must see to Ruth."

I am not a reticent person, but the sight of the boys—Stephen in bed and sleepily smiling good night, John respectfully standing but sneaking an envious glance at his less respectful friend—wrenched me almost to tears. I did not trust myself to say that I was very glad to offer them my son's bed for as long as they chose to stay in the Manor of Roses.

I could only say, "Sleep as late as you like. Sarah can fix you breakfast at any hour."

"You're very kind," said Stephen. "But tomorrow, I think, we must get an early start for London."

"London!" I cried. "But your wounds haven't healed!"

"They were just scratches, really, and now you've cured them with your medicine. If we stayed, we might *never* want to go."

"I might never want you to go."

"But don't you see, Lady Mary, we have to fight for Jerusalem."

"You expect to succeed where kings have failed? Frederick Barbarossa? Richard the Lion-Hearted? Two little boys without a weapon between them!"

"We're not little boys," he protested. "I'm a young swain—fifteen winters old—and John here is a—stripling who will grow like a bindweed. Aren't you, John?"

"Grow, anyway," said John without enthusiasm. "But I don't see why we have to leave in the morning."

"Because of Ruth."

"And Ruth is your guardian angel?" I asked with an irony lost on the boy.

"Yes. Already she's saved our lives."

"Has she, Stephen? Has she? Sleep now. We'll talk tomorrow. I want to tell you about my own son."

I returned to the solar heavy of foot. It was well for Ruth that she had changed to a nightdress, joined the window seats with the necessary stool, and retired to bed in a tumble of cushions. Now, she was feigning sleep, but forgetting to mimic the slow, deep breaths of the true sleeper. Well, I could question her tomorrow. One thing I knew: she would lead my boys on no unholy Crusade.

A chill in the air awakened me. It was not unusual for a hot summer day to grow wintry at night. I rose, lit a candle, and found additional coverlets for myself and Ruth. Her face seemed afloat in her golden hair: decapitated, somehow, or drowned.

I thought of the boys, shivering in the draft of their glassless window. I had not remembered to draw the canopy of their bed. In my linen nightdress and my pointed satin slippers which, like all the footwear expected of English ladies, cruelly pinched my toes, I passed through the hall and then the kitchen, tiptoed among the pallets of Sarah and her children stretched near the oven, and climbed a staircase whose steepness resembled a ladder.

Lifting aside a coarse leather curtain, I stood in the doorway of my son's room and looked at the boys. They had fallen asleep without extinguishing the pewter lamp which hung from a rod beside their bed. The bearskin covered their chins, and their bodies had met for warmth in the middle of the bed. I leaned above them and started to spread my coverlet. John, who was closer to me, opened his eyes and smiled.

"Mother," he said.

"Mary," I said, sitting on the edge of the bed.

"That's what I meant."

"I'm sorry I woke you."

"I'm glad. You came to bring us a coverlet, didn't you?"

"Yes. Won't we wake your brother?"

His smile broadened; he liked my acceptance of Stephen as his brother and equal. "Not our voices. Only if I got out of bed. Then he would feel me gone. But once he's asleep, he never hears anything, unless it's one of his hounds."

"You're really going tomorrow?"

"I don't want to go. I don't think Stephen does either. It's Ruth's idea. She whispered to him in the solar, when you and I were talking. But I heard her just the same. She said they must get to London. She said it was why she had come, and why she had saved us from the Mandrakes."

"Why won't she trust me, John?"

"I think she's afraid of you. Of what you might guess."

"What is there to guess?"

There was fear in his eyes. He looked at Stephen, asleep, and then at me. "I think that Ruth is a Mandrake. One who has passed."

I flinched. I had thought a thief, adventuress, harlot, carrier of the plague, but nothing so terrible as a Mandrake. Though fear was a brand in my chest, I spoke quietly. I did not want to judge her until he had made his case. He might be a too imaginative child, frightened by the forest and now bewildered with sleep. He was only twelve. And yet, from what I had seen, I had thought him singularly rational for his years. Stephen, one might have said, would wake in the night and babble of Mandrake girls. Never John. Not without reason, at least.

"Why do you think that, John?"

His words cascaded like farthings from a purse cut by a pickpocket, swift, confused at times, and yet with a thread of logic which made me share his suspicions. Ruth's mysterious arrival in the Mithraeum. Her vague answers and her claim to forgetfulness. Her lore of the forest. Her shock and disgust when he and Stephen had told her about the Mandrake hunters. Her strangely successful bargain with the crucifix.

"And they kept their word," he said. "Even when they thought Stephen and I had killed one of their babies. It was as if they let us go so that she could *use* us."

"It's true they're Christians," I said. "I've found their stone crosses in the woods around my Manor. They might have felt bound by their word.

An oath to a savage, especially a Christian savage, can be a sacred thing. Far more sacred than to some of our own Crusaders, who have sacked the towns of their sworn friends. Ruth may have told you the truth about the crucifix."

"I know," he said. "I know. It's wicked of me to suspect her. She's always been kind to me. She brought me strawberries in the forest once! And Stephen worships her. But I had to tell you, didn't I? She might have passed when she was a small child. Grown up in a village. But someone became suspicious. She fled to the forest. Took shelter in the Mithraeum where Stephen and I found her. You see, if I'm right—"

"We're all in danger. You and Stephen most of all. You have been exposed to her visitations. We shall have to learn the truth before you leave this house."

"You mean we must wound her? But if she passed a long time ago, we would have to cut her to the bone."

"We wouldn't so much as scratch her. We would simply confront her with an accusation. Suppose she is a Mandrake. Either she knew already when she first met you or else her people told her in the forest. Told her with pride: 'See, we have let you grow soft and beautiful in the town!' Tomorrow we shall demand proof of her innocence. Innocent, she will offer herself to the knife. The offer alone will suffice. But a true Mandrake will surely refuse such a test, and then we will know her guilt."

"It's rather like trial by combat, isn't it?" he said at last. "God condemns the guilty. Pricks him with conscience until he loses the fight. But this way, there won't be a combat, just a trial. God will make Ruth reveal her guilt or innocence."

"And you and I will be His instruments. Nothing more."

"And if she's guilty?"

"We'll send her into the forest and let her rejoin her people."

"It will break Stephen's heart."

"It will save his life. Save him from Ruth—and from going to London. Without his angel, do you think he'll still persist in his foolish Crusade? He will stay here with you and me. The Manor of Roses has need of two fine youths."

"You won't make him a servant because he's a villein? His ancestors were Saxon earls when mine were pirates."

"Mine were pirates too. Bloodthirsty ones, at that. No, you and Stephen shall both be my sons. You adopted him. Why shouldn't I?"

"You know," he said, "when you first spoke to us at the hedge—after we had come from the forest—you said we'd come to the Manor of Roses. At first I thought you meant the *manner* of roses. Without the capitals."

"Did you, John?"

"Yes. And it's quite true. Of the house, I mean, and you. The manner of roses."

"But I have thorns to protect the ones I love. Ruth will feel them to-morrow." I knelt beside him and touched my lips to his cheek. It was not as if I were kissing him for the first time, but had kissed him every night for—how many years?—the years of my son when he rode to London.

"You're crying," he said.

"It's the smoke from the lamp. It has stung my eyes."

He clung to my neck, no longer a boy, but a small child I could almost feed at my breast.

"I like your hair when it's loose," he said. "It's like a halo that comes all the way to your shoulders."

He fell asleep in my arms.

V

I woke to the twittering of sparrows. Their little shapes flickered against the windowpanes, and for once I regretted the glass. I would have liked them to flood the room with their unmelodious chirpings and share in my four-walled, raftered safety. Minikin beings, they reveled in the sun, noisily, valiantly, yet prey to eagle and hawk from the wilderness of sky, and the more they piped defiance, the more they invited death.

But other sparrows were not beyond my help.

I rose and dressed without assistance. I did not call Sarah's daughters to comb my hair and exclaim, "But it's like black samite!" and fasten the sleeves above my wrists and burden my fingers with jade and tourmaline. I did not wish to awaken Ruth. I dreaded the confrontation.

Encased from the tip of my toes to the crest of my hair—amber and green in wimple, robe, gloves, stocking, and slippers—I walked into the courtyard and sat on a bench among my herbs, lulled by the soft scent of lavender, but not from my hesitations; piqued by the sharp pungency of tarragon but not to pride in what I must ask of Ruth.

The sun was high as a bell tower before the sounds from the solar told me that the children had waked and met. Ruth and Stephen were belaboring John when I entered the room. Stephen looked liberated in his breechclout, and Ruth disported herself in his green tunic, the one he had worn reluctantly to my feast, but without the *chausses* or the cape. They were telling John that he ought to follow their example and dress for the woods.

"You're white as a sheep this morning," chided Stephen. "Your shoulders need the sun."

John, engulfed by his cape and tunic, might have been ten instead of twelve. I pitied the child. He would have to side with me against his friends. He returned my smile with a slight nod of his head, as if to say, "It must be now."

Stephen's voice was husky with gratitude. "Lady Mary, we must leave you and make our way to London. You've fed us and given us a roof, and we won't forget you. In a dark forest, you have been our candle. Your gifts—the drums and rebec—will help us to earn our passage to the Holy Land."

"Knights and abbots will throw you pennies," I said. "Robbers will steal them. It will take you a long time to earn your passage."

"But that's why we have to go! To start earning. And when we come back this way, we'll bring you a Saracen shield to hang above your hearth." He kissed my hand with a rough, impulsive tenderness. An aura of camphor wreathed him from yesterday's bath. He had combed his hair in a fringe across his forehead, like jonquils above his bluer-than-larkspur eyes. I thought how the work of the comb would soon be spoiled, the petals wilted by the great forest, tangled with cobwebs, matted perhaps with blood.

"Before you go, I think you should know the nature of your company."

His eyes widened into a question. The innocence of them almost shook my resolve. "John? But he's my friend! If you mean he's very young, you ought to have seen him fight the Mandrake."

"Ruth."

"Ruth is an angel." He made the statement as one might say, "I believe in God."

"You want her to be an angel. But is she, Stephen? Ask her."

He turned to Ruth for confirmation. "You said you came from the sky, didn't you?"

"I said I didn't remember." She stared at the Persian carpet and seemed to be counting the polygons or reading the cryptic letters woven into the border.

"But you said you remembered falling a great distance."

"There are other places to fall than out of the sky."

John spoke at last. "But you remembered things." His voice seemed disembodied. It might have come from the vault of a deep Mithraeum. "About the forest. Where to find the wild strawberries. How to weave a cup out of rushes. How to escape from the Mandrakes."

"Ruth," I said. "Tell them who you are. Tell me. We want to know."

She began to tremble. "I don't know. I don't know." I was ready to pity her when she told the truth.

I walked to the aumbry with slow, deliberate steps. In spite of my silken slippers, I placed each foot as if I were crushing a mite which threatened my roses. I opened the doors, knelt, and reached to the lowest shelf for a Saracen poniard, its ivory hilt emblazoned with sapphires in the shape of a running gazelle. The damascene blade was very sharp: steel inlaid with threads of silver.

There was steel in my voice as I said, "You are not to leave my house till I know who you are. I accepted you as a guest and friend. Now I have reason to believe that you are dangerous. To the boys, if not to me."

"You would harm me, Lady Mary?" She shrank from the light of the window and joined the shadows near the hearth. I half expected her to dwindle into a spider and scuttle to safety among the dark rafters.

"I would ask you to undergo a test."

She said, "You think I am a Mandrake."

"I think you must show us that you are not a Mandrake." I walked toward her with the poniard. "My husband killed the Saracen who owned this blade. Wrestled him for it. Drove it into his heart. You see, the point is familiar with blood. It will know what to do."

"Lady Mary!" It was Stephen who stepped between us; charged, I should say, like an angry stag, and almost took the blade in his chest. "What are you saying, Lady Mary?"

"Ask her," I cried. "Ask her! Why does she fear the knife? Because it will prove her guilt!"

He struck my hand and the poniard fell to the floor. He gripped my shoulders. "Witch! You have blasphemed an angel!"

Anger had drained me—indignation, doubts. I drooped in his punishing hands. I wanted to sleep.

John awoke from his torpor and beat on his friend with desperate fists. "It's true, it's true! You must let her go!"

Stephen unleashed a kick like a javelin hurled from an arbalest. I forgot the poniard, forgot to watch the girl. All I could see was John as he struck the doors of the aumbry and sank, winded and groaning, to the floor. Twisting from Stephen's fingers, I knelt to the wounded boy and took him in my arms.

"I'm not hurt," he gasped. "But Ruth . . . the poniard . . ."

I saw the flash of light on the blade in Ruth's hand. Stephen swayed on his feet, a stag no longer, now a bear chained in a pit, baited by some, fed by others—how can he tell his tormenters from his friends? Wildly he stared from the boy he had hurt to the girl he had championed. Ruth walked toward me with soundless feet and eyes as cold as hornstones under a stream. She might have been dead.

The poniard flashed between us. I threw up my hands for defense of myself and John. She brought the blade down sharply against her own hand, the mount of the palm below her thumb. I heard—I actually heard—the splitting of flesh, the rasp of metal on bone. The blade must have cut through half of her hand before it lodged in the bone, and then she withdrew it without a cry, with a sharp, quick jerk, like a fisherman removing a hook, and stretched her fingers to display her wound. The flesh parted to reveal white bone, and crimson blood, not in the least resinous, swelled to fill the part. She smiled at me with triumph but without malice, a young girl who had vindicated herself before an accuser more than twice her years.

"Did you think I meant to hurt you?" she said almost playfully and then, seeing her blood as it reddened the carpet, winced and dropped the poniard.

Stephen steadied her into the chair by the hearth and pressed her palm to staunch the flow.

"You are an evil woman." He glared at me. "Your beauty is a lie. It hides an old heart."

"Both of your friends are in pain," I said. "It isn't a time for curses."

He looked at John in my arms and stiffened as if he would drop Ruth's hand and come to his friend.

"No. Stay with Ruth." I helped John across the room to a seat in the window; the tinted panes ruddied his pale cheeks. "He will be all right. Ruth is in greater need. Let me tend her, Stephen."

"You shan't touch her."

Ruth spoke for herself. "The pain is very sharp. Can you ease it, Lady Mary?"

I treated the wound with a tincture of opium and powdered rose petals and swaddled her hand with linen. John rose from the window and stood behind me, in silent attendance on Ruth—and in atonement. Stephen, an active boy denied a chance to act, stammered to his friends: "Forgive me, both of you. It was my Crusade, wasn't it? I brought you to this."

Ruth's face was as white as chalk-rubbed parchment awaiting the quill of a monk. Her smile was illumination. "But you see, Stephen, Lady Mary was right to a point. I am no more an angel than you are. Less, in fact. You're a dreamer. I'm a liar. I've lied to you from the start, as Lady Mary guessed. That's why I couldn't trust her—because I saw that she couldn't trust me. My name isn't Ruth, it's Madeleine. I didn't come from heaven but the Castle of the Boar, three miles from your own kennels. My father was noble of birth, brother to the Boar. But he hated the life of a knight— the hunts, the feasts, the joustings—and most of all, the Crusades without God's blessing. He left his brother's castle to live as a scholar in Chichester, above a butcher's shop. He earned his bread by copying manuscripts or reading the stars. It was he who taught me my languages—English and Norman French and Latin—and just as if I were a boy, the lore of the stars, the sea, and the forest. He also taught me to play the rebec and curtsy and use a spoon at the table. 'Someday,' he said, 'you will marry a knight, a gentle one, I hope, if such still exist, and you have to be able to talk to him about a man's interests, and also delight him with the ways of a woman. Then he won't ride off to fight in a foolish Crusade, as most men do because of ignorant wives.' He taught me well and grew as poor as a

Welshman. When he died of the plague last year, he left me pennies instead of pounds, and no relatives except my uncle, the Boar, who despised my father and took me into his castle only because I was brought to him by an abbot from Chichester.

"But the Boar was recently widowed, and he had a taste for women. Soon I began to please him. I think I must have grown—how shall I say it?—riper, more womanly. He took me hawking and praised my lore of the forest. I sat beside him at banquets, drank his beer, laughed at his bawdy tales, and almost forgot my Latin. But after a feast one night he followed me to the chapel and said unspeakable things. My own uncle! I hit him with a crucifix from the altar. No one stopped me when I left the castle. No one knew the master was not at his prayers! But where could I go? Where but Chichester? Perhaps the abbot would give me shelter.

"But John, as I passed near your father's castle I heard a rider behind me. I ducked in a thicket of gorse and tumbled down some stairs into a dark vault. You see, I did have a kind of fall, though not from Heaven. I was stiff and tired and scared, and I fell asleep and woke up to hear Stephen proclaiming me an angel and talking about London and the Holy Land. London! Wasn't that better than Chichester? Further away from my uncle? Stephen, I let you think me an angel because I was tired of men and their lust. I had heard stories about you even at the castle—your way with a wench. After I knew you, though, I *wanted* your way. You weren't at all the boy in the stories, but kind and trusting. But I couldn't admit my lie and lose your respect.

"As for the crucifix you found in my hands, I had stolen it from my uncle. He owed me *something,* I felt. I had heard him say it was worth a knight's ransom. I hoped to sell it and buy a seamstress shop and marry a fine gentleman who brought me stockings to mend. When I traded it to the Mandrakes, it was just as I said. They kept their promise for the sake of their faith. You see, they were much more honest than I have been."

Stephen was very quiet. I had seen him pressed for words but never for gestures, the outstretched hand, the nod, the smile. I wanted to ease the silence with reassurances and apologies. But Ruth was looking to Stephen; it was he who must speak.

"Now I'm just another wench to you," she said with infinite wistfulness. "I should have told you the truth. Let you have your way. This way, I've nothing at all."

He thought for a long time before he spoke, and the words he found were not an accusation. "I think a part of me never really took you for an angel. At least, not after the first. I'm not good enough to deserve a guardian from Heaven. Besides, you stirred me like a girl of flesh and blood. But I wanted a reason for running away. An excuse and a hope. I lacked courage, you see. It's a fearful thing for a villein to leave his master. John's father could have me killed, or cut off my hands and feet. So I lied to myself: an angel had come to guide me! We were both dishonest, Ruth—Madeleine."

"Ruth. That's the name you gave me."

"Ruth, we can still go to London. Without any lies between us." Gestures returned to him; he clasped her shoulders with the deference of a brother (and looked to John: "My arms are not yet filled."). "But Lady Mary, it was cruel of you to find the truth in such a way."

"She never meant to touch Ruth," said John. "Only to test her. It was things I told Lady Mary that made her suspicious."

"John, John," said Ruth, walking to him and placing her swaddled hand on his arm. "I know you've never liked me. You saw through my tale from the first. You thought I wanted your friend. You were right, of course. I wouldn't trade him for Robin Hood, if Robin were young again and lord of the forest! But I never wished you ill. You were his chosen brother. How could I love him without loving you? I wanted to say, 'Don't be afraid of losing Stephen to me. It was you he loved first. If I take a part of his heart, it won't be a part that belongs to you. Can't you see, John, that the heart is like the catacombs of the old Christians? You can open a second chamber without closing the first. Trust your friend to have chambers for both of us.' But I said nothing. It would have shown me to be a girl instead of an angel."

"You're coming with us, John?" asked Stephen doubtfully. "I didn't mean to hurt you. It was like the time you stepped on my dog. But you forgave me then."

"There's no reason now why any of you should go," I said.

"There's no reason for us to stay."

"You'll go on a Crusade without a guardian angel?"

"We'll walk to London and then—who knows? Venice, Baghdad, Cathay! Maybe it was just to run away I wanted, and not to save Jerusalem." He pressed John between his big hands. "You *are* coming, aren't you, brother?"

"No," said John. "No, Stephen. Lady Mary needs me."

"So does Stephen," said Ruth.

"Stephen is strong. I was never any use to him. Just the one he protected."

"Someday," said Ruth, "you'll realize that needing a person is the greatest gift you can give him."

"I need all of you," I said. "Stay here. Help me. Let me help you. London killed my son. It's a city forsaken by God."

Stephen shook his head. "We have to go, Ruth and I. The Boar might follow her here. She hurt his pride as well as his skull and stole his crucifix."

John said, "I'm going to stay."

I packed them provisions of bread, beer, and salted bacon, gave them the Saracen poniard to use against thieves or sell in London, and strapped the rebec and kettledrums on their backs.

"You must have a livelihood in London," I said, when Stephen wanted to leave the instruments with John.

I walked with Stephen and Ruth to the wicket and gave them directions for finding the road: "Walk a mile to the east. . . . Look for the chestnut tree with a hole like a door in the trunk. . . ."

But Stephen was looking over his shoulder for John.

"He stayed in the solar," I said. "He loves you too much to say goodbye."

"Or too little. Why else is he staying with you?"

"The world is a harsh place, Stephen. Harsher than the forest, and without any islands like the Manor of Roses." How could I make him understand that God had given me John in return for the son I had lost to the Devil?

"I would be his island," said Stephen, his big frame shaken with sobs.

"Never mind," said Ruth. "Never mind. We'll come back for him, Stephen." And then to me: "My lady, we thank you for your hospitality." She curtsied and kissed my hand with surprising warmth.

I said, "May an angel truly watch over you."

They marched toward the forest as proud and straight as Vikings, in spite of their wounds and their burdens. No more tears for Stephen. Not a backward look. London. Baghdad. Cathay!

It was then that I saw the face in the dense foliage, a bleached moon in a dusk of tangled ivy.

"Ruth, Stephen," I started to call. "You are being watched!"

But she had no eye for the children. She was watching me. I had seen her several times in the forest. Something of curiosity—no, of awe—distinguished her from the gray, anonymous tribe. Perhaps it was she who had left the crosses around my estate, like charms to affright the Devil. She had never threatened me. Once I had run from her. Like a wraith of mist before the onslaught of sunlight, she had wasted into the trees. I had paused and watched her with shame and pity.

Now, I walked toward her, compelled by a need which surpassed my fear. "I won't hurt you," I said. I was deathly afraid. Her friends could ooze from the trees and envelop me before I could cry for help. "I won't hurt you," I repeated. "I only want to talk to you."

The rank vegetable scent of her clogged my nostrils. I had always felt that the rose and the Mandrake represented the antitheses of the forest: grace and crookedness. Strange, though, now that I looked at her closely for the first time, she was like a crooked tree mistreated by many weathers; a natural object unanswerable to human concepts of beauty and ugliness.

Dredging archaic words from memories of old books, I spoke with soft emphasis. "Tell me," I said. "Why do you watch my house—my mead-hall? Is it treasure-rich to you? Broad-gabled?"

She caught my meaning at once. "Not mead-hall."

"What, then? The roses perhaps? You may pick some if you like."

"Bantling."

"Bantling? *In my house?*"

She knelt and seized my hand and pressed her hairy lips against my knuckles.

"Here," she said.

I flung my hands to my ears as if I had heard a Mandrake shriek in the night. It was I who had shrieked. I fled . . . I fled. . . .

His eyes were closed; he rested against a cushion embroidered with children playing Hoodman Blind. He rose from his seat when he heard me enter the room.

"They're gone?"

"What? What did you say, John?"

"Stephen and Ruth are gone?"

"Yes."

He came toward me. "You're pale, Lady Mary. Don't be sad for me. I wanted to stay."

I said quietly, "I think you should go with your friends. They asked me to send you after them."

He blinked his eyes. The lids looked heavy and gray. "But I am staying to protect you. To be your son. You said—"

"It was really Stephen I wanted. You're only a little boy. Stephen is a young man. I would have taught him to be a gentleman and a knight. But now that he's gone, what do I need with a skinny child of twelve?"

"But I don't ask to be loved like Stephen!"

I caught him between my hands, and his lean, hard-muscled shoulders, the manhood stirring within him, belied my taunts.

"Go to him," I cried. "Now, John, now! You'll lose him if you wait!"

Pallor drained from his face, like pain routed by opium. "Lady Mary," he whispered. "I think I understand. You *do* love me, don't you? Enough to let me go. So much—"

I dropped my hands from his shoulders. I must not touch him. I must not kiss him. "So much. So much. . . ."

Beyond the hedge, he turned and waved to me, laughing, and ran to catch his friends. Before he could reach the woods, Stephen blazed from the trees.

"I waited," he cried. "I knew you would come!"

The boys embraced in such a swirl of color, of whirling bodies and clattering kettledrums, that the fair might have come to London Town! Then, arm in arm, with Ruth, they entered the woods.

> *Summer is a-comin' in,*
> *Loud sing cuckoo. . . .*

I, also, entered the woods. For a long time I knelt before one of the stone crosses left by the Mandrakes—set like a bulwark between enormous oaks to thwart whatever of evil, griffins, wolves, men, might threaten my house. My knees sank through the moss to ache against stone; my lips were dry of prayer. I knelt, waiting.

I did not turn when the vegetable scent of her was a palpable touch. I said, "Would you like to live with me in the mead-hall?"

Her cry was human; anguish born of ecstasy. I might have said, "Would you like to see the Holy Grail?"

"Serve you?"

"Help me. You and your friends. Share with me."

Slowly, I leaned to the shy, tentative fingers which loosened my hair and spread my tresses, as one spreads a fine brocade to admire its weave and the delicacy of its figures.

"Bantling," she said. "Madonna-beautiful." What had John said? "I love your hair when it's loose. It's like a halo. . . ." Roses and I have this in common: we have both been judged too kindly by the softness of our petals.

"I must go now. Those in the mead-hall would not welcome you. I shall have to send them away. For your sake—and theirs. Tomorrow I will meet you here and take you back with me."

Earth, the mother of roses, has many children.

ACKNOWLEDGMENTS

I wish to express with gratitude a large debt to *A History of Everyday Things in England: 1066–1499* by Marjorie and C. H. B. Quennell, and *The Crusades* by Henry Treece. The songs quoted in my story are modernized versions of anonymous Old and Middle English lyrics.

ROGER ZELAZNY

Death and the Executioner

Like a number of other writers, the late Roger Zelazny began publishing in 1962 in the pages of Cele Goldsmith's *Amazing*. This was the so-called "Class of '62," whose membership also included Thomas M. Disch, Keith Laumer, and Ursula K. Le Guin. Everyone in that "class" eventually achieved prominence, but some of them would achieve it faster than others, and Zelazny's subsequent career was one of the most meteoric in the history of SF. The first Zelazny story to attract wide notice was "A Rose for Ecclesiastes," published in 1963 (it was later selected by vote of the SFWA membership as one of the best SF stories of all time). By the end of that decade, he had won two Nebula Awards and two Hugo Awards and was widely regarded as one of the two most important American SF writers of the sixties (the other was Samuel R. Delany). By the end of the 1970s, although his critical acceptance as an important science fiction writer had dimmed, his long series of novels about the enchanted land of Amber—beginning with *Nine Princes in Amber*—had made him one of the most popular and best-selling fantasy writers of our time, and inspired fan clubs and fanzines worldwide.

Zelazny's approach to fantasy was similar to the brisk, wise-cracking, anachronistic slant of the de Camp and Pratt "Harold Shea" stories such as *The Incomplete Enchanter,* but in a somewhat different key, with less emphasis on whimsy (very few authors, with the exception of de Camp and Pratt, T. H. White, and Lewis Carroll, were ever really able to use whimsy successfully) and more emphasis on action and on dramatic—and often quite theatrical—showdowns between immensely powerful adversaries. Still, the Zelazny hero (who was often fundamentally the same person, whether he was called Corwin or Conrad or Sam) faces his supernatural foes with genial good sense, unperturbed calm, and a store of self-deprecating humor, always quick with a quip or a wry witticism, and although the Zelazny hero *himself* is almost always a being of immense power and resources (which must help in maintaining your *sangfroid* when confronting fearsome demons and monsters), he frequently defeats his enemies by outwitting them rather than by the brute use of either physical might or magical potency. In fact, the typical Zelazny hero, in both fantasy and science fiction, can usually be thought of as a more benign and genial version of the Trickster, a wry, pipe-smoking Coyote, who, although he sometimes admits to being scared or bewildered, is usually several moves ahead of his opponents all the way to the end of the game.

The multivolume *Amber* series, of course, is probably Zelazny's most important sustained contribution to fantasy, although it's worth noting that the first few volumes of the series were published as science fiction novels by an established science fiction line. By the time of Zelazny's death, however, the *Amber* books seemed much more centrally categorizable as fantasy, although the story line would occasionally touch bases with our modern-day Earth, or employ some high-tech gadget, almost as though Zelazny was deliberately trying to muddy the waters . . . which indeed perhaps he *was,* as there are fantasy elements in almost all of his "science fiction" books and science fictional elements in almost all of his "fantasy" books, and it's difficult to believe that these weren't deliberate aesthetic choices on Zelazny's part. Indeed, Zelazny's *other* sustained fantasy series—actually launched before the *Amber* books—an uncompleted sequence of stories about the adventures of Dilvish the Damned (collected in *Dilvish, the Damned),* is much more firmly and unambiguously centered at the heart of Sword & Sorcery, but is also, perhaps as a result, considerably less interesting and successful; Zelazny himself seemed to lose interest in it for long stretches at a time, producing only one novel—*The Changing Land*—and a few stories in the sequence throughout the last few decades of his life. One could argue that Zelazny's most popular, successful, and influential singleton novel, *Lord of Light,* although also ostensibly a science fiction novel, functions as well as a fantasy novel as it does as an SF novel; in fact, the book probably makes *more* logical sense as a fantasy than it does as a plausible science fiction scenario, and I can't help but wonder if it is an example of an author "disguising" a fantasy book as science fiction in order to make it saleable under the market conditions of the time—although again, this may also be just another example of Zelazny, with his Trickster hat on, deliberately blurring the borderlines between the two genres, perhaps smiling at the thought of some future critic trying to sort things out.

Whatever the truth of that, the vivid, suspenseful, and evocative story that follows, one of a sequence of individually published magazine stories that were later melded into *Lord of Light,* certainly *feels* like fantasy—and, considered as fantasy, is a lyrical, inventive, and gorgeously colored one, one that demonstrates that, although we all have an Appointment with Death, some of us are considerably more reluctant to *go* than others, and put up a good deal more of a fight . . . perhaps enough of a fight to give even Death himself pause.

Zelazny won another Nebula and Hugo Award in 1976 for his novella "Home Is the Hangman," another Hugo in 1982 for his story "Unicorn Variation" and one in 1986 for his novella "24 Views of Mt. Fuji, by Hokusai," and a final Hugo in 1987 for his story "Permafrost." His other books, in addition to the multi-volume *Amber* series, include *This Immortal, The Dream Master, Isle of the Dead, Jack of Shadows, Eye of Cat, Doorways in the Sand, Today We Choose Faces, Bridge of Ashes, To Die in Italbar, Roadmarks, Changeling, Madwand,* and *A Night in the Lonesome October,* and the collections *Four for Tomorrow, The Doors of His Face, the Lamps of His Mouth and Other Stories, The Last Defender of Camelot, Unicorn Variations,* and *Frost & Fire.* Among his last books are two collaborative novels, *A Farce to Be Reckoned With,* with Robert Sheckley, and *Wilderness,* with Gerald Hausman, and, as editor, two anthologies, *Wheel of Fortune* and *Warriors of Blood and Dream.* Zelazny died in 1995.

> *There is no disappearing of the true Dhamma*
> *until a false Dhamma arises in the world.*
> *When the false Dhamma arises, he makes the*
> *true Dhamma to disappear.*
> —Samyutta-nikaya (II, 224)

Near the city of Alundil there was a rich grove of blue-barked trees, having purple foliage like feathers. It was famous for its beauty and the shrinelike peace of its shade. It had been the property of the merchant Vasu until his conversion, at which time he had presented it to the teacher variously known as Mahasamatman, Tathagatha and the Enlightened One. In that wood did this teacher abide with his followers, and when they walked forth into the town at midday their begging bowls never went unfilled.

There was always a large number of pilgrims about the grove. The believers, the curious and those who preyed upon the others were constantly passing through it. They came by horseback, they came by boat, they came on foot.

Alundil was not an overly large city. It had its share of thatched huts, as well as wooden bungalows; its main roadway was unpaved and rutted; it had two large bazaars and many small ones; there were wide fields of grain, owned by the Vaisyas, tended by the Sudras, which flowed and rippled, blue-green, about the city; it had many hostels (though none so fine as the legendary hostel of Hawkana, in far Mahartha), because of the constant passage of travelers; it had its holy men and its storytellers; and it had its Temple.

The Temple was located on a low hill near the center of town, enormous gates on each of its four sides. These gates, and the walls about them, were filled with layer upon layer of decorative carvings, showing musicians and dancers, warriors and demons, gods and goddesses, animals and artists, lovemakers and half-people, guardians and devas. These gates led into the first courtyard, which held more walls and more gates, leading in turn into the second courtyard. The first courtyard contained a little bazaar, where offerings to the gods were sold. It also housed numerous small shrines dedicated to the lesser deities. There were begging beggars, meditating holy men, laughing children, gossiping women, burning incenses, singing birds, gurgling purification tanks and humming pray-o-mats to be found in this courtyard at any hour of the day.

The inner courtyard, though, with its massive shrines dedicated to the major deities, was a focal point of religious intensity. People chanted or shouted prayers, mumbled verses from the Vedas, or stood, or knelt, or lay prostrate before huge stone images, which often were so heavily garlanded with flowers, smeared with red *kumkum* paste and surrounded by heaps of offerings that it was impossible to tell which deity was so immersed in tangible adoration. Periodically, the horns of the Temple were blown, there was a moment's hushed appraisal of their echo and the clamor began again.

And none would dispute the fact that Kali was queen of this Temple. Her tall, white-stone statue, within its gigantic shrine, dominated the inner courtyard. Her faint smile, perhaps contemptuous of the other gods and their worshipers, was, in its way, as arresting as the chained grins of the skulls she wore for a necklace. She held daggers in her hands; and poised in mid-step she stood, as though deciding whether to dance before or slay those who came to her shrine. Her lips were full, her eyes were wide. Seen by torchlight, she seemed to move.

It was fitting, therefore, that her shrine faced upon that of Yama, god of Death. It had been decided, logically enough, by the priests and architects, that he was best suited of all the deities to spend every minute of the day facing her, matching his unfaltering death-gaze against her own, returning her half smile with his twisted one. Even the most devout generally made a detour rather than pass between the two shrines; and after dark their section of the courtyard was always the abode of silence and stillness, being untroubled by late worshipers.

From out of the north, as the winds of spring blew across the land, there came the one called Rild. A small man, whose hair was white, though his years were few—Rild, who wore the dark trappings of a pilgrim, but about whose forearm, when they found him lying in a ditch with the fever, was wound the crimson strangling cord of his true profession: Rild.

Rild came in the spring, at festival-time, to Alundil of the blue-green fields, of the thatched huts and the bungalows of wood, of unpaved roadways and many hostels, of bazaars, and holy men and storytellers, of the great religious revival and its Teacher, whose reputation had spread far across the land—to Alundil of the Temple, where his patron goddess was queen.

Festival-time.

Twenty years earlier, Alundil's small festival had been an almost exclusively local affair. Now, though, with the passage of countless travelers, caused by the presence of the Enlightened One, who taught the Way of the Eightfold Path, the Festival of Alundil attracted so many pilgrims that local accommodations were filled to overflowing. Those who possessed tents could charge a high fee for their rental. Stables were rented out for human occupancy. Even bare pieces of land were let as camping sites.

Alundil loved its Buddha. Many other towns had tried to entice him away from his purple grove: Shengodu, Flower of the Mountains, had offered him a palace and harem to come bring his teaching to the slopes. But the Enlightened One did not go to the mountain. Kannaka, of the Serpent River, had offered him elephants and ships, a town house and a country villa, horses and servants, to come and preach from its wharves. But the Enlightened One did not go to the river.

The Buddha remained in his grove and all things came to him. With the passage of years the festival grew larger and longer and more elaborate, like a well-fed dragon, scales all a-shimmer. The local Brahmins did not approve of the antiritualistic teachings of the Buddha, but his presence filled their coffers to overflowing; so they learned to live in his squat shadow, never voicing the word *tirthika*—heretic.

So the Buddha remained in his grove and all things came to him, including Rild.

Festival-time.

The drums began in the evening on the third day.

On the third day, the massive drums of the *kathakali* began their rapid thunder. The miles-striding staccato of the drums carried across the fields to the town, across the town, across the purple grove and across the wastes of marshland that lay behind it. The drummers, wearing white *mundus,* bare to the waist, their dark flesh glistening with perspiration, worked in shifts, so strenuous was the mighty beating they set up; and never was the flow of sound broken, even as the new relay of drummers moved into position before the tightly stretched heads of the instruments.

As darkness arrived in the world, the travelers and townsmen who had begun walking as soon as they heard the chatter of the drums began to arrive at the festival field, large as a battlefield of old. There they found places and waited for the night to deepen and the drama to begin, sipping the sweet-smelling tea that they purchased at the stalls beneath the trees.

A great brass bowl of oil, tall as a man, wicks hanging down over its edges, stood in the center of the field. These wicks were lighted, and torches flickered beside the tents of the actors.

The drumming, at close range, was deafening and hypnotic, the rhythms complicated, syncopated, insidious. As midnight approached, the devotional chanting began, rising and falling with the drumbeat, working a net about the senses.

There was a brief lull as the Enlightened One and his monks arrived, their yellow robes near-orange in the flamelight. But they threw back their cowls and seated themselves cross-legged upon the ground. After a time, it was only the chanting and the voices of the drums that filled the minds of the spectators.

When the actors appeared, gigantic in their makeup, ankle bells jangling as their feet beat the ground, there was no applause, only rapt attention. The *kathakali* dancers were famous, trained from their youth in acrobatics as well as the ages-old patterns of the classical dance, knowing the nine distinct movements of the neck and of the eyeballs and the hundreds of hand positions required to reenact the ancient epics of love and battle, of the encounters of gods and demons, of the valiant fights and bloody treacheries of tradition. The musicians shouted out the words of the stories as the actors, who never spoke, portrayed the awesome exploits of Rama and of the Pandava brothers. Wearing makeup of green and red, or black and stark white, they stalked across the field, skirts billowing, their mirror-sprinkled halos glittering in the light of the lamp. Occasionally, the lamp would flare or sputter, and it was as if a nimbus of holy or unholy light played about their heads, erasing entirely the sense of the event, causing the spectators to feel for a moment that they themselves were the illusion, and that the great-bodied figures of the cyclopean dance were the only real things in the world.

The dance would continue until daybreak, to end with the rising of the sun. Before daybreak, however, one of the wearers of the saffron robe arrived from the direction of town, made his way through the crowd and spoke into the ear of the Enlightened One.

The Buddha began to rise, appeared to think better of it and reseated himself. He gave a message to the monk, who nodded and departed from the field of the festival.

The Buddha, looking imperturbable, returned his attention to the drama. A monk seated nearby noted that he was tapping his fingers upon the ground, and he decided that the Enlightened One must be keeping time with the drumbeats, for it was common knowledge that he was above such things as impatience.

When the drama had ended and Surya the sun pinked the skirts of Heaven above the eastern rim of the world, it was as if the night just passed had held the crowd prisoner within a tense and frightening dream, from which they were just now released, weary, to wander this day.

The Buddha and his followers set off walking immediately, in the direction of the town. They did not pause to rest along the way, but passed through Alundil at a rapid but dignified gait.

When they came again to the purple grove, the Enlightened One instructed his monks to take rest, and he moved off in the direction of a small pavilion located deep within the wood.

The monk who had brought the message during the drama sat within the pavilion. There he tended the fever of the traveler he had come upon in the marshes, where he walked often to better meditate upon the putrid condition his body would assume after death.

Tathagatha studied the man who lay upon the sleeping mat. His lips were thin and pale; he had a high forehead, high cheekbones, frosty eyebrows, pointed ears; and Tathagatha guessed that when those eyelids rose, the eyes revealed would be of a faded blue or gray. There was a quality of—translucency?—fragility perhaps, about his unconscious form, which might have been caused partly by the fevers that racked his body, but which could not be attributed entirely to them. The small man did not give the impression of being one who would bear the thing that Tathagatha now raised in his hands. Rather, on first viewing, he might seem to be a very old man. If one granted him a second look, and realized then that his colorless hair and his slight frame did not signify advanced age, one might then be struck by something childlike about his appearance. From the condition of his complexion, Tathagatha doubted that he need shave very often. Perhaps a slightly mischievous pucker was now hidden somewhere between his cheeks and the corners of his mouth. Perhaps not, also.

The Buddha raised the crimson strangling cord, which was a thing borne only by the holy executioners of the goddess Kali. He fingered its silken length, and it passed like a serpent through his hand, clinging slightly. He did not doubt but that it was intended to move in such a manner about his throat. Almost unconsciously, he held it and twisted his hands through the necessary movements.

Then he looked up at the wide-eyed monk who had watched him, smiled his imperturbable smile and laid the cord aside. With a damp cloth, the monk wiped the perspiration from the pale brow.

The man on the sleeping mat shuddered at the contact, and his eyes snapped open. The madness of the fever was in them and they did not truly see, but Tathagatha felt a sudden jolt at their contact.

Dark, so dark they were almost jet, and it was impossible to tell where the pupil ended and the iris began. There was something extremely unsettling about eyes of such power in a body so frail and effete.

He reached out and stroked the man's hands, and it was like touching steel, cold and impervious. He drew his fingernail sharply across the back of the right hand. No scratch or indentation marked its passage, and his nail fairly slid, as though across a pane of glass. He squeezed the man's thumbnail and released it. There was no sudden change of color. It was as though these hands were dead or mechanical things.

He continued his examination. The phenomenon ended somewhat above the wrists, occurred again in other places. His hands, breast, abdomen, neck and portions of his back had soaked within the death bath, which gave this special unyielding power. Total immersion would, of course, have proved fatal; but as it was, the man had traded some of his tactile sensitivity for the equivalent of invisible gauntlets, breastplate, neck-piece and back armor of steel. He was indeed one of the select assassins of the terrible goddess.

"Who else knows of this man?" asked the Buddha.

"The monk Simha," replied the other, "who helped me bear him here."

"Did he see"—Tathagatha gestured with his eyes toward the crimson cord—"that?" he inquired.

The monk nodded.

"Then go fetch him. Bring him to me at once. Do not mention anything of this to anyone, other than that a pilgrim was taken ill and we are tending him here. I will personally take over his care and minister to his illness."

"Yes, Illustrious One."

The monk hurried forth from the pavilion.

Tathagatha seated himself beside the sleeping mat and waited.

It was two days before the fever broke and intelligence returned to those dark eyes. But during those two days, anyone who passed by the pavilion might have heard the voice of the Enlightened One droning on and on, as though he addressed his sleeping charge. Occasionally, the man himself mumbled and spoke loudly, as those in a fever often do.

On the second day, the man opened his eyes suddenly and stared upward. Then he frowned and turned his head.

"Good morning, Rild," said Tathagatha.

"You are . . .?" asked the other, in an unexpected baritone.

"One who teaches the way of liberation," he replied.

"The Buddha?"

"I have been called such."

"Tathagatha?"

"This name, too, have I been given."

The other attempted to rise, failed, settled back. His eyes never left the placid countenance. "How is it that you know my name?" he finally asked.

"In your fever you spoke considerably."

"Yes, I was very sick, and doubtless babbling. It was in that cursed swamp that I took the chill."

Tathagatha smiled. "One of the disadvantages of traveling alone is that when you fall there is none to assist you."

"True," acknowledged the other, and his eyes closed once more and his breathing deepened.

Tathagatha remained in the lotus posture, waiting.

When Rild awakened again, it was evening. "Thirsty," he said.

Tathagatha gave him water. "Hungry?" he asked.

"No, not yet. My stomach would rebel."

He raised himself up onto his elbows and stared at his attendant. Then he sank back upon the mat. "You are the one," he announced.

"Yes," replied the other.

"What are you going to do?"

"Feed you, when you say you are hungry."

"I mean, after that."

"Watch as you sleep, lest you lapse again into the fever."

"That is not what I meant."

"I know."

"After I have eaten and rested and recovered my strength—what then?"

Tathagatha smiled as he drew the silken cord from somewhere beneath his robe. "Nothing," he replied, "nothing at all," and he draped the cord across Rild's shoulder and withdrew his hand.

The other shook his head and leaned back. He reached up and fingered the length of crimson. He twined it about his fingers and then about his wrist. He stroked it.

"It is holy," he said, after a time.

"So it would seem."

"You know its use, and its purpose?"

"Of course."

"Why then will you do nothing at all?"

"I have no need to move or to act. All things come to me. If anything is to be done, it is you who will do it."

"I do not understand."

"I know that, too."

The man stared into the shadows overhead. "I will attempt to eat now," he announced.

Tathagatha gave him broth and bread, which he managed to keep down. Then he drank more water, and when he had finished he was breathing heavily.

"You have offended Heaven," he stated.

"Of that, I am aware."

"And you have detracted from the glory of a goddess, whose supremacy here has always been undisputed."

"I know."

"But I owe you my life, and I have eaten your bread . . ."

There was no reply.

"Because of this, I must break a most holy vow," finished Rild. "I cannot kill you, Tathagatha."

"Then I owe my life to the fact that you owe me yours. Let us consider the life-owing balanced."

Rild uttered a short chuckle. "So be it," he said.

"What will you do, now that you have abandoned your mission?"

"I do not know. My sin is too great to permit me to return. Now I, too, have offended against Heaven, and the goddess will turn away her face from my prayers. I have failed her."

"Such being the case, remain here. You will at least have company in damnation."

"Very well," agreed Rild. "There is nothing else left to me."

He slept once again, and the Buddha smiled.

In the days that followed, as the festival wore on, the Enlightened One preached to the crowds who passed through the purple grove. He spoke of the unity of all things, great and small, of the law of cause, of becoming and dying, of the illusion of the world, of the spark of the *atman,* of the way of salvation through renunciation of the self and union with the whole; he spoke of realization and enlightenment, of the meaninglessness of the Brahmins' rituals, comparing their forms to vessels empty of content. Many listened, a few heard and some remained in the purple grove to take up the saffron robe of the seeker.

And each time he taught, the man Rild sat nearby, wearing his black garments and leather harness, his strange dark eyes ever upon the Enlightened One.

Two weeks after his recovery, Rild came upon the teacher as he walked through the grove in meditation. He fell into step beside him, and after a time he spoke.

"Enlightened One, I have listened to your teachings, and I have listened well. Much have I thought upon your words."

The other nodded.

"I have always been a religious man," he stated, "or I would not have been selected for the post I once occupied. After it became impossible for me to fulfill my mission, I felt a great emptiness. I had failed my goddess, and life was without meaning for me."

The other listened, silently.

"But I have heard your words," he said, "and they have filled me with a kind of joy. They have shown me another way to salvation, a way which I feel to be superior to the one I previously followed."

The Buddha studied his face as he spoke.

"Your way of renunciation is a strict one, which I feel to be good. It suits my needs. Therefore, I request permission to be taken into your community of seekers, and to follow your path."

"Are you certain," asked the Enlightened One, "that you do not seek merely to punish yourself for what has been weighing upon your conscience as a failure, or a sin?"

"Of that I am certain," said Rild. "I have held your words within me and felt the truth which they contain. In the service of the goddess have I slain more men than purple fronds upon yonder bough. I am not even counting women and children. So I am not easily taken in by words, having heard too many, voiced in all tones of speech—words pleading, arguing, cursing. But your words move me, and they are superior to the teachings of the Brahmins. Gladly would I become your executioner, dispatching for you your enemies with a saffron cord—or with a blade, or pike, or with my hands, for I am proficient with all weapons, having spent three lifetimes learning their use—but I know that such is not your way. Death and life are as one to you, and you do not seek the destruction of your enemies. So I request entrance to your Order. For me, it is not so difficult a thing as it would be for another. One must renounce home and family, origin and property. I lack these things. One must renounce one's own will, which I have already done. All I need now is the yellow robe."

"It is yours," said Tathagatha, "with my blessing."

Rild donned the robe of a buddhist monk and took to fasting and meditating. After a week, when the festival was near to its close, he departed into the town with his begging bowl, in the company of the other monks. He did not return with them, however. The day wore on into evening, the evening into darkness. The horns of the Temple had already sounded the last notes of the *nagaswaram,* and many of the travelers had since departed the festival.

For a long while, the Enlightened One walked the woods, meditating. Then he, too, vanished.

Down from the grove, with the marshes at its back, toward the town of Alundil, above which lurked the hills of rock and around which lay the blue-green fields, into the town of Alundil, still astir with travelers, many of them at the height of their revelry, up the streets of Alundil toward the hill with its Temple, walked the Buddha.

He entered the first courtyard, and it was quiet there. The dogs and children and beggars had gone away. The priests slept. One drowsing attendant sat behind a bench at the bazaar. Many of the shrines were now empty, the statues having been borne within. Before several of the others, worshipers knelt in late prayer.

He entered the inner courtyard. An ascetic was seated on a prayer mat before the statue of Ganesha. He, too, seemed to qualify as a statue, making no visible movements. Four oil lamps flickered about the yard, their dancing light serving primarily to accentuate the shadows that lay upon most of the shrines. Small votive lights cast a faint illumination upon some of the statues.

Tathagatha crossed the yard and stood facing the towering figure of Kali, at whose feet a tiny lamp blinked. Her smile seemed a plastic and moving thing, as she regarded the man before her.

Draped across her outstretched hand, looped once about the point of her dagger, lay a crimson strangling cord.

Tathagatha smiled back at her, and she seemed almost to frown at that moment.

"It is a resignation, my dear," he stated. "You have lost this round."

She seemed to nod in agreement.

"I am pleased to have achieved such a height of recognition in so short a period of time," he continued. "But even if you had succeeded, old girl, it would have done you little good. It is too late now. I have started something which you cannot undo. Too many have heard the ancient words. You had thought they were lost, and so did I. But we were both wrong. The religion by which you rule is very ancient, goddess, but my protest is also that of a venerable tradition. So call me a protestant, and remember—now I am more than a man. Good night."

He left the Temple and the shrine of Kali, where the eyes of Yama had been fixed upon his back.

It was many months before the miracle occurred, and when it did, it did not seem a miracle, for it had grown up slowly about them.

Rild, who had come out of the north as the winds of spring blew across the land, wearing death upon his arm and the black fire within his eyes— Rild, of the white brows and pointed ears—spoke one afternoon, after the spring had passed, when the long days of summer hung warm beneath the Bridge of the Gods. He spoke, in that unexpected baritone, to answer a question asked him by a traveler.

The man asked him a second question, and then a third.

He continued to speak, and some of the other monks and several pilgrims gathered about him. The answers following the questions, which now came from all of them, grew longer and longer, for they became parables, examples, allegories.

Then they were seated at his feet, and his dark eyes became strange pools, and his voice came down as from Heaven, clear and soft, melodic and persuasive.

They listened, and then the travelers went their way. But they met and spoke with other travelers upon the road, so that, before the summer had passed, pilgrims coming to the purple grove were asking to meet this disciple of the Buddha's, and to hear his words also.

Tathagatha shared the preaching with him. Together, they taught of the Way of the Eightfold Path, the glory of Nirvana, the illusion of the world and the chains that the world lays upon a man.

And then there were times when even the soft-spoken Tathagatha listened to the words of his disciple, who had digested all of the things he had preached, had meditated long and fully upon them and now, as though he had found entrance to a secret sea, dipped with his steel-hard hand into places of hidden waters, and then sprinkled a thing of truth and beauty upon the heads of the hearers.

Summer passed. There was no doubt now that there were two who had received enlightenment: Tathagatha and his small disciple, whom they called Sugata. It was even said that Sugata was a healer, and that when his eyes shone strangely and the icy touch of his hands came upon a twisted limb, that limb grew straight again. It was said that a blind man's vision had suddenly returned to him during one of Sugata's sermons.

There were two things in which Sugata believed: the Way of Salvation and Tathagatha, the Buddha.

"Illustrious One," he said to him one day, "my life was empty until you revealed to me the True Path. When you received your enlightenment, before you began your teaching, was it like a rush of fire and the roaring of water and you everywhere and a part of everything—the clouds and the trees, the animals in the forest, all people, the snow on the mountaintop and the bones in the field?"

"Yes," said Tathagatha.

"I, also, know the joy of all things," said Sugata.

"Yes, I know," said Tathagatha.   •

"I see now why once you said that all things come to you. To have brought such a doctrine into the world—I can see why the gods were envious. Poor gods! They are to be pitied. But you know. You know all things."

Tathagatha did not reply.

* * *

When the winds of spring blew again across the land, the year having gone full cycle since the arrival of the second Buddha, there came one day from out of the heavens a fearful shrieking.

The citizens of Alundil turned out into their streets to stare up at the sky. The Sudras in the fields put by their work and looked upward. In the great Temple on the hill there was a sudden silence. In the purple grove beyond the town, the monks turned their heads.

It paced the heavens, the one who was born to rule the wind. . . . From out of the north it came—green and red, yellow and brown. . . . Its glide was a dance, its way was the air. . . .

There came another shriek, and then the beating of mighty pinions as it climbed past clouds to become a tiny dot of black.

And then it fell, like a meteor, bursting into flame, all of its colors blazing and burning bright, as it grew and grew, beyond all belief that anything could live at that size, that pace, that magnificence. . . .

Half spirit, half bird, legend darkening the sky.

Mount of Vishnu, whose beak smashes chariots.

The Garuda Bird circled above Alundil.

Circled, and passed beyond the hills of rock that stood behind the city.

"Garuda!" The word ran through the town, the fields, the Temple, the grove.

If he did not fly alone; it was known that only a god could use the Garuda Bird for a mount.

There was silence. After those shrieks and that thunder of pinions, voices seemed naturally to drop to a whisper.

The Enlightened One stood upon the road before the grove, his monks moving about him, facing in the direction of the hills of rock.

Sugata came to his side and stood there. "It was but a spring ago . . ." he said.

Tathagatha nodded.

"Rild failed," said Sugata. "What new thing comes from Heaven?"

The Buddha shrugged.

"I fear for you, my teacher," he said. "In all my lifetimes, you have been my only friend. Your teaching has given me peace. Why can they not leave you alone? You are the most harmless of men, and your doctrine the gentlest. What ill could you possibly bear them?"

The other turned away.

At that moment, with a mighty beating of the air and a jagged cry from its opened beak, the Garuda Bird rose once more above the hills. This time, it did not circle over the town, but climbed to a great height in the heavens and swept off to the north. Such was the speed of its passing that it was gone in a matter of moments.

"Its passenger has dismounted and remains behind," suggested Sugata.

The Buddha walked within the purple grove.

*   *   *

He came from beyond the hills of stone, walking.

He came to a passing place through stone, and he followed this trail, his red leather boots silent on the rocky path.

Ahead, there was a sound of running water, from where a small stream cut across his way. Shrugging his blood-bright cloak back over his shoulders, he advanced upon a bend in the trail, the ruby head of his scimitar gleaming in his crimson sash.

Rounding a corner of stone, he came to a halt.

One waited ahead, standing beside the log that led across the stream.

His eyes narrowed for an instant, then he moved forward again.

It was a small man who stood there, wearing the dark garments of a pilgrim, caught about with a leather harness from which was suspended a short, curved blade of bright steel. This man's head was closely shaven, save for a small lock of white hair. His eyebrows were white above eyes that were dark, and his skin was pale; his ears appeared to be pointed.

The traveler raised his hand and spoke to this man, saying, "Good afternoon, pilgrim."

The man did not reply, but moved to bar his way, positioning himself before the log that led across the stream.

"Pardon me, good pilgrim, but I am about to cross here and you are making my passage difficult," he stated.

"You are mistaken, Lord Yama, if you think you are about to pass here," replied the other.

The One in Red smiled, showing a long row of even, white teeth. "It is always a pleasure to be recognized," he acknowledged, "even by one who conveys misinformation concerning other matters."

"I do not fence with words," said the man in black.

"Oh?" The other raised his eyebrows in an expression of exaggerated inquiry. "With what then do you fence, sir? Surely not that piece of bent metal you bear."

"None other."

"I took it for some barbarous prayer-stick at first. I understand that this is a region fraught with strange cults and primitive sects. For a moment, I took you to be a devotee of some such superstition. But if, as you say, it is indeed a weapon, then I trust you are familiar with its use?"

"Somewhat," replied the man in black.

"Good, then," said Yama, "for I dislike having to kill a man who does not know what he is about. I feel obligated to point out to you, however, that when you stand before the Highest for judgment, you will be accounted a suicide."

The other smiled faintly.

"Any time that you are ready, deathgod, I will facilitate the passage of your spirit from out its fleshy envelope."

"One more item only, then," said Yama, "and I shall put a quick end to conversation. Give me a name to tell the priests, so that they shall know for whom they offer the rites."

"I renounced my final name but a short while back," answered the other. "For this reason, Kali's consort must take his death of one who is name-less."

"Rild, you are a fool," said Yama, and drew his blade.

The man in black drew his.

"And it is fitting that you go unnamed to your doom. You betrayed your goddess."

"Life is full of betrayals," replied the other, before he struck. "By opposing you now and in this manner, I also betray the teachings of my new master. But I must follow the dictates of my heart. Neither my old name nor my new do therefore fit me, nor are they deserved—so call me by no name!"

Then his blade was fire, leaping everywhere, clicking, blazing.

Yama fell back before this onslaught, giving ground foot by foot, moving only his wrist as he parried the blows that fell about him.

Then, after he had retreated ten paces, he stood his ground and would not be moved. His parries widened slightly, but his ripostes became more sudden now, and were interspersed with feints and unexpected attacks.

They swaggered blades till their perspiration fell upon the ground in showers; and then Yama began to press the attack, slowly forcing his opponent into a retreat. Step by step, he recovered the ten paces he had given.

When they stood again upon the ground where the first blow had been struck, Yama acknowledged, over the clashing of steel, "Well have you learned your lessons, Rild! Better even than I had thought! Congratulations!"

As he spoke, his opponent wove his blade through an elaborate double feint and scored a light touch that cut his shoulder, drawing blood that immediately merged with the color of his garment.

At this, Yama sprang forward, beating down the other's guard, and delivered a blow to the side of his neck that might have decapitated him.

The man in black raised his guard, shaking his head, parried another attack and thrust forward, to be parried again himself.

"So, the death bath collars your throat," said Yama. "I'll seek entrance elsewhere, then," and his blade sang a faster song, as he tried for a low-line thrust.

Yama unleashed the full fury of that blade, backed by the centuries and the masters of many ages. Yet, the other met his attacks, parrying wider and wider, retreating faster and faster now, but still managing to hold him off as he backed away, counterthrusting as he went.

He retreated until his back was to the stream. Then Yama slowed and made comment:

"Half a century ago," he stated, "when you were my pupil for a brief time, I said to myself, 'This one has within him the makings of a master.' Nor was I wrong, Rild. You are perhaps the greatest swordsman raised up in all the ages I can remember. I can almost forgive apostasy when I witness your skill. It is indeed a pity . . .'"

He feinted then a chest cut, and at the last instant moved around the parry so that he lay the edge of his weapon high upon the other's wrist.

Leaping backward, parrying wildly and cutting at Yama's head, the man in black came into a position at the head of the log that lay above the crevice that led down to the stream.

"Your hand, too, Rild! Indeed, the goddess is lavish with her protection. Try this!"

The steel screeched as he caught it in a bind, nicking the other's bicep as he passed about the blade.

"Aha! There's a place she missed!" he cried. "Let's try for another!"

Their blades bound and disengaged, feinted, thrust, parried, riposted.

Yama met an elaborate attack with a stop-thrust, his longer blade again drawing blood from his opponent's upper arm.

Yama met an elaborate attack with a stop-thrust, his longer blade again drawing blood from his opponent's upper arm.

The man in black stepped up upon the log, swinging a vicious head cut, which Yama beat away. Pressing the attack then even harder, Yama forced him to back out upon the log and then he kicked at its side.

The other jumped backward, landing upon the opposite bank. As soon as his feet touched ground, he, too, kicked out, causing the log to move.

It rolled, before Yama could mount it, slipping free of the banks, crashing down into the stream, bobbing about for a moment, and then following the water trail westward.

"I'd say it is only a seven- or eight-foot jump, Yama! Come on across!" cried the other.

The deathgod smiled. "Catch your breath quickly now, while you may," he stated. "Breath is the least appreciated gift of the gods. None sing hymns to it, praising the good air, breathed by king and beggar, master and dog alike. But, oh to be without it! Appreciate each breath, Rild, as though it were your last—for that one, too, is near at hand!"

"You are said to be wise in these matters, Yama," said the one who had been called Rild and Sugata. "You are said to be a god, whose kingdom is death and whose knowledge extends beyond the ken of mortals. I would question you, therefore, while we are standing idle."

Yama did not smile his mocking smile, as he had to all his opponent's previous statements. This one had a touch of ritual about it.

"What is it that you wish to know? I grant you the death-boon of a question."

Then, in the ancient words of the *Katha Upanishad*, the one who had been called Rild and Sugata chanted:

" 'There is doubt concerning a man when he is dead. Some say he still exists. Others say he does not. This thing I should like to know, taught by you.' "

Yama replied with the ancient words, " 'On this subject even the gods have their doubts. It is not easy to understand, for the nature of the *atman* is a subtle thing. Ask me another question. Release me from this boon!' "

" 'Forgive me if it is foremost in my mind, oh Death, but another teacher such as yourself cannot be found, and surely there is no other boon which I crave more at this moment.' "

" 'Keep your life and go your way,' " said Yama, plunging his blade again into his sash. " 'I release you from your doom. Choose sons and grandsons; choose elephants, horses, herds of cattle and gold. Choose any other boon—fair maidens, chariots, musical instruments. I shall give them unto you and they shall wait upon you. But ask me not of death.' "

" 'Oh Death,' " sang the other, " 'these endure only till tomorrow. Keep your maidens, horses, dances and songs for yourself. No boon will I accept but the one which I have asked—tell me, oh Death, of that which lies beyond life, of which men and the gods have their doubts.' "

Yama stood very still and he did not continue the poem. "Very well, Rild," he said, his eyes locking with the other's, "but it is not a kingdom subject to words. I must show you."

They stood, so, for a moment; and then the man in black swayed. He threw his arm across his face, covering his eyes, and a single sob escaped his throat.

When this occurred, Yama drew his cloak from his shoulders and cast it like a net across the stream.

Weighted at the hems for such a maneuver, it fell, netlike, upon his opponent.

As he struggled to free himself, the man in black heard rapid footfalls and then a crash, as Yama's blood-red boots struck upon his side of the stream. Casting aside the cloak and raising his guard, he parried Yama's new attack. The ground behind him sloped upward, and he backed farther and farther, to where it steepened, so that Yama's head was no higher than his belt. He then struck down at his opponent. Yama slowly fought his way uphill.

"Deathgod, deathgod," he chanted, "forgive my presumptuous question, and tell me you did not lie."

"Soon you shall know," said Yama, cutting at his legs.

Yama struck a blow that would have run another man through, cleaving his heart. But it glanced off his opponent's breast.

When he came to a place where the ground was broken, the small man kicked, again and again, sending showers of dirt and gravel down upon his opponent. Yama shielded his eyes with his left hand, but then larger pieces of stone began to rain down upon him. These rolled on the ground, and, as several came beneath his boots, he lost his footing and fell, slipping backward down the slope. The other kicked at heavy rocks then, even dislodging a boulder and following it downhill, his blade held high.

Unable to gain his footing in time to meet the attack, Yama rolled and slid back toward the stream. He managed to brake himself at the edge of the crevice, but he saw the boulder coming and tried to draw back out of its way. As he pushed at the ground with both hands, his blade fell into the waters below.

With his dagger, which he drew as he sprang into a stumbling crouch, he managed to parry the high cut of the other's blade. The boulder splashed into the stream.

Then his left hand shot forward, seizing the wrist that had guided the blade. He slashed upward with the dagger and felt his own wrist taken.

They stood then, locking their strength, until Yama sat down and rolled to his side, thrusting the other from him.

Still, both locks held, and they continued to roll from the force of that thrust. Then the edge of the crevice was beside them, beneath them, above them. He felt the blade go out of his hand as it struck the stream bed.

When they came again above the surface of the water, gasping for breath, each held only water in his hands.

"Time for the final baptism," said Yama, and he lashed out with his left hand.

The other blocked the punch, throwing one of his own.

They moved to the left with the waters, until their feet struck upon rock and they fought, wading, along the length of the stream.

It widened and grew more shallow as they moved, until the waters swirled about their waists. In places, the banks began to fall nearer the surface of the water.

Yama landed blow after blow, both with his fists and the edges of his hands; but it was as if he assailed a statue, for the one who had been Kali's holy executioner took each blow without changing his expression, and he returned them with twisting punches of bone-breaking force. Most of these blows were slowed by the water or blocked by Yama's guard, but one landed between his rib cage and hipbone and another glanced off his left shoulder and rebounded from his cheek.

Yama cast himself into a backstroke and made for shallower water.

The other followed and sprang upon him, to be caught in his impervious midsection by a red boot, as the front of his garment was jerked forward and down. He continued on, passing over Yama's head, to land upon his back on a section of shale.

Yama rose to his knees and turned, as the other found his footing and drew a dagger from his belt. His face was still impassive as he dropped into a crouch.

For a moment their eyes met, but the other did not waver this time.

"Now can I meet your death-gaze, Yama," he stated, "and not be stopped by it. You have taught me too well!"

And as he lunged, Yama's hands came away from his waist, snapping his wet sash like a whip about the other's thighs.

He caught him and locked him to him as he fell forward, dropping the blade; and with a kick he bore them both back into deeper water.

"None sing hymns to breath," said Yama. "But, oh to be without it!"

Then he plunged downward, bearing the other with him, his arms like steel loops about his body.

Later, much later, as the wet figure stood beside the stream, he spoke softly and his breath came in gasps:

"You were—the greatest—to be raised up against me—in all the ages I can remember. . . . It is indeed a pity . . ."

Then, having crossed the stream, he continued on his way through the hills of stone, walking.

Entering the town of Alundil, the traveler stopped at the first inn he came to. He took a room and ordered a tub of water. He bathed while a servant cleaned his garments.

Before he had his dinner, he moved to the window and looked down into the street. The smell of slizzard was strong upon the air, and the babble of many voices arose from below.

People were leaving the town. In the courtyard at his back, preparations for the departure of a morning caravan were being made. This night marked the end of the spring festival. Below him in the street, businessmen were still trading, mothers were soothing tired children and a local prince was returning with his men from the hunt, two fire-roosters strapped to the back of a skittering slizzard. He watched a tired prostitute discussing something with a priest, who appeared to be even more tired, as he kept shaking his head and finally walked away. One moon was already high in the heavens—seen as golden through the Bridge of the Gods—and a second, smaller moon had just appeared above the horizon. There was a cool tingle in the evening air, bearing to him, above the smells of the city, the scents of the growing things of spring: the small shoots and the tender grasses, the clean smell of the blue-green spring wheat, the moist ground, the roiling freshet. Leaning forward, he could see the Temple that stood upon the hill.

He summoned a servant to bring his dinner in his chamber and to send for a local merchant.

He ate slowly, not paying especial attention to his food, and when he had finished, the merchant was shown in.

The man bore a cloak full of samples, and of these he finally decided upon a long, curved blade and a short, straight dagger, both of which he thrust into his sash.

Then he went out into the evening and walked along the rutted main street of the town. Lovers embraced in doorways. He passed a house where mourners were wailing for one dead. A beggar limped after him for half a block, until he turned and glanced into his eyes, saying, "You are not lame," and then the man hurried away, losing himself in a crowd that was passing. Overhead, the fireworks began to burst against the sky, sending long, cherry-colored streamers down toward the ground. From the Temple came the sound of the gourd horns playing the *nagaswaram* music. A man stumbled from out a doorway, brushing against him, and he broke the man's wrist as he felt his hand fall upon his purse. The man uttered a curse and called for help, but he pushed him into the drainage ditch and walked on, turning away his two companions with one dark look.

At last, he came to the Temple, hesitated a moment and passed within.

He entered the inner courtyard behind a priest who was carrying in a small statue from an outer niche.

He surveyed the courtyard, then quickly moved to the place occupied by the statue of the goddess Kali. He studied her for a long while, drawing his blade and placing it at her feet. When he picked it up and turned away, he saw that the priest was watching him. He nodded to the man, who immediately approached and bade him a good evening.

"Good evening, priest," he replied.

"May Kali sanctify your blade, warrior."

"Thank you. She has."

The priest smiled. "You speak as if you knew that for certain."

"And that is presumptuous of me, eh?"

"Well, it may not be in the best of taste."

"Nevertheless, I felt her power come over me as I gazed upon her shrine."

The priest shuddered. "Despite my office," he stated, "that is a feeling of power I can do without."

"You fear her power?"

"Let us say," said the priest, "that despite its magnificence, the shrine of Kali is not so frequently visited as are those of Lakshmi, Sarasvati, Shakti, Sitala, Ratri and the other less awesome goddesses."

"But she is greater than any of these."

"And more terrible."

"So? Despite her strength, she is not an unjust goddess."

The priest smiled. "What man who has lived for more than a score of years desires justice, warrior? For my part, I find mercy infinitely more attractive. Give me a forgiving deity any day."

"Well taken," said the other, "but I am, as you say, a warrior. My own nature is close to hers. We think alike, the goddess and I. We generally agree on most matters. When we do not, I remember that she is also a woman."

"I live here," said the priest, "and I do not speak that intimately of my charges, the gods."

"In public, that is," said the other. "Tell me not of priests. I have drunk with many of you, and know you to be as blasphemous as the rest of mankind."

"There is a time and place for everything," said the priest, glancing back at Kali's statue.

"Aye, aye. Now tell me why the base of Yama's shrine has not been scrubbed recently. It is dusty."

"It was cleaned but yesterday, but so many have passed before it since then that it has felt considerable usage."

The other smiled. "Why then are there no offerings laid at his feet, no remains of sacrifices?"

"No one gives flowers to Death," said the priest. "They just come to look and go away. We priests have always felt the two statues to be well situated. They make a terrible pair, do they not? Death, and the mistress of destruction?"

"A mighty team," said the other. "But do you mean to tell me that no one makes sacrifice to Yama? No one at all?"

"Other than we priests, when the calendar of devotions requires it, and an occasional townsman, when a loved one is upon the deathbed and has been refused direct incarnation—other than these, no, I have never seen sacrifice made to Yama, simply, sincerely, with goodwill or affection."

"He must feel offended."

"Not so, warrior. For are not all living things, in themselves, sacrifices to Death?"

"Indeed, you speak truly. What need has he for their goodwill or affection? Gifts are unnecessary, for he takes what he wants."

"Like Kali," acknowledged the priest. "And in the cases of both deities have I often sought justification for atheism. Unfortunately, they manifest themselves too strongly in the world for their existence to be denied effectively. Pity."

The warrior laughed. "A priest who is an unwilling believer! I like that. It tickles my funny bone! Here, buy yourself a barrel of soma—for sacrificial purposes."

"Thank you, warrior. I shall. Join me in a small libation now—on the Temple?"

"By Kali, I will!" said the other. "But a small one only."

He accompanied the priest into the central building and down a flight of stairs into the cellar, where a barrel of soma was tapped and two beakers drawn.

"To your health and long life," he said, raising it.

"To your morbid patrons—Yama and Kali," said the priest.

"Thank you."

They gulped the potent brew, and the priest drew two more. "To warm your throat against the night."

"Very good."

"It is a good thing to see some of these travelers depart," said the priest. "Their devotions have enriched the Temple, but they have also tired the staff considerably."

"To the departure of the pilgrims!"

"To the departure of the pilgrims!"

They drank again.

"I thought that most of them came to see the Buddha," said Yama.

"That is true," replied the priest, "but on the other hand, they are not anxious to antagonize the gods by this. So, before they visit the purple grove, they generally make sacrifice or donate to the Temple for prayers."

"What do you know of the one called Tathagatha, and of his teachings?"

The other looked away. "I am a priest of the gods and a Brahmin, warrior. I do not wish to speak of this one."

"So, he has gotten to you, too?"

"Enough! I have made my wishes known to you. It is not a subject on which I will discourse."

"It matters not—and will matter less shortly. Thank you for the soma. Good evening, priest."

"Good evening, warrior. May the gods smile upon your path."

"And yours also."

Mounting the stairs, he departed the Temple and continued on his way through the city, walking.

When he came to the purple grove, there were three moons in the heavens, small camplights behind the trees, pale blossoms of fire in the sky above the town, and a breeze with a certain dampness in it stirring the growth about him.

He moved silently ahead, entering the grove.

When he came into the lighted area, he was faced with row upon row of motionless, seated figures. Each wore a yellow robe with a yellow cowl drawn over the head. Hundreds of them were seated so, and not one uttered a sound.

He approached the one nearest him.

"I have come to see Tathagatha, the Buddha," he said.

The man did not seem to hear him.

"Where is he?"

The man did not reply.

He bent forward and stared into the monk's half-closed eyes. For a moment, he glared into them, but it was as though the other was asleep, for the eyes did not even meet with his.

Then he raised his voice, so that all within the grove might hear him: "I have come to see Tathagatha, the Buddha," he said. "Where is he?" It was as though he addressed a field of stones.

"Do you think to hide him in this manner?" he called out. "Do you think that because you are many, and all dressed alike, and because you will not answer me, that for these reasons I cannot find him among you?"

There was only the sighing of the wind, passing through from the back of the grove. The light flickered and the purple fronds stirred.

He laughed. "In this, you may be right," he admitted. "But you must move sometime, if you intend to go on living—and I can wait as long as any man."

Then he seated himself upon the ground, his back against the blue bark of a tall tree, his blade across his knees.

Immediately, he was seized with drowsiness. His head nodded and jerked upward several times. Then his chin came to rest upon his breast and he snored.

Was walking, across a blue-green plain, the grasses bending down to form a pathway before him. At the end of this pathway was a massive tree, a tree such as did not grow upon the world, but rather held the world together with its roots, and with its branches reached up to utter leaves among the stars.

At its base sat a man, cross-legged, a faint smile upon his lips. He knew this man to be the Buddha, and he approached and stood before him.

"Greetings, oh Death," said the seated one, crowned with a rose-hued aureole that was bright in the shadow of the tree.

Yama did not reply, but drew his blade.

The Buddha continued to smile, and as Yama moved forward he heard a sound like distant music.

He halted and looked about him, his blade still upraised.

They came from all quarters, the four Regents of the world, come down from Mount Sumernu: the Master of the North advanced, followed by his Yakshas, all in gold, mounted on yellow horses, bearing shields that blazed with golden light; the Angel of the South came on, followed by his hosts, the Kumbhandas, mounted upon blue steeds and bearing sapphire shields; from the East rode the Regent whose horsemen carry shields of pearl, and who are clad all in silver; and from the West there came the One whose Nagas mounted blood-red horses, were clad all in red and held before them shields of coral. Their hooves did not appear to touch the grasses, and the only sound in the air was the music, which grew louder.

"Why do the Regents of the world approach?" Yama found himself saying.

"They come to bear my bones away," replied the Buddha, still smiling.

The four Regents drew rein, their hordes at their backs, and Yama faced them.

"You come to bear his bones away," said Yama, "but who will come for yours?"

The Regents dismounted.

"You may not have this man, oh Death," said the Master of the North, "for he belongs to the world, and we of the world will defend him."

"Hear me, Regents who dwell upon Sumernu," said Yama, taking his Aspect upon him. "Into your hands is given the keeping of the world, but Death takes whom he will from out the world, and whenever he chooses. It is not given to you to dispute my Attributes, or the ways of their working."

The four Regents moved to a position between Yama and Tathagatha.

"We do dispute your way with this one, Lord Yama. For in his hands he holds the destiny of our world. You may touch him only after having overthrown the four Powers."

"So be it," said Yama. "Which among you will be first to oppose me?"

"I will," said the speaker, drawing his golden blade.

Yama, his Aspect upon him, sheared through the soft metal like butter and laid the flat of his scimitar along the Regent's head, sending him sprawling upon the ground.

A great cry came up from the ranks of the Yakshas, and two of the golden horsemen came forward to bear away their leader. Then they turned their mounts and rode back into the North.

"Who is next?"

The Regent of the East came before him, bearing a straight blade of silver and a net woven of moonbeams. "I," he said, and he cast with the net.

Yama set his foot upon it, caught it in his fingers, jerked the other off balance. As the Regent stumbled forward, he reversed his blade and struck him in the jaw with its pommel.

Two silver warriors glared at him, then dropped their eyes, as they bore their Master away to the East, a discordant music trailing in their wake.

"Next!" said Yama.

Then there came before him the burly leader of the Nagas, who threw down his weapons and stripped off his tunic, saying, "I will wrestle with you, deathgod."

Yama laid his weapons aside and removed his upper garments.

All the while this was happening, the Buddha sat in the shade of the great tree, smiling, as though the passage of arms meant nothing to him.

The Chief of the Nagas caught Yama behind the neck with his left hand, pulling his head forward. Yama did the same to him; and the other did then twist his body, casting his right arm over Yama's left shoulder and behind his neck, locking it then tight about his head, which he now drew down hard against his hip, turning his body as he dragged the other forward.

Reaching up behind the Naga Chief's back, Yama caught his left shoulder in his left hand and then moved his right hand behind the Regent's knees, so that he lifted both his legs off the ground while drawing back upon his shoulder.

For a moment he held this one cradled in his arms like a child, then raised him up to shoulder level and dropped away his arms.

When the Regent struck the ground, Yama fell upon him with his knees and rose again. The other did not.

When the riders of the West had departed, only the Angel of the South, clad all in blue, stood before the Buddha.

"And you?" asked the deathgod, raising his weapons again.

"I will not take up weapons of steel or leather or stone, as a child takes up toys, to face you, god of death. Nor will I match the strength of my body against yours," said the Angel. "I know I will be bested if I do these things, for none may dispute you with arms."

"Then climb back upon your blue stallion and ride away," said Yama, "if you will not fight."

The Angel did not answer, but cast his blue shield into the air, so that it spun like a wheel of sapphire, growing larger and larger as it hung above them.

Then it fell to the ground and began to sink into it, without a sound, still growing as it vanished from sight, the grasses coming together again above the spot where it had struck.

"And what does that signify?" asked Yama.

"I do not actively contest. I merely defend. Mine is the power of passive opposition. Mine is the power of life, as yours is the power of death. While you can destroy anything I send against you, you cannot destroy everything, oh Death. Mine is the power of the shield, but not the sword. Life will oppose you, Lord Yama, to defend your victim."

The Blue One turned then, mounted his blue steed and rode into the South, the Kumbhandas at his back. The sound of the music did not go with him, but remained in the air he had occupied.

Yama advanced once more, his blade in his hand. "Their efforts came to naught," he said. "Your time is come."

He struck forward with his blade.

The blow did not land, however, as a branch from the great tree fell between them and struck the scimitar from his grasp.

He reached for it and the grasses bent to cover it over, weaving themselves into a tight, unbreakable net.

Cursing, he drew his dagger and struck again.

One mighty branch bent down, came swaying before his target, so that his blade was imbedded deeply in its fibers. Then the branch lashed again skyward, carrying the weapon with it, high out of reach.

The Buddha's eyes were closed in meditation and his halo glowed in the shadows.

Yama took a step forward, raising his hands, and the grasses knotted themselves about his ankles, holding him where he stood.

He struggled for a moment, tugging at their unyielding roots. Then he stopped and raised both hands high, throwing his head far back, death leaping from his eyes.

"Hear me, oh Powers!" he cried. "From this moment forward, this spot shall bear the curse of Yama! No living thing shall ever stir again upon this ground! No bird shall sing, nor snake slither here! It shall be barren and stark, a place of rocks and shifting sand! Not a spear of grass shall ever be upraised from here against the sky! I speak this curse and lay this doom upon the defenders of my enemy!"

The grasses began to wither, but before they had released him there came a great splintering, cracking noise, as the tree whose roots held together the world and in whose branches the stars were caught, as fish in a net, swayed forward, splitting down its middle, its uppermost limbs tearing apart the sky, its roots opening chasms in the ground, its leaves falling like blue-green rain about him. A massive section of its trunk toppled toward him, casting before it a shadow dark as night.

In the distance, he still saw the Buddha, seated in meditation, as though unaware of the chaos that erupted about him.

Then there was only blackness and a sound like the crashing of thunder.

Yama jerked his head, his eyes springing open.

He sat in the purple grove, his back against the bole of a blue tree, his blade across his knees.

Nothing seemed to have changed.

The rows of monks were seated, as in meditation, before him. The breeze was still cool and moist and the lights still flickered as it passed.

Yama stood, knowing then, somehow, where he must go to find that which he sought.

He moved past the monks, following a well-beaten path that led far into the interior of the wood.

He came upon a purple pavilion, but it was empty.

He moved on, tracing the path back to where the wood became a wilderness. Here, the ground was damp and a faint mist sprang up about him. But the way was still clear before him, illuminated by the light of the three moons.

The trail led downward, the blue and purple trees growing shorter and more twisted here than they did above. Small pools of water, with floating patches of leprous, silver scum, began to appear at the sides of the trail. A marshland smell came to his nostrils, and the wheezing of strange creatures came out of clumps of brush.

He heard the sound of singing, coming from far up behind him, and he realized that the monks he had left were now awake and stirring about the grove. They had finished with the task of combining their thoughts to force upon him the vision of their leader's invincibility. Their chanting was probably a signal, reaching out to—

There!

He was seated upon a rock in the middle of a field, the moonlight falling full upon him.

Yama drew his blade and advanced.

When he was about twenty paces away, the other turned his head.

"Greetings, oh Death," he said.

"Greetings, Tathagatha."

"Tell me why you are here."

"It has been decided that the Buddha must die."

"That does not answer my question, however. Why have you come here?"

"Are you not the Buddha?"

"I have been called Buddha, and Tathagatha, and the Enlightened One, and many other things. But, in answer to your question, no, I am not the Buddha. You have already succeeded in what you set out to do. You slew the real Buddha this day."

"My memory must indeed be growing weak, for I confess that I do not remember doing this thing."

"The real Buddha was named by us Sugata," replied the other. "Before that, he was known as Rild."

"Rild!" Yama chuckled. "You are trying to tell me that he was more than an executioner whom you talked out of doing his job?"

"Many people are executioners who have been talked out of doing their jobs," replied the one on the rock. "Rild gave up his mission willingly and became a follower of the Way. He was the only man I ever knew to really achieve enlightenment."

"Is this not a pacifistic religion, this thing you have been spreading?"

"Yes."

Yama threw back his head and laughed. "Gods! Then it is well you are not preaching a militant one! Your foremost disciple, enlightenment and all, near had my head this afternoon!"

A tired look came over the Buddha's wide countenance. "Do you think he could actually have beaten you?"

Yama was silent a moment, then, "No," he said.

"Do you think he knew this?"

"Perhaps," Yama replied.

"Did you not know one another prior to this day's meeting? Have you not seen one another at practice?"

"Yes," said Yama. "We were acquainted."

"Then he knew your skill and realized the outcome of the encounter."

Yama was silent.

"He went willingly to his martyrdom, unknown to me at the time. I do not feel that he went with real hope of beating you."

"Why, then?"

"To prove a point."

"What point could he hope to prove in such a manner?"

"I do not know. I only know that it must be as I have said, for I knew him. I have listened too often to his sermons, to his subtle parables, to believe that he would do a thing such as this without a purpose. You have slain the true Buddha, deathgod. You know what *I* am."

"Siddhartha," said Yama, "I know that you are a fraud. I know that you are not an Enlightened One. I realize that your doctrine is a thing which could have been remembered by any among the First. You chose to resurrect it, pretending to be its originator. You decided to spread it, in hopes of raising an opposition to the religion by which the true gods rule. I admire the effort. It was cleverly planned and executed. But your biggest mistake, I feel, is that you picked a pacifistic creed with which to oppose an active one. I am curious why you did this thing, when there were so many more appropriate religions from which to choose."

"Perhaps I was just curious to see how such a countercurrent would flow," replied the other.

"No, Sam, that is not it," answered Yama. "I feel it is only part of a larger plan you have laid, and that for all these years—while you pretended to be a saint and preached sermons in which you did not truly believe yourself—you have been making other plans. An army, great in space, may offer opposition in a brief span of time. One man, brief in space, must spread his opposition across a period of many years if he is to have a chance of succeeding. You are aware of this, and now that you have sown the seeds of this stolen creed, you are planning to move on to another phase of opposition. You are trying to be a one-man antithesis to Heaven, opposing the will of the gods across the years, in many ways and from behind many masks. But it will end here and now, false Buddha."

"Why, Yama?" he asked.

"It was considered quite carefully," said Yama. "We did not want to make you a martyr, encouraging more than ever the growth of this thing you have been teaching. On the other hand, if you were not stopped, it would still continue to grow. It was decided, therefore, that you must meet your end at the hands of an agent of Heaven—thus showing which religion is the stronger. So, martyr or no, Buddhism will be a second-rate religion henceforth. That is why you must now die the real death."

"When I asked 'Why?' I meant something different. You have answered the wrong question. I meant, why have *you* come to do this thing, Yama? Why have you, master of arms, master of sciences, come as lackey to a crew of drunken body-changers, who are not qualified to polish your blade or wash out your test tubes? Why do you, who might be the freest spirit of us all, demean yourself by serving your inferiors?"

"For that, your death shall not be a clean one."

"Why? I did but ask a question, which must have long since passed through more minds than my own. I did not take offense when you called me a false Buddha. I know what I am. Who are you, deathgod?"

Yama placed his blade within his sash and withdrew a pipe, which he had purchased at the inn earlier in the day. He filled its bowl with tobacco, lit it, and smoked.

"It is obvious that we must talk a little longer, if only to clear both our minds of questions," he stated, "so I may as well be comfortable." He seated himself upon a low rock. "First, a man may in some ways be superior to his fellows and still serve them, if together they serve a common cause which is greater than any one man. I believe that I serve such a cause, or I would not be doing it. I take it that you feel the same way concerning what you do, or you would not put up with this life of miserable asceticism—though I note that you are not so gaunt as your followers. You were offered godhood some years ago in Mahartha, as I recall, and you mocked Brahma, raided the Palace of Karma, and filled all the pray-machines of the city with slugs . . ."

The Buddha chuckled. Yama joined him briefly and continued, "There are no Accelerationists remaining in the world, other than yourself. It is a dead issue, which should never have become an issue in the first place. I do have a certain respect for the manner in which you have acquitted yourself over the years. It has even occurred to me that if you could be made to realize the hopelessness of your present position, you might still be persuaded to join the hosts of Heaven. While I did come here to kill you, if you can be convinced of this now and give me your word upon it, promising to end your foolish fight, I will take it upon myself to vouch for you. I will take you back to the Celestial City with me, where you may now accept that which you once refused. They will harken to me, because they need me."

"No," said Sam, "for I am not convinced of the futility of my position, and I fully intend to continue the show."

The chanting came down from the camp in the purple grove. One of the moons disappeared beyond the treetops.

"Why are your followers not beating the bushes, seeking to save you?"

"They would come if I called, but I will not call. I do not need to."

"Why did they cause me to dream that foolish dream?"

The Buddha shrugged.

"Why did they not arise and slay me as I slept?"

"It is not their way."

"You might have, though, eh? If you could get away with it? If none would know the Buddha did it?"

"Perhaps," said the other. "As you know, the personal strengths and weaknesses of a leader are no true indication of the merits of his cause."

Yama drew upon his pipe. The smoke wreathed his head and eddied away to join the fogs, which were now becoming more heavy upon the land.

"I know we are alone here, and you are unarmed," said Yama.

"We are alone here. My traveling gear is hidden farther along my route."

"Your traveling gear?"

"I have finished here. You guessed correctly. I have begun what I set out to begin. After we have finished our conversation, I will depart."

Yama chuckled. "The optimism of a revolutionary always gives rise to a sense of wonder. How do you propose to depart? On a magic carpet?"

"I shall go as other men go."

"That is rather condescending of you. Will the powers of the world rise up to defend you? I see no great tree to shelter you with its branches. There is no clever grass to seize at my feet. Tell me how you will achieve your departure?"

"I'd rather surprise you."

"What say we fight? I do not like to slaughter an unarmed man. If you actually do have supplies cached somewhere nearby, go fetch your blade. It is better than no chance at all. I've even heard it said that Lord Sid-dhartha was, in his day, a formidable swordsman."

"Thank you, no. Another time, perhaps. But not this time."

Yama drew once more upon his pipe, stretched, and yawned. "I can think of no more questions then, which I wish to ask you. It is futile to argue with you. I have nothing more to say. Is there anything else that you would care to add to the conversation?"

"Yes," said Sam. "What's she like, that bitch Kali? There are so many different reports that I'm beginning to believe she is all things to all men—"

Yama hurled the pipe, which struck him upon the shoulder and sent a shower of sparks down his arm. His scimitar was a bright flash about his head as he leapt forward.

When he struck the sandy stretch before the rock, his motion was arrested. He almost fell, twisted himself perpendicularly and remained standing. He struggled, but could not move.

"Some quicksand," said Sam, "is quicker than other quicksand. Fortunately, you are settling into that of the slower sort. So you have considerable time yet remaining at your disposal. I would like to prolong the conversation, if I thought I had a chance of persuading you to join with me. But I know that I do not—no more than you could persuade me to go to Heaven."

"I will get free," said Yam softly, not struggling. "I will get free somehow, and I will come after you again."

"Yes," said Sam, "I feel this to be true. In fact, in a short while I will instruct you how to go about it. For the moment, however, you are something every preacher longs for—a captive audience, representing the opposition. So, I have a brief sermon for you, Lord Yama."

Yama hefted his blade, decided against throwing it, thrust it again into his sash.

"Preach on," he said, and he succeeded in catching the other's eyes.

Sam swayed where he sat, but he spoke again:

"It is amazing," he said, "how that mutant brain of yours generated a mind capable of transferring its powers to any new brain you choose to occupy. It has been years since I last exercised my one ability, as I am at this moment—but it, too, behaves in a similar manner. No matter what body I inhabit, it appears that my power follows me into it also. I understand it is still that way with most of us. Sitala, I hear, can control temperatures for a great distance about her. When she assumes a new body, the power accompanies her into her new nervous system, though it comes only weakly at first. Agni, I know, can set fire to objects by staring at them for a period of time and willing that they burn. Now, take for example the death-gaze you are at this moment turning upon me. Is it not amazing how you keep this gift about you in all times and places, over the centuries? I have often wondered as to the physiological basis for the phenomenon. Have you ever researched the area?"

"Yes," said Yama, his eyes burning beneath his dark brows.

"And what is the explanation? A person is born with an abnormal brain, his psyche is later transferred to a normal one and yet his abnormal abilities are not destroyed in the transfer. Why does this thing happen?"

"Because you really have only one body-image, which is electrical as well as chemical in nature. It begins immediately to modify its new physiological environment. The new body has much about it which it treats rather like a disease, attempting to cure it into being the old body. If the body which you now inhabit were to be made physically immortal, it would someday come to resemble your original body."

"How interesting."

"That is why the transferred power is weak at first, but grows stronger as you continue occupancy. That is why it is best to cultivate an Attribute, and perhaps to employ mechanical aids, also."

"Well. That is something I have often wondered about. Thank you. By the way, keep trying with your death-gaze—it is painful, you know. So that is something, anyway. Now, as to the sermon—a proud and arrogant man, such as yourself—with an admittedly admirable quality of didacticism about him—was given to doing research in the area of a certain disfiguring and degenerative disease. One day he contracted it himself. Since he had not yet developed a cure for the condition, he did take time out to regard himself in a mirror and say, 'But on *me* it does look good.' You are such a man, Yama. You will not attempt to fight your condition. Rather, you are proud of it. You betrayed yourself in your fury, so I know that I speak the truth when I say that the name of your disease is Kali. You would not give power into the hands of the unworthy if that woman did not bid you do it. I knew her of old, and I am certain that she has not changed. She cannot love a man. She cares only for those who bring her gifts of chaos. If ever you cease to suit her purposes, she will put you aside, deathgod. I do not say this because we are enemies, but rather as one man to another. I know. Believe me, I do. Perhaps it is unfortunate that you were never really young, Yama, and did not know your first love in the days of spring. . . . The moral, therefore, of my sermon on this small mount is this—even a mirror will not show you yourself, if you do not wish to see. Cross her once to try the truth of my words, even in a small matter, and see how quickly she responds, and in what fashion. What will you do if your own weapons are turned against you, Death?"

"You have finished speaking now?" asked Yama.

"That's about it. A sermon is a warning, and you have been warned."

"Whatever your power, Sam, I see that it is at this moment proof against my death-gaze. Consider yourself fortunate that I am weakened—"

"I do indeed, for my head is about to split. Damn your eyes!"

"One day I will try your power again, and even if it should still be proof against my own, you will fall on that day. If not by my Attribute, then by my blade."

"If that is a challenge, I choose to defer acceptance. I suggest that you do try my words before you attempt to make it good."

At this point, the sand was halfway up Yama's thighs.

Sam sighed and climbed down from his perch.

"There is only one clear path to this rock, and I am about to follow it away from here. Now, I will tell you how to gain your life, if you are not too proud. I have instructed the monks to come to my aid, here at this place, if they hear a cry for help. I told you earlier that I was not going to call for help, and that is true. If, however, you begin calling out for aid with that powerful voice of yours, they shall be here before you sink too much farther. They will bring you safely to firm ground and will not try to harm you, for such is their way. I like the thought of the god of death being saved by the monks of Buddha. Good night, Yama, I'm going to leave you now."

Yama smiled. "There will be another day, oh Buddha," he stated. "I can wait for it. Flee now as far and as fast as you can. The world is not large enough to hide you from my wrath. I will follow you, and I will teach you of the enlightenment that is pure hellfire."

"In the meantime," said Sam, "I suggest you solicit aid of my followers or learn the difficult art of mudbreathing."

He picked his way across the field, Yama's eyes burning into his back.

When he reached the trail, he turned. "And you may want to mention in Heaven," he said, "that I was called out of town on a business deal."

Yama did not reply.

"I think I am going to make a deal for some weapons," he finished, "some rather special weapons. So when you come after me, bring your girlfriend along. If she likes what she sees, she may persuade you to switch sides."

Then he struck the trail and moved away through the night, whistling, beneath a moon that was white and a moon that was golden.

R. A. LAFFERTY

The Configuration of the North Shore

R. A. Lafferty started writing in 1960, at the relatively advanced age (for a new writer, anyway) of forty-six, and in the years before his retirement in 1987, he published some of the freshest and funniest short stories ever written, almost all of them dancing on the borderlines between fantasy, science fiction, and the tall tale in its most boisterous and quintessentially American of forms.

Lafferty has published memorable novels that stand up quite well today—among the best of them are *Past Master, The Devil Is Dead, The Reefs of Earth,* the historical novel *Okla Hannali,* and the totally unclassifiable (a fantasy novel *disguised as* a non-fiction historical study, perhaps?) *The Fall of Rome*—but it was the prolific stream of short stories he began publishing in 1960 that would eventually establish his reputation. Stories like "Slow Tuesday Night," "Thus We Frustrate Charlemagne," "Hog-Belly Honey," "The Hole on the Corner," "All Pieces of a River Shore," "Among the Hairy Earthmen," "Seven Day Terror," "Continued on Next Rock," "All But the Words," and many others, are among the most original and pyrotechnic stories of our times.

Almost any of those stories would have served for this anthology, even those published ostensibly as science fiction—but I finally settled on the story that follows. It's one of Lafferty's least-known and least-reprinted, but a little gem regardless that demonstrates all of Lafferty's virtues: folksy exuberance, a singing lyricism of surprising depth and power, outlandish imagination, a store of offbeat erudition matched only by Avram Davidson, and a strong, shaggy sense of humor unrivaled by anyone.

His short work has been gathered in the landmark collection *Nine Hundred Grandmothers,* as well as in *Strange Doings, Does Anyone Else Have Something Further to Add?, Golden Gate and Other Stories,* and *Ringing Changes.* Some of his work is available only in small press editions—like the very strange novel *Archipelago,* or *My*

Heart Leaps Up, which was serialized as a sequence of chapbooks—but his other novels available in trade editions (although many of them are long out of print) include, *Fourth Mansions, Arrive at Easterwine, Space Chantey,* and *The Flame Is Green.* Lafferty won the Hugo Award in 1973 for his story "Eurema's Dam," and in 1990 received the World Fantasy Award, the prestigious Life Achievement Award. His most recent books are the collections *Lafferty in Orbit* and *Iron Star.*

The patient was named John Miller.

The analyst was named Robert Rousse.

Two men.

The room was cluttered with lighting, testing, and recording equipment. It held several sets of furniture that conferred together in small groups, sofas, easy chairs, business chairs, desks, couches, coffee tables, and two small bars. There were books, and there was a shadow booth. The pictures on the walls were of widely different sorts.

One setting. Keep it simple, and be not distracted by indifferent details.

"I have let my business go down," Miller said. "My wife says that I have let her down. My sons say that I have turned into a sleepy stranger. Everybody agrees that I've lost all ambition and judgment. And yet I *do* have a stirring ambition. I am not able, however, to put it into words."

"We'll put it into words, Miller, either yours or mine," Rousse said. "Slip up on it right now! Quickly, what is the stirring ambition?"

"To visit the Northern Shore, and to make the visit stick."

"How does one get to this Northern Shore, Miller?"

"That's the problem. I can locate it only very broadly on the globe. Sometimes it seems that it should be off the eastern tip of New Guinea, going north from the D'Entrecasteaux Islands and bypassing Trobriand; again I feel that it is off in the Molucca Passage toward Talaud; and again it should be a little further south, coming north out of the Banda Sea by one of the straats. But I have been in all those waters without finding any clue to it. And the maps show unacceptable land or open sea wherever I try to set it."

"How long?"

"About twenty-five years."

"All in what we might call the Outer East Indies and dating from your own time in that part of the world, in World War II. When did it become critical?"

"It was always critical, but I worked around it. I built up my business and my family and led a pleasant and interesting life. I was able to relegate the Thing to my normal sleeping hours. Now I slow down a little and have less energy. I have trouble keeping both sets of things going."

"Can you trace the impression of the North Shore to anything? Transfigured early memory of some striking sea view? Artform-triggered intuition? Can you trace any roots to the evocative dream?"

"I had an inland childhood, not even a striking lake view in it. And yet the approach to the North Shore is always by a way recognized from early childhood. I don't believe that I have any intuition at all, nor any sense of art forms. It is simply a continuing dream that brings me almost to it. I am rounding a point, and the North Shore will be just beyond that point. Or I have left ship and wade through the shallows; and then I have only a narrow (but eerie) neck of land to traverse to reach the North Shore. Or I am, perhaps, on the North Shore itself and going through fog to the place of importance, and I will have the whole adventure as soon as the fog clears a little; but it doesn't. I've been on the verge of discovering it all a thousand times."

"All right. Lie down and go to dreaming, Miller. We will try to get you past that verge. Dream, and we record it."

"It isn't that easy, Rousse. There's always preliminaries to be gone through. First there is a setting and sound and smell of a place near the surf and a tide booming. This watery background then grows fainter; but it remains behind it all. And then there is a little anteroom dream, a watery dream that is not the main one. The precursor dream comes and goes, sharp and clear, and it has its own slanted pleasure. And only then am I able to take up the journey to the North Shore."

"All right, Miller, we will observe the amenities. Dream your dreams in their proper order. Lie easy there. Now the shot. The recorders and the shadow booth are waiting."

Shadow booths reproduced dreams in all dimensions and senses, so much so that often a patient on seeing a playback of his own dream was startled to find that an impression, which he would have said could be in no way expressed, was quite well expressed in shadow or color or movement or sound or odor. The shadow booth of the analyst Rousse was more than a basic booth, as he had incorporated many of his own notions into it. It reproduced the dreams of his patients very well, though to some extent through his own eyes and presuppositions.

First was given the basic, and Rousse realized that for his patient Miller this was New Guinea, and more particularly Black Papua, the stark mountain land full of somber spooky people. It was night; the area seemed to be about fifty yards from the surf, but every boom and sigh was audible. And there was something else: the tide was booming underground; the ocean permeated the land. Guinea, the mountain that is an island, was a mountain full of water. The roots of the mountain move and sigh; the great boulders squeak when the hammer of the tide hits them; and on the inside of the cliffs, the water level rises. There is the feeling of being on a very large ship, a ship a thousand miles long.

"He has captured the Earth-Basic well," the analyst Rousse said. Then the basic faded back a bit, and the precursor dream began.

It was in a flat-bottomed rowboat from some old camping trip. He was lying on his back in the bottom of the boat, and it was roped to a stump or tree and was rocking just a little in the current. And here was another mountain full of water, but an inland one of much less bulk, and the ice-cold springs ran out of its sides and down its piney shoulders to the shingle of the creek bank. Fish jumped in the dark, and blacksnakes slid down the hill to drink. Bullfrogs echoed, and hoot owls made themselves known; and far away dogs and men were out possuming, with the baying carrying over the miles. Then the boy remembered what he must do, and in his dream he unroped the boat and shoved into the stream and ran his trot line. From every hook he took a fish as long as his arm till the boat was full and nearly swamped.

And from the last hook of all, he took a turtle as big as a wagon wheel. He would not have been able to get it into the boat had not the turtle helped by throwing a booted leg over the side and heaving himself in. For by this time it was not so much a turtle but more like someone the boy knew. Then he talked for a while with the turtle that was not exactly a turtle anymore. The turtle had a sack of Bull Durham and the boy had papers, so they rolled and smoked and watched the night clouds slide overhead. One of them was named Thinesta and one was named Shonge, which chased the first and would soon have him treed or caught, if they did not run into the mountain or the moon first.

"Boy, this is the life!" said the turtle. "Boy, this is the life!" said the boy.

"He's a poet," said Rousse, and this puzzled him. He knew himself to be a cultured man, and he knew that Miller wasn't.

Then the little precursor dream slid away, and there began the tortuous and exhilarating journey to the North Shore. It was coming around a point in an old windjammer on which all the men were dead except the dreamer. The dead men were grinning and were happy enough in their own way. They had lashed themselves to rails and davits and such before they had died. "They didn't want it bad enough," the dreamer said, "but they won't mind me going ahead with it." But the point was devilish hard to turn. There came on wind and driving spray so that the ship shuddered. There was only ashen light as of false dawn. There was great strain. The dreamer struggled, and Rousse (caught up in the emotion of it) became quite involved and would have been in despair if it were not for the ultimate hope that took hold of him.

A porpoise whistled loudly, and at that moment they rounded the point. But it was a false point, and the true point was still up ahead. Yet the goal was now more exciting than ever. Yet both the current and the wind were against them. Rousse was a practical man. "We will not make it tonight," he said. "We had better heave to in this little cove and hold onto what advantage we have gained. We can make it the next time from here." "Aye, we'll tie up in the little cove," one of the dead men said, "we'll make it on the next sortie." "We will make it *now,*" the dreamer swore. He jammed the windjammer and refused to give up.

It was very long and painful, and they did not make it that night, or that afternoon in the analyst's office. When the dream finally broke, both Miller and Rousse were trembling with the effort—and the high hope was set again into the future.

"That's it," Miller said. "Sometimes I come closer. There is something in it that makes it worthwhile. I have to get there."

"We should have tied up in the cove," Rousse said. "We'll have blown backwards some ways, but it can't be helped. I seem to be a little too much in empathy with this thing, Miller. I can see how it is quite real to you. Analysis, as you may not know, has analogs in many of the sciences. In Moral Theology, which I count a science, the analog is Ultimate Compensation. I am sure that I can help you. I have already helped you, Miller. Tomorrow we will go much further with it."

The tomorrow session began very much the same. It was Guinea again, the Earth Basic, the Mountain Spook Land, the Fundament permeated with Chaos which is the Sea. It boomed and sighed and trembled to indicate that there are black and sea-green spirits in the basic itself. Then the basic adjusted itself into the background, and the precursor dream slid in.

The boy, the dreamer was in a canoe. It was night, but the park lights were on, and the lights of the restaurants and little beer gardens along the way. The girl was with him in the canoe; she had green eyes and a pleasantly crooked mouth. Well, it was San Antonio on the little river that runs through the parkways and under the bridges. Then they were beyond the parkway and out of town. There were live-oak trees overhanging the water, and beards of Spanish moss dragged the surface as though they were drifting through a cloud made up of gossamer and strands of old burlap.

"We've come a thousand miles," the girl said, "and it costs a dollar a mile for the canoe. If you don't have that much money we'll have to keep the canoe; the man won't take it back unless we pay him." "I have the money, but we might want to save it to buy breakfast when we cross the Mississippi," the boy said. The girl's name was Ginger, and she strummed on a stringed instrument that was spheroid; it revolved as she played and changed colors like a jukebox. The end of the canoe paddle shone like a star and left streaks of cosmic dust on the night water as the boy dipped it.

They crossed the Mississippi, and were in a world that smelled of wet sweet clover and very young catfish. The boy threw away the paddle and kissed Ginger. It felt as though she were turning him inside out, drawing him into her completely. And suddenly she bit him hard and deep with terrible teeth, and he could smell the blood running down his face when he pushed her away. He pushed her out of the canoe and she sank down and down. The underwater was filled with green light and he watched her as she sank. She waved to him and called up in a burst of bubbles. "That's all right. I was tired of the canoe anyhow. I'll walk back." "Damn you, Ginger, why didn't you tell me you weren't people?" the dreamer asked.

"It is ritual, it is offering, the little precursor dreams that he makes," Rousse said.

Then the precursor dream glided away like the canoe itself, and the main thing gathered once more to mount the big effort. It was toward the North Shore once more, but not in a windjammer. It was in a high hooting steamship that rode with nine other ships in splendid array through one of the straats out of what, in concession to the world, they had let be called the Banda Sea.

"We come to the edge of the world now," the dreamer said, "and only I will know the way here." "It is *not* the edge of the world," one of the seamen said. "See, here is the map, and here we are on it. As you can see, it is a long way to the edge of the world." "The map is wrong," the dreamer said, "let me fix it." He tore the map in two. "Look now," the dreamer pointed, "are we not now at the edge of the world?" All saw that they were; whereupon all the seamen began to jump off the ship, and tried to swim back to safety. And the other ships of the array, one by one, up-ended themselves and plunged into the abyss at the edge of the water. This really was the edge of the world, and the waters rushed over it.

But the dreamer knew the secret of this place, and he had faith. Just in time he saw it, right where he knew it must be, a narrow wedge of high water extending beyond the edge of the world. The ship sailed out on this narrow wedge, very precariously. "For the love of God be careful!" Rousse gasped. "Oh hell, I'm becoming too involved in a patient's dream." Well, it *was* a pretty nervous go there. So narrow was the wedge that the ship seemed to be riding on nothing; and on both sides was bottomless space and the sound of water rushing into it and falling forever. The sky also had ended—it does not extend beyond the world. There was no light, but only ashen darkness. And the heavy wind came up from below on both sides.

Nevertheless, the dreamer continued on and on until the wedge became too narrow to balance the ship. "I will get out and walk," the dreamer said, and he did. The ship upended itself and plunged down into bottomless space; and the dreamer was walking, as it were, on a rope of water, narrower than his boots, narrow as a rope indeed. It was, moreover, very slippery, and the sense of depth below was sickening. Even Rousse trembled and broke into cold sweat from the surrogate danger of it.

But the dreamer still knew the secret. He saw, far ahead, where the sky began again, and there is no sky over a void. And after continuing some further distance on the dangerous way, he saw where the land began again, a true land mass looming up ahead.

What was dimly seen, of course, was the back side of the land mass, and a stranger coming onto it would not guess its importance. But the dreamer knew that one had only to reach it and turn the point to be on the North Shore itself.

The excitement of the thing to come communicated itself, and at that very moment the watery rope widened to a path. It was still slippery and dangerous, it still had on each side of it depths so deep that a thousand miles would be only an inch. And then for the first time the dreamer realized the fearsomeness of the thing he was doing. "But I always knew I could walk on water if things got bad enough," he said. It was a tricky path, but it was a path that a man could walk on.

"Keep on! Keep on!" Rousse shouted. "We're almost there!" "There's a break in the path," said Miller the dreamer, and there was. It wasn't a hundred feet from the land mass, it wasn't a thousand feet to the turning of the point and the arrival at the North Shore itself. But there was a total break. Opposite them, on the dim land mass, was an emperor penguin.

"You have to wait till we get it fixed," the penguin said. "My brothers have gone to get more water to fix it with. It will be tomorrow before we get it fixed." "I'll wait," the dreamer shouted.

But Rousse saw something that the dreamer did not see, that nobody else had ever seen before. He looked at the shape of the new sky that is always above the world and is not above the abyss. From the configuration of the sky he read the Configuration of the Northern Shore. He gasped with unbelief. Then the dream broke.

"It may be only the quest-in-itself motif," Rousse lied, trying to control himself and to bring his breathing back to normal. "And then, there might, indeed, be something at the end of it. I told you, Miller, that analysis has its parallels in other sciences. Well, it can borrow devices from them also. We will borrow the second-stage platform from the science of rocketry."

"You've turned into a sly man, Rousse," Miller said. "What's taken hold of you suddenly? What is it that you're not saying?"

"What I am saying, Miller, is that we will use it tomorrow. When the dream has reached its crest and just before it breaks up, we'll cut in a second-stage booster. I've done it before with lesser dreams. We are going to see this thing to the end tomorrow."

"All right."

"It will take some special rigging," Rousse told himself when Miller was gone. "And I'll have to gather a fair amount of information and shape it up. But it will be worth it. I am thinking of the second stage shot in another sense, and I might just be able to pull it off. This isn't the quest-in-itself at all. I've seen plenty of them. I've seen the false a thousand times. Let me not now fumble the real! This is the Ultimate Arrival Nexus that takes a man clean out of himself. It is the Compensation. If it were not achieved in one life in a million, then none of the other lives would have been worthwhile. Somebody has to win to keep the gamble going. There has to be a grand prize behind it all. I've seen the shape of it in that second sky. I'm the one to win it."

Then Rousse busied himself against the following day. He managed some special rigging. He gathered a mass of information and shaped it up. He incorporated these things into the shadow booth. He canceled a number of appointments. He was arranging that he could take some time off, a day, a month, a year, a lifetime if necessary.

The tomorrow session began very much the same, except for some doubts on the part of the patient Miller. "I said it yesterday, and I say it again," Miller grumbled. "You've turned sly on me, man. What is it?" "All analysts are sly, Miller, it's the name of our trade. Get with it now. I promise that we will get you past the verge today. We are going to see this dream through to its end."

There was the Earth Basic again. There was the Mountain booming full of water, the groaning of the rocks, and the constant adjusting and readjusting of the world on its uneasy foundation. There was the salt spray, the salt of the Earth that leavens the lump. There were the crabs hanging onto the wet edge of the world.

Then the Basic muted itself, and the precursor dream slid in, the ritual fish.

It was a rendezvous of ships and boats in an immensity of green islands scattered in a purple-blue sea. It was a staging area for both ships and islands; thence they would travel in convoys to their proper positions, but here they were all in a jumble. There were LST's and Jay Boats, cargo ships and little packets. There were old sailing clippers with topgallants and moonscrapers full of wind, though they were at anchor. There was much moving around, and it was easy to step from the ships to the little green islands (if they were islands, some of them were no more than rugs of floating moss, but they did not sink) and back again onto the ships. There were sailors and seamen and pirates shooting craps together on the little islands. Bluejackets and bandits would keep jumping from the ships down to join the games, and then others would leave them and hop to other islands.

Piles of money of rainbow colors and of all sizes were everywhere. There were pesos and pesetas and pesarones. There were crowns and coronets and rix-dollars. There were gold certificates that read "Redeemable only at Joe's Marine Bar Panama City." There were guilders with the Queen's picture on them, and half-guilders with the Jack's picture on them. There were round coins with square holes in them, and square coins with round holes. There was stage money and invasion money, and comic money from the Empires of Texas and Louisiana. And there were bales of real frogskins, green and sticky, which were also current.

"Commodore," one of the pirates said, "get that boat out of the way or I'll ram it down your throat." "I don't have any boat," said the dreamer. "I'm not a commodore; I'm an army sergeant; I'm supposed to guard this box for the lieutenant." Oh hell, he didn't even have a box. What had happened to the box? "Commodore," said the pirate, "get that boat out of the way or I'll cut off your feet."

He did cut off his feet. And this worried the boy, the dreamer, since he did not know whether it was in the line of duty or if he would be paid for his feet. "I don't know which boat you mean," he told the pirate. "Tell me which boat you mean and I'll try to move it. "Commodore," the pirate said, "move this boat or I'll cut your hands off." He did cut his hands off. "This isn't getting us anywhere," the dreamer said, "tell me which boat you want moved." "If you don't know your own boat by now, I ought to slit your gullet," the pirate said. He did slit his gullet. It was harder to breathe after that, and the boy worried more. "Sir, you're not even a pirate in my own outfit. You ought to get one of the sailors to move the boat for you. I'm an army sergeant and I don't even know how to move a boat."

The pirate pushed him down in a grave on one of the green islands and covered him up. He was dead now and it scared him. This was not at all like he thought it would be. But the green dirt was transparent and he could still see the salty dogs playing cards and shooting craps all around him. "If that boat isn't moved," the pirate said, "you're going to be in real trouble." "Oh, let him alone," one of the dice players said. So he let him alone.

"It's ritual sacrifice he offers," Rousse said. "He brings the finest gift he can make every time. I will have to select a top one from the files for my own Precursor."

Then it was toward the North Shore again as the Precursor Dream faded.

It was with a big motor launch now, as big as a yacht, half as big as a ship. The craft was very fast when called on to be. It would have to be, for it was going through passes that weren't there all the time. Here was a seacliff, solid and without a break. But to one who knows the secret there *is* a way through. Taken at morning half-light and from a certain angle there was a passage through. The launch made it, but barely. It was a very close thing, and the cliffs ground together again behind it. And there behind was the other face of the seacliff, solid and sheer. But the ocean ahead was different, for they had broken with the map and with convention in finding a passage where there was none. There were now great groupings of islands and almost-islands. But some of them were merely sargasso-type weed islands, floating clumps; and some of then were only floating heaps of pumice and ash from a volcano that was now erupting.

How to tell the true land from the false? The dreamer threw rocks at all the islands. If the islands were of weed or pumice or ash they would give but a dull sound. But if they were real land they would give a solid ringing sound to the thrown rock. Most of them were false islands, but now one rang like iron.

"It is a true island," said the dreamer, "it is named Pulo Bakal." And after the launch had gone a great way through the conglomerate, one of the islands rang like solid wood to the thrown rock. "It is a true island," said the dreamer, "it is named Pulo Kaparangan."

And finally there was a land that rang like gold, or almost like it (like cracked gold really) to the thrown rock. "It is true land, I think it is," said the dreamer. "It is named Pulo Ginto, I think it is. It should be the land itself, and its North Shore should be the Shore Itself. But it is spoiled this day. The sound was cracked. I don't want it as much as I thought I did. It's been tampered with."

"This is it," Rousse urged the dreamer. "Quickly now, right around the point and you are there. We can make it this time."

"No, there's something wrong with it. I don't want it the way it is. I'll just wake up and try it some other time."

"Second stage called for," Rousse cried. He did certain things with electrodes and with a needle into Miller's left rump, and sent him reeling back into the dream. "We'll make it," Rousse encouraged. "We're there. It's everything you've sought."

"No, no, the light's all wrong. The sound was cracked. What we are coming to—oh no no, it's ruined, it's ruined forever. You robbed me of it."

What they came to was that little canal off the River and into the Sixth Street Slip to the little wharf where barges used to tie up by the Consolidated Warehouse. And it was there that Miller stormed angrily onto the rotten wooden wharf, past the old warehouse, up the hill three blocks and past his own apartment house, to the left three blocks and up and into the analyst's office, and there the dream and the reality came together.

"You've robbed me, you filthy fool," Miller sputtered, waking up in blithering anger. "You've spoiled it forever. I'll not go back to it. It isn't there anymore. What a crass thing to do."

"Easy, easy, Miller. You're cured now, you know. You can enter onto your own full life again. Have you never heard the most beautiful parable ever, about the boy who went around the world in search of the strangest thing of all, and came to his own home at the end, and it so transfigured that he hardly knew it?"

"It's a lie, is what it is. Oh, you've cured me, and you get your fee. And slyness is the name of your game. May somebody someday rob you of the ultimate thing!"

"I hope not, Miller."

Rousse had been making his preparations for a full twenty-four hours. He had canceled appointments and phased out and transferred patients. He would not be available to anyone for some time, he did not know for how long a time.

He had his hideout, an isolated point on a wind-ruffled lake. He needed no instrumentation. He believed he knew the direct way into it.

"It's the real thing," he told himself. "I've seen the shape of it, accidentally in the dream sky that hung over it. Billions of people have been on the earth, and not a dozen have been to it; and not one would bother to put it into words. 'I have seen such things—' said Aquinas. 'I have seen such things—' said John of the Cross. 'I have seen such things—' said Plato. And they all lived out the rest of their lives in a glorious daze.

"It is too good for a peasant like Miller. I'll grab it myself."

It came easy. An old leather couch is as good a craft as any to go there. First the Earth Basic and the Permeating Ocean, that came natural on the wind-ruffled point of the lake. Then the ritual offering, the Precursor Dream. Rousse had thrown a number of things into this: a tonal piece by Gideon Styles, an old seascape by Grobin that had a comic and dreamlike quality, Lyall's curious sculpture "Moon Crabs," a funny sea tale by McVey and a poignant one by Gironella. It was pretty good. Rousse understood this dream business.

Then the Precursor Dream was allowed to fade back. And it was off toward the North Shore by a man in the finest craft ever dreamed up, by a man who knew just what he wanted, "The Thing Itself," by a man who would give all the days of his life to arrive at it.

Rousse understood the approaches and the shoals now; he had studied them thoroughly. He knew that, however different they had seemed each time in the dreams of Miller, they were always essentially the same. He took the land right at the first rounding of the point, leaping clear and letting his launch smash on the rocks.

"There will be no going back now," he said, "it was the going back that always worried Miller, that caused him to fail." The cliffs here appeared forbidding, but Rousse had seen again and again the little notch in the high purple of them, the path over. He followed the path with high excitement and cleared the crest.

"Here Basho walked, here Aquin, here John de Yepes," he proclaimed, and he came down toward the North Shore itself, with the fog over it beginning to lift.

"You be false captain with a stolen launch," said a small leviathan off shore.

"No, no, I dreamed the launch myself," Rousse maintained. "I'll not be stopped."

"I will not stop you," said the small leviathan. "The launch is smashed, and none but I know that you are false captain."

Why, it was clearing now! The land began to leap out in its richness, and somewhere ahead was a glorious throng. In the throat of a pass was a monokeros, sleek and brindled.

"None passes here and lives," said the monokeros.

"I pass," said Rousse.

He passed through, and there was a small moan behind him.

"What was that?" he asked.

"You died," said the monokeros.

"Oh, so I'm dead on my couch, am I? It won't matter. I hadn't wanted to go back."

He went forward over the ensorceled and pinnacled land, hearing the rakish and happy throng somewhere ahead.

"I must not lose my way now," said Rousse. And there was a stele, standing up and telling him the way with happy carved words.

Rousse read it, and he entered the shore itself.

And all may read and enter.

The stele, the final marker, was headed:

Which None May Read and Return

And the words on it—
And the words—
And the words—

Let go! You're holding on! You're afraid! Read it and take it. It is *not* blank!
It's carved clear and bright.
Read it and enter.

You're afraid.

GEORGE ALEC EFFINGER

Two Sadnesses

Perhaps *the* hot young writer of the 1970s, George Alec Effinger has subsequently maintained a reputation as one of the most creative innovators in SF, and one of the genre's finest short-story writers. His first novel, *What Entropy Means to Me,* is considered a cult classic in some circles. His most popular novel is probably the gritty and fascinating *When Gravity Fails,* a finalist for the Hugo Award in 1987. His short story "Schrödinger's Kitten," set in the same *milieu,* went on to win both the Hugo Award and a Nebula Award in 1988. His many other books include the novels *A Fire in the Sun* and *The Exile Kiss* (the sequels to *When Gravity Fails*), *The Wolves of Memory, The Bird of Time, Those Gentle Voices, Utopia 3,* and *Heroics,* and his large body of stylish, funny, and sometimes surrealistic short stories have been gathered in the collections *Mixed Feelings, Irrational Numbers, Idle Pleasures,* and *The Old Funny Stuff.* Effinger lives in New Orleans.

When he sets himself to it, Effinger can produce some of the funniest short fiction ever written, putting him in the select company of people like R. A. Lafferty, Robert Sheckley, Howard Waldrop, John Sladek, and Avram Davidson. The bittersweet fantasy that follows, however, though certainly wry and satirical, is considerably more poignant than it is funny. It is, in fact, very aptly named.

I

It was one of those warm, summery afternoons where you *know* that Something Grand is going to happen, but the only problem is whether you ought to go out to meet it or not, or wait around your house to be pleasantly surprised. Waiting around the house has its points, for you can always say, "Yes, well, perhaps it would be better, *if* Something Grand is to happen *today,* to *me, here,* it may be better to Have A Bit Of A Snack just in case. In case Something Grand *does* happen, so that I won't be left All At Sea, as it were."

But going out to look for S.G. has just as many good points, because then you could take A Bit Of A Snack along with you on the search, and you always stood the chance of running into Rabbit or Piglet on the way. It certainly was better to have Something Grand happen with Piglet watching, than to have it alone in your house, as Grand as that may be to tell about afterward. And this is what decided the case. Bear made himself a honey and honey sandwich and set out carelessly, purely by chance in the direction of Piglet's house.

It was one of those summery afternoons out of doors, also. Bear walked along through the Forest happily, not actually laughing-happy but sort of smiling and humming as if he didn't know *for sure* about that Something. The tall trees of the Forest waved in the wind, as if they didn't know *for sure,* either, and Bear took that as a Good Sign and felt even Grander. He walked for a while, and after a time to his surprise he found himself in front of Piglet's house.

"Ho," thought Bear, "why, here I am at Piglet's, and my sandwich seems to have been left behind. Perhaps Piglet may have found it somewhere, or one like it, and we can discuss *that,* of course, and who knows but that Something might happen?"

Piglet lived in the middle of the Forest in a large beech tree. The front door to the house had neither bell cord nor knocker, as did some of the other, more elegant houses in the Forest. Piglet was always surprised and delighted whenever someone came to visit *him,* but first he stood in the middle of his large room and quivered, not exactly knowing what to expect. He was not the bravest animal in the Forest, and a simple knock on the door was enough to set him quivering, until he actually answered the call and discovered one of his very good friends. Thus it was that Bear generally called to him first, before knocking. "Piglet?" he would cry. "It's just me, Bear, your friend. I'm going to knock on your door so that you'll know that I've come to visit."

Then he would knock, and Piglet would quiver anyway. When at last he opened the door to his house he would say, "Bear! Come in! You gave me quite a start." And Bear would come in.

This morning, though, Bear stopped before he shouted to Piglet in the beech tree. His mouth opened but he didn't say anything, and his brown paw stopped in the air, because over his head in the sky he saw Something. It looked like a flock of little silver birds, or a swarm of big silver bees. Bear frowned to himself, because he could remember some other interesting times that he had had with bees. These silver bees were flying by very fast, and they buzzed so loudly that when he called out to Piglet, Bear couldn't hear his own voice.

Very soon the noise from the silver bees faded away, and Bear knocked on Piglet's door. The door didn't open; instead, Bear heard Piglet's voice from inside. "Oh, Bear!" he squealed. "It's you! Come in!" Bear opened the door to Piglet's house and went in. He couldn't see Piglet anywhere, but he did see a very suspicious quivering beneath a rug on the floor.

"I suppose you heard the buzzing of those silver bees," said Bear, as Piglet appeared from under the rug.

"Why, yes," said Piglet, his ears still pink. "I think I heard it when I was . . . I was . . . I was looking for something that I might have lost underneath this rug." He was *still* quivering.

"I see," said Bear.

"Silver bees, you say?" said Piglet.

Bear rubbed his nose, unsure that the Something Grand could be anywhere in Piglet's room, because the room looked exactly the way it had always looked. "Yes," he said.

"They must have been awfully big bees to make such a noise."

"Yes, I suppose." Bear was beginning to think of suggesting a trip to see Owl, whom they hadn't visited since yesterday.

"I wonder what sort of hive they live in. It must be bigger than any that we've *ever* seen in the Forest," said Piglet as he patted the rug flat, taking out all the Piglet-shaped folds.

Now Bear is not known among his friends, who all love him dearly nevertheless, for having the sharpest wits in the Forest. Indeed, he is the one to whom even the simplest Plans of Operation must be explained, and usually more than once. But Bear knew bees, and he knew beehives, being a bear. And so he thought that the silver bees should, indeed, have a great big hive. And, the idea trickled through, a great big hive must have a great deal of HONEY. Now it was plain to see that a Great Deal of Honey would be Something Grand on any occasion. Bear was very proud to have solved the mystery ever so quickly, and even before anyone else knew that there *was* a mystery, completely by himself (although Piglet had maybe helped just the least bit). The only thing that remained was to get the honey out of the hive, which was always a problem that needed a Careful Scheme.

"Let us go see Owl," announced Bear after this bit of thinking. It had made him quite tired and unable to come up with a Careful Scheme, too. "Perhaps you have some provisions about, and then we could be all set in case Something Grand happens *before* we get to Owl's, so that we should be able to tell him all about it. And then, if Something Grand *doesn't* happen, we shouldn't be too disappointed."

"Is Something Grand to happen today?" asked Piglet, who really hadn't had the same feeling that morning, and certainly not after the buzzing of the silver bees had shaken up his house.

"Well, one never knows that it will, for sure," said Bear, looking for a moment as if he really did have a prodigious brain in there after all, "but, again, one never knows that it won't, either, on the other hand. In either case, a Bit of Lunch is the safest way." And then he looked like the same dear old Bear.

So Bear and Piglet set out for Owl's house. Bear was thinking that he would like that Something Grand to happen *before* they reached Owl's, because, with Piglet, he already had to give half away, and, should Owl join in the venture, the Something must be further divided. Not, he hastily interrupted himself, that he was so selfish that he didn't want his friends to enjoy his Good Fortune, but rather that the more people who were in on the adventure originally, the less of an appreciative audience he could expect afterward, just in the event that some celebrative poem might suggest itself to him.

The sun lit the beeches and firs of the Forest perfectly, just the way Bear had been taught that the sun ought to on such a summery day. The clouds were small and quick, and were having their own Important Business in the very blue sky. The familiar path unfolded like an old and especially favorite story.

And then the bees returned. Some flew overhead so high that the sun made tiny, bright stars of them, and some flew by closer, so that they screeched louder than anything Bear or Piglet had ever heard. Piglet quivered, and held tight to Bear, who realized that he would have to Be Stout for them both but didn't want to. The bees seemed to spit at them as they flew past, and the ground jumped up in straight little rows, like spouting teakettles going *thitt! thitt! thitt! thitt! thitt! thitt!* around them. Sometimes the rows of flying dirt and grass would lead to a tree, and then instead of a *thitt!* there would be a *thokk!* and a piece of the tree would fly off over their heads.

Just before they got to Owl's house they found Owl, lying on the ground as if he had fallen asleep before reaching his bed. He thrashed as though he were having bad dreams, flapping his ruffled wings against the ground. He wouldn't talk except in very small, un-Owl-like noises, and Bear and Piglet decided that he may have been hit by one of the *thitts* or maybe a *thokk*. The best thing seemed to be to carry him home and put him to bed. Bear said that they might be able to fix him up A Bit Of A Snack, which looked like a good idea all 'round.

When they got to Owl's house they put him to bed, and he rested there very quietly, without any of his usual pronouncements. Bear and Piglet found this very strange. Bear explained that it was a day for Something Grand, and not at all a day for Being Still and Mysterious. Unless, Bear thought to himself, unless you were part of some large and secret Something Grand that you didn't want to tell anyone (like Bear) about yet. Bear smiled to himself proudly for figuring out Owl's secret. Two puzzles solved already, before lunchtime! In any event, Owl said nothing and did not seem to move in his bed.

After a time, during which Piglet had fixed them a small and rather in-complete sort of Snack, the bees came back again. Bear and Piglet watched them from Owl's window. The bees did not fly so high as before, and looked larger even than any birds that they had ever seen. The bees roared as they flew, and Bear and Piglet were frightened even though they were in old Owl's home right in the middle of their own Forest. Silver eggs dropped from the bees, and when they fell to the ground they burst into huge, boiling, orange and black clouds of flame. Bear watched silently; Piglet was suddenly nowhere to be found. With every flash of fire there was a horrible thunder that shook the tree that was Owl's home.

After a time the bees went away. Bear stood by the window, watching the flaming trees shrivel and fall. There was a knock on Owl's door, and a voice called out hoarsely. Bear recognized it as belonging to the gray Donkey. He opened the door for Donkey, and felt a flash of heat from the raging fires outside.

"Hullo, Bear."

"Hullo, Donkey."

"Looks like a busy morning. We're always having Busy Mornings whenever I specially decide to have a little nap. But I don't suppose a nap is very important if everyone else decides to have a Busy Morning." He indicated the burning Forest with a flick of his floppy ears. "Is that your idea? If it is, it certainly busied up the morning. It looks like it will use up most of the afternoon as well. Not that I mind, you understand, I can see how you might forget to notify me; but I would like to schedule that nap *sometime*."

"No, Donkey, I don't think that is my idea," said Bear, feeling just a lit-tle guilty because he knew that he did have that Something Grand feel-ing. But he wasn't at all sure that this was the sort of Grand Something that he was looking forward to.

"I was standing around in my little part of the bracken," said Donkey. "You know how my little part is more or less marshy and wet and cold and altogether unpleasant. Not that I'm complaining, you see, but *some-one* has to live there, I suppose, while the rest of you live out here in the really comfortable places. And I don't really mind. But, as I was saying, there I was, eating my thistles (which are hardly delicious, but that *is* all that I have, and I'm not one to complain), when this group of men came running through, splashing around in my stream, turning my little yard into a perfect swamp, if you like swamps, which I don't particularly, es-pecially in my own living room. And I tried to be civil, as much as I can be to men, but do they listen? Why, they do not. They point their ma-chines and start making a horrible racket, and my little spot of home is torn to pieces. Now, it's not the most attractive spot in the Forest, I'll be the first to admit that, but it *is* home to me, and I was pretty upset when they started knocking it all to bits. But they looked like they were having such a good time running around and shouting and pointing their fingers and blasting away that I decided that I would just come over here and sit awhile." And Donkey did sit, flopping in a corner of Owl's parlor with a sullen expression, and he didn't say another word.

After a time there was a series of *whumps!* After each *whump!* there would be a terrible clap of thunder and a large part of the Forest would disappear in a black cloud, leaving only a smoking hole. Bear watched this silently, his hands clasped behind his back, until the *whumps!* went away, too. Then the men that Donkey had seen arrived, running around in front of Owl's house and shouting. Some of them had metal tanks strapped on their backs, and these men began to spray more fire from long hoses attached to the tanks. Soon all the gorse and brush in this part of the wood was afire, and the larger trees were beginning to catch, too. Bear thought for a moment about his other friends in the other parts of the Forest.

"Did you see Rabbit on your way here?" he asked Donkey.

"Yes," said Donkey.

"Oh. Perhaps he will come here, too."

"You know that I am hardly an expert in these matters," said Donkey, "but I am of the opinion that Rabbit will not be coming."

"Oh," said Bear. The men outside were rapidly chopping away at whatever of the standing saplings and trees remained. "Perhaps Christ—"

The guns of the men drowned out Bear's voice. He stood by the window and watched; Donkey sat in his corner. Piglet was still off Somewhere, doing Something. During a sudden lull in the noise Bear turned from the window.

"I think that I know what we need," he said. "If only Christ—"

"As I said before," said Donkey, "I'm not the most experienced member of our little band. But I am sure, I am very, *very* sure, that he will not be coming either."

Bear stared at him sadly for some time, until a crash behind him made them all start. Something had been thrown through the window. It was a rough, gray-green object with a handle. In the few seconds before it went off there was a strange silence, during which they could all hear the distant chuttering of the helicopters.

II

The summer had very definitely come to its conclusion, running smack into autumn, as it has its way of doing; Mole thought to himself that it was very fortunate indeed that he and Water Rat had managed to finish up this bit of adventure before the really cold weather set in. Now was the time for steaming tea in china cups, and cedar shakes crackling in the fire, and, above all else, *stories* about adventuring. But Mole knew that mucking about the countryside on strange errands had its season, and that time was not autumn. The short breather that Nature in her wisdom permits between the fevers of the warm weather and the sleepy contemplation of winter was for only one thing: sitting comfortably, dry and warm in Ratty's snug rooms at River Bank, planning the excursion of next year.

And as the year found its way to its end, so did this particular day. The sun was going down through the carmine sky, and the late afternoon was so absolutely lovely, in a purely autumn and unhurried way, that both animals kept their own counsel, as if by unspoken mutual consent fearing to disturb that fragile beauty that they thought had passed, too, with the pleasanter temperatures. "It is like this every year," thought the Mole. "Autumn *is* such a wonderful time of year, there is really nothing else quite like it. And the trees now are really without their equal in the sameness of the summer's colors! Why do I always seem to forget that autumn is, after all, my favorite season?" Perhaps the Rat was thinking the same thoughts, for after a time the Mole could hear him whispering his poetry words, about pumpkins and frost and that sort of thing.

As the twilight deepened around the pair while they crossed a meadow yet some distance from their goal, the Rat stopped still in his tracks. "Mole, my good friend and true companion," he said, "it is October." Rat bent back his silky head and gazed silently into the sky, which was growing bluer and darker blue, and already a star or two had edged into view. "Where does the year go?" And then he moved on, his hands clasped behind his back, or shoved into the shallow pockets of his thin coat.

At the other side of the meadow they found a low, broken-backed fence of timber and, as there did not appear to be a gate, the Mole stood on the lowest beam and vaulted over. Rat made as to follow but, before he grasped the topmost timber, he turned and looked out across the field that next they would cross. He paused for a moment, and Mole knew that he could expect a bit of poetry. And so the Rat recited:

> *"Tears, idle tears, I know not what they mean,*
> *Tears from the depth of some divine despair*
> *Rise in the heart, and gather to the eyes,*
> *In looking on the happy autumn-fields,*
> *And thinking of the days that are no more."*

"Hmmm," said the Mole, moved but unsure if he were glad or totally melancholy. "Quite lovely, but not without its proper weight of sensibility."

"Tennyson," said the Rat.

"Hmmm." And this was all that was said for a longish period of time, as they made their way over the field of stalks of last summer's corn. The field was set off on the farther side by another barrier like the one that they previously had crossed. They passed over, and were in a large coppice of mountain ash.

"It will take but one good shower to loose these leaves at last," said the Rat. "Then the rowan will stand winter-bare, and we will be left for a time with nothing to remind us of the summer but the cry of the jay."

"Ratty," said the Mole in a small voice, "might I ask of you the least favor?"

"Certainly, Mole. You ought to know that you are my dearest of friends."

"Why, if you please, it is nothing, actually. But you keep saying the *most* saddening things, so that while I am going along thinking about how wonderful it will be to find River Bank once more, and about how delightful everything will be when we're all tucked in at home again, you say something to make me feel all tumbled about inside and downright *abandoned*. Sometimes I want to stop right here, or turn around and *look* for our lost summer. Certainly it is autumn, and winter is coming on. There's no use saying that it isn't. But it's happened to us before, and I do *so* wish that you could talk of spring and punting about in the boat for the first time of the new season, or at least, if it must be autumn, then how lovely it is to see Orion again. Because it is hard, it is so hard to be sad and in unfamiliar territory at the same time." This was a rather long speech for the poor Mole, but he was always so affected by poetry. And of course Ratty understood, and thoughtfully made his comments to cheer his companion.

And thus the stand of rowan was passed, and more relics of fields, and open meads where the eyes of animals glared like little glass marbles from the clumps of brown grass. It was night now, no use at all trying to call it "evening," and Mole, whose habits had been set in his later life at retiring early and rising with the sun, began to feel uncomfortable. Even one as adventured as he, who had seen more odd things than ever he could have dreamed in his parochial molish youth, was glad that he was not alone beneath the watchful gaze of the diamond stars. He walked with his head tucked down and his short, stubby arms held at his sides; every once in a while he stumbled, as upon an unseen clod of dirt or half-buried stone, and fell against Water Rat, mumbling apologies and feeling grateful for the solid presence of his friend.

The Mole's thoughts were exclusively of home; he employed the memories of long-out-of-sight friends and out-of-mind, familiar objects to hold back both the pressing darkness and the insistent, cold wind. But the home of his reveries was not always River Bank, where he had gone to live upon discovering the joys of riverside life and meeting River Bank's most generous and gentle tenant, the Water Rat. No, the cozy fires that he imagined burned as often as not in his own relinquished place at Mole End.

The more he thought, the cozier the picture became, until he was just on the point of asking the Rat if they might stop there for the night, rather than going on to River Bank. It *was* very late, of course, and it *was* getting colder and colder. Mole's hands were nearly without sensation, and his poor feet were *his* only by virtue of their aching. He knew that there was a small supply of food left in his rooms (mainly a tin of Danish bacon and some capers); a small but sufficient supper might be coaxed from his forsaken pantry. It would be nice to stop by again; it had been so long, and perhaps the detour would be advisable, just to check that all was still in order. And then the trip to River Bank could be continued after a good rest, and perhaps something more undiscovered would appear for a bit of breakfast, although—

"—Beyond that hedge, I should think," said the Water Rat.

"Eh?" said Mole, who realized that the Rat had stopped by the wayside and had been speaking to him for no little time. "I'm sorry, Ratty, but perhaps my ears are a little numb, too."

"I merely suggested that, as I calculate, your very nice Mole End should be in a field very near, perhaps just on the other side of the hedge on that knoll, there. It would be a convenience to spend the night there tonight, for I, at least, have just about had a full time of it. That is, of course, if the plan meets with your approval. I should hate to invite myself around in this way, except that I *am* so infernally exhausted. However, if you would rather remain with our original—"

"Oh, remarkable, Ratty!" cried Mole. "Have you been eavesdropping on my secretest thoughts? Oh, thank you, I would so like to see my old home again." The two companions discussed their situation further, and agreed to pass the night at Mole End, although it would not be as comfortable as had they pressed on to River Bank. The next day would be one of cleaning and tidying up after their long absence, and also of the happy chore of visiting their friends and spending tea, dinner, and supper regaling them with the history of their adventures. The Mole and the Rat began to feel better, warmer inside if not out, and both knew that welcome tingle of anticipation. At last, they were coming home.

The Mole could hardly control his excitement as he topped the low rise and passed through an opening in the hedgerow. It was far too dark to see, but (if Ratty's estimate were correct) he ought to be able to smell the first fair indications of his old neighborhood. And there they were! His nose twitched with pleasure as he scented those familiar signals. But they were arriving somewhat muffled, as though buried under strange and unknown smells. The Mole strained his eyes to try to aid his bewildered nose, but of course all that he could see was a bright glow before him.

"Is that morning already?" he asked.

"No," said Rat, his voice peculiarly grim.

"Because I didn't think that the night had passed so quickly. We must have come much farther than ever we thought. Or else this quite proves my theory that the time you spend asleep is actually less than the equal number of daylight hours," said the Mole, chuckling at his very small joke.

"No, we've been heading west for some time, in any event."

They walked toward the light, upon a curious hard black surface. The ground had been made flat and smooth, and covered over with some material. It was this that the Mole's nose could not identify. As they came closer it became evident that the light was originating from a group of shining lamps placed high on poles. These were situated about the queer field in widely spaced rows.

"Your home ought to be right about here," said the Rat, indicating a spot on the blacktop between two painted yellow lines.

"It looks as though I have a bit of work," said the Mole unhappily. "They seem to have covered over my tunnel." He set to immediately, trying with his freezing paws to get through the pavement to his warm little burrow.

"Oh, Ratty, it . . . won't . . . *dig!*" And the gasping Mole sat down on the blacktop, tears forming in his tiny eyes. The Rat was stricken by the sadness of his friend, and thought that Mole should at least make another attempt, if only because that seemed so much more positive a plan than nocturnal and earnest lamentation. So the Mole turned to once more, working even harder but with the same lack of success. The hard surface of the parking lot resisted his most practiced efforts.

"What are we to do, Ratty?"

"We'll continue on, of course. It would have been pleasant to stay here, but River Bank isn't an impossible distance. So buck up; we'll have you all tucked in soon enough."

"But that was my *home!*" said the distressed Mole.

"You'll live with me officially, now. So remember to mind your muddy feet." But the Water Rat was not so unconcerned as he would have his companion believe. He was nearly as sick at heart as the Mole to find the least trace of Mole End obliterated; animals take only one spot for their home, not like we larger folk who may move about several times before finding one last resting place in our dotage. And animals invest in their single residences all the security and love that they hold in their smaller but wiser selves. Thus it takes a major disruption of life, such as that experienced by the Mole when he turned out his solitary existence for the new and exciting life at River Bank, to enable an animal to quit his chosen home. The Rat was wise enough to know this, and he also knew that it could serve no purpose to let his friend languish in despair.

In accordance then with their revised schedule, the Mole and Water Rat turned south, heading across the lot toward the river. It was quite impossible for either to walk along without picturing in his private and gloomy thoughts the beautiful spot of greenery that had been removed to allow the pavement's unsightly intrusion. At the far end of the lot, where once had been a border of low hedges and, beyond that, a row of slender poplars, the Rat could make out the dim lines of a huge, square, dark building. He said nothing to the sorrowful Mole, but waited instead until they were close enough to investigate at first hand. He suspected another of Toad's ephemeral and ill-advised schemes, but surely even Toad had enough romance and enough sense to prevent him from cementing over the countryside.

The building was quite monstrous, and ugly in an efficient sort of way that indicated that it was some sort of factory.

"How long were we gone?" asked the Mole in a hurt tone of voice.

"Much too long, it would seem," said the Rat.

"Toad?"

"I'm not certain. It would be like his old self to catch on to a seemingly easy moneymaking proposition, and then ruin everyone for miles around. But, of course, to be fair we'll make inquiries in the morning."

"Not many folks around anymore to ask," said a new voice. The Mole and the Water Rat turned around, startled. The voice belonged to a rather small and hungry-looking weasel. He nodded in recognition of the two returned travelers, although neither Mole nor Rat knew him by name.

"Toad's gone, himself," said the weasel.

"Old Toad, gone?" said the Mole.

"Yes, sir. Had a spell of warmish weather along about the end of June. One of those still days, not a breath of air to be had; lot of smoke from this factory just hung there, thicker than fog. Some of the older folk couldn't do it. Apoplexy or something, Mr. Badger called it."

"You mean Toad's passed away?" asked the Rat, astonished.

"Yes, sir."

"Silly old Toad . . ."

"Good old Toad . . . dead?"

There was a shocked silence. After a time the weasel spoke again.

"And then, when they built those new homes across the water, a good many fine weasels and others lost theirs. When they tore down the Wild Wood, that is. Most everybody that I grew up with has left the neighborhood entirely. Gone east, I suppose."

"They tore down the Wild Wood?" asked Mole in his very small voice.

"And Badger?" asked Rat.

"Well, that is, Mr. Badger got caught up in a load of concrete. When they were putting in those new homes."

"*Badger?*" cried the Rat. He was sorely smitten; the Mole just stood, confused, with his long snout wavering in the night air. After a time the Rat roused himself enough to wish the weasel a good evening and grab

Mole's elbow. The two travelers hurried off, following a large corrugated-metal pipe toward the river a short distance away.

At the water's edge the conduit ended. From its open maw poured a sluggish and foul-smelling stream. The river itself seemed slow-moving and evil.

"What have they done to my river?" cried the Rat. He stared across in the gloom, but he could not make out the night-shrouded features of his house. After a bit of a search he located the small boat that had been left tied up on the Mole's side of the water so many months previously. The Rat allowed Mole to enter, meanwhile undoing the knotted painter. He threw the line into the boat and pushed off, stepping into the river to do so. The water felt oily and unpleasant, and the Rat shuddered as he hopped into the skiff and grabbed the oars. He rowed in silence, and the Mole was similarly lost in his own thoughts. On the other side Mole leaped out and hauled the boat to shore, where the Rat joined him after shipping the oars.

River Bank was ruined. The outside of the dwelling was coated with a thick, sludgy layer that had seeped inside and spoiled everything: furniture, books, food stores, everything. Rat viewed the scene with growing anger and frustration, but remained quiet. Finally he took the Mole's elbow once again.

"Come along, old friend. It's obvious that we can't stay here, either."

"Where shall we go, Ratty? We have nowhere to go."

"And nothing to take with us. That's fine, I suppose; a new start, new beginnings. Although we're both a bit far along for that sort of thing. But, what's done is done, and no use being resentful. Let us leave soon, while I still have the strength of this impulse, and before I truthfully realize that everything I've ever had is wasted and made into rubbish."

So they took to the water, following the course of the stream and the cold night wind. The Rat took the first turn at rowing while the Mole drowsed. Then they switched; Mole rowed and Water Rat failed in his resolve to stay awake and hunt for a likely place to spend the night. The Rat dropped off to sleep, and the Mole's rowing grew slower and slower as he, too, fell fast asleep. They were both awakened some time later by the lurching of the boat in the strong current.

"Oh, Mole," said the Rat accusingly, *"have* you lost the oars? Where? Just now?"

"I don't know, Ratty! I suppose that I've drifted off to sleep, and I don't know just when I dropped the oars. Where are we? Oh, I'm so sorry, but I'm just so tired!"

"I don't know where we are, my very good Mole. I'm sorry for speaking to you in that unkind way. I don't recognize any of this shoreline that we're passing, so I assume that we've both been getting back a good share of the night's rest that we have cheated ourselves of so far. It looks as if our adventures *aren't* over yet."

The river had grown broader and stronger than they had ever seen it. The boat and its two weary passengers followed helplessly wherever it led them. The Rat must have dozed again, for he was awakened by the Mole's excited cry.

"Rat, do you see? The dawn, now for sure. At least we won't be traveling in the dark any longer. Oh, how glad I will be to see the sun!"

But Mole was incorrect once more; it was not the sun. The fierce, ruddy glow on the river ahead was caused by artificial means, though not as before in the parking lot. As the crippled rowboat sped nearer in the river's grasp, it became clear to the Water Rat that the light was from a great fire. Indeed, up ahead the thick, orange water of the river itself was blazing in a towering wall of flame.

POUL ANDERSON

The Tale of Hauk

One of the most acclaimed and most prolific writers in science fiction, Poul Anderson made his first sale in 1947, and in the course of his subsequent fifty-year career has published almost a hundred books (in several different fields, as Anderson has written historical novels, fantasies, and mysteries, in addition to SF), sold hundreds of short pieces to every conceivable market, and won seven Hugo Awards, three Nebula Awards, and the Tolkien Memorial Award for life achievement.

Although Anderson is best known as a writer of "hard science fiction" and fast-paced intergalactic adventure tales, he has always loved fantasy, and has published a good deal of it, some quite influential. His best known fantasy novel is probably *Three Hearts and Three Lions,* a whimsical *"Unknown-*style" deliberately anachronistic fantasy along the lines of de Camp and Pratt's *The Incomplete Enchanter,* but with a somewhat harder adventure edge to it, as though one of the de Camp and Pratt stories had been cross-bred with a Sword & Sorcery swashbuckler such as one of Robert E. Howard's *Conan* books; it was followed decades later by a semi-sequel, *Midsummer Tempest.* The more typical Anderson fantasy story, though, abandons the whimsy and explores the harsh, bleak, unrelenting, frequently violent territory of Norse mythology and folklore—his explorations of that *milieu* include *Hrolf Kraki's Saga, The Broken Sword, The Golden Horn, The Road of the Sea Horse, The Sign of the Raven,* and short stories such as "The Peat Bog" and "The Valor of Cappen Varra" . . . and the chilling story that follows, which tells the story of a most unwelcome houseguest, one who will *not* go away, no matter how many times you ask him to . . .

Anderson's books include, among *many* others, *The High Crusade, The Enemy Stars, Brain Wave, Tau Zero, The Night Face, Orion Shall Rise, The Shield of Time, The Time Patrol,* and *The People of the Wind,* as well as the two multivolume series of novels about his two most popular characters, Dominic Flandry and Nicholas van Rijn. His short work has been collected in *The Queen of Air and Darkness and Other Stories, Guardians of Time, The Earth Book of Stormgate, Fantasy, The Unicorn Trade* (with Karen Anderson), *Past Times, Time Patrolman,* and *Explorations.* Among his most recent books are the novels *The Boat of a Million Years, Harvest of Stars,* and *The Stars Are Also Fire.* Anderson lives in Orinda, California, with his wife (and fellow writer) Karen.

A man called Geirolf dwelt on the Great Fjord in Raumsdal. His father was Bui Hardhand, who owned a farm inland near the Dofra Fell. One year Bui went in viking to Finnmark and brought back a woman he dubbed Gydha. She became the mother of Geirolf. But because Bui already had children by his wife, there would be small inheritance for this by-blow.

Folk said uncanny things about Gydha. She was fair to see, but spoke little, did no more work than she must, dwelt by herself in a shack out of sight of the garth, and often went for long stridings alone on the upland heaths, heedless of cold, rain, and rovers. Bui did not visit her often. Her son Geirolf did. He too was a moody sort, not much given to playing with others, quick and harsh of temper. Big and strong, he went abroad with his father already when he was twelve, and in the next few years won the name of a mighty though ruthless fighter.

Then Gydha died. They buried her near her shack, and it was whispered that she spooked around it of nights. Soon after, walking home with some men by moonlight from a feast at a neighbor's, Bui clutched his breast and fell dead. They wondered if Gydha had called him, maybe to accompany her home to Finnmark, for there was no more sight of her.

Geirolf bargained with his kin and got the price of a ship for himself. Thereafter he gathered a crew, mostly younger sons and a wild lot, and fared west. For a long while he harried Scotland, Ireland, and the coasts south of the Channel, and won much booty. With some of this he bought his farm on the Great Fjord. Meanwhile he courted Thyra, a daughter of the yeoman Sigtryg Einarsson, and got her.

They had one son early on, Hauk, a bright and lively lad. But thereafter five years went by until they had a daughter who lived, Unn, and two years later a boy they called Einar. Geirolf was in viking every summer, and sometimes wintered over in the Westlands. Yet he was a kindly father, whose children were always glad to see him come roaring home. Very tall and broad in the shoulders, he had long red-brown hair and a full beard around a broad blunt-nosed face whose eyes were ice blue and slanted. He liked fine clothes and heavy gold rings, which he also lavished on Thyra.

Then the time came when Geirolf said he felt poorly and would not fare elsewhere that season. Hauk was fourteen years old and had been wild to go. "I'll keep my promise to you as well as may be," Geirolf said, and sent men asking around. The best he could do was get his son a bench on a ship belonging to Ottar the Wide-Faring from Haalogaland in the north, who was trading along the coast and meant to do likewise overseas.

Hauk and Ottar took well to each other. In England, the man got the boy prime-signed so he could deal with Christians. Though neither was baptized, what he heard while they wintered there made Hauk thoughtful. Next spring they fared south to trade among the Moors, and did not come home until late fall.

Ottar was Geirolf's guest for a while, though he scowled to himself when his host broke into fits of deep coughing. He offered to take Hauk along on his voyages from now on and start the youth toward a good livelihood.

"You a chapman—the son of a viking?" Geirolf sneered. He had grown surly of late.

Hauk flushed. "You've heard what we did to those vikings who set on *us*," he answered.

"Give our son his head," was Thyra's smiling rede, "or he'll take the bit between his teeth."

The upshot was that Geirolf grumbled agreement, and Hauk fared off. He did not come back for five years.

Long were the journeys he took with Ottar. By ship and horse, they made their way to Uppsala in Svithjodh, thence into the wilderness of the Keel after pelts; amber they got on the windy strands of Jutland, salt herring along the Sound; seeking beeswax, honey, and tallow, they pushed beyond Holmgard to the fair at Kiev; walrus ivory lured them past North Cape, through bergs and floes to the land of the fur-clad Biarmians; and they bore many goods west. They did not hide that the wish to see what was new to them drove them as hard as any hope of gain.

In those days King Harald Fairhair went widely about in Norway, bringing all the land under himself. Lesser kings and chieftains must either plight faith to him or meet his wrath; it crushed whomever would stand fast. When he entered Raumsdal, he sent men from garth to garth as was his wont, to say he wanted oaths and warriors.

"My older son is abroad," Geirolf told these, "and my younger still a stripling. As for myself—" He coughed, and blood flecked his beard. The king's men did not press the matter.

But now Geirolf's moods grew ever worse. He snarled at everybody, cuffed his children and housefolk, once drew a dagger and stabbed to death a thrall who chanced to spill some soup on him. When Thyra reproached him for this, he said only, "Let them know I am not altogether hallowed out. I can still wield blade." And he looked at her so

threateningly from beneath his shaggy brows that she, no coward, withdrew in silence.

A year later, Hauk Geirolfsson returned to visit his parents.

That was on a chill fall noontide. Whitecaps chopped beneath a
whistling wind and cast spindrift salty onto lips. Clifftops on either side
of the fjord were lost in mist. Above blew cloud wrack like smoke. Hauk's
ship, a wide-beamed knorr, rolled, pitched, and creaked as it beat its way
under sail. The owner stood in the bows, wrapped in a flame-red cloak,
an uncommonly big young man, yellow hair tossing around a face akin
to his father's, weatherbeaten though still scant of beard. When he saw
the arm of the fjord that he wanted to enter, he pointed with a spear at
whose head he had bound a silk pennon. When he saw Disafoss pouring in a white stream down the blue-gray stone wall to larboard, and beyond the waterfall at the end of that arm lay his old home, he shouted
for happiness.

Geirolf had rich holdings. The hall bulked over all else, heavy-timbered,
brightly painted, dragon heads arching from rafters and gables. Elsewhere around the yard were cookhouse, smokehouse, bathhouse, store-
houses, workshop, stables, barns, women's bower. Several cabins for
hirelings and their families were strewn beyond. Fishing boats lay on
the strand near a shed which held the master's dragonship. Behind
the steading, land sloped sharply upward through a narrow dale, where
fields were walled with stones grubbed out of them and now stubbled after
harvest. A bronze-leaved oakenshaw stood untouched not far from the
buildings; and a mile inland, where hills humped themselves toward the
mountains, rose a darkling wall of pinewood.

Spearheads and helmets glimmered ashore. But men saw it was a single craft bound their way, white shield on the mast. As the hull slipped
alongside the little wharf, they lowered their weapons. Hauk sprang from
bow to dock in a single leap and whooped.

Geirolf trod forth. "Is that you, my son?" he called. His voice was
hoarse from coughing; he had grown gaunt and sunken-eyed; the ax that
he bore shivered in his hand.

"Yes, father, yes, home again," Hauk stammered. He could not hide his
shock.

Maybe this drove Geirolf to anger. Nobody knew; he had become impossible to get along with. "I could well-nigh have hoped otherwise," he
rasped. "An unfriend would give me something better than straw-death."

The rest of the men, housecarls and thralls alike, flocked about Hauk
to bid him welcome. Among them was a burly, grizzled yeoman whom
he knew from aforetime, Leif Egilsson, a neighbor come to dicker for a
horse. When he was small, Hauk had often wended his way over a woodland trail to Leif's garth to play with the children there.

He called his crew to him. They were not just Norse, but had among them Danes, Swedes, and English, gathered together over the years as he found them trustworthy. "You brought a mickle for me to feed," Geirolf said. Luckily, the wind bore his words from all but Hauk. "Where's your master Ottar?"

The young man stiffened. "He's my friend, never my master," he answered. "This is my own ship, bought with my own earnings. Ottar abides in England this year. The West Saxons have a new king, one Alfred, whom he wants to get to know."

"Time was when it was enough to know how to get sword past a Westman's shield," Geirolf grumbled.

Seeing peace down by the water, women and children hastened from the hall to meet the newcomers. At their head went Thyra. She was tall and deep-bosomed; her gown blew around a form still straight and freely striding. But as she neared, Hauk saw that the gold of her braids was dimmed and sorrow had furrowed her face. Nonetheless she kindled when she knew him. "Oh, thrice welcome, Hauk!" she said low. "How long can you bide with us?"

After his father's greeting, it had been in his mind to say he must soon be off. But when he spied who walked behind his mother, he said, "We thought we might be guests here the winter through, if that's not too much of a burden."

"Never—" began Thyra. Then she saw where his gaze had gone, and suddenly she smiled.

Alfhild Leifsdottir had joined her widowed father on this visit. She was two years younger than Hauk, but they had been glad of each other as playmates. Today she stood a maiden grown, lissome in a blue wadmal gown, heavily crowned with red locks above great green eyes, straight nose, and gently curved mouth. Though he had known many a woman, none struck him as being so fair.

He grinned at her and let his cloak flap open to show his finery of broidered, fur-lined tunic, linen shirt and breeks, chased leather boots, gold on arms and neck and sword-hilt. She paid them less heed than she did him when they spoke.

Thus Hauk and his men moved to Geirolf's hall. He brought plentiful gifts, there was ample food and drink, and their tales of strange lands—their songs, dances, games, jests, manners—made them good housefellows in these lengthening nights.

Already on the next morning, he walked out with Alfhild. Rain had cleared the air, heaven and fjord sparkled, wavelets chuckled beneath a cool breeze from the woods. Nobody else was on the strand where they went.

"So you grow mighty as a chapman, Hauk," Alfhild teased. "Have you never gone in viking . . . only once, only to please your father?"

"No," he answered gravely. "I fail to see what manliness lies in falling on those too weak to defend themselves. We traders must be stronger and more war-skilled than any who may seek to plunder us." A thick branch of driftwood, bleached and hardened, lay nearby. Hauk picked it up and snapped it between his hands. Two other men would have had trouble doing that. It gladdened him to see Alfhild glow at the sight. "Nobody has tried us twice," he said.

They passed the shed where Geirolf's dragon lay on rollers. Hauk opened the door for a peek at the remembered slim shape. A sharp whiff from the gloom within brought his nose wrinkling. "Whew!" he snorted. "Dry rot."

"Poor *Fireworm* has long lain idle," Alfhild sighed. "In later years, your father's illness has gnawed him till he doesn't even see to the care of his ship. He knows he will never take it a-roving again."

"I feared that," Hauk murmured.

"We grieve for him on our own garth too," she said. "In former days, he was a staunch friend to us. Now we bear with his ways, yes, insults that would make my father draw blade on anybody else."

"That is dear of you," Hauk said, staring straight before him. "I'm very thankful."

"You have not much cause for that, have you?" she asked. "I mean, you've been away so long . . . Of course, you have your mother. She's borne the brunt, stood like a shield before your siblings—" She touched her lips. "I talk too much."

"You talk as a friend," he blurted. "May we always be friends."

They wandered on, along a path from shore to fields. It went by the shaw. Through boles and boughs and falling leaves, they saw Thor's image and altar among the trees. "I'll make offering here for my father's health," Hauk said, "though truth to tell, I've more faith in my own strength than in any gods."

"You have seen lands where strange gods rule," she nodded.

"Yes, and there too, they do not steer things well," he said. "It was in a Christian realm that a huge wolf came raiding flocks, on which no iron would bite. When it took a baby from a hamlet near our camp, I thought I'd be less than a man did I not put an end to it."

"What happened?" she asked breathlessly, and caught his arm.

"I wrestled it barehanded—no foe of mine was ever more fell—and at last broke its neck." He pulled back a sleeve to show scars of terrible bites. "Dead, it changed into a man they had outlawed that year for his evil deeds. We burned the lich to make sure it would not walk again, and there-after the folk had peace. And . . . we had friends, in a country otherwise wary of us."

She looked on him in the wonder he had hoped for.

Erelong she must return with her father. But the way between the garths was just a few miles, and Hauk often rode or skied through the woods. At home, he and his men helped do what work there was, and gave merriment where it had long been little known.

Thyra owned this to her son, on a snowy day when they were by themselves. They were in the women's bower, whither they had gone to see a tapestry she was weaving. She wanted to know how it showed against those of the Westlands; he had brought one such, which hung above the benches in the hall. Here, in the wide quiet room, was dusk, for the day outside had become a tumbling whiteness. Breath steamed from lips as the two of them spoke. It smelled sweet; both had drunk mead until they could talk freely.

"You did better than you knew when you came back," Thyra said. "You blew like spring into this winter of ours. Einar and Unn were withering; they blossom again in your nearness."

"Strangely has our father changed," Hauk answered sadly. "I remember once when I was small, how he took me by the hand on a frost-clear night, led me forth under the stars, and named for me the pictures in them, Thor's Wain, Freyja's Spindle—how wonderful he made them, how his deep slow laughterful voice filled the dark."

"A wasting illness draws the soul inward," his mother said. "He . . . has no more manhood . . . and it tears him like fangs that he will die helpless in bed. He must strike out at someone, and here we are."

She was silent a while before she added: "He will not live out the year. Then you must take over."

"I must be gone when weather allows," Hauk warned. "I promised Ottar."

"Return as soon as may be," Thyra said. "We have need of a strong man, the more so now when yonder King Harald would reave their freehold rights from yeomen."

"It would be well to have a hearth of my own." Hauk stared past her, toward the unseen woods. Her worn face creased in a smile.

Suddenly they heard yells from the yard below. Hauk ran out onto the gallery and looked down. Geirolf was shambling after an aged carl named Atli. He had a whip in his hand and was lashing it across the white locks and wrinkled cheeks of the man, who could not run fast either and who sobbed.

"What is this?" broke from Hauk. He swung himself over the rail, hung, and let go. The drop would at least have jarred the wind out of most. He, though, bounced from where he landed, ran behind his father, caught hold of the whip and wrenched it from Geirolf's grasp. "What are you doing?"

Geirolf howled and struck his son with a doubled fist. Blood trickled from Hauk's mouth. He stood fast. Atli sank to hands and knees and fought not to weep.

"Are you also a heelbiter of mine?" Geirolf bawled.

"I'd save you from your madness, father," Hauk said in pain. "Atli followed you to battle ere I was born—he dandled me on his knee—and he's a free man. What has he done, that you'd bring down on us the anger of his kinfolk?"

"Harm not the skipper, young man," Atli begged. "I fled because I'd sooner die than lift hand against my skipper."

"Hell swallow you both!" Geirolf would have cursed further, but the coughing came on him. Blood drops flew through the snowflakes, down onto the white earth, where they mingled with the drip from the heads of Hauk and Atli. Doubled over, Geirolf let them half lead, half carry him to his shut-bed. There he closed the panel and lay alone in darkness.

"What happened between you and him?" Hauk asked.

"I was fixing to shoe a horse," Atli said into a ring of gaping onlookers. "He came in and wanted to know why I'd not asked his leave. I told him 'twas plain Kolfaxi needed new shoes. Then he hollered, 'I'll show you I'm no log in the woodpile!' and snatched yon whip off the wall and took after me." The old man squared his shoulders. "We'll speak no more of this, you hear?" he ordered the household.

Nor did Geirolf, when next day he let them bring him some broth.

For more reasons than this, Hauk came to spend much of his time at Leif's garth. He would return in such a glow that even the reproachful looks of his young sister and brother, even the sullen or the weary greeting of his father, could not dampen it.

At last, when lengthening days and quickening blood bespoke seafarings soon to come, that happened which surprised nobody. Hauk told them in the hall that he wanted to marry Alfhild Leifsdottir, and prayed Geirolf press the suit for him. "What must be, will be," said his father, a better grace than awaited. Union of the families was clearly good for both.

Leif Egilsson agreed, and Alfhild had nothing but aye to say. The betrothal feast crowded the whole neighborhood together in cheer. Thyra hid the trouble within her, and Geirolf himself was calm if not blithe.

Right after, Hauk and his men were busking themselves to fare. Regardless of his doubts about gods, he led in offering for a safe voyage to Thor, Aegir, and St. Michael. But Alfhild found herself a quiet place alone, to cut runes on an ash tree in the name of Freyja.

When all was ready, she was there with the folk of Geirolf's stead to see the sailors off. That morning was keen, wind roared in trees and skirled between cliffs, waves ran green and white beneath small flying clouds. Unn could not but hug her brother who was going, while Einar gave him a handclasp that shook. Thyra said, "Come home hale and early, my son." Alfhild mostly stored away the sight of Hauk. Atli and others of the household mumbled this and that.

Geirolf shuffled forward. The cane on which he leaned rattled among the stones of the beach. He was hunched in a hairy cloak against the sharp air. His locks fell tangled almost to the coal-smoldering eyes. "Father, farewell," Hauk said, taking his free hand.

"You mean 'fare far,' don't you?" Geirolf grated. " 'Fare far and never come back.' You'd like that, wouldn't you? But we will meet again. Oh, yes, we will meet again."

Hauk dropped the hand. Geirolf turned and sought the house. The rest behaved as if they had not heard, speaking loudly, amidst yelps of laughter, to overcome those words of foreboding. Soon Hauk called his orders to begone.

Men scrambled aboard the laden ship. Its sail slatted aloft and filled, the mooring lines were cast loose, the hull stood out to sea. Alfhild waved until it was gone from sight behind the bend where Disafoss fell.

The summer passed—plowing, sowing, lambing, calving, farrowing, hoeing, reaping, flailing, butchering—rain, hail, sun, stars, loves, quarrels, births, deaths—and the season wore toward fall. Alfhild was seldom at Geirolf's garth, nor was Leif; for Hauk's father grew steadily worse. After midsummer he could no longer leave his bed. But often he whispered, between lung-tearing coughs, to those who tended him, "I would kill you if I could."

On a dark day late in the season, when rain roared about the hall and folk and hounds huddled close to fires that hardly lit the gloom around, Geirolf awoke from a heavy sleep. Thyra marked it and came to him. Cold and dankness gnawed their way through her clothes. The fever was in him like a brand. He plucked restlessly at his blanket, where he half sat in his short shut-bed. Though flesh had wasted from the great bones, his fingers still had strength to tear the wool. The mattress rustled under him. "Straw-death, straw-death," he muttered.

Thyra laid a palm on his brow. "Be at ease," she said.

It dragged from him: "You'll not be rid . . . of me . . . so fast . . . by straw-death." An icy sweat broke forth and the last struggle began.

Long it was, Geirolf's gasps and the sputtering flames the only noises within that room, while rain and wind ramped outside and night drew in. Thyra stood by the bedside to wipe the sweat off her man, blood and spittle from his beard. A while after sunset, he rolled his eyes back and died.

Thyra called for water and lamps. She cleansed him, clad him in his best, and laid him out. A drawn sword was on his breast.

In the morning, thralls and carls alike went forth under her orders. A hillock stood in the fields about half a mile inland from the house. They dug a grave chamber in the top of this, lining it well with timber. "Won't you bury him in his ship?" asked Atli.

"It is rotten, unworthy of him," Thyra said. Yet she made them haul it to the barrow, around which she had stones to outline a hull. Meanwhile folk readied a grave-ale, and messengers bade neighbors come.

When all were there, men of Geirolf's carried him on a litter to his resting place and put him in, together with weapons and a jar of Southland coins. After beams had roofed the chamber, his friends from aforetime took shovels and covered it well. They replaced the turfs of sere grass, leaving the hillock as it had been save that it was now bigger. Einar Thorolfsson kindled his father's ship. It burned till dusk, when the horns of the new moon stood over the fjord. Meanwhile folk had gone back down to the garth to feast and drink. Riding home next day, well gifted by Thyra, they told each other that this had been an honorable burial.

The moon waxed. On the first night that it rose full, Geirolf came again.

A thrall named Kark had been late in the woods, seeking a strayed sheep. Coming home, he passed near the howe. The moon was barely above the pines; long shivery beams of light ran on the water, lost themselves in shadows ashore, glinted wanly anew where a bedewed stone wall snaked along a stubblefield. Stars were few. A great stillness lay on the land, not even an owl hooted, until all at once dogs down in the garth began howling. It was not the way they howled at the moon; across the mile between, it sounded ragged and terrified. Kark felt the chill close in around him, and hastened toward home.

Something heavy trod the earth. He looked around and saw the bulk of a huge man coming across the field from the barrow. "Who's that?" he called uneasily. No voice replied, but the weight of those footfalls shivered through the ground into his bones. Kark swallowed, gripped his staff, and stood where he was. But then the shape came so near that moonlight picked out the head of Geirolf. Kark screamed, dropped his weapon, and ran.

Geirolf followed slowly, clumsily behind.

Down in the garth, light glimmered red as doors opened. Folk saw Kark running, gasping for breath. Atli and Einar led the way out, each with a torch in one hand, a sword in the other. Little could they see beyond the wild flame-gleam. Kark reached them, fell, writhed on the hard-beaten clay of the yard, and wailed.

"What is it, you lackwit?" Atli snapped, and kicked him. Then Einar pointed his blade.

"A stranger—" Atli began.

Geirolf rocked into sight. The mould of the grave clung to him. His eyes stared unblinking, unmoving, blank in the moonlight, out of a gray face whereon the skin crawled. The teeth in his tangled beard were dry. No breath smoked from his nostrils. He held out his arms, crook-fingered.

"Father!" Einar cried. The torch hissed from his grip, flickered weakly at his feet, and went out. The men at his back jammed the doorway of the hall as they sought its shelter.

"The skipper's come again," Atli quavered. He sheathed his sword, though that was hard when his hand shook, and made himself step forward. "Skipper, d'you know your old shipmate Atli?"

The dead man grabbed him, lifted him, and dashed him to earth. Einar heard bones break. Atli jerked once and lay still. Geirolf trod him and Kark underfoot. There was a sound of cracking and rending. Blood spurted forth.

Blindly, Einar swung blade. The edge smote but would not bite. A wave of grave-chill passed over him. He whirled and bounded back inside.

Thyra had seen. "Bar the door," she bade. The windows were already shuttered against frost. "Men, stand fast. Women, stoke up the fires."

They heard the lich groping about the yard. Walls creaked where Geirolf blundered into them. Thyra called through the door, "Why do you wish us ill, your own household?" But only those noises gave answer. The hounds cringed and whined.

"Lay iron at the doors and under every window," Thyra commanded. "If it will not cut him, it may keep him out."

All that night, then, folk huddled in the hall. Geirolf climbed onto the roof and rode the ridgepole, drumming his heels on the shakes till the whole building boomed. A little before sunrise, it stopped. Peering out by the first dull dawnlight, Thyra saw no mark of her husband but his deep-sunken footprints and the wrecked bodies he had left.

"He grew so horrible before he died," Unn wept. "Now he can't rest, can he?"

"We'll make him an offering," Thyra said through her weariness. "It may be we did not give him enough when we buried him."

Few would follow her to the howe. Those who dared, brought along the best horse on the farm. Einar, as the son of the house when Hauk was gone, himself cut its throat after a sturdy man had given the hammer-blow. Carls and wenches butchered the carcass, which Thyra and Unn cooked over a fire in whose wood was blent the charred rest of the dragonship. Nobody cared to eat much of the flesh or broth. Thyra poured what was left over the bones, upon the grave.

Two ravens circled in sight, waiting for folk to go so they could take the food. "Is that a good sign?" Thyra sighed. "Will Odin fetch Geirolf home?"

That night everybody who had not fled to neighboring steads gathered in the hall. Soon after the moon rose, they heard the footfalls come nearer and nearer. They heard Geirolf break into the storehouse and worry the laid-out bodies of Atli and Kark. They heard him kill cows in the barn. Again he rode the roof.

In the morning Leif Egilsson arrived, having gotten the news. He found Thyra too tired and shaken to do anything further. "The ghost did not take your offering," he said, "but maybe the gods will."

In the oakenshaw, he led the giving of more beasts. There was talk of a thrall for Odin, but he said that would not help if this did not. Instead, he saw to the proper burial of the slain, and of those kine which nobody would dare eat. That night he abode on the farm.

And Geirolf came back. Throughout the darkness, he tormented the home which had been his.

"I will bide here one more day," Leif said next sunrise. "We all need rest—though ill is it that we must sleep during daylight when we've so much readying for winter to do."

By that time, some other neighborhood men were also on hand. They spoke loudly of how they would hew the lich asunder.

"You know not what you boast of," said aged Grim the Wise. "Einar smote, and he strikes well for a lad, but the iron would not bite. It never will. Ghost-strength is in Geirolf, and all the wrath he could not set free during his life."

That night folk waited breathless for moonrise. But when the gnawed shield climbed over the pines, nothing stirred. The dogs, too, no longer seemed cowed. About midnight, Grim murmured into the shadows, "Yes, I thought so. Geirolf walks only when the moon is full."

"Then tomorrow we'll dig him up and burn him!" Leif said.

"No," Grim told them. "That would spell the worst of luck for every-body here. Don't you see, the anger and unpeace which will not let him rest, those would be forever unslaked? They could not but bring doom on the burners."

"What then can we do?" Thyra asked dully.

"Leave this stead," Grim counselled, "at least when the moon is full."

"Hard will that be," Einar sighed. "Would that my brother Hauk were here."

"He should have returned erenow," Thyra said. "May we in our woe never know that he has come to grief himself."

In truth, Hauk had not. His wares proved welcome in Flanders, where he bartered for cloth that he took across to England. There Ottar greeted him, and he met the young King Alfred. At that time there was no war going on with the Danes, who were settling into the Danelaw and thus in need of household goods. Hauk and Ottar did a thriving business among them. This led them to think they might do as well in Iceland, whither Norse folk were moving who liked not King Harald Fairhair. They made a voyage to see. Foul winds hampered them on the way home. Hence fall was well along when Hauk's ship returned.

The day was still and cold. Low overcast turned sky and water the hue of iron. A few gulls cruised and mewed, while under them sounded creak and splash of oars, swearing of men, as the knorr was rowed. At the end of the fjord-branch, garth and leaves were tiny splashes of color, lost against rearing cliffs, brown fields, murky wildwood. Straining ahead from afar, Hauk saw that a bare handful of men came down to the shore, moving listlessly more than watchfully. When his craft was unmistakable, though, a few women—no youngsters—sped from the hall as if they could not wait. Their cries came to him more thin than the gulls'.

Hauk lay alongside the dock. Springing forth, he called merrily, "Where is everybody? How fares Alfhild?" His words lost themselves in silence. Fear touched him. "What's wrong?"

Thyra trod forth. Years might have gone by during his summer abroad, so changed was she. "You are barely in time," she said in an unsteady tone. Taking his hands, she told him how things stood.

Hauk stared long into emptiness. At last, "Oh, no," he whispered. "What's to be done?"

"We hoped you might know that, my son," Thyra answered. "The moon will be full tomorrow night."

His voice stumbled. "I am no wizard. If the gods themselves would not lay this ghost, what can I do?"

Einar spoke, in the brashness of youth: "We thought you might deal with him as you did with the werewolf."

"But that was—No, I cannot!" Hauk croaked. "Never ask me."

"Then I fear we must leave," Thyra said. "For aye. You see how many have already fled, thrall and free alike, though nobody else has a place for them. We've not enough left to farm these acres. And who would buy them of us? Poor must we go, helpless as the poor ever are."

"Iceland—" Hauk wet his lips. "Well, you shall not want while I live." Yet he had counted on this homestead, whether to dwell on or sell.

"Tomorrow we move over to Leif's garth, for the next three days and nights," Thyra said.

Unn shuddered. "I know not if I can come back," she said. "This whole past month here, I could hardly ever sleep." Dulled skin and sunken eyes bore her out.

"What else would you do?" Hauk asked.

"Whatever I can," she stammered, and broke into tears. He knew: wedding herself too young to whoever would have her dowryless, poor though the match would be—or making her way to some town to turn whore, his little sister.

"Let me think on this," Hauk begged. "Maybe I can hit on something."

His crew were also daunted when they heard. At eventide they sat in the hall and gave only a few curt words about what they had done in foreign parts. Everyone lay down early on bed, bench, or floor, but none slept well.

Before sunset, Hauk had walked forth alone. First he sought the grave of Atli. "I'm sorry, dear old friend," he said. Afterward he went to Geirolf's howe. It loomed yellow-gray with withered grass wherein grinned the skull of the slaughtered horse. At its foot were strewn the charred bits of the ship, inside stones which outlined a greater but unreal hull. Around reached stubblefields and walls, hemmed in by woods on one side and water on the other, rock lifting sheer beyond. The chill and the quiet had deepened.

Hauk climbed to the top of the barrow and stood there a while, head bent downward. "Oh, father," he said, "I learned doubt in Christian lands. What's right for me to do?" There was no answer. He made a slow way back to the dwelling.

All were up betimes next day. It went slowly over the woodland path to Leif's, for animals must be herded along. The swine gave more trouble than most. Hauk chuckled once, not very merrily, and remarked that at least this took folk's minds off their sorrows. He raised no mirth.

But he had Alfhild ahead of him. At the end of the way, he sprinted shouting into the yard. Leif owned less land than Geirolf, his buildings were smaller and fewer, most of his guests must house outdoors in sleeping bags. Hauk paid no heed. "Alfhild!" he called. "I'm here!"

She left the dough she was kneading and sped to him. They hugged each other hard and long, in sight of the whole world. None thought that shame, as things were. At last she said, striving not to weep, "How we've longed for you! Now the nightmare can end."

He stepped back. "What mean you?" he uttered slowly, knowing full well.

"Why—" She was bewildered. "Won't you give him his second death?"

Hauk gazed past her for some heartbeats before he said: "Come aside with me."

Hand in hand, they wandered off. A meadow lay hidden from the garth by a stand of aspen. Elsewhere around, pines speared into a sky that today was bright. Clouds drifted on a nipping breeze. Far off, a stag bugled.

Hauk spread feet apart, hooked thumbs in belt, and made himself meet her eyes. "You think over-highly of my strength," he said.

"Who has more?" she asked. "We kept ourselves going by saying you would come home and make things good again."

"What if the drow is too much for me?" His words sounded raw through the hush. Leaves dropped yellow from their boughs.

She flushed. "Then your name will live."

"Yes—" Softly he spoke the words of the High One:

> *"Kine die, kinfolk die,*
> *and so at last oneself.*
> *This I know that never dies;*
> *how dead men's deeds are deemed."*

"You will do it!" she cried gladly.

His head shook before it drooped. "No. I will not. I dare not."

She stood as if he had clubbed her.

"Won't you understand?" he began.

The wound he had dealt her hopes went too deep. "So you show your-self a nithing!"

"Hear me," he said, shaken. "Were the lich anybody else's—"

Overwrought beyond reason, she slapped him and choked, "The gods bear witness, I give them my holiest oath, never will I wed you unless you do this thing. See, by my blood I swear." She whipped out her dag-ger and gashed her wrist. Red rills coursed out and fell in drops on the fallen leaves.

He was aghast. "You know not what you say. You're too young, you've been too sheltered. *Listen.*"

She would have fled from him, but he gripped her shoulders and made her stand. "Listen," went between his teeth. "Geirolf is still my father—my father who begot me, reared me, named the stars for me, weaponed me to make my way in the world. How can I fight him? Did I slay him, what horror would come upon me and mine?"

"O-o-oh," broke from Alfhild. She sank to the ground and wept as if to tear loose her ribs.

He knelt, held her, gave what soothing he could. "Now I know," she mourned. "Too late."

"Never," he murmured. "We'll fare abroad if we must, take new land, make new lives together."

"No," she gasped. "Did I not swear? What doom awaits an oath-breaker?"

Then he was long still. Heedlessly though she had spoken, her blood lay in the earth, which would remember.

He too was young. He straightened. "I will fight," he said.

Now she clung to him and pleaded that he must not. But an iron calm had come over him. "Maybe I will not be cursed," he said. "Or maybe the curse will be no more than I can bear."

"It will be mine too, I who brought it on you," she plighted herself.

Hand in hand again, they went back to the garth. Leif spied the hag-gard look on them and half guessed what had happened. "Will you fare to meet the drow, Hauk?" he asked. "Wait till I can have Grim the Wise brought here. His knowledge may help you."

"No," said Hauk. "Waiting would weaken me. I go this night."

Wide eyes stared at him—all but Thyra's; she was too torn.

Toward evening he busked himself. He took no helm, shield, or byrnie, for the dead man bore no weapons. Some said they would come along, armored themselves well, and offered to be at his side. He told them to follow him, but no farther than to watch what happened. Their iron would be of no help, and he thought they would only get in each other's way, and his, when he met the over-human might of the drow. He kissed Alfhild, his mother, and his sister, and clasped hands with his brother, bidding them stay behind if they loved him.

Long did the few miles of path seem, and gloomy under the pines. The sun was on the world's rim when men came out in the open. They looked past fields and barrow down to the empty garth, the fjordside cliffs, the water where the sun lay as half an ember behind a trail of blood. Clouds hurried on a wailing wind through a greenish sky. Cold struck deep. A wolf howled.

"Wait here," Hauk said.

"The gods be with you," Leif breathed.

"I've naught tonight but my own strength," Hauk said. "Belike none of us ever had more."

His tall form, clad in leather and wadmal, showed black athwart the sunset as he walked from the edge of the woods, out across plowland toward the crouching howe. The wind fluttered his locks, a last brightness until the sun went below. Then for a while the evenstar alone had light.

Hauk reached the mound. He drew sword and leaned on it, waiting. Dusk deepened. Star after star came forth, small and strange. Clouds blowing across them picked up a glow from the still unseen moon.

It rose at last above the treetops. Its ashen sheen stretched gashes of shadow across earth. The wind loudened.

The grave groaned. Turves, stones, timbers swung aside. Geirolf shambled out beneath the sky. Hauk felt the ground shudder under his weight. There came a carrion stench, though the only sign of rotting was on the dead man's clothes. His eyes peered dim, his teeth gnashed dry in a face at once well remembered and hideously changed. When he saw the living one who waited, he veered and lumbered thitherward.

"Father," Hauk called. "It's I, your eldest son."

The drow drew nearer.

"Halt, I beg you," Hauk said unsteadily. "What can I do to bring you peace?"

A cloud passed over the moon. It seemed to be hurtling through heaven. Geirolf reached for his son with fingers that were ready to clutch and tear. "Hold," Hauk shrilled. "No step farther."

He could not see if the gaping mouth grinned. In another stride, the great shape came well-nigh upon him. He lifted his sword and brought it singing down. The edge struck truly, but slid aside. Geirolf's skin heaved, as if to push the blade away. In one more step, he laid grave-cold hands around Hauk's neck.

Before that grip could close, Hauk dropped his useless weapon, brought his wrists up between Geirolf's, and mightily snapped them apart. Nails left furrows, but he was free. He sprang back, into a wrestler's stance.

Geirolf moved in, reaching. Hauk hunched under those arms and himself grabbed waist and thigh. He threw his shoulder against a belly like rock. Any live man would have gone over, but the lich was too heavy.

Geirolf smote Hauk on the side. The blows drove him to his knees and thundered on his back. A foot lifted to crush him. He rolled off and found his own feet again. Geirolf lurched after him. The hastening moon linked their shadows. The wolf howled anew, but in fear. Watching men gripped spearshafts till their knuckles stood bloodless.

Hauk braced his legs and snatched for the first hold, around both of Geirolf's wrists. The drow strained to break loose and could not; but neither could Hauk bring him down. Sweat ran moon-bright over the son's cheeks and darkened his shirt. The reek of it was at least a living smell in his nostrils. Breath tore at his gullet. Suddenly Geirolf wrenched so hard that his right arm tore from between his foe's fingers. He brought that hand against Hauk's throat. Hauk let go and slammed himself backward before he was throttled.

Geirolf stalked after him. The drow did not move fast. Hauk sped behind and pounded on the broad back. He seized an arm of Geirolf's and twisted it around. But the dead cannot feel pain. Geirolf stood fast. His other hand groped about, got Hauk by the hair, and yanked. Live men can hurt. Hauk stumbled away. Blood ran from his scalp into his eyes and mouth, hot and salt.

Geirolf turned and followed. He would not tire. Hauk had no long while before strength ebbed. Almost, he fled. Then the moon broke through to shine full on his father. "You . . . shall not . . . go on . . . like that," Hauk mumbled while he snapped after air.

The drow reached him. They closed, grappled, swayed, stamped to and fro, in wind and flickery moonlight. Then Hauk hooked an ankle behind Geirolf's and pushed. With a huge thud, the drow crashed to earth. He dragged Hauk along.

Hauk's bones felt how terrible was the grip upon him. He let go his own hold. Instead, he arched his back and pushed himself away. His clothes ripped. But he burst free and reeled to his feet.

Geirolf turned over and began to crawl up. His back was once more to Hauk. The young man sprang. He got a knee hard in between the shoulderblades, while both his arms closed on the frosty head before him.

He hauled. With the last and greatest might that was in him, he hauled. Blackness went in tatters before his eyes.

There came a loud snapping sound. Geirolf ceased pawing behind him. He sprawled limp. His neck was broken, his jawbone wrenched from the skull. Hauk climbed slowly off him, shuddering. Geirolf stirred, rolled, half rose. He lifted a hand toward Hauk. It traced a line through the air and a line growing from beneath that. Then he slumped and lay still.

Hauk crumpled too.

"Follow me who dare!" Leif roared, and went forth across the field. One by one, as they saw nothing move ahead of them, the men came after. At last they stood hushed around Geirolf—who was only a harmless dead man now, though the moon shone bright in his eyes—and on Hauk, who had begun to stir.

"Bear him carefully down to the hall," Leif said. "Start a fire and tend it well. Most of you, take from the woodpile and come back here. I'll stand guard meanwhile . . . though I think there is no need."

And so they burned Geirolf there in the field. He walked no more.

In the morning, they brought Hauk back to Leif's garth. He moved as if in dreams. The others were too awestruck to speak much. Even when Alfhild ran to meet him, he could only say, "Hold clear of me. I may be under a doom."

"Did the drow lay a weird on you?" she asked, spear-stricken.

"I know not," he answered. "I think I fell into the dark before he was wholly dead."

"What?" Leif well-nigh shouted. "You did not see the sign he drew?"

"Why, no," Hauk said. "How did it go?"

"Thus. Even afar and by moonlight, I knew." Leif drew it.

"That is no ill-wishing!" Grim cried. "That's naught but the Hammer."

Life rushed back into Hauk. "Do you mean what I hope?"

"He blessed you," Grim said. "You freed him from what he had most dreaded and hated—his straw-death. The madness in him is gone, and he has wended hence to the world beyond."

Then Hauk was glad again. He led them all in heaping earth over the ashes of his father, and in setting things right on the farm. That winter, at the feast of Thor, he and Alfhild were wedded. Afterward he became well thought of by King Harald, and rose to great wealth. From him and Alfhild stem many men whose names are still remembered. Here ends the tale of Hauk the Ghost Slayer.

Manatee Gal Ain't You Coming Out Tonight

Here's another story by Avram Davidson, whose "The Golem"
appeared earlier in this anthology. Many a Grand Master pro-
duces weak or inferior work in the last few years of his life, but
in this, as in so much else, Davidson was far from typical–in fact,
toward the end of his long career, Davidson produced some of
his *best* work ever, in a series of stories–that started appearing in
the last years of the 1970s and continued through to the early
1990s (the last of them was published in 1993, just before his
death)–that detail the strange adventures of Jack Limekiller.

The Limekiller stories are set against the lushly evocative
background of "British Hidalgo," Davidson's vividly realized,
richly imagined version of one of those tiny, eccentric Central
American nations that exist in near-total isolation on the edge of
the busy twentieth-century world . . . a place somehow at once
flamboyant and languorous, where strange things can–and *do*–
happen . . .

. . . as the brilliant story that follows, one of the best of the
Limekiller tales, and one of the best fantasies of the 1970s, will
amply demonstrate!

The Cupid Club was the only waterhole on the Port Cockatoo waterfront.
To be sure, there were two or three liquor booths back in the part where
the tiny town ebbed away into the bush. But they were closed for siesta,
certainly. And they sold nothing but watered rum and warm soft drinks
and loose cigarettes. Also, they were away from the breezes off the Bay
which kept away the flies. In British Hidalgo gnats were flies, mosquitoes
were flies, sand-flies–worst of all–were flies–*flies* were also flies: and if anyone were inclined to question this nomenclature, there was the unques-
tionable fact that mosquito itself was merely Spanish for little fly.

It was not really cool in the Cupid Club (Alfonso Key, prop.,
LICENSED TO SELL WINE, SPIRITS, BEER, ALE, CYDER AND
PERRY). But it was certainly less hot than outside. Outside the sun

burned the Bay, turning it into molten sparkles. Limekiller's boat stood at mooring, by very slightly raising his head he could see her, and every so often he did raise it. There wasn't much aboard to tempt thieves, and there weren't many thieves in Port Cockatoo, anyway. On the other hand, what was aboard the *Sacarissa* he could not very well spare; and it only took one thief, after all. So every now and then he did raise his head and make sure that no small boat was out by his own. No skiff or dory.

Probably the only thief in town was taking his own siesta.

"Nutmeg P'int," said Alfonso Key. "You been to Nutmeg P'int?"

"Been there."

Every place needs another place to make light fun of. In King Town, the old colonial capital, it was Port Cockatoo. Limekiller wondered what it was they made fun of, down at Nutmeg Point.

"What brings it into your mind, Alfonso?" he asked, taking his eyes from the boat. All clear. Briefly he met his own face in the mirror. Wasn't much of a face, in his own opinion. Someone had once called him "Young Count Tolstoy." Wasn't much point in shaving, anyway.

Key shrugged. "Sometimes somebody goes down there, goes up the river, along the old bush trails, buys carn. About now, you know, mon, carn bring good price, up in King Town."

Limekiller knew that. He often did think about that. He could quote the prices Brad Welcome paid for corn: white corn, yellow corn, cracked and ground. "I know," he said. "In King Town they have a lot of money and only a little corn. Along Nutmeg River they have a lot of corn and only a little money. Someone who brings down money from the Town can buy corn along the Nutmeg. Too bad I didn't think of that before I left."

Key allowed himself a small sigh. He knew that it wasn't any lack of thought, and that Limekiller had had no money before he left, or, likely, he wouldn't have left. "May-be they trust you down along the Nutmeg. They trust old Bob Blaine. Year after year he go up the Nutmeg, he go up and down the bush trail, he buy carn on credit, bring it bock up to King *Town*."

Off in the shadow at the other end of the barroom someone began to sing, softly.

> *W'ol' Bob Blaine, he done gone.*
> *W'ol' Bob Blaine, he done gone.*
> *Ahl, ahl me money gone—*
> *Gone to Spahnish Hidalgo . . .*

In King Town, Old Bob Blaine had sold corn, season after season. Old Bob Blaine had bought salt, he had bought shotgun shells, canned milk, white flour, cotton cloth from the Turkish merchants. Fishhooks, sweet candy, rubber boots, kerosene, lamp *chim*ney. Old Bob Blaine had returned and paid for corn in kind—not, to be sure, immediately after selling the corn. Things did not move that swiftly even today, in British Hidalgo, and certainly had not Back When. Old Bob Blaine returned with the merchandise on his next buying trip. It was more convenient, he did not have to make so many trips up and down the mangrove coast. By and by it must almost have seemed that he was paying in advance, when he came, buying corn down along the Nutmeg River, the boundary between the Colony of British Hidalgo and the country which the Colony still called Spanish Hidalgo, though it had not been Spain's for a century and a half.

"Yes mon," Alfonso Key agreed. "Only, that one last time, he *not* come bock. They say he buy one marine engine yard, down in Republican waters."

"I heard," Limekiller said, "that he bought a garage down there."

The soft voice from the back of the bar said, "No, mon. Twas a coconut walk he bought. Yes, mon."

Jack wondered why people, foreign people, usually, sometimes complained that it was difficult to get information in British Hidalgo. In his experience, information was the easiest thing in the world, there—all the information you wanted. In fact, sometimes you could get more than you wanted. Sometimes, of course, it was contradictory. Sometimes it was outright wrong. But that, of course, was another matter.

"Anybody else ever take up the trade down there?" Even if the information, the answer, if there was an answer, even if it were negative, what difference would it make?

"No," said Key. "No-body. May-be you try, eh, Jock? May-be they trust you."

There was no reason why the small cultivators, slashing their small cornfields by main force out of the almighty bush and then burning the slash and then planting corn in the ashes, so to speak—maybe they would trust him, even though there was no reason *why* they should trust him. Still . . . Who knows . . . They might. They just might. Well . . . some of them just might. For a moment a brief hope rose in his mind.

"Naaa . . . I haven't even got any crocus sacks." There wasn't much point in any of it after all. Not if he'd have to tote the corn wrapped up in his shirt. The jute sacks were fifty cents apiece in local currency; they were as good as money, sometimes even better than money.

Key, who had been watching rather unsleepingly as these thoughts were passing through Jack's mind, slowly sank back in his chair. "Ah," he said, very softly. "You haven't got any crocus sack."

"Een de w'ol' days," the voice from the back said, "every good 'oman, she di know which bush yerb good fah wyes, fah kid-ney, which bush yerb good fah heart, which bush yerb good fah fever. But ahl of dem good w'ol' 'omen, new, dey dead, you see. Yes mon. Ahl poss ahway. No-body know bush medicine nowadays. Only *bush-doc-tor*. And dey very few, sah, very few."

"What you say, Captain Cudgel, you not bush *doc*-tor you w'own self? Nah true, Coptain?"

Slowly, almost reluctantly, the old man answered. "Well sah. Me know few teeng. Fah true. Me know few teeng. Not like in w'ol' days. In w'ol' days, me dive fah conch. Yes mon. Fetch up plan-ty conch. De sahlt wah-tah hort me eyes, take bush-yerb fah cure dem. But nomah. No, mon. Me no dive no mah. Ahl de time, me wyes hort, stay out of strahng sun now . . . Yes mon . . ."

Limekiller yawned, politely, behind his hand. To make conversation, he repeated something he had heard. "They say some of the old-time people used to get herbs down at Cape Manatee."

Alfonso Key flashed him a look. The old man said, a different note suddenly in his voice, different from the melancholy one of a moment before, "Mon-ah-*tee*. Mon-ah-*tee* is hahf-*mon,* you know, sah. Fah true. Yes sah, mon-ah-*tee* is hahf-*mon*. Which reason de lah w'only allow you to tehk one mon-ah-*tee* a year."

Covertly, Jack felt his beer. Sure enough, it was warm. Key said, "Yes, but who even bother nowadays? The leather is so tough you can't even sole a boot with it. And you dasn't bring the meat up to the Central Market in King *Town,* you *know*."

The last thing on Limekiller's mind was to apply for a license to shoot manatee, even if the limit were one a week. "How come?" he asked. "How come you're not?" King Town. King Town was the reason that he was down in Port Cockatoo. There was no money to be made here, now. But there was none to be lost here, either. His creditors were all in King Town, though if they wanted to, they could reach him even down here. But it would hardly be worth anyone's while to fee a lawyer to come down and feed him during the court session. Mainly, though, it was a matter of, Out of sight, somewhat out of mind. And, anyway—who knows? The Micawber Principle was weaker down here than up in the capital. But still and all: something might turn up.

"Because, they say it is because Manatee have teats like a woman."

"One time, you know, one time dere is a mahn who mehk mellow wit ah mon-ah-tee, yes, sah. And hahv pickney by mon-ah-tee." It did seem that the old man had begun to say something more, but someone else said, *"Ha-ha-ha!"* And the same someone else next said, in a sharp, all-but-demanding voice, "Shoe *shine?* Shoe *shine?*"

"I don't have those kind of shoes," Limekiller told the boy.

"Suede *brush?* Suede *brush?*"

Still no business being forthcoming, the bootblack withdrew, muttering.

Softly, the owner of the Cupid Club murmured, "That is one bod bob-boon."

Limekiller waited, then he said, "I'd like to hear more about that, Captain Cudgel . . ."

But the story of the man who "made mellow" with a manatee and fathered a child upon her would have to wait, it seemed, upon another occasion. Old Captain Cudgel had departed, via the back door. Jack decided to do the same, via the front.

The sun, having vexed the Atlantic coast most of the morning and afternoon, was now on its equal way towards the Pacific. The Bay of Hidalgo stretched away on all sides, out to the faint white line which marked the barrier reef, the great coral wall which had for so long safeguarded this small, almost forgotten nation for the British Crown and the Protestant Religion. To the south, faint and high and blue against the lighter blue of the sky, however faint, darker: Pico Guapo, in the Republic of Hidalgo. Faint, also, though recurrent, was Limekiller's thought that he might, just might, try his luck down there. His papers were in order. Port Cockatoo was a Port of Entry and of Exit. The wind was free.

But from day to day, from one hot day to another hot day, he kept putting the decision off.

He nodded politely to the District Commissioner and the District Medical Officer and was nodded to, politely, in return. A way down the front street strolled white-haired Mr. Stuart, who had come out here in The Year Thirty-Nine, to help the war effort, and had been here ever since: too far for nodding. Coming from the market shed where she had been buying the latest eggs and ground-victuals was good Miss Gwen; if she saw him she would insist on giving him his supper at her boardinghouse on credit: her suppers (her breakfasts and lunches as well) were just fine. But he had debts enough already. So, with a sigh, and a fond recollection of her fried fish, her country-style chicken, and her candied breadfruit, he sidled down the little lane, and he avoided Miss Gwen.

One side of the lane was the one-story white-painted wooden building with the sign DENDRY WASHBURN, LICENCED TO SELL DRUGS AND POISONS, the other side of the lane was the one-story white-painted wooden building where Captain Cumberbatch kept shop. The lane itself was paved with the crushed decomposed coral called pipeshank—and, indeed, the stuff did look like so much busted-up clay pipe stems. At the end of the lane was a small wharf and a flight of steps, at the bottom of the steps was his skiff.

He poled out to his boat, where he was greeted by his first mate, Skippy, an off-white cat with no tail. Skippy was very neat, and always used the ashes of the caboose: and if Jack didn't remember to sweep them *out* of the caboose as soon as they had cooled, and off to one side, why, that was his own carelessness, and no fault of Skippy's.

"All clear?" he asked the small tiger, as it rubbed against his leg. The small tiger growled something which might have been "Portuguese man o'war off the starboard bow at three bells," or "Musket-men to the futtock-shrouds," or perhaps only, "Where in the Hell have *you* been, all day, you creep?"

"Tell you what, Skip," as he tied the skiff, untied the *Sacarissa,* and, taking up the boat's pole, leaned against her in a yo-heave-ho manner; "let's us bugger off from this teeming tropical metropolis and go timely down the coast . . . say, to off Crocodile Creek, lovely name, proof there really is no Chamber of Commerce in these parts . . . then take the dawn tide and drop a line or two for some grunts or jacks or who knows what . . . sawfish, maybe . . . maybe . . . *some*thing to go with the rice and beans to-morrow . . . Corn what we catch but can't eat," he grunted, leaned, hastily released his weight and grabbed the pole up from the sucking bottom, dropped it on deck, and made swift shift to raise sail; *slap/slap/* . . . and then he took the tiller.

"And *thennn* . . . Oh, shite and onions, *I* don't know. Out to the Welsh-man's Cayes, maybe."

"Harebrained idea if ever I heard one," the first mate growled, trying to take Jack by the left greattoe. "Why don't you cut your hair and shave that beard and get a job and get drunk, like any decent, civilized son of a bitch would do?"

The white buildings and red roofs and tall palms wavering along the front street, the small boats riding and reflecting, the green mass of the bush behind: all contributed to give Port Cockatoo and environs the look and feel of a South Sea Island. Or, looked at from the viewpoint of another culture, the District Medical Officer (who was due for a retirement which he would not spend in his natal country), said that Port Cockatoo was *"gemütlich."* It was certainly a quiet and a gentle and undemanding sort of place.

But, somehow, it did not seem the totally ideal place for a man not yet thirty, with debts, with energy, with uncertainties, and with a thirty-foot boat.

A bright star slowly detached itself from the darkening land and swam up and up and then stopped and swayed a bit. This was the immense kerosene lamp which was nightly swung to the top of the great flagpole in the Police yard; it could be seen, the local Baymen assured J. Limekiller, as far out as Serpent Caye . . . Serpent Caye, the impression was, lay hard upon the very verge of the known and habitable earth, beyond which the River Ocean probably poured its stream into The Abyss.

Taking the hint, Limekiller took his own kerosene lamp, by no means immense, lit it, and set it firmly between two chocks of wood. Technically, there should have been two lamps and of different colors. But the local vessels seldom showed any lights at all. "He see me forst, he blow he conch-*shell;* me see *he* forst, me blow *my* conch-shell." And if neither saw the other. "Well, we suppose to meet each othah . . ." And if they didn't? Well, there was Divine Profidence—hardly any lives were lost from such misadventures: unless, of course, someone was drunk.

The dimlight lingered and lingered to the west, and then the stars started to come out. It was time, Limekiller thought, to stop for the night.

He was eating his rice and beans and looking at the chart when he heard a voice nearby saying, "Sheep a-high!"

Startled, but by no means alarmed, he called out, "Come aboard!"

What came aboard first was a basket, then a man. A man of no great singularity of appearance, save that he was lacking one eye. "Me name," said the man, "is John Samuel, barn in dis very Colony, me friend, and hence ah subject of de Queen, God bless hah." Mr. Samuel was evidently a White Creole, a member of a class never very large, and steadily dwindling away: sometimes by way of absorption into the non-White majority, sometimes by way of emigration, and sometimes just by way of Death the Leveler. "I tehks de libahty of bringing you some of de forst fruits of de sile," said John S.

"Say, mighty thoughtful of you, Mr. Samuel, care for some rice and beans?—My name's Jack Limekiller."

"—to weet, sour*sop,* bread*fruit,* oh-*ronge,* coco*nut*—what I care for, Mr. Limekiller, is some *rum. Rum* is what I has come to beg of you. De hond of mon, sah, has yet to perfect any medicine de superior of *rum.*"

Jack groped in the cubbyhold. "What about all those bush medicines down at Cape Manatee? he asked, grunting. There was supposed to be a small bottle, a *chaparita,* as they called it. Where—Oh. It must be . . . No. Then it must be . . .

Mr. Samuel rubbed the grey bristles on his strong jaw. "I does gront you, sah, de vertue of de country yerba. But you must steep de *yerba* een de *rum,* sah. Yes mon."

Jack's fingers finally found the bottle and his one glass and his one cup and poured. Mr. Samuel said nothing until he had downed his, and then gave a sigh of satisfaction. Jack, who had found a mawmee-apple in the basket of fruit, nodded as he peeled it. The flesh was tawny, and reminded him of wintergreen.

After a moment, he decided that he didn't want to finish his rum, and, with a questioning look, passed it over to his guest. It was pleasant there on the open deck, the breeze faint but sufficient, and comparatively few flies of any sort had cared to make the voyage from shore. The boat swayed gently, there was no surf to speak of, the waves of the Atlantic having spent themselves, miles out, upon the reef; and only a few loose items of gear knocked softly as the vessel rose and fell upon the soft bosom of the inner bay.

"Well sah," said Mr. Samuel, with a slight smack of his lips, "I weesh to acknowledge your generosity. I ahsked you to wahk weet me wan mile, and you wahk weet me twain." Something splashed in the water, and he looked out, sharply.

"Shark?"

"No, mon. Too far een-shore." His eyes gazed out where there was nothing to be seen.

"Porpoise, maybe. Turtle. Or a stingray . . ."

After a moment, Samuel said, "Suppose to be ah tortle." He turned back and gave Limekiller a long, steady look.

Moved by some sudden devil, Limekiller said, "I hope, Mr. Samuel, that you are not about to tell me about some Indian caves or ruins, full of gold, back in the bush, which you are willing to go shares on with me and all I have to do is put up the money—because, you see, Mr. Samuel, I haven't got any money." And added, "Besides, they tell me it's illegal and that all those things belong to the Queen."

Solemnly, Samuel said, "God save de Queen." Then his eyes somehow seemed to become wider, and his mouth as well, and a sound like hissing steam escaped him, and he sat on the coaming and shook with almost-silent laughter. Then he said, "I sees dot you hahs been ahproached ahlready. No sah. No such teeng. My proposition eenclude only two quality: Expedition. Discretion." And he proceded to explain that what he meant was that Jack should, at regular intervals, bring him supplies in small quantities and that he would advance the money for this and pay a small amount for the service. Delivery was to be made at night. And nothing was to be said about it, back at Port Cockatoo, or anywhere else.

Evidently Jack Limekiller wasn't the only one who had creditors.

"Anything else, Mr. Samuel?"

Samuel gave a deep sigh. "Ah, mon, I would like to sogjest dat you breeng me out ah woman . . . but best no. Best not . . . not yet . . . Oh, Mon, I om so lustful, ahlone out here, eef you tie ah rottlesnake down fah me I weel freeg eet!"

"Well, Mr. Samuel, the fact is, I will not tie a rattlesnake down for you, or up for you, for any purpose at all. However, I will keep my eyes open for a board with a knothole in it."

Samuel guffawed. Then he got up, his machete slap-flapping against his side, and with a few more words, clambered down into his dory—no plank-boat, in these waters, but a dugout—and began to paddle. Bayman, bushman, the machete was almost an article of clothing, though there was nothing to chop out here on the gentle waters of the bay. There was a splash, out there in the darkness, and a cry—Samuel's voice—

"Are you all right out there?" Limekiller called.

"Yes mon . . ." faintly. "Fine . . . bloddy Oxville tortle . . ."

Limekiller fell easily asleep. Presently he dreamed of seeing a large Hawksbill turtle languidly pursuing John Samuel, who languidly evaded the pursuit. Later, he awoke, knowing that he knew what had awakened him, but for the moment unable to name it. The awakeners soon enough identified themselves. Manatees. Sea cows. The most harmless creatures God ever made. He drowsed off again, but again and again he lightly awoke and always he could hear them sighing and sounding.

Early up, he dropped his line, made a small fire in the sheet-iron caboose set in its box of sand, and put on the pot of rice and beans to cook in co-conut oil. The head and tail of the first fish went into a second pot, the top of the double boiler, to make fish-tea, as the chowder was called; when they were done, he gave them to Skippy. He fried the fillets with sliced breadfruit, which had as near no taste of its own as made no matter, but was a great extender of tastes. The second fish he cut and corned—that is, he spread coarse salt on it: there was nothing else to do to preserve it in this hot climate, without ice, and where the art of smoking fish was not known. And more than those two he did not bother to take, he had no license for commercial fishing, could not sell a catch in the market, and the "sport" of taking fish he could neither eat nor sell, and would have to throw back, was a pleasure which eluded his understanding.

It promised to be a hot day and it kept its promise, and he told himself, as he often did on hot, hot days, that it beat shoveling snow in Toronto.

He observed a vacant mooring towards the south of town, recollected that it always had been vacant, and so, for no better reason than that, he tied up to it. Half of the remainder of his catch came ashore with him. This was too far south for any plank houses or tin roofs. Port Cockatoo at both ends straggled out into "trash houses," as they were called—sides of wild cane allowing the cooling breezes to pass, and largely keeping out the brute sun; roofs of thatch, usually of the bay or cohune palm. The people were poorer here than elsewhere in this town where no one at all by North American standards was rich, but "trash" had no reference to that: *Loppings, twigs, and leaves of trees, bruised sugar cane, corn husks, etc.,* his dictionary explained.

An old, old woman in the ankle-length skirts and the kerchief of her generation stood in the doorway of her little house and looked, first at him, then at his catch. And kept on looking at it. All the coastal people of Hidalgo were fascinated by fish: rice and beans was the staple dish, but fish was the roast beef, the steak, the chicken, of this small, small coun-try which had never been rich and was now—with the growing depletion of its mahogany and rosewood—even poorer than ever. Moved, not so much by conscious consideration of this as by a sudden impulse, he held up his hand and what it was holding. "Care for some corned fish, Grandy?"

Automatically, she reached out her tiny, dark hand, all twisted and withered, and took it. Her lips moved. She looked from the fish to him and from him to the fish; asked, doubtfully, "How much I have for you?"— meaning, how much did she owe him.

"Your prayers," he said, equally on impulse.

Her head flew up and she looked at him full in the face, then. "T'ank you, Buckra," she said. "And I weel do so. I weel pray for you." And she went back into her trash house.

Up the dusty, palm-lined path a ways, just before it branched into the cemetery road and the front street, he encountered Mr. Stuart—white-haired, learned, benevolent, deaf, and vague—and wearing what was surely the very last sola topee in everyday use in the Western Hemisphere (and perhaps, what with one thing and another, in the Eastern, as well).

"Did you hear the baboons last night?" asked Mr. Stuart.

Jack knew that "baboons," hereabouts, were howler monkeys. Even their daytime noises, a hollow and repetitive *Rrrr-Rrrr-Rrrr,* sounded uncanny enough; as for their nighttime wailings—

"I was anchored offshore, down the coast, last night," he explained. "All I heard were the manatees."

Mr. Stuart looked at him with faint, grey eyes, smoothed his long moustache. "Ah, *those* poor chaps," he said. "They've slipped back down the scale . . . much *too* far down, I expect, for any quick return. Tried to help them, you know. Tried the Herodotus method. Carthaginians. Mute trade, you know. Set out some bright red cloth, put trade-goods on, went away. Returned. Things were knocked about, as though animals had been at them. *Some* of the items were gone, though. But nothing left in return. Too bad, oh yes, too bad . . ." His voice died away into a low moan, and he shook his ancient head. In another moment, before Jack could say anything, or even think of anything to say, Mr. Stuart had flashed him a smile of pure friendliness, and was gone. A bunch of flowers was in one hand, and the path he took was the cemetery road. He had gone to visit one of "the great company of the dead, which increase around us as we grow older."

From this mute offering, laid also upon the earth, nothing would be expected in return. There are those whom we do not see and whom we do not desire that they should ever show themselves at all.

The shop of Captain Cumberbatch was open. The rules as to what stores or offices were open and closed at which times were exactly the opposite of the laws of the Medes and the Persians. The time to go shopping was when one saw the shop open. Any shop. They opened, closed, opened, closed . . . And as to why stores with a staff of only one closed so often, why, they closed not only to allow the proprietor to siesta, they also closed to allow him to eat. It was no part of the national culture for Ma to send Pa's "tea" for Pa to eat behind the counter: Pa came home. Period. And as for establishments with a staff of more than one, why could the staff not have taken turns? Answer: De baas, of whatsoever race, creed, or color, might trust an employee with his life, but he would never trust his employee with his cash or stock, never, never, never.

Captain Cumberbatch had for many years puffed up and down the coast in his tiny packet-and-passenger boat, bringing cargo merchandise for the shopkeepers of Port Caroline, Port Cockatoo, and—very, very semi-occasionally—anywhere else as chartered. But some years ago he had swallowed the anchor and set up business as shopkeeper in Port Cockatoo. And one day an epiphany of sorts had occurred: Captain Cumberbatch had asked himself why he should bring cargo for others to sell and/or why he should pay others to bring cargo for he himself to sell. Why should he not bring his own cargo and sell it himself?

The scheme was brilliant as it was unprecedented. And indeed it had but one discernable flaw: Whilst Captain Cumberbatch was at sea, he could not tend shop to sell what he had shipped. And while he was tending his shop he could not put to sea to replenish stock. And, tossing ceaselessly from the one horn of this dilemma to the other, he often thought resentfully of the difficulties of competing with such peoples as the Chinas, Turks, and 'Paniards, who—most unfairly—were able to trust the members of their own families to mind the store.

Be all this as it may, the shop of Captain Cumberbatch was at this very moment open, and the captain himself was leaning upon his counter and smoking a pipe.

"Marneen, Jock. Hoew de day?"

"Bless God."

"Forever and ever, ehhh-men."

A certain amount of tinned corned beef and corned-beef hash, of white sugar (it was nearer grey), of bread (it was dead white, as unsuitable an item of diet as could be designed for the country and the country would have rioted at the thought of being asked to eat dark), salt, lamp-oil, tea, tinned milk, cheese, were packed and passed across the worn counter; a certain amount of national currency made the same trip in reverse.

As for the prime purchaser of the items, Limekiller said nothing. That was part of the Discretion.

Outside again, he scanned the somnolent street for any signs that anyone might have—somehow—arrived in town who might want to charter a boat for . . . well, for anything. Short of smuggling, there was scarcely a purpose for which he would have not chartered the *Sacarissa*. It was not that he had an invincible repugnance to the midnight trade, there might well be places and times where he would have considered it. But Government, in British Hidalgo (here, as elsewhere in what was left of the Empire, the definite article was conspicuously absent: "Government will do this," they said—or, often as not, "Government will not do this") had not vexed him in any way and he saw no reason to vex it. And, furthermore, he had heard many reports of the accommodations at the Queen's Hotel, as the King Town "gaol" was called: and they were uniformly unfavorable.

But the front street was looking the same as ever, and, exemplifying, as ever, the observation of The Preacher, that there was no new thing under the sun. So, with only the smallest of sighs, he had started for the Cupid Club, when the clop . . . clop of hooves made him look up. Coming along the street was the horse-drawn equivalent of a pickup truck. The back was open, and contained a few well-filled crocus sacks and some sawn timber; the front was roofed, but open at the sides; and for passengers it had a white-haired woman and a middle-aged man. It drew to a stop.

"Well, young man. And who are *you?*" the woman asked. Some elements of the soft local accent overlaid her speech, but underneath was something else, something equally soft, but different. Her "Man" was not *mon,* it was *mayun,* and her "you" was more like *yiewu.*

He took off his hat. "Jack Limekiller is my name, ma'am."

"Put it right back on, Mr. Limekiller. I do appreciate the gesture, but it has already been gestured, now. Draft dodger, are you?"

That was a common guess. Any North American who didn't fit into an old and familiar category—tourist, sport fisherman, sport huntsman, missionary, businessman—was assumed to be either a draft dodger or a trafficker in "weed" . . . or maybe both. "No, ma'am. I've served my time and, anyway, I'm a Canadian, and we don't have a draft."

"Well," she said, "doesn't matter even if you are, I don't *cay*-uh. Now, sir, I am Amelia Lebedee. And this is my nephew, Tom McFee." Tom smiled a faint and abstract smile, shook hands. He was sun-dark and had a slim moustache and he wore a felt hat which had perhaps been crisper than it was now. Jack had not seen many men like Tom McFee in Canada, but he had seen many men like Tom McFee in the United States. Tom McFee sold crab in Baltimore. Tom McFee managed the smaller cotton gin in a two-gin town in Alabama. Tom McFee was foreman at the shrimp-packing plant in one of the Florida Parishes in Louisiana. And Tom McFee was railroad freight agent in whatever dusty town in Texas it was that advertised itself as "Blue Vetch Seed Capital of the World."

"We are carrying you off to Shiloh for lunch," said Amelia, and a handsome old woman she was, and sat up straight at the reins. "So you just climb up in. Tom will carry you back later, when he goes for some more of this wood. Land! You'd think it was *teak,* they cut it so slow. Instead of pine."

Limekiller had no notion who or what or where Shiloh was, although it clearly could not be very far, and he could think of no reason why he should not go there. So in he climbed.

"Yes," said Amelia Lebedee, "the war wiped us out completely. So we came down here and we planted sugar, yes, we planted sugar and we made sugar for, oh, most eighty years. But we didn't move with the times, and so that's all over with now. We plant most anything *but* sugar nowadays. And when we see a new and a civilized face, we plant them down at the table." By this time the wagon was out of town. The bush to either side of the road looked like just bushtype bush to Jack. But to Mrs. Lebedee each acre had an identity of its own. "That was the Cullens' place," she'd say. And, "The Robinsons lived there. Beautiful horses, they had. Nobody has horses anymore, just us. Yonder used to be the Simmonses. Part of the house is still standing, but, land!—you can't see it from the road anymore. They've gone back. Most everybody has gone back, who hasn't died off . . ." For a while she said nothing. The road gradually grew narrower, and all three of them began thoughtfully to slap at "flies."

A bridge now appeared and they rattled across it, a dark-green stream rushing below. There was a glimpse of an old grey house in the archaic, universal-tropical style, and then the bush closed in again. "And *they*-uh," Miss Amelia gestured, backwards, "is Texas. Oh, what a fine place that was, in its day! Nobody lives there, now. Old Captain Rutherford, the original settler, he was with Hood. *Gen*eral Hood, I mean."

It all flashed on Jack at once, and it all came clear, and he wondered that it had not been clear from the beginning. They were now passing through the site of the old Confederate colony. There had been such in Venezuela, in Colombia, even in Brazil; for all he knew, there might still be. But this one here in Hidalgo, it had not been wiped out in a year or two, like the Mormon colonies in Mexico—there had been no Revolution here, no gringo-hating Villistas—it had just ebbed away. Tiny little old B.H., "a country," as someone (who?) had said, "which you can put your arms around," had put its arms around the Rebel refugees . . . its thin, green arms . . . and it had let them clear the bush and build their houses . . . and it had waited . . . and waited . . . and, as, one by one, the Southern American families had "died out" or "gone back," why, as easy as easy, the bush had slipped back. And, for the present, it seemed like it was going to stay back. It had, after all, closed in after the Old Empire Mayans had so mysteriously left, and that was a thousand years ago. What was a hundred years, to the bush?

The house at Shiloh was small and neat and trim and freshly painted, and one end of the veranda was undergoing repairs. There had been no nonsense, down here, of reproducing any of the ten thousand imitations of Mount Vernon. A neatly-mowed lawn surrounded the house; in a moment, as the wagon made its last circuit, Jack saw that the lawnmowers were a small herd of cattle. A line of cedars accompanied the road, and Miss Amelia pointed to a gap in the line. "That tree that was there," she said, calmly, "was the one that fell on my husband and on John Samuel. It had been obviously weakened in the hurricane, you know, and they went over to see how badly—that was a mistake. John Samuel lost his left eye and my husband lost his life."

Discretion . . . Would it be indiscreet to ask—? He asked.

"How long ago was this, Miss Amelia?" All respectable women down here were "Miss," followed by the first name, regardless of marital state.

"It was ten years ago, come September," she said. "Let's go in out of the sun, now, and Tom will take care of the horse."

In out of the sun was cool and neat and, though shady, the living room-dining room was as bright as fresh paint and flowered wallpaper—the only wallpaper he had seen in the colony—could make it. There were flowers in vases, too, fresh flowers, not the widely-popular plastic ones. Somehow the Bayfolk did not make much of flowers.

For lunch there was heart-of-palm, something not often had, for a palm had to die to provide it, and palms were not idly cut down; there was the vegetable pear, or chayote, here called cho-cho; venison chops, tomato with okra; there was cashew wine, made from the fruit of which the Northern Lands know only the seed, which they ignorantly call "nut." And, even, there was coffee, not powdered ick, not grown-in-Brazil-shipped-to-the-United-States-roasted-ground-canned-shipped-to-Hidalgo-coffee, but actual local coffee. Here, where coffee grew with no more care than weeds, hardly anyone except the Indians bothered to grow it, and what *they* grew, *they* used.

"Yes," Miss Amelia said, "it can be a very good life here. It is necessary to work, of course, but the work is well-rewarded, oh, not in terms of large sums of money, but in so many other ways. But it's coming to an end. There is just no way that working this good land can bring you all the riches you see in the moving pictures. And that is what they all want, and dream of, all the young people. And there is just no way they are going to get it."

Tom McFee made one of his rare comments. *"I* don't dream of any white Christmas," he said. "I am staying here, where it is always green. I told Malcolm Stuart that."

Limekiller said, "I was just talking to him this morning, myself. But I couldn't understand what he was talking about . . . something about trying to trade with the manatees . . ."

The Shiloh people, clearly, had no trouble understanding what Stuart had been talking about; they did not even think it was particularly bizarre. "Ah, those poor folks down at Mantee," said Amelia Lebedee; "—now, mind you, I mean *Mantee,* Cape Mantee, I am *not* referring to the people up on Man*a*tee River and the Lagoons, who are just as civilized as you and I: I mean *Cape* Mantee, which is its correct name, you know—"

"Where the medicine herbs grew?"

"Why, yes, Mr. Limekiller. Where they grew. As I suppose they still do. No one really knows, of course, *what* still grows down at Cape Mantee, though Nature, I suppose, would not change her ways. It was the hurricanes, you see. The War Year hurricanes. Until then, you know, Government had kept a road open, and once a month a police constable would ride down and, well, at least, take a look around. Not that any of the people there would ever bring any of their troubles to the police. They were . . . well, how should I put it? Tom, how would *you* put it?"

Tom thought a long moment. "Simple. They were always simple."

What he meant by "simple," it developed, was simpleminded. His aunt did not entirely agree with that. They gave that impression, the Mantee people, she said, but that was only because their ways were so different. "There is a story," she said, slowly, and, it seemed to Jack Limekiller, rather reluctantly, "that a British man-of-war took a Spanish slave ship. I don't know when this would have been, it was well before we came down and settled here. Well before The War. Our own War, I mean. It was a small Spanish slaver and there weren't many captives in her. As I understand it, between the time that Britain abolished slavery and the dreadful Atlantic slave trade finally disappeared, if slavers were taken anywhere near Africa, the British would bring the captives either to Saint Helena or Sierra Leone, and liberate them there. But this one was taken fairly near the American coast. I suppose she was heading for Cuba. So the British ship brought them *here.* To British Hidalgo. And the people were released down at Cape Mantee, and told they could settle there and no one would 'vex' them, as they say here."

Where the slaves had come from, originally, she did not know, but she thought the tradition was that they had come from somewhere well back in the African interior. Over the course of the many subsequent years, some had trickled into the more settled parts of the old colony. "But some of them just stayed down there," she said. "Keeping up their own ways."

"Too much intermarrying," Tom offered.

"So the Bayfolk say. The Bayfolk were always, *I* think, rather afraid of them. None of them would ever go there alone. And, after the hurricanes, when the road went out, and the police just couldn't get there, none of the Bayfolk would go there at *all.* By sea, I mean. You must remember, Mr. Limekiller, that in the 1940s this little colony was very much as it was in the 1840s. There were no airplanes. There wasn't one single highway. When I say there used to be a road to Mantee, you mustn't think it was a road such as we've got between Port Cockatoo and Shiloh."

Limekiller, thinking of the dirt road between Port Cockatoo and Shiloh, tried to think what the one between Port Cockatoo and the region behind Cape Mantee must have been like. Evidently a trail, nothing more, down which an occasional man on a mule might make his way, boiling the potato-like fruit of the breadnut tree for his food and feeding his mule the leaves: a trail that had to be "chopped," had to be "cleaned" by machete-work, at least twice a year, to keep the all-consuming bush from closing over it the way the flesh closes over a cut. An occasional trader, an occasional buyer or gatherer of chicle or herbs or hides, an occasional missioner or medical officer, at infrequent intervals would pass along this corridor in the eternal jungle.

And then came a hurricane, smashing flat everything in its path. And the trail vanished. And the trail was never recut. British Hidalgo had probably never been high on any list of colonial priorities at the best of times. During the War of 1939–1945, they may have forgotten all about it in London. Many of Hidalgo's able-bodied men were off on distant fronts. An equal number had gone off to cut the remaining forests of the Isle of Britain, to supply anyway a fraction of the wood which was then impossible to import. Nothing could be spared for Mantee and its people; in King Town, Mantee was deemed as distant as King Town was in London. The p.c. never went there again. No missioner ever returned. Neither had a medical officer or nurse. Nor any trader. No one. Except for Malcolm Stuart . . .

"He did try. Of course, he had his own concerns. During the War he had his war work. Afterwards, he took up a block of land a few miles back from here, and he had his hands full with that. And then, after, oh, I don't remember how many years of stories, stories—there is no television here, you know, and few people have time for books—stories about the Mantee people, well, he decided he had to go have a look, see for himself, you know."

Were the Mantee people really eating raw meat and raw fish? He would bring them matches. Had they actually reverted to the use of stone for tools? He would bring them machetes, axes, knives. And . . . as for the rest of it . . . the rest of the rather awful and certainly very odd stories . . . he would see for himself.

But he had seen nothing. There had been nothing to see. That is, nothing which he could be sure he had seen. Perhaps he had thought that he had seen some few things which he had not cared to mention to Jack, but had spoken of to the Shiloh people.

They, however, were not about to speak of it to Jack.

"Adventure," said Amelia Lebedee, dismissing the matter of Mantee with a sigh. "Nobody wants the adventure of cutting bush to plant yams. They want the adventure of nightclubs and large automobiles. They see it in the moving pictures. And you, Mr. Limekiller, what is it that *you*

want?—coming, having come, from the land of nightclubs and large automobiles . . ."

The truth was simple. "I wanted the adventure of sailing a boat with
white sails through tropic seas," he said. "I saw it in the moving pictures.
I never had a nightclub but I had a large automobile, and I sold it and
came down here and bought the boat. And, well, here I am."

They had talked right through the siesta time. Tom McFee was ready,
now, to return for the few more planks which the sawmill might—or might
not—have managed to produce since the morning. It was time to stand
up now and to make thanks and say good-bye. "Yes," said Amelia Lebedee,
pensively "Here we are. Here we all are. We are all here. And some of us
are more content being here than others."

Half past three at the Cupid Club. On Limekiller's table, the usual single bottle of beer. Also, the three chaparitas of rum which he had bought—
but they were in a paper bag, lest the sight of them, plus the fact that he
could invite no one to drink of them, give rise to talk that he was "mean."
Behind the bar, Alfonso Key. In the dark, dark back, slowly sipping a
lemonade (all soft drinks were "lemonade"—coke was lemonade, straw-
berry pop was lemonade, ginger stout was lemonade . . . sometimes,
though not often, for reasons inexplicable, there was also lemon-flavored
lemonade)—in the dark rear part of the room, resting his perpetually sore
eyes, was old Captain Cudgel.

"Well, how you spend the night, Jock?" Alfonso ready for a tale of
amour, ready with a quip, a joke.

"Oh, just quietly. Except for the manatees." Limekiller, saying this, had
a sudden feeling that he had said all this before, been all this before, was
caught on the moebius strip which life in picturesque Port Cockatoo had
already become, caught, caught, never would be released. *Adventure!* Hah!

At this point, however, a slightly different note, a slightly different comment from the old, old man.

"Een Eedalgo," he said, dolefully, "de monatee hahv no leg, mon. Bec-
ahs Eedalgo ees a smahl coun-*tree,* ahn every-teeng smahl. Every-teeng
weak. Now, een Ahfrica, mon, de monatee *does* hahv leg."

Key said, incredulous, but still respectful, "What you tell we, Captain
Cudgel? *What?*" His last word, pronounced in the local manner of using
it as a particular indication of skepticism, of criticism, of denial, seemed
to have at least three *T*s at the end of it; he repeated "Wh*attt?*"

"Yes, mon. Yes sah. Een Ahfrica, de monatee hahv *leg,* mon. Eet be ah
poerful beast, een Ahfrica, come up on de *lond,* mon."

"I tell you. *Me* di hear eet befoah. Een Ahfrica," he repeated, doggedly,
"de monatee hahv leg, de monatee be ah poerful beast, come up on de
lond, mon, no lahf, mon—"

"Me no di lahf, sah—"

"–de w'ol' people, dey tell me so, fah true."

Alfonso Key gave his head a single shake, gave a single click of his tongue, gave Jack a single look.

Far down the street, the bell of the Church of Saint Benedict the Moor sounded. Whatever time it was marking had nothing to do with Greenwich Meridian Time or any variation thereof.

The weak, feeble old voice resumed the thread of conversation. "Me grahndy di tell me dot she grahndy di tell *she*. Motta hav foct, eet me grahndy di give me me name, b'y. Cudgel. Ahfrica name. Fah true. Fah True."

A slight sound of surprise broke Limekiller's silence. He said, "Excuse me, Captain. Could it have been 'Cudjoe' . . . maybe?"

For a while he thought that the question had either not been heard or had, perhaps, been resented. Then the old man said, "Eet could be so. Sah, eet might be so. Lahng, lahng time ah-go . . . Me Christian name, Pe-tah. Me w'ol'grahndy she say. 'Pickney: you hahv ah Christian name, Pe-tah. But me give you Ahfrica name, too. Cahdjo. No fah-get, pickney?' Time poss, time poss, de people dey ahl cahl me 'Cudgel,' you see, sah. So me fah-get . . . Sah, hoew you know dees teeng, sah?"

Limekiller said that he thought he had read it in a book. The old captain repeated the word, lengthening it in his local speech. "Ah boook, sah. To t'eenk ahv dot. Een ah boook. Me w'own name een ah boook." By and by he departed as silently as always.

In the dusk a white cloth waved behind the thin line of white beach. He took off his shirt and waved back. Then he transferred the groceries into the skiff and, as soon as it was dark and he had lit and securely fixed his lamp, set about rowing ashore. By and by a voice called out, "Mon, where de Hell you gweyn? You keep on to de right, you gweyn wine up een *Sponeesh* Hidalgo: Mah to de lef, mon: mah to de *lef!*" And with such assistances, soon enough the skiff softly scraped the beach.

Mr. John Samuel's greeting was, "You bring de rum?" The rum put in his hand, he took up one of the sacks, gestured Limekiller towards the other. "Les go timely, noew," he said. For a moment, in what was left of the dimmest dimlight, Jack thought the man was going to walk straight into an enormous tree: instead, he walked across the enormous roots and behind the tree. Limekiller followed the faint white patch of shirt bobbing in front of him. Sometimes the ground was firm, sometimes it went squilchy, sometimes it was simply running water–shallow, fortunately– sometimes it felt like gravel. The bush noises were still fairly soft. A rustle. He hoped it was only a wish-willy lizard, or a bamboo-chicken–an iguana–and not a yellow-jaw, that snake of which it was said . . . but this was no time to remember scare stories about snakes.

Without warning–although what sort of warning there could have been was a stupid question, anyway–there they were. Gertrude Stein, returning to her old hometown after an absence of almost forty years, and finding the old home itself demolished, had observed (with a lot more objectivity than she was usually credited with) that there was no *there,* there. The *there,* here, was simply a clearing, with a very small fire, and a *ramada:* four poles holding up a low thatched roof. John Samuel let his sack drop. "Ahnd noew," he said, portentously, "let us broach de rum."

After the chaparita had been not only broached but drained, for the second time that day Limekiller dined ashore. The cooking was done on a raised fire-hearth of clay and sticks, and what was cooked was a breadfruit, simply strewn, when done, with sugar; and a gibnut. To say that the gibnut, or paca, is a rodent, is perhaps—though accurate—unfair: it is larger than a rabbit, and it eats well. After that Samuel made black tea and laced it with more rum. After that he gave a vast belch and a vast sigh. "Can you play de bon*joe?*" he next asked.

"Well . . . I have been known to try . . ."

The lamp flared and smoked. Samuel adjusted it . . . somewhat. . . . He got up and took a bulky object down from a peg on one of the roof-poles. It was a sheet of thick plastic, laced with rawhide thongs, which he laboriously unknotted. Inside that was a deerskin. And inside *that,* an ordinary banjo case, which contained an ordinary, if rather old and worn, banjo.

"Mehk I hear ah sahng . . . ah sahng ahv *you* country."

What song should he make him hear? No particularly Canadian song brought itself to mind. Ah well, he would dip down below the border just a bit . . . His fingers strummed idly on the strings. The words grew, the tune grew, he lifted up what some (if not very many) had considered a not-bad-baritone, and began to sing and play.

> *Manatee gal, ain't you coming out tonight,*
> *Coming out tonight, coming out tonight?*
> *Oh, Manatee gal, ain't you coming out tonight,*
> *To dance by the light of the—*

An enormous hand suddenly covered his own and pressed it down. The tune subsided into a jumble of chords, and an echo, and a silence.

"Mon, mon, you not do me right. I no di say, 'Mehk I hear a sahng ahv *you* country?'" Samuel, on his knees, breathed heavily. His breath was heavy with rum and his voice was heavy with reproof . . . and with a something else for which Limekiller had no immediate name. But, friendly it was not.

Puzzled more than apologetic, Jack said, "Well, it *is* a North American song, anyway. It was an old Erie Canal song. It—Oh. I'll be damned. Only it's supposed to go, *'Buffalo gal, ain't you coming out tonight,'* And I dunno what made me change it, what difference does it make?"

"What different? What different it mehk? Ah, Christ me King! You lee' buckra b'y, you not know w'ehnnah-teeng?"

It was all too much for Limekiller. The last thing he wanted was anything resembling an argument, here in the deep, dark bush, with an all-but-stranger. Samuel having lifted his heavy hand from the instrument, Limekiller, moved by a sudden spirit, began.

> *Amazing grace, how sweet the sound,*
> *To save a wretch like me.*

With a rough catch of his breath, Samuel muttered, "Yes. Yes. Dot ees good. Go on, b'y. No stop."

> *I once was halt, but now can walk:*
> *Was blind, but now I see . . .*

He sang the beautiful old hymn to the end: and, by that time, if not overpowered by Grace, John Samuel—having evidently broached the second and the third chaparita—was certainly overpowered: and it did not look as though the dinner guest was going to get any kind of guided tour back to the shore and the skiff. He sighed and he looked around him. A bed rack had roughly been fixed up, and its lashings were covered with a few deer hides and an old Indian blanket. Samuel not responding to any shakings or urgings, Limekiller, with a shrug and a "Well what the hell," covered him with the blanket as he lay upon the ground. Then, having rolled up the sacks the supplies had come in and propped them under his head, Limekiller disposed himself for slumber on the hides. Some lines were running through his head and he paused a moment to consider what they were. What they were, they were, *From ghoulies and ghosties, long leggedy feasties, and bugges that go* boomp *in the night, Good Lord, deliver us.* With an almost absolute certainty that this was not the Authorized Version or Text, he heard himself give a grottle and a snore and knew he was fallen asleep.

He awoke to slap heartily at some flies, and the sound perhaps awoke the host, who was heard to mutter and mumble. Limekiller leaned over. "What did you say?"

The lines said, Limekiller learned that he had heard them before.

"Eef you tie ah rottlesnake doewn fah me, I weel freeg eet."

"I yield," said Limekiller, "to any man so much hornier than myself. Produce the snake, sir, and I will consider the rest of the matter."

The red eye of the expiring fire winked at him. It was still winking at him when he awoke from a horrid nightmare of screams and thrashings-about, in the course of which he had evidently fallen or had thrown himself from the bed rack to the far side. Furthermore, he must have knocked against one of the roof-poles in doing so, because a good deal of the thatch had landed on top of him. He threw it off, and, getting up, began to apologize.

"Sorry if I woke you, Mr. Samuel. I don't know what—" There was no answer, and looking around in the faint light of the fire, he saw no one.

"Mr. Samuel? Mr. *Samuel?* John? oh, hey, *Johhn!?* . . ."

No answer. If the man had merely gone out to "ease himself," as the Bayfolk delicately put it, he would have surely been near enough to answer. No one in the colony engaged in strolling in the bush at night for fun. "Son of a bitch," he muttered. He felt for and found his matches, struck one, found the lamp, lit it, looked around.

There was still no sign of John Samuel, but what there were signs of was some sort of horrid violence. Hastily he ran his hands over himself, but, despite his fall, despite part of the roof having fallen on him, he found no trace of blood.

All the blood which lay around, then, must have been—could only have been—John Samuel's blood.

All the screaming and the sounds of something—or some things—heavily thrashing around, they had not been in any dream. They had been the sounds of truth.

And as for what else he saw, as he walked, delicate as Agag, around the perimeter of the clearing, he preferred not to speculate.

There was a shotgun and there were shells. He put the shells into the chambers and he stood up, weapon in his hand, all the rest of the night.

"Now, if it took you perhaps less than an hour to reach the shore, and if you left immediately, how is it that you were so long in arriving at Port?" The District Commissioner asked. He asked politely, but he did ask. He asked a great many questions, for, in addition to his other duties, he was the Examining Magistrate.

"Didn't you observe the wind, D. C.? Ask anyone who was out on the water yesterday. I spent most of the day tacking—"

Corporal Huggin said, softly, from the wheel, "That would be correct, Mr. Blossom."

They were in the police boat, the *George* . . . once, Jack had said to P.C. Ed Huggin, "For George VI, I suppose?" and Ed, toiling over the balky and antique engine, his clear tan skin smudged with grease, had scowled, and said, "More for bloody George III, you ask *me* . . ." At earliest daylight, yesterday, Limekiller, red-eyed and twitching, had briefly cast around in the bush near the camp, decided that, ignorant of bush lore as he was, having not even a compass, let alone a pair of boots or a snakebite kit, it would have been insane to attempt any explorations. He found his way along the path, found his skiff tied up, and had rowed to his boat.

Unfavorable winds had destroyed his hope of getting back to Port Cockatoo in minimum time: it had been night when he arrived.

The police had listened to his story, had summoned Mr. Florian Blossom, the District Commissioner; all had agreed that "No purpose would be served by attempting anything until next morning." They had taken his story down, word by word, and by hand–if there was an official stenographer anywhere in the country, Limekiller had yet to hear of it–and by longhand, too; and in their own accustomed style and method, too, so that he was officially recorded as having said things such as: *Awakened by loud sounds of distress, I arose and hailed the man known to me as John Samuel. Upon receiving no response,* etcetera.

After Jack had signed the statement, and stood up, thinking to return to his boat, the District Commissioner said, "I believe that they can accommodate you with a bed in the Unmarried Police Constables' Quarters, Mr. Limekiller. Just for the night."

He looked at the official. A slight shiver ran up and down him. "Do you mean that I am a prisoner?"

"Certainly not, Mr. Limekiller. No such thing."

"You know, if I had wanted to, I could have been in Republican waters by now."

Mr. Blossom's politeness never flagged. "We realize it and we take it into consideration, Mr. Limekiller. But if we are all of us here together it will make an early start in the morning more efficacious."

Anyway, Jack was able to shower, and Ed Huggins loaned him clean clothes. Of course they had not gotten an early start in the morning. Only fishermen and sandboatmen got early starts. Her Majesty's Government moved at its accustomed pace. In the police launch, besides Limekiller, was P.C. Huggin, D.C. Blossom, a very small and very black and very wiry man called Harlow the Hunter, Police Sergeant Ruiz, and whitehaired Dr. Rafael, the District Medical Officer.

"I wouldn't have been able to come at all, you know," he said to Limekiller, "except my assistant has returned from his holidays a day earlier. Oh, there is so much to see in this colony! Fascinating, fascinating!"

D.C. Blossom smiled. "Doctor Rafael is a famous antiquarian, you know, Mr. Limekiller. It was he who discovered the grave*stone* of my three or four times great-grand-sir and-grandy."

Sounds of surprise and interest–polite on Limekiller's part, gravestones perhaps not being what he would have most wished to think of–genuine on the part of everyone else, ancestral stones not being numerous in British Hidalgo.

"Yes, Yes," Dr. Rafael agreed. "Two years ago I was on *my* holidays, and I went out to St. Saviour's Caye . . . well, to what is left of St. Saviour's Caye after the last few hurricanes. You can imagine what is left of the old settlement. Oh, the Caye is dead, it is like a skeleton, bleached and bare!"

Limekiller felt he could slightly gladly have tipped the medico over the side and watched the bubbles; but, unaware, on the man went. "—so, difficult though it was making my old map agree with the present outlines, still, I did find the site of the old burial ground, and I cast about and I prodded with my iron rod, and I felt stone underneath the sand, and I dug!"

More sounds of excited interest. Digging in the sand on the bit of ravished sand and coral where the ancient settlement had been—but was no more—was certainly of more interest than digging for yams on the fertile soil of the mainland. And, even though they already knew that it was not a chest of gold, still, they listened and they murmured *oh* and *ah*. "The letters were still very clear, I had no difficulty reading them. *Sacred to the memory of Ferdinando Rousseau, a native of Guernsey, and of Marianna his Wife, a native of Mandingo, in Africa.* Plus a poem in three stanzas, of which I have deposited a copy in the National Archives, and of course I have a copy myself and a third copy I offered to old Mr. Ferdinand Rousseau in King Town—"

Smiling, Mr. Blossom asked, "And what he tell you, then, Doctor?"

Dr. Rafael's smile was a trifle rueful. "He said, 'Let the dead bury their dead'—" The others all laughed. Mr. Ferdinand Rousseau was evidently known to all of them. "—and he declined to take it. Well, I was aware that Mr. Blossom's mother was a cousin of Mr. Rousseau's mother—" ("Double-cousin," said Mr. Blossom.)

Said Mr. Blossom, "And the doctor has even been there, too, to that country. I don't mean Guernsey; in Africa, I mean; not true, Doctor?"

Up ahead, where the coast thrust itself out into the blue, blue Bay, Jack thought he saw the three isolated palms which were his landmark. But there was no hurry. He found himself unwilling to hurry anything at all.

Doctor Rafael, in whose voice only the slightest trace of alien accent still lingered, said that after leaving Vienna, he had gone to London, in London he had been offered and had accepted work in a British West African colonial medical service. "I was just a bit surprised that the old gravestone referred to Mandingo as a country, there is no such country on the maps today, but there are such a people."

"What they like, Doc-tah? What they like, thees people who dey mehk some ahv Mr. Blossom ahn-*ces*-tah?"

There was another chuckle. This one had slight overtones.

The DMO's round, pink face furrowed in concentration among memories a quarter of a century old. "Why," he said, "they are like elephants. They never forget."

There was a burst of laughter. Mr. Blossom laughed loudest of them all. Twenty-five years earlier he would have asked about Guernsey; today . . .

Harlow the Hunter, his question answered, gestured towards the shore.

A slight swell had come up, the blue was flecked, with bits of white. "W'over dere, suppose to be wan ahv w'ol' Bob Blaine cahmp, in de w'ol' days."

"Filthy fellow," Dr. Rafael said, suddenly, concisely.

"Yes sah." Harlow agreed. "He was ah lewd fellow, fah true, fah true. What he use to say, he use to say, 'Eef you tie ah rottle-snehk doewn fah me, I weel freeg eet . . .' "

Mr. Blossom leaned forward. "Something the matter, Mr. Limekiller?"

Mr. Limekiller did not at that moment feel like talking. Instead, he lifted his hand and pointed towards the headland with the three isolated palms.

"Cape Man'tee, Mr. Limekiller? What about it?"

Jack cleared his throat. "I thought that was farther down the coast . . . according to my chart . . ."

Ed Huggin snorted. "Chart! Washington chart copies London chart and London chart I think must copy the original *chart* made by old Captain Cook. *Chart!*" He snorted again.

Mr. Florian Blossom asked, softly, "Do you recognize your landfall, Mr. Limekiller? I suppose it would not be at the cape itself, which is pure mangrove bog and does not fit the description which you gave us . . ."

Mr. Limekiller's eyes hugged the coast. Suppose he couldn't *find* the goddamned place? Police and Government wouldn't like that at all. Every ounce of fuel had to be accounted for. Chasing the wild goose was not approved. He might find an extension of his stay refused when next he went applying for it. He might even find himself officially listed as a Proscribed Person, trans.: haul ass, Jack, and don't try coming back. And he realized that he did not want that at all, at all. The whole coast looked the same to him, all of a sudden. And then, all of a sudden, it didn't . . . somehow. There was something about that solid-seeming mass of bush–

"I think there may be a creek. Right there."

Harlow nodded. "Yes mon. Is a creek. Right dere."

And right there, at the mouth of the creek–in this instance, meaning not a stream, but an inlet–Limekiller recognized the huge tree. And Harlow the Hunter recognized something else. "Dot mark suppose to be where Mr. Limekiller drah up the skiff."

"Best we ahl put boots *on,*" said Sergeant Ruiz, who had said not a word until now. They all put boots on. Harlow shouldered an axe. Ruiz and Huggin took up machetes. Dr. Rafael had, besides his medical bag, a bundle of what appeared to be plastic sheets and crocus sacks. "You doesn't mind to cahry ah shovel, Mr. Jock?" Jack decided that he could think of a number of things he had rather carry: but he took the thing. And Mr. Blossom carefully picked up an enormous camera, with tripod. The Governments of His and/or Her Majesties had never been known for throwing money around in these parts; the camera could hardly have dated back to George III but was certainly earlier than the latter part of the reign of George V.

"You must lead us, Mr. Limekiller." The District Commissioner was not grim. He was not smiling. He was grave.

Limekiller nodded. Climbed over the sprawling trunk of the tree. Suddenly remembered that it had been night when he had first come this way, that it had been from the other direction that he had made his way the next morning, hesitated. And then Harlow the Hunter spoke up.

"Eef you pleases, Mistah Blossom. I believes I knows dees pahth bettah."

And, at any rate, he knew it well enough to lead them there in less time, surely, than Jack Limekiller could have.

Blood was no longer fresh and red, but a hundred swarms of flies suddenly rose to show where the blood had been. Doctor Rafael snipped leaves, scooped up soil, deposited his take in containers.

And in regard to other evidence, whatever it was evidence of, for one thing, Mr. Blossom handed the camera over to Police Corporal Huggin, who set up his measuring tape, first along one deep depression and photographed it; then along another . . . another . . . another . . .

"Mountain-cow," said the District Commissioner. He did not sound utterly persuaded.

Harlow shook his head. "No, Mistah Florian. No sah. No, no."

"Well, if not a tapir: what?"

Harlow shrugged.

Something heavy had been dragged through the bush. And it had been dragged by something heavier . . . something much, much heavier . . . It was horridly hot in the bush, and every kind of "fly" seemed to be ready and waiting for them: sand-fly, bottle fly, doctor-fly. They made unavoidable noise, but whenever they stopped, the silence closed in on them. No wild parrot shrieked. No "baboons" rottled or growled. No warree grunted or squealed. Just the waiting silence of the bush. Not friendly. Not hostile. Just indifferent.

And when they came to the little river (afterwards, Jack could not even find it on the maps) and scanned the opposite bank and saw nothing, the District Commissioner said, "Well, Harlow. What you think?"

The wiry little man looked up and around. After a moment he nodded, plunged into the bush. A faint sound, as of someone—or of something?—Then Ed Huggin pointed. Limekiller would never even have noticed that particular tree was there; indeed, he was able to pick it out now only because a small figure was slowly but surely climbing it. The tree was tall, and it leaned at an angle—old enough to have experienced the brute force of a hurricane, strong enough to have survived, though bent.

Harlow called something Jack did not understand, but he followed the others, splashing down the shallows of the river. The river slowly became a swamp. Harlow was suddenly next to them. "Eet not fah," he muttered.

Nor was it.

What there was of it.

An eye in a monstrously swollen head winked at them. Then an insect leisurely crawled out, flapped its horridly-damp wings in the hot and humid air, and sluggishly flew off. There was no wink. There was no eye.

"Mr. Limekiller," said District Commissioner Blossom, "I will now ask you if you identify this body as that of the man known to you as John Samuel."

"It's him. Yes sir."

But was as though the commissioner had been holding his breath and had now released it. "Well, well," he said. "And he was supposed to have gone to Jamaica and died there. I never heard he'd come back. Well, he is dead now, for true."

But little Doctor Rafael shook his snowy head. "He is certainly dead. And he is certainly not John Samuel."

"Why—" Limekiller swallowed bile, pointed. "Look. The eye is missing, John Samuel lost that eye when the tree fell—"

"Ah, yes, young man. John Samuel did. *But not that eye.*"

The bush was not so silent now. Every time the masses and masses of flies were waved away, they rose, buzzing, into the heavy, squalid air. Buzzing, hovered. Buzzing, returned.

"Then who in the Hell—?"

Harlow wiped his face on his sleeve. "Well, sah. I cahn tell you. Lord hahv mercy on heem. Eet ees Bob Blaine."

There was a long outdrawn *ahhh* from the others. Then Ed Huggin said, "But Bob Blaine had both his eyes."

Harlow stopped, picked a stone from the river bed, with dripping hand threw it into the bush . . . one would have said, at random. With an ugly croak, a buzzard burst up and away. Then Harlow said something, as true—and as dreadful—as it was unarguable. "He not hahv either of them, noew."

By what misadventure and in what place Bob Blaine had lost one eye whilst alive and after decamping from his native land, no one knew and perhaps it did not matter. He had trusted on "discretion" not to reveal his hideout, there at the site of his old bush-camp. But he had not trusted to it one hundred percent. Suppose that Limekiller were, deceitfully or accidentally, to let drop the fact that a man was camping out there. A man with only one eye. What was the man's name? John Samuel. What? John *Samuel* . . . Ah. Then John Samuel had not, after all, died in Jamaica, according to report. Report had been known to be wrong before. John Samuel alive, then. No big thing. Nobody then would have been moved to go down there to check up.—Nobody, now, knew why Bob Blaine had returned. Perhaps he had made things too hot for himself, down in "Republican waters"—where hot water could be so very much hotter than back here. Perhaps some day a report would drift back up, and it might be a true report or it might be false or it might be a mixture of both.

As for the report, the official, Government one, on the circumstances surrounding the death of Roberto Blaine, a.k.a. Bob Blaine . . . as for Limekiller's statement and the statements of the District Commissioner and the District Medical Officer and the autopsy and the photographs: why, that had all been neatly transcribed and neatly (and literally) laced with red tape, and forwarded up the coast to King Town. And as to what happened to it there—

"What do you think they will do about it, Doctor?"

Rafael's rooms were larger, perhaps, than a bachelor needed. But they were the official quarters for the DMO, and so the DMO lived in them. The wide floors gleamed with polish. The spotless walls showed, here a shield, there a paddle, a harpoon with barbed head, the carapace of a huge turtle, a few paintings. The symmetry and conventionality of it all was slightly marred by the bookcases which were everywhere, against every wall, adjacent to desk and chairs. And all were full, crammed, overflowing.

Doctor Rafael shrugged. "Perhaps the woodlice will eat the papers," he said. "Or the roaches, or the *wee-wee* ants. The mildew. The damp. Hurricane . . . This is not a climate which helps preserve the history of men. I work hard to keep my own books and papers from going that way. But I am not Government, and Government lacks time and money and personnel, and . . . perhaps, also . . . Government has so many, many things pressing upon it . . . Perhaps, too, Government lacks interest."

"What were those tracks, Doctor Rafael?"

Doctor Rafael shrugged.

"You do know, don't you?"

Doctor Rafael grimaced.

"Have you seen them, or anything like them, before?"

Doctor Rafael, very slowly, very slowly nodded.

"Well . . . for God's sake . . . can you even give me a, well a *hint?* I mean: that was a rather rotten experience for me, you know. And—"

The sunlight, kept at bay outside, broke in through a crack in the jalousies, sun making the scant white hair for an instant ablaze: like the brow of Moses. Doctor Rafael got up and busied himself with a fresh lime and the sweetened lime juice and the gin and ice. He was rapt in this task, like an ancient apothecary mingling strange unguents and syrups. Then he gave one of the gimlets to his guest and from one he took a long, long pull.

"You see. I have two years to go before my retirement. The pension, well, it is not spectacular, but I have no complaint. I will be able to rest.

Not for an hour, or an evening . . . an evening! only on my holidays, once a year, do I even have an evening all my own!—Well. You may imagine how I look forward. And I am not going to risk premature and enforced retirement by presenting Government with an impossible situation. One which wouldn't be its fault, anyway. By insisting on impossible things. By demonstrating—"

He finished his drink. He gave Jack a long, shrewd look.

"So I have nothing more to say . . . about *that*. If they want to believe, up in King Town, that the abominable Bob Blaine was mauled by a crocodile, let them. If they prefer to make it a jaguar or even a tapir, why, that is fine with Robert Rafael, M.D., DMO. It might be, probably, the first time in history that anybody anywhere was killed by a tapir, but that is not my affair. The matter is, so far as I am concerned, so far—in fact—as *you* and I are concerned—over.

"Do you understand?"

Limekiller nodded. At once the older man's manner changed. "I have many, many books, as you can see. Maybe some of them would be of interest to you. Pick any one you like. Pick one at random." So saying, he took a book from his desk and put it in Jack's hands. It was just a book-looking book. It was, in fact, volume II of the Everyman edition of Plutarch's Lives. There was a wide card, of the kind on which medical notes or records are sometimes made, and so Jack Limekiller opened the book at that place.

seasons, as the gods sent them, seemed natural to him. The Greeks that inhabited Asia were very much pleased to see the great lords and governors of Persia, with all the pride, cruelty, and

"Well, now, what the Hell," he muttered. The card slipped, he clutched. He glanced at it. He put down vol. II of the Lives and he sat back and read the notes on the card.

It is in the nature of things [they began] for men, in a new country and faced with new things, to name them after old, familiar things. Even when resemblance unlikely. Example: *Mountain-cow* for tapir. ("Tapir" from Tupi Indian *tapira*, big beast.) Example: Mawmee-*apple* not apple at all. Ex.: *Sea-cow* for manatee. Early British settlers not entomologists. Quest.: Whence word *manatee?* From Carib? Perhaps. After the British, what other people came to this corner of the world? Ans.: Black people. Calabars, Ashantee, Mantee, Mandingo. Re last two names. Related peoples. Named after totemic animal. *Also,* not likely? *likely*—named unfamiliar animals after familiar (i.e., familiar in Africa) animals. Mantee, Mandee-hippo. Refer legend.

Limekiller's mouth fell open. "Oh, my God!" he groaned. In his ear now, he heard the old, old, quavering voice of Captain Cudgel (once Cudjoe): *"Mon, een Ahfrica, de mon-ah-tee hahv leg, I tell you. Een Ahfrica eet be ah poerful beast, come up on de lond, I tell you . . . de w'ol' people, dey tell me so, fah true . . ."*

He heard the old voice, repeating the old words, no longer even half-understood: but, in some measure, at least half-true.

Refer legend of were-animals, universal. Were-wolf, were-tiger, were-shark, were-dolphin. Quest.: Were-manatee?

"Mon-ah-tee ees hahlf ah mon . . . hahv teats like a womahn . . . Dere ees wahn mon, mehk mellow weet mon-ah-tee, hahv pickney by mon-ah-tee . . ."

And he heard another voice saying, not only once, saying, *"Mon, eef you tie ah rottlesnake doewn fah me, I weel freeg eet . . ."*

He thought of the wretched captives in the Spanish slave ship, set free to fend for themselves in a bush by far wilder than the one left behind. Few, to begin with, fewer as time went on; marrying and intermarrying, no new blood, no new thoughts. And, finally, the one road in to them, destroyed. Left alone. Left quite alone. Or . . . almost . . .

He shuddered.

How desperate for refuge must Blaine have been, to have sought to hide himself anywhere near Cape Mantee—

And what miserable happenstance had brought he himself, Jack Limekiller, to improvise on that old song that dreadful night?—And what had he called up out of the darkness . . . out of the bush . . . out of the mindless present which was the past and future and the timeless tropical forever? . . .

There was something pressing gently against his finger, something on the other side of the card. He turned it over. A clipping from a magazine had been roughly pasted there.

Valentry has pointed out that, despite a seeming resemblance to such aquatic mammals as seals and walrus, the manatee is actually more closely related anatomically to the elephant.

. . . out of the bush . . . out of the darkness . . . out of the mindless present which was also the past and the timeless tropical forever . . .

"They are like elephants. They never forget."

"Ukh," he said, though clenched teeth. "My God. Uff. Jesus . . ."

The card was suddenly, swiftly, snatched from his hands. He looked up still in a state of shock, to see Doctor Rafael tearing it into pieces.

"Doña 'Sana!"

A moment. Then the housekeeper, old, all in white. "Doctór?"

"Burn this."

A moment passed. Just the two of them again. Then Rafael, in a tone which was nothing but kindly, said, "Jack, you are still young and you are still healthy. My advice to you: Go away. Go to a cooler climate. One with cooler ways and cooler memories." The old woman called something from the back of the house. The old man sighed. "It is the summons to supper," he said. "Not only must I eat in haste because I have my clinic in less than half an hour, but suddenly-invited guests make Doña 'Sana very nervous. Good night, then, Jack."

Jack had had two gin drinks. He felt that he needed two more. At least two more. Or, if not gin, rum. Beer would not do. He wanted to pull the blanket of booze over him, awfully, awfully quickly. He had this in his mind as though it were a vow as he walked up the front street towards the Cupid Club.

Someone hailed him, someone out of the gathering dusk.

"Jock! Hey, mon, Jock! Hey, b'y! Where you gweyn so fahst? Bide, b'y, bide a bit!"

The voice was familiar. It was that of Harry Hazeed, his principal creditor in King Town. Ah, well. He had had his chance, Limekiller had. He could have gone on down the coast, down into the Republican waters, where the Queen's writ runneth not. Now it was too late.

"Oh, hello, Harry," he said, dully.

Hazeed took him by the hand. Took him by both hands. "Mon, show me where is your boat? She serviceable? She is? Good: Mon, you don't hear de news: Welcome's warehouse take fire and born up! Yes, mon. Ahl de carn in King *Town* born up! No carn ah-tahl: No tortilla, no empinada, no tamale, no carn-*cake!* Oh, mon, how de people going to punish! Soon as I hear de news, I drah me money from de bonk, I buy ahl de crocus sock I can find, I jump on de pocket-*boat*—and here I am, oh, mon, I pray fah you . . . I pray I fine you!"

Limekiller shook his head. It had been one daze, one shock after another. The only thing clear was that Harry Hazeed didn't seem angry. "You no understond?" Hazeed cried. "Mon! We going take your boat, we going doewn to Nutmeg P'int, we going to buy carn, mon! We going to buy ahl de carn dere is to buy! Nevah mine dat lee' bit money you di owe me, b'y! We going make plenty money, mon! And we going make de cultivators plenty money, too! What you theenk of eet, Jock, me b'y? Eh? Hey? What you theenk?"

Jack put his forefinger in his mouth, held it up. The wind was in the right quarter. The wind would, if it held up, and, somehow, it felt like a wind which would hold up, the wind would carry them straight and clear to Nutmeg Point: the clear, clean wind in the clear and starry night.

Softly, he said—and, old Hazeed leaning closer to make the words out, Limekiller said them again, louder, "I think it's great. Just great. I think it's great."

T. H. WHITE

The Troll

Born in 1906, the late T. H. White was perhaps the most talented and widely acclaimed creator of whimsical fantasy since Lewis Carroll, and probably did more to mold the popular image of King Arthur and Merlin than any other writer since Twain. Although he published other well-received fantasy novels such as *Mistress Masham's Repose* and *The Elephant and the Kangaroo,* White's major work—and the work on which almost all of his present-day reputation rests—was the massive Arthurian tetralogy, *The Once and Future King.* Begun in 1939 with the publication of the first volume, *The Sword in the Stone* (itself well known as an individual novel, and later made into a not-terribly-successful Disney animated film), the tetralogy was published in an omnibus volume in 1958, became a nationwide best-seller, inspired the musical *Camelot,* one of the most popular shows in the history of Broadway, and later was made into a big-budget (and quite dreadful) movie of the same name. Gloriously eccentric and impressively erudite, full of whimsy and delightful anachronism, hilarious and melancholy by turns, poetically written and peopled with psychologically complex and compassionately drawn characters, *The Once and Future King* is probably one of the two or three best fantasies of the last half of the twentieth century, and is surpassed for widespread impact only by J. R. R. Tolkien's *Lord of the Rings.* (As an example of its influence, most subsequent fantasy books and stories that handle Arthurian themes take for *granted* the idea that Merlin (or Merlyn, as White spelled it) is living his life backward through time—although that trope is not found in Mallory, Tennyson, or Twain, but only in White's work. It has become *part* of the ongoing Merlin legend, with most subsequent writers not even realizing where they've picked it up from, and you can't ask for a much better demonstration of influence than that!)

T. H. White died in 1964. *The Book of Merlyn,* a postscript to

The Once and Future King, was published posthumously in 1980.

White was not prolific at short lengths, and most of his stories are gathered in the collection *The Maharajah, and Other Stories.* White's strengths as a writer did not desert him at shorter lengths, though, as you will see in the wry story that follows, which shows that, even in the carpeted, comfortable, and luxurious halls of a modern hotel, a leopard does not change its spots, nor a troll its nature . . .

"My father," said Mr. Marx, "used to say that an experience like the one I am about to relate was apt to shake one's interest in mundane matters. Naturally he did not expect to be believed, and he did not mind whether he was or not. He did not himself believe in the supernatural, but the thing happened, and he proposed to tell it as simply as possible. It was stupid of him to say that it shook his faith in mundane matters, for it was just as mundane as anything else. Indeed, the really frightening part about it was the horribly tangible atmosphere in which it took place. None of the outlines wavered in the least. The creature would have been less remarkable if it had been less natural. It seemed to overcome the usual laws without being immune to them.

"My father was a keen fisherman, and used to go to all sorts of places for his fish. On one occasion he made Abisko his Lapland base, a comfortable railway hotel, one hundred and fifty miles within the Arctic Circle. He traveled the prodigious length of Sweden (I believe it is as far from the south of Sweden to the north, as it is from the south of Sweden to the south of Italy) in the electric railway, and arrived tired out. He went to bed early, sleeping almost immediately, although it was bright daylight outside, as it is in those parts throughout the night at that time of the year. Not the least shaking part of his experience was that it should all have happened under the sun.

"He went to bed early, and slept, and dreamed. I may as well make it clear at once, as clear as the outlines of that creature in the northern sun, that his story did not turn out to be a dream in the last paragraph. The division between sleeping and waking was abrupt, although the feeling of both was the same. They were both in the same sphere of horrible absurdity, though in the former he was asleep and in the latter almost terribly awake. He tried to be asleep several times.

"My father always used to tell one of his dreams, because it somehow seemed of a piece with what was to follow. He believed that it was a consequence of the thing's presence in the next room. My father dreamed of blood.

"It was the vividness of the dreams that was impressive, their minute detail and horrible reality. The blood came through the keyhole of a locked door which communicated with the next room. I suppose the two rooms had originally been designed en suite. It ran down the door panel with a viscous ripple, like the artificial one created in the conduit of Trumpington Street. But it was heavy, and smelled. The slow welling of it sopped the carpet and reached the bed. It was warm and sticky. My father woke up with the impression that it was all over his hands. He was rubbing his first two fingers together, trying to rid them of the greasy adhesion where the fingers joined.

"My father knew what he had got to do. Let me make it clear that he was now perfectly wide awake, but he knew what he had got to do. He got out of bed, under this irresistible knowledge, and looked through the keyhole into the next room.

"I suppose the best way to tell the story is simply to narrate it, without an effort to carry belief. The thing did not require belief. It was not a feeling of horror in one's bones, or a misty outline, or anything that needed to be given actuality by an act of faith. It was as solid as a wardrobe. You don't have to believe in wardrobes. They are there, with corners.

"What my father saw through the keyhole in the next room was a Troll. It was eminently solid, about eight feet high, and dressed in brightly ornamented skins. It had a blue face, with yellow eyes, and on its head there was a woolly sort of nightcap with a red bobble on top. The features were Mongolian. Its body was long and sturdy, like the trunk of a tree. Its legs were short and thick, like the elephant's feet that used to be cut off for umbrella stands, and its arms were wasted: little rudimentary members like the forelegs of a kangaroo. Its head and neck were very thick and massive. On the whole, it looked like a grotesque doll.

"That was the horror of it. Imagine a perfectly normal golliwog (but without the association of a Christie minstrel) standing in the corner of a room, eight feet high. The creature was as ordinary as that, as tangible, as stuffed, and as ungainly at the joints: but it could move itself about.

"The Troll was eating a lady. Poor girl, she was tightly clutched to its breast by those rudimentary arms, with her head on a level with its mouth. She was dressed in a nightdress which had crumpled up under her armpits, so that she was a pitiful naked offering, like a classical picture of Andromeda. Mercifully, she appeared to have fainted.

"Just as my father applied his eye to the keyhole, the Troll opened its mouth and bit off her head. Then, holding the neck between the bright blue lips, he sucked the bare meat dry. She shriveled, like a squeezed orange, and her heels kicked. The creature had a look of thoughtful ecstasy. When the girl seemed to have lost succulence as an orange she was lifted into the air. She vanished in two bites. The Troll remained leaning against the wall, munching patiently and casting its eyes about it with a vague benevolence. Then it leaned forward from the low hips, like a jackknife folding in half, and opened its mouth to lick the blood up from the carpet. The mouth was incandescent inside, like a gas fire, and the blood evaporated before its tongue, like dust before a vacuum cleaner. It straightened itself, the arms dangling before it in patient uselessness, and fixed its eyes upon the keyhole.

"My father crawled back to bed, like a hunted fox after fifteen miles. At first it was because he was afraid that the creature had seen him through the hole, but afterward it was because of his reason. A man can attribute many nighttime appearances to the imagination, and can ultimately persuade himself that creatures of the dark did not exist. But this was an appearance in a sunlit room, with all the solidity of a wardrobe and unfortunately almost none of its possibility. He spent the first ten minutes making sure that he was awake, and the rest of the night trying to hope that he was asleep. It was either that, or else he was mad.

"It is not pleasant to doubt one's sanity. There are no satisfactory tests. One can pinch oneself to see if one is asleep, but there are no means of determining the other problem. He spent some time opening and shutting his eyes, but the room seemed normal and remained unaltered. He also soused his head in a basin of cold water, without result. Then he lay on his back, for hours, watching the mosquitoes on the ceiling.

"He was tired when he was called. A bright Scandinavian maid admitted the full sunlight for him and told him that it was a fine day. He spoke to her several times, and watched her carefully, but she seemed to have no doubts about his behavior. Evidently, then, he was not badly mad: and by now he had been thinking about the matter for so many hours that it had begun to get obscure. The outlines were blurring again, and he determined that the whole thing must have been a dream or a temporary delusion, something temporary, anyway, and finished with; so that there was no good in thinking about it longer. He got up, dressed himself fairly cheerfully, and went down to breakfast.

"These hotels used to be run extraordinarily well. There was a hostess always handy in a little office off the hall, who was delighted to answer any questions, spoke every conceivable language, and generally made it her business to make the guests feel at home. The particular hostess at Abisko was a lovely creature into the bargain. My father used to speak to her a good deal. He had an idea that when you had a bath in Sweden one of the maids was sent to wash you. As a matter of fact this sometimes used to be the case, but it was always an old maid and highly trusted. You had to keep yourself underwater and this was supposed to confer a cloak of invisibility. If you popped your knee out she was shocked. My father had a dim sort of hope that the hostess would be sent to bathe him one day: and I dare say he would have shocked her a good deal. However, this is beside the point. As he passed through the hall something prompted him to ask about the room next to his. Had anybody, he inquired, taken number 23?

" 'But, yes,' said the lady manager with a bright smile, twenty-three is taken by a doctor professor from Uppsala and his wife, such a charming couple!'

"My father wondered what the charming couple had been doing, whilst the Troll was eating the lady in the nightdress. However, he decided to think no more about it. He pulled himself together, and went in to breakfast. The professor was sitting in an opposite corner (the manageress had kindly pointed him out), looking mild and shortsighted, by himself. My father thought he would go out for a long climb on the mountains, since exercise was evidently what his constitution needed.

"He had a lovely day. Lake Torne blazed a deep blue below him, for all its thirty miles, and the melting snow made a lacework of filigree around the tops of the surrounding mountain basin. He got away from the stunted birch trees, and the mossy bogs with the reindeer in them, and the mosquitoes, too. He forded something that might have been a temporary tributary of the Abiskojokk, having to take off his trousers to do so and tucking his shirt up around his neck. He wanted to shout, bracing himself against the glorious tug of the snow water, with his legs crossing each other involuntarily as they passed, and the boulders turning under his feet. His body made a bow wave in the water, which climbed and feathered on his stomach, on the upstream side. When he was under the opposite bank a stone turned in earnest, and he went in. He came up, shouting with laughter, and made out loud a remark which has since become a classic in my family. 'Thank God,' he said, 'I rolled up my sleeves.' He wrung out everything as best he could, and dressed again in the wet clothes, and set off up the shoulder of Niakatjavelk. He was dry and warm again in half a mile. Less than a thousand feet took him over the snow line, and there, crawling on hands and knees, he came face-to-face with what seemed to be the summit of ambition. He met an ermine. They were both on all fours, so that there was a sort of equality about the encounter, especially as the ermine was higher up than he was. They looked at each other for a fifth of a second, without saying anything, and then the ermine vanished. He searched for it everywhere in vain, for the snow was only patchy. My father sat down on a dry rock, to eat his well-soaked luncheon of chocolate and rye bread.

"Life is such unutterable hell, solely because it is sometimes beautiful. If we could only be miserable all the time, if there could be no such things as love or beauty or faith or hope, if I could be absolutely certain that my love would never be returned: how much more simple life would be. One could plod through the Siberian salt mines of existence without being bothered about happiness. Unfortunately the happiness is there. There is always the chance (about eight hundred and fifty to one) that another heart will come to mine. I can't help hoping, and keeping faith, and loving beauty. Quite frequently I am not so miserable as it would be wise to be. And there, for my poor father sitting on his boulder above the snow, was stark happiness beating at the gates.

"The boulder on which he was sitting had probably never been sat upon before. It was a hundred and fifty miles within the Arctic Circle, on a mountain five thousand feet high, looking down on a blue lake. The lake was so long that he could have sworn it sloped away at the ends, proving to the naked eye that the sweet earth was round. The railway line and the half-dozen houses of Abisko were hidden in the trees. The sun was warm on the boulder, blue on the snow, and his body tingled smooth from the spate water. His mouth watered for the chocolate, just behind the tip of his tongue.

"And yet, when he had eaten the chocolate—perhaps it was heavy on his stomach—there was the memory of the Troll. My father fell suddenly into a black mood, and began to think about the supernatural. Lapland was beautiful in the summer, with the sun sweeping around the horizon day and night, and the small tree leaves twinkling. It was not the sort of place for wicked things. But what about the winter? A picture of the Arctic night came before him, with the silence and the snow. Then the legendary wolves and bears snuffled at the far encampments, and the nameless winter spirits moved on their darkling courses. Lapland had always been associated with sorcery, even by Shakespeare. It was at the outskirts of the world that the Old Things accumulated, like driftwood around the edges of the sea. If one wanted to find a wise woman, one went to the rims of the Hebrides; on the coast of Brittany one sought the mass of St. Secaire. And what an outskirt Lapland was! It was an outskirt not only of Europe, but of civilization. It had no boundaries. The Lapps went with the reindeer, and where the reindeer were, was Lapland. Curiously indefinite region, suitable to the indefinite things. The Lapps were not Christians. What a fund of power they must have had behind them, to resist the march of mind. All through the missionary centuries they had held to something: something had stood behind them, a power against Christ. My father realized with a shock that he was living in the age of the reindeer, a period contiguous to the mammoth and the fossil.

"Well, this was not what he had come out to do. He dismissed the nightmares with an effort, got up from his boulder, and began to scramble back to his hotel. It was impossible that a professor from Abisko could become a troll.

"As my father was going in to dinner that evening the manageress stopped him in the hall.

" 'We have had a day so sad,' she said. 'The poor Dr. Professor has disappeared his wife. She has been missing since last night. The Dr. Professor is inconsolable.'

"My father then knew for certain that he had lost his reason.

"He went blindly to dinner, without making any answer, and began to eat a thick sour-cream soup that was taken cold with pepper and sugar. The professor was still sitting in his corner, a sandy-headed man with thick spectacles and a desolate expression. He was looking at my father, and my father, with a soup spoon halfway to his mouth, looked at him. You know that eye-to-eye recognition, when two people look deeply into each other's pupils, and burrow to the soul? It usually comes before love. I mean the clear, deep, milk-eyed recognition expressed by the poet Donne. Their eyebeams twisted and did thread their eyes upon a double string. My father recognized that the professor was a troll, and the professor recognized my father's recognition. Both of them knew that the professor had eaten his wife.

"My father put down his soup spoon, and the professor began to grow. The top of his head lifted and expanded, like a great loaf rising in an oven; his face went red and purple, and finally blue, the whole ungainly upperworks began to sway and topple toward the ceiling. My father looked about him. The other diners were eating unconcernedly. Nobody else could see it, and he was definitely mad at last. When he looked at the Troll again, the creature bowed. The enormous superstructure inclined itself toward him from the hips, and grinned seductively.

"My father got up from his table experimentally, and advanced toward the Troll, arranging his feet on the carpet with excessive care. He did not find it easy to walk, or to approach the monster, but it was a question of his reason. If he was mad, he was mad; and it was essential that he should come to grips with the thing, in order to make certain.

"He stood before it like a small boy, and held out his hand, saying, 'Good evening.'

" 'Ho! Ho!' said the Troll, 'little mannikin. And what shall I have for my supper tonight?'

"Then it held out its wizened furry paw and took my father by the hand.

"My father went straight out of the dining-room, walking on air. He found the manageress in the passage and held out his hand to her.

" 'I am afraid I have burned my hand,' he said. 'Do you think you could tie it up?'

"The manageress said, 'But it is a very bad burn. There are blisters all over the back. Of course, I will bind it up at once.'

"He explained that he had burned it on one of the spirit lamps at the sideboard. He could scarcely conceal his delight. One cannot burn oneself by being insane.

" 'I saw you talking to the Dr. Professor,' said the manageress, as she was putting on the bandage. 'He is a sympathetic gentleman, is he not?'

"The relief about his sanity soon gave place to other troubles. The Troll had eaten its wife and given him a blister, but it had also made an unpleasant remark about its supper that evening. It proposed to eat my father. Now very few people can have been in a position to decide what to do when a troll earmarks them for its next meal. To begin with, although it was a tangible troll in two ways, it had been invisible to the other diners. This put my father in a difficult position. He could not, for instance, ask for protection. He could scarcely go to the manageress and say, 'Professor Skal is an odd kind of werewolf, ate his wife last night, and proposes to eat me this evening.' He would have found himself in a loony bin at once. Besides, he was too proud to do this, and still too confused. Whatever the proofs and blisters, he did not find it easy to believe in professors that turned into trolls. He had lived in the normal world all his life, and, at his age, it was difficult to start learning afresh. It would have been quite easy for a baby, who was still coordinating the world, to cope with the troll situation: for my father, not. He kept trying to fit it in somewhere, without disturbing the universe. He kept telling himself that it was nonsense: one did not get eaten by professors. It was like having a fever, and telling oneself that it was all right, really, only a delirium, only something that would pass.

"There was that feeling on the one side, the desperate assertion of all the truths that he had learned so far, the tussle to keep the world from drifting, the brave but intimidated refusal to give in or to make a fool of himself.

"On the other side there was stark terror. However much one struggled to be merely deluded, or hitched up momentarily in an odd packet of space-time, there was panic. There was the urge to go away as quickly as possible, to flee the dreadful Troll. Unfortunately the last train had left Abisko, and there was nowhere else to go.

"My father was not able to distinguish these trends of thought. For him they were at the time intricately muddled together. He was in a whirl. A proud man, and an agnostic, he stuck to his muddled guns alone. He was terribly afraid of the Troll, but he could not afford to admit its existence. All his mental processes remained hung up, whilst he talked on the terrace, in a state of suspended animation, with an American tourist who had come to Abisko to photograph the Midnight Sun.

"The American told my father that the Abisko railway was the northernmost electric railway in the world, that twelve trains passed through it every day traveling between Uppsala and Narvik, that the population of Abo was 12,000 in 1862, and that Gustavus Adolphus ascended the throne of Sweden in 1611. He also gave some facts about Greta Garbo.

"My father told the American that a dead baby was required for the mass of St. Secaire, that an elemental was a kind of mouth in space that sucked at you and tried to gulp you down, that homeopathic magic was practiced by the aborigines of Australia, and that a Lapland woman was careful at her confinement to have no knots or loops about her person, lest these should make the delivery difficult.

"The American, who had been looking at my father in a strange way for some time, took offense at this and walked away; so that there was nothing for it but to go to bed.

"My father walked upstairs on willpower alone. His faculties seemed to have shrunk and confused themselves. He had to help himself with the banister. He seemed to be navigating himself by wireless, from a spot about a foot above his forehead. The issues that were involved had ceased to have any meaning, but he went on doggedly up the stairs, moved forward by pride and contrariety. It was physical fear that alienated him from his body, the same fear that he had felt as a boy, walking down long corridors to be beaten. He walked firmly up the stairs.

"Oddly enough, he went to sleep at once. He had climbed all day and been awake all night and suffered emotional extremes. Like a condemned man, who was to be hanged in the morning, my father gave the whole business up and went to sleep.

"He was woken at midnight exactly. He heard the American on the terrace below his window, explaining excitedly that there had been a cloud on the last two nights at 11:58, thus making it impossible to photograph the Midnight Sun. He heard the camera click.

"There seemed to be a sudden storm of hail and wind. It roared at his windowsill, and the window curtains lifted themselves taut, pointing horizontally into the room. The shriek and rattle of the tempest framed the window in a crescendo of growing sound, an increasing blizzard directed toward himself. A blue paw came over the sill.

"My father turned over and hid his head in the pillow. He could feel the doomed head dawning at the window and the eyes fixing themselves upon the small of his back. He could feel the places physically, about four inches apart. They itched. Or else the rest of his body itched, except those places. He could feel the creature growing into the room, glowing like ice, and giving off a storm. His mosquito curtains rose in its afflatus, uncovering him, leaving him defenseless. He was in such an ecstasy of terror that he almost enjoyed it. He was like a bather plunging for the first tine into freezing water and unable to articulate. He was trying to yell, but all he could do was to throw a series of hooting noises from his paralyzed lungs. He became a part of the blizzard. The bedclothes were gone. He felt the Troll put out its hands.

"My father was an agnostic, but, like most idle men, he was not above having a bee in his bonnet. His favorite bee was the psychology of the Catholic Church. He was ready to talk for hours about psychoanalysis and the confession. His greatest discovery had been the rosary.

"The rosary, my father used to say, was intended solely as a factual occupation which calmed the lower centers of the mind. The automatic telling of the beads liberated the higher centers to meditate upon the mysteries. They were a sedative, like knitting or counting sheep. There was no better cure for insomnia than a rosary. For several years he had given up deep breathing or regular counting. When he was sleepless he lay on his back and told his beads, and there was a small rosary in the pocket of his pyjama coat.

"The Troll put out its hands, to take him around the waist. He became completely paralyzed, as if he had been winded. The Troll put its hands upon the beads.

"They met, the occult forces, in a clash above my father's heart. There was an explosion, he said, a quick creation of power. Positive and negative. A flash, a beam. Something like the splutter with which the antenna of a tram meets its overhead wires again, when it is being changed about.

"The Troll made a high squealing noise, like a crab being boiled, and began rapidly to dwindle in size. It dropped my father and turned about, and ran wailing, as if it had been terribly burned, for one window. Its color waned as its size decreased. It was one of those air toys now, that expire with a piercing whistle. It scrambled over the windowsill, scarcely larger than a little child, and sagging visibly.

"My father leaped out of bed and followed it to the window. He saw it drop on the terrace like a toad, gather itself together, stumble off, staggering and whistling like a bat, down the valley of the Abiskojokk.

"My father fainted.

"In the morning the manageress said, 'There has been such a terrible tragedy. The poor Dr. Professor was found this morning in the lake. The worry about his wife had certainly unhinged his mind.'

"A subscription for the wreath was started by the American, to which my father subscribed five shillings; and the body was shipped off next morning, on one of the twelve trains that travel between Uppsala and Narvik every day."

The Sleep of Trees

One of the most distinguished of modern fantasists, Jane Yolen has been compared to writers such as Oscar Wilde and Charles Perrault, and has been called "the Hans Christian Andersen of the Twentieth Century." Primarily known for her work for children and young adults, Yolen has produced more than a hundred books, including novels, collections of short stories, poetry collections, picture books, biographies, and a book of essays on folklore and fairy tales. She has received the Golden Kite Award and the World Fantasy Award, and has been a finalist for the National Book Award. In recent years, she has also been writing more adult-oriented fantasy, work that has appeared in collections such as *Tales of Wonder, Neptune Rising: Songs and Tales of the Undersea Folk, Dragonfield and Other Stories,* and *Merlin's Booke,* and in novels such as *Cards of Grief, Sister Light, Sister Dark,* and *White Jenna.* She lives with her family in Massachusetts.

Dryads, tree-spirits, are hardly the most fearsome or formidable of mythological creatures, usually portrayed in sentimental paintings as beautiful young women in diaphanous gowns—still, as the wry story that follows suggests, if you *do* happen to encounter one, it might be wise to treat her with a certain measure of *respect . . .*

> *"Never invoke the gods unless you really*
> *want them to appear. It annoys them very much."*
> —*Chesterton*

It had been a long winter. Arrhiza had counted every line and blister on the inside of the bark. Even the terrible binding power of the heartwood rings could not contain her longings. She desperately wanted spring to come so she could dance free, once again, of her tree. At night she looked up and through the spiky winter branches counted the shadows of early birds crossing the moon. She listened to the mewling of buds making their slow, painful passage to the light. She felt the sap veins pulse sluggishly around her. All the signs were there, spring was coming, spring was near, yet still there was no spring.

She knew that one morning, without warning, the rings would loosen and she would burst through the bark into her glade. It had happened every year of her life. But the painful wait, as winter slouched towards its dismal close, was becoming harder and harder to bear.

When Arrhiza had been younger, she had always slept the peaceful, uncaring sleep of trees. She would tumble, half-awake, through the bark and onto the soft, fuzzy green earth with the other young dryads, their arms and legs tangling in that first sleepy release. She had wondered then that the older trees released their burdens with such stately grace, the dryads and the meliade sending slow green praises into the air before the real Dance began. But she wondered no longer. Younglings simply slept the whole winter dreaming of what they knew best: roots and bark and the untroubling dark. But aging conferred knowledge, dreams change. Arrhiza now slept little and her waking, as her sleep, was filled with sky.

She even found herself dreaming of birds. Knowing trees were the honored daughters of the All Mother, allowed to root themselves deep into her flesh, knowing trees were the treasured sisters of the Huntress, allowed to unburden themselves into her sacred groves, Arrhiza envied birds. She wondered what it would be like to live apart from the land, to travel at will beyond the confines of the glade. Silly creatures though birds were, going from egg to earth without a thought, singing the same messages to one another throughout their short lives, Arrhiza longed to fly with one, passengered within its breast. A bird lived but a moment, but what a moment that must be.

Suddenly realizing her heresy, Arrhiza closed down her mind lest she share thoughts with her tree. She concentrated on the blessings to the All Mother and Huntress, turning her mind from sky to soil, from flight to the solidity of roots.

And in the middle of her prayer, Arrhiza fell out into spring, as surprised as if she were still young. She tumbled against one of the birch, her nearest neighbor, Phyla of the white face. Their legs touched, their hands brushing one another's thighs.

Arrhiza turned toward Phyla. "Spring comes late," she sighed, her breath caressing Phyla's budlike ear.

Phyla rolled away from her, pouting. "You make Spring Greeting sound like a complaint. It is the same every year." She sat up with her back to Arizona and stretched her arms. Her hands were outlined against the evening sky, the second and third fingers slotted together like a leaf. Then she turned slowly towards Arrhiza, her woods-green eyes unfocused. In the soft, filtered light her body gleamed whitely and the darker patches were mottled beauty marks on her breasts and sides. She was up to her feet in a single fluid movement and into the Dance.

Arrhiza watched, still full-length on the ground, as one after another the dryads and meliades rose and stepped into position, circling, touching, embracing, moving apart. The cleft of their legs flashed pale signals around the glade.

Rooted to their trees, the hamadryads could only lean out into the Dance. They swayed to the lascivious pipings of spring. Their silver-green hair, thick as vines, eddied around their bodies like water.

Arrhiza watched it all but still did not move. How long she had waited for this moment, the whole of the deep winter, and yet she did not move. What she wanted was more than this, this entering into the Dance on command. She wanted to touch, to walk, to run, even to dance when she alone desired it. But then her blood was singing, her body pulsating; her limbs stretched upward answering the call. She was drawn towards the others and, even without willing it, Arrhiza was into the Dance.

Silver and green, green and gold, the grove was a smear of color and wind as she whirled around and around with her sisters. Who was touched and who the toucher; whose arm, whose thigh was pressed in the Dance, it did not matter. The Dance was all. Drops of perspiration, sticky as sap, bedewed their backs and ran slow rivulets to the ground. The Dance *was* the glade, *was* the grove. There was no stopping, no starting, for a circle has no beginning or end.

Then suddenly a hunter's horn knifed across the meadow. It was both discordant and sweet, sharp and caressing at once. The Dance did not stop but it dissolved. The Huntress was coming, the Huntress was here.

And then She was in the middle of them all, straddling a moon-beam, the red hem of Her saffron hunting tunic pulled up to expose muscled thighs. Seven hounds lay growling at Her feet. She reached up to Her hair and in one swift, savage movement, pulled at the golden cords that bound it up. Her hair cascaded like silver and gold leaves onto Her shoulders and crept in tendrils across Her small, perfect breasts. Her heart-shaped face, with its crescent smile, was both innocent and corrupt; Her eyes as dark blue as a storm-coming sky. She dismounted the moon shaft and turned around slowly, as if displaying Herself to them all, but She was the Huntress, and She was doing the hunting. She looked into their faces one at a time, and the younger ones looked back, both eager and afraid.

Arrhiza was neither eager nor afraid. Twice already she had been the chosen one, torn laughing and screaming from the glade, brought for a night to the moon's dark side. The pattern of the Huntress's mouth was burned into her throat's hollow, Her mark, just as Her words were still in Arrhiza's ears. "You are mine. Forever. If you leave me, I will kill you, so fierce is my love." It had been spoken each time with a kind of passion, in between kisses, but the words, like the kisses, were as cold and distant and pitiless as the moon.

The Huntress walked around the circle once again, pausing longest before a young meliade, Pyrena of the apple blossoms. Under that gaze Pyrena seemed both to wither and to bloom. But the Huntress shook Her head and Her mouth formed the slightest moue of disdain. Her tongue flicked out and was caught momentarily between flawless teeth. Then She clicked to the hounds who sprang up. Mounting the moonbeam again, She squeezed it with Her thighs and was gone, riding to another grove.

The moment She disappeared, the glade was filled with breathy gossip.

"Did you see . . ." began Dryope. Trembling with projected pleasure, she turned to Pyrena. "The Huntress looked at you. Truly looked. Next time it *will* be you. I *know* it will."

Pyrena wound her fingers through her hair, letting fall a cascade of blossoms that perfumed the air. She shrugged but smiled a secret, satisfied smile.

Arrhiza turned abruptly and left the circle. She went back to her tree. Sluggishly the softened heartwood rings admitted her and she leaned into them, closed her eyes, and tried to sleep though she knew that in spring no true sleep would come.

She half-dreamed of clouds and birds, forcing them into her mind, but really she was hearing a buzzing. Sky, she murmured to herself, remember sky.

"Oh trees, fair and flourishing, on the high hills They stand, lofty. The Deathless sacred grove . . ."

Jeansen practiced his Homeric supplication, intoning carefully through his nose. The words as they buzzed through his nasal passages tickled. He sneezed several times rapidly, a light punctuation to the verses. Then he continued:

". . . The Deathless sacred grove Men call them, and with iron never cut."

He could say the words perfectly now, his sounds rounded and full. The newly learned Greek rolled off his tongue. He had always been a fast study. Greek was his fifth language, if he counted Esperanto. He could even, on occasion, feel the meanings that hid behind the ancient poetry, but as often the meanings slid away, slippery little fish and he the incompetent angler.

He had come to Greece because he wanted to be known as the American Olivier, the greatest classical actor the States had ever produced. He told interviewers he planned to learn Greek—classic Greek, not the Greek of the streets—to show them Oedipus from the amphitheaters where it had first been played. He would stand in the groves of Artemis, he had said, and call the Goddess to him in her own tongue. One columnist even suggested that with his looks and voice and reputation she would be crazy not to come. If she did, Jeansen thought to himself, smiling, I wouldn't treat her with any great distance. The goddesses like to play at shopgirls; the shopgirls, goddesses. And they all, he knew only too well, liked grand gestures.

And so he had traveled to Greece, not the storied isles of Homer but the fume-clogged port of Pyreus, where a teacher with a mouthful of broken teeth and a breath only a harpy could love had taught him. But mouth and breath aside, he was a fine teacher and Jeansen a fine learner. Now he was ready. Artemis first, a special for PBS, and then the big movie. Oedipus starring *the* Jeansen Forbes.

Only right now all he could feel was the buzz of air, diaphragm against lungs, lungs to larynx, larynx to vocal chords, a mechanical vibration. Buzz, buzz, buzz.

He shook his head as if to clear it, and the well-cut blond hair fell perfectly back in place. He reached a hand up to check it, then looked around the grove slowly, admiringly. The grass was long, uncut, but trampled down. The trees—he had not noticed it at first—were a strange mixture: birch and poplar, apple and oak. He was not a botanist, but it seemed highly unlikely that such a mix would have simply sprung up. Perhaps they had been planted years and years ago. *Note to himself, check on that.*

This particular grove was far up on Mount Cynthus, away from any roads and paths. He had stumbled on it by accident. Happy accident. But it was perfect, open enough for reenacting some of the supplicatory dances and songs, but the trees thick enough to add mystery. The guide book said that Cynthus had once been sacred to the Huntress, virgin Artemis, Diana of the moon. He liked that touch of authenticity. Perhaps her ancient worshippers had first seeded the glade. Even if he could not find the documentation, he could suggest it in such a way as to make it sound true enough.

Jeansen walked over to one birch, a young tree, slim and gracefully bending. He ran his hands down its white trunk. He rubbed a leaf between his fingers and considered the camera focusing on the action. He slowed the movement to a sensuous stroking. *Close-up of hand and leaf, full frame.*

Next to the birch was an apple, so full of blossoms there was a small fall of petals puddling the ground. He pushed them about tentatively with his boot. Even without wind, more petals drifted from the tree to the ground. *Long tracking shot as narrator kicks through the pile of white flowers, lap dissolve to a single blossom.*

Standing back from the birch and the apple tree, tall and unbending, was a mature oak. It looked as if it were trying to keep the others from getting close. Its reluctance to enter the circle of trees made Jeansen move over to it. Then he smiled at his own fancies. He was often, he knew, too fanciful, yet such invention was also one of his great strengths as an actor. He took off his knapsack and set it down at the foot of the oak like an offering. Then he turned and leaned against the tree, scratching between his shoulder blades with the rough bark. *Long shot of man in grove, move in slowly for tight close-up. Voice-over.*

But when the fate of death is drawing near, First wither on the earth the beauteous trees. The bark around them wastes, the branches fall, And the Nymph's soul, at the same moment, leaves The sun's fair light.

He let two tears funnel down his cheeks. Crying was easy. He could call upon tears whenever he wanted to, even before a word was spoken in a scene. They meant nothing anymore. *Extremely tight shot on tear, then slow dissolve to . . .*

A hand touched his face, reaching around him from behind. Startled, Jeansen grabbed at the arm, held, and turned.

"Why do you water your face?"

He stared. It was a girl, scarcely in her teens, with the clearest complexion he had ever seen and flawless features, except for a crescent scar at her throat which somehow made the rest more perfect. His experienced eyes traveled quickly down her body. She was naked under a light green chiffon shift. He wondered where they had gotten her, what she wanted. A part in the special?

"Why do you water your face?" she asked again. Then this time she added, "You are a man." It was almost a question. She moved around before him and knelt unselfconsciously.

Jeansen suddenly realized she was speaking ancient Greek. He had thought her English with that skin. But the hair was black with blue-green highlights. Perhaps she *was* Greek.

He held her face in his hands and tilted it up so that she met him eye to eye. The green of her eyes was unbelievable. He thought they might be lenses, but saw no telltale double impression in the eye.

Jeansen chose his words with care, but first he smiled, the famous slow smile printed on posters and magazine covers. "You," he said, pronouncing the Greek with gentle precision, his voice carefully low and tremulous, "you are a goddess."

She leaped up and drew back, holding her hands before her. "No, no," she cried, her voice and body registering such fear that Jeansen rejected it at once. This was to be a classic play, not a horror flick.

But even if she couldn't act, she was damned beautiful. He closed his eyes for a moment, imprinting her face on his memory. And he thought for a moment of her pose, the hands held up. There had been something strange about them. She had too many—or too few—fingers. He opened his eyes to check them, and she was gone.

"Damned bit players," he muttered at last, angry to have wasted so much time on her. He took the light tent from his pack and set it up. Then he went to gather sticks for a fire. It could get pretty cold in the mountains in early spring, or so he had been warned.

From the shelter of the tree, Arrhiza watched the man. He moved gracefully, turning, gesturing, stooping. His voice was low and full of music and he spoke the prayers with great force. Why had she been warned that men were coarse, unfeeling creatures? He was far more beautiful then any of the worshippers who came cautiously at dawn in their black-beetle dresses, creeping down the paths like great nicophorus from the hidden chambers of earth, to lift their year-scarred faces to the sky. They brought only jars of milk, honey, and oil, but he came bringing a kind of springy joy. And had he not wept when speaking of the death of trees, the streams from his eyes as crystal as any that ran near the grove? Clearly this man was neither coarse nor unfeeling.

A small breeze stirred the top branches, and Arrhiza glanced up for a moment, but even the sky could not hold her interest today. She looked back at the stranger, who was pulling oddments from his pack. He pounded small nails into the earth, wounding it with every blow, yet did not fear its cries.

Arrhiza was shocked. What could he be doing? Then she realized he was erecting a dwelling of some kind. It was unthinkable—yet this stranger had thought it. No votary would dare stay in a sacred grove past sunfall, dare carve up the soil on which the trees of the Huntress grew. To even think of being near when the Dance began was a desecration. And to see the Huntress, should She visit this glade at moonrise, was to invite death. Arrhiza shivered. She was well-schooled in the history of Acteon, torn by his own dogs for the crime of spying upon Her.

Yet this man was unafraid. As he worked, he raised his voice—speaking, laughing, weeping, singing. He touched the trees with bold, unshaking hands. It was the trees, not the man, who trembled at his touch. Arrhiza shivered again, remembering the feel of him against the bark, the muscles hard under the fabric of his shirt. Not even the Huntress had such a back.

Then perhaps, she considered, this fearless votary was not a man at all. Perhaps he was a god come down to tease her, test her, take her by guile or by force. Suddenly, she longed to be wooed.

"You are a goddess," he had said. And it had frightened her. Yet only a god would dare such a statement. Only a god, such as Eros, might take time to woo. She would wait and let the night reveal him. If he remained untouched by the Huntress and unafraid, she would know.

Jeansen stood in front of the tent and watched the sun go down. It seemed to drown itself in blood, the sky bathed in an elemental red that was only slowly leeched out. Evening, however, was an uninteresting entre-act. He stirred the coals on his campfire and climbed into the tent. *Lap dissolve . . .*

Lying in the dark, an hour later, still sleepless, he thought about the night. He often went camping by himself in the California mountains, away from the telephone and his fans. *Intercut other campsites.* He knew enough to carry a weapon against marauding mountain lions or curious bears. But the silence of this Greek night was more disturbing than all the snufflings and howlings in the American dark. He had never heard anything so complete before—no crickets, no wind, no creaking of trees.

He turned restlessly and was surprised to see that the tent side facing the grove was backlit by some kind of diffused lighting. Perhaps it was the moon. It had become a screen, and shadow women seemed to dance across it in patterned friezes. It had to be a trick of his imagination, trees casting silhouettes. Yet without wind, how did they move?

As he watched, the figures came more and more into focus, clearly women. This was no trick of imagination, but of human proposing. If it was one of the columnists or some of his erstwhile friends . . . Try to frighten him, would they? He would give them a good scare instead.

He slipped into his khaki shorts and found the pistol in his pack. Moving stealthily, he stuck his head out of the tent. And froze.

Instead of the expected projector, he saw real women dancing, silently beating out a strange exotic rhythm. They touched, stepped, circled. There was no music that he could hear, yet not one of them misstepped. And each was as lovely as the girl he had met in the grove.

Jeansen wondered briefly if they were local girls hired for an evening's work. But they were each so incredibly beautiful, it seemed unlikely they could all be from any one area. Then suddenly realizing it didn't matter, that he could simply watch and enjoy it, Jeansen chuckled to himself. It was the only sound in the clearing. He settled back on his haunches and smiled.

The moon rose slowly as if reluctant to gain the sky. Arrhiza watched it silver the landscape. Tied to its rising, she was pulled into the Dance.

Yet as she danced a part of her rested still within the tree, watching. And she wondered. Always before, without willing it, she was wholly a part of the Dance. Whirling, stepping along with the other dryads, their arms, her arms; their legs, her legs. But now she felt as cleft as a tree struck by a bolt. The watching part of her trembled in anticipation.

Would the man emerge from his hasty dwelling? Would he prove himself a god? She watched and yet she dared not watch, each turn begun and ended with the thought, the fear.

And then his head appeared between the two curtains of his house, his bare shoulders, his bronzed and muscled chest. His face registered first a kind of surprise, then a kind of wonder, and at last delight. There was no fear. He laughed and his laugh was more powerful than the moon. It drew her to him and she danced slowly before her god.

Setting: moonlit glade. 30–35 girls dancing. No Busby Berkley kicklines, please. Try for a frenzied yet sensuous native dance. Robbins? Tharp? Ailey? Absolutely no dirndls. Light makeup. No spots. Diffused light. Music: an insistent pounding, feet on grass. Maybe a wild piping. Wide shot of entire dance then lap dissolve to single dancer. She begins to slow down, dizzy with anticipation, dread. Her god has chosen her . . .

Jeansen stood up as one girl turned slowly around in front of him and held out her arms. He leaned forward and caught her up, drew her to him.

A god is different, thought Arrhiza, as she fell into his arms. They tumbled onto the fragrant grass.

He was soft where the Huntress was hard, hard where She was soft. His smell was sharp, of earth and mold; Hers was musk and air.

"Don't leave," he whispered, though Arrhiza had made no movement to go. "I swear I'll kill myself if you leave." He pulled her gently into the canvas dwelling.

She went willingly though she knew that a god would say no such thing. Yet knowing he was but a man, she stayed and opened herself under him, drew him in, felt him shudder above her, then heavily fall. There was thunder outside the dwelling and the sound of dogs growling. Arrhiza heard it all and, hearing, did not care. The Dance outside had ended abruptly. She breathed gently in his ear, "It is done."

He grunted his acceptance and rolled over onto his side, staring at nothing, but a hero's smile playing across his face. Arrhiza put her hand over his mouth to silence him and he brought up his hand to hers. He counted the fingers with his own and sighed. It was then that the lightning struck, breaking her tree, her home, her heart, her life.

She was easy, Jeansen thought. Beautiful and silent and easy, the best sort of woman. He smiled into the dark. He was still smiling when the tree fell across the tent, bringing the canvas down around them and crushing three of his ribs. A spiky branch pierced his neck, ripping the larynx. He pulled it out frantically and tried to scream, tried to breathe. A ragged hissing of air through the hole was all that came out. He reached for the girl and fainted.

Three old women in black dresses found him in the morning. They pushed the tree off the tent, off Jeansen, and half carried, half dragged him down the mountainside. They found no girl.

He would live, the doctor said through gold and plaster teeth, smiling proudly.

Live. Jeansen turned the word over in his mind, bitterer than any tears. In Greek or in English, the word meant little to him now. *Live.* His handsome face unmarred by the fallen tree seemed to crack apart with the effort to keep from crying. He shaped the word with his lips but no sound passed them. Those beautiful, melodious words would never come again. His voice had leaked out of his neck with his blood.

Camera moves in silently for a tight close-up. Only sounds are routine hospital noises; and mounting over them to an overpowering cacophony is a steady, harsh, rasping breathing, as credits roll.

Howard Waldrop

God's Hooks!

Howard Waldrop has been called "the resident Weird Mind of his generation," and he has one of the most individual and quirky voices (and visions) in letters today. Nobody but Howard could possibly have written one of Howard's stories; in most cases, nobody but *Howard* could possibly even have *thought* of them. Nor is any one Waldrop story ever much like any previous Waldrop story, and in that respect (as well as in the *panache* and pungency of the writing, the sweep of imagination, and the depth of offbeat erudition), he resembles those other two great Uniques, R. A. Lafferty and Avram Davidson.

Waldrop is widely considered to be one of the best short-story writers in the business, and has produced some of the best short work of the last few decades, including such flamboyantly unclassifiable stories as "Mary Margaret Road-Grader," "Flying Saucer Rock & Roll," "Ike at the Mike," "Save a Place in the Lifeboat for Me," "Man Mountain Gentian," "Fair Game," "The Lions Are Asleep This Night," "Heirs of the Perisphere," "He-We-Await," "Do Ya, Do Ya, Wanna Dance?", "Night of the Cooters," and many others. His famous story "The Ugly Chickens," which can be found in my *Modern Classics of Science Fiction,* won both the Nebula Award and the World Fantasy Award in 1981.

For a while in the middle 1970s, Waldrop was being talked about as the progenitor of a subgenre of fantasy called "Outlaw Fantasy," but creating a literary movement out of the work of one eccentric genius alone is difficult, and little is heard of "Outlaw Fantasy" these days, although echoes of it are still to be found in the work of Neal Barrett, Jr., Don Webb, and Joe R. Lansdale; for a while in the mid-eighties, "Outlaw Fantasy" seemed to be evolving into what has been called "cowpunk," a cross between gonzo fantasy and the Western, but that subgenre also seems to have faded. Meanwhile, resolutely ignoring all such matters, Waldrop continues to produce his own eclectic and unclassifiable work, just as he had before. In the end, perhaps all that can usefully be said about a Waldrop Story, as far as classification is concerned, is that it is a Waldrop Story.

Waldrop's work has been gathered in three collections: *Howard Who?*, *All About Strange Monsters of the Recent Past: Neat Stories by Howard Waldrop,* and *Night of the Cooters: More Neat Stories by Howard Waldrop,* with more collections in the works. Waldrop is also the author of the novel *The Texas-Israeli War: 1999,* in collaboration with Jake Saunders, and of two solo novels, *Them Bones* and *A Dozen Tough Jobs.* He is at work on a new novel, tentatively entitled *I, John Mandeville.* After spending many years as one of the best-known residents of Austin, Texas, Waldrop recently moved, and now lives in a small town outside of Seattle, Washington.

In the delightful story that follows, he takes us along on one of the most unusual fishing expeditions of all time, for the biggest fish of all . . .

They were in the End of the World Tavern at the bottom of Great Auk Street.

The place was crowded, noisy. As patrons came in, they paused to kick their boots on the floor and shake the cinders from their rough clothes.

The air smelled of wood smoke, singed hair, heated and melted glass.

"Ho!" yelled a man at one of the noisiest tables to his companions, who were dressed more finely than the workmen around them. "Here's old Izaak now, come up from Staffordshire."

A man in his seventies, dressed in brown with a wide white collar, bagged pants, and cavalier boots, stood in the doorway. He took off his high-brimmed hat and shook it against his pantsleg.

"Good evening, Charles, Percy, Mr. Marburton," he said, his gray eyes showing merry above his full white mustache and Vandyke beard.

"Father Izaak," said Charles Cotton, rising and embracing the older man. Cotton was wearing a new-style wig, whose curls and ringlets flowed onto his shoulders.

"Mr. Peale, if you please, sherry all round," yelled Cotton to the innkeeper. The older man seated himself.

"Sherry's dear," said the innkeep, "though our enemy, the King of France, is sending two ships' consignments this fortnight. The Great Fire has worked wonders."

"What matters the price when there's good fellowship?" asked Cotton.

"Price is All," said Marburton, a melancholy round man.

"Well, Father Izaak," said Charles, turning to his friend, "how looks the house on Chancery Lane?"

"Praise to God, Charles, the Fire burnt but the top floor. Enough remains to rebuild, if decent timbers can be found. Why, the lumbermen are selling green wood most expensive, and finding ready buyers."

"Their woodchoppers are working day and night in the north, since good King Charles gave them leave to cut his woods down," said Percy, and drained his glass.

"They'll not stop till all England's flat and level as Dutchman's land," said Marburton.

"If they're not careful, they'll play hob with the rivers," said Cotton.

"And the streams," said Izaak.

"And the ponds," said Percy.

"Oh, the fish!" said Marburton.

All four sighed.

"Ah, but come!" said Izaak. "No joylessness here! I'm the only one to suffer from the Fire at this table. We'll have no long faces till April! Why, there's tench and dace to be had, and pickerel! What matters the salmon's in his Neptunian rookery? Who cares that trout burrow in the mud, and bite not from coat of soot and cinders? We've the roach and the gudgeon!"

"I suffered from the Fire," said Percy.

"What? Your house lies to east," said Izaak.

"My book was at bindery at the Office of Stationers. A neighbor brought me a scorched and singed bundle of title pages. They fell sixteen miles west o' town, like snow, I suppose."

Izaak winked at Cotton. "Well, Percy, that can be set aright soon as the Stationers reopen. What you need is something right good to eat." He waved to the barkeep, who nodded and went outside to the kitchen. "I was in early and prevailed on Mr. Peale to fix a supper to cheer the dourest disposition. What with shortages, it might not pass for kings, but we are not so high. Ah, here it comes!"

Mr. Peale returned with a huge, round platter. High and thick, it smelled of fresh-baked dough, meat, and savories. It looked like a crooked pond. In a line around the outside, halves of whole pilchards stuck out, looking up at them with wide eyes, as if they had been struggling to escape being cooked.

"Oh, Izaak!" said Percy, tears of joy springing to his eyes. "A star-gazey pie!"

Peale beamed with pleasure. "It may not be the best," he said, "but it's the End o' the World!" He put a finger alongside his nose and laughed. He took great pleasure in puns.

The four men at the table fell to, elbows and pewter forks flying.

They sat back from the table, full. They said nothing for a few minutes, and stared out the great bow window of the tavern. The shop across the way blocked the view. They could not see the ruins of London which stretched–charred, black, and still smoking–from the Tower to the Temple. Only the waterfront in that great length had been spared.

On the fourth day of that Great Fire, the King had given orders to blast with gunpowder all houses in the way of the flames. It had been done, creating the breaks that, with a dying wind, had brought it under control and saved the city.

"What the city has gone through this past year!" said Percy. "It's lucky, Izaak, that you live down country, and have not suffered till now."

"They say the Fire didn't touch the worst of the Plague districts," said Marburton. "I would imagine that such large crowds milling and looking for shelter will cause another one this winter. Best we should all leave the city before we drop dead in our steps."

"Since the comet of December, year before last, there's been nothing but talk of doom on everyone's lips," said Cotton.

"Apocalypse talk," said Percy.

"Like as not it's right," said Marburton.

They heard the clanging bell of a crier at the next cross street.

The tavern was filling in the late-afternoon light. Carpenters, tradesmen covered with soot, a few soldiers all soiled came in.

"Why, the whole city seems full of chimney sweeps," said Percy.

The crier's clanging bell sounded, and he stopped before the window of the tavern.

"New edict from His Majesty Charles II to be posted concerning rebuilding of the city. New edict from Council of Aldermen on rents and leases, to be posted. An Act concerning movements of trade and shipping to new quays to become law. Assize Courts sessions to begin September 27, please God. Foreign nations to send all manner of aid to the City. Murder on New Ogden Street, felon apprehended in the act. Portent of Doom, monster fish seen in Bedford."

As one, the four men leaped from the table, causing a great stir, and ran outside to the crier.

"See to the bill, Charles," said Izaak, handing him some coins. "We'll meet at nine o' the clock at the Ironmongers' Company yard. I must go see to my tackle."

"If the man the crier sent us to spoke right, there'll be no other fish like it in England," said Percy.

"Or the world," said Marburton, whose spirits had lightened considerably.

"I imagine the length of the fish has doubled with each county the tale passed through," said Izaak.

"It'll take stout tackle," said Percy. "Me for my strongest salmon rod."

"I for my twelve-hair lines," said Marburton.

"And me," said Izzak, "to new and better angles."

The Ironmongers' Hall had escaped the Fire with only the loss of its roof. There were a few workmen about, and the Company secretary greeted Izaak cordially.

"Brother Walton," he said, "what brings you to town?" They gave each other the secret handshake and made The Sign.

"To look to my property on Chancery Lane, and the Row," he said. "But now, is there a fire in the forge downstairs?"

Below the Company Hall was a large workroom, where the more adventurous of the ironmongers experimented with new processes and materials.

"Certain there is," said the secretary. "We've been making new nails for the roof timbers."

"I'll need the forge for an hour or so. Send me down the small black case from my lockerbox, will you?"

"Oh, Brother Walton," asked the secretary. "Off again to some pellucid stream?"

"I doubt," said Walton. "But to fish, nonetheless."

Walton was in his shirt, sleeves rolled up, standing in the glow of the forge. A boy brought down the case from the upper floor, and now Izaak opened it, and took out three long gray-black bars.

"Pump away, boy," he said to the young man near the bellows, "and there's a copper in it for you."

Walton lovingly placed the metal bars, roughened by pounding years before, into the coals. Soon they began to glow redly as the teenaged boy worked furiously on the bellows-sack. He and Walton were covered with sweat.

"Lovely color, now," said the boy.

"To whom are you prenticed?" asked Walton.

"To the Company, sir."

"Ah," said Walton. "Ever seen angles forged?"

"No, sir, mostly hinges and buckles, nails like. Sir Abram Jones sometimes puddles his metal here. I have to work most furious when he's here. I sometimes don't like to see him coming."

Walton winked conspiratorially. "You're right, the metal reaches a likeable ruddy hue. Do you know what this metal is?"

"Cold iron, wasn't it? Ore beaten out?"

"No iron like you've seen, or me much either. I've saved it for nineteen years. It came from the sky, and was given to me by a great scientific man at whose feet it nearly fell."

"No!" said the boy. "I heard tell of stones falling from the sky."

"I assure you, he assured me it did. And now," said Izaak, gripping the smallest metal bar with great tongs and taking it to the anvil, "we shall tease out the fishhook that is hidden away inside."

Sparks and clanging filled the basement.

They were eight miles out of northern London before the air began to smell more of September than of Hell. Two wagons jounced along the road toward Bedford, one containing the four men, the other laden with tackle, baggage, and canvas.

"This is rough enough," said Cotton. "We could have sent for my coach!"

"And lost four hours," said Marburton. "These fellows were idle enough, and Izaak wanted an especially heavy cart for some reason. Izaak, you've been most mysterious. We saw neither your tackles nor your baits."

"Suffice to say, they are none too strong nor none too delicate for the work at hand."

Away from the town, there was a touch of coming autumn in the air.

"We might find nothing there," said Marburton, whose spirits had sunk again. "Or some damnably small salmon."

"Why then," said Izaak, "we'll have Bedfordshire to our own, and all of September, and perhaps an inn where the smell of lavender is in the sheets and there are twenty printed ballads on the wall!"

"Hmmph!" said Marburton.

At noon of the next day, they stopped to water the horses and eat.

"I venture to try the trout in this stream," said Percy.

"Come, come," said Cotton. "Our goal is Bedford, and we seek Leviathan himself! Would you tempt sport by angling here?"

"But a brace of trouts would be fine now."

"Have some more cold mutton," said Marburton. He passed out bread and cheese and meat all around. The drivers tugged their forelocks to him and put away their rougher fare.

"How far to Bedford?" asked Cotton of the driver called Humphrey.

"Ten miles, sir, more or less. We should have come farther but, what with the Plague, the roads haven't been worked in above a year."

"I'm bruised through and through," said Marburton.

Izaak was at the stream, relieving himself against a tree.

"Damn me!" said Percy. "Did anyone leave word where I was bound?"

Marburton laughed. "Izaak sent word to all our families. Always considerate."

"Well, he's become secretive enough. All those people following him a-angling since his book went back to the presses the third time. Ah, books!" Percy grew silent.

"What, still lamenting your loss?" asked Izaak, returning. "What you need is singing, the air, sunshine. Are we not Brothers of the Angle, out a-fishing? Come, back into the carts! Charles, start us off on 'Tom o' the Town.' "

Cotton began to sing, in a clear sweet voice, the first stanza. One by one the others joined, their voices echoing under the bridge. The carts pulled back on the roads. The driver of the baggage cart sang with them. They went down the rutted Bedford road, September all about them, the long summer after the Plague over, their losses, heartaches all gone, all deep thoughts put away. The horses clopped time to their singing.

Bedford was a town surrounded by villages, where they were stared at when they went through. The town was divided neatly in two by the double-gated bridge over the River Ouse.

After the carts crossed the bridge, they alighted at the doorway of a place called the Topsy-Turvey Inn, whose sign above the door was a world globe turned arse-over-teakettle.

The people who stood by the inn were all looking up the road, where a small crowd had gathered around a man who was preaching from a stump.

"I think," said Cotton, as they pulled their baggage from the cart, "that we're in Dissenter country."

"Of that I'm sure," said Walton. "But once we Anglicans were on the outs and they'd say the same of us."

One of the drivers was listening to the man preach. So was Marburton.

The preacher was dressed in somber clothes. He stood on a stump at two cross streets. He was stout and had brown-red hair that glistened in the sun. His mustache was an unruly wild thing on his lip, but his beard was a neat red spike on his chin. He stood with his head uncovered, a great worn clasp Bible under his arm.

"London burned clean through," he was saying. "Forty-three parish churches razed. Plagues! Fires! Signs in the skies of the sure and certain return of Christ. The Earth swept clean by God's loving mercy. I ask you sinners to repent for the sake of your souls."

A man walking by on the other side of the street slowed, listened, stopped.

"Oh, this is Tuesday!" he yelled to the preacher. "Save your rantings for the Sabbath, you old jailbird!"

A few people in the crowd laughed, but others shushed him.

"In my heart," said the man on the stump, "it is always the Sabbath as long as there are sinners among you."

"Ah, a fig to your damned sneaking disloyal NonConformist drivel!" said the heckler, holding his thumb up between his fingers.

"Wasn't I once as you are now?" asked the preacher. "Didn't I curse and swear, play at tipcat, ring bells, cause commotion wherever I went? Didn't God's forgiving Grace . . . ?"

A constable hurried up.

"Here, John," he said to the stout preacher. "There's to be no sermons, you know that!" He waved his staff of office. "And I charge you all under the Act of 13 Elizabeth 53 to go about your several businesses."

"Let him go on, Harry," yelled a woman. "He's got words for sinners."

"I can't argue that. I can only tell you the law. The sheriff's about on dire business, and he'd have John back in jail and the jailer turned out in a trice. Come down off the stump, man."

The stout man waved his arms. "We must disperse, friends. The Sabbath meeting will be at . . ."

The constable clapped his hands over his ears and turned his back until the preacher finished giving directions to some obscure clearing in a woods. The red-haired man stepped down.

Walton had been listening and staring at him, as had the others. Izaak saw that the man had a bag of his tools of the trade with him. He was obviously a coppersmith or brazier, his small anvils, tongs, and taphammers identifying him as such. But he was no ironmonger, so Walton was not duty-bound to be courteous to him.

"Damnable Dissenters indeed," said Cotton. "Come, Father Izaak, let's to this hospitable inn."

A crier appeared at the end of the street. "Town meeting. Town meeting. All free men of the Town of Bedford and its villages to be in attendance. Levies for the taking of the Great Fish. Four of the clock in the town hall."

"Well," said Marburton, "that's where we shall be."

They returned to the inn at dusk.

"They're certainly going at this thing full-tilt," said Percy. "Nets, pikes, muskets."

"If those children had not been new to the shire, they wouldn't have tried to angle there."

"And wouldn't have been eaten and mangled," said Marburton.

"A good thing the judge is both angler and reader," said Cotton. "Else Father Walton wouldn't have been given all the morrow to prove our mettle against this great scaly beast."

"If it have scales," said Marburton.

"I fear our tackle is not up to it," said Percy.

"Didn't Father Walton always say that an angler stores up his tackle against the day he needs it? I'll wager we get good sport out of this before it's over."

"And the description of the place! In such a narrow defile, the sunlight touches it but a few hours a day. For what possible reason would children fish there?"

"You're losing your faith, Marburton. I've seen you up to your whiskers in the River Lea, snaggling for salmon under a cutbank."

"But I, praise God, know what I'm about."

"I suppose," said Izaak, seating himself, "that the children thought so too."

They noticed the stout Dissenter preacher had come in and was talking jovially with his cronies. He lowered his voice and looked toward their table.

Most of the talk around Walton was of the receding Plague, the consequences of the Great Fire on the region's timber industry, and other matters of report.

"I expected more talk of the fish," said Percy.

"To them," said Cotton, "it's all the same. Just another odious county task, like digging a new canal or hunting down a heretic. They'll be in holiday mood day after tomorrow."

"They strike me as a cheerless lot," said Percy.

"Cheerless, but efficient. I'd hate to be the fish."

"You think we won't have it to gaff long before the workmen arrive?"

"I have my doubts," said Marburton.

"But you always do."

Next morning, the woods became thick and rank on the road they took out of town. The carts bounced in the ruts. The early sun was lost in the mists and the trees. The road rose and fell again into narrow valleys.

"Someone is following us," said Percy, getting out his spyglass.

"Probably a pedlar out this way," said Cotton, straining his eyes at the pack on the man's back.

"I've seen no cottages," said Marburton. He was taking kinks out of his fishing line.

Percy looked around him. "What a godless-looking place."

The trees were more stunted, thicker. Quick shapes, which may have been grouse, moved among their twisted boles. An occasional cry, unknown to the four anglers, came from the depths of the woods. A dull boom, as of a great door closing, sounded from far away. The horses halted, whinnying, their nostrils flared.

"In truth," said Walton from where he rested against a cushion, "I feel myself some leagues beyond Christendom."

The gloom deepened. Green was gone now, nothing but grays and browns met the eye. The road was a rocky rut. The carts rose, wheels teetering on stone, and agonizingly fell. Humphrey and the other driver swore great blazing oaths.

"Be so abusive as you will," said Cotton to them, "but take not the Lord's name in vain, for we are Christian men."

"As you say," Humphrey tugged his forelock.

The trees reached overhead, the sky was obscured. An owl swept over, startling them. Something large bolted away, feet drumming on the high bank over the road.

Percy and Cotton grew quiet. Walton talked, of lakes, streams, of summer. Seeing the others grow moody, he sang a quiet song. A driver would sometimes curse.

A droning, flapping sound grew louder, passed to their right, veered away. The horses shied then, trying to turn around in the road, almost upsetting the carts. They refused to go on.

"We'll have to tether them here," said Humphrey. "Besides, Your Lordship, I think I see water at the end of the road."

It was true. In what dim light there was, they saw a darker sheen down below.

"We must take the second cart down there, Charles," said Walton, "even if we must push it ourselves."

"We'll never make it," said Percy.

"Whatever for?" asked Cotton. "We can take our tackle and viands down there."

"Not my tackle," said Walton.

Marburton just sighed.

They pushed and pulled the second cart down the hill; from the front they kept it from running away on the incline, from the back to get it over stones the size of barrels. It was stuck.

"I can't go on," said Marburton.

"Surely you can," said Walton.

"Your cheerfulness is depressing," said Percy.

"Be that as it may. Think trout, Marburton. Think salmon!"

Marburton strained against the recalcitrant wheel. The cart moved forward a few inches.

"See, see!" said Walton. "A foot's good as a mile!"

They grunted and groaned.

They stood panting at the edge of the mere. The black sides of the valley lifted to right and left like walls. The water itself was weed-choken, scummy, and smelled of the sewer ditch. Trees came down to its very edges. Broken and rotted stumps dotted the shore. Mist rose from the water in fetid curls.

Sunlight had not yet come to the bottom of the defile. To left and right, behind, all lay in twisted woody darkness. The valley rose like a hand around them.

Except ahead. There was a break, with no trees at the center of the cleft. Through it they saw, shining and blue-purple against the cerulean of the sky, the far-off Chiltern Hills.

"Those," said a voice behind them, and they jumped and turned and saw the man with the pack. It was the stout red-haired preacher of the day before. "Those are the Delectable Mountains," he said.

"And this is the Slough of Despond."

He built a small lean-to some hundred feet from them.

The other three anglers unloaded their gear and began to set it up.

"What, Father Walton? Not setting up your poles?" asked Charles Cotton.

"No, no," said Izaak, studying the weed-clotted swamp with a sure eye. "I'll let you young ones try your luck first."

Percy looked at the waters. "The fish most likely a carp or other rough type," he said. "No respectable fish could live in this mire. I hardly see room for anything that could swallow a child."

"It is Leviathan," said the preacher from his shelter. "It is the Beast of Babylon, which shall rise in the days before Antichrist. These woods are beneath his sway."

"What do you want?" asked Cotton.

"To dissuade you, and the others who will come, from doing this. It is God's will these things come to pass."

"Oh, Hell and damn!" said Percy.

"Exactly," said the preacher.

Percy shuddered involuntarily. Daylight began to creep down to the mere's edge. With the light, the stench from the water became worse.

"You're not doing very much to stop us," said Cotton. He was fitting together an eighteen-foot rod of yew, fir, and hazelwood.

"When you raise Leviathan," said the preacher, "then will I begin to preach." He took a small cracked pot from his large bag, and began to set up his anvil.

Percy's rod had a butt as thick as a man's arm. It tapered throughout its length to a slender reed. The line was made of plaited, dyed horsehair, twelve strands at the pole end, tapering to nine. The line was forty feet long. Onto the end of this, he fastened a sinker and a hook as long as a crooked little finger.

"Where's my baits? Oh, here they are." He reached into a bag filled with wet moss, pulled out a gob of worms, and threaded seven or eight, their ends wriggling, onto the hook.

The preacher had started a small fire. He was filling an earthen pot with solder. He paid very little attention to the anglers.

Percy and Marburton, who was fishing with a shorter but thicker rod, were ready before Cotton.

"I'll take this fishy spot here," said Percy, "and you can have that grown-over place there." He pointed beyond the preacher.

"We won't catch anything," said Marburton suddenly and pulled the bait from his hook and threw it into the water. Then he walked back to the cart and sat down, and shook.

"Come, come," said Izaak. "I've never seen you so discouraged, even after fishless days on the Thames."

"Never mind me," said Marburton. Then he looked down at the ground. "I shouldn't have come all this way. I have business in the city. There are no fish here."

Cajoling could not get him up again. Izaak's face became troubled. Marburton stayed put.

"Well, I'll take the fishy spot then," said Cotton, tying onto his line an artificial fly of green with hackles the size of porcupine quills.

He moved past the preacher.

"I'm certain to wager you'll get no strikes on that gaudy bird's wing," said Percy.

"There is no better fishing than angling fine and far off," answered Cotton. "Heavens, what a stink!"

"This is the place," said the preacher without looking up, "where all the sins of mankind have been flowing for sixteen hundred years. Not twenty thousand cartloads of earth could fill it up."

"Prattle," said Cotton.

"Prattle it may be," said the preacher. He puddled solder in a sandy ring. Then he dipped the pot in it. "It stinks from mankind's sins, nonetheless."

"It stinks from mankind's bowels," said Cotton.

He made two backcasts with his long rod, letting more line out the wire guide at the tip each time. He placed the huge fly gently on the water sixty feet away.

"There are no fish about," said Percy, down the mire's edge. "Not even gudgeon."

"Nor snakes," said Cotton. "What does this monster eat?"

"Miscreant children," said the preacher. "Sin feeds on the young."

Percy made a clumsy cast into some slime-choked weeds.

His rod was pulled from his hands and flew across the water. A large dark shape blotted the pond's edge and was gone.

The rod floated to the surface and lay still. Percy stared down at his hands in disbelief. The pole came slowly in toward shore, pushed by the stinking breeze.

Cotton pulled his fly off the water, shook his line, and walked back toward the cart.

"That's all for me, too," he said. They turned to Izaak. He rubbed his hands together gleefully, making a show he did not feel.

The preacher was grinning.

"Call the carters down," said Walton. "Move the cart to the very edge of the mere."

While they were moving the wagon with its rear facing the water, Walton went over to the preacher.

"My name is Izaak Walton," he said, holding out his hand. The preacher took it formally.

"John Bunyan, mechanic-preacher," said the other.

"I hold no man's religious beliefs against him, if he be an honest man, or an angler. My friends are not of like mind, though they be both fishermen and honest."

"Would that Parliament were full of such as yourself," said Bunyan. "I took your hand, but I am dead set against what you do."

"If not us," said Walton, "then the sheriff with his powder and pikes."

"I shall prevail against them, too. This is God's warning to mankind. You're a London man. You've seen the Fire, the Plague?"

"London is no place for honest men. I'm of Stafford."

"Even you see London as a place of sin," said Bunyan. "You have children?"

"I have two, by second wife," said Walton. "Seven others died in infancy."

"I have four," Bunyan said. "One born blind." His eyes took on a faraway look. "I want them to fear God, in hope of eternal salvation."

"As do we all," said Walton.

"And this monster is warning to mankind of the coming rains of blood and fire and the fall of stars."

"Either we shall take it, or the townsmen will come tomorrow."

"I know them all," said Bunyan. "Mr. Nurse-nickel, Mr. By-your-Leave, Mr. Cravenly-Crafty. Do ye not feel your spirits lag, your backbone fail? They'll not last long as you have."

Walton had noticed his own lassitude, even with the stink of the slough goading him. Cotton, Percy and Marburton, finished with the cart, were sitting disconsolately on the ground. The swamp had brightened some; the blazing blue mountain ahead seemed inches away. But the woods were dark, the defile precipitous, the noises loud as before.

"It gets worse after dark," said the preacher. "I beg you, take not the fish."

"If you stop the sheriff, he'll have you in prison."

"It's prison from which I come," said Bunyan. "To jail I shall go back, for I know I'm right."

"Do your conscience," said Walton, "for that way lies salvation."

"Amen!" said Bunyan, and went back to his pots.

* * *

Percy, Marburton, and Charles Cotton watched as Walton set up his tackle. Even with flagging spirits, they were intrigued. He'd had the carters peg down the trace poles of the wagon. Then he sectioned together a rod like none they had seen before. It was barely nine feet long, starting big as a smith's biceps, ending in a fine end. It was made of many split laths glued seamlessly together. On each foot of its length past the handle were iron guides bound with wire. There was a hole in the handle of the rod, and now Walton reached in the wagon and took out a shining metal wheel.

"What's that, a squirrel cage?" asked Percy.

They saw him pull line out from it. It clicked with each turn. There was a handle on the wheel, and a peg at the bottom. He put the peg through the hole in the handle and fastened it down with an iron screw.

He threaded the line, which was thick as a pen quill, through the guides, opened the black case, and took out the largest of the hooks he'd fashioned.

On the line he tied a strong wire chain, and affixed a sinker to one end and the hook on the other.

He put the rod in the wagon seat and climbed down to the back and opened his bait box and reached in.

"Come, my pretty," he said, reaching. He took something out, white, segmented, moving. It filled his hand.

It was a maggot that weighed half a pound.

"I had them kept down a cistern behind a shambles," said Walton. He lifted the bait to show them. "Charles, take my line after I bait the angle; make a handcast into the edge of those stumps yonder. As I was saying, take your gentles, put them in a cool well, feed them on liver or pork for the summer. They'll eat and grow and not change to flies, for the changing of one so large kills it. Keep them well fed; put them into wet moss before using them. I feared the commotion and flames had collapsed the well. Though the butcher shop was gone, the baits were still fat and lively."

As he said the last word, he plunged the hook through the white flesh of the maggot.

It twisted and oozed onto his hand. He opened a small bottle. "And dowse it with camphire oil just before the cast." They smelled the pungent liquid as he poured it. The bait went into a frenzy.

"Now, Charles," he said, pulling off fifty feet of line from the reel. Cotton whirled the weighted hook around and around his head. "Be so kind as to tie this rope to my belt and the cart, Percy," said Walton.

Percy did so. Cotton made the hand-cast, the pale globule hitting the water and sinking.

"Do as I have told you," said Walton, "and you shall not fail to catch the biggest fish."

Something large between the eyes swallowed the hook and five feet of line.

"And set the hook sharply, and you shall have great sport." Walton, seventy years old, thin of build, stood in the seat, jerked far back over his head, curving the rod in a loop.

The waters of the slough exploded, they saw the shallow bottom and a long dark shape, and the fight was on.

The preacher stood up from his pots, opened his clasp Bible, and began to preach in a loud strong voice.

"Render to Caesar," he said: Walton flinched and put his back into turning the fish, which was heading toward the stumps. The reel's clicks were a buzz. Bunyan raised his voice: "Those things which are Caesar's, and to God those things which are God's."

"Oh, shut up!" said Cotton. "The man's got trouble enough!"

The wagon creaked and began to lift off the ground. The rope and belt cut into Walton's flesh. His arms were nearly pulled from their sockets. Sweat sprang to his forehead like curds through a cheesecloth. He gritted his teeth and pulled.

The pegs lifted from the ground.

Bunyan preached on.

The sunlight faded, though it was late afternoon. The noise from the woods grew louder. The blue hills in the distance became flat, gray. The whole valley leaned over them, threatening to fall over and kill them. Eyes shined in the deeper woods.

Walton had regained some line in the last few hours. Bunyan preached on, pausing long enough to light a horn lantern from his fire.

After encouraging Walton at first, Percy, Marburton and Cotton had become quiet. The sounds were those of Bunyan's droning voice, screams from the woods, small pops from the fire, and the ratcheting of the reel.

The fish was fighting him on the bottom. He'd had no sight of it yet since the strike. Now the water was becoming a flat black sheet in the failing light. It was no salmon or trout or carp. It must be a pike or eel or some other toothed fish. Or a serpent. Or cuttlefish, with squiddy arms to tear the skin from a man.

Walton shivered. His arms were numb, his shoulders a tight aching band. His legs where he braced against the footrest quivered with fatigue. Still he held, even when the fish ran to the far end of the swamp. If he could keep it away from the snags, he could wear it down. The fish turned, the line slackened, Walton pumped the rod up and down. He regained the lost line. The water hissed as the cording cut through it. The fish headed for the bottom.

Tiredly, Walton heaved, turned the fish. The wagon creaked.

"Blessed are they that walk in the path of righteousness," said Bunyan.

The ghosts came in over the slough straight at them. Monkey-demons began to chatter in the woods. Eyes peered from the bole of every tree. Bunyan's candle was the only light. Something walked heavily on a limb at the woods' edge, bending it. Marburton screamed and ran up the road.

Percy was on his feet. Ghosts and banshees flew at him, veering away at the last instant.

"You have doubts," said Bunyan to him. "You are assailed. You think yourself unworthy."

Percy trotted up the stony road, ragged shapes fluttering in the air behind him, trying to tug his hair. Skeletons began to dance across the slough, acting out pantomimes of life, death, and love. The Seven Deadly Sins manifested themselves.

Hell yawned opened to receive them all.

Then the sun went down.

"Before you join the others, Charles," said Walton, pumping the rod, "cut away my coat and collar."

"You'll freeze," said Cotton, but climbed into the wagon and cut the coat up the back and down the sleeves. It and the collar fell away.

"Good luck, Father Walton," he said. Something plucked at his eyes. "We go to town for help."

"Be honest and trustworthy all the rest of your days," said Izaak Walton. Cotton looked stunned. Something large ran down from the woods, through the wagon, and up into the trees. Cotton ran up the hill. The thing loped after him.

Walton managed to gain six inches on the fish.

Grinning things sat on the taut line. The air was filled with meteors: burning, red, thick as snow. Huge worms pushed themselves out of the ground, caught and ate demons, then turned inside out. The demons flew away.

Everything in the darkness had claws and horns.

"And lo! the seventh seal was broken, and there was quietness on the earth for the space of half an hour," read Bunyan.

He had lit his third candle.

Walton could see the water again. A little light came from somewhere behind him. The noises of the woods diminished. A desultory ghost or skeleton flitted grayly by. There was a calm in the air.

The fish was tiring. Walton did not know how long he had fought on, or with what power. He was a human ache, and he wanted to sleep. He was nodding.

"The townsmen come," said Bunyan. Walton stole a fleeting glance behind him. Hundreds of people came quietly and cautiously through the woods, some extinguishing torches as he watched.

Walton cranked in another ten feet of line. The fish ran, but only a short way, slowly, and Walton reeled him back. It was still a long way out, still another hour before he could bring it to gaff. Walton heard low talk, recognized Percy's voice. He looked back again. The people had pikes, nets, a small cannon. He turned, reeled the fish, fighting it all the way.

"You do not love God!" said Bunyan suddenly, shutting his Bible.

"Yes I do!" said Walton, pulling as hard as he could. He gained another foot. "I love God as much as you."

"You do not!" said Bunyan. "I see it now."

"I love God!" yelled Walton and heaved the rod.

A fin broke the frothing water.

"In your heart, where God can see from his high throne, you lie!" said Bunyan.

Walton reeled and pulled. More fin showed. He quit cranking.

"God forgive me!" said Walton. "It's fishing I love."

"I thought so," said Bunyan. Reaching in his pack, he took out a pair of tin snips and cut Walton's line.

Izaak fell back in the wagon.

"John Bunyan, you son of a bitch!" said the sheriff. "You're under arrest for hampering the King's business. I'll see you rot."

Walton watched the coils of line on the surface slowly sink into the brown depths of the Slough of Despond.

He began to cry, fatigue and numbness taking over his body.

"I denied God," he said to Cotton. "I committed the worst sin." Cotton covered him with a blanket.

"Oh, Charles, I denied God."

"What's worse," said Cotton, "you lost the fish."

Percy and Marburton helped him up. The carters hitched the wagons, the horses now docile. Bunyan was being ridden back to jail by constables, his tinker's bag clanging against the horse's side.

They put the crying Walton into the cart, covered him more, climbed in. Some farmers helped them get the carts over the rocks.

Walton's last view of the slough was of resolute and grim-faced men staring at the water and readying their huge grapples, their guns, their cruel hooked nets.

They were on the road back to town. Walton looked up into the trees, devoid of ghosts and demons. He caught a glimpse of the blue Chiltern Hills.

"Father Izaak," said Cotton. "Rest now. Think of spring. Think of clear water, of leaping trout."

"My dreams will be haunted by God the rest of my days," he said tiredly. Walton fell asleep.

He dreamed of clear water, leaping trouts.

This story is for Chad Oliver, Punisher of Trouts.

LUCIUS SHEPARD

The Man Who Painted the Dragon Griaule

Although Lucius Shepard's work in general probably leans more toward horror than fantasy, the brilliant story that follows was one of the most popular and talked-about pieces of fantasy short fiction of the 1980s, and was followed by other related (and also well-received stories) such as "The Scalehunter's Beautiful Daughter" and "The Father of Stones." It takes place in a land dominated by the immobile but still-living body of an immense, mountain-huge dragon, enchanted into stillness in some sorcerous battle in the unimaginably distant past, so long ago that forests and villages have sprung up along the dragon's mountainous flanks. But, as we shall see, even into the lifetime of such a creature, change must come—sometimes even change of the most elemental and revolutionary sort . . .

Lucius Shepard was perhaps the most popular and influential new writer of the 1980s, rivaled for that title only by William Gibson, Connie Willis, and Kim Stanley Robinson. Shepard won the John W. Campbell Award in 1985 as the year's Best New Writer, and few years since have gone by without him adorning the final ballot for one major award or another, and often for several. In 1987, he won the Nebula Award for his landmark novella "R & R"; in 1988, he picked up a World Fantasy Award for his monumental short-story collection *The Jaguar Hunter,* following it in 1992 with a second World Fantasy Award for his second collection, *The Ends of the Earth;* and in 1993 he won the Hugo Award for his novella "Barnacle Bill the Spacer." His novels include *Green Eyes,* the best-selling *Life during Wartime, Kalimantan,* and *The Golden.* He's currently at work on a mainstream novel, *Family Values.* Born in Lynchburg, Virginia, he now lives in Seattle, Washington.

" . . . *Other than the Sichi Collection, Cattanay's only surviving works are to be found in the Municipal Gallery at Regensburg, a group of eight oils-on-*

canvas, most notable among them being Woman with Oranges. *These paintings constitute his portion of a student exhibition hung some weeks after he had left the city of his birth and traveled south to Teocinte, there to present his proposal to the city fathers; it is unlikely he ever learned of the disposition of his work, and even more unlikely that he was aware of the general critical indifference with which it was received. Perhaps the most interesting of the group to modern scholars, the most indicative as to Cattanay's later preoccupations, is the* Self Portrait, *painted at the age of twenty-eight, a year before his departure.*

"The majority of the canvas is a richly varnished black in which the vague shapes of floorboards are presented, barely visible. Two irregular slashes of gold cross the blackness, and within these we can see a section of the artist's thin features and the shoulder panel of his shirt. The perspective given is that we are looking down at the artist, perhaps through a tear in the roof, and that he is looking up at us, squinting into the light, his mouth distorted by a grimace born of intense concentration. On first viewing the painting, I was struck by the atmosphere of tension that radiated from it. It seemed I was spying upon a man imprisoned within a shadow having two golden bars, tormented by the possibilities of light beyond the walls. And though this may be the reaction of the art historian, not the less knowledgeable and therefore more trustworthy response of the gallery-goer, it also seemed that this imprisonment was self-imposed, that he could have easily escaped his confine; but that he had realized a feeling of stricture was an essential fuel to his ambition, and so had chained himself to this arduous and thoroughly unreasonable chore of perception. . . ."

—from *Meric Cattanay: The Politics of Conception*
by Reade Holland, Ph.D.

I

In 1853, in a country far to the south, in a world separated from this one by the thinnest margin of possibility, a dragon named Griaule dominated the region of the Carbonales Valley, a fertile area centering upon the town of Teocinte and renowned for its production of silver, mahogany, and indigo. There were other dragons in those days, most dwelling on the rocky islands west of Patagonia—tiny, irascible creatures, the largest of them no bigger than a swallow. But Griaule was one of the great Beasts who had ruled an age. Over the centuries he had grown to stand 750 feet high at the midback, and from the tip of his tail to his nose he was 6,000 feet long. (It should be noted here that the growth of dragons was due not to caloric intake, but to the absorption of energy derived from the passage of time.) Had it not been for a miscast spell, Griaule would have died millennia before. The wizard entrusted with the task of slaying him—

knowing his own life would be forfeited as a result of the magical back-wash—had experienced a last-second twinge of fear, and, diminished by this ounce of courage, the spell had flown a mortal inch awry. Though the wizard's whereabouts were unknown, Griaule had remained alive. His heart had stopped, his breath stilled, but his mind continued to seethe, to send forth the gloomy vibrations that enslaved all who stayed for long within range of his influence.

This dominance of Griaule's was an elusive thing. The people of the valley attributed their dour character to years of living under his mental shadow, yet there were other regional populations who maintained a harsh face to the world and had no dragon on which to blame the condition; they also attributed their frequent raids against the neighboring states to Griaule's effect, claiming to be a peaceful folk at heart—but again, was this not human nature? Perhaps the most certifiable proof of Griaule's primacy was the fact that despite a standing offer of a fortune in silver to anyone who could kill him, no one had succeeded. Hundreds of plans had been put forward, and all had failed, either through inanition or impracticality. The archives of Teocinte were filled with schematics for enormous steam-powered swords and other such improbable devices, and the architects of these plans had every one stayed too long in the valley and become part of the disgruntled populace. And so they went on with their lives, coming and going, always returning, bound to the valley, until one spring day in 1853, Meric Cattanay arrived and proposed that the dragon be painted.

He was a lanky young man with a shock of black hair and a pinched look to his cheeks; he affected the loose trousers and shirt of a peasant, and waved his arms to make a point. His eyes grew wide when listening, as if his brain were bursting with illumination, and at times he talked incoherently about "the conceptual statement of death by art." And though the city fathers could not be sure, though they allowed for the possibility that he simply had an unfortunate manner, it seemed he was mocking them. All in all, he was not the sort they were inclined to trust. But, because he had come armed with such a wealth of diagrams and charts, they were forced to give him serious consideration.

"I don't believe Griaule will be able to perceive the menace in a process as subtle as art," Meric told them. "We'll proceed as if we were going to illustrate him, grace his side with a work of true vision, and all the while we'll be poisoning him with the paint."

The city fathers voiced their incredulity, and Meric waited impatiently until they quieted. He did not enjoy dealing with these worthies. Seated at their long table, sour-faced, a huge smudge of soot on the wall about their heads like an ugly thought they were sharing, they reminded him of the Wine Merchants Association in Regensburg, the time they had rejected his group portrait.

"Paint can be deadly stuff," he said after their muttering had died down. "Take vert Veronese, for example. It's derived from oxide of chrome and barium. Just a whiff would make you keel over. But we have to go about it seriously, create a real piece of art. If we just slap paint on his side, he might see through us."

The first step in the process, he told them, would be to build a tower of scaffolding, complete with hoists and ladders, that would brace against the supraocular plates above the dragon's eye; this would provide a direct route to a seven-hundred-foot-square loading platform and base station behind the eye. He estimated it would take eighty-one thousand board feet of lumber, and a crew of ninety men should be able to finish construction within five months. Ground crews accompanied by chemists and geologists would search out limestone deposits (useful in priming the scales) and sources of pigments, whether organic or minerals such as azurite and hematite. Other teams would be set to scraping the dragon's side clean of algae, peeled skin, any decayed material, and afterward would laminate the surface with resins.

"It would be easier to bleach him with quicklime," he said. "But that way we lose the discolorations and ridges generated by growth and age, and I think what we'll paint will be defined by those shapes. Anything else would look like a damn tattoo!"

There would be storage vats and mills: edge-runner mills to separate pigments from crude ores, ball mills to powder the pigments, pug mills to mix them with oil. There would be boiling vats and calciners—fifteen-foot-high furnaces used to produce caustic lime for sealant solutions.

"We'll build most of them atop the dragon's head for purposes of access," he said. "On the frontoparital plate." He checked some figures. "By my reckoning, the plate's about 350 feet wide. Does that sound accurate?"

Most of the city fathers were stunned by the prospect, but one managed a nod, and another asked, "How long will it take for him to die?"

"Hard to say," came the answer. "Who knows how much poison he's capable of absorbing. It might just take a few years. But in the worst instance, within forty or fifty years, enough chemicals will have seeped through the scales to have weakened the skeleton, and he'll fall in like an old barn."

"Forty years!" exclaimed someone. "Preposterous!"

"Or fifty." Meric smiled. "That way we'll have time to finish the painting." He turned and walked to the window and stood gazing out at the white stone houses of Teocinte. This was going to be the sticky part, but if he read them right, they would not believe in the plan if it seemed too easy. They needed to feel they were making a sacrifice, that they were nobly bound to a great labor. "If it does take forty or fifty years," he went on, "the project will drain your resources. Timber, animal life, minerals. Everything will be used up by the work. Your lives will be totally changed. But I guarantee you'll be rid of him."

The city fathers broke into an outraged babble.

"Do you really want to kill him?" cried Meric, stalking over to them and planting his fists on the table. "You've been waiting centuries for someone to come along and chop off his head or send him up in a puff of smoke. That's not going to happen! There is no easy solution. But there is a practical one, an elegant one. To use the stuff of the land he dominates to destroy him. It will *not* be easy, but you *will* be rid of him. And that's what you want, isn't it?"

They were silent, exchanging glances, and he saw that they now believed he could do what he proposed and were wondering if the cost was too high.

"I'll need five hundred ounces of silver to hire engineers and artisans," said Meric. "Think it over. I'll take a few days and go see this dragon of yours . . . inspect the scales and so forth. When I return, you can give me your answer."

The city fathers grumbled and scratched their heads, but at last they agreed to put the question before the body politic. They asked for a week in which to decide and appointed Jarcke, who was the mayoress of Hangtown, to guide Meric to Griaule.

The valley extended seventy miles from north to south, and was enclosed by jungled hills whose folded sides and spiny backs gave rise to the idea that beasts were sleeping beneath them. The valley floor was cultivated into fields of bananas and cane and melons, and where it was not cultivated, there were stands of thistle palms and berry thickets and the occasional giant fig brooding sentinel over the rest. Jarcke and Meric tethered their horses a half hour's ride from town and began to ascend a gentle incline that rose into the notch between two hills. Sweaty and short of breath, Meric stopped a third of the way up; but Jarcke kept plodding along, unaware he was no longer following. She was by nature as blunt as her name—a stump beer keg of a woman with a brown, weathered face. Though she appeared to be ten years older than Meric, she was nearly the same age. She wore a gray robe belted at the waist with a leather band that held four throwing knives, and a coil of rope was slung over her shoulder.

"How much further?" called Meric.

She turned and frowned. "You're standin' on his tail. Rest of him's around back of the hill."

A pinprick of chill bloomed in Meric's abdomen, and he stared down at the grass, expecting it to dissolve and reveal a mass of glittering scales.

"Why don't we take the horses?" he asked.

"Horses don't like it up here." She grunted with amusement. "Neither do most people, for that matter." She trudged off.

Another twenty minutes brought them to the other side of the hill high above the valley floor. The land continued to slope upward, but more gently than before. Gnarled, stunted oaks pushed up from thickets of chokecherry, and insects sizzled in the weeds. They might have been walking on a natural shelf several hundred feet across; but ahead of them, where the ground rose abruptly, a number of thick, greenish black columns broke from the earth. Leathery folds hung between them, and these were encrusted with clumps of earth and brocaded with mold. They had the look of a collapsed palisade and the ghosted feel of ancient ruins.

"Them's the wings," said Jarcke. "Mostly they's covered, but you can catch sight of 'em off the edge, and up near Hangtown there's places where you can walk under 'em . . . but I wouldn't advise it."

"I'd like to take a look off the edge," said Meric, unable to tear his eyes away from the wings; though the surfaces of the leaves gleamed in the strong sun, the wings seemed to absorb the light, as if their age and strangeness were proof against reflection.

Jarcke led him to a glade in which tree ferns and oaks crowded together and cast a green gloom, and where the earth sloped sharply downward. She lashed her rope to an oak and tied the other end around Meric's waist. "Give a yank when you want to stop, and another when you want to be hauled up," she said, and began paying out the rope, letting him walk backward against her pull.

Ferns tickled Meric's neck as he pushed through the brush, and the oak leaves pricked his cheeks. Suddenly he emerged into bright sunlight. On looking down, he found his feet were braced against a fold of the dragon's wing, and on looking up, he saw that the wing vanished beneath a mantle of earth and vegetation. He let Jarcke lower him a dozen feet more, yanked, and gazed off northward along the enormous swell of Griaule's side.

The swells were hexagonals thirty feet across and half that distance high; their basic color was a pale greenish gold, but some were whitish, draped with peels of dead skin, and others were overgrown by viridian moss, and the rest were scrolled with patterns of lichen and algae that resembled the characters of a serpentine alphabet. Birds had nested in the cracks, and ferns plumed from the interstices, thousands of them lifting in the breeze. It was a great hanging garden whose scope took Meric's breath away—like looking around the curve of a fossil moon. The sense of all the centuries accreted in the scales made him dizzy, and he found he could not turn his head, but could only stare at the panorama, his soul shriveling with a comprehension of the timelessness and bulk of this creature to which he clung like a fly. He lost perspective on the scene—Griaule's side was bigger than the sky, possessing its own potent gravity, and it seemed completely reasonable that he should be able to walk out along it and suffer no fall. He started to do so, and Jarcke, mistaking the strain on the rope for signal, hauled him up, dragging him across the wing, through the dirt and ferns, and back into the glade. He lay speechless and gasping at her feet.

"Big 'un, ain't he," she said, and grinned.

After Meric had gotten his legs under him, they set off toward Hangtown; but they had not gone a hundred yards, following a trail that wound through the thickets, before Jarcke whipped out a knife and hurled it at a raccoon-sized creature that leaped out in front of them.

"Skizzer," she said, kneeling beside it and pulling the knife from its neck. "Calls 'em that 'cause they hisses when they runs. They eats snakes, but they'll go after children what ain't careful."

Meric dropped down next to her. The skizzer's body was covered with short black fur, but its head was hairless, corpse-pale, the skin wrinkled as if it had been immersed too long in water. Its face was squinty-eyed, flat-nosed, with a disproportionately large jaw that hinged open to expose a nasty set of teeth.

"They's the dragon's critters," said Jarcke. "Used to live in his bunghole." She pressed one of its paws, and claws curved like hooks slid forth. "They'd hang around the lip and drop on other critters what wandered in. And if nothing' wandered in . . ." She pried out the tongue with her knife—its surface was studded with jagged points like the blade of a rasp. "Then they'd lick Griaule clean for their supper."

Back in Teocinte, the dragon had seemed to Meric a simple thing, a big lizard with a tick of life left inside, the residue of a dim sensibility; but he was beginning to suspect that this tick of life was more complex than any he had encountered.

"My gram used to say," Jarcke went on, "that the old dragons could fling themselves up to the sun in a blink and travel back to their own world, and when they come back, they'd bring the skizzers and all the rest with 'em. They was immortal, she said. Only the young ones came here 'cause later on they grew too big to fly on Earth." She made a sour face. "Don't know as I believe it."

"Then you're a fool," said Meric.

Jarcke glanced up at him, her hand twitching toward her belt.

"How can you live here and *not* believe it!" he said, surprised to hear himself so fervently defending a myth. "God! This . . ." He broke off, noticing the flicker of a smile on her face.

She clucked her tongue, apparently satisfied by something. "Come on," she said. "I want to be at the eye before sunset."

The peaks of Griaule's folded wings, completely overgrown by grass and shrubs and dwarfish trees, formed two spiny hills that cast a shadow over Hangtown and the narrow lake around which it sprawled. Jarcke said the lake was a stream flowing off the hill behind the dragon, and that it drained away through the membranes of his wing and down onto his shoulder. It was beautiful beneath the wing, she told him. Ferns and waterfalls. But it was reckoned an evil place. From a distance the town looked picturesque—rustic cabins, smoking chimneys. As they approached, however, the cabins resolved into dilapidated shanties with missing boards and broken windows; suds and garbage and offal floated in the shallows of the lake. Aside from a few men idling on the stoops, who squinted at Meric and nodded glumly at Jarcke, no one was about. The grass blades stirred in the breeze, spiders scuttled under the shanties, and there was an air of torpor and dissolution.

Jarcke seemed embarrassed by the town. She made no attempt at introductions, stopping only long enough to fetch another coil of rope from one of the shanties, and as they walked between the wings, down through the neck spines—a forest of greenish gold spikes burnished by the lowering sun—she explained how the townsfolk grubbed a livelihood from Griaule. Herbs gathered on his back were valued as medicine and charms, as were the peels of dead skin; the artifacts left by previous Hangtown generations were of some worth to various collectors.

"Then there's scale hunters," she said with disgust. "Henry Sichi from Port Chantay'll pay good money for pieces of scale, and though it's bad luck to do it, some'll have a go at chippin' off the loose 'uns." She walked a few paces in silence. "But there's others who've got better reasons for livin' here."

The frontal spike above Griaule's eyes was whorled at the base like a narwhal's horn and curved back toward the wings. Jarcke attached the ropes to eyebolts drilled into the spike, tied one about her waist, the other about Meric's; she cautioned him to wait, and rappelled off the side. In a moment she called for him to come down. Once again he grew dizzy as he descended; he glimpsed a clawed foot far below, mossy fangs jutting from an impossibly long jaw; and then he began to spin and bash against the scales. Jarcke gathered him in and helped him sit on the lip of the socket.

"Damn!" she said, stamping her foot.

A three-foot-long section of the adjoining scale shifted slowly away. Peering close, Meric saw that while in texture and hue it was indistinguishable from the scale, there was a hairline division between it and the surface. Jarcke, her face twisted in disgust, continued to harry the thing until it moved out of reach.

"Call 'em flakes," she said when he asked what it was. "Some kind of insect. Got a long tube that they pokes down between the scales and sucks the blood. See there?" She pointed off to where a flock of birds were wheeling close to Griaule's side; a chip of pale gold broke loose and went tumbling down to the valley. "Birds pry 'em off, let 'em bust open, and eats the innards." She hunkered down beside him and after a moment asked, "You really think you can do it?"

"What? You mean kill the dragon?"

She nodded.

"Certainly," he said, and then added, lying, "I've spent years devising the method."

"If all the paint's goin' to be atop his head, how're you goin' to get it to where the paintin's done?"

"That's no problem. We'll pipe it to wherever it's needed."

She nodded again. "You're a clever fellow," she said; and when Meric, pleased, made as if to thank her for the compliment, she cut in and said, "Don't mean nothin' by it. Bein' clever ain't an accomplishment. It's just somethin' you come by, like bein' tall." She turned away, ending the conversation.

Meric was weary of being awestruck, but even so he could not help marveling at the eye. By his estimate it was seventy feet long and fifty feet high, and it was shuttered by an opaque membrane that was unusually clear of algae and lichen, glistening, with vague glints of color visible behind it. As the westering sun reddened and sank between two distant hills, the membrane began to quiver and then split open down the center. With the ponderous slowness of a theater curtain opening, the halves slid apart to reveal the glowing humor. Terrified by the idea that Griaule could see him, Meric sprang to his feet, but Jarcke restrained him.

"Stay still and watch," she said.

He had no choice—the eye was mesmerizing. The pupil was slit and featureless black, but the humor . . . he had never seen such fiery blues and crimsons and golds. What had looked to be vague glints, odd refractions of the sunset, he now realized were photic reactions of some sort. Fairy rings of light developed deep within the eye, expanded into spooked shapes, flooded the humor, and faded—only to be replaced by another and another. He felt the pressure of Griaule's vision, his ancient mind, pouring through him, and as if in response to this pressure, memories bubbled up in his thoughts. Particularly sharp ones. The way a bowlful of brush water had looked after freezing over during a winter's night—a delicate, fractured flower of murky yellow. An archipelago of orange peels that his girl had left strewn across the floor of the studio. Sketching atop Jokenam Hill one sunrise, the snow-capped roofs of Regensburg below pitched at all angles like broken paving stones, and silver shafts of the sun striking down through a leaden overcast. It was as if these things were being drawn forth for his inspection. Then they were washed away by what also seemed a memory, though at the same time it was wholly unfamiliar. Essentially, it was a landscape of light, and he was plunging through it, up and up. Prisms and lattices of iridescent fire bloomed around him, and everything was a roaring fall into brightness, and finally he was clear into its white furnace heart, his own heart swelling with the joy of his strength and dominion.

It was dusk before Meric realized the eye had closed. His mouth hung open, his eyes ached from straining to see, and his tongue was glued to his palate. Jarcke sat motionless, buried in shadow.

"Th . . ." He had to swallow to clear his throat of mucus. "This is the reason you live here, isn't it?"

"Part of the reason," she said. "I can see things comin' way up here. Things to watch out for, things to study on."

She stood and walked to the lip of the socket and spat off the edge; the valley stretched out gray and unreal behind her, the folds of the hills barely visible in the gathering dusk.

"I seen you comin'," she said.

A week later, after much exploration, much talk, they went down into Teocinte. The town was a shambles—shattered windows, slogans painted on the walls, glass and torn banners and spilled food littering the streets— as if there had been both a celebration and a battle. Which there had. The city fathers met with Meric in the town hall and informed him that his plan had been approved. They presented him a chest containing five hundred ounces of silver and said that the entire resources of the community were at his disposal. They offered a wagon and a team to transport him and the chest to Regensburg and asked if any of the preliminary work could be begun during his absence.

Meric hefted one of the silver bars. In its cold gleam he saw the object of his desire—two, perhaps three years of freedom, of doing the work he wanted and not having to accept commissions. But all that had been confused. He glanced at Jarcke; she was staring out the window, leaving it to him. He set the bar back in the chest and shut the lid.

"You'll have to send someone else," he said. And then, as the city fathers looked at each other askance, he laughed and laughed at how easily he had discarded all his dreams and expectations.

"*. . . It had been eleven years since I had been to the valley, twelve since work had begun on the painting, and I was appalled by the changes that had taken place. Many of the hills were scraped brown and treeless, and there was a general dearth of wildlife. Griaule, of course, was most changed. Scaffolding hung from his back; artisans, suspended by webworks of ropes, crawled over his side; and all the scales to be worked had either been painted or primed. The tower rising to his eye was swarmed by laborers, and at night the calciners and vats atop his head belched flame into the sky, making it seem there was a mill town in the heavens. At his feet was a brawling shantytown populated by prostitutes, workers, gamblers, ne'er-do-wells of every sort, and sol-*

diers: the burdensome cost of the project had encouraged the city fathers of
Teocinte to form a regular militia, which regularly plundered the adjoining
states and had posted occupation forces to some areas. Herds of frightened animals milled in the slaughtering pens, waiting to be rendered into oils and pigments. Wagons filled with ores and vegetable products rattled in the streets. I
myself had brought a cargo of madder roots from which a rose tint would be
derived.

"It was not easy to arrange a meeting with Cattanay. While he did none
of the actual painting, he was always busy in his office consulting with engineers and artisans, or involved in some other part of the logistical process. When
at last I did meet with him, I found he had changed as drastically as Griaule. His hair had gone gray, deep lines scored his features, and his right shoulder had a peculiar bulge at its midpoint—the product of a fall. He was amused
by the fact that I wanted to buy the painting, to collect the scales after Griaule's death, and I do not believe he took me at all seriously. But the woman
Jarcke, his constant companion, informed him that I was a responsible businessman, that I had already bought the bones, the teeth, even the dirt beneath
Griaule's belly (this I eventually sold as having magical properties).

" 'Well,' said Cattanay, 'I suppose someone has to own them.'

"He led me outside, and we stood looking at the painting.

" 'You'll keep them together?' he asked.

"I said, 'Yes.'

" 'If you'll put that in writing,' he said, 'then they're yours.'

"Having expected to haggle long and hard over the price, I was flabbergasted; but I was even more flabbergasted by what he said next.

" 'Do you think it's any good?' he asked.

"Cattanay did not consider the painting to be the work of his imagination; he felt he was simply illuminating the shapes that appeared on Griaule's
side and was convinced that once the paint was applied, new shapes were produced beneath it, causing him to make constant changes. He saw himself as
an artisan more than a creative artist. But to put his question into perspective, people were beginning to flock from all over the world and marvel at
the painting. Some claimed they saw intimations of the future in its gleaming
surface; others underwent transfiguring experiences; still others—artists themselves—attempted to capture something of the work on canvas, hopeful of establishing reputations merely by being competent copyists of Cattanay's art. The
painting was nonrepresentational in character, essentially a wash of pale gold
spread across the dragon's side; but buried beneath the laminated surface were
a myriad tints of iridescent color that, as the sun passed through the heavens
and the light bloomed and faded, solidified into innumerable forms and figures that seemed to flow back and forth. I will not try to categorize these forms,
because there was no end to them; they were as varied as the conditions under
which they were viewed. But I will say that on the morning I met with Cattanay, I—who was the soul of the practical man, without a visionary bone in

*my body—felt as though I were being whirled away into the painting, up
through geometries of light, latticeworks of rainbow color that built the way
the edges of a cloud build, past orbs, spirals, wheels of flame. . . ."*
—from *This Business of Griaule*
by Henry Sichi

II

There had been several women in Meric's life since he arrived in the valley; most had been attracted by his growing fame and his association with
the mystery of the dragon, and most had left him for the same reasons,
feeling daunted and unappreciated. But Lise was different in two respects.
First, because she loved Meric truly and well; and second, because she
was married—albeit unhappily—to a man named Pardiel, the foreman of
the calciner crew. She did not love him as she did Meric, yet she respected
him and felt obliged to consider carefully before ending the relationship.
Meric had never known such an introspective soul. She was twelve years
younger than he, tall and lovely, with sun-streaked hair and brown eyes
that went dark and seemed to turn inward whenever she was pensive.
She was in the habit of analyzing everything that affected her, drawing
back from her emotions and inspecting them as if they were a clutch of
strange insects she had discovered crawling on her skirt. Though her pen-
chant for self-examination kept her from him, Meric viewed it as a kind
of baffling virtue. He had the classic malady and could find no fault with
her. For almost a year they were as happy as could be expected; they
talked long hours and walked together, and on those occasions when Pardiel worked double shifts and was forced to bed down by his furnaces,
they spent the nights making love in the cavernous spaces beneath the
dragon's wing.

It was still reckoned an evil place. Something far worse than skizzers
or flakes was rumored to live there, and the ravages of this creature were
blamed for every disappearance, even that of the most malcontented la-
borer. But Meric did not give credence to the rumors. He half-believed
Griaule had chosen him to be his executioner and that the dragon would
never let him be harmed; and besides, it was the only place where they
could be assured of privacy.

A crude stair led under the wing, handholds and steps hacked from
the scales—doubtless the work of scale hunters. It was a treacherous passage, six hundred feet above the valley floor; but Lise and Meric were secured by ropes, and over the months, driven by the urgency of passion,
they adapted to it. Their favorite spot lay fifty feet in (Lise would go no
farther; she was afraid even if he was not), near a waterfall that trickled
over the leathery folds, causing them to glisten with a mineral brilliance.

It was eerily beautiful, a haunted gallery. Peels of dead skin hung down from the shadows like torn veils of ectoplasm; ferns sprouted from the vanes, which were thicker than cathedral columns; swallows curved through the black air. Sometimes, lying with her hidden by a tuck of the wing, Meric would think the beating of their hearts was what really animated the place, that the instant they left, the water ceased flowing and the swallows vanished. He had an unshakable faith in the transforming power of their affections, and one morning as they dressed, preparing to return to Hangtown, he asked her to leave with him.

"To another part of the valley?" She laughed sadly. "What good would that do? Pardiel would follow us."

"No," he said. "To another country. Anywhere far from here."

"We can't," she said, kicking at the wing. "Not until Griaule dies. Have you forgotten?"

"We haven't tried."

"Others have."

"But we'd be strong enough. I know it!"

"You're a romantic," she said gloomily, and stared out over the slope of Griaule's back at the valley. Sunrise had washed the hills to crimson, and even the tips of the wings were glowing a dull red.

"Of course I'm a romantic!" He stood, angry. "What the hell's wrong with that?"

She sighed with exasperation. "You wouldn't leave your work," she said. "And if we did leave, what work would you do? Would . . ."

"Why must everything be a problem in advance!" he shouted. "I'll tattoo elephants! I'll paint murals on the chests of giants, I'll illuminate whales! Who else is better qualified?"

She smiled, and his anger evaporated.

"I didn't mean it that way," she said. "I just wondered if you could be satisfied with anything else."

She reached out her hand to be pulled up, and he drew her into an embrace. As he held her, inhaling the scent of vanilla water from her hair, he saw a diminutive figure silhouetted against the backdrop of the valley. It did not seem real—a black homunculus—and even when it began to come forward, growing larger and larger, it looked less a man than a magical keyhole opening in a crimson set hillside. But Meric knew from the man's rolling walk and the hulking set of his shoulders that it was Pardiel; he was carrying a long-handled hook, one of those used by artisans to maneuver along the scales.

Meric tensed, and Lise looked back to see what had alarmed him. "Oh, my God!" she said, moving out of the embrace.

Pardiel stopped a dozen feet away. He said nothing. His face was in shadow, and the hook swung lazily from his hand. Lise took a step toward him, then stepped back and stood in front of Meric as if to shield

him. Seeing this, Pardiel let out an inarticulate yell and charged, slashing
with the hook. Meric pushed Lise aside and ducked. He caught a brimstone whiff of the calciners as Pardiel rushed past and went sprawling,
tripped by some irregularity in the scale. Deathly afraid, knowing he was
no match for the foreman, Meric seized Lise's hand and ran deeper under
the wing. He hoped Pardiel would be too frightened to follow, leery of
the creature that was rumored to live there; but he was not. He came after
them at a measured pace, tapping the hook against his leg.

Higher on Griaule's back, the wing was dimpled downward by hundreds of bulges, and this created a maze of small chambers and tunnels
so low that they had to crouch to pass along them. The sound of their
breathing and the scrape of their feet were amplified by the enclosed spaces
and Meric could no longer hear Pardiel. He had never been this deep before. He had thought it would be pitch-dark; but the lichen and algae ad-
hering to the wing were luminescent and patterned every surface, even
the scales beneath them, with whorls of blue and green fire that shed a
sickly radiance. It was as if they were giants crawling through a universe
whose starry matter had not yet congealed into galaxies and nebulas. In
the wan light, Lise's face—turned back to him now and again—was teary
and frantic; and then, as she straightened, passing into still another chamber, she drew in breath with a shriek.

At first Meric thought Pardiel had somehow managed to get ahead of
them; but on entering he saw that the cause of her fright was a man
propped in a sitting position against the far wall. He looked mummified.
Wisps of brittle hair poked up from his scalp, the shapes of his bones were
visible through his skin, and his eyes were empty holes. Between his legs
was a scatter of dust where his genitals had been. Meric pushed Lise toward the next tunnel, but she resisted and pointed to the man.

"His eyes," she said, horror-struck.

Though the eyes were mostly a negative black, Meric now realized they
were shot through by opalescent flickers. He felt compelled to kneel beside the man—it was a sudden, motiveless urge that gripped him, bent him
to its will, and released him a second later. As he rested his hand on the
scale, he brushed a massive ring that was lying beneath the shrunken fingers. Its stone was black, shot through by flickers identical to those within
the eyes, and incised with the letter *S*. He found his gaze was deflected
away from both the stone and the eyes, as if they contained charges repellent to the senses. He touched the man's withered arm; the flesh was
rock-hard, petrified. But alive. From that brief touch he gained an impression of the man's life, of gazing for centuries at the same patch of unearthly fire, of a mind gone beyond mere madness into a perverse rapture, a meditation upon some foul principle. He snatched back his hand
in revulsion.

There was a noise behind them, and Meric jumped up, pushing Lise into the next tunnel. "Go right," he whispered. "We'll circle back toward the stair." But Pardiel was too close to confuse with such tactics, and their flight became a wild chase, scrambling, falling, catching glimpses of Pardiel's smoke-stained face, until finally—as Meric came to a large chamber—he felt the hook bite into his thigh. He went down, clutching at the wound, pulling the hook loose. The next moment Pardiel was atop him; Lise appeared over his shoulder, but he knocked her away and locked his fingers in Meric's hair and smashed his head against the scale. Lise screamed, and white lights fired through Meric's skull. Again his head was smashed down. And again. Dimly, he saw Lise struggling with Pardiel, saw her shoved away, saw the hook raised high and the foreman's mouth distorted by a grimace. Then the grimace vanished. His jaw dropped open and he reached behind him as if to scratch his shoulder blade. A line of dark blood eeled from his mouth and he collapsed, smothering Meric beneath his chest. Meric heard voices. He tried to dislodge the body, and the effects drained the last of his strength. He whirled down through a blackness that seemed as negative and inexhaustible as the petrified man's eyes.

Someone had propped his head on their lap and was bathing his brow with a damp cloth. He assumed it was Lise, but when he asked what had happened, it was Jarcke who answered saying, "Had to kill him." His head throbbed, his leg throbbed even worse, and his eyes would not focus. The peels of dead skin hanging overhead appeared to be writhing. He realized they were out near the edge of the wing.

"Where's Lise?"

"Don't worry," said Jarcke. "You'll see her again." She made it sound like an indictment.

"Where is she?"

"Sent her back to Hangtown. Won't do you two bein' seen hand in hand the same day Pardiel's missin'."

"She wouldn't have left . . ." He blinked, trying to see her face; the lines around her mouth were etched deep and reminded him of the patterns of lichen on the dragon's scale. "What did you do?"

"Convinced her it was best," said Jarcke. "Don't you know she's just foolin' with you?"

"I've got to talk with her." He was full of remorse, and it was unthinkable that Lise should be bearing her grief alone; but when he struggled to rise, pain lanced through his leg.

"You wouldn't get ten feet," she said. "Soon as your head's clear, I'll help you to the stairs."

He closed his eyes, resolving to find Lise the instant he got back to Hangtown—together they would decide what to do. The scale beneath him was cool, and that coolness was transmitted to his skin, his flesh, as if he were merging with it, becoming one of its ridges.

"What was the wizard's name?" he asked after a while, recalling the petrified man, the ring and its incised letter. "The one who tried to kill Griaule. . . ."

"Don't know as I ever heard it," said Jarcke. "But I reckon it's him back there."

"You saw him?"

"I was chasin' a scale hunter once what stole some rope, and I found him instead. Pretty miserable sort, whoever he is."

Her fingers trailed over his shoulder—a gentle, treasuring touch. He did not understand what it signaled, being too concerned with Lise, with the terrifying potentials of all that had happened; but years later, after things had passed beyond remedy, he cursed himself for not having understood.

At length Jarcke helped him to his feet, and they climbed up to Hangtown, to bitter realizations and regrets, leaving Pardiel to the birds or the weather or worse.

". . . *It seems it is considered irreligious for a woman in love to hesitate or examine the situation, to do anything other than blindly follow the impulse of her emotions. I felt the brunt of such an attitude—people judged it my fault for not having acted quickly and decisively one way or another. Perhaps I was overcautious. I do not claim to be free of blame, only innocent of sacrilege. I believe I might have eventually left Pardiel—there was not enough in the relationship to sustain happiness for either of us. But I had good reason for cautious examination. My husband was not an evil man, and there were matters of loyalty between us.*

"*I could not face Meric after Pardiel's death, and I moved to another part of the valley. He tried to see me on many occasions, but I always refused. Though I was greatly tempted, my guilt was greater. Four years later, after Jarcke died—crushed by a runaway wagon—one of her associates wrote and told me Jarcke had been in love with Meric, that it had been she who had informed Pardiel of the affair, and that she may well have staged the murder. The letter acted somewhat to expiate my guilt, and I weighed the possibility of seeing Meric again. But too much time had passed, and we had both assumed other lives. I decided against it. Six years later, when Griaule's influence had weakened sufficiently to allow emigration, I moved to Port Chantay. I did not hear from Meric for almost twenty years after that, and then one day I received a letter, which I will reproduce in part.*

"'. . . *My old friend from Regensburg, Louis Dardano, has been living here for the past few years, engaged in writing my biography. The narrative has a breezy feel, like a tale being told in a tavern, which—if you recall my telling you how this all began—is quite appropriate. But on reading it, I am amazed my life has had such a simple shape. One task, one passion. God, Lise! Seventy years old, and I still dream of you. And I still think of what happened that morning under the wing. Strange, that it has taken me all this time to realize it was not Jarcke, not you or I who were culpable, but Griaule. How obvious it seems now. I was leaving, and he needed me to complete the expression on his side, his dream of flying, of escape, to grant him the death of his desire. I am certain you will think I have leaped to this assumption, but I remind you that it has been a leap of forty years' duration. I know Griaule, know his monstrous subtlety. I can see it at work in every action that has taken place in the valley since my arrival. I was a fool not to understand that his powers were at the heart of our sad conclusion.'*

"'The army now runs everything here, as no doubt you are aware. It is rumored they are planning a winter campaign against Regensburg. Can you believe it! Their fathers were ignorant, but this generation is brutally stupid. Otherwise, the work goes well and things are as usual with me. My shoulder aches, children stare at me on the street, and it is whispered I am mad . . .'"

—from *Under Griaule's Wing*
by Lise Claverie

III

Acne-scarred, lean, arrogant, Major Hauk was a very young major with a limp. When Meric had entered, the major had been practicing his signature—it was a thing of elegant loops and flourishes, obviously intended to have a place in posterity. As he strode back and forth during their conversation, he paused frequently to admire himself in the window glass, settling the hang of his red jacket or running his fingers along the crease of his white trousers. It was the new style of uniform, the first Meric had seen at close range, and he noted with amusement the dragons embossed on the epaulets. He wondered if Griaule was capable of such an irony, if his influence was sufficiently discreet to have planted the idea for this comic opera apparel in the brain of some general's wife.

". . . not a question of manpower," the major was saying, "but of . . ." He broke off, and after a moment cleared his throat.

Meric, who had been studying the blotches on the backs of his hands, glanced up; the cane that had been resting against his knee slipped and clattered to the floor.

"A question of *matériel*," said the major firmly. "The price of antimony, for example . . ."

"Hardly use it anymore," said Meric. "I'm almost done with the mineral reds."

A look of impatience crossed the major's face. "Very well," he said; he stopped to his desk and shuffled through some papers. "Ah! Here's a bill for a shipment of cuttlefish from which you derive . . ." He shuffled more papers.

"Syrian brown," said Meric gruffly. "I'm done with that, too. Golds and violets are all I need anymore. A little blue and rose." He wished the man would stop badgering him; he wanted to be at the eye before sunset.

As the major continued his accounting, Meric's gaze wandered out the window. The shantytown surrounding Griaule had swelled into a city and now sprawled across the hills. Most of the buildings were permanent, wood and stone, and the cant of the roofs, the smoke from the factories around the perimeter, put him in mind of Regensburg. All the natural beauty of the land had been drained into the painting. Blackish gray rain clouds were muscling up from the east, but the afternoon sun shone clear and shed a heavy gold radiance on Griaule's side. It looked as if the sunlight were an extension of the gleaming resins, as if the thickness of the paint were becoming infinite. He let the major's voice recede to a buzz and followed the scatter and dazzle of the images; and then, with a start, he realized the major was sounding him out about stopping the work.

The idea panicked him at first. He tried to interrupt, to raise objections but the major talked through him, and as Meric thought it over, he grew less and less opposed. The painting would never be finished, and he was tired. Perhaps it was time to have done with it, to accept a university post somewhere and enjoy life for a while.

"We've been thinking about a temporary stoppage," said Major Hauk. "Then if the winter campaign goes well . . ." He smiled. "If we're not visited by plague and pestilence, we'll assume things are in hand. Of course we'd like your opinion."

Meric felt a surge of anger toward this smug little monster. "In my opinion, you people are idiots," he said. "You wear Griaule's image on your shoulders, weave him on your flags, and yet you don't have the least comprehension of what that means. You think it's just a useful symbol. . . ."

"Excuse me," said the major stiffly.

"The hell I will!" Meric groped for his cane and heaved up to his feet. "You see yourselves as conquerors. Shapers of destiny. But all your rapes and slaughters are Griaule's expressions. *His* will. You're every bit as much his parasites as the skizzers."

The major sat, picked up a pen, and began to write.

"It astounds me," Meric went on, "that you can live next to a miracle, a source of mystery, and treat him as if he were an oddly shaped rock."

The major kept writing.

"What are you doing?" asked Meric.

"My recommendation," said the major without looking up.

"Which is?"

"That we initiate stoppage at once."

They exchanged hostile stares, and Meric turned to leave; but as he took hold of the doorknob, the major spoke again.

"We owe you so much," he said; he wore an expression of mingled pity and respect that further irritated Meric.

"How many men have you killed, Major?" he asked, opening the door.

"I'm not sure. I was in the artillery. We were never able to be sure."

"Well, I'm sure of my tally," said Meric. "It's taken me forty years to amass it. Fifteen hundred and ninety-three men and women. Poisoned, scaled, broken by falls, savaged by animals. Murdered. Why don't we—you and I—just call it even."

Though it was a sultry afternoon, he felt cold as he walked toward the tower—an internal cold that left him light-headed and weak. He tried to think what he would do. The idea of a university post seemed less appealing away from the major's office; he would soon grow weary of worshipful students and in-depth dissections of his work by jealous academics. A man hailed him as he turned into the market. Meric waved but did not stop, and heard another man say, *"That's* Cattanay?" (That ragged old ruin?)

The colors of the market were too bright, the smells of charcoal cookery too cloying, the crowds too thick, and he made for the side streets, hobbling past one-room stucco houses and tiny stores where they sold cooking oil by the ounce and cut cigars in half if you could not afford a whole one. Garbage, tornados of dust and flies, drunks with bloody mouths. Somebody had tied wires around a pariah dog—a bitch with slack teats; the wires had sliced into her flesh, and she lay panting in an alley mouth, gaunt ribs flecked with pink lather, gazing into nowhere. She, thought Meric, and not Griaule, should be the symbol of their flag.

As he rode the hoist up the side of the tower, he fell into his old habit of jotting down notes for the next day. *What's that cord of wood doing on level five? Slow leak of chrome yellow from pipes on level twelve.* Only when he saw a man dismantling some scaffolding did he recall Major Hauk's recommendation and understand that the order must already have been given. The loss of his work struck home to him then, and he leaned against the railing, his chest constricted and his eyes brimming. He straightened, ashamed of himself. The sun hung in a haze of iron-colored light low above the western hills, looking red and bloated and vile as a vulture's ruff. That polluted sky was his creation as much as was the painting, and it would be good to leave it behind. Once away from the valley, from all the influences of the place, he would be able to consider the future.

A young girl was sitting on the twentieth level just beneath the eye. Years before, the ritual of viewing the eye had grown to cultish proportions; there had been group chanting and praying and discussions of the experience. But these were more practical times, and no doubt the young men and women who had congregated here were now manning administrative desks somewhere in the burgeoning empire. They were the ones about whom Dardano should write; they, and all the eccentric characters who had played roles in this slow pageant. The gypsy woman who had danced every night by the eye, hoping to charm Griaule into killing her faithless lover—she had gone away satisfied. The man who had tried to extract one of the fangs—nobody knew what had become of him. The scale hunters, the artisans. A history of Hangtown would be a volume in itself.

The walk had left Meric weak and breathless; he sat down clumsily beside the girl, who smiled. He could not remember her name, but she came often to the eye. Small and dark, with an inner reserve that reminded him of Lise. He laughed inwardly—most women reminded him of Lise in some way.

"Are you all right?" she asked, her brow wrinkled with concern.

"Oh, yes," he said; he felt a need for conversation to take his mind off things, but he could think of nothing more to say. She was so young! All freshness and gleam and nerves.

"This will be my last time," she said. "At least for a while. I'll miss it." And then, before he could ask why, she added, "I'm getting married tomorrow, and we're moving away."

He offered congratulations and asked her who was the lucky fellow.

"Just a boy." She tossed her hair, as if to dismiss the boy's importance; she gazed up at the shuttered membrane. "What's it like for you when the eye opens?" she asked.

"Like everyone else," he said. "I remember . . . memories of my life. Other lives, too." He did not tell her about Griaule's memory of flight; he had never told anyone except Lise about that.

"All those bits of souls trapped in there," she said, gesturing at the eye. "What do they mean to him? Why does he show them to us?"

"I imagine he has his purposes, but I can't explain them."

"Once I remembered being with you," said the girl, peeking at him shyly through a dark curl. "We were under the wing."

He glanced at her sharply. "Tell me."

"We were . . . together," she said, blushing. "Intimate, you know. I was very afraid of the place, of the sounds and shadows. But I loved you so much, it didn't matter. We made love all night, and I was surprised because I thought that kind of passion was just in stories, something people had invented to make up for how ordinary it really was. And in the morning even that dreadful place had become beautiful, with the wing tips glowing red and the waterfall echoing . . ." She lowered her eyes. "Ever since I had that memory, I've been a little in love with you."

"Lise," he said, feeling helpless before her.

"Was that her name?"

He nodded and put a hand to his brow, trying to pinch back the emotions that flooded him.

"I'm sorry." Her lips grazed his cheek, and just that slight touch seemed to weaken him further. "I wanted to tell you how she felt in case she hadn't told you herself. She was very troubled by something, and I wasn't sure she had."

She shifted away from him, made uncomfortable by the intensity of his reaction, and they sat without speaking. Meric became lost in watching how the sun glazed the scales to reddish gold, how the light was channeled along the ridges in molten streams that paled as the day wound down. He was startled when the girl jumped to her feet and backed toward the hoist.

"He's dead," she said wonderingly.

Meric looked at her, uncomprehending.

"See?" She pointed at the sun, which showed a crimson sliver above the hill. "He's dead," she repeated, and the expression on her face flowed between fear and exultation.

The idea of Griaule's death was too large for Meric's mind to encompass, and he turned to the eye to find a counterproof—no glints of color flickered beneath the membrane. He heard the hoist creak as the girl headed down, but he continued to wait. Perhaps only the dragon's vision had failed. No. It was likely not a coincidence that work had been officially terminated today. Stunned, he sat staring at the lifeless membrane until the sun sank below the hills; then he stood and went over to the hoist. Before he could throw the switch, the cables thrummed—somebody heading up. Of course. The girl would have spread the news, and all the Major Hauks and their underlings would be hurrying to test Griaule's reflexes. He did not want to be here when they arrived, to watch them pose with their trophy like successful fishermen.

It was hard work climbing up to the frontoparietal plate. The ladder swayed, the wind buffeted him, and by the time he clambered onto the plate, he was giddy, his chest full of twinges. He hobbled forward and leaned against the rust-caked side of a boiling vat. Shadowy in the twilight, the great furnaces and vats towered around him, and it seemed this system of fiery devices reeking of cooked flesh and minerals was the actual machinery of Griaule's thought materialized above his skull. Energyless, abandoned. They had been replaced by more efficient equipment down below, and it had been—what was it?—almost five years since they were last used. Cobwebs veiled a pyramid of firewood; the stairs leading to the rims of the vats were crumbling. The plate itself was scarred and coated with sludge.

"Cattanay!"

Someone shouted from below, and the top of the ladder trembled. God, they were coming after him! Bubbling over with congratulations and plans for testimonial dinners, memorial plaques, specially struck medals. They would have him draped in bunting and bronzed and covered with pigeon shit before they were done. All these years he had been among them, both their slave and their master, yet he had never felt at home. Leaning heavily on his cane, he made his way past the frontal spike—blackened by years of oily smoke—and down between the wings to Hangtown. It was a ghost town, now. Weeds overgrowing the collapsed shanties; the lake a stinking pit, drained after some children had drowned in the summer of '91. Where Jarcke's home had stood was a huge pile of animal bones, taking a pale shine from the half-light. Wind keened through the tattered shrubs.

"Meric!" "Cattanay."

The voices drew closer.

Well, there was one place where they would not follow.

The leaves of the thickets were speckled with mold and brittle, flaking away as he brushed them. He hesitated at the top of the scale hunters' stair. He had no rope. Though he had done the climb unaided many times, it had been quite a few years. The gusts of wind, the shouts, the sweep of the valley and the lights scattered across it like diamonds on gray velvet—it all seemed a single inconstant medium. He heard the brush crunch behind him, more voices. To hell with it! Gritting his teeth against a twinge of pain in his shoulder, hooking his cane over his belt, he inched onto the stair and locked his fingers in the handholds. The wind whipped his clothes and threatened to pry him loose and send him pinwheeling off. Once he slipped; once he froze, unable to move backward or forward. But at last he reached the bottom and edged upslope until he found a spot flat enough to stand.

The mystery of the place suddenly bore in upon him, and he was afraid. He half-turned to the stair, thinking he would go back to Hangtown and accept the hurly-burly. But a moment later he realized how foolish a thought that was. Waves of weakness poured through him, his heart hammered, and white dazzles flared in his vision. His chest felt heavy as iron. Rattled, he went a few steps forward, the cane pocking the silence. It was too dark to see more than outlines, but up ahead was the fold of wing where he and Lise had sheltered. He walked toward it, intent on revisiting it; then he remembered the girl beneath the eye and understood that he had already said that good-bye. And it *was* good-bye—that he understood vividly. He kept walking. Blackness looked to be welling from the wing joint, from the entrances to the maze of luminous tunnels where they had stumbled onto the petrified man. Had it really been the old wizard, doomed by magical justice to molder and live on and on? It made sense. At least it accorded with what happened to wizards who slew their dragons.

"Griaule?" he whispered to the darkness, and cocked his head, half-expecting an answer. The sound of his voice pointed up the immensity of the great gallery under the wing, the emptiness, and he recalled how vital a habitat it had once been. Flakes shifting over the surface, skizzers, peculiar insects fuming in the thickets, the glum populace of Hangtown, waterfalls. He had never been able to picture Griaule fully alive–that kind of vitality was beyond the powers of the imagination. Yet he wondered if by some miracle the dragon were alive now, flying up through his golden night to the sun's core. Or had that merely been a dream, a bit of tissue glittering deep in the cold tons of his brain? He laughed. Ask the stars for their first names, and you'd be more likely to receive a reply.

He decided not to walk any farther–it was really no decision. Pain was spreading through his shoulder so intense he imagined it must be glowing inside. Carefully, carefully, he lowered himself and lay propped on an elbow, hanging onto the cane. Good, magical wood. Cut from a hawthorn atop Griaule's haunch. A man had once offered him a small fortune for it. Who would claim it now? Probably old Henry Sichi would snatch it for his museum, stick it in a glass case next to his boots. What a joke! He decided to lie flat on his stomach, resting his chin on an arm–the stony coolness beneath acted to muffle the pain. Amusing, how the range of one's decision dwindled. You decided to paint a dragon, to send hundreds of men searching for malachite and cochineal beetles, to love a woman, to heighten an undertone here and there, and finally to position your body a certain way. He seemed to have reached the end of the process. What next? He tried to regulate his breathing, to ease the pressure on his chest. Then, as something rustled out near the wing joint, he turned on his side. He thought he detected movement, a gleaming blackness flowing toward him . . . or else it was only the haphazard firing of his nerves playing tricks with his vision. More surprised than afraid, wanting to see, he peered into the darkness and felt his heart beating erratically against the dragon's scale.

"*. . . It's foolish to draw simple conclusions from complex events, but I suppose there must be both moral and truth to this life, these events. I'll leave that to the gadflies. The historians, the social scientists, the expert apologists for reality. All I know is that he had a fight with his girlfriend over money and walked out. He sent her a letter saying he had gone south and would be back in a few months with more money than she could ever spend. I had no idea what he'd done. The whole thing about Griaule had just been a bunch of us sitting around the Red Bear, drinking up my pay–I'd sold an article–and somebody said, 'Wouldn't it be great if Dardano didn't have to write articles, if we didn't have to paint pictures that color-coordinated with people's furniture or slave at getting the gooey smiles of little nieces and nephews just right?' All sorts of improbable moneymaking schemes were put forward. Rob-*

beries, kidnappings. Then the idea of swindling the city fathers of Teocinte came up, and the entire plan was fleshed out in minutes. Scribbled on napkins, scrawled on sketchpads. A group effort. I keep trying to remember if anyone got a glassy look in their eye, if I felt a cold tendril of Griaule's thought stirring my brains. But I can't. It was a half hour's sensation, nothing more. A drunken whimsy, an art-school metaphor. Shortly thereafter, we ran out of money and staggered into the streets. It was snowing—big wet flakes that melted down our collars. God, we were drunk! Laughing, balancing on the icy railing of the University Bridge. Making faces at the bundled-up burghers and their fat ladies who huffed and puffed past, spouting steam and never giving us a glance, and none of us—not even the burghers—knowing that we were living our happy ending in advance. . . ."

—from *The Man Who Painted The Dragon Griaule*
by Louis Dardano

For Jamie and Laura

GENE WOLFE

A Cabin on the Coast

The Little People are known to have the power to grant wishes
of all sorts, but it is always dangerous for mortals to try to bargain with them. Often they will give you what you ask for, but
always for a *price* . . . and sometimes the price will turn out to be
a *higher* one than you were willing to pay . . .

Gene Wolfe is perceived by many critics to be one of the best—
perhaps the best—SF and fantasy writers working today. His most
acclaimed work is the tetralogy *The Book of the New Sun*—technically
science fiction, but which *feels* enough like fantasy to appeal to most
fantasy readers—individual volumes of which have won the Nebula Award, the World Fantasy Award, and the John W. Campbell
Memorial Award. His other books include the classic fantasy novels *Peace* and *The Devil in a Forest,* both recently re-released, as well
as *Soldier of the Mist, Free Live Free, Soldier of Arête, There Are Doors,
Castleview, Pandora by Holly Hollander,* and *The Urth of the New Sun.*
His short fiction has been collected in *The Island of Doctor Death and
Other Stories and Other Stories, Gene Wolfe's Book of Days, The Wolfe Archipelago,* the recent World Fantasy Award–winning collection *Storeys
from the Old Hotel,* and *Endangered Species.* His most recent books are
part of a popular new series, including *Nightside the Long Sun, The
Lake of the Long Sun,* and *Caldé of the Long Sun.* He has just published
a new novel, *Exodus from the Long Sun.*

It might have been a child's drawing of a ship. He blinked, and blinked
again. There were masts and sails, surely. One stack, perhaps another. If
the ship were really there at all. He went back to his father's beach cottage, climbed the five wooden steps, wiped his feet on the coco mat.

Lissy was still in bed, but awake, sitting up now. It must have been the
squeaking of the steps, he thought. Aloud he said, "Sleep good?"

He crossed the room and kissed her. She caressed him and said, "You
shouldn't go swimming without a suit, dear wonderful swimmer. How
was the Pacific?"

"Peaceful. Cold. It's too early for people to be up, and there's nobody within a mile of here anyway."

"Get into bed then. How about the fish?"

"Salt water makes the sheets sticky. The fish have seen them before." He went to the corner, where a showerhead poked from the wall. The beach cottage—Lissy called it a cabin—had running water of the sometimes and rusty variety.

"They might bite 'em off. Sharks, you know. Little ones."

"Castrating woman." The shower coughed, doused him with icy spray, coughed again.

"You look worried."

"No."

"Is it your dad?"

He shook his head, then thrust it under the spray, fingers combing his dark, curly hair.

"You think he'll come out here? Today?"

He withdrew, considering. "If he's back from Washington, and he knows we're here."

"But he couldn't know, could he?"

He turned off the shower and grabbed a towel, already damp and a trifle sandy. "I don't see how."

"Only he might guess." Lissy was no longer smiling. "Where else could we go? Hey, what did we do with my underwear?"

"Your place. Your folks'. Any motel."

She swung long, golden legs out of bed, still holding the sheet across her lap. Her breasts were nearly perfect hemispheres, except for the tender protrusions of their pink nipples. He decided he had never seen breasts like that. He sat down on the bed beside her. "I love you very much," he said. "You know that?"

It made her smile again. "Does that mean you're coming back to bed?"

"If you want me to."

"I want a swimming lesson. What will people say if I tell them I came here and didn't go swimming."

He grinned at her. "That it's that time of the month."

"You know what you are? You're filthy!" She pushed him. "Absolutely filthy! I'm going to bite your ears off." Tangled in the sheet, they fell off the bed together. "There they are!"

"There what are?"

"My bra and stuff. We must have kicked them under the bed. Where are our bags?"

"Still in the trunk. I never carried them in."

"Would you get mine? My swimsuit's in it."

"Sure," he said.

"And put on some pants!"

"My suit's in my bag too." He found his trousers and got the keys to the Triumph. Outside the sun was higher, the chill of the fall morning nearly gone. He looked for the ship and saw it. Then it winked out like a star.

That evening they made a fire of driftwood and roasted the big, greasy Italian sausages he had brought from town, making giant hot dogs by clamping them in French bread. He had brought red supermarket wine too; they chilled it in the Pacific. "I never ate this much in my life," Lissy said.

"You haven't eaten anything yet."

"I know, but just looking at this sandwich would make me full if I wasn't so hungry." She bit off the end. "Cuff tough woof."

"What?"

"Castrating woman. That's what you called me this morning, Tim. Now *this* is a castrating woman."

"Don't talk with your mouth full."

"You sound like my mother. Give me some wine. You're hogging it."

He handed the bottle over. "It isn't bad, if you don't object to a complete lack of character."

"I sleep with you, don't I?"

"I have character, it's just all rotten."

"You said you wanted to get married."

"Let's go. You can finish that thing in the car."

"You drank half the bottle. You're too high to drive."

"Bullshoot."

Lissy giggled. "You just said bullshoot. Now *that's* character!"

He stood up. "Come on, let's go. It's only five hundred miles to Reno. We can get married there in the morning."

"You're serious, aren't you?"

"If you are."

"Sit down."

"You were testing me," he said. "That's not fair, now is it?"

"You've been so worried all day. I wanted to see if it was about me—if you thought you'd made a terrible mistake."

"We've made a mistake," he said. "I was trying to fix it just now."

"You think your dad is going to make it rough for you—"

"Us."

"—for us because it might hurt him in the next election."

He shook his head. "Not that. All right, maybe partly that. But he means it too. You don't understand him."

"I've got a father myself."

"Not like mine. Ryan was almost grown-up before he left Ireland. Taught by nuns and all that. Besides, I've got six older brothers and two sisters. You're the oldest kid. Ryan's probably at least fifteen years older than your folks."

"Is that really his name? Ryan Neal?"

"His full name is Timothy Ryan Neal, the same as mine. I'm Timothy, Junior. He used Ryan when he went into politics because there was another Tim Neal around then, and we've always called me Tim to get away from the Junior."

"I'm going to call him Tim again, like the nuns must have when he was young. Big Tim. You're Little Tim."

"Okay with me. I don't know if Big Tim is going to like it."

Something was moving, it seemed, out where the sun had set. Something darker against the dark horizon.

"What made you Junior anyway? Usually it's the oldest boy."

"He didn't want it, and would never let Mother do it. But she wanted to, and I was born during the Democratic convention that year."

"He had to go, of course."

"Yeah, he had to go, Lissy. If you don't understand that, you don't understand politics at all. They hoped I'd hold off for a few days, and what the hell, Mother'd had eight with no problems. Anyway he was used to it—he was the youngest of seven boys himself. So she got to call me what she wanted."

"But then she died." The words sounded thin and lonely against the pounding of the surf.

"Not because of that."

Lissy upended the wine bottle; he saw her throat pulse three times. "Will I die because of that, Little Tim?"

"I don't think so." He tried to think of something gracious and comforting. "If we decide we want children, that's the risk I have to take."

"*You* have to take? Bullshoot."

"That both of us have to take. Do you think it was easy for Ryan, raising nine kids by himself?"

"You love him, don't you?"

"Sure I love him. He's my father."

"And now you think you might be ruining things for him. For my sake."

"That's not why I want us to be married, Lissy."

She was staring into the flames; he was not certain she had even heard him. "Well, now I know why his pictures look so grim. So gaunt."

He stood up again. "If you're through eating . . ."

"You want to go back to the cabin? You can screw me right here on the beach—there's nobody here but us."

"I didn't mean that."

"Then why go in there and look at the walls? Out here we've got the fire and the ocean. The moon ought to be up pretty soon."

"It would be warmer."

"With just that dinky little kerosene stove? I'd rather sit here by the fire. In a minute I'm going to send you off to get me some more wood. You can run up to the cabin and get a shirt too if you want to."

"I'm okay."

"Traditional roles. Big Tim must have told you all about them. The woman has the babies and keeps the home fires burning. You're not going to end up looking like him though, are you, Little Tim?"

"I suppose so. He used to look just like me."

"Really?"

He nodded. "He had his picture taken just after he got into politics. He was running for ward committeeman, and he had a poster made. We've still got the picture, and it looks like me with a high collar and a funny hat."

"She knew, didn't she?" Lissy said. For a moment he did not understand what she meant. "Now go and get some more wood. Only don't wear yourself out, because when you come back we're going to take care of that little thing that's bothering you, and we're going to spend the night on the beach."

When he came back she was asleep, but he woke her carrying her up to the beach cottage.

Next morning he woke up alone. He got up and showered and shaved, supposing that she had taken the car into town to get something for breakfast. He had filled the coffeepot and put it on before he looked out the shore-side window and saw the Triumph still waiting near the road.

There was nothing to be alarmed about, of course. She had awakened before he had and gone out for an early dip. He had done the same thing himself the morning before. The little patches of green cloth that were her bathing suit were hanging over the back of a rickety chair, but then they were still damp from last night. Who would want to put on a damp, clammy suit? She had gone in naked, just as he had.

He looked out the other window, wanting to see her splashing in the surf, waiting for him. The ship was there, closer now, rolling like a derelict. No smoke came from its clumsy funnel and no sails were set, but dark banners hung from its rigging. Then there was no ship, only wheeling gulls and the empty ocean. He called her name, but no one answered.

He put on his trunks and a jacket and went outside. A wind had smoothed the sand. The tide had come, obliterating their fire, reclaiming the driftwood he had gathered.

For two hours he walked up and down the beach, calling, telling himself there was nothing wrong. When he forced himself not to think of Lissy dead, he could only think of the headlines, the ninety seconds of ten o'clock news, how Ryan would look, how Pat—all his brothers—would look at him. And when he turned his mind from that, Lissy was dead again, her pale hair snarled with kelp as she rolled in the surf, green crabs feeding from her arms.

He got into the Triumph and drove to town. In the little brick station he sat beside the desk of a fat cop and told his story.

The fat cop said, "Kid, I can see why you want us to keep it quiet."

Tim said nothing. There was a paperweight on the desk—a baseball of white glass.

"You probably think we're out to get you, but we're not. Tomorrow we'll put out a missing persons report, but we don't have to say anything about you or the senator in it, and we won't."

"Tomorrow?"

"We got to wait twenty-four hours, in case she should show up. That's the law. But kid—" The fat cop glanced at his notes.

"Tim."

"Right. Tim. She ain't going to show up. You got to get yourself used to that."

"She could be . . ." Without wanting to, he let it trail away.

"Where? You think she snuck off and went home? She could walk out to the road and hitch, but you say her stuff's still there. Kidnapped? Nobody could have pulled her out of bed without waking you up. Did you kill her?"

"No!" Tears he could not hold back were streaming down his cheeks.

"Right. I've talked to you and I don't think you did. But you're the only one that could have. If her body washes up, we'll have to look into that."

Tim's hands tightened on the wooden arms of the chair. The fat cop pushed a box of tissues across the desk.

"Unless it washes up, though, it's just a missing person, okay? But she's dead, kid, and you're going to have to get used to it. Let me tell you what happened." He cleared his throat.

"She got up while you were still asleep, probably about when it started to get light. She did just what you thought she did—went out for a nice refreshing swim before you woke up. She went out too far, and probably she got a cramp. The ocean's cold as hell now. Maybe she yelled, but if she did she was too far out, and the waves covered it up. People think drowners holler like fire sirens, but they don't—they don't have that much air. Sometimes they don't make any noise at all."

Tim stared at the gleaming paperweight.

"The current here runs along the coast—you probably know that. Nobody ought to go swimming without somebody else around, but sometimes it seems like everybody does it. We lose a dozen or so a year. In maybe four or five cases we find them. That's all."

* * *

The beach cottage looked abandoned when he returned. He parked the Triumph and went inside and found the stove still burning, his coffee perked to tar. He took the pot outside, dumped the coffee, scrubbed the pot with beach sand and rinsed it with salt water. The ship, which had been invisible through the window of the cottage, was almost plain when he stood waist deep. He heaved the coffeepot back to shore and swam out some distance, but when he straightened up in the water, the ship was gone.

Back inside he made fresh coffee and packed Lissy's things in her suitcase. When that was done, he drove into town again. Ryan was still in Washington, but Tim told his secretary where he was. "Just in case anybody reports me missing," he said.

She laughed. "It must be pretty cold for swimming."

"I like it," he told her. "I want to have at least one more long swim."

"All right, Tim. When he calls, I'll let him know. Have a good time."

"Wish me luck," he said, and hung up. He got a hamburger and more coffee at a Jack-in-the-Box and went back to the cottage and walked a long way along the beach.

He had intended to sleep that night, but he did not. From time to time he got up and looked out the window at the ship, sometimes visible by moonlight, sometimes only a dark presence in the lower night sky. When the first light of dawn came, he put on his trunks and went into the water.

For a mile or more, as well as he could estimate the distance, he could not see it. Then it was abruptly close, the long oars like the legs of a water spider, the funnel belching sparks against the still-dim sky, sparks that seemed to become new stars.

He swam faster then, knowing that if the ship vanished he would turn back and save himself, knowing too that if it only retreated before him, retreated forever, he would drown. It disappeared behind a cobalt wave, reappeared. He sprinted and grasped at the sea-slick shaft of an oar, and it was like touching a living being. Quite suddenly he stood on the deck, with no memory of how he came there.

Bare feet pattered on the planks, but he saw no crew. A dark flag lettered with strange script flapped aft, and some vague recollection of a tour of a naval ship with his father years before made him touch his forehead. There was a sound that might have been laughter or many other things. The captain's cabin would be aft too, he thought. He went there, bracing himself against the wild roll, and found a door.

Inside, something black crouched upon a dais. "I've come for Lissy," Tim said.

There was no reply, but a question hung in the air. He answered it almost without intending to. "I'm Timothy Ryan Neal, and I've come for Lissy. Give her back to me."

A light, it seemed, dissolved the blackness. Cross-legged on the dais, a slender man in tweeds sucked at a long clay pipe. "It's Irish, are ye?" he asked.

"American," Tim said.

"With such a name? I don't believe ye. Where's yer feathers?"

"I want her back," Tim said again.

"An' if ye don't get her?"

"Then I'll tear this ship apart. You'll have to kill me or take me too."

"Spoken like a true son of the ould sod," said the man in tweeds. He scratched a kitchen match on the sole of his boot and lit his pipe. "Sit down, will ye? I don't fancy lookin' up like that. It hurts me neck. Sit down, and 'tis possible we can strike an agreement."

"This is crazy," Tim said. "The whole thing is crazy."

"It is that," the man in tweeds replied. "An' there's much, much more comin'. Ye'd best brace for it, Tim me lad. Now sit down."

There was a stout wooden chair behind Tim where the door had been. He sat. "Are you about to tell me you're a leprechaun? I warn you, I won't believe it."

"Me? One o' them scamperin', thievin', cobblin', little misers? I'd shoot meself. Me name's Daniel O'Donoghue, King o' Connaught. Do ye believe that, now?"

"No," Tim said.

"What would ye believe then?"

"That this is—some way, somehow—what people call a saucer. That you and your crew are from a planet of another sun."

Daniel laughed. " 'Tis a close encounter you're havin', is it? Would ye like to see me as a tiny green man wi' horns like a snail's? I can do that too."

"Don't bother."

"All right, I won't, though, 'tis a good shape. A man can take it and be whatever he wants, one o' the People o' Peace or a bit o' a man from Mars. I've used it for both, and there's nothin' better."

"You took Lissy," Tim said.

"And how would ye be knowin' that?"

"I thought she'd drowned."

"Did ye now?"

"And that this ship—or whatever it is—was just a sign, an omen. I talked to a policeman and he as good as told me, but I didn't really think about what he said until last night, when I was trying to sleep."

"Is it a dream yer havin'? Did ye ever think on that?"

"If it's a dream, it's still real," Tim said doggedly. "And anyway, I saw your ship when I was awake, yesterday and the day before."

"Or yer dreamin' now ye did. But go on wi' it."

"He said Lissy couldn't have been abducted because I was in the same bed, and that she'd gone out for a swim in the morning and drowned. But she could have been abducted, if she had gone out for the swim first. If someone had come for her with a boat. And she wouldn't have drowned, because she didn't swim good enough to drown. She was afraid of the water. We went in yesterday, and even with me there, she would hardly go in over her knees. So it was you."

"Yer right, ye know," Daniel said. He formed a little steeple of his fingers. " 'Twas us."

Tim was recalling stories that had been read to him when he was a child. "Fairies steal babies, don't they? And brides. Is that why you do it? So we'll think that's who you are?"

"Bless ye, 'tis true," Daniel told him. " 'Tis the Fair Folk we are. The jinn o' the desert too, and the saucer riders ye say ye credit, and forty score more. Would ye be likin' to see me wi' me goatskin breeches and me panpipe?" He chuckled. "Have ye never wondered why we're so much alike the world over? Or thought that we don't always know just which shape's the best for a place, so the naiads and the dryads might as well be the ladies o' the Deeny Shee? Do ye know what the folk o' the Barb'ry Coast call the hell that's under their sea?"

Tim shook his head.

"Why, 'tis Domdaniel. I wonder why that is, now. Tim, ye say ye want this girl."

"That's right."

"An' ye say there'll be trouble and plenty for us if ye don't have her. But let me tell ye now that if ye don't get her, wi' our blessin' to boot, ye'll drown.—Hold your tongue, can't ye, for 'tis worse than that.—If ye don't get her wi' our blessin', 'twill be seen that ye were drownin' now. Do ye take me meaning?"

"I think so. Close enough."

"Ah, that's good, that is. Now here's me offer. Do ye remember how things stood before we took her?"

"Of course."

"They'll stand so again, if ye but do what I tell ye. 'Tis yourself that will remember, Tim Neal, but she'll remember nothin'. An' the truth of it is, there'll be nothin' to remember, for it'll all be gone, every stick of it. This policeman ye spoke wi', for instance. Ye've me word that ye will not have done it."

"What do I have to do?" Tim asked.

"Service. Serve us. Do whatever we ask of ye. We'd sooner have a broth of a girl like yer Lissy than a great hulk of a lad like yerself, but then, too, we'd sooner be havin' one that's willin', for the unwillin' girls are everywhere—I don't doubt but ye've seen it yerself. A hundred years, that's all we ask of ye. 'Tis short enough, like Doyle's wife. Will ye do it?"

"And everything will be the same, at the end, as it was before you took Lissy?"

"Not everythin', I didn't say that. Ye'll remember, don't ye remember me sayin' so? But for her and all the country round, why 'twill be the same."

"All right," Tim said. "I'll do it."

" 'Tis a brave lad ye are. Now I'll tell ye what I'll do. I said a hundred years, to which ye agreed—"

Tim nodded.

"—but I'll have no unwillin' hands about me boat, nor no ungrateful ones neither. I'll make it twenty. How's that? Sure and I couldn't say fairer, could I?"

Daniel's figure was beginning to waver and fade; the image of the dark mass Tim had seen first hung about it like a cloud.

"Lay yerself on yer belly, for I must put me foot upon yer head. Then the deal's done."

The salt ocean was in his mouth and his eyes. His lungs burst for breath. He revolved in the blue chasm of water, tried to swim, at last exploded gasping into the air.

The King had said he would remember, but the years were fading already. Drudging, dancing, buying, spying, prying, waylaying and betraying when he walked in the world of men. Serving something that he had never wholly understood. Sailing foggy seas that were sometimes of this earth. Floating among the constellations. The years and the slaps and the kicks were all fading, and with them (and he rejoiced in it) the days when he had begged.

He lifted an arm, trying to regain his old stroke, and found that he was very tired. Perhaps he had never really rested in all those years. Certainly, he could not recall resting. Where was he? He paddled listlessly, not knowing if he were swimming away from land, if he were in the center of an ocean. A wave elevated him, a long, slow swell of blue under the gray sky. A glory—the rising or perhaps the setting sun—shone to his right. He swam toward it, caught sight of a low coast.

He crawled onto the sand and lay there for a time, his back struck by drops of spray like rain. Near his eyes, the beach seemed nearly black. There were bits of charcoal, fragments of half-burned wood. He raised his head, pushing away the earth, and saw an empty bottle of greenish glass nearly buried in the wet sand.

When he was able at last to rise, his limbs were stiff and cold. The dawnlight had become daylight, but there was no warmth in it. The beach cottage stood only about a hundred yards away, one window golden with sunshine that had entered from the other side, the walls in shadow. The red Triumph gleamed beside the road.

At the top of a small dune he turned and looked back out to sea. A black freighter with a red and white stack was visible a mile or two out, but it was only a freighter. For a moment he felt a kind of regret, a longing for a part of his life that he had hated but that was now gone forever. I will never be able to tell her what happened, he thought. And then, Yes, I will, if only I let her think I'm just making it up. And then, No wonder so many people tell so many stories. Good-bye to all that.

The steps creaked under his weight, and he wiped the sand from his feet on the coco mat. Lissy was in bed. When she heard the door open she sat up, then drew up the sheet to cover her breasts.

"Big Tim," she said. "You did come. Tim and I were hoping you would."

When he did not answer, she added, "He's out having a swim, I think. He should be around in a minute."

And when he still said nothing: "We're—Tim and I—we're going to be married."

JAMES P. BLAYLOCK

Paper Dragons

Here's one of the strangest and most strangely beautiful stories
you are ever likely to read: as evocative, melancholy, and mysterious as a paper dragon soaring against the darkening sky of
evening . . .

James P. Blaylock was born in Long Beach, California, and
now lives in Orange, California. He made his first sale to the
now-defunct semiprozine *Unearth,* and subsequently became one
of the most popular, literate, and wildly eclectic fantasists of the
1980s and 1990s. "Paper Dragons" won him a World Fantasy
Award in 1986. His critically acclaimed novels–often a quirky
blend of different genres (SF, fantasy, nineteenth-century mainstream novels, horror, romance, ghost stories, mystery, adventure) that would seem doomed to clash, but which in Blaylock's
whimsically affectionate hands somehow do *not*–include *The Last
Coin, Land of Dreams, The Digging Leviathan, Homunculus, Lord
Kelvin's Machine, The Elfin Ship, The Disappearing Dwarf, The Magic
Spectacles, The Stone Giant,* and *The Paper Grail.* His most recent
book is the novel *All the Bells on Earth.*

Strange things are said to have happened in this world–some are said to
be happening still–but half of them, if I'm any judge, are lies. There's no
way to tell sometimes. The sky above the north coast has been flat gray
for weeks–clouds thick overhead like carded wool not fifty feet above the
ground, impaled on the treetops, on redwoods and alders and hemlocks.
The air is heavy with mist that lies out over the harbor and the open
ocean, drifting across the tip of the pier and breakwater now and again,
both of them vanishing into the gray so that there's not a nickel's worth
of difference between the sky and the sea. And when the tide drops, and
the reefs running out toward the point appear through the fog, covered
in the brown bladders and rubber leaves of kelp, the pink lace of algae,
and the slippery sheets of sea lettuce and eel grass, it's a simple thing to
imagine the dark bulk of the fish that lie in deep-water gardens and angle

up toward the pale green of shallows to feed at dawn.

There's the possibility, of course, that winged things, their counterparts if you will, inhabit dens in the clouds, that in the valleys and caverns of the heavy, low skies live unguessed beasts. It occurs to me sometimes that if without warning a man could draw back that veil of cloud that obscures the heavens, snatch it back in an instant, he'd startle a world of oddities aloft in the skies: balloon things with hovering little wings like the fins of pufferfish, and spiny, leathery creatures, nothing but bones and teeth and with beaks half again as long as their ribby bodies.

There have been nights when I was certain I heard them, when the clouds hung in the treetops and foghorns moaned off the point and water dripped from the needles of hemlocks beyond the window onto the tin roof of Filby's garage. There were muffled shrieks and the airy flapping of distant wings. On one such night when I was out walking along the bluffs, the clouds parted for an instant and a spray of stars like a reeling carnival shone beyond, until, like a curtain slowly drawing shut, the clouds drifted up against each other and parted no more. I'm certain I glimpsed something—a shadow, the promise of a shadow—dimming the stars. It was the next morning that the business with the crabs began.

I awoke, late in the day, to the sound of Filby hammering at something in his garage—talons, I think it was, copper talons. Not that it makes much difference. It woke me up. I don't sleep until an hour or so before dawn. There's a certain bird, Lord knows what sort, that sings through the last hour of the night and shuts right up when the sun rises. Don't ask me why. Anyway, there was Filby smashing away some time before noon. I opened my left eye, and there atop the pillow was a blood-red hermit crab with eyes on stalks, giving me a look as if he were proud of himself, waving pincers like that. I leaped up. There was another, creeping into my shoe, and two more making away with my pocket watch, dragging it along on its fob toward the bedroom door.

The window was open and the screen was torn. The beasts were clambering up onto the woodpile and hoisting themselves in through the open window to rummage through my personal effects while I slept. I pitched them out, but that evening there were more—dozens of them, bent beneath the weight of seashells, dragging toward the house with an eye to my pocket watch.

It was a migration. Once every hundred years, Dr. Jensen tells me, every hermit crab in creation gets the wanderlust and hurries ashore. Jensen camped on the beach in the cove to study the things. They were all heading south like migratory birds. By the end of the week there was a tiresome lot of them afoot—millions of them to hear Jensen carry on— but they left my house alone. They dwindled as the next week wore out, and seemed to be straggling in from deeper water and were bigger and bigger: The size of a man's fist at first, then of his head, and then a giant, vast as a pig, chased Jensen into the lower branches of an oak. On Friday there were only two crabs, both of them bigger than cars. Jensen went home gibbering and drank himself into a stupor. He was there on Saturday though; you've got to give him credit for that. But nothing appeared. He speculates that somewhere off the coast, in a deep-water chasm a hundred fathoms below the last faded colors is a monumental beast, blind and gnarled from spectacular pressures and wearing a seashell overcoat, feeling his way toward shore.

At night sometimes I hear the random echoes of far-off clacking, just the misty and muted suggestion of it, and I brace myself and stare into the pages of an open book, firelight glinting off the cut crystal of my glass, countless noises out in the foggy night among which is the occasional clack clack clack of what might be Jensen's impossible crab, creeping up to cast a shadow in the front porch lamplight, to demand my pocket watch. It was the night after the sighting of the pig-sized crabs that one got into Filby's garage—forced the door apparently—and made a hash out of his dragon. I know what you're thinking. I thought it was a lie too. But things have since fallen out that make me suppose otherwise. He did, apparently, know Augustus Silver. Filby was an acolyte; Silver was his master. But the dragon business, they tell me, isn't merely a matter of mechanics. It's a matter of perspective. That was Filby's downfall.

There was a gypsy who came round in a cart last year. He couldn't speak, apparently. For a dollar he'd do the most amazing feats. He tore out his tongue, when he first arrived, and tossed it onto the road. Then he danced on it and shoved it back into his mouth, good as new. Then he pulled out his entrails—yards and yards of them like sausage out of a machine—then jammed them all back in and nipped shut the hole he'd torn in his abdomen. It made half the town sick, mind you, but they paid to see it. That's pretty much how I've always felt about dragons. I don't half believe in them, but I'd give a bit to see one fly, even if it were no more than a clever illusion.

But Filby's dragon, the one he was keeping for Silver, was a ruin. The crab—I suppose it was a crab—had shredded it, knocked the wadding out of it. It reminded me of one of those stuffed alligators that turns up in curiosity shops, all eaten to bits by bugs and looking sad and tired, with its tail bent sidewise and a clump of cotton stuffing shoved through a tear in its neck.

Filby was beside himself. It's not good for a grown man to carry on so. He picked up the shredded remnant of a dissected wing and flagellated himself with it. He scourged himself, called himself names. I didn't know him well at the time, and so watched the whole weird scene from my kitchen window: His garage door banging open and shut in the wind, Filby weeping and howling through the open door, storming back and forth, starting and stopping theatrically, the door slamming shut and slicing off the whole embarrassing business for thirty seconds or so and then sweeping open to betray a wailing Filby scrabbling among the debris on the garage floor—the remnants of what had once been a flesh-and-blood dragon, as it were, built by the ubiquitous Augustus Silver years before. Of course I had no idea at the time. Augustus *Silver,* after all. It almost justifies Filby's carrying on. And I've done a bit of carrying on myself since, although as I said, most of what prompted the whole business has begun to seem suspiciously like lies, and the whispers in the foggy night, the clacking and whirring and rush of wings, has begun to sound like thinly disguised laughter, growing fainter by the months and emanating from nowhere, from the clouds, from the wind and fog. Even the occasional letters from Silver himself have become suspect.

Filby is an eccentric. I could see that straightaway. How he finances his endeavors is beyond me. Little odd jobs, I don't doubt—repairs and such. He has the hands of an archetypal mechanic: spatulate fingers, grime under the nails, nicks and cuts and scrapes that he can't identify. He has only to touch a heap of parts, wave his hands over them, and the faint rhythmic stirrings of order and pattern seem to shudder through the cross-members of his workbench. And here an enormous crab had gotten in, and in a single night had clipped apart a masterpiece, a wonder, a thing that couldn't be tacked back together. Even Silver would have pitched it out. The cat wouldn't want it.

Filby was morose for days, but I knew he'd come out of it. He'd be mooning around the house in a slump, poking at yesterday's newspapers, and a glint of light off a copper wire would catch his eye. The wire would suggest something. That's how it works. He not only has the irritating ability to coexist with mechanical refuse; it speaks to him too, whispers possibilities.

He'd be hammering away some morning soon—damn all crabs—piecing together the ten thousand silver scales of a wing, assembling the jeweled bits of a faceted eye, peering through a glass at a spray of fine wire spun into a braid that would run up along the spinal column of a creature which, when released some misty night, might disappear within moments into the clouds and be gone. Or so Filby dreamed. And I'll admit it: I had complete faith in him, in the dragon that he dreamed of building.

In the early spring, such as it is, some few weeks after the hermit crab business, I was hoeing along out in the garden. Another frost was unlikely. My tomatoes had been in for a week, and an enormous green worm with spines had eaten the leaves off the plants. There was nothing left but stems, and they were smeared up with a sort of slime. Once when I was a child I was digging in the dirt a few days after a rain, and I unearthed a finger-sized worm with the face of a human being. I buried it. But this tomato worm had no such face. He was pleasant, in fact, with little piggy eyes and a smashed-in sort of nose, as worm noses go. So I pitched him over the fence into Filby's yard. He'd climb back over—there was no doubting it. But he'd creep back from anywhere, from the moon. And since that was the case—if it was inevitable—then there seemed to be no reason to put him too far out of his way, if you follow me. But the plants were a wreck. I yanked them out by the roots and threw them into Filby's yard too, which is up in weeds anyway, but Filby himself had wandered up to the fence like a grinning gargoyle, and the clump of a half-dozen gnawed vines flew into his face like a squid. That's not the sort of thing to bother Filby though. He didn't mind. He had a letter from Silver mailed a month before from points south.

I was barely acquainted with the man's reputation then. I'd heard of him—who hasn't? And I could barely remember seeing photographs of a big, bearded man with wild hair and a look of passion in his eye, taken when Silver was involved in the mechano-vivisectionist's league in the days when they first learned the truth about the mutability of matter. He and three others at the university were responsible for the brief spate of unicorns, some few of which are said to roam the hills hereabouts, interesting mutants, certainly, but not the sort of wonder that would satisfy Augustus Silver. He appeared in the photograph to be the sort who would leap headlong into a cold pool at dawn and eat bulgur wheat and honey with a spoon.

And here was Filby, ridding himself of the remains of ravaged tomato plants, holding a letter in his hand, transported. A letter from the master! He'd been years in the tropics and had seen a thing or two. In the hills of the eastern jungles he'd sighted a dragon with what was quite apparently a bamboo rib cage. It flew with the xylophone clacking of wind chimes, and had the head of an enormous lizard, the pronged tail of a devilfish, and clockwork wings built of silver and string and the skins of carp. It had given him certain ideas. The best dragons, he was sure, would come from the sea. He was setting sail for San Francisco. Things could be purchased in Chinatown—certain "necessaries," as he put it in his letter to Filby. There was mention of perpetual motion, of the building of an immortal creature knitted together from parts of a dozen beasts.

I was still waiting for the issuance of that last crab, and so was Jensen. He wrote a monograph, a paper of grave scientific accuracy in which he postulated the correlation between the dwindling number of the creatures and the enormity of their size. He camped on the cliffs above the sea with his son Bumby, squinting through the fog, his eye screwed to the lens of a special telescope—one that saw things, as he put it, particularly clearly—and waiting for the first quivering claw of the behemoth to thrust up out of the gray swells, cascading water, draped with weeds, and the bearded face of the crab to follow, drawn along south by a sort of migratory magnet toward heaven alone knows what. Either the crab passed away down the coast hidden by mists, or Jensen was wrong—there hasn't been any last crab.

The letter from Augustus Silver gave Filby wings, as they say, and he flew into the construction of his dragon, sending off a letter east in which he enclosed forty dollars, his unpaid dues in the Dragon Society. The tomato worm, itself a wingless dragon, crept back into the garden four days later and had a go at a half-dozen fresh plants, nibbling lacy arabesques across the leaves. Flinging it back into Filby's yard would accomplish nothing. It was a worm of monumental determination. I put him into a jar—a big, gallon pickle jar, empty of pickles, of course—and I screwed onto it a lid with holes punched in. He lived happily in a little garden of leaves and dirt and sticks and polished stones, nibbling on the occasional tomato leaf.

I spent more and more time with Filby, watching, in those days after the arrival of the first letter, the mechanical bones and joints and organs of the dragon drawing together. Unlike his mentor, Filby had almost no knowledge of vivisection. He had an aversion to it, I believe, and as a consequence his creations were almost wholly mechanical—and almost wholly unlikely. But he had such an aura of certainty about him, such utter and uncompromising conviction that even the most unlikely project seemed inexplicably credible.

I remember one Saturday afternoon with particular clarity. The sun had shone for the first time in weeks. The grass hadn't been alive with slugs and snails the previous night—a sign, I supposed, that the weather was changing for the drier. But I was only half right. Saturday dawned clear. The sky was invisibly blue, dotted with the dark specks of what might have been sparrows or crows flying just above the treetops, or just as easily something else, something more vast—dragons, let's say, or the peculiar denizens of some very distant cloud world. Sunlight poured through the diamond panes of my bedroom window, and I swear I could hear the tomato plants and onions and snow peas in my garden unfurling, hastening skyward. But around noon great dark clouds roiled in over the Coast Range, their shadows creeping across the meadows and redwoods, picket fences, and chaparral. A spray of rain sailed on the freshening offshore breeze, and the sweet smell of ozone rose from the pavement of Filby's driveway, carrying on its first thin ghost an unidentifiable sort of promise and regret: the promise of wonders pending, regret for the bits and pieces of lost time that go trooping away like migratory hermit crabs, inexorably, irretrievably into the mists.

So it was a Saturday afternoon of rainbows and umbrellas, and Filby, still animate at the thought of Silver's approach, showed me some of his things. Filby's house was a marvel, given over entirely to his collections. Carven heads whittled of soapstone and ivory and ironwood populated the rooms, the strange souvenirs of distant travel. Aquaria bubbled away, thick with water plants and odd, mottled creatures: spotted eels and leaf fish, gobies buried to their noses in sand, flatfish with both eyes on the same side of their heads, and darting anableps that had the wonderful capacity to see above and below the surface of the water simultaneously and so, unlike the mundane fish that swam beneath, were inclined toward philosophy. I suggested as much to Filby, but I'm not certain he understood. Books and pipes and curios filled a half-dozen cases, and star charts hung on the walls. There were working drawings of some of Silver's earliest accomplishments, intricate swirling sketches covered over with what were to me utterly meaningless calculations and commentary.

On Monday another letter arrived from Silver. He'd gone along east on the promise of something very rare in the serpent line—an elephant trunk snake, he said, the lungs of which ran the length of its body. But he was coming to the west coast, that much was sure, to San Francisco. He'd be here in a week, a month, he couldn't be entirely sure. A message would come. Who could say when? We agreed that I would drive the five hours south on the coast road into the city to pick him up: I owned a car.

Filby was in a sweat to have his creature built before Silver's arrival. He wanted so badly to hear the master's approval, to see in Silver's eyes the brief electricity of surprise and excitement. And I wouldn't doubt for a moment that there was an element of envy involved. Filby, after all, had languished for years at the university in Silver's shadow, and now he was on the ragged edge of becoming a master himself.

So there in Filby's garage, tilted against a wall of rough-cut fir studs and redwood shiplap, the shoulders, neck, and right wing of the beast sat in silent repose, its head a mass of faceted pastel crystals, piano wire, and bone clutched in the soft rubber grip of a bench vise. It was on Friday, the morning of the third letter, that Filby touched the bare ends of two microscopically thin copper rods, and the eyes of the dragon rotated on their axis, very slowly, blinking twice, surveying the cramped and dimly lit garage with an ancient, knowing look before the rods parted and life flickered out.

Filby was triumphant. He danced around the garage, shouting for joy, cutting little capers. But my suggestion that we take the afternoon off, perhaps drive up to Fort Bragg for lunch and a beer, was met with stolid refusal. Silver, it seemed, was on the horizon. I was to leave in the morning. I might, quite conceivably, have to spend a few nights waiting. One couldn't press Augustus Silver, of course. Filby himself would work on the dragon. It would be a night and day business, to be sure. I determined to take the tomato worm along for company, as it were, but the beast had dug himself into the dirt for a nap.

This business of my being an emissary of Filby struck me as dubious when I awoke on Saturday morning. I was a neighbor who had been ensnared in a web of peculiar enthusiasm. Here I was pulling on heavy socks and stumbling around the kitchen, tendrils of fog creeping in over the sill, the hemlocks ghostly beyond dripping panes, while Augustus Silver tossed on the dark Pacific swell somewhere off the Golden Gate, his hold full of dragon bones. What was I to say to him beyond, "Filby sent me." Or something more cryptic: "Greetings from Filby." Perhaps in these circles one merely winked or made a sign or wore a peculiar sort of cap with a foot-long visor and a pyramid-encased eye embroidered across the front. I felt like a fool, but I had promised Filby. His garage was alight at dawn, and I had been awakened once in the night by a shrill screech, cut off sharply and followed by Filby's cackling laughter and a short snatch of song.

I was to speak to an old Chinese named Wun Lo in a restaurant off Washington. Filby referred to him as "the connection." I was to introduce myself as a friend of Captain Augustus Silver and wait for orders. Orders—what in the devil sort of talk was that? In the dim glow of lamplight the preceding midnight such secret talk seemed sensible, even satisfactory; in the chilly dawn it was risible.

It was close to six hours into the city, winding along the tortuous road, bits and pieces of it having fallen into the sea on the back of winter rains. The fog rose out of rocky coves and clung to the hillsides, throwing a gray veil over dew-fed wildflowers and shore grasses. Silver fencepickets loomed out of the murk with here and there the skull of a cow or a goat impaled atop, and then the quick passing of a half-score of mailboxes on posts, rusted and canted over toward the cliffs along with twisted cypresses that seemed on the verge of flinging themselves into the sea.

Now and again, without the least notice, the fog would disappear in a twinkling, and a clear mile of highway would appear, weirdly sharp and crystalline in contrast to its previous muted state. Or an avenue into the sky would suddenly appear, the remote end of which was dipped in opalescent blue and which seemed as distant and unattainable as the end of a rainbow. Across one such avenue, springing into clarity for perhaps three seconds, flapped the ungainly bulk of what might have been a great bird, laboring as if against a stiff, tumultuous wind just above the low-lying fog. It might as easily have been something else, much higher. A dragon? One of Silver's creations that nested in the dense emerald fog forests of the Coast Range? It was impossible to tell, but it seemed, as I said, to be struggling—perhaps it was old—and a bit of something, a fragment of a wing, fell clear of it and spun dizzily into the sea. Maybe what fell was just a stick being carried back to the nest of an ambitious heron. In an instant the fog closed, or rather the car sped out of the momentary clearing, and any opportunity to identify the beast, really to study it, was gone. For a moment I considered turning around, going back, but it was doubtful that I'd find that same bit of clarity, or that if I did, the creature would still be visible. So I drove on, rounding bends between redwood-covered hills that might have been clever paintings draped along the ghostly edge of Highway One, the hooks that secured them hidden just out of view in the mists above. Then almost without warning the damp asphalt issued out onto a broad highway and shortly thereafter onto the humming expanse of the Golden Gate Bridge.

Some few silent boats struggled against the tide below. Was one of them the ship of Augustus Silver, slanting in toward the Embarcadero? Probably not. They were fishing boats from the look of them, full of shrimp and squid and bug-eyed rock cod. I drove to the outskirts of Chinatown and parked, leaving the car and plunging into the crowd that swarmed down Grant and Jackson and into Portsmouth Square.

It was Chinese New Year. The streets were heavy with the smell of almond cookies and fog, barbecued duck and gunpowder, garlic and seaweed. Rockets burst overhead in showers of barely visible sparks, and one, teetering over onto the street as the fuse burned, sailed straightaway up Washington, whirling and glowing and fizzing into the wall of a curio shop, then dropping lifeless onto the sidewalk as if embarrassed at its own antics. The smoke and pop of firecrackers, the milling throng, and the nagging senselessness of my mission drove me along down Washington until I stumbled into the smoky open door of a narrow, three-story restaurant. Sam Wo it was called.

An assortment of white-garmented chefs chopped away at vegetables. Woks hissed. Preposterous bowls of white rice steamed on the counter. A fish head the size of a melon blinked at me out of a pan. And there, at a small table made of chromed steel and rubbed formica, sat my contact. It had to be him. Filby had been wonderfully accurate in his description. The man had a gray beard that wagged on the tabletop and a suit of similar color that was several sizes too large, and he spooned up clear broth in such a mechanical, purposeful manner that his eating was almost ceremonial. I approached him. There was nothing to do but brass it out. "I'm a friend of Captain Silver," I said, smiling and holding out a hand. He bowed, touched my hand with one limp finger, and rose. I followed him into the back of the restaurant.

It took only a scattering of moments for me to see quite clearly that my trip had been entirely in vain. Who could say where Augustus Silver was? Singapore? Ceylon? Bombay? He'd had certain herbs mailed east just two days earlier. I was struck at once with the foolishness of my position. What in the world was I doing in San Francisco? I had the uneasy feeling that the five chefs just outside the door were having a laugh at my expense, and that old Wun Lo, gazing out toward the street, was about to ask for money—a fiver, just until payday. I was a friend of Augustus Silver, wasn't I?

My worries were temporarily arrested by an old photograph that hung above a tile-faced hearth. It depicted a sort of weird shantytown somewhere on the north coast. There was a thin fog, just enough to veil the surrounding countryside, and the photograph had clearly been taken at dusk, for the long, deep shadows thrown by strange hovels slanted away landward into the trees. The tip of a lighthouse was just visible on the edge of the dark Pacific, and a scattering of small boats lay at anchor beneath. It was puzzling, to be sure—doubly so, because the lighthouse, the spit of land that swerved round toward it, the green bay amid cypress and eucalyptus was, I was certain, Point Reyes. But the shantytown, I was equally certain, didn't exist, couldn't exist.

The collection of hovels tumbled down to the edge of the bay, a long row of them that descended the hillside like a strange gothic stairway, and all of them, I swear it, were built in part of the ruins of dragons, of enormous winged reptiles—tin and copper, leather and bone. Some were stacked on end, tilted against each other like card houses. Some were perched atop oil drums or upended wooden pallets. Here was nothing but a broken wing throwing a sliver of shade; there was what appeared to be a tolerably complete creature, lacking, I suppose, whatever essential parts had once served to animate it. And standing alongside a cooking pot with a man who could quite possibly have been Wun Lo himself was Augustus Silver.

His beard was immense—the beard of a hill wanderer, of a prospector lately returned from years in unmapped goldfields, and that beard and broad-brimmed felt hat, his Oriental coat and the sharp glint of arcane knowledge that shone from his eyes, the odd harpoon he held loosely in his right hand, the breadth of his shoulders—all those bits and pieces seemed almost to deify him, as if he were an incarnation of Neptune just out of the bay, or a wandering Odin who had stopped to drink flower-petal tea in a queer shantytown along the coast. The very look of him abolished my indecision. I left Wun Lo nodding in a chair, apparently having forgotten my presence.

Smoke hung in the air of the street. Thousands of sounds—a cacophony of voices, explosions, whirring pinwheels, Oriental music—mingled into a strange sort of harmonious silence. Somewhere to the northwest lay a village built of the skins of dragons. If nothing else—if I discovered nothing of the arrival of Augustus Silver—I would at least have a look at the shantytown in the photograph. I pushed through the crowd down Washington, oblivious to the sparks and explosions. Then almost magically, like the Red Sea, the throng parted and a broad avenue of asphalt opened before me. Along either side of the suddenly clear street were grinning faces, frozen in anticipation. A vast cheering arose, a shouting, a banging on Chinese cymbals and tooting on reedy little horns. Rounding the corner and rushing along with the maniacal speed of an express train, careered the leering head of a paper dragon, lolling back and forth, a wild rainbow mane streaming behind it. The body of the thing was half a block long, and seemed to be built of a thousand layers of the thinnest sort of pastel-colored rice paper, sheets and sheets of it threatening to fly loose and dissolve in the fog. A dozen people crouched within, racing along the pavement, the whole lot of them yowling and chanting as the crowd closed behind and in a wave pressed along east toward Kearny, the tumult and color muting once again into silence.

The rest of the afternoon had an air of unreality to it, which, strangely, deepened my faith in Augustus Silver and his creations, even though all rational evidence seemed to point squarely in the opposite direction. I drove north out of the city, cutting off at San Rafael toward the coast, toward Point Reyes and Inverness, winding through the green hillsides as the sun traveled down the afternoon sky toward the sea. It was shortly before dark that I stopped for gasoline.

The swerve of shoreline before me was a close cousin of that in the photograph, and the collected bungalows on the hillside could have been the ghosts of the dragon shanties, if one squinted tightly enough to confuse the image through a foliage of eyelashes. Perhaps I've gotten that backward; I can't at all say anymore which of the two worlds had substance and which was the phantom.

A bank of fog had drifted shoreward. But for that, perhaps I could have made out the top of the lighthouse and completed the picture. As it was I could see only the gray veil of mist wisping in on a faint onshore breeze. At the gas station I inquired after a map. Surely, I thought, somewhere close by, perhaps within eyesight if it weren't for the fog, lay my village. The attendant, a tobacco-chewing lump of engine oil and blue paper towels, hadn't heard of it—the dragon village, that is. He glanced sideways at me. A map hung in the window. It cost nothing to look. So I wandered into a steel and glass cubicle, cold with rust and sea air, and studied the map. It told me little. It had been hung recently; the tape holding its corners hadn't yellowed or begun to peel. Through an open doorway to my right was the dim garage where a Chinese mechanic tinkered with the undercarriage of a car on a hoist.

I turned to leave just as the hovering fog swallowed the sun, casting the station into shadow. Over the dark Pacific swell the mists whirled in the sea wind, a trailing wisp arching skyward in a rush, like surge-washed tidepool grasses or the waving tail of an enormous misty dragon, and for a scattering of seconds the last faint rays of the evening sun shone out of the tattered fog, illuminating the old gas pumps, the interior of the weathered office, the dark, tool-strewn garage.

The map in the window seemed to curl at the corners, the tape suddenly brown and dry. The white background tinted into shades of antique ivory and pale ocher, and what had been creases in the paper appeared, briefly, to be hitherto unseen roads winding out of the redwoods toward the sea.

It was the strange combination, I'm sure, of the evening, the dying sun, and the rising fog that for a moment made me unsure whether the mechanic was crouched in his overalls beneath some vast and finny automobile spawned of the peculiar architecture of the early sixties, or instead worked beneath the chrome and iron shell of a tilted dragon, frozen in flight above the greasy concrete floor, and framed by tiers of heater hoses and old dusty tires.

Then the sun was gone. Darkness fell within moments, and all was as it had been. I drove slowly north through the village. There was, of course, no shantytown built of castaway dragons. There were nothing but warehouses and weedy vacant lots and the weathered concrete and tin of an occasional industrial building. A tangle of small streets comprised of odd, tumbledown shacks, some few of them on stilts as if awaiting a flood of apocalyptic proportions. But the shacks were built of clapboard and asphalt shingles—there wasn't a hint of a dragon anywhere, not even the tip of a rusted wing in the jimsonweed and mustard.

I determined not to spend the night in a motel, although I was tempted to, on the off chance that the fog would dissipate and the watery coastal moonbeams would wash the coastline clean of whatever it was—a trick of sunlight or a trick of fog—that had confused me for an instant at the gas station. But as I say, the day had, for the most part, been unprofitable, and the thought of being twenty dollars out of pocket for a motel room was intolerable.

It was late—almost midnight—when I arrived home, exhausted. My tomato worm slept in his den. The light still burned in Filby's garage, so I wandered out and peeked through the door. Filby sat on a stool, his chin in his hands, staring at the dismantled head of his beast. I suddenly regretted having looked in; he'd demand news of Silver, and I'd have nothing to tell him. The news—or rather the lack of news—seemed to drain the lees of energy from him. He hadn't slept in two days. Jensen had been round hours earlier babbling about an amazingly high tide and of his suspicion that the last of the crabs might yet put in an appearance. Did Filby want to watch on the beach that night? No, Filby didn't. Filby wanted only to assemble his dragon. But there was something not quite right—some wire or another that had gotten crossed, or a gem that had been miscut—and the creature wouldn't respond. It was so much junk.

I commiserated with him. Lock the door against Jensen's crab, I said, and wait until dawn. It sounded overmuch like a platitude, but Filby, I think, was ready to grasp at any reason, no matter how shallow, to leave off his tinkering.

The two of us sat up until the sun rose, drifting in and out of maudlin reminiscences and debating the merits of a stroll down to the bluffs to see how Jensen was faring. The high tide, apparently, was accompanied by a monumental surf, for in the spaces of meditative silence I could just hear the rush and thunder of long breakers collapsing on the beach. It seemed unlikely to me that there would be giant crabs afoot.

The days that followed saw no break in the weather. It continued dripping and dismal. No new letters arrived from Augustus Silver. Filby's dragon seemed to be in a state of perpetual decline. The trouble that plagued it receded deeper into it with the passing days, as if it were mocking Filby, who groped along in its wake, clutching at it, certain in the morning that he had the problem securely by the tail, morose that same afternoon that it had once again slipped away. The creature was a perfect wonder of separated parts. I'd had no notion of its complexity. Hundreds of those parts, by week's end, were laid out neatly on the garage floor, one after another in the order they'd been dismantled. Concentric circles of them expanded like ripples on a pond, and by Tuesday of the following week masses of them had been swept into coffee cans that sat here and there on the bench and floor. Filby was declining, I could see that. That week he spent less time in the garage than he had been spending there in a single day during the previous weeks, and he slept instead long hours in the afternoon.

I still held out hope for a letter from Silver. He was, after all, out there somewhere. But I was plagued with the suspicion that such a letter might easily contribute to certain of Filby's illusions—or to my own—and so prolong what with each passing day promised to be the final deflation of those same illusions. Better no hope, I thought, than impossible hope, than ruined anticipation.

But late in the afternoon, when from my attic window I could see Jensen picking his way along the bluffs, carrying with him a wood and brass telescope, while the orange glow of a diffused sun radiated through the thinned fog over the sea, I wondered where Silver was, what strange seas he sailed, what rumored wonders were drawing him along jungle paths that very evening.

One day he'd come, I was sure of it. There would be patchy fog illuminated by ivory moonlight. The sound of Eastern music, of Chinese banjos and copper gongs would echo over the darkness of the open ocean. The fog would swirl and part, revealing a universe of stars and planets and the aurora borealis dancing in transparent color like the thin rainbow light of paper lanterns hung in the windswept sky. Then the fog would close, and out of the phantom mists, heaving on the groundswell, his ship would sail into the mouth of the harbor, slowly, cutting the water like a ghost, strange sea creatures visible in the phosphorescent wake, one by one dropping away and returning to sea as if having accompanied the craft across ten thousand miles of shrouded ocean. We'd drink a beer, the three of us, in Filby's garage. We'd summon Jensen from his vigil.

But as I say, no letter came, and all anticipation was so much air. Filby's beast was reduced to parts—a plate of broken meats, as it were. The idea of it reminded me overmuch of the sad bony remains of a Thanksgiving turkey. There was nothing to be done. Filby wouldn't be placated. But the fog, finally, had lifted. The black oak in the yard was leafing out and the tomato plants were knee-high and luxuriant. My worm was still asleep, but I had hopes that the spring weather would revive him. It wasn't, however, doing a thing for Filby. He stared long hours at the salad of debris, and when in one ill-inspired moment I jokingly suggested he send to Detroit for a carburetor, he cast me such a savage look that I slipped out again and left him alone.

On Sunday afternoon a wind blew, slamming Filby's garage door until the noise grew tiresome. I peeked in, aghast. There was nothing in the heaped bits of scrap that suggested a dragon, save one dismantled wing, the silk and silver of which was covered with greasy handprints. Two cats wandered out. I looked for some sign of Jensen's crab, hoping, in fact, that some such rational and concrete explanation could be summoned to explain the ruin. But Filby, alas, had quite simply gone to bits along with his dragon. He'd lost whatever strange inspiration it was that propelled him. His creation lay scattered, not two pieces connected. Wires and fuses were heaped amid unidentifiable crystals, and one twisted bit of elaborate machinery had quite clearly been danced upon and lay now cold and dead, half hidden beneath the bench. Delicate thises and thats sat mired in a puddle of oil that scummed half the floor.

Filby wandered out, adrift, his hair frazzled. He'd received a last letter. There were hints in it of extensive travel, perhaps danger. Silver's visit to the west coast had been delayed again. Filby ran his hand backward through his hair, oblivious to the harrowed result the action effected. He had the look of a nineteenth-century Bedlam lunatic. He muttered something about having a sister in McKinleyville, and seemed almost illuminated when he added, apropos of nothing, that in his sister's town, deeper into the heart of the north coast, stood the tallest totem pole in the world. Two days later he was gone. I locked his garage door for him and made a vow to collect his mail with an eye toward a telling, exotic postmark. But nothing so far has appeared. I've gotten into the habit of spending the evening on the beach with Jensen and his son Bumby, both of whom still hold out hope for the issuance of the last crab. The spring sunsets are unimaginable. Bumby is as fond of them as I am, and can see comparable whorls of color and pattern in the spiral curve of a seashell or in the peculiar green depths of a tidepool.

In fact, when my tomato worm lurched up out of his burrow and unfurled an enormous gauzy pair of mottled brown wings, I took him along to the seaside so that Bumby could watch him set sail, as it were.

The afternoon was cloudless and the ocean sighed on the beach. Perhaps the calm, insisted Jensen, would appeal to the crab. But Bumby by then was indifferent to the fabled crab. He stared into the pickle jar at the half-dozen circles of bright orange dotting the abdomen of the giant sphinx moth that had once crept among my tomato plants in a clever disguise. It was both wonderful and terrible, and held a weird fascination for Bumby, who tapped at the jar, making up and discarding names.

When I unscrewed the lid, the moth fluttered skyward some few feet and looped around in a crazy oval, Bumby charging along in its wake, then racing away in pursuit as the monster hastened south. The picture of it is as clear to me now as rainwater: Bumby running and jumping, kicking up glinting sprays of sand, outlined against the sheer rise of mossy cliffs, and the wonderful moth just out of reach overhead, luring Bumby along the afternoon beach. At last it was impossible to say just what the diminishing speck in the china-blue sky might be—a tiny winged creature silhouetted briefly on the false horizon of our little cove, or some vast flying reptile swooping over the distant ocean where it fell away into the void, off the edge of the flat earth.

Tanith Lee

Into Gold

Tanith Lee is one of the best known and most prolific of modern fantasists, with over forty books to her credit, including (among many others) *The Birthgrave, Drinking Sapphire Wine, Don't Bite the Sun, Night's Master, The Storm Lord, Sung in Shadow, Volkhavaar, Anackire, Night Sorceries, The Black Unicorn,* and *The Blood of Roses,* and the collections *Tamastara, The Gorgon, Dreams of Dark and Light,* and *The Forests of the Night.* Her short story "Elle Est Trois (La Mort)" won a World Fantasy Award in 1984 and her brilliant collection of retold folk tales, *Red as Blood,* was also a finalist that year, in the Best Collection category. Her most recent books are the collection *Nightshades* and the novel *Vivia.*

Lee's work is usually intense, vivid, gorgeously colored, richly sensuous, and erotically charged, and the compelling story that follows is no exception, as she takes us to the tumultuous days after the fall of the Roman Empire, to a remote border outpost left isolated by the retreat of the Legions, for a scary and passionate tale of intrigue, obsession, vaunting ambition, and love.

I

Up behind Danuvius, the forests are black, and so stiff with black pork, black bears, and black-grey wolves, a man alone will feel himself jostled. Here and there you come on a native village, pointed houses of thatch with carved wooden posts, and smoke thick enough to cut with your knife. All day the birds call, and at night the owls come out. There are other things of earth and darkness, too. One ceases to be surprised at what may be found in the forests, or what may stray from them on occasion.

One morning, a corn-king emerged, and pleased us all no end. There had been some trouble, and some of the stores had gone up in flames. The ovens were standing empty and cold. It can take a year to get goods overland from the River, and our northern harvest was months off.

The old fort, that had been the palace then for twelve years, was built on high ground. It looked out across a mile of country strategically cleared of trees, to the forest cloud and a dream of distant mountains. Draco had called me up to the roof-walk, where we stood watching these mountains glow and fade, and come and go. It promised to be a fine day, and I had been planning a good long hunt, to exercise the men and give the bread-less bellies solace. There is also a pine-nut meal they grind in the villages, accessible to barter. The loaves were not to everyone's taste, but we might have to come round to them. Since the armies pulled away, we had learned to improvise. I could scarcely remember the first days. The old men told you, everything, anyway, had been going down to chaos even then. Draco's father, holding on to a commander's power, assumed a prince's title which his orphaned warriors were glad enough to concede him. Discipline is its own ritual, and drug. As, lands and seas away from the center of the world caved in, soldier-fashion, they turned builders. They made the road to the fort, and soon began on the town, shoring it, for eternity, with strong walls. Next, they opened up the country, and got trade rights seen to that had gone by default for decades. There was plenty of skirmishing as well to keep their swords bright. When the Comman-der died of a wound got fighting the Blue-Hair Tribe, a terror in those days, not seen for years since, Draco became the Prince in the Palace. He was eighteen then, and I five days older. We had known each other nearly all our lives, learned books and horses, drilled, hunted together. Though he was born elsewhere, he barely took that in, coming to this life when he could only just walk. For myself, I am lucky, perhaps, I never saw the Mother of Cities, and so never hanker after her, or lament her downfall.

That day on the roof-walk, certainly, nothing was further from my mind. Then Draco said, *"There* is something."

His clear-water eyes saw detail quicker and more finely than mine. When I looked, to me still it was only a blur and fuss on the forest's edge, and the odd sparkling glint of things catching the early sun.

"Now, Skorous, do you suppose . . . ?" said Draco.

"Someone has heard of our misfortune, and considerably changed his route," I replied.

We had got news a week before of a grain-caravan, but too far west to be of use. Conversely, it seemed, the caravan had received news of our fire. "Up goes the price of bread," said Draco.

By now I was sorting it out, the long rigmarole of mules and baggage-wagons, horses and men. He traveled in some style. Truly, a corn-king, profiting always because he was worth his weight in gold amid the wilds of civilization. In Empire days, he would have weighed rather less.

We went down, and were in the square behind the east gate when the sentries brought him through. He left his people out on the parade be-fore the gate, but one wagon had come up to the gateway, presumably his own, a huge conveyance, a regular traveling house, with six oxen in the shafts. Their straps were spangled with what I took for brass. On the side-leathers were pictures of grindstones and grain done in purple and yellow. He himself rode a tall horse, also spangled. He had a slim, snaky look, an Eastern look, with black brows and fawn skin. His fingers and ears were remarkable for their gold. And suddenly I began to wonder about the spangles. He bowed to Draco, the War-Leader and Prince. Then, to be quite safe, to me.

"Greetings, Miller," I said.

He smiled at this coy honorific.

"Health and greetings, Captain. I think I am welcome?"

"My prince," I indicated Draco, "is always hospitable to wayfarers."

"Particularly to those with wares, in time of dearth."

"Which dearth is that?"

He put one golden finger to one golden earlobe.

"The trees whisper. This town of the Iron Shields has no bread."

Draco said mildly, "You should never listen to gossip."

I said, "If you've come out of your way, that would be a pity."

The Corn-King regarded me, not liking my arrogance—though I never saw the Mother of Cities, I have the blood—any more than I liked his slink and glitter.

As this went on, I gambling and he summing up the bluff, the tail of my eye caught another glimmering movement, from where his house wagon waited at the gate. I sensed some woman must be peering round the flap, the way the Eastern females do. The free girls of the town are prouder, even the wolf-girls of the brothel, and aristocrats use a veil only as a sunshade. Draco's own sisters, though decorous and well brought-up, can read and write, each can handle a light chariot, and will stand and look a man straight in the face. But I took very little notice of the fleeting apparition, except to decide it too had gold about it. I kept my sight on my quarry, and presently he smiled again and drooped his eye-lids, so I knew he would not risk calling me, and we had won. "Perhaps," he said, "there might be a little consideration of the detour I, so foolishly, erroneously, made."

"We are always glad of fresh supplies. The fort is not insensible to its isolation. Rest assured."

"Too generous," he said. His eyes flared. But politely he added, "I have heard of your town. There is great culture here. You have a library, with scrolls from Hellas, and Semitic Byblos—I can read many tongues, and would like to ask permission of your lord to visit among his books."

I glanced at Draco, amused by the fellow's cheek, though all the East thinks itself a scholar. But Draco was staring at the wagon. Something worth a look, then, which I had missed.

"And we have excellent baths," I said to the Corn-King, letting him know in turn that the Empire's lost children think all the scholarly East to be also unwashed.

By midday, the whole caravan had come in through the walls and arranged itself in the marketplace, near the temple of Mars. The temple priests, some of whom had been serving with the Draconis Regiment when it arrived, old, old men, did not take to this influx. In spring and summer, traders were in and out the town like flies, and native men came to work in the forges and the tannery or with the horses, and built their muddy thatch huts behind the unfinished law-house—which huts winter rain always washed away again when their inhabitants were gone. To such events of passage the priests were accustomed. But this new show displeased them. The chief Salius came up to the fort, attended by his slaves, and argued a while with Draco. Heathens, said the priest, with strange rituals, and dirtiness, would offend the patron god of the town. Draco seemed preoccupied.

I had put off the hunting party, and now stayed to talk the Salius into a better humor. It would be a brief nuisance, and surely, they had been directed to us by the god himself, who did not want his warlike sons to go hungry? I assured the priest that, if the foreigners wanted to worship their own gods, they would have to be circumspect. Tolerance of every religious rag, as we knew, was unwise. They did not, I thought, worship Iusa. There would be no abominations. I then vowed a boar to Mars, if I could get one, and the dodderer tottered, pale and grim, away.

Meanwhile, the grain was being seen to. The heathen god-offenders had sacks and jars of it, and ready flour besides. It seemed a heavy chancy load with which to journey, goods that might spoil if at all delayed, or if the weather went against them. And all that jangling of gold besides. They fairly bled gold. I had been right in my second thought on the bridle-decorations, there were even nuggets and bells hung on the wagons, and gold flowers; and the oxen had gilded horns. For the men, they were ringed and buckled and roped and tied with it. It was a marvel.

When I stepped over to the camp near sunset, I was on the lookout for anything amiss. But they had picketed their animals couthly enough, and the dazzle-fringed, clink-bellied wagons stood quietly shadowing and gleaming in the westered light. Columns of spicy smoke rose, but only from their cooking. Boys dealt with that, and boys had drawn water from the well; neither I nor my men had seen any women.

Presently I was conducted to the Corn-King's wagon. He received me before it, where woven rugs, and cushions stitched with golden discs, were strewn on the ground. A tent of dark purple had been erected close by. With its gilt-tasseled sides all down, it was shut as a box. A disc or two more winked yellow from the folds. Beyond, the plastered colonnades, the stone Mars Temple, stood equally closed and eyeless, refusing to see.

The Miller and I exchanged courtesies. He asked me to sit, so I sat. I was curious.

"It is pleasant," he said, "to be within safe walls."

"Yes, you must be often in some danger," I answered.

He smiled, secretively now. "You mean our wealth? It is better to display than to hide. The thief kills, in his hurry, the man who conceals his gold. I have never been robbed. They think, Ah, this one shows all his riches. He must have some powerful demon to protect him."

"And is that so?"

"Of course," he said.

I glanced at the temple, and then back at him, meaningly. He said, "Your men drove a hard bargain for the grain and the flour. And I have been docile. I respect your gods, Captain. I respect all gods. That, too, is a protection."

Some drink came. I tasted it cautiously, for Easterners often eschew wine and concoct other disgusting muck. In the forests they ferment thorn berries, or the milk of their beasts, neither of which methods makes such a poor beverage, when you grow used to it. But of the Semites one hears all kinds of things. Still, the drink had a sweet hot sizzle that made me want more, so I swallowed some, then waited to see what else it would do to me.

"And your lord will allow me to enter his library?" said the Corn-King, after a host's proper pause.

"That may be possible," I said. I tried the drink again. "How do you manage without women?" I added, "You'll have seen the House of the Mother, with the she-wolf painted over the door? The girls there are fastidious and clever. If your men will spare the price, naturally."

The Corn-King looked at me, with his liquid man-snake's eyes, aware of all I said which had not been spoken.

"It is true," he said at last, "that we have no women with us."

"Excepting your own wagon."

"My daughter," he said.

I had known Draco, as I have said, almost all my life. He was for me what no other had ever been; I had followed his star gladly and without question, into scrapes, and battles, through very fire and steel. Very rarely would he impose on me some task I hated, loathed. When he did so it was done without design or malice, as a man sneezes. The bad times were generally to do with women. I had fought back to back with him, but I did not care to be his pander. Even so, I would not refuse. He had stood in the window that noon, looking at the black forest, and said in a dry low voice, carelessly apologetic, irrefutable, "He has a girl in that wagon. Get her for me." "Well, she may be his–" I started off. He cut me short. "Whatever she is. He sells things. He is accustomed to selling." "And if he won't?" I said. Then he looked at me, with his high-colored, translucent eyes. "Make him," he said, and next laughed, as if it were nothing at all, this choice mission. I had come out thinking glumly, she has witched him, put the Eye on him. But I had known him lust like this before. Nothing would do then but he must have. Women had never been that way for me. They were available, when one needed them. I like to this hour to see them here and there, *our* women, straight-limbed, graceful, clean. In the perilous seasons I would have died defending his sisters, as I would have died to defend him. That was that. It was a fact, the burning of our grain had come about through an old grievance, an idiot who kept score of something Draco had done half a year ago, about a native girl got on a raid.

I put down the golden cup, because the drink was going to my head. They had two ways, Easterners, with daughters. One was best left unspoken. The other kept them locked and bolted virgin. Mercurius bless the dice. Then before I could say anything, the Miller put my mind at rest.

"My daughter," he said, "is very accomplished. She is also very beautiful, but I speak now of the beauty of learning and art."

"Indeed. Indeed."

The sun was slipping over behind the walls. The far mountains were steeped in dyes. This glamour shone behind the Corn-King's head, gold in the sky for him, too. And he said, "Amongst other matters, she has studied the lore of Khemia—Old Aegyptus, you will understand."

"Ah, yes?"

"Now I will confide in you," he said. His tongue flickered on his lips. Was it forked? The damnable drink had fuddled me after all, that, and a shameful relief. "The practice of the Al-Khemia contains every science and sorcery. She can read the stars, she can heal the hurts of man. But best of all, my dear Captain, my daughter has learned the third great secret of the Tri-Magae."

"Oh, yes, indeed?"

"She can," he said, "change all manner of materials into gold."

II

"Sometimes, Skorous," Draco said, "you are a fool."

"Sometimes I am not alone in that."

Draco shrugged. He had never feared honest speaking. He never asked more of a title than his own name. But those two items were, in themselves, significant. He was what he was, a law above the law. The heart-legend of the City was down, and he a prince in a forest that ran all ways forever.

"What do you think then she will do to me? Turn me into metal, too?"

We spoke in Greek, which tended to be the palace mode for private chat. It was fading out of use in the town.

"I don't believe in that kind of sorcery," I said.

"Well, he has offered to have her show us. Come along."

"It will be a trick."

"All the nicer. Perhaps he will find someone for you, too."

"I shall attend you," I said, "because I trust none of them. And fifteen of my men around the wagon."

"I must remember not to groan," he said, "or they'll be splitting the leather and tumbling in on us with swords."

"Draco," I said, "I'm asking myself why he boasted that she had the skill?"

"All that gold: They didn't steal it or cheat for it. A witch *made* it for them."

"I have heard of the Al-Khemian arts."

"Oh yes," he said. "The devotees make gold, they predict the future, they raise the dead. She might be useful. Perhaps I should marry her. Wait till you see her," he said. "I suppose it was all prearranged. He will want paying again."

When we reached the camp, it was midnight. Our torches and theirs opened the dark, and the flame outside the Mars Temple burned faint. There were stars in the sky, no moon.

We had gone to them at their request, since the magery was intrinsic, required utensils, and was not to be moved to the fort without much effort. We arrived like a bridal procession. The show was not after all to be in the wagon, but the tent. The other Easterners had buried themselves from view. I gave the men their orders and stood them conspicuously about. Then a slave lifted the tent's purple drapery a chink and squinted up at us. Draco beckoned me after him, no one demurred. We both went into the pavilion.

To do that was to enter the East head-on. Expensive gums were burning with a dark hot perfume that put me in mind of the wine I had had earlier. The incense burners were gold, tripods on leopards' feet, with swags of golden ivy. The floor was carpeted soft, like the pelt of some beast, and beast-skins were hung about—things I had not seen before, some of them, maned and spotted, striped and scaled, and some with heads and jewelry eyes and the teeth and claws gilded. Despite all the clutter of things, of polished mirrors and casks and chests, cushions and dead animals, and scent, there was a feeling of great space within that tent. The ceiling of it stretched taut and high, and three golden wheels depended, with oil lights in little golden boats. The wheels turned idly now this way, now that, in a wind that came from nowhere and went to nowhere, a demon wind out of a desert. Across the space, wide as night, was an opaque dividing curtain, and on the curtain, a long parchment. It was figured with another mass of images, as if nothing in the place should be spare. A tree went up, with two birds at the roots, a white bird with a raven-black head, a soot-black bird with the head of an ape. A snake twined the tree too, round and round, and ended looking out of the lower branches where yellow fruit hung. The snake had the face of a maiden, and flowing hair. Above sat three figures, judges of the dead from Aegyptus, I would have thought, if I had thought about them, with a balance, and wands. The sun and the moon stood over the tree.

I put my hand to the hilt of my sword, and waited. Draco had seated himself on the cushions. A golden jug was to hand, and a cup. He reached forward, poured the liquor and made to take it, before—reluctantly—I snatched the vessel. "Let me, first. Are you mad?"

He reclined, not interested as I tasted for him, then let him have the cup again.

Then the curtain parted down the middle and the parchment with it, directly through the serpent tree. I had expected the Miller, but instead what entered was a black dog with a collar of gold. It had a wolf's shape, but more slender, and with a pointed muzzle and high carven pointed ears. Its eyes were also black. It stood calmly, like a steward, regarding us, then stepped aside and lay down, its head still raised to watch. And next the woman Draco wanted came in.

To me, she looked nothing in particular. She was pleasantly made, slim, but rounded, her bare arms and feet the color of amber. Over her head, to her breast, covering her hair and face like a dusky smoke, was a veil, but it was transparent enough you saw through it to black locks and black aloe eyes, and a full tawny mouth. There was only a touch of gold on her, a rolled torque of soft metal at her throat, and one ring on her right hand. I was puzzled as to what had made her glimmer at the edge of my sight before, but perhaps she had dressed differently then, to make herself plain.

She bowed Easternwise to Draco, then to me. Then, in the purest Greek I ever heard, she addressed us.

"Lords, while I am at work, I must ask that you will please be still, or else you will disturb the currents of the act and so impair it. Be seated," she said to me, as if I had only stood till then from courtesy. Her eyes were very black, black as the eyes of the jackal-dog, blacker than the night. Then she blinked, and her eyes flashed. The lids were painted with gold. And I found I had sat down.

What followed I instantly took for an hallucination, induced by the incense, and by other means less perceptible. That is not to say I did not think she was a witch. There was something of power to her I never met before. It pounded from her, like heat, or an aroma. It did not make her beautiful for me, but it held me quiet, though I swear never once did I lose my grip either on my senses or my sword.

First, and quite swiftly, I had the impression the whole tent blew upward, and we were in the open in fact, under a sky of a million stars that blazed and crackled like diamonds. Even so, the golden wheels stayed put, up in the sky now, and they spun, faster and faster, until each was a solid golden O of fire, three spinning suns in the heaven of midnight.

(I remember I thought flatly, We have been spelled. So what now? But in its own way, my stoicism was also suspect. My thoughts in any case flagged after that.)

There was a smell of lions, or of a land that had them. Do not ask me how I know, I never smelled or saw them, or such a spot. And there before us all stood a slanting wall of brick, at once much larger than I saw it, and smaller than it was. It seemed even so to lean into the sky. The woman raised her arms. She was apparent now as if rinsed all over by gilt, and one of the great stars seemed to sear on her forehead.

Forms began to come and go, on the lion-wind. If I knew then what they were, I forgot it later. Perhaps they were animals, like the skins in the tent, though some had wings.

She spoke to them. She did not use Greek anymore. It was the language of Khem, presumably, or we were intended to believe so. A liquid tongue, an Eastern tongue, no doubt.

Then there were other visions. The ribbed stems of flowers, broader than ten men around, wide petals pressed to the ether. A rainbow of mist that arched over, and touched the earth with its feet and its brow. And other mirages, many of which resembled effigies I had seen of the gods, but they walked.

The night began to close upon us slowly, narrowing and coming down. The stars still raged overhead and the gold wheels whirled, but some sense of enclosure had returned. As for the sloped angle of brick it had huddled down into a sort of oven, and into this the woman was placing, with extreme care—of all things—long sceptres of corn, all brown and dry and withered, blighted to straw by some harvest like a curse.

I heard her whisper then. I could not hear what.

Behind her, dim as shadows, I saw other women, who sat weaving, or who toiled at the grindstone, and one who shook a rattle upon which rings of gold sang out. Then the vision of these women was eclipsed. Something stood there, between the night and the Eastern witch. Tall as the roof, or tall as the sky, bird-headed maybe, with two of the stars for eyes. When I looked at this, this ultimate apparition, my blood froze and I could have howled out loud. It was not common fear, but terror, such as the worst reality has never brought me, though sometimes subtle nightmares do.

Then there was a lightning, down the night. When it passed, we were enclosed in the tent, the huge night of the tent, and the brick oven burned before us, with a thin harsh fume coming from the aperture in its top.

"Sweet is truth," said the witch, in a wild and passionate voice, all music, like the notes of the gold rings on the rattle. "O Lord of the Word. The Word is, and the Word makes all things to be."

Then the oven cracked into two pieces, it simply fell away from itself, and there on a bank of red charcoal, which died to clinker even as I gazed at it, lay a sheaf of golden corn. *Golden* corn, smiths' work. It was pure and sound and rang like a bell when presently I went to it and struck it and flung it away.

The tent had positively resettled all around us. It was there. I felt queasy and stupid, but I was in my body and had my bearings again, the sword hilt firm to my palm, though it was oddly hot to the touch, and my forehead burned, sweatless, as if I too had been seethed in a fire. I had picked up the goldwork without asking her anything. She did not prevent me, nor when I slung it off.

When I looked up from that, she was kneeling by the curtain, where the black dog had been and was no more. Her eyes were downcast under her veil. I noted the torque was gone from her neck and the ring from her finger. Had she somehow managed her trick that way, melting gold on to the stalks of mummified corn—No, lunacy. Why nag at it? It was *all* a deception.

But Draco lay looking at her now, burned up by another fever. It was her personal gold he wanted.

"Out, Skorous," he said to me. "Out, now." Slurred and sure.

So I said to her, through my blunted lips and woollen tongue, "Listen carefully, girl. The witchery ends now. You know what he wants, and how to see to that, I suppose. Scratch him with your littlest nail, and you die."

Then, without getting to her feet, she looked up at me, only the second time. She spoke in Greek, as at the start. In the morning, when I was better able to think, I reckoned I had imagined what she said. It had seemed to be: "He is safe, for I desire him. It is my choice. If it were not my choice and my desire, where might you hide yourselves, and live?"

We kept watch round the tent, in the Easterners' camp, in the marketplace, until the ashes of the dawn. There was not a sound from anywhere, save the regular quiet passaging of sentries on the walls, and the cool black forest wind that turned grey near sunrise.

At sunup, the usual activity of any town began. The camp stirred and let its boys out quickly to the well to avoid the town's women. Some of the caravaners even chose to stroll across to the public lavatories, though they had avoided the bathhouse.

An embarrassment came over me, that we should be standing there, in the foreigners' hive, to guard our prince through his night of lust. I looked sharply, to see how the men were taking it, but they had held together well. Presently Draco emerged. He appeared flushed and tumbled, very nearly shy, like some girl just out of a love-bed.

We went back to the fort in fair order, where he took me aside, thanked me, and sent me away again.

Bathed and shaved, and my fast broken, I began to feel more sanguine. It was over and done with. I would go down to the temple of Father Jupiter and give him something—why, I was not exactly sure. Then get my boar for Mars. The fresh-baked bread I had just eaten was tasty, and maybe worth all the worry.

Later, I heard the Miller had taken himself to our library and been let in. I gave orders he was to be searched on leaving. Draco's grandfather had started the collection of manuscripts, there were even scrolls said to have been rescued from Alexandria. One could not be too wary.

In the evening, Draco called me up to his writing-room.

"Tomorrow," he said, "the Easterners will be leaving us."

"That's good news," I said.

"I thought it would please you. Zafra, however, is to remain. I'm taking her into my household."

"Zafra," I said.

"Well, they call her that. For the yellow-gold. Perhaps not her name. That might have been *Nefra*—Beautiful . . ."

"Well," I said, "if you want."

"Well," he said, "I never knew you before to be jealous of one of my women."

I said nothing, though the blood knocked about in my head. I had noted before, he had a woman's tongue himself when he was put out. He was a spoiled brat as a child, I have to admit, but a mother's early death, and the life of a forest fortress, pared most of it from him.

"The Corn-King is not her father," he said now. "She told me. But he's stood by her as that for some years. I shall send him something, in recompense."

He waited for my comment that I was amazed nothing had been asked for. He waited to see how I would jump. I wondered if he had paced about here, planning how he would put it to me. Not that he was required to. Now he said: "We gain, Skorous, a healer and diviner. Not just my pleasure at night."

"Your pleasure at night is your own affair. There are plenty of girls about, I would have thought, to keep you content. As for anything else she can or cannot do, all three temples, particularly the Women's Temple, will be up in arms. The Salius yesterday was only a sample. Do you think they are going to let some yellow-skinned harlot divine for you? Do you think that men who get hurt in a fight will want her near them?"

"You would not, plainly."

"No, I would not. As for the witchcraft, we were drugged and made monkeys of. An evening's fun is one thing."

"Yes, Skorous," he said. "Thanks for your opinion. Don't sulk too long. I shall miss your company."

An hour later, he sent, so I was informed, two of the scrolls from the library to the Corn-King in his wagon. They were two of the best, Greek, one transcribed by the hand, it was said, of a very great king. They went in a silver box, with jewel inlay. Gold would have been tactless, under the circumstances.

Next day she was in the palace. She had rooms on the women's side. It had been the apartment of Draco's elder sister, before her marriage. He treated this one as nothing less than a relative from the first. When he was at leisure, on those occasions when the wives and women of his officers dined with them, there was she with him. When he hunted, she went with him, too, not to have any sport, but as a companion, in a litter between two horses that made each hunt into a farce from its onset. She was in his bed each night, for he did not go to her, her place was solely hers: The couch his father had shared only with his mother. And when he wanted advice, it was she who gave it to him. He called on his soldiers and his priests afterwards. Though he always did so call, nobody lost face. He was wise and canny, she must have told him how to be at long last. And the charm he had always had. He even consulted me, and made much of me before everyone, because, very sensibly he realized, unless he meant to replace me, it would be foolish to let the men see I no longer counted a feather's weight with him. Besides, I might get notions of rebellion. I had my own following, my own men who would die for me if they thought me wronged. Probably that angered me more than the rest, that he might have the idea I would forego my duty and loyalty, forget my honor, and try to pull him down. I could no more do that than put out one of my own eyes.

Since we lost our homeland, since we lost, more importantly, the spine of the Empire, there had been a disparity, a separation of men. Now I saw it, in those bitter golden moments after she came among us. He had been born in the Mother of Cities, but she had slipped from his skin like water. He was a new being, a creature of the world, that might be anything, of any country. But, never having seen the roots of me, they yet had me fast. I was of the old order. I would stand until the fire had me, rather than tarnish my name, and my heart.

Gradually, the fort and town began to fill with gold. It was very nearly a silly thing. But we grew lovely and we shone. The temples did not hate her, as I had predicted. No, for she brought them glittering vessels, and laved the gods' feet with rare offerings, and the sweet spice also of her gift burned before Mars, and the Father, and the Mother, so every holy place smelled like Aegyptus, or Judea, or the brothels of Babylon for all I knew.

She came to walk in the streets with just one of the slaves at her heels, bold, the way our ladies did, and though she never left off her veil, she dressed in the stola and the palla, all clasped and cinched with the tiniest amounts of gold, while gold flooded everywhere else, and everyone looked forward to the summer heartily, for the trading. The harvest would be wondrous too. Already there were signs of astounding fruition. And in the forest, not a hint of any restless tribe, or any ill wish.

They called her by the name *Zafra*. They did not once call her "Easterner." One day, I saw three pregnant women at the gate, waiting for Zafra to come out and touch them. She was lucky. Even the soldiers had taken no offense. The old Salius had asked her for a balm for his rheumatism. It seemed the balm had worked.

Only I, then, hated her. I tried to let it go. I tried to remember she was only a woman, and, if a sorceress, did us good. I tried to see her as voluptuous and enticing, or as homely and harmless. But all I saw was some shuttered-up, close, fermenting thing, like mummy-dusts reviving in a tomb, or the lion-scent, and the tall shadow that had stood between her and the night, bird-headed, the Lord of the Word that made all things, or unmade them. What was she, under her disguise? Draco could not see it. Like the black dog she had kept, which walked by her on a leash, well-mannered and gentle, and which would probably tear out the throat of anyone who came at her with mischief on his mind—Under her honeyed wrappings, was it a doll of straw or gold, or a viper?

Eventually, Draco married her. That was no surprise. He did it in the proper style, with sacrifices to the Father, and all the forms, and a feast that filled the town. I saw her in colors then, that once, the saffron dress, the Flammeus, the fire-veil of the bride, and her face bare, and painted up like a lady's, pale, with rosy cheeks and lips. But it was still herself, still the Eastern Witch.

And dully that day, as in the tent that night, I thought, So what now?

III

In the late summer, I picked up some talk, among the servants in the palace. I was by the well-court, in the peach arbor, where I had paused to look at the peaches. They did not always come, but this year we had had one crop already, and now the second was blooming. As I stood there in the shade, sampling the fruit, a pair of the kitchen men met below by the well, and stayed to gossip in their argot. At first I paid no heed, then it came to me what they were saying, and I listened with all my ears.

When one went off, leaving the other, old Ursus, to fill his dipper, I came down the stair and greeted him. He started, and looked at me furtively.

"Yes, I heard you," I said. "But tell me, now."

I had always put a mask on, concerning the witch, with everyone but Draco, and afterwards with him too. I let it be seen I thought her nothing much, but if she was his choice, I would serve her. I was careful never to speak slightingly of her to any—since it would reflect on his honor— even to men I trusted, even in wine. Since he had married her, she had got my duty, too, unless it came to vie with my duty to him.

But Ursus had the servant's way, the slave's way, of holding back bad news for fear it should turn on him. I had to repeat a phrase or two of his own before he would come clean.

It seemed that some of the women had become aware that Zafra, a sorceress of great power, could summon to her, having its name, a mighty demon. Now she did not sleep every night with Draco, but in her own apartments, sometimes things had been glimpsed, or heard—

"Well, Ursus," I said, "you did right to tell me. But it's a lot of silly women's talk. Come, you're not going to give it credit?"

"The flames burn flat on the lamps, and change color," he mumbled. "And the curtain rattled, but no one there. And Eunike says she felt some form brush by her in the corridor—"

"That is enough," I said. "Women will always fancy something is happening, to give themselves importance. You well know that. Then there's hysteria and they can believe and say anything. We are aware she has arts, and the science of Aegyptus. But demons are another matter."

I further admonished him and sent him off. I stood by the well, pondering. Rattled curtains, secretive forms—it crossed my thoughts she might have taken a lover, but it did not seem in keeping with her shrewdness. I do not really believe in such beasts as demons, except what the brain can bring forth. Then again, her brain might be capable of many things.

It turned out I attended Draco that evening, something to do with one of the villages that traded with us, something he still trusted me to understand. I asked myself if I should tell him about the gossip. Frankly, when I had found out—the way you always can—that he lay with her less frequently, I had had a sort of hope, but there was a qualm, too, and when the trade matter was dealt with, he stayed me over the wine, and he said: "You may be wondering about it, Skorous. If so, yes. I'm to be given a child."

I knew better now than to scowl. I drank a toast, and suggested he might be happy to have got a boy on her.

"She says it will be a son."

"Then of course, it will be a son."

And, I thought, it may have her dark-yellow looks. It may be a magus too. And it will be your heir, Draco. My future Prince, and the master of the town. I wanted to hurl the wine cup through the wall, but I held my hand and my tongue, and after he had gone on a while trying to coax me to thrill at the joy of life, I excused myself and went away.

It was bound to come. It was another crack in the stones. It was the way of destiny, and of change. I wanted not to feel I must fight against it, or desire to send her poison, to kill her or abort her, or tear it, her womb's fruit, when born, in pieces.

For a long while I sat on my sleeping-couch and allowed my fury to sink down, to grow heavy and leaden, resigned, defeated.

When I was sure of that defeat, I lay flat and slept.

In sleep, I followed a demon along the corridor in the women's quarters, and saw it melt through her door. It was tall, long-legged, with the head of a bird, or perhaps of a dog. A wind blew, lion-tanged. I was under a tree hung thick with peaches, and a snake looked down from it with a girl's face framed by a flaming bridal-veil. Then there was a spinning fiery wheel, and golden corn flew off clashing from it. And next I saw a glowing oven, and on the red charcoal lay a child of gold, burning and gleaming and asleep.

When I woke with a jump it was the middle of the night, and someone had arrived, and the slave was telling me so.

Summer went to winter, and soon enough the snows came. The trading and the harvests had shored us high against the cruelest weather, we could sit in our towers and be fat, and watch the wolves howl through the white forests. They came to the very gates that year. There were some odd stories, that wolf-packs had been fed of our bounty, things left for them, to tide them over. Our own she-wolves were supposed to have started it, the whorehouse girls. But when I mentioned the tale to one of them, she flared out laughing.

I recall that snow with an exaggerated brilliance, the way you sometimes do with time that precedes an illness, or a deciding battle. Albino mornings with the edge of a broken vase, the smoke rising from hearths and temples, or steaming with the blood along the snow from the sacrifices of Year's Turn. The Wolf Feast with the races, and later the ivies and vines cut for the Mad Feast, and the old dark wine got out, the torches, and a girl I had in a shed full of hay and pigs; and the spate of weddings that come after, very sensibly. The last snow twilights were thick as soup with blueness. Then spring, and the forest surging up from its slough, the first proper hunting, with the smell of sap and crushed freshness spraying out as if one waded in a river.

Draco's child was born one spring sunset, coming forth in the bloody golden light, crying its first cry to the evening star. It was a boy, as she had said.

I had kept even my thoughts off from her after that interview in her chamber. My feelings had been confused and displeasing. It seemed to me she had in some way tried to outwit me, throw me down. Then I had felt truly angry, and later, oddly shamed. I avoided, where I could, all places where I might have to see her. Then she was seen less, being big with the child.

After the successful birth all the usual things were done. In my turn, I beheld the boy. He was straight and flawlessly formed, with black hair, but a fair skin; he had Draco's eyes from the very start. So little of the mother. Had she contrived it, by some other witch's art, knowing that when at length we had to cleave to him, it would be Draco's line we wished to see? No scratch of a nail, there, none.

Nor had there been any more chat of demons. Or they made sure I never intercepted it.

I said to myself, She is a matron now, she will wear to our ways. She has borne him a strong boy.

But it was no use at all.

She was herself, and the baby was half of her.

They have a name now for her demon, her genius in the shadowlands of witchcraft. A scrambled name that does no harm. They call it, in the town's argot: *Rhamthibiscan*.

We claim so many of the Greek traditions; they know of Rhadaman-thys from the Greek. A judge of the dead, he is connectable to Thot of Aegyptus, the Thrice-Mighty Thrice-Mage of the Al-Khemian Art. And because Thot the Ibis-Headed and Anpu the Jackal became mingled in it, along with Hermercurius, Prince of Thieves and Whores—who is too the guide of lost souls—an ibis and a dog were added to the brief itinerary. Rhadamanthys-Ibis-Canis. The full name, even, has no power. It is a muddle, and a lie, and the invocation says: *Sweet is Truth*. Was it, though, ever sensible to claim to know what truth might be?

IV

"They know of her, and have sent begging for her. She's a healer and they're sick. It's not unreasonable. She isn't afraid. I have seen her close an open wound by passing her hands above it. Yes, Skorous, perhaps she only made me see it, and the priests to see it, and the wounded man. But he recovered, as you remember. So I trust her to be able to cure these people and make them love us even better. She herself is immune to illness. Yes, Skorous, she only thinks she is. However, thinking so has apparently worked wonders. She was never once out of sorts with the child. The midwives were amazed—or not amazed, maybe—that she seemed to have no pain during the birth. Though they told me she wept when the child was

put into her arms. Well, so did I." Draco frowned. He said, "So we'll let
her do it, don't you agree, let her go to them and heal them. We may yet
be able to open this country, make something of it, one day. Anything
that is useful in winning them."

"She will be taking the child with her?"

"Of course. He's not weaned yet, and she won't let another woman
nurse him."

"Through the forests. It's three days' ride away, this village. And then
we hardly know the details of the sickness. If your son—"

"He will be with his mother. She has never done a foolish thing."

"You let this bitch govern you. Very well. But don't risk the life of your
heir, since your heir is what you have made him, this half-breed brat—"

I choked off the surge in horror. I had betrayed myself. It seemed to
me instantly that I had been made to do it. *She* had made me. All the stored
rage and impotent distrust, all the bitter frustrated *guile*—gone for nothing in a couple of sentences.

But Draco only shrugged, and smiled. He had learned to contain himself these past months. Her invaluable aid, no doubt, her rotten honey.

He said, "She has requested that, though I send a troop with her to
guard her in our friendly woods, you, Skorous, do not go with them."

"I see."

"The reason which she gave was that, although there is no danger in
the region at present, your love and spotless commitment to my well-being
preclude you should be taken from my side." He put the smile away and
said, "But possibly, too, she wishes to avoid your close company for so
long, knowing as she must do you can barely keep your fingers from her
throat. Did you know, Skorous," he said, and now it was the old Draco,
I seemed somehow to have hauled him back, "that the first several
months, I had her food always tasted. I thought you would try to see to
her. I was so very astounded you never did. Or did you have some other,
more clever plan, that failed?"

I swallowed the bile that had come into my mouth. I said, "You forget,
Sir, if I quit you I have no other battalion to go to. The Mother of Cities
is dead. If I leave your warriors, I am nothing. I am one of the scores who
blow about the world like dying leaves, soldiers' sons of the lost Empire.
If there were an option, I would go at once. There is none. You've spat
in my face, and I can only wipe off the spit."

His eyes fell from me, and suddenly he cursed.

"I was wrong, Skorous. You would never have—"

"No, Sir. Never. Never in ten million years. But I regret you think I
might. And I regret she thinks so. Once she was your wife, she could expect no less from me than I give one of your sisters."

"That bitch," he said, repeating for me my error, woman-like, "her half-
breed brat—damn you, Skorous. He's my son."

"I could cut out my tongue that I said it. It's more than a year of holding it back before all others, I believe. Like vomit, Sir. I could not keep it down any longer."

"Stop saying *Sir* to me. You call her *Domina*. That's sufficient."

His eyes were wet. I wanted to slap him, the way you do a vicious stupid girl who claws at your face. But he was my prince, and the traitor was myself.

Presently, thankfully, he let me get out.

What I had said was true, if there had been any other life to go to that was thinkable—but there was not, anymore. So, she would travel into the forest to heal, and I, faithful and unshakable, I would stay to guard him. And then she would come back. Year in and out, mist and rain, snow and sun. And bear him other brats to whom, in due course, I would swear my honor over. I had better practice harder, not to call her anything but *Lady*.

Somewhere in the night I came to myself and I knew. I saw it accurately, what went on, what was to be, and what I, so cunningly excluded, must do. Madness, they say, can show itself like that. Neither hot nor cold, with a steady hand, and every faculty honed bright.

The village with the sickness had sent its deputation to Draco yesterday. They had grand and blasphemous names for *her*, out there. She had said she must go, and at first light today would set out. Since the native villagers revered her, she might have made an arrangement with them, some itinerant acting as messenger. Or even, if the circumstance were actual, she could have been biding for such a chance. Or she herself had sent the malady to ensure it.

Her gods were the gods of her mystery. But the Semitic races have a custom ancient as their oldest altars, of giving a child to the god.

Perhaps Draco even knew—no, unthinkable. How then could she explain it? An ancient, a straying, bears, wolves, the sickness after all . . . And she could give him other sons. She was like the magic oven of the Khemian Art. Put in, take out. So easy.

I got up when it was still pitch black and announced to my body-slave and the man at the door I was off hunting, alone. There was already a rumor of an abrasion between the Prince and his Captain. Draco himself would not think unduly of it, Skorous raging through the wood, slicing pigs. I could be gone the day before he considered.

I knew the tracks pretty well, having hunted them since I was ten. I had taken boar spears for the look, but no dogs. The horse I needed, but she was forest-trained and did as I instructed.

I lay off the thoroughfare, like an old fox, and let the witch's outing come down, and pass me. Five men were all the guard she had allowed, a cart with traveling stuff, and her medicines in a chest. There was one of her women, the thickest in with her, I thought, Eunike, riding on a mule. And Zafra herself, in the litter between the horses.

When they were properly off, I followed. There was no problem in the world. We moved silently and they made a noise. Their horses and mine were known to each other, and where they snuffed a familiar scent, thought nothing of it. As the journey progressed, and I met here and there with some native in the trees, he hailed me cheerily, supposing me an outrider, a rear guard. At night I bivouacked above them; at sunrise their first rustlings and throat-clearings roused me. When they were gone we watered at their streams, and once I had a burned sausage forgotten in the ashes of their cookfire.

The third day, they came to the village. From high on the mantled slope, I saw the greetings and the going in, through the haze of foul smoke. The village did have a look of ailing, something in its shades and colors, and the way the people moved about. I wrapped a cloth over my nose and mouth before I sat down to wait.

Later, in the dusk, they began to have a brisker look. The witch was making magic, evidently, and all would be well. The smoke condensed and turned yellow from their fires as the night closed in. When full night had come, the village glowed stilly, enigmatically, cupped in the forest's darkness. My mental wanderings moved towards the insignificance, the smallness, of any lamp among the great shadows of the earth. A candle against the night, a fire in winter, a life flickering in eternity, now here, now gone forever.

But I slept before I had argued it out.

Inside another day, the village was entirely renewed. Even the rusty straw thatch glinted like gold. She had worked her miracles. Now would come her own time.

A couple of the men had kept up sentry-go from the first evening out, and last night, patrolling the outskirts of the huts, they had even idled a minute under the tree where I was roosting. I had hidden my mare half a mile off, in a deserted bothy I had found, but tonight I kept her near, for speed. And this night, too, when one of them came up the slope, making his rounds, I softly called his name.

He went to stone. I told him smartly who I was, but when I came from cover, his sword was drawn and eyes on stalks.

"I'm no forest demon," I said. Then I asked myself if he was alarmed for other reasons, a notion of the scheme Draco had accused me of. Then again, here and now, we might have come to such a pass. I needed a witness. I looked at the soldier, who saluted me slowly. "Has she cured them all?" I inquired. I added for his benefit, "Zafra."

"Yes," he said. "It was—worth seeing."

"I am sure of that. And how does the child fare?"

I saw him begin to conclude maybe Draco had sent me after all. "Bonny," he said.

"But she is leaving the village, with the child–" I had never thought she would risk her purpose among the huts, as she would not in the town, for all her hold on them. "Is that tonight?"

"Well, there's the old woman, she won't leave her own place, it seems."

"So Zafra told you?"

"Yes. And said she would go. It's close. She refused the litter and only took Carus with her. No harm. These savages are friendly enough–"

He ended, seeing my face.

I said, "She's gone already?"

"Yes, Skorous. About an hour–"

Another way from the village? But I had watched, I had skinned my eyes–pointlessly. Witchcraft could manage anything.

"And the child with her," I insisted.

"Oh, she never will part from the child, Eunike says–"

"Damn Eunike." He winced at me, more than ever uncertain. "Listen," I said, and informed him of my suspicions. I did not say the child was half East, half spice and glisten and sins too strange to speak. I said *Draco's son.* And I did not mention sacrifice. I said there was some chance Zafra might wish to mutilate the boy for her gods. It was well known, many of the Eastern religions had such rites. The soldier was shocked, and disbelieving. His own mother–? I said, to her kind, it was not a deed of dishonor. She could not see it as we did. All the while we debated, my heart clutched and struggled in my side, I sweated. Finally he agreed we should go to look. Carus was there, and would dissuade her if she wanted to perform such a disgusting act. I asked where the old woman's hut was supposed to be, and my vision filmed a moment with relief when he located it for me as that very bothy where I had tethered my horse the previous night. I said, as I turned to run that way, "There's no old woman there. The place is a ruin."

We had both won at the winter racing, he and I. It did not take us long to achieve the spot. A god, I thought, must have guided me to it before, so I knew how the land fell. The trees were densely packed as wild grass, the hut wedged between, and an apron of bared weedy ground about the door where once the household fowls had pecked. The moon would enter there, too, but hardly anywhere else. You could come up on it, cloaked in forest and night. Besides, she had lit her stage for me. As we pushed among the last phalanx of trunks, I saw there was a fire burning, a sullen throb of red, before the ruin's gaping door.

Carus stood against a tree. His eyes were wide and beheld nothing. The other man punched him and hissed at him, but Carus was far off. He breathed and his heart drummed, but that was all.

"She's witched him," I said. Thank Arean Mars and Father Jupiter she had. It proved my case outright. I could see my witness thought this too. We went on stealthily, and stopped well clear of the tree-break, staring down.

Then I forgot my companion. I forgot the manner in which luck at last had thrown my dice for me. What I saw took all my mind.

It was like the oven of the hallucination in the tent, the thing she had made, yet open, the shape of a cauldron. Rough mud brick, smoothed and curved, and somehow altered. Inside, the fire burned. It had a wonderful color, the fire, rubies, gold. To look at it did not seem to hurt the eyes, or dull them. The woman stood the other side of it, and her child in her grasp. Both appeared illumined into fire themselves, and the darkness of garments, of hair, the black gape of the doorway, of the forest and the night, these had grown warm as velvet. It is a sight often seen, a girl at a brazier or a hearth, her baby held by, as she stirs a pot, or throws on the kindling some further twig or cone. But in her golden arm the golden child stretched out his hands to the flames. And from her moving palm fell some invisible essence I could not see but only feel.

She was not alone. Others had gathered at her fireside. I was not sure of them, but I saw them, if only by their great height which seemed to rival the trees. A warrior there, his metal faceplate and the metal ribs of his breast just glimmering, and there a young woman, garlands, draperies and long curls, and a king who was bearded, with a brow of thunder and eyes of light, and near him another, a musician with wings starting from his forehead—they came and went as the fire danced and bowed. The child laughed, turning his head to see them, the deities of his father's side.

Then Zafra spoke the Name. It was so soft, no sound at all. And yet the roots of the forest moved at it. My entrails churned. I was on my knees. It seemed as though the wind came walking through the forest, to fold his robe beside the ring of golden red. I cannot recall the Name. It was not any of those I have written down, nor anything I might imagine. But it was the true one, and he came in answer to it. And from a mile away, from the heaven of planets, out of the pit of the earth, his hands descended and rose. He touched the child and the child was quiet. The child slept.

She drew Draco's son from his wrapping as a shining sword is drawn from the scabbard. She raised him up through the dark, and then she lowered him, and set him down in the holocaust of the oven, into the bath of flame, and the fires spilled up and covered him.

No longer on my knees, I was running. I plunged through black waves of heat, the amber pungence of incense, and the burning breath of lions. I yelled as I ran. I screamed the names of all the gods, and knew them powerless in my mouth, because I said them wrongly, knew them not, and so they would not answer. And then I ran against the magic, the Power, and broke through it. It was like smashing air. Experienced—inexperienceable.

Sword in hand, in the core of molten gold, I threw myself on, wading, smothered, and came to the cauldron of brick, the oven, and dropped the sword and thrust in my hands and pulled him out—

He would be burned, he would be dead, a blackened little corpse, such as the Semite Karthaginians once made of their children, incinerating them in line upon line of ovens by the shores of the Inner Sea—

But I held in my grip only a child of jewel-work, of poreless perfect gold, and I sensed his gleam run into my hands, through my wrists, down my arms like scalding water to my heart.

Someone said to me, then, with such gentle sadness, "Ah Skorous. Ah, Skorous."

I lay somewhere, not seeing. I said, "Crude sorcery, to turn the child, too, into gold."

"No," she said. "Gold is only the clue. For those things which are alive, laved by the flame, it is life. It is immortal and imperishable life. And you have torn the spell, which is all you think it to be. You have robbed him of it."

And then I opened my eyes, and I saw her. There were no others, no Other, they had gone with the tearing. But she—She was no longer veiled. She was very tall, so beautiful I could not bear to look at her, and yet, could not take my eyes away. And she was golden. She was golden not in the form of metal, but as a dawn sky, as fire, and the sun itself. Even her black eyes—were of gold, and her midnight hair. And the tears she wept were stars.

I did not understand, but I whispered, "Forgive me. Tell me how to make it right."

"It is not to be," she said. Her voice was a harp, playing through the forest. "It is never to be. He is yours now, no longer mine. Take him. Be kind to him. He will know his loss all his days, all his mortal days. And never know it."

And then she relinquished her light, as a coal dies. She vanished.

I was lying on the ground before the ruined hut, holding the child close to me, trying to comfort him as he cried, and my tears fell with his. The place was empty and hollow as if its very heart had bled away.

The soldier had run down to me, and was babbling. She had tried to immolate the baby, he had seen it, Carus had woken and seen it also. And, too, my valor in saving the boy from horrible death.

As one can set oneself to remember most things, so one can study to forget. Our sleeping dreams we dismiss on waking. Or, soon after.

They call her now, the Greek Woman. Or the Semite Witch. There has begun, in recent years, to be a story she was some man's wife, and in the end went back to him. It is generally thought she practiced against the child and the soldiers of her guard killed her.

Draco, when I returned half-dead of the fever I had caught from the contagion of the ruinous hut—where the village crone had died, it turned out, a week before—hesitated for my recovery, and then asked very little. A dazzle seemed to have lifted from his sight. He was afraid at what he might have said and done under the influence of sorceries and drugs. "Is it a fact, what the men say? She put the child into a fire?" "Yes," I said. He had looked at me, gnawing his lips. He knew of Eastern rites, he had heard out the two men. And, long, long ago, he had relied only on me. He appeared never to grieve, only to be angry. He even sent men in search for her: A bitch who would burn her own child—let her be caught and suffer the fate instead.

It occurs to me now that, contrary to what they tell us, one does not age imperceptibly, finding one evening, with cold dismay, the strength has gone from one's arm, the luster from one's heart. No, it comes at an hour, and is seen, like the laying down of a sword.

When I woke from the fever, and saw his look, all imploring on me, the look of a man who has gravely wronged you, not meaning to, who says: But I was blind—that was the hour, the evening, the moment when life's sword of youth was removed from my hand, and with no protest I let it go.

Thereafter the months moved away from us, the seasons, and next the years.

Draco continued to look about him, as if seeking the evil Eye that might still hang there, in the atmosphere. Sometimes he was partly uneasy, saying he too had seen her dog, the black jackal. But it had vanished at the time she did, though for decades the woman Eunike claimed to meet it in the corridor of the women's quarters.

He clung to me, then, and ever since he has stayed my friend; I do not say, my suppliant. It is in any event the crusty friendship now of the middle years, where once it was the flaming blazoned friendship of childhood, the envious love of young men.

We share a secret, he and I, that neither has ever confided to the other. He remains uncomfortable with the boy. Now the princedom is larger, its borders fought out wider, and fortressed in, he sends him often away to the fostering of soldiers. It is I, without any rights, none, who love her child.

He is all Draco, to look at, but for the hair and brows. We have a dark-haired strain ourselves. Yet there is a sheen to him. They remark on it. What can it be? A brand of the gods—(They make no reference, since she has fallen from their favor, to his mother.) A light from within, a gloss, of gold. Leaving off his given name, they will call him for that effulgence more often, Ardorius. Already I have caught the murmur that he can draw iron through stone, yes, yes, they have seen him do it, though I have not. (From Draco they conceal such murmurings, as once from me.) He, too, has a look of something hidden, some deep and silent pain, as if he knows, as youth never does, that men die, and love, that too.

To me, he is always courteous, and fair. I can ask nothing else. I am, to him, an adjunct of his life. I should perhaps be glad that it should stay so.

In the deep nights, when summer heat or winter snow fill up the forest, I recollect a dream, and think how I robbed him, the child of gold. I wonder how much, how much it will matter, in the end.

BRUCE STERLING

Flowers of Edo

One of the most powerful and innovative new talents to come
along in recent years, Bruce Sterling sold his first story in 1976,
and has since sold stories to *Universe, Omni, Asimov's Science Fiction,
The Magazine of Fantasy & Science Fiction, Lone Star Universe,* and elsewhere. Sterling is often thought of as purely a writer of "hard
science fiction," and made most of his reputation as one of the
leaders of the Cyberpunk movement—but, in fact, he writes a
good deal of fantasy as well, including such distinctive and
quirky pieces as "Telliamed," "Dinner at Audoghast," "The
Sword of Damocles," and "The Little Magic Shop." Sterling's fantasy shares with his science fiction a keen eye for the details of
social behavior, a dangerously dry and deadpan sense of humor,
a fondness for the grotesque underbelly of life, a wry appreciation of weird juxtapositions (the more outrageous and incongruous the better), and a love of obscure and nearly forgotten
historical milieu (all of which have caused him to be listed occasionally as an "Outlaw Fantasist," along with his colleagues
Howard Waldrop and Neal Barrett, Jr.). Here, for instance, he
takes us to nineteenth-century Japan in the days just after its first
contact with Europeans—a milieu as strange and mysterious as
any alien planet, in Sterling's gifted hands—for a lively and fascinating tale of an ex-samurai who finds he must do battle, quite
literally, with the demons of Progress.

As a science fiction writer, Bruce Sterling first attracted serious attention in the eighties with a series of stories set in his exotic "Shaper/Mechanist" future (a complex and disturbing future
where warring political factions struggle to control the shape of
human destiny), and by the end of the decade had established
himself, with novels such as the complex and Stapledonian *Schis-
matrix* and the well-received *Islands in the Net* (as well as with his
editing of the influential anthology *Mirrorshades: The Cyberpunk Anthology* and the infamous critical magazine *Cheap Truth*) as perhaps

the prime driving force behind the revolutionary Cyberpunk movement in science fiction (rivaled for that title only by his friend and collaborator, William Gibson), and also as one of the best new hard science fiction writers to enter the field in some time. His other books include the novels *The Artificial Kid* and *Involution Ocean,* a novel in collaboration with William Gibson, *The Difference Engine,* and the landmark collections *Crystal Express* and *Globalhead.* His most recent books are two new novels, *Heavy Weather* and *Holy Fire,* and a critically acclaimed nonfiction study of First Amendment issues in the world of computer networking, *The Hacker Crackdown: Law and Disorder on the Electronic Frontier.* He lives with his family in Austin, Texas.

Autumn. A full moon floated over old Edo, behind the thinnest haze of high cloud. It shone like a geisha's night-lamp through an old mosquito net. The sky was antique browned silk.

Two sweating runners hauled an iron-wheeled rickshaw south, toward the Ginza. This was Kabukiza District, its streets bordered by low tile-roofed wooden shops. These were modest places: coopers, tobacconists, cheap fabric shops where the acrid reek of dye wafted through reed blinds and paper windows. Behind the stores lurked a maze of alleys, crammed with townsmen's wooden hovels, the walls festooned with morning glories, the tinder-dry thatched roofs alive with fleas.

It was late. Kabukiza was not a geisha district, and honest workmen were asleep. The muddy streets were unlit, except for moonlight and the rare upstairs lamp. The runners carried their own lantern, which swayed precariously from the rickshaw's drawing-pole. They trotted rapidly, dodging the worst of the potholes and puddles. But with every lurching dip, the rickshaw's strings of brass bells jumped and rang.

Suddenly the iron wheels grated on smooth red pavement. They had reached the New Ginza. Here, the air held the fresh alien smell of mortar and brick.

The amazing New Ginza had buried its old predecessor. For the Flowers of Edo had killed the Old Ginza. To date, this huge disaster had been the worst, and most exciting, fire of the Meiji Era. Edo had always been proud of its fires, and the Old Ginza's fire had been a real marvel. It had raged for three days and carried right down to the river.

Once they had mourned the dead, the Edokko were ready to rebuild. They were always ready. Fires, even earthquakes, were nothing new to them. It was a rare building in Low City that escaped the Flowers of Edo for as long as twenty years.

But this was Imperial Tokyo now, and not the Shogun's old Edo anymore. The Governor had come down from High City in his horse-drawn coach and looked over the smoldering ruins of Ginza. Low City towns-

men still talked about it—how the Governor had folded his arms—like this—
with his wrists sticking out of his Western frock coat. And how he had
frowned a mighty frown. The Edo townsmen were getting used to those
unsettling frowns by now. Hard, no-nonsense, modern frowns, with the
brows drawn low over cold eyes that glittered with Civilization and Enlightenment.

So the Governor, with a mighty wave of his modern frock-coated arm,
sent for his foreign architects. And the Englishmen had besieged the district with their charts and clanking engines and tubs full of brick and mortar. The very heavens had rained bricks upon the black and flattened
ruins. Great red hills of brick sprang up—were they houses, people wondered, were they buildings at all? Stories spread about the foreigners and
their peculiar homes. The long noses, of course—necessary to suck air
through the stifling brick walls. The pale skin—because bricks, it was said,
drained the life and color out of a man. . . .

The rickshaw drew up short with a final brass jingle. The older rickshawman spoke, panting, "Far enough, gov?"

"Yeah, this'll do," said one passenger, piling out. His name was Encho
Sanyutei. He was the son and successor of a famous vaudeville comedian
and, at thirty-five, was now a well-known performer in his own right. He
had been telling his companion about the Ginza Bricktown, and his
folded arms and jutting underlip had cruelly mimicked Tokyo's Governor.

Encho, who had been drinking, generously handed the older man a
pocketful of jingling copper sen. "Here, pal," he said. "Do something about
that cough, will ya?" The runners bowed, not bothering to overdo it. They
trotted off toward the nearby Ginza crowd, hunting another fare.

Parts of Tokyo never slept. The Yoshiwara District, the famous Night-
less City of geishas and rakes, was one of them. The travelers had just
come from Asakusa District, another sleepless place: a brawling, vibrant
playground of bars, Kabuki theaters, and vaudeville joints.

The Ginza Bricktown never slept either. But the air here was different.
It lacked that earthy Low City workingman's glow of sex and entertainment. Something else, something new and strange and powerful, drew
the Edokko into the Ginza's iron-hard streets.

Gaslights. They stood hissing on their black foreign pillars, blasting a
pitiless moon-drowning glare over the crowd. There were eighty-five of
the appalling wonders, stretching arrow-straight across the Ginza, from
Shiba all the way to Kyobashi.

The Edokko crowd beneath the lights was curiously silent. Drugged
with pitiless enlightenment, they meandered down the hard, gritty street
in high wooden clogs, or low leather shoes. Some wore hakama skirts and
jinbibaori coats, others modern pipe-legged trousers, with top hats and
bowlers.

The comedian Encho and his big companion staggered drunkenly toward the lights, their polished leather shoes squeaking merrily. To the Tokyo modernist, squeaking was half the fun of these foreign-style shoes. Both men wore inserts of "singing leather" to heighten the effect.

"I don't like their attitudes," growled Encho's companion. His name was Onogawa, and until the Emperor's Restoration, he had been a samurai. But Imperial decree had abolished the wearing of swords, and Onogawa now had a post in a trading company. He frowned, and dabbed at his nose, which had recently been bloodied and was now clotting. "It's all too free and easy with these modern rickshaws. Did you see those two runners? They looked into our faces, just as bold as tomcats."

"Relax, will you?" said Encho. "They were just a couple of street runners. Who cares what they think? The way you act, you'd think they were Shogun's Overseers." Encho laughed freely and dusted off his hands with a quick, theatrical gesture. Those grim, spying Overseers, with their merciless canons of Confucian law, were just a bad dream now. Like the Shogun, they were out of business.

"But your face is known all over town," Onogawa complained. "What if they gossip about us? Everyone will know what happened back there."

"It's the least I could do for a devoted fan," Encho said airily.

Onogawa had sobered up a bit since his street fight in Asakusa. A scuffle had broken out in the crowd after Encho's performance—a scuffle centered on Onogawa, who had old acquaintances he would have preferred not to meet. But Encho, appearing suddenly in the crowd, had distracted Onogawa's persecutors and gotten Onogawa away.

It was not a happy situation for Onogawa, who put much stock in his own dignity, and tended to brood. He had been born in Satsuma, a province of radical samurai with stern unbending standards. But ten years in the capital had changed Onogawa, and given him an Edokko's notorious love for spectacle. Somewhat shamefully, Onogawa had become completely addicted to Encho's sidesplitting skits and impersonations.

In fact, Onogawa had been slumming in Asakusa vaudeville joints at least twice each week, for months. He had a wife and small son in a modest place in Nihombashi, a rather straitlaced High City district full of earnest young bankers and civil servants on their way up in life. Thanks to old friends from his radical days, Onogawa was an officer in a prosperous trading company. He would have preferred to be in the army, of course, but the army was quite small these days, and appointments were hard to get.

This was a major disappointment in Onogawa's life, and it had driven him to behave strangely. Onogawa's long-suffering in-laws had always warned him that his slumming would come to no good. But tonight's event wasn't even a geisha scandal, the kind men winked at or even admired. Instead, he had been in a squalid punch-up with low-class commoners.

And he had been rescued by a famous commoner, which was worse. Onogawa couldn't bring himself to compound his loss of face with gratitude. He glared at Encho from under the brim of his bowler hat. "So where's this fellow with the foreign booze you promised?"

"Patience," Encho said absently. "My friend's got a little place here in Bricktown. It's private, away from the street." They wandered down the Ginza, Encho pulled his silk top hat low over his eyes, so he wouldn't be recognized.

He slowed as they passed a group of four young women, who were gathered before the modern glass window of a Ginza fabric shop. The store was closed, but the women were admiring the tailor's dummies. Like the dummies, the women were dressed with daring modernity, sporting small Western parasols, cutaway riding coats in brilliant purple, and sweeping foreign skirts over large, jutting bustles. "How about that, eh?" said Encho as they drew nearer. "Those foreigners sure like a rump on a woman, don't they?"

"Women will wear anything," Onogawa said, struggling to loosen one pinched foot inside its squeaking shoe. "Plain kimono and obi are far superior."

"Easier to get into, anyway," Encho mused. He stopped suddenly by the prettiest of the women, a girl who had let her natural eyebrows grow out, and whose teeth, unstained with old-fashioned tooth-blacking, gleamed like ivory in the gaslight.

"Madame, forgive my boldness," Encho said. "But I think I saw a small kitten run under your skirt."

"I beg your pardon?" the girl said in a flat Low City accent.

Encho pursed his lips. Plaintive mewing came from the pavement. The girl looked down, startled, and raised her skirt quickly almost to the knee. "Let me help," said Encho, bending down for a better look. "I see the kitten! It's climbing up inside the skirt!" He turned. "You'd better help me, older brother! Have a look up in there."

Onogawa, abashed, hesitated. More mewing came. Encho stuck his entire head under the woman's skirt. "There it goes! It wants to hide in her false rump!" The kitten squealed wildly. "I've got it!" the comedian cried. He pulled out his doubled hands, holding them before him. "There's the rascal now, on the wall!" In the harsh gaslight, Encho's knotted hands cast the shadowed figure of a kitten's head against the brick.

Onogawa burst into convulsive laughter. He doubled over against the wall, struggling for breath. The women stood shocked for a moment. Then they all ran away, giggling hysterically. Except for the victim of Encho's joke, who burst into tears as she ran.

"Wah," Encho said alertly. "Her husband." He ducked his head, then jammed the side of his hand against his lips and blew. The street rang with a sudden trumpet blast. It sounded so exactly like the trumpet of a Tokyo omnibus that Onogawa himself was taken in for a moment. He glanced wildly up and down the Ginza prospect, expecting to see the omnibus driver, horn to his lips, reining up his team of horses.

Encho grabbed Onogawa's coat sleeve and hauled him up the street before the rest of the puzzled crowd could recover. "This way!" They pounded drunkenly up an ill-lit street into the depths of Bricktown. Onogawa was breathless with laughter. They covered a block, then Onogawa pulled up, gasping. "No more," he wheezed, wiping tears of hilarity. "Can't take another . . . ha ha ha . . . step!"

"All right," Encho said reasonably, "but not here." He pointed up. "Don't you know better than to stand under those things?" Black telegraph wires swayed gently overhead.

Onogawa, who had not noticed the wires, moved hastily out from under them. "Kuwabara, kuwabara," he muttered—a quick spell to avert lightning. The sinister magic wires were all over Bricktown, looping past and around the thick, smelly buildings.

Everyone knew why the foreigners put their telegraph wires high up on poles. It was so the demon messengers inside could not escape to wreak havoc amongst decent folk. These ghostly, invisible spirits flew along the wires as fast as swallows, it was said, carrying their secret spells of Christian black magic. Merely standing under such a baleful influence was inviting disaster.

Encho grinned at Onogawa. "There's no danger as long as we keep moving," he said confidently. "A little exposure is harmless. Don't worry about it."

Onogawa drew himself up. "Worried? Not a bit of it." He followed Encho down the street.

The stonelike buildings seemed brutal and featureless. There were no homey reed blinds or awnings in those outsized windows, whose sheets of foreign glass gleamed like an animal's eyeballs. No cozy porches, no bamboo wind chimes or cricket cages. Not even a climbing tendril of Edo morning glory, which adorned even the worst and cheapest city hovels. The buildings just sat there, as mute and threatening as cannonballs. Most were deserted. Despite their fireproof qualities and the great cost of their construction, they were proving hard to rent out. Word on the street said those red bricks would suck the life out of a man—give him beriberi, maybe even consumption.

Bricks paved the street beneath their shoes. Bricks on the right of them, bricks on their left, bricks in front of them, bricks in back. Hundreds of them, thousands of them. Onogawa muttered to the smaller man. "Say. What *are* bricks, exactly? I mean, what are they made of?"

"Foreigners make 'em," Encho said, shrugging. "I think they're a kind of pottery."

"Aren't they unhealthy?"

"People say that," Encho said, "but foreigners live in them and I haven't noticed any shortage of foreigners lately." He drew up short. "Oh, here's my friend's place. We'll go around the front. He lives upstairs."

They circled the two-story building and looked up. Honest old-fashioned light, from an oil lamp, glowed against the curtains of an upstairs window. "Looks like your friend's still awake," Onogawa said, his voice more cheery now.

Encho nodded. "Taiso Yoshitoshi doesn't sleep much. He's a little highstrung. I mean, peculiar." Encho walked up to the heavy, ornate front door, hung foreign-style on large brass hinges. He yanked a bellpull.

"Peculiar," Onogawa said. "No wonder, if he lives in a place like this." They waited.

The door opened inward with a loud squeal of hinges. A man's disheveled head peered around it. Their host raised a candle in a cheap tin holder. "Who is it?"

"Come on, Taiso," Encho said impatiently. He pursed his lips again. Ducks quacked around their feet.

"Oh! It's Encho-san, Encho Sanyutei. My old friend. Come in, do."

They stepped inside into a dark landing. The two visitors stopped and unlaced their leather shoes. In the first-floor workshop, beyond the landing, the guests could dimly see bound bales of paper, a litter of tool chests and shallow trays. An apprentice was snoring behind a shrouded woodblock press. The damp air smelled of ink and cherry-wood shavings.

"This is Mr. Onogawa Azusa," Encho said. "He's a fan of mine, down from High City. Mr. Onogawa, this is Taiso Yoshitoshi. The popular artist, one of Edo's finest."

"Oh, Yoshitoshi the artist!" said Onogawa, recognizing the name for the first time. "Of course! The wood-block print peddler. Why, I bought a whole series of yours, once. *Twenty-eight Infamous Murders with Accompanying Verses.*"

"Oh," said Yoshitoshi. "How kind of you to remember my squalid early efforts." The ukiyo-e print artist was a slight, somewhat pudgy man, with stooped, rounded shoulders. The flesh around his eyes looked puffy and discolored. He had close-cropped hair parted in the middle and wide, fleshy lips. He wore a printed cotton house robe, with faded bluish sunbursts, or maybe daisies, against a white background. "Shall we go upstairs, gentlemen? My apprentice needs his sleep."

They creaked up the wooden stairs to a studio lit by cheap pottery oil lamps. The walls were covered with hanging prints, while dozens more lay rolled, or stacked in corners, or piled on battered bookshelves. The windows were heavily draped and tightly shut. The naked brick walls seemed to sweat, and a vague reek of mildew and stale tobacco hung in the damp, close air.

The window against the far wall had a secondhand set of exterior shutters nailed to its inner sill. The shutters were bolted. "Telegraph wires outside," Yoshitoshi explained, noticing the glances of his guests. The artist gestured vaguely at a couple of bedraggled floor cushions. "Please."

The two visitors sat, struggling politely to squeeze some comfort from the mashed and threadbare cushions. Yoshitoshi knelt on a thicker cushion beside his worktable, a low bench of plain pine with ink stick, grinder, and water cup. A bamboo tool jar on the table's corner bristled with assorted brushes, as well as compass and ruler. Yoshitoshi had been working; a sheet of translucent rice paper was pinned to the table, lightly and precisely streaked with ink.

"So," Encho said, smiling and waving one hand at the artist's penurious den. "I heard you'd been doing pretty well lately. This place has certainly improved since I last saw it. You've got real bookshelves again. I bet you'll have your books back in no time."

Yoshitoshi smiled sweetly. "Oh—I have so many debts . . . the books come last. But yes, things are much better for me now. I have my health again. And a studio. And one apprentice, Toshimitsu, came back to me. He's not the best of the ones I lost, but he's honest at least."

Encho pulled a short foreign briar-pipe from his coat. He opened the ornate tobacco-bag on his belt, an embroidered pouch that was the pride of every Edo man-about-town. He glanced up casually, stuffing his pipe. "Did that Kabuki gig ever come to anything?"

"Oh, yes," said Yoshitoshi, sitting up straighter. "I painted bloodstains on the armor of Onoe Kikugoro the Fifth. For his role in *Kawanakajima Island.* I'm very grateful to you for arranging that."

"Wait, I saw that play," said Onogawa, surprised and pleased. "Say, those were wonderful bloodstains. Even better than the ones in that murder print, *Kasamori Osen Carved Alive by Her Stepfather.* You did that print too, am I right?" Onogawa had been studying the prints on the wall, and the familiar style had jogged his memory. "A young girl yanked backwards by a maniac with a knife, big bloody handprints all over her neck and legs. . . ."

Yoshitoshi smiled. "You liked that one, Mr. Onogawa?"

"Well," Onogawa said, "it was certainly a fine effort for what it was." It wasn't easy for a man in Onogawa's position to confess a liking for mere commoner art from Low City. He dropped his voice a little. "Actually, I had quite a few of your pictures, in my younger days. Ten years ago, just before the Restoration." He smiled, remembering. "I had the *Twenty-eight Murders,* of course. And some of the *One Hundred Ghost Stories.* And a few of the special editions, now that I think of it. Like Tamigoro blowing his head off with a rifle. Especially good sprays of blood in that one."

"Oh, I remember that one," Encho volunteered. "That was back in the old days, when they used to sprinkle the bloody scarlet ink with powdered mica. For that deluxe bloody gleaming effect!"

"Too expensive now," Yoshitoshi said sadly.

Encho shrugged. "Remember *Naosuke Gombei Murders His Master*? With the maniac servant standing on his employer's chest, ripping the man's face off with his hands alone?" The comedian cleverly mimed the murderer's pinching and wrenching, along with loud sucking and shredding sounds.

"Oh, yes!" said Onogawa. "I wonder whatever happened to my copy of it?" He shook himself. "Well, it's not the sort of thing you can keep in the house, with my age and position. It might give the children nightmares. Or the servants ideas." He laughed.

Encho had stuffed his short pipe; he lit it from a lamp. Onogawa, preparing to follow suit, dragged his long iron-bound pipe from within his coat sleeve. "How wretched," he cried. "I've cracked my good pipe in the scuffle with those hooligans. Look, it's ruined."

"Oh, is that a smoking pipe?" said Encho. "From the way you used it on your attackers, I thought it was a simple bludgeon."

"I certainly would not go into the Low City without self-defense of some kind," Onogawa said stiffly. "And since the new government has seen fit to take our swords away, I'm forced to make do. A pipe is an ignoble weapon. But as you saw tonight, not without its uses."

"Oh, no offense meant, sir," said Encho hastily. "There's no need to be formal here among friends! If I'm a bit harsh of tongue I hope you'll forgive me, as it's my livelihood! So! Why don't we all have a drink and relax, eh?"

Yoshitoshi's eye had been snagged by the incomplete picture on his drawing table. He stared at it raptly for a few more seconds, then came to with a start. "A drink! Oh!" He straightened up. "Why, come to think of it, I have something very special, for gentlemen like yourselves. It came from Yokohama, from the foreign trade zone." Yoshitoshi crawled rapidly across the floor, his knees skidding inside the cotton robe, and threw open a dented wooden chest. He unwrapped a tall glass bottle from a wad of tissue and brought it back to his seat, along with three dusty sake cups.

The bottle had the flawless symmetrical ugliness of foreign manufacture. It was full of amber liquid, and corked. A paper label showed the grotesquely bearded face of an American man, framed by blocky foreign letters.

"Who's that?" Onogawa asked, intrigued. "Their king?"

"No, it's the face of the merchant who brewed it," Yoshitoshi said with assurance. "In America, merchants are famous. And a man of the merchant class can even become a soldier. Or a farmer, or priest, or anything he likes."

"Hmmph," said Onogawa, who had gone through a similar transition himself and was not at all happy about it. "Let me see." He examined the printed label closely. "Look how this foreigner's eyes bug out. He looks like a raving lunatic!"

Yoshitoshi stiffened at the term. An awkward moment of frozen silence seeped over the room. Onogawa's gaffe floated in midair among them, until its nature became clear to everyone. Yoshitoshi had recovered his health recently, but his illness had not been a physical one. No one had to say anything, but the truth slowly oozed its way into everyone's bones and liver. At length, Onogawa cleared his throat. "I mean, of course, that there's no accounting for the strange looks of foreigners."

Yoshitoshi licked his fleshy lips and the sudden gleam of desperation slowly faded from his eyes. He spoke quietly.

"Well, my friends in the Liberal Party have told me all about it. Several of them have been to America and back, and they speak the language, and can even read it. If you want to know more, you can read their national newspaper, the *Lamp of Liberty,* for which I am doing illustrations."

Onogawa glanced quickly at Encho. Onogawa, who was not a reading man, had only vague notions as to what a "liberal party" or a "national newspaper" might be. He wondered if Encho knew better. Apparently the comedian did, for Encho looked suddenly grave.

Yoshitoshi rattled on. "One of my political friends gave me this bottle, which he bought in Yokohama, from Americans. The Americans have many such bottles there—a whole warehouse. Because the American Shogun, Generalissimo Guranto, will be arriving next year to pay homage to our Emperor. And the Guranto, the 'Puresidento,' is especially fond of this kind of drink! Which is called borubona, from the American prefecture of Kentukki."

Yoshitoshi twisted the cork loose and dribbled bourbon into all three cups. "Shouldn't we heat it first?" Encho said.

"This isn't sake, my friend. Sometimes they even put ice in it!"

Onogawa sipped carefully and gasped. "What a bite this has! It burns the tongue like Chinese peppers." He hesitated. "Interesting, though."

"It's good!" said Encho, surprised. "If sake were like an old stone lantern, then this borubona would be gaslight! Hot and fierce!" He tossed back the rest of his cup. "It's a pity there's no pretty girl to serve us our second round."

Yoshitoshi did the honors, filling their cups again. "This serving girl," Onogawa said. "She would have to be hot and fierce too—like a tigress."

Encho lifted his brows. "You surprise me. I thought you were a family man, my friend."

A warm knot of bourbon in Onogawa's stomach was reawakening an evening's worth of sake. "Oh, I suppose I seem settled enough now. But you should have known me ten years ago, before the Restoration. I was quite the tough young radical in those days. You know, we really thought we could change the world. And perhaps we did!"

Encho grinned, amused. "So! You were a shishi?"

Onogawa had another sip. "Oh, yes!" He touched the middle of his back. "I had hair down to here, and I never washed! Touch money? Not a one of us! We'd have died first! No, we lived in rags and ate plain brown rice from wooden bowls. We just went to our kendo schools, practiced swordsmanship, decided what old fool we should try to kill next. . . ." Onogawa shook his head ruefully. The other two were listening with grave attention.

The bourbon and the reminiscing had thawed Onogawa out. The lost ideals of the Restoration rose up within him irresistibly. "I was the despair of my family," he confided. "I abandoned my clan and my daimyo. We shishi radicals, you know, we believed only in our swords and the Emperor. Sonno joi! Remember that slogan?" Onogawa grinned, the tears of mono no aware, the pathos of lost things, coming to his eyes.

"Sonno joi! The very streets used to ring with it. 'Revere the Emperor, destroy the foreigners!' We wanted the Emperor restored to full and unconditional power! We demanded it in the streets! Because the Shogun's men were acting like frightened old women. Frightened of the black ships, the American black warships with their steam and cannon. Admiral Perry's ships."

"It's pronounced 'Peruri,' " Encho corrected gently.

"Peruri, then . . . I admit, we shishi went a bit far. We had some bad habits. Like threatening to commit hara-kiri unless the townsfolk gave us food. That's one of the problems we faced because we refused to touch money. Some of the shopkeepers still resent the way we shishi used to push them around. In fact that was the cause of tonight's incident after your performance, Encho. Some rude fellows with long memories."

"So that was it," Encho said. "I wondered."

"Those were special times," Onogawa said. "They changed me, they changed everything. I suppose everyone of this generation knows where they were, and what they were doing, when the foreigners arrived in Edo Bay."

"I remember," said Yoshitoshi. "I was fourteen and an apprentice at Kuniyoshi's studio. And I'd just done my first print. *The Heike Clan Sink to Their Horrible Doom in the Sea.*"

"I saw them dance once," Encho said. "The American sailors, I mean."

"Really?" said Onogawa.

Encho cast a storyteller's mood with an irresistible gesture. "Yes, my father, Entaro, took me. The performance was restricted to the Shogun's court officials and their friends, but we managed to sneak in. The foreigners painted their faces and hands quite black. They seemed ashamed of their usual pinkish color, for they also painted broad white lines around

their lips. Then they all sat on chairs together in a row, and one at a time
they would stand up and shout dialogue. A second foreigner would answer, and they would all laugh. Later two of them strummed on strange
round-bodied samisens, with long thin necks. And they sang mournful
songs, very badly. Then they played faster songs and capered and danced,
kicking out their legs in the oddest way, and flinging each other about.
Some of the Shogun's counselors danced with them." Encho shrugged.
"It was all very odd. To this day I wonder what it meant."

"Well," said Onogawa. "Clearly they were trying to change their appearance and shape, like foxes or badgers. That seems clear enough."

"That's as much as saying they're magicians," Encho said, shaking his
head. "Just because they have long noses, doesn't mean they're mountain goblins. They're men—they eat, they sleep, they want a woman. Ask
the geishas in Yokohama if that's not so." Encho smirked. "Their real
power is in the spirits of copper wires and black iron and burning coal.
Like our own Tokyo-Yokohama Railway that the hired English built for
us. You've ridden it, of course?"

"Of course!" Onogawa said proudly. "I'm a modern sort of fellow."

"That's the sort of power we need today. Civilization and Enlightenment. When you rode the train, did you see how the backward villagers
in Omori come out to pour water on the engine? To cool it off, as if the
railway engine were a tired horse!" Encho shook his head in contempt.

Onogawa accepted another small cup of bourbon. "So they pour
water," he said judiciously. "Well, I can't see that it does any harm."

"It's rank superstition!" said Encho. "Don't you see, we have to learn
to deal with those machine-spirits, just as the foreigners do. Treating them
as horses can only insult them. Isn't that so, Taiso?"

Yoshitoshi looked up guiltily from his absentminded study of his latest
drawing. "I'm sorry, Encho-san, you were saying?"

"What's that you're working on? May I see?" Encho crept nearer.

Yoshitoshi hastily plucked out pins and rolled up his paper. "Oh, no,
no, you wouldn't want to see this one just yet. It's not ready. But I can
show you another recent one. . . ." He reached to a nearby stack and dexterously plucked a printed sheet from the unsteady pile. "I'm calling this
series *Beauties of the Seven Nights.*"

Encho courteously held up the print so that both he and Onogawa
could see it. It showed a woman in her underrobe; she had thrown her
scarlet-lined outer kimono over a nearby screen. She had both natural and
artificial eyebrows, lending a double seductiveness to her high forehead.
Her mane of jet black hair had a killing little wispy fringe at the back of
the neck; it seemed to cry out to be bitten. She stood at some lucky man's
doorway, bending to blow out the light of a lantern in the hall. And her
tiny, but piercingly red mouth was clamped down over a roll of paper towels.

"I get it!" Onogawa said. "That beautiful whore is blowing out the light so she can creep into some fellow's bed in the dark! And she's taking those handy paper towels in her teeth to mop up with, after they're through playing mortar-and-pestle."

Encho examined the print more closely. "Wait a minute," he said. "This caption reads 'Her Ladyship Yanagihara Aiko.' This is an Imperial lady-in-waiting!"

"Some of my newspaper friends gave me the idea," Yoshitoshi said, nodding. "Why should prints always be of tiresome, stale old actors and warriors and geishas? This is the modern age!"

"But this print, Taiso . . . it clearly implies that the Emperor sleeps with his ladies-in-waiting."

"No, just with Lady Yanagihara Aiko," Yoshitoshi said reasonably. "After all, everyone knows she's his special favorite. The rest of the Seven Beauties of the Imperial Court are drawn, oh, putting on their makeup, arranging flowers, and so forth." He smiled. "I expect big sales from this series. It's very topical, don't you think?"

Onogawa was shocked. "But this is rank scandalmongering! What happened to the good old days, with the nice gouts of blood and so on?"

"No one buys those anymore!" Yoshitoshi protested. "Believe me, I've tried everything! I did *A Yoshitoshi Miscellany of Figures from Literature*. Very edifying, beautifully drawn classical figures, the best. It died on the stands. Then I did *Raving Beauties at Tokyo Restaurants*. Really hot girls, but old-fashioned geishas done in the old style. Another total waste of time. We were dead broke, not a copper piece to our names! I had to pull up the floorboards of my house for fuel! I had to work on fabric designs—two yen for a week's work! My wife left me! My apprentices walked out! And then my health . . . my brain began to . . . I had nothing to eat . . . nothing . . . But . . . But that's all over now."

Yoshitoshi shook himself, dabbed sweat from his pasty upper lip, and poured another cup of bourbon with a steady hand. "I changed with the times, that's all. It was a hard lesson, but I learned it. I call myself Taiso now, Taiso, meaning 'Great Rebirth.' Newspapers! That's where the excitement is today! *Tokyo Illustrated News* pays plenty for political cartoons and murder illustrations. They do ten thousand impressions at a stroke. My work goes everywhere—not just Edo, the whole nation. The nation, gentlemen!" He raised his cup and drank. "And that's just the beginning. The *Lamp of Liberty* is knocking them dead! The Liberal Party committee has promised me a raise next year, and my own rickshaw."

"But I like the old pictures," Onogawa said.

"Maybe you do, but you don't buy them," Yoshitoshi insisted. "Modern people want to see what's happening now! Take an old theme picture—Yorimitsu chopping an ogre's arm off, for instance. Draw a thing like that today and it gets you nowhere. People's tastes are more refined

today. They want to see real cannonballs blowing off real arms. Like my
eyewitness illustrations of the Battle of Ueno. A sensation! People don't
want print peddlers anymore. 'Journalist illustrator'—that's what they call
me now."

"Don't laugh," said Encho, nodding in drunken profundity. "You
should hear what they say about me. I mean the modern writer fellows,
down from the University. They come in with their French novels under
their arms, and their spectacles and slicked-down hair, and all sit in the
front row together. So I tell them a vaudeville tale or two. Am I 'spinning
a good yarn'? Not anymore. They tell me I'm 'creating naturalistic prose
in a vigorous popular vernacular.' They want to publish me in a book."
He sighed and had another drink. "This stuff's poison, Taiso. My head's
spinning."

"Mine, too," Onogawa said. An autumn wind had sprung up outside.
They sat in doped silence for a moment. They were all much drunker
than they had realized. The foreign liquor seemed to bubble in their
stomachs like tofu fermenting in a tub.

The foreign spirits had crept up on them. The very room itself seemed
drunk. Wind sang through the telegraph wires outside Yoshitoshi's shuttered window. A low eerie moan.

The moan built in intensity. It seemed to creep into the room with them.
The walls hummed with it. Hair rose on their arms.

"Stop that!" Yoshitoshi said suddenly. Encho stopped his ventriloquial
moaning, and giggled. "He's trying to scare us," Yoshitoshi said. "He loves
ghost stories."

Onogawa lurched to his feet. "Demon in the wires," he said thickly. "I
heard it moaning at us." He blinked, red-faced, and staggered to the shuttered window. He fumbled loudly at the lock, ignoring Yoshitoshi's
protests, and flung it open.

Moonlit wire clustered at the top of a wooden pole, in plain sight a few
feet away. It was a junction of cables, and leftover coils of wire dangled
from the pole's crossarm like thin black guts. Onogawa flung up the case-
ment with a bang. A chilling gust of fresh air entered the stale room, and
the prints danced on the walls. "Hey, you foreign demon!" Onogawa
shouted. "Leave honest men in peace!"

The artist and entertainer exchanged unhappy glances. "We drank too
much," Encho said. He lurched to his knees and onto one unsteady foot.
"Leave off, big fellow. What we need now. . . ." He belched. "Women,
that's what."

But the air outside the window seemed to have roused Onogawa. "We
didn't ask for you!" he shouted. "We don't need you! Things were fine
before you came, demon! You and your foreign servants . . ." He turned
half around, looking red-eyed into the room. "Where's my pipe? I've a
mind to give these wires a good thrashing."

He spotted the pipe again, stumbled into the room and picked it up. He lost his balance for a moment, then brandished the pipe threateningly. "Don't do it," Encho said, getting to his feet. "Be reasonable. I know some girls in Asakusa, they have a piano. . . ." He reached out.

Onogawa shoved him aside. "I've had enough!" he announced. "When my blood's up, I'm a different man! Cut them down before they attack first, that's my motto! Sonno joi!"

He lurched across the room toward the open window. Before he could reach it there was a sudden hiss of steam, like the breath of a locomotive. The demon, its patience exhausted by Onogawa's taunts, gushed from its wire. It puffed through the window, a gray gaseous thing, its lumpy misshapen head glaring furiously. It gave a steam-whistle roar, and its great lantern eyes glowed.

All three men screeched aloud. The armless, legless monster, like a gray cloud on a tether, rolled its glassy eyes at all of them. Its steel teeth gnashed, and sparks showed down its throat. It whistled again and made a sudden gnashing lurch at Onogawa.

But Onogawa's old sword training had soaked deep into his bones. He leapt aside reflexively, with only a trace of stagger, and gave the thing a smart overhead riposte with his pipe. The demon's head bonged like an iron kettle. It began chattering angrily, and hot steam curled from its nose. Onogawa hit it again. Its head dented. It winced, then glared at the other men.

The townsmen quickly scrambled into line behind their champion. "Get him!" Encho shrieked. Onogawa dodged a halfhearted snap of teeth and bashed the monster across the eye. Glass cracked and the bowl flew from Onogawa's pipe.

But the demon had had enough. With a grumble and crunch like dying gearworks, it retreated back toward its wires, sucking itself back within them, like an octopus into its hole. It vanished, but hissing sparks continued to drip from the wire.

"You humiliated it!" Encho said, his voice filled with awe and admiration. "That was amazing!"

"Had enough, eh!" shouted Onogawa furiously, leaning on the sill. "Easy enough mumbling your dirty spells behind our backs! But try an Imperial warrior face-to-face, and it's a different story! Hah!"

"What a feat of arms!" said Yoshitoshi, his pudgy face glowing. "I'll do a picture, *Onogawa Humiliates a Ghoul*. Wonderful!"

The sparks began to travel down the wire, away from the window. "It's getting away!" Onogawa shouted. "Follow me!"

He shoved himself from the window and ran headlong from the studio. He tripped at the top of the stairs, but did an inspired shoulder-roll and landed on his feet at the door. He yanked it open.

Encho followed him headlong. They had no time to lace on their leather shoes, so they kicked on the wooden clogs of Yoshitoshi and his apprentice and dashed out. Soon they stood under the wires, where the little nest of sparks still clung. "Come down here, you rascal," Onogawa demanded. "Show some fighting honor, you skulking wretch!"

The thing moved back and forth, hissing, on the wire. More sparks dripped. It dodged back and forth, like a cornered rat in an alley. Then it made a sudden run for it.

"It's heading south!" said Onogawa. "Follow me!"

They ran in hot pursuit, Encho bringing up the rear, for he had slipped his feet into the apprentice's clogs and the shoes were too big for him.

They pursued the thing across the Ginza. It had settled down to head-long running now, and dropped fewer sparks.

"I wonder what message it carries," panted Encho.

"Nothing good, I'll warrant," said Onogawa grimly. They had to strug-gle to match the thing's pace. They burst from the southern edge of the Ginza Bricktown and into the darkness of unpaved streets. This was Shiba District, home of the thieves' market and the great Zojoji Temple. They followed the wires. "Aha!" cried Onogawa. "It's heading for Shin-bashi Railway Station and its friends the locomotives!"

With a determined burst of speed, Onogawa outdistanced the thing and stood beneath the path of the wire, waving his broken pipe frantically. "Whoa! Go back!"

The thing slowed briefly, well over his head. Stinking flakes of ash and sparks poured from it, raining down harmlessly on the ex-samurai. Ono-gawa leapt aside in disgust, brushing the filth from his derby and frock coat. "Phew!"

The thing rolled on. Encho caught up with the larger man. "Not the locomotives," the comedian gasped. "We can't face those."

Onogawa drew himself up. He tried to dust more streaks of filthy ash from his soiled coat. "Well, I think we taught the nasty thing a lesson, anyway."

"No doubt," said Encho, breathing hard. He went green suddenly, then leaned against a nearby wooden fence, clustered with tall autumn grass. He was loudly sick.

They looked about themselves. Autumn. Darkness. And the moon. A pair of cats squabbled loudly in an adjacent alley.

Onogawa suddenly realized that he was brandishing, not a sword, but a splintered stick of ironbound bamboo. He began to tremble. Then he flung the thing away with a cry of disgust. "They took our swords away," he said. "Let them give us honest soldiers our swords back. We'd make short work of such foreign foulness. Look what it did to my coat, the filthy creature. It defiled me."

"No, no," Encho said, wiping his mouth. "You were incredible! A reg-ular Shoki the Demon Queller."

"Shoki," Onogawa said. He dusted his hat against his knee. "I've seen drawings of Shoki. He's the warrior demigod, with a red face and a big sword. Always hunting demons, isn't he? But he doesn't know there's a little demon hiding on the top of his own head."

"Well, a regular Yoshitsune, then," said Encho, hastily grasping for a better compliment. Yoshitsune was a legendary master of swordsmanship. A national hero without parallel.

Unfortunately, the valorous Yoshitsune had ended up riddled with arrows by the agents of his treacherous half-brother, who had gone on to rule Japan. While Yoshitsune and his high ideals had to put up with a shadow existence in folklore. Neither Encho nor Onogawa had to mention this aloud, but the melancholy associated with the old tale seeped into their moods. Their world became heroic and fatal. Naturally all the bourbon helped.

"We'd better go back to Bricktown for our shoes," Onogawa said.

"All right," Encho said. Their feet had blistered in the commandeered clogs, and they walked back slowly and carefully.

Yoshitoshi met them in his downstairs landing. "Did you catch it?"

"It made a run for the railroads," Encho said. "We couldn't stop it; it was way above our heads." He hesitated. "Say. You don't suppose it will come back here, do you?"

"Probably," Yoshitoshi said. "It lives in that knot of cables outside the window. That's why I put the shutters there."

"You mean you've seen it before?"

"Sure, I've seen it," Yoshitoshi muttered. "In fact I've seen lots of things. It's my business to see things. No matter what people say about me."

The others looked at him, stricken. Yoshitoshi shrugged irritably. "The place has atmosphere. It's quiet and no one bothers me here. Besides, it's cheap."

"Aren't you afraid of the demon's vengeance?" Onogawa said.

"I get along fine with that demon," Yoshitoshi said. "We have an understanding. Like neighbors anywhere."

"Oh," Encho said. He cleared his throat. "Well, ah, we'll be moving on, Taiso. It was good of you to give us the borubona." He and Onogawa stuffed their feet hastily into their squeaking shoes. "You keep up the good work, pal, and don't let those political fellows put anything over on you. Their ideas are weird, frankly. I don't think the government's going to put up with that kind of talk."

"Someday they'll have to," Yoshitoshi said.

"Let's go," Onogawa said, with a sidelong glance at Yoshitoshi. The two men left.

Onogawa waited until they were well out of earshot. He kept a wary eye on the wires overhead. "Your friend certainly is a weird one," he told the comedian. "What a night!"

Encho frowned. "He's gonna get in trouble with that visionary stuff. The nail that sticks up gets hammered down, you know." They walked into the blaze of artificial gaslight. The Ginza crowd had thinned out considerably.

"Didn't you say you knew some girls with a piano?" Onogawa said.

"Oh, right!" Encho said. He whistled shrilly and waved at a distant two-man rickshaw. "A piano. You won't believe the thing; it makes amazing sounds. And what a great change after those dreary geisha samisen routines. So whiny and thin and wailing and sad! It's always, 'Oh, How Piteous Is A Courtesan's Lot,' and 'Let's Stab Each Other To Prove You Really Love Me.' Who needs that old-fashioned stuff? Wait till you hear these gals pound out some 'opera' and 'waltzes' on their new machine."

The rickshaw pulled up with a rattle and a chime of bells. "Where to, gentlemen?"

"Asakusa," said Encho, climbing in.

"It's getting late," Onogawa said reluctantly. "I really ought to be getting back to the wife."

"Come on," said Encho, rolling his eyes. "Live a little. It's not like you're just cheating on the little woman. These are high-class modern girls. It's a cultural experience."

"Well, all right," said Onogawa. "If it's cultural."

"You'll learn a lot," Encho promised.

But they had barely covered a block when they heard the sudden frantic ringing of alarm bells, far to the south.

"A fire!" Encho yelled in glee. "Hey, runners, stop! Fifty sen if you get us there while it's still spreading!"

The runners wheeled in place and set out with a will. The rickshaw rocked on its axle and jangled wildly. "This is great!" Onogawa said, clutching his hat. "You're a good fellow to know, Encho. It's nothing but excitement with you!"

"That's the modern life!" Encho shouted. "One wild thing after another."

They bounced and slammed their way through the darkened streets until the sky was lit with fire. A massive crowd had gathered beside the Shinagawa Railroad Line. They were mostly low-class townsmen, many half-dressed. It was a working-class neighborhood in Shiba District, east of Atago Hill. The fire was leaping merrily from one thatched roof to another.

The two men jumped from their rickshaw. Encho shouldered his way immediately through the crowd. Onogawa carefully counted out the fare. "But he said fifty sen," the older rickshawman complained. Onogawa clenched his fist, and the men fell silent.

The firemen had reacted with their usual quick skill. Three companies of them had surrounded the neighborhood. They swarmed like ants over the roofs of the undamaged houses nearest the flames. As usual, they did not attempt to fight the flames directly. That was a hopeless task in any case, for the weathered graying wood, paper shutters, and reed blinds flared up like tinder, in great blossoming gouts.

Instead, they sensibly relied on firebreaks. Their hammers, axes, and crowbars flew as they destroyed every house in the path of the flames. Their skill came naturally to them, for, like all Edo firemen, they were also carpenters. Special bannermen stood on the naked ridgepoles of the disintegrating houses, holding their company's ensigns as close as possible to the flames. This was more than bravado; it was good business. Their reputations, and their rewards from a grateful neighborhood, depended on this show of spirit and nerve.

Some of the crowd, those whose homes were being devoured, were weeping and counting their children. But most of the crowd was in a fine holiday mood, cheering for their favorite fire teams and laying bets.

Onogawa spotted Encho's silk hat and plowed after him. Encho ducked and elbowed through the press, Onogawa close behind. They crept to the crowd's inner edge, where the fierce blaze of heat and the occasional falling wad of flaming straw had established a boundary.

A fireman stood nearby. He wore a knee-length padded fireproof coat with a pattern of printed blocks. A thick protective headdress fell stiffly over his shoulders, and long padded gauntlets shielded his forearms to the knuckles. An apprentice in similar garb was soaking him down with a pencil-thin gush of water from a bamboo hand-pump. "Stand back, stand back," the fireman said automatically, then looked up. "Say, aren't you Encho the comedian? I saw you last week."

"That's me," Encho shouted cheerfully over the roar of flame. "Good to see you fellows performing for once."

The fireman examined Onogawa's ash-streaked frock coat. "You live around here, big fella? Point out your house for me, we'll do what we can."

Onogawa frowned. Encho broke in hastily. "My friend's from uptown! A High City company man!"

"Oh," said the fireman, rolling his eyes.

Onogawa pointed at a merchant's tile-roofed warehouse, a little closer to the tracks. "Why aren't you doing anything about that place? The fire's headed right for it!"

"That's one of merchant Shinichi's," the fireman said, narrowing his eyes. "We saved a place of his out in Kanda District last month! And he gave us only five yen."

"What a shame for him," Encho said, grinning.

"It's full of cotton cloth, too," the fireman said with satisfaction. "It's gonna go up like a rocket."

"How did it start?" Encho said.

"Lightning, I hear," the fireman said. "Some kind of fireball jumped off the telegraph lines."

"Really?" Encho said in a small voice.

"That's what they say," shrugged the fireman. "You know how things are. Always tall stories. Probably some drunk knocked over his sake kettle, then claimed to see something. No one wants the blame."

"Right," Onogawa said carefully.

The fire teams had made good progress. There was not much left to do now except admire the destruction. "Kind of beautiful, isn't it?" the fireman said. "Look how that smoke obscures the autumn moon." He sighed happily. "Good for business, too. I mean the carpentry business, of course." He waved his gauntleted arm at the leaping flames. "We'll get this worn-out trash out of here and build something worthy of a modern city. Something big and expensive with long-term construction contracts."

"Is that why you have bricks printed on your coat?" Onogawa asked.

The fireman looked down at the block printing on his dripping cotton armor. "They do look like bricks, don't they?" He laughed. "That's a good one. Wait'll I tell the crew."

Dawn rose above old Edo. With red-rimmed eyes, the artist Yoshitoshi stared, sighing, through his open window. Past the telegraph wires, billowing smudge rose beyond the Bricktown rooftops. Another Flower of Edo reaching the end of its evanescent life.

The telegraph wires hummed. The demon had returned to its tangled nest outside the window. "Don't tell, Yoshitoshi," it burbled in its deep humming voice.

"Not me," Yoshitoshi said. "You think I want them to lock me up again?"

"I keep the presses running," the demon whined. "Just you deal with me. I'll make you famous, I'll make you rich. There'll be no more slow dark shadows where townsmen have to creep with their heads down. Everything's brightness and speed with me, Yoshitoshi. I can change things."

"Burn them down, you mean," Yoshitoshi said.

"There's power in burning," the demon hummed. "There's beauty in the flames. When you give up trying to save the old ways, you'll see the beauty. I want you to serve me, you Japanese. You'll do it better than the clumsy foreigners, once you accept me as your own. I'll make you all rich. Edo will be the greatest city in the world. You'll have light and music at a finger's touch. You'll step across oceans. You'll be as gods."

"And if we don't accept you?"

"You will! You must! I'll burn you until you do. I told you that, Yoshitoshi. When I'm stronger, I'll do better than these little flowers of Edo.

I'll open seeds of Hell above your cities. Hell-flowers taller than mountains! Red blooms that eat a city in a moment."

Yoshitoshi lifted his latest print and unrolled it before the window. He had worked on it all night; it was done at last. It was a landscape of pure madness. Beams of frantic light pierced a smoldering sky. Winged locomotives, their bellies fattened with the eggs of white-hot death, floated like maddened blowflies above a corpse-white city. "Like this," he said.

The demon gave a gloating whir. "Yes! Just as I told you. Now show it to them. Make them understand that they can't defeat me. Show them all!"

"I'll think about it," Yoshitoshi said. "Leave me now." He closed the heavy shutters.

He rolled the drawing carefully into a tube. He sat at his worktable again, and pulled an oil lamp closer. Dawn was coming. It was time to get some sleep.

He held the end of the paper tube above the lamp's little flame. It browned at first, slowly, the brand-new paper turning the rich antique tinge of an old print, a print from the old days when things were simpler. Then a cigar-ring of smoldering red encircled its rim, and blue flame blossomed. Yoshitoshi held the paper up, and flame ate slowly down its length, throwing smoky shadows.

Yoshitoshi blew and watched his work flare up, cherry-blossom white and red. It hurt to watch it go, and it felt good. He savored the two feelings for as long as he could. Then he dropped the last flaming inch of paper in an ashtray. He watched it flare and smolder until the last of the paper became a ghost-curl of gray.

"It'd never sell," he said. Absently, knowing he would need them tomorrow, he cleaned his brushes. Then he emptied the ink-stained water over the crisp dark ashes.

URSULA K. LE GUIN

Buffalo Gals, Won't You Come Out Tonight

Ursula K. Le Guin is probably one of the best known and most universally respected writers in the world today, and has been highly influential in the development both of modern fantasy and of modern science fiction. In the fantasy genre, her 1968 novel *A Wizard of Earthsea* (published initially as a Young Adult novel, perhaps because no one knew what else to do with it) would be deeply influential on future generations of High Fantasy writers, and it would be followed by several sequels, including *The Tombs of Atuan* and *The Farthest Shore,* which won the National Book Award for children's literature. Another novel in the "Earthsea" universe, *Tehanu,* won her a Nebula Award in 1990.

In science fiction, Le Guin's famous novel *The Left Hand of Darkness* may have been the most influential SF novel of its decade, and shows every sign of becoming one of the enduring classics of the genre—even ignoring the rest of Le Guin's work, the impact of this one novel alone on science fiction has been incalculably strong. *The Left Hand of Darkness* won both the Hugo and Nebula Awards in 1969, and Le Guin's monumental novel *The Dispossessed* followed suit a few years later. Le Guin has also won three other Hugo Awards and two Nebula Awards for her short fiction. Her other novels include *Planet of Exile, The Lathe of Heaven, City of Illusions, Rocannon's World, Searoad,* and the controversial multimedia novel *Always Coming Home.* Her elegant short work has been collected in *The Wind's Twelve Quarters, Orsinian Tales, The Compass Rose, Buffalo Gals and Other Animal Presences,* and *A Fisherman of the Inland Sea.* Her most recent book is a new collection, *Four Ways to Forgiveness.*

Le Guin has also been an important critic in the science fiction and fantasy fields, publishing two landmark volumes of nonfiction, *The Language of the Night* and *Dancing at the End of the World.* In the former, she notes that she herself makes no rigorous distinction between fantasy and science fiction, and so it follows that much of Le Guin's work is hard to classify and determinedly resists pigeonholing. Other works of hers that are overtly fantasy include the *The Beginning Place,* a novel that explores the boundaries of Faërie and the everyday world, and a handful of finely crafted short fantasies such as "The White Donkey," "Horse Camp," "The Barrow," "The Wife's Story", and the evocative and somberly lyrical story that follows, in which she tells us about a little girl lost in a strange and mysterious way, a way in which no one has ever been lost before . . .

I

"You fell out of the sky," the coyote said.

Still curled up tight, lying on her side, her back pressed against the overhanging rock, the child watched the coyote with one eye. Over the other eye she kept her hand cupped, its back on the dirt.

"There was a burned place in the sky, up there alongside the rimrock, and then you fell out of it," the coyote repeated, patiently, as if the news was getting a bit stale. "Are you hurt?"

She was all right. She was in the plane with Mr. Michaels, and the motor was so loud she couldn't understand what he said even when he shouted, and the way the wind rocked the wings was making her feel sick, but it was all right. They were flying to Canyonville. In the plane.

She looked. The coyote was still sitting there. It yawned. It was a big one, in good condition, its coat silvery and thick. The dark tear-line from its long yellow eye was as clearly marked as a tabby cat's.

She sat up, slowly, still holding her right hand pressed to her right eye.

"Did you lose an eye?" the coyote asked, interested.

"I don't know," the child said. She caught her breath and shivered. "I'm cold."

"I'll help you look for it," the coyote said. "Come on! If you move around you won't have to shiver. The sun's up."

Cold lonely brightness lay across the falling land, a hundred miles of sagebrush. The coyote was trotting busily around, nosing under clumps of rabbit-brush and cheatgrass, pawing at a rock. "Aren't you going to look?" it said, suddenly sitting down on its haunches and abandoning the search. "I knew a trick once where I could throw my eyes way up into a tree and see everything from up there, and then whistle, and they'd come back into my head. But that goddamn bluejay stole them, and when I whistled nothing came. I had to stick lumps of pine pitch into my head so I could see anything. You could try that. But you've got one eye that's OK, what do you need two for? Are you coming, or are you dying there?"

The child crouched, shivering.

"Well, come if you want to," said the coyote, yawned again, snapped at a flea, stood up, turned, and trotted away among the sparse clumps of rabbit-brush and sage, along the long slope that stretched on down and down into the plain streaked across by long shadows of sagebrush. The slender, grey-yellow animal was hard to keep in sight, vanishing as the child watched.

She struggled to her feet, and without a word, though she kept saying in her mind, "Wait, please wait," she hobbled after the coyote. She could not see it. She kept her hand pressed over the right eye socket. Seeing with one eye there was no depth; it was like a huge, flat picture. The coyote suddenly sat in the middle of the picture, looking back at her, its mouth open, its eyes narrowed, grinning. Her legs began to steady and her head did not pound so hard, though the deep, black ache was always there. She had nearly caught up to the coyote when it trotted off again. This time she spoke. "Please wait!" she said.

"OK," said the coyote, but it trotted right on. She followed, walking downhill into the flat picture that at each step was deep.

Each step was different underfoot; each sage bush was different, and all the same. Following the coyote she came out from the shadow of the rimrock cliffs, and the sun at eye level dazzled her left eye. Its bright warmth soaked into her muscles and bones at once. The air, that all night had been so hard to breathe, came sweet and easy.

The sage bushes were pulling in their shadows and the sun was hot on the child's back when she followed the coyote along the rim of a gully. After a while the coyote slanted down the undercut slope and the child scrambled after, through scrub willows to the thin creek in its wide sandbed. Both drank.

The coyote crossed the creek, not with a careless charge and splashing like a dog, but singlefoot and quiet like a cat; always it carried its tail low. The child hesitated, knowing that wet shoes make blistered feet, and then waded across in as few steps as possible. Her right arm ached with the effort of holding her hand up over her eye. "I need a bandage," she said to the coyote. It cocked its head and said nothing. It stretched out its forelegs and lay watching the water, resting but alert. The child sat down nearby on the hot sand and tried to move her right hand. It was glued to the skin around her eye by dried blood. At the little tearing-away pain, she whimpered; though it was a small pain it frightened her. The coyote came over close and poked its long snout into her face. Its strong, sharp smell was in her nostrils. It began to lick the awful, aching blindness, cleaning and cleaning with its curled, precise, strong, wet tongue, until the child was able to cry a little with relief, being comforted. Her head was bent close to the grey-yellow ribs, and she saw the hard nipples, the whitish belly-fur. She put her arm around the she-coyote, stroking the harsh coat over back and ribs.

"OK," the coyote said, "let's go!" And set off without a backward glance. The child scrambled to her feet and followed. "Where are we going?" she said, and the coyote, trotting on down along the creek, answered, "On down along the creek . . ."

There must have been a while she was asleep while she walked, because she felt like she was waking up, but she was walking along, only in a different place. She didn't know how she knew it was different. They were still following the creek, though the gully was flattened out to nothing much, and there was still sagebrush range as far as the eye could see. The eye—the good one—felt rested. The other one still ached, but not so sharply, and there was no use thinking about it. But where was the coyote?

She stopped. The pit of cold into which the plane had fallen reopened and she fell. She stood falling, a thin whimper making itself in her throat.

"Over here!"

The child turned. She saw a coyote gnawing at the half-dried-up carcass of a crow, black feathers sticking to the black lips and narrow jaw.

She saw a tawny-skinned woman kneeling by a campfire, sprinkling something into a conical pot. She heard the water boiling in the pot, though it was propped between rocks, off the fire. The woman's hair was yellow and grey, bound back with a string. Her feet were bare. The up-turned soles looked as dark and hard as shoe soles, but the arch of the foot was high, and the toes made two neat curving rows. She wore blue jeans and an old white shirt. She looked over at the girl. "Come on, eat crow!" she said. The child slowly came toward the woman and the fire, and squatted down. She had stopped falling and felt very light and empty; and her tongue was like a piece of wood stuck in her mouth.

Coyote was now blowing into the pot or basket or whatever it was. She reached into it with two fingers, and pulled her hand away shaking it and shouting, "Ow! Shit! Why don't I ever have any spoons?" She broke off a dead twig of sagebrush, dipped it into the pot, and licked it. "Oh, boy," she said. "Come on!"

The child moved a little closer, broke off a twig, dipped. Lumpy pink-ish mush clung to the twig. She licked. The taste was rich and delicate.

"What is it?" she asked after a long time of dipping and licking.

"Food. Dried salmon mush," Coyote said. "It's cooling down." She stuck two fingers into the mush again, this time getting a good load, which she ate very neatly. The child, when she tried, got mush all over her chin. It was like chopsticks, it took practice. She practiced. They ate turn and turn until nothing was left in the pot but three rocks. The child did not ask why there were rocks in the mush-pot. They licked the rocks clean. Coyote licked out the inside of the potbasket, rinsed it once in the creek, and put it onto her head. It fit nicely, making a conical hat. She pulled off her blue jeans. "Piss on the fire!" she cried, and did so, standing straddling it. "Ah, steam between the legs!" she said. The child, embarrassed, thought she was supposed to do the same thing, but did not want to, and did not. Bare-assed, Coyote danced around the dampened fire, kicking her long thin legs out and singing,

> *"Buffalo gals, won't you come out tonight,*
> *Come out tonight, come out tonight,*
> *Buffalo gals, won't you come out tonight,*
> *And dance by the light of the moon?"*

She pulled her jeans back on. The child was burying the remains of the fire in creek-sand, heaping it over, seriously, wanting to do right. Coyote watched her.

"Is that you?" she said. "A Buffalo Gal? What happened to the rest of you?"

"The rest of me?" The child looked at herself, alarmed.

"All your people."

"Oh. Well, Mom took Bobbie, he's my little brother, away with Uncle Norm. He isn't really my uncle, or anything. So Mr. Michaels was going there anyway so he was going to fly me over to my real father, in Canyonville. Linda, my stepmother, you know, she said it was OK for the summer anyhow if I was there, and then we could see. But the plane."

In the silence the girl's face became dark red, then greyish white. Coyote watched, fascinated. "Oh," the girl said, "Oh—Oh—Mr. Michaels—he must be—Did the—"

"Come on!" said Coyote, and set off walking.

The child cried, "I ought to go back—"

"What for?" said Coyote. She stopped to look round at the child, then went on faster. "Come on, Gal!" She said it as a name; maybe it was the child's name, Myra, as spoken by Coyote. The child, confused and despairing, protested again, but followed her. "Where are we going? Where *are* we?"

"This is my country," Coyote answered, with dignity, making a long, slow gesture all round the vast horizon. "I made it. Every goddam sage bush."

And they went on. Coyote's gait was easy, even a little shambling, but she covered the ground; the child struggled not to drop behind. Shadows were beginning to pull themselves out again from under the rocks and shrubs. Leaving the creek, they went up a long, low, uneven slope that ended away off against the sky in rimrock. Dark trees stood one here, another way over there; what people called a juniper forest, a desert forest, one with a lot more between the trees than trees. Each juniper they passed smelled sharply, cat-pee smell the kids at school called it, but the child liked it; it seemed to go into her mind and wake her up. She picked off a juniper berry and held it in her mouth, but after a while spat it out. The aching was coming back in huge black waves, and she kept stumbling. She found that she was sitting down on the ground. When she tried to get up her legs shook and would not go under her. She felt foolish and frightened, and began to cry.

"We're home!" Coyote called from way on up the hill.

The child looked with her one weeping eye, and saw sagebrush, juniper, cheatgrass, rimrock. She heard a coyote yip far off in the dry twilight.

She saw a little town up under the rimrock, board houses, shacks, all unpainted. She heard Coyote call again, "Come on, pup! Come on, Gal, we're home!" She could not get up, so she tried to go on all fours, the long way up the slope to the houses under the rimrock. Long before she got there, several people came to meet her. They were all children, she thought at first, and then began to understand that most of them were grown people, but all were very short; they were broad-bodied, fat, with fine, delicate hands and feet. Their eyes were bright. Some of the women helped her stand up and walk, coaxing her, "It isn't much farther, you're doing fine." In the late dusk lights shone yellow-bright through doorways and through unchinked cracks between boards. Wood smoke hung sweet in the quiet air. The short people talked and laughed all the time, softly, "Where's she going to stay?"–"Put her in with Robin, they're all asleep a!ready!"–"Oh, she can stay with us."

The child asked hoarsely, "Where's Coyote?"

"Out hunting," the short people said.

A deeper voice spoke: "Somebody new has come into town?"

"Yes, a new person," one of the short men answered.

Among these people the deep-voiced man bulked impressive; he was broad and tall, with powerful hands, a big head, a short neck. They made way for him respectfully. He moved very quietly, respectful of them also. His eyes when he stared down at the child were amazing. When he blinked, it was like the passing of a hand before a candle-flame.

"It's only an owlet," he said. "What have you let happen to your eye, new person?"

"I was–We were flying–"

"You're too young to fly," the big man said in his deep, soft voice. "Who brought you here?"

"Coyote."

And one of the short people confirmed: "She came here with Coyote, Young Owl."

"Then maybe she should stay in Coyote's house tonight," the big man said.

"It's all bones and lonely in there," said a short woman with fat cheeks and a striped shirt. "She can come with us."

That seemed to decide it. The fat-cheeked woman patted the child's
arm and took her past several shacks and shanties to a low, windowless
house. The doorway was so low even the child had to duck down to enter.
There were a lot of people inside, some already there and some crowding in after the fat-cheeked woman. Several babies were fast asleep in
cradle-boxes in corners. There was a good fire, and a good smell, like
toasted sesame seeds. The child was given food, and ate a little, but her
head swam and the blackness in her right eye kept coming across her left
eye so she could not see at all for a while. Nobody asked her name or
told her what to call them. She heard the children call the fat-cheeked
woman Chipmunk. She got up courage finally to say, "Is there somewhere
I can go to sleep, Mrs. Chipmunk?"

"Sure, come on," one of the daughters said, "in here," and took the child
into a back room, not completely partitioned off from the crowded front
room, but dark and uncrowded. Big shelves with mattresses and blankets
lined the walls. "Crawl in!" said Chipmunk's daughter, patting the child's
arm in the comforting way they had. The child climbed onto a shelf, under
a blanket. She laid down her head. She thought, "I didn't brush my
teeth."

II

She woke; she slept again. In Chipmunk's sleeping room it was always
stuffy, warm, and half-dark, day and night. People came in and slept and
got up and left, night and day. She dozed and slept, got down to drink
from the bucket and dipper in the front room, and went back to sleep and
doze.

She was sitting up on the shelf, her feet dangling, not feeling bad anymore, but dreamy, weak. She felt in her jeans pockets. In the left front
one was a pocket comb and a bubblegum wrapper, in the right front, two
dollar bills and a quarter and a dime.

Chipmunk and another woman, a very pretty dark-eyed plump one,
came in. "So you woke up for your dance!" Chipmunk greeted her, laughing, and sat down by her with an arm around her.

"Jay's giving you a dance," the dark woman said. "He's going to make
you all right. Let's get you all ready!"

There was a spring up under the rimrock, that flattened out into a pool
with slimy, reedy shores. A flock of noisy children splashing in it ran off
and left the child and the two women to bathe. The water was warm on
the surface, cold down on the feet and legs. All naked, the two soft-voiced
laughing women, their round bellies and breasts, broad hips and buttocks
gleaming warm in the late afternoon light, sluiced the child down, washed
and stroked her limbs and hands and hair, cleaned around the cheekbone

and eyebrow of her right eye with infinite softness, admired her, sudsed her, rinsed her, splashed her out of the water, dried her off, dried each other off, got dressed, dressed her, braided her hair, braided each other's hair, tied feathers on the braid-ends, admired her and each other again, and brought her back down into the little straggling town and to a kind of playing field or dirt parking lot in among the houses. There were no streets, just paths and dirt, no lawns and gardens, just sagebrush and dirt. Quite a few people were gathering or wandering around the open place, looking dressed up, wearing colorful shirts, print dresses, strings of beads, earrings. "Hey there, Chipmunk, Whitefoot!" they greeted the women.

A man in new jeans, with a bright blue velveteen vest over a clean, faded blue workshirt, came forward to meet them, very handsome, tense, and important. "All right, Gal!" he said in a harsh, loud voice, which startled among all these soft-speaking people. "We're going to get that eye fixed right up tonight! You just sit down here and don't worry about a thing." He took her wrist, gently despite his bossy, brassy manner, and led her to a woven mat that lay on the dirt near the middle of the open place. There, feeling very foolish, she had to sit down, and was told to stay still. She soon got over feeling that everybody was looking at her, since nobody paid her more attention than a checking glance or, from Chipmunk or Whitefoot and their families, a reassuring wink. Every now and then Jay rushed over to her and said something like, "Going to be as good as new!" and went off again to organize people, waving his long blue arms and shouting.

Coming up the hill to the open place, a lean, loose, tawny figure—and the child started to jump up, remembered she was to sit still, and sat still, calling out softly, "Coyote! Coyote!"

Coyote came lounging by. She grinned. She stood looking down at the child. "Don't let that Bluejay fuck you up, Gal," she said, and lounged on.

The child's gaze followed her, yearning.

People were sitting down now over on one side of the open place, making an uneven half-circle that kept getting added to at the ends until there was nearly a circle of people sitting on the dirt around the child, ten or fifteen paces from her. All the people wore the kind of clothes the child was used to, jeans and jeans-jackets, shirts, vests, cotton dresses, but they were all barefoot, and she thought they were more beautiful than the people she knew, each in a different way, as if each one had invented beauty. Yet some of them were also very strange: thin black shining people with whispery voices, a long-legged woman with eyes like jewels. The big man called Young Owl was there, sleepy-looking and dignified, like Judge Mc-Cown who owned a sixty-thousand acre ranch; and beside him was a woman the child thought might be his sister, for like him she had a hook nose and big, strong hands; but she was lean and dark, and there was a crazy look in her fierce eyes. Yellow eyes, but round, not long and slanted like Coyote's. There was Coyote sitting yawning, scratching her armpit, bored. Now somebody was entering the circle: a man, wearing only a kind of kilt and a cloak painted or beaded with diamond shapes, dancing to the rhythm of the rattle he carried and shook with a buzzing fast beat. His limbs and body were thick yet supple, his movements smooth and pouring. The child kept her gaze on him as he danced past her, around her, past again. The rattle in his hand shook almost too fast to see, in the other hand was something thin and sharp. People were singing around the circle now, a few notes repeated in time to the rattle, soft and tuneless. It was exciting and boring, strange and familiar. The Rattler wove his dancing closer and closer to her, darting at her. The first time she flinched away, frightened by the lunging movement and by his flat, cold face with narrow eyes, but after that she sat still, knowing her part. The dancing went on, the singing went on, till they carried her past boredom into a floating that could go on forever.

Jay had come strutting into the circle, and was standing beside her. He couldn't sing, but he called out, "Hey! Hey! Hey! Hey!" in his big, harsh voice, and everybody answered from all round, and the echo came down from the rimrock on the second beat. Jay was holding up a stick with a ball on it in one hand, and something like a marble in the other. The stick was a pipe: he got smoke into his mouth from it and blew it in four directions and up and down and then over the marble, a puff each time. Then the rattle stopped suddenly, and everything was silent for several breaths. Jay squatted down and looked intently into the child's face, his head cocked to one side. He reached forward, muttering something in time to the rattle and the singing that had started up again louder than before; he touched the child's right eye in the black center of the pain. She flinched and endured. His touch was not gentle. She saw the marble, a dull yellow ball like beeswax, in his hand; then she shut her seeing eye and set her teeth.

"There!" Jay shouted. "Open up. Come on! Let's see!"

Her jaw clenched like a vise, she opened both eyes. The lid of the right one stuck and dragged with such a searing white pain that she nearly threw up as she sat there in the middle of everybody watching.

"Hey, can you see? How's it work? It looks great!" Jay was shaking her arm, railing at her. "How's it feel? Is it working?"

What she saw was confused, hazy, yellowish. She began to discover, as everybody came crowding around peering at her, smiling, stroking and patting her arms and shoulders, that if she shut the hurting eye and looked with the other, everything was clear and flat; if she used them both, things were blurry and yellowish, but deep.

There, right close, was Coyote's long nose and narrow eyes and grin.

"What is it, Jay?" she was asking peering at the new eye. "One of mine you stole that time?"

"It's pine pitch," Jay shouted furiously. "You think I'd use some stupid secondhand coyote eye? I'm a doctor!"

"Ooooh, ooooh, a doctor," Coyote said. "Boy, that is one ugly eye. Why didn't you ask Rabbit for a rabbit-dropping? That eye looks like shit." She put her lean face yet closer, till the child thought she was going to kiss her; instead, the thin, firm tongue once more licked accurate across the pain, cooling, clearing. When the child opened both eyes again the world looked pretty good.

"It works fine," she said.

"Hey!" Jay yelled. "She says it works fine! It works fine, she says so! I told you! What'd I tell you?" He went off waving his arms and yelling. Coyote had disappeared. Everybody was wandering off.

The child stood up, stiff from long sitting. It was nearly dark; only the long west held a great depth of pale radiance. Eastward the plains ran down into night.

Lights were on in some of the shanties. Off at the edge of town somebody was playing a creaky fiddle, a lonesome chirping tune.

A person came beside her and spoke quietly: "Where will you stay?"

"I don't know," the child said. She was feeling extremely hungry. "Can I stay with Coyote?"

"She isn't home much," the soft-voiced woman said. "You were staying with Chipmunk, weren't you? Or there's Rabbit or Jackrabbit, they have families . . ."

"Do you have a family?" the girl asked, looking at the delicate, soft-eyed woman.

"Two fawns," the woman answered, smiling. "But I just came into town for the dance."

"I'd really like to stay with Coyote," the child said after a little pause, timid, but obstinate.

"OK, that's fine. Her house is over here." Doe walked along beside the child to a ramshackle cabin on the high edge of town. No light shone from inside. A lot of junk was scattered around the front. There was no step up to the half-open door. Over the door a battered pine board, nailed up crooked, said BIDE-A-WEE.

"Hey, Coyote? Visitors," Doe said. Nothing happened.

Doe pushed the door farther open and peered in. "She's out hunting, I guess. I better be getting back to the fawns. You going to be OK? Anybody else here will give you something to eat—you know . . . OK?"

"Yeah. I'm fine. Thank you," the child said.

She watched Doe walk away through the clear twilight, a severely elegant walk, small steps, like a woman in high heels, quick, precise, very light.

Inside Bide-A-Wee it was too dark to see anything and so cluttered that she fell over something at every step. She could not figure out where or how to light a fire. There was something that felt like a bed, but when she lay down on it, it felt more like a dirty-clothes pile, and smelt like one. Things bit her legs, arms, neck, and back. She was terribly hungry. By smell she found her way to what had to be a dead fish hanging from the ceiling in one corner. By feel she broke off a greasy flake and tasted it. It was smoked dried salmon. She ate one succulent piece after another until she was satisfied, and licked her fingers clean. Near the open door starlight shone on water in a pot of some kind; the child smelled it cautiously, tasted it cautiously, and drank just enough to quench her thirst, for it tasted of mud and was warm and stale. Then she went back to the bed of dirty clothes and fleas, and lay down. She could have gone to Chipmunk's house, or other friendly households; she thought of that as she lay forlorn in Coyote's dirty bed. But she did not go. She slapped at fleas until she fell asleep.

Along in the deep night somebody said, "Move over, pup," and was warm beside her.

Breakfast, eaten sitting in the sun in the doorway, was dried-salmon-powder mush. Coyote hunted, mornings and evenings, but what they ate was not fresh game but salmon, and dried stuff, and any berries in season. The child did not ask about this. It made sense to her. She was going to ask Coyote why she slept at night and waked in the day like humans, instead of the other way round like coyotes, but when she framed the question in her mind she saw at once that night is when you sleep and day when you're awake; that made sense too. But one question she did ask, one hot day when they were lying around slapping fleas.

"I don't understand why you all look like people," she said.

"We are people."

"I mean, people like me, humans."

"Resemblance is in the eye," Coyote said. "How is that lousy eye, by the way?"

"It's fine. But—like you wear clothes—and live in houses—with fires and stuff—"

"That's what you think . . . If that loudmouth Jay hadn't horned in, I could have done a really good job."

The child was quite used to Coyote's disinclination to stick to any one subject, and to her boasting. Coyote was like a lot of kids she knew, in some respects. Not in others.

"You mean what I'm seeing isn't true? Isn't real—like on TV, or something?"

"No," Coyote said. "Hey, that's a tick on your collar." She reached over, flicked the tick off, picked it up on one finger, bit it, and spat out the bits.

"Yecch!" the child said. "So?"

"So, to me you're basically greyish yellow and run on four legs. To that lot—" she waved disdainfully at the warren of little houses next down the hill—"you hop around twitching your nose all the time. To Hawk, you're an egg, or maybe getting pinfeathers. See? It just depends on how you look at things. There are only two kinds of people."

"Humans and animals?"

"No. The kind of people who say, 'There are two kinds of people' and the kind of people who don't." Coyote cracked up, pounding her thigh and yelling with delight at her joke. The child didn't get it, and waited.

"OK," Coyote said. "There's the first people, and then the others. That's the two kinds."

"The first people are—?"

"Us, the animals . . . and things. All the old ones. You know. And you pups, kids, fledglings. All first people."

"And the—others?"

"Them," Coyote said. "You know. The others. The new people. The ones who came." Her fine, hard face had gone serious, rather formidable. She glanced directly, as she seldom did, at the child, a brief gold sharpness. "We were here," she said. "We were always here. We are always here. Where we are is here. But it's their country now. They're running it . . . Shit, even I did better!"

The child pondered and offered a word she had used to hear a good deal: "They're illegal immigrants."

"Illegal!" Coyote said, mocking, sneering. "Illegal is a sick bird. What the fuck's illegal mean? You want a code of justice from a coyote? Grow up, kid!"

"I don't want to."

"You don't want to grow up?"

"I'll be the other kind if I do."

"Yeah. So," Coyote said, and shrugged. "That's life." She got up and went around the house, and the child heard her pissing in the backyard.

A lot of things were hard to take about Coyote as a mother. When her boyfriends came to visit, the child learned to go stay with Chipmunk or the Rabbits for the night, because Coyote and her friend wouldn't even wait to get on the bed but would start doing that right on the floor or even out in the yard. A couple of times Coyote came back late from hunting with a friend, and the child had to lie up against the wall in the same bed and hear and feel them doing that right next to her. It was something like fighting and something like dancing, with a beat to it, and she didn't mind too much except that it made it hard to stay asleep.

Once she woke up and one of Coyote's friends was stroking her stomach in a creepy way. She didn't know what to do, but Coyote woke up and realized what he was doing, bit him hard, and kicked him out of bed.

He spent the night on the floor, and apologized next morning—"Aw, hell, Ki, I forgot the kid was there, I thought it was you—"

Coyote, unappeased, yelled, "You think I don't got any standards? You think I'd let some coyote rape a kid in my bed?" She kicked him out of the house, and grumbled about him all day. But a while later he spent the night again, and he and Coyote did that three or four times.

Another thing that was embarrassing was the way Coyote peed anywhere, taking her pants down in public. But most people here didn't seem to care. The thing that worried the child most, maybe, was when Coyote did number two anywhere and then turned around and talked to it. That seemed so awful. As if Coyote was—the way she often seemed, but really wasn't—crazy.

The child gathered up all the old dry turds from around the house one day while Coyote was having a nap, and buried them in a sandy place near where she and Bobcat and some of the other people generally went and did and buried their number twos.

Coyote woke up, came lounging out of Bide-A-Wee, rubbing her hands through her thick, fair, greyish hair and yawning, looked all around once with those narrow eyes, and said, "Hey! Where are they?" Then she shouted, "Where are you? Where are you?"

And a faint, muffled chorus came from over in the sandy draw, "Mommy! Mommy! We're here!"

Coyote trotted over, squatted down, raked out every turd, and talked with them for a long time. When she came back she said nothing, but the child, red-faced and heart pounding, said, "I'm sorry I did that."

"It's just easier when they're all around close by," Coyote said, washing her hands (despite the filth of her house, she kept herself quite clean, in her own fashion).

"I kept stepping on them," the child said, trying to justify her deed.

"Poor little shits," said Coyote, practicing dance-steps.

"Coyote," the child said timidly. "Did you ever have any children? I mean real pups?"

"Did I? Did I have children? Litters! That one that tried feeling you up, you know? that was my son. Pick of the litter . . . Listen, Gal. Have daughters. When you have anything, have daughters. At least they clear out."

III

The child thought of herself as Gal, but also sometimes as Myra. So far as she knew, she was the only person in town who had two names. She had to think about that, and about what Coyote had said about the two kinds of people; she had to think about where she belonged. Some persons in town made it clear that as far as they were concerned she didn't and never would belong there. Hawk's furious stare burned through her; the Skunk children made audible remarks about what she smelled like. And though Whitefoot and Chipmunk and their families were kind, it was the generosity of big families, where one more or less simply doesn't count. If one of them, or Cottontail, or Jackrabbit, had come upon her in the desert lying lost and half-blind, would they have stayed with her, like Coyote? That was Coyote's craziness, what they called her craziness. She wasn't afraid. She went between the two kinds of people, she crossed over. Buck and Doe and their beautiful children weren't really afraid, because they lived so constantly in danger. The Rattler wasn't afraid, because he was so dangerous. And yet maybe he was afraid of her, for he never spoke, and never came close to her. None of them treated her the way Coyote did. Even among the children, her only constant playmate was one younger than herself, a preposterous and fearless little boy called Horned Toad Child. They dug and built together, out among the sagebrush, and played at hunting and gathering and keeping house and holding dances, all the great games. A pale, squatty child with fringed eyebrows, he was a self-contained but loyal friend; and he knew a good deal for his age.

"There isn't anybody else like me here," she said, as they sat by the pool in the morning sunlight.

"There isn't anybody much like me anywhere," said Horned Toad Child.

"Well, you know what I mean."

"Yeah . . . There used to be people like you around, I guess."

"What were they called?"

"Oh—people. Like everybody . . ."

"But where do my people live? They have towns. I used to live in one. I don't know where they are, is all. I ought to find out. I don't know where my mother is now, but my daddy's in Canyonville. I was going there when."

"Ask Horse," said Horned Toad Child, sagaciously. He had moved away from the water, which he did not like and never drank, and was plaiting rushes.

"I don't know Horse."

"He hangs around the butte down there a lot of the time. He's waiting till his uncle gets old and he can kick him out and be the big honcho. The old man and the women don't want him around till then. Horses are weird. Anyway, he's the one to ask. He gets around a lot. And his people came here with the new people, that's what they say, anyhow."

Illegal immigrants, the girl thought. She took Horned Toad's advice, and one long day when Coyote was gone on one of her unannounced and unexplained trips, she took a pouchful of dried salmon and salmonberries and went off alone to the flat-topped butte miles away in the southwest.

There was a beautiful spring at the foot of the butte, and a trail to it with a lot of footprints on it. She waited there under willows by the clear pool, and after a while Horse came running, splendid, with copper-red skin and long, strong legs, deep chest, dark eyes, his black hair whipping his back as he ran. He stopped, not at all winded, and gave a snort as he looked at her. "Who are you?"

Nobody in town asked that—ever. She saw it was true: Horse had come here with her people, people who had to ask each other who they were.

"I live with Coyote," she said, cautiously.

"Oh, sure, I heard about you," Horse said. He knelt to drink from the pool, long deep drafts, his hands plunged in the cool water. When he had drunk he wiped his mouth, sat back on his heels, and announced, "I'm going to be king."

"King of the Horses?"

"Right! Pretty soon now. I could lick the old man already, but I can wait. Let him have his day," said Horse, vainglorious, magnanimous. The child gazed at him, in love already, forever.

"I can comb your hair, if you like," she said.

"Great!" said Horse, and sat still while she stood behind him, tugging her pocket comb through his coarse, black, shining, yard-long hair. It took a long time to get it smooth. She tied it in a massive ponytail with willowbark when she was done. Horse bent over the pool to admire himself. "That's great," he said. "That's really beautiful!"

"Do you ever go . . . where the other people are?" she asked in a low voice.

He did not reply for long enough that she thought he wasn't going to; then he said, "You mean the metal places, the glass places? The holes? I go around them. There are all the walls now. There didn't used to be so many. Grandmother said there didn't used to be any walls. Do you know Grandmother?" he asked naively, looking at her with his great dark eyes.

"Your grandmother?"

"Well, yes—Grandmother—You know. Who makes the web. Well, anyhow. I know there's some of my people, horses, there. I've seen them across the walls. They act really crazy. You know, we brought the new people here. They couldn't have got here without us, they only have two legs, and they have those metal shells. I can tell you that whole story. The King has to know the stories."

"I like stories a lot."

"It takes three nights to tell it. What do you want to know about them?"

"I was thinking that maybe I ought to go there. Where they are."

"It's dangerous. Really dangerous. You can't go through–they'd catch you."

"I'd just like to know the way."

"I know the way," Horse said, sounding for the first time entirely adult and reliable; she knew he did know the way. "It's a long run for a colt." He looked at her again. "I've got a cousin with different-color eyes," he said, looking from her right to her left eye. "One brown and one blue. But she's an Appaloosa."

"Bluejay made the yellow one," the child explained. "I lost my own one. In the . . . when . . . You don't think I could get to those places?"

"Why do you want to?"

"I sort of feel like I have to."

Horse nodded. He got up. She stood still.

"I could take you, I guess," he said.

"Would you? When?"

"Oh, now, I guess. Once I'm King I won't be able to leave, you know. Have to protect the women. And I sure wouldn't let my people get anywhere near those places!" A shudder ran right down his magnificent body, yet he said, with a toss of his head, "They couldn't catch me, of course, but the others can't run like I do . . ."

"How long would it take us?"

Horse thought a while. "Well, the nearest place like that is over by the red rocks. If we left now we'd be back here around tomorrow noon. It's just a little hole."

She did not know what he meant by "a hole," but did not ask.

"You want to go?" Horse said, flipping back his ponytail.

"OK," the girl said, feeling the ground go out from under her.

"Can you run?"

She shook her head. "I walked here, though."

Horse laughed, a large, cheerful laugh. "Come on," he said, and knelt and held his hands backturned like stirrups for her to mount to his shoulders. "What do they call you?" he teased, rising easily, setting right off at a jogtrot. "Gnat? Fly? Flea?"

"Tick, because I stick!" the child cried, gripping the willowbark tie of the black mane, laughing with delight at being suddenly eight feet tall and traveling across the desert without even trying, like the tumbleweed, as fast as the wind.

Moon, a night past full, rose to light the plains for them. Horse jogged easily on and on. Somewhere deep in the night they stopped at a Pygmy Owl camp, ate a little, and rested. Most of the owls were out hunting, but an old lady entertained them at her campfire, telling them tales about the ghost of a cricket, about the great invisible people, tales that the child heard interwoven with her own dreams as she dozed and half-woke and dozed again. Then Horse put her up on his shoulders and on they went at a tireless slow lope. Moon went down behind them, and before them the sky paled into rose and gold. The soft night wind was gone; the air was sharp, cold, still. On it, in it, there was a faint, sour smell of burning. The child felt Horse's gait change, grow tighter, uneasy.

"Hey, Prince!"

A small, slightly scolding voice: the child knew it, and placed it as soon as she saw the person sitting by a juniper tree, neatly dressed, wearing an old black cap.

"Hey, Chickadee!" Horse said, coming round and stopping. The child had observed, back in Coyote's town, that everybody treated Chickadee with respect. She didn't see why. Chickadee seemed an ordinary person, busy and talkative like most of the small birds, nothing like so endearing as Quail or so impressive as Hawk or Great Owl.

"You're going on that way?" Chickadee asked Horse.

"The little one wants to see if her people are living there," Horse said, surprising the child. Was that what she wanted?

Chickadee looked disapproving, as she often did. She whistled a few notes thoughtfully, another of her habits, and then got up. "I'll come along."

"That's great," Horse said, thankfully.

"I'll scout," Chickadee said, and off she went, surprisingly fast, ahead of them, while Horse took up his steady long lope.

The sour smell was stronger in the air.

Chickadee halted, way ahead of them on a slight rise, and stood still. Horse dropped to a walk, and then stopped. "There," he said in a low voice.

The child stared. In the strange light and slight mist before sunrise she could not see clearly, and when she strained and peered she felt as if her left eye were not seeing at all. "What is it?" she whispered.

"One of the holes. Across the wall—see?"

It did seem there was a line, a straight, jerky line drawn across the sagebrush plain, and on the far side of it—nothing? Was it mist? Something moved there—"It's cattle!" she said. Horse stood silent, uneasy. Chickadee was coming back towards them.

"It's a ranch," the child said. "That's a fence. There's a lot of Herefords." The words tasted like iron, like salt in her mouth. The things she named wavered in her sight and faded, leaving nothing—a hole in the world, a burned place like a cigarette burn. "Go closer!" she urged Horse. "I want to see."

And as if he owed her obedience, he went forward, tense but unquestioning.

Chickadee came up to them. "Nobody around," she said in her small, dry voice, "but there's one of those fast turtle things coming."

Horse nodded, but kept going forward.

Gripping his broad shoulders, the child stared into the blank, and as if Chickadee's words had focused her eyes, she saw again: the scattered whitefaces, a few of them looking up with bluish, rolling eyes—the fences—over the rise a chimneyed house-roof and a high barn—and then in the distance something moving fast, too fast, burning across the ground straight at them at terrible speed. "Run!" she yelled to Horse, "run away! Run!" As if released from bonds he wheeled and ran, flat out, in great reaching strides, away from sunrise, the fiery burning chariot, the smell of acid, iron, death. And Chickadee flew before them like a cinder on the air of dawn.

IV

"Horse?" Coyote said. "That prick? Cat food!"

Coyote had been there when the child got home to Bide-A-Wee, but she clearly hadn't been worrying about where Gal was, and maybe hadn't even noticed she was gone. She was in a vile mood, and took it all wrong when the child tried to tell her where she had been.

"If you're going to do damn fool things, next time do 'em with me, at least I'm an expert," she said, morose, and slouched out the door. The child saw her squatting down, poking an old, white turd with a stick, trying to get it to answer some question she kept asking it. The turd lay obstinately silent. Later in the day the child saw two coyote men, a young one and a mangy-looking older one, loitering around near the spring, looking over at Bide-A-Wee. She decided it would be a good night to spend somewhere else.

The thought of the crowded rooms of Chipmunk's house was not attractive. It was going to be a warm night again tonight, and moonlit. Maybe she would sleep outside. If she could feel sure some people wouldn't come around, like the Rattler . . . She was standing indecisive halfway through town when a dry voice said, "Hey, Gal."

"Hey, Chickadee."

The trim, black-capped woman was standing on her doorstep shaking out a rug. She kept her house neat, trim like herself. Having come back across the desert with her the child now knew, though she still could not have said, why Chickadee was a respected person.

"I thought maybe I'd sleep out tonight," the child said, tentative.

"Unhealthy," said Chickadee. "What are nests for?"

"Mom's kind of busy," the child said.

"Tsk!" went Chickadee, and snapped the rug with disapproving vigor. "What about your little friend? At least they're decent people."

"Horny-toad? His parents are so shy . . ."

"Well. Come in and have something to eat, anyhow," said Chickadee.

The child helped her cook dinner. She knew now why there were rocks in the mush-pot.

"Chickadee," she said, "I still don't understand, can I ask you? Mom said it depends who's seeing it, but still, I mean if I see you wearing clothes and everything like humans, then how come you cook this way, in baskets, you know, and there aren't any—any of the things like they have—there where we were with Horse this morning?"

"I don't know," Chickadee said. Her voice indoors was quite soft and pleasant. "I guess we do things the way they always were done. When your people and my people lived together, you know. And together with everything else here. The rocks, you know. The plants and everything." She looked at the basket of willowbark, fernroot and pitch, at the blackened rocks that were heating in the fire. "You see how it all goes together . . .?"

"But you have fire—That's different—"

"Ah!" said Chickadee, impatient, "you people! Do you think you invented the sun?"

She took up the wooden tongs, plopped the heated rocks into the water-filled basket with a terrific hiss and steam and loud bubblings. The child sprinkled in the pounded seeds, and stirred.

Chickadee brought out a basket of fine blackberries. They sat on the newly-shaken-out rug, and ate. The child's two-finger scoop technique with mush was now highly refined.

"Maybe I didn't cause the world," Chickadee said, "but I'm a better cook than Coyote."

The child nodded, stuffing.

"I don't know why I made Horse go there," she said, after she had stuffed. "I got just as scared as him when I saw it. But now I feel again like I have to go back there. But I want to stay here. With my, with Coyote. I don't understand."

"When we lived together it was all one place," Chickadee said in her slow, soft home-voice. "But now the others, the new people, they live apart. And their places are so heavy. They weigh down on our place, they press on it, draw it, suck it, eat it, eat holes in it, crowd it out . . . Maybe after a while longer there'll only be one place again, their place. And none of us here. I knew Bison, out over the mountains. I knew Antelope right here. I knew Grizzly and Greywolf, up west there. Gone. All gone. And the salmon you eat at Coyote's house, those are the dream salmon, those are the true food; but in the rivers, how many salmon now? The rivers that were red with them in spring? Who dances, now, when the First

Salmon offers himself? Who dances by the river? Oh, you should ask Coyote about all this. She knows more than I do! But she forgets . . . She's hopeless, worse than Raven, she has to piss on every post, she's a terrible housekeeper . . ." Chickadee's voice had sharpened. She whistled a note or two, and said no more.

After a while the child asked very softly, "Who is Grandmother?"

"Grandmother," Chickadee said. She looked at the child, and ate several blackberries thoughtfully. She stroked the rug they sat on.

"If I built the fire on the rug, it would burn a hole in it," she said. "Right? So we build the fire on sand, on dirt . . . Things are woven together. So we call the weaver the Grandmother." She whistled four notes, looking up the smokehole. "After all," she added, "maybe all this place, the other places too, maybe they're all only one side of the weaving, I don't know. I can only look with one eye at a time, how can I tell how deep it goes?"

Lying that night rolled up in a blanket in Chickadee's backyard, the child heard the wind soughing and storming in the cottonwoods down in the draw, and then slept deeply, weary from the long night before. Just at sunrise she woke. The eastern mountains were a cloudy dark red as if the level light shone through them as through a hand held before the fire. In the tobacco patch—the only farming anybody in this town did was to raise a little wild tobacco—Lizard and Beetle were singing some kind of growing song or blessing song, soft and desultory, huh-huh-huh-huh, huh-huh-huh-huh, and as she lay warm-curled on the ground the song made her feel rooted in the ground, cradled on it and in it, so where her fingers ended and the dirt began she did not know, as if she were dead, but she was wholly alive, she was the earth's life. She got up dancing, left the blanket folded neatly on Chickadee's neat and already empty bed, and danced up the hill to Bide-A-Wee. At the half-open door she sang,

> "*Danced with a gal with a hole in her stocking*
> *And her knees kept a knocking and her toes kept a rocking,*
> *Danced with a gal with a hole in her stocking,*
> *Danced by the light of the moon!*"

Coyote emerged, tousled and lurching, and eyed her narrowly. "Sheeeoot," she said. She sucked her teeth and then went to splash water all over her head from the gourd by the door. She shook her head and the water drops flew. "Let's get out of here," she said. "I have had it. I don't know what got into me. If I'm pregnant again, at my age, oh, shit. Let's get out of town. I need a change of air."

In the foggy dark of the house, the child could see at least two coyote men sprawled snoring away on the bed and floor. Coyote walked over to the old white turd and kicked it. "Why didn't you stop me?" she shouted.

"I *told* you," the turd muttered sulkily.

"Dumb shit," Coyote said. "Come on, Gal. Let's go. Where to?" She didn't wait for an answer. "I know. Come on!"

And she set off through town at that lazy-looking rangy walk that was so hard to keep up with. But the child was full of pep, and came dancing, so that Coyote began dancing too, skipping and pirouetting and fooling around all the way down the long slope to the level plains. There she slanted their way off northeastward. Horse Butte was at their backs, getting smaller in the distance.

Along near noon the child said, "I didn't bring anything to eat."

"Something will turn up," Coyote said, "sure to." And pretty soon she turned aside, going straight to a tiny grey shack hidden by a couple of half-dead junipers and a stand of rabbit-brush. The place smelled terrible. A sign on the door said: FOX. PRIVATE. NO TRESPASSING!—but Coyote pushed it open, and trotted right back out with half a small smoked salmon. "Nobody home but us chickens!" she said, grinning sweetly.

"Isn't that stealing?" the child asked, worried.

"Yes," Coyote answered, trotting on.

They ate the fox-scented salmon by a dried-up creek, slept a while, and went on.

Before long the child smelled the sour burning smell, and stopped. It was as if a huge, heavy hand had begun pushing her chest, pushing her away, and yet at the same time as if she had stepped into a strong current that drew her forward, helpless.

"Hey, getting close!" Coyote said, and stopped to piss by a juniper stump.

"Close to what?"

"Their town. See?" She pointed to a pair of sage-spotted hills. Between them was an area of greyish blank.

"I don't want to go there."

"We won't go all the way in. No way! We'll just get a little closer and look. It's fun," Coyote said, putting her head on one side, coaxing. "They do all these weird things in the air."

The child hung back.

Coyote became businesslike, responsible. "We're going to be very careful," she announced. "And look out for big dogs, OK? Little dogs I can handle. Make a good lunch. Big dogs, it goes the other way. Right? Let's go, then."

Seemingly as casual and lounging as ever, but with a tense alertness in the carriage of her head and the yellow glance of her eyes, Coyote led off again, not looking back; and the child followed.

All around them the pressures increased. It was if the air itself was pressing on them, as if time was going too fast, too hard, not flowing but pounding, pounding, pounding, faster and harder till it buzzed like Rattler's rattle. Hurry, you have to hurry! everything said, there isn't time! everything said. Things rushed past screaming and shuddering. Things turned, flashed, roared, stank, vanished. There was a boy—he came into focus all at once, but not on the ground: he was going along a couple of inches above the ground, moving very fast, bending his legs from side to side in a kind of frenzied swaying dance, and was gone. Twenty children sat in rows in the air all singing shrilly and then the walls closed over them. A basket no a pot no a can, a garbage can, full of salmon smelling wonderful no full of stinking deerhides and rotten cabbage stalks, keep out of it, Coyote! Where was she?

"Mom!" the child called. "Mother!"—standing a moment at the end of an ordinary small-town street near the gas station, and the next moment in a terror of blanknesses, invisible walls, terrible smells and pressures and the overwhelming rush of Time straight forward rolling her helpless as a twig in the race above a waterfall. She clung, held on trying not to fall— "Mother!"

Coyote was over by the big basket of salmon, approaching it, wary, but out in the open, in the full sunlight, in the full current. And a boy and a man borne by the same current were coming down the long, sage-spotted hill behind the gas station, each with a gun, red hats, hunters, it was killing season. "Hell, will you look at that damn coyote in broad daylight big as my wife's ass," the man said, and cocked aimed shot all as Myra screamed and ran against the enormous drowning torrent. Coyote fled past her yelling, "Get out of here!" She turned and was borne away.

Far out of sight of that place, in a little draw among low hills, they sat and breathed air in searing gasps until after a long time it came easy again.

"Mom, that was *stupid*," the child said furiously.

"Sure was," Coyote said. "But did you see all that food!"

"I'm not hungry," the child said sullenly. "Not till we get all the way away from here."

"But they're your folks," Coyote said. "All yours. Your kith and kin and cousins and kind. Bang! Pow! There's Coyote! Bang! There's my wife's ass! Pow! There's anything—BOOOOM! Blow it away, man! BOOOOOOM!"

"I want to go home," the child said.

"Not yet," said Coyote. "I got to take a shit." She did so, then turned to the fresh turd, leaning over it. "It says I have to stay," she reported, smiling.

"It didn't say anything! I was listening!"

"You know how to understand? You hear everything, Miss Big Ears? Hears all—Sees all with her crummy gummy eye—"

"You have pine-pitch eyes too! You told me so!"

"That's a story," Coyote snarled. "You don't even know a story when you hear one! Look, do what you like, it's a free country. I'm hanging around here tonight. I like the action." She sat down and began patting her hands on the dirt in a soft four-four rhythm and singing under her breath, one of the endless tuneless songs that kept time from running too fast, that wove the roots of trees and bushes and ferns and grass in the web that held the stream in the streambed and the rock in the rock's place and the earth together. And the child lay listening.

"I love you," she said.

Coyote went on singing.

Sun went down the last slope of the west and left a pale green clarity over the desert hills.

Coyote had stopped singing, She sniffed. "Hey," she said. "Dinner." She got up and moseyed along the little draw. "Yeah," she called back softly. "Come on!"

Stiffly, for the fear-crystals had not yet melted out of her joints, the child got up and went to Coyote. Off to one side along the hill was one of the lines, a fence. She didn't look at it. It was OK. They were outside it.

"Look at that!"

A smoked salmon, a whole chinook, lay on a little cedar-bark mat. "An offering! Well, I'll be darned!" Coyote was so impressed she didn't even swear. "I haven't seen one of these for years! I thought they'd forgotten!"

"Offering to who?"

"Me! Who else? Boy, *look* at that!"

The child looked dubiously at the salmon.

"It smells funny."

"How funny?"

"Like burned."

"It's smoked, stupid! Come on."

"I'm not hungry."

"OK. It's not your salmon anyhow. It's mine. My offering, for me. Hey, you people! You people over there! Coyote thanks you! Keep it up like this and maybe I'll do some good things for you too!"

"Don't, don't yell, Mom! They're not that far away—"

"They're all my people," said Coyote with a great gesture, and then sat down cross-legged, broke off a big piece of salmon, and ate.

Evening Star burned like a deep, bright pool of water in the clear sky. Down over the twin hills was a dim suffusion of light, like a fog. The child looked away from it, back at the star.

"Oh," Coyote said. "Oh, shit."

"What's wrong?"

"That wasn't so smart, eating that," Coyote said, and then held herself and began to shiver, to scream, to choke—her eyes rolled up, her long arms and legs flew out jerking and dancing, foam spurted out between her clenched teeth. Her body arched tremendously backwards, and the child, trying to hold her, was thrown violently off by the spasms of her limbs.

The child scrambled back and held the body as it spasmed again, twitched, quivered, went still.

By moonrise Coyote was cold. Till then there had been so much warmth under the tawny coat that the child kept thinking maybe she was alive, maybe if she just kept holding her, keeping her warm, she would recover, she would be all right. She held her close, not looking at the black lips drawn back from the teeth, the white balls of the eyes. But when the cold came through the fur as the presence of death, the child let the slight, stiff corpse lie down on the dirt.

She went nearby and dug a hole in the stony sand of the draw, a shallow pit. Coyote's people did not bury their dead, she knew that. But her people did. She carried the small corpse to the pit, laid it down, and covered it with her blue and white bandanna. It was not large enough; the four stiff paws stuck out. The child heaped the body over with sand and rocks and a scurf of sagebrush and tumbleweed held down with more rocks. She also went to where the salmon had lain on the cedar mat, and finding the carcass of a lamb heaped dirt and rocks over the poisoned thing. Then she stood up and walked away without looking back.

At the top of the hill she stood and looked across the draw toward the misty glow of the lights of the town lying in the pass between the twin hills.

"I hope you all die in pain," she said aloud. She turned away and walked down into the desert.

V

It was Chickadee who met her, on the second evening, north of Horse Butte.

"I didn't cry," the child said.

"None of us do," said Chickadee. "Come with me this way now. Come into Grandmother's house."

It was underground, but very large, dark and large, and the Grandmother was there at the center, at her loom. She was making a rug or blanket of the hills and the black rain and the white rain, weaving in the lightning. As they spoke she wove.

"Hello, Chickadee. Hello, New Person."

"Grandmother," Chickadee greeted her.

The child said, "I'm not one of them."

Grandmother's eyes were small and dim. She smiled and wove. The shuttle thrummed through the warp.

"Old Person, then," said Grandmother. "You'd better go back there now, Granddaughter. That's where you live."

"I lived with Coyote. She's dead. They killed her."

"Oh, don't worry about Coyote!" Grandmother said, with a little huff of laughter. "She gets killed all the time."

The child stood still. She saw the endless weaving.

"Then I—Could I go back home—to her house—?"

"I don't think it would work," Grandmother said. "Do you, Chickadee?"

Chickadee shook her head once, silent.

"It would be dark there now, and empty, and fleas . . . You got outside your people's time, into our place; but I think that Coyote was taking you back, see. Her way. If you go back now, you can still live with them. Isn't your father there?"

The child nodded.

"They've been looking for you."

"They have?"

"Oh, yes, ever since you fell out of the sky. The man was dead, but you weren't there—they kept looking."

"Serves him right. Serves them all right," the child said. She put her hands up over her face and began to cry terribly, without tears.

"Go on, little one, Granddaughter," Spider said. "Don't be afraid. You can live well there. I'll be there too, you know. In your dreams, in your ideas, in dark corners in the basement. Don't kill me, or I'll make it rain . . ."

"I'll come around," Chickadee said. "Make gardens for me."

The child held her breath and clenched her hands until her sobs stopped and let her speak.

"Will I ever see Coyote?"

"I don't know," the Grandmother replied.

The child accepted this. She said, after another silence, "Can I keep my eye?"

"Yes. You can keep your eye."

"Thank you, Grandmother," the child said. She turned away then and started up the night slope towards the next day. Ahead of her in the air of dawn for a long way a little bird flew, black-capped, light-winged.

ROBERT SAMPSON

A Gift of the People

Sometimes in the cold dead middle of the night, we may get the uneasy intuition that our tidy rational world is surrounded by Powers old and strange and implacable, remorseless creatures who swim and flicker subliminally around us, vanishing at the turn of a head. If we're lucky, we'll never actually see these Powers. If we're really lucky, we'll never have to *meet* them . . .

The late Robert Sampson, a veteran pulp-era author who had sold to *Planet Stories* and *Weird Tales,* in recent years retired from NASA's Marshall Space Flight Center and began to revitalize his career with a number of sales to the top short fiction markets in both the science fiction and mystery fields. In mystery, he won the Edgar Award for the best story of 1986. In the science fiction genre, his stories appeared in *Full Spectrum, Strange Plasma, Asimov's Science Fiction,* and elsewhere. His most recent book was *Dangerous Horizons,* a study of famous series characters of the pulp magazine era. He lived for many years in Huntsville, Alabama, and died in 1993 at the age of sixty-five.

My brother Ted was eight when he first saw the People. I suppose it was for the first time. He never talked much, especially about that. When he saw them, if he saw them, he was at the bottom of Lake Olwanee, about twenty seconds from drowning. I had teased him into that mess, so it was not something I even wanted to talk about, either.

Olwanee, in northern Ohio, is a sprawling, mud-bottomed lake with a dark-pebble beach that agonized our feet. About seventy feet offshore floated a raft, its black timber riding clustered oil drums. It was beyond comfortable swimming distance and was therefore a challenge. Whatever was nearly out of reach, I felt obligated to strain after.

I insisted that Ted swim with me out to the raft.

He didn't want to, having more sense than I did, even then. I was two years older and, as I recall, I shamed him into the attempt—not from any need of company but from the silent pulsing of rivalry that spreads its dark under so many family relationships.

Limping across the beach, we plunged into water the color and temperature of iced coffee. The raft was distant, black, and ominously tilted. Ted thrashed furiously toward it, arms pounding up spray, his head rigidly lifted, like the head of a scouting turtle.

After a bitter struggle, he flailed to the raft. His fingers locked hard on the slippery timbers and there he huddled, shaking, white-faced, gulping air. He had fought his way out by sheer will. Even to me, it was apparent he could not fight his way back.

Eventually he tried.

The years overlay this incident with a spurious inevitability, as if events could have happened only this way. But, like so much else, events seem inevitable only when you stare straight at what happened, ignoring the motives behind.

Ted tried for shore. Halfway there, his splashing stopped. Very quietly, he submerged.

From the raft, I saw the pale glimmer of his body dwindle through the clear black water. Guilt shocked me. I had wanted him to fail, I suppose, without ever considering the consequences of failure.

No one else noticed that he had gone down. I hurled off the raft and swam furiously to where he had vanished. Not a bubble marked the spot. I surface dived, eyes open, swimming steeply away from the light. The water seemed to open all around me, black and deep and hollow, as if I swam downward through the ceiling of a liquid room, immensely empty. I descended through layers of increasing cold. Pressure closed around me. Light left the water and I could see nothing.

Then, entirely without warning, my hands plunged into a chilled silk of mud.

I jerked away in horror. As I did so, my left hand lightly grazed cold skin. I clutched and missed. I spread my arms and found nothing and groped at random through that lightless place tasting of stirred mud.

I was confused and needed air. I lashed about, scared and disoriented within that darkness.

And blundered full against his small, cold figure, sitting upright, arms locked about his knees.

I clutched him with both hands, squeezing unmercifully, and drove both feet against the mud. My legs sank in to the knees. In a frenzy, I kicked loose. The mud taste thickened in the water. Mindless, angry, horrified, I kicked frantically. Slowly we wallowed upward. Anguish gripped my chest. Beneath, the mud waited for our return.

It was black, then not so black. I was mad for air. The water grayed, then transformed itself to opaque white, softly warm, and we burst into the light.

Afterward we sprawled loose-limbed on the beach stones. I felt the violence in my heart, and, at the edge of my sight, in all that sun, dark mist wavered.

But no one had noticed. Past us stormed a pack of kids, howling after a yellow ball. Not one of them knew. It had all happened right beside them, sixteen feet away—the blind search above the mud, the despairing struggle upward. As close to those kids as the skins on their bodies. But not one of them knew.

Finally I asked him, "How come you just sat there?"

"Was watching them."

"Watching who?"

"People."

"People" was a favored word. He used it with casual ambiguity to mean swimmers or weeds or fish or fleets of boats. The imprecision bothered neither of us.

He added in his thin voice, "They watched but they wouldn't come."

I said, "Nobody saw us. You shut up."

He rolled over to stare at me with uncomprehending eyes. "You hit the People. They went away."

Then he slammed me hard on one shoulder and scrambled up and tottered off toward the car.

Eventually Ted learned to swim—although in an indoor swimming pool. He had developed a distaste for the water of lakes and streams. He prowled warily at the banks of these, studying their currents with calculating eyes.

"Swimming doesn't bother you, does it?" he asked, many vacations later.

We lounged in a boat that slowly drifted across the weed beds of Indian Lake. Ahead of our prow, swarms of brightly patched red and yellow turtles scattered wildly.

I said, "In lakes and stuff? No. Should it?"

"Look at all that down there." He motioned toward the green-brown banks of weeds that rose like cliffs in the transparent water. "Weeds, turtles, all that stuff."

"You can stay out of the weeds."

"I was just thinking," he said. "Suppose there's something in there looking at you. Watching. Lying back where they can see and you can't, all quiet. Not curious, not mad, just watching you and the way you move and waiting till you go someplace else. Just patient and quiet and part of the water, sort of."

"What? Fish?"

"No, not that."

I sensed that he had told me something of importance and I had not understood. In some annoyance, I snapped, "What you talking about, watching?"

"I don't know," he said. "It was just a sort of feeling I had. A kind of idea. I don't like swimming much."

We grew up and grew apart. Twenty-five years of education and military service separated us. The parents died and Ted married. So did I, although that was a mistake. We settled into the flow of time, I in Texas with NASA, Bill in Pennsylvania as an associate college professor.

We did not write much. We were separated by more than geography. The Ted and Ray Madison who were joined, as children, by blood ties and silent competition, were separated, as adults, by the same factors. We indulged our separation carefully, as if aware of what closer relations might incubate.

In early June, I took off a week to visit him. I had been at NASA headquarters in Washington, as a mainly silent handler of viewgraphs and printed handouts showing wonderfully high shuttle launch rates, supported by personnel who never got tired, never encountered technical problems, and needed no spare parts. This was in 1985, before the ethereal palace of mission planning splintered against reality.

Ted and his wife Barbara owned a small farmhouse just outside of Peter's Ford. This is one of those tiny Pennsylvania towns with narrow streets and worn red or white brick buildings crowding against the sidewalk, their windows masked by interior curtains. They resemble rows of faces with their eyes shut.

You crept through town at thirty miles an hour (radar enforced) until, with no warning, the town fell away. You came at once among fields rolling leisurely across shallow hills.

This was worn country, old country, rubbed by time, concealing a million years' worth of death beneath its gentle fields. Behind fat clusters of willows along Happyjack Creek showed lines of blue mountains, as lovely and ominous as an endgame in chess.

I followed a gravel road between fields of young corn. Far overhead, a hawk watched from its spiral against a hot blue sky. The road rose around a knoll and circled a small brown and white house, full of windows. Bulky trees shielded it from the fields.

I stopped the car and stepped out. The shaded air smelled sweetly cool. I could hear nothing. No wind, no birds, no creak of limb or flutter of leaf. My footsteps grated loudly as I walked to the house and rapped on the screen.

"Hey, Ted."

No one answered.

Far overhead, limbs and leaves interlocked in ascending layers through which blazed bright bits of sky. I stood at the bottom of a clear, dim well of light as transparent as water, listening to the silence.

The screen door banged when I entered the house. The kitchen smelled of onions and wax, and on the walls gleamed copper food molds. I called again and got no answer and moved, watchful and soft-footed into the next room.

This was a brown and gold living room, full of light. It was as neatly ordered as a small girl dressed for Sunday school. Well-used furniture crowded against stuffed bookcases. On the pale walls matted watercolors glowed soft rose, blue, pale green. Their mood was calm. The technique was pure Barbara: she favored partially drawn outlines touched by color. It was delicate work that looked like the tag end of a dream.

I stood listening intently, although there was nothing to listen to. "This place," I said loudly, "is like the Marie Celeste." And moved to the baby grand piano by a double window. A transcription of Handel's *Water Music* stood open on a rack above the keyboard.

When I touched the keys, the piano emitted an unexpected bellow of sound. I jumped, scowled, looked at the music. Handel instantly defeated me. Closing the *Water Music,* I rooted through a stack of 1930s sheet music, searching for simplicity.

At the bottom of the pile, under a copy of "Muddy River Moan," I found a folded watercolor. It was a study of light and shadow along a stream. From the water stared a transparent man, evidently stretched among white stones. It was hard to tell. His body melted into shadow. Except for the figure, which was irritatingly indistinct, it was a nice piece of work. Barbara's name was scribbled in the lower right-hand corner.

After tucking the watercolor back under the music, I sat and listened. Caught myself listening. Stood up violently and padded through the hush of the back door.

Outside, the sense of being watched was powerful, the quiet intolerable. High overhead, layered leaves quivered, liquid and unstable as flowing water. Some sort of small gray animal slowly crept along a high branch, like the silent sliding of a gray fingertip. I could not see it clearly. It flowed out of sight and I had the curious feeling that it stopped behind the leaves to look down at me.

From the road rang a clear feminine voice: "Hey, Ray. Here I am."

I jumped less than a foot and stepped down to greet Barbara.

She was a tall girl, lean and square-faced, with a lot of flying brown hair. She wore jeans and a color-smudged old shirt with the tail out, and carried a wooden painter's box. "I was down at the creek," she said, kissing me. "You're early. Lordy, isn't it hot? When'd you get in?"

"Just a while ago. Thought you were all lost in the woods."

"How do you like the place? Isn't it lovely?"

A bird shrilled. Overhead a limb jerked as a squirrel scuttled along it and a twig clicked against the top of my car. In the distance, I heard the lament of cattle.

"Listen to that bird," I said.

"Place is full of birds. Wait till you hear them in the morning. Let's get a drink. Where's your bag?"

Inside, in the living room, I settled into a gold chair and watched her snap open the wooden box and rustle out her sketches. "Ted hates me going down to the creek to paint. But it's so pretty."

"What's the matter with the creek? Quicksand?"

"No. It's shallow. Stony. Look here."

She showed me her sketches–white stones and sun on a shallow skin of water. No transparent figures.

"Very nice," I said, listening to the birds outside the window.

"Ted don't like the creek. He's got this thing." Her long fingers made a complicated movement in the air. "I try not to worry him. But it's so silly. He almost drowned once, didn't he?"

"Once." I told her about my heroic rescue, leaving out the sibling rivalry and my panic under the dark water. "I suppose he's got a right to be funny about water."

"He swims okay," she said. "He just worries. . . ." Again the curious finger gestures suggesting complexity. "Anyhow, it's a real pest. Here I am, right in the middle of a drawing cycle. You know–daybreak to dusk on the creek." Her voice sounded diminished. "I guess he's afraid I might fall in."

"He's got funny in his old age," I said.

"It isn't very funny," she said, and the talk shifted to other things.

At four o'clock, the screen door slammed and Ted burst into the living room, his long face beaming. "Well, I'll be doggonned, you did come, didn't you."

He had become a tall lean man with a wide mouth. Gray scattered the edges of his hair. He was long-bodied, long-armed and, unlike his brother, had not thickened around the waist.

He beat joyously on my shoulder with a hand. "I was going to be early, but the computer flopped. The computer always flops. Damn fool thing. A computer's a box full of half-right information that it feeds you in one-minute bursts, surrounded by hours of downtime."

"Just like ours," I said, looking at him.

"Ahhhhhh, you dern scientist."

Behind the graying hair, the faintly worn face, the strange long body, I saw the familiar brother of yesterday, still eager, still protecting his vulnerability with chatter, expressing himself in broad, clumsy gestures. I wondered if I seemed as strange to him as he did to me.

He dropped his briefcase, kissed Barbara, beamed at me.

"When'd you get in? Did Barb show you around? I got to work a couple of hours tomorrow, then I'm off all weekend. How do you like this place?"

"Nice and quiet," I said. "I was admiring Barbara's watercolors."

"I have some new ones," she said, not quite defiantly. She thrust them out.

Animation went out of his face. "The creek, huh? It's pretty." Ghosts of past disagreements edged his voice.

She smiled up at him, innocent as a cat. "The light was just right."

"That's nice," he said.

He laid the watercolors carefully on the table and did not look at them again. We talked of other things—of birds and orbital flight, term papers and county history. Through it all you could feel the presence of the watercolors, a point of vague unease, like a tiny cut in the skin. A very tiny cut. But enough to make them carefully cheerful with each other and over-enthusiastic with me.

After dark, Ted and I ambled down the road to admire Jupiter and Venus in the same sector of sky. Above us, leaves hissed with wind, as if water rushed at us across sand.

"Yeah," he said, "we're sorta far out here. I'd like to be over on the other side of town. But it seems our inescapable destiny to have this house and live in this house and love this house and never ever escape from this house. About six generations of Barb's family owned this area. She grew up here and we bought it from her parents. They still farm it. It's okay. I'm just not too crazy about it."

"Too close to the creek?"

His head moved sharply, his expression masked by shadow. "Barb said something, huh?"

"No. You were never too crazy about water."

"I guess not," he said slowly, thinking about it. "Especially deep water. Not that the creek is all that deep. Isn't Happyjack Creek a great name? It's only about six inches, usually."

"You can drown in an inch when your luck's out."

"I expect I'm nuts," he said. "Barb thinks I'm nuts. About the creek."

I hardly knew what to say to this stranger-brother. He stood in the darkness, head tipped back, listening to the hissing of the wind. The house lights quivered behind the tossing leaves and between that distant yellow light and our eyes hung shapeless masses of blackness, alive with movement, shadows slipping within shadows.

I saw that he was looking out toward Jupiter. He said, "I come out here a lot at night. It's quite likely extremely self-indulgent, morally. Do you ever get the feeling that we're living on the outside of reality? Walking around preoccupied with ourselves. And just a hand away, the real world goes on. We're of no importance to the real world. We're just an unimportant transient. The living part of reality is someplace else."

"Sure," I said, "I feel that way every time I go to Washington."

He broke into a sharp laugh. "You violate my sense of melodramatic doom."

We walked slowly back to the house, our feet crunching the gravel. Nothing lay behind the shadows. We stepped through them quite easily and came under the trees. But when I looked back, the place where we had talked was dense with darkness.

I went to sleep in a strange bedroom and just as always woke immediately. The pillow felt too flat and the bed too high and the mattress pressed at unfamiliar points, comfortable but not my own. I adjusted myself and heard their voices through the near wall.

It was not possible to understand much. His voice, then hers, a soft blur of sound, rising to a few clear words, then fading to a rhythmic blur, so that you caught the cadence of speech without the sense of it, the sound the fish hear as the fishermen talk while baiting their hooks.

". . . must not," his voice said. And again, ". . . dangerous. I asked you not . . ." And once, "Don't look for them."

Her voice answering, softer yet clearer, holding anger and pity, ". . . all my life . . . There's nothing. I know you're worried. Ask Ray. Thought too long about. Nothing. Nothing . . ."

It was shameful to listen but I listened, prying at their privacy, feeling as if the act of listening exposed me to the silent derision of those intelligences watching from a concealed place.

Their voices stopped. I covered myself. Wind among the leaves like water flowing among white rocks. I slept without dreams.

By the time I pried myself out of bed the next morning, Ted had left for work. As I entered the kitchen, sweet with the odor of hot ham and biscuits, Barbara was snapping up her painting box.

"Can you make out all alone here for a couple of hours?" she asked. "I got maybe an hour's light left. Ted's gone."

"Let me make a sandwich and I'll walk down with you. I want to see the Forbidden Creek."

"Ha!" she said. "It doesn't make me nervous. I've looked at that creek all my life. . . ."

I had found a foam cup in the cupboard and was pouring it full of coffee. ". . . and never saw the People," I said.

The painting box banged loudly as she dropped it on the table. I saw the darkness under her eyes from not enough sleep, the gossamer lines of strain at the corners of eyes and lips. She looked wary and alert.

She asked, "When did he tell you?"

"He never did. I sort of worked it out over the years."

"Oh, God," she cried, "it's been that long?"

"Let's walk on down to the creek," I said. "I'll tell you on the way."

We descended through open woods. Sunlight barred the slope with streaks of gray shadow, and small white flowers, like vanilla flecks, were scattered under hickory and walnut. The air smelled sweetly cool.

I said, "It's a way of looking at things. Here we are in the middle of reality. It's solid and concrete. It has specific odors and colors. You can feel it and measure it. That's reality. But every now and then you see something else. Say you're in these woods and you look up through the branches toward a cloud. You see that the angle of the branches, a cluster of leaves, a bit of that cloud combine to make up the outline of a face. Take a step forward and the face vanishes. It doesn't exist. It's just a suggestion, a bunch of fortuitous factors. Maybe you look into the water and see weeds and a pebble and a ripple. And maybe that sort of suggests a human shape. If you move, the perspective changes, and it disappears."

"So you get to thinking. Wouldn't it be funny if these shapes in trees and water aren't illusions. They might be like reflections of something real. Someplace else. Maybe realities at a different angle to us, each one throwing off its own reflections."

"But that isn't real," she said, setting down her painting box. Flat white stones scattered along a strip of sandy mud. Beyond slipped a shallow sheet of water, whispering across light tan rock.

"It isn't real to us."

Crisp snaps as she released the catches of the painting box. "That's sick, Ray. He believes it's real. Something physical, out there in the water. He says you can see them."

"Maybe you can if you look at them right."

Scowling faintly, she set up the easel, opened the sketchbook, began wetting her paints. At last she said, "I've tried. I can't see them. I keep thinking, this time I'm going to see them, too."

"Maybe his imagination runs away with him."

"You're not being any help."

That was so obviously true I felt a small convulsion of anger. She could read the problem as well as I could—Ted was showing obsessive symptoms of some kind. "There's really not very much I can do."

"You're really cold, aren't you," she snapped, swinging around at me.

I said, "No, I'm not. I just don't know what to tell you. Maybe he ought to see a doctor."

She swept color across the page, her brush darting and jabbing. "Let's not quarrel," she said finally, eyes on her work. "I don't know what to do either."

"Don't look too hard at the water," I said.

It was the wrong moment for a joke. Her lips clamped together. She did not look at or speak to me again. After a few minutes, I excused myself. I might as well have said good-bye to one of the white rocks.

I went away from the creek, angling along the base of the hill. Finally I came out on the gravel road and walked slowly up to the house through full sunshine. When I got under the trees, it was silent again. Silent. No sound. No bird cry. No breeze. Nothing.

It scared the fool out of me. I went in and had some coffee and fiddled around in the house, listening and furious with myself for listening. There was no sound in that terrible place, nothing at all but the pressure of silence. I could see no movement along the upper limbs. I even went out and looked.

Prancing across the kitchen, loudly elated, Ted tossed down his briefcase. "So you finally got up. I had a great morning. Did a ton of stuff. Next Saturday, I'll do it all over again. Great life. Where's Barb?"

I said, "Haven't seen her since morning."

That swiveled his eyes to mine. "Painting?"

"Yeah."

"Creek?"

"Yeah."

Exuberance went away. He grew taller and graver. "I guess maybe we better wander down there and remind her it's lunchtime."

"You go ahead. I'll fix up some sandwiches." I was not eager to see Barbara again so soon.

"Come on along. I'm using you shamelessly, if you want to know. You're my buffer. Every time the creek's involved, we get into a snapping match." He tugged gently on my arm in the old way I remembered from years back. "Humor me."

We stepped out the back door into an uneasy filigree of leaf shadow, gray and white on the pale gravel. The sky was stacked with broken clouds. Ted strode rapidly off across the parking area, not waiting for me.

When I caught up with him, I said, "I feel like a fool saying it, but maybe you ought to ease up on Barbara about that creek."

He glanced at me with that sudden stab of intelligence I found so disconcerting. "You mean Barb's worried about my intellectual vagaries?"

"Well, she doesn't know how nutty you can be."

We walked quickly down the sharp slanted road, the air sweet with leaves and warm dust, walking where the shadows had moved last night.

He said lightly, "Just like when we were kids. You'd never listen."

"I had to listen to you. You never told me anything right out."

He said quite sharply, "Did I have to? You're not that thickheaded. You know exactly what I mean. Whenever I get near water—you know how it was."

"Down and down," I said.

"Right down among 'em, every time."

The road swerved right toward disciplined fields lined with corn. Bearing left, we entered woods where no line was straight and the hill concealed its surface under last year's leaves. Ahead, dense green foliage clustered along the creek.

I said, "So you saw dreams in water."

"Not dreams. Entities."

"I never saw them."

"It's a way you have to look," he told me. "You can't expect to see them just by staring. I don't mean they're incorporeal. It's just a different way of looking."

"I never found out how."

"I did. It was natural. I just did it."

He glanced toward me over his shoulder, a graying man, belief hollow in his eyes. He grinned. "You see what a crazy you raised, Ray. A water psychic."

"Maybe you've got a special talent. So why worry about Barbara?"

"She wants to see. That's the problem."

Keeping my voice uninflected, I said, "Maybe they don't want her."

"Maybe they haven't made up their minds."

Crossing a narrow field, we entered under the trees. The light became a clear soft gray and the air smelled darkly of water and wet stone. Waist-high weeds slapped at us as we followed a worn track along the creek bank.

Ted's long stride broke into a trot. "Barb!" he called.

We burst out into the flat place by the creek. Near the water stood the easel, a watercolor propped on the crossbar. Her painting box lay open on the rock. Her shoes and socks were scattered by the creek edge. A single slim footprint showed in the sandy mud. Blurred impressions lined out under the still water. Perhaps they were footprints, lost where the rock began in midstream.

"Dear God!" Ted said.

He darted into the creek. He ran splashing through ankle-deep water to the center, his arms and legs in exaggerated motion, looking absurdly like a child at play.

I looked at the shore, the footprint, the shoes. I thought, *Fraud,* and did not believe.

He stared at me in blank confusion, then raced downstream, bent over to peer into the shallow water.

I stepped to the easel, sure that the watercolor would contain some alien thing. And, yes, it did. There, in delicately rendered water, floated a tiny, partially formed eye.

It was a setup, then, arranged to shock. In a moment he would find clothing in the stream, evidence that she had been entrapped. That the People had called. That she had walked guilelessly into the water, and walking dissolved, and dissolving vanished.

She would be watching us from someplace close. I began methodical checking of the low foliage, searching for the glint of skin and intent eye.

Downstream, Ted uttered a harsh bark of sound.

He would have found clothing.

The moment of horror, now. Pause for maximum effect. Pause and pause. The revelation—Now.

Nothing happened.

Upstream toward me came Ted, picking his steps, holding himself tall. He threw down the sodden blouse, the jeans, the bra. Clear water ran from blue and white cloth.

"Where is she?" he asked.

I said nothing.

"I thought it was a gag," he said. "I looked at the shoes, the footprint. I said, 'Oh, hell, they're ribbing me. They're putting me on.' Only you're not, are you?"

"No."

"The timing was wrong," he said. "When she didn't pop out of the bushes and laugh, that's when I knew it wasn't a joke."

This precise re-creation of my own thoughts had the effect of shutting off my brain entirely. I could think of nothing to say.

"Oh, hell," he said, and slowly stepped past the saturated clothing to stare at the watercolor on the easel. I heard his breath hiss. He hadn't missed the eye, either.

"She's probably up at the house waiting for us," I said.

His head shook very slowly right and left, eyes slit, as if the movement gave him pain. "We better look for her down here."

We looked.

We ranged the creek, splashing its length down, searching its length up, bending to peer into shallow pools, poking into deep cuts under banks matted with blackberry that left delicate dots and lines of blood etched on our skin, moving with the sound of water, waiting for laughter and her voice, seeing sunlight unsteady on the shallows, the sudden panicked dart of a crawdad, the shapes of leaves against the late afternoon light, the sudden animal scuttle through underbrush that brought us erect, taut with expectation.

Nothing and no one.

And finally, Ted standing bent in a calm pool, head strained forward, regarding the pebbled bottom, his face anguished.

I saw his right leg swing. He kicked the water savagely, three times. Kick, kick, kick.

"Give her back!" he shouted. "Let her go!"

* * *

When evening came, we returned to the open area where the easel stood. I squatted down beside Ted in the dusk. Neither of us spoke. We waited together, listening to water mutter among the stones. The creek, dim in the larger dark, stretched hugely away.

He said in a small clear voice, "You needn't stay."

"I will."

"Taking care of the stupid younger brother."

I said, "You shouldn't do this all alone."

"How else can you do anything?"

Limbs stirred against a vague sky.

After a long pause, he said in a rapid monotone, "I've always seen them. They didn't particularly care about me. I don't know why. In Ohio, in that lake, when I was way underwater down in the mud, they came looking. Watching me drown. They didn't care. Their way. Not malicious. Just indifferent. When you came down, they scattered. It was dark but I saw them somehow or other. You never did. You were just as indifferent as they were. Only it was different with you. You always kind of looked right through me. You never saw me either, you know. You really didn't care. I figured that out. I carried that all alone—you, and seeing the People—and that was pretty bad later, when nobody else saw them. How I wanted you to see them. But you never did."

It was work to keep my voice level. "I couldn't see. I don't have the gift."

"Gift! Lord protect us from such ill-considered gifts. The People must be all over, you know. Everywhere. A completely unidentified species. Millions of them. All the free water. Think how they swarm in the Mississippi. Think of the Nile."

His voice lifted, stumbling with intensity.

"Millions. And I'm the only one to see. I'm a lunatic in a special way. Oh, my God, you don't know how horrible it is to know that. And now this with Barb. How do I deal with this? She's out there. She's . . ."

Sound shut off. The flutter of leaves, frog sound, the rasp of small night creatures, creek sound. All stopped, as if a key had been turned.

Ted's fingers chewed into my arm.

"Listen," he barked. "Listen."

Silence pressed against us with physical force.

He demanded savagely, "You hear that?"

"What?"

"For God's sake," he said, "for God's sake, that's her voice."

He leaped up and plunged toward the creek.

I called, "Wait for me."

"No. No, don't you come. Please. If you come, they'll never let me see her."

"Ted, I don't want to have to drag you out."

"You won't have to. I promise you."

He strode quickly away into the creek, the beam of his flashlight bobbing ahead of him. As he moved off through the shallow creek water, the sound of splashing abruptly faded and became remote. It was as if he passed through some sound-absorbent medium. He moved a few feet off and sounded a hundred yards away. Then there was no sound at all. I watched him slip downstream like the shadow of a ghost. The enveloping silence made me feel vaguely sick.

I knelt on the stones, calculating how long to wait before following. The soundlessness made it hard to judge. He would be able to hear me following a long way behind and that he would count as betrayal.

I was intensely aware that we had come to one of those points where your actions, in a very brief time, can permanently alter the way you regard each other. It's easy to fumble. It requires such care. You have to handle yourself with the delicacy of a surgeon cutting along a nerve.

While I crouched, coldly disturbed, watching the intermittent glimmer of his light, I became aware of my own voice.

It whispered, "He hears. I don't. Same thing."

At first I didn't register the meaning of that. Then I felt a light shock of understanding as it made sense.

Sensitives, the pair of us.

We sensed the same thing in different ways. It was two sides of the same experience. Where he heard the calling voice, I heard silence.

Either way it meant the same thing. It meant that the People had come, the flowing, watching People of Happyjack Creek.

No sooner had I repeated that over to myself a couple of times, trying to understand by repetition, than I realized I could no longer see Ted's light. It was time to follow. But when I started to move, I could not. The thought of stepping into that water and perhaps putting my foot on one of the People turned my muscles to mush.

So there I huddled, completely amazed at myself, grinding my fingers together, while Ted sloshed downstream, the light jittering ahead of him, listening to Barbara's voice calling from God knows where, saying God knows what.

Shame dragged me erect. I forced myself up into a silence as thick as felt slabs, my back flinching horribly at the darkness behind. I took a tentative step forward, feeling cold water flooding into my shoes, and the darkness came down on me, a thousand tons of it. With no warning at all, it became the way it had been under that Ohio lake, my legs sunk in icy mud and no air.

The fear pours up through you, stunning the nerves and penetrating the muscles. If you run, it runs with you. But you don't dare run. Running creates its own pursuit. It is one of the rules that you must face fear

at once, head-on. You clamp your teeth and stand and look at it and endure.

I switched off the flashlight and let night come down.

When the light went out, I almost fell over. Panic bent me. It was pretty
bad. I felt that I was standing on a tongue in an open mouth. I felt the
creek banks behind stir and concentrate, preparing to close on me in one
whispering rush, vine, stone, dirt, and water clamping shut.

All this, I suppose, was direct attack by the People. I suppose. I don't
know. I do know there were some terrible moments and I resisted them,
body stiff and eyes shut, because you have to resist. I endured.

The way you endure, you get through one second. When that is over,
you get through the next one. And so the seconds go. No matter how bad
it is, you hang on one second more, because if you run, you know you
will remember running later and then the shame will come and that will
be worse than standing, enduring, with the mouth around you and the
banks moving behind.

After a long while I got my shoulders back and my head up, although
it was terror to move. You come back to yourself a sensation at a time.
First, cold water in the shoes. Next, the smell of night leaves. After that,
the shirt plastered against your back, the feel of clenched fingers.

I got my eyes open.

Gray sky showed behind blurred limbs. Beyond them hung a dusting
of stars.

The ferocity of the night had softened. I saw that the darkness was
streaked by variations of light, gray, black, pale silver. I could make out
clumps of bushes and the intricate interweaving of limbs. These were familiar, ordinary, natural shapes, the way they had always been.

Finally I punched on the light and, concentrating hard, began to move.
My body felt wooden and uncontrollable. It seemed to take a year to go
fifty feet.

As I blundered slowly downstream through that nasty silence, a small
glow flickered behind foliage far down the creek. It wavered like a trace
of moonlight, then went out. I could imagine that a flashlight had been
waved briefly, the beam crossing overhead limbs. I could think of no reason for that, and anxiety pressed me forward like the push of a hand.

The creek bent sharply right around bushy shallows. My light grazed
cliffs to the left, black water at their base. White and brown rock chunks
littered the stream. From the right bank, a muddy bed of gravel tongued
into the creek. On the tongue lay Ted's flashlight pointing its beam
serenely across the water.

He lay on the far side of the gravel, stretched out in a shallow pool.

My light touched his pale body. He had thrown off his clothing and
lay with lifted head, staring into the water.

As my light came on him, a thick ripple seemed to rise close to his face and rolled away from him across the shallows. It might have marked the passage of a large fish or muskrat.

Darting forward, I jabbed my light at the ripple. But there was only water, inches deep, quite transparent. It concealed nothing and contained nothing.

The ripple slipped smoothly to the far shore and flattened away.

As it did so, sound returned. It was like being struck from all sides at once. Water rustled and night creatures cried and I heard the rasp of my own breathing. The sounding world pulsed all around, as terrifying as the silence.

I flopped down in the water beside Ted. He turned his head slowly, bringing his face into the glare of the flashlight. It was a still, blank face, smoothed of hope.

"They came," he said. "But they didn't want me."

Reaching down, I set my arm across his frigid shoulders.

"It's okay," I said.

"I tried to go to them. But there wasn't any way."

His voice was low and calm, without excitement, without cadence, the voice of a stone figure speaking with a kind of precise indifference.

I gripped his shoulders hard. It was as if a door in me had opened that I had never realized was closed. He was valuable and of enormous worth. I felt amazement that this extraordinary person was my brother.

He remained motionless under my arm.

"There is no use waiting," he said in that uninflected voice.

I looked down sharply at him then and saw what the People had taken. There was no warmth in him. His passionless eyes remained fixed on me and they found nothing to judge, neither guilt nor virtue. He was stripped of both. The processes of his life, I saw, proceeded without such human ambiguities.

"We'll wait a little bit," I said to him, through my shock.

We waited. But the People did not return.

We never saw Barbara again, either.

Missolonghi 1824

One of the most acclaimed and respected authors of our day, John Crowley is perhaps best known for his fat and fanciful novel about the sometimes dangerous interactions between Faërie and our own everyday world, *Little, Big,* which won the prestigious World Fantasy Award. His other novels include *Beasts, The Deep, Engine Summer, Ægypt,* and a collection, *Novelty.* His most recent books are *Antiquities,* a collection, and a new novel, *Love and Sleep.* His short fiction has appeared in *Omni, Asimov's Science Fiction, Elsewhere, Shadows,* and *Whispers.* He lives in the Berkshire Hills of western Massachusetts.

Crowley doesn't write many short stories, but when he does, they are usually worth waiting for—as is the subtle and lyrical story that follows, in which a man of the smugly rational nineteenth-century "modern" world has a curious and unsettling encounter with a survivor of Ancient Times. . . .

The English milord took his hands from the boy's shoulders, discomfited but unembarrassed. "No?" he said. "No. Very well, I see, I see; you must forgive me then . . ."

The boy, desperate not to have offended the Englishman, clutched at the milord's tartan cloak and spoke in a rush of Romaic, shaking his head and near tears.

"No, no, my dear," the milord said. "It's not at all your fault; you have swept me into an impropriety. I misunderstood your kindness, that is all, and it is you who must forgive me."

He went, with his odd off-kilter and halting walk, to his couch, and re-clined there. The boy stood erect in the middle of the room, and (switching to Italian) began a long speech about his deep love and respect for the noble lord, who was as dear as life itself to him. The noble lord watched him in wonder, smiling. Then he held out a hand to him: "Oh, no more, no more. You see it is just such sentiments as those that misled me. Really, I swear to you, I misunderstood and it shan't happen again. Only you mustn't stand there preaching at me, don't; come sit by me at least. Come."

The boy, knowing that a dignified coldness was often the safest demeanor to adopt when offers like the milord's were made to him, came and stood beside his employer, hands behind his back.

"Well," the milord said, himself adopting a more serious mien. "I'll tell you what. If you will not stand there like a stick, if you will put back on your usual face—sit, won't you?—then . . . then what shall I do? I shall tell you a story."

Immediately the boy melted. He sat, or squatted, near his master—not on the couch, but on a rag of carpet on the floor near it. "A story," he said. "A story of what, of what?"

"Of what, of what," said the Englishman. He felt the familiar night pains beginning within, everywhere and nowhere. "If you will just trim the lamp," he said, "and open a jar of that Hollands gin there, and pour me a cup with some *limonata,* and then put a stick on the fire—then we will have 'of what, of what.' "

The small compound was dark now, though not quiet; in the courtyard could still be heard the snort and stamp of horses arriving, the talk of his Suliote soldiers and the petitioners and hangers-on around the cookfires there, talk that could turn to insults, quarrels, riot, or dissolve in laughter. Insofar as he could, the noble foreign lord on whom all of them depended had banished them from this room: here, he had his couch, and the table where he wrote—masses of correspondence, on gold-edged crested paper to impress, or on plain paper to explain (endless the explanations, the cajolings, the reconcilings these Greeks demanded of him); and another pile of papers, messy large sheets much marked over, stanzas of a poem it had lately been hard for him to remember he was writing. Also on the table amid the papers, not so incongruous as they would once have struck him, were a gilt dress-sword, a fantastical crested helmet in the Grecian style, and a Manton's pistol.

He sipped the gin the boy had brought him, and said: "Very well. A story." The boy knelt again on his carpet, dark eyes turned up, eager as a hound: and the poet saw in his face that hunger for tales (what boy his age in England would show it, what public-school boy or even carter's or ploughman's lad would show it?), the same eagerness that must have been in the faces gathered around the fire by which Homer spoke. He felt almost abashed by the boy's open face: he could tell him anything, and be believed.

"Now this would have happened," he said, "I should think, in the year of your birth, or very near; and it happened not a great distance from this place, down in the Morea, in a district that was once called, by your own ancestors a long time ago, Arcadia."

"Arcadia," the boy said in Romaic.

"Yes. You've been there?"

He shook his head.

"Wild and strange it was to me then. I was very young, not so many years older than you are now, hard as it may be for you to imagine I was ever so. I was traveling, traveling because—well, I knew not why; for the sake of traveling, really, though that was hard to explain to the Turks, who do not travel for pleasure, you know, only for gain. I did discover why I traveled, though: that's part of this story. And a part of the story of how I come to be here in this wretched marsh, with you, telling you of it.

"You see, in England, where the people are chiefly hypocrites, and thus easily scandalized, the offer that I just foolishly made to you, my dear, should it have become public knowledge, would have got both us, but chiefly me, in a deal of very hot water. When I was young there was a fellow hanged for doing such things, or rather for being caught at it. Our vices are whoring and drink, you see; other vices are sternly punished.

"And yet it was not that which drove me abroad; nor was it the ladies either—that would come later. No—I think it was the weather, above all." He tugged the tartan more closely around him. "Now, this winter damp; this rain today, every day this week; these fogs. Imagine if they never stopped: summer and winter, the same, except that in winter it is . . . well, how am I to explain an English winter to you? I shall not try.

"As soon as I set foot on these shores, I knew I had come home. I was no citizen of England gone abroad. No: this was my land, my clime, my air. I went upon Hymettus and heard the bees. I climbed to the Acropolis (which Lord Elgin was just conspiring to despoil; he wanted to bring the statues to England, to teach the English sculpture—the English being as capable of sculpture as you, my dear, are of skating). I stood within the grove sacred to Apollo at Claros: except there is no grove there now, it is nothing but dust. You, Loukas, and your fathers have cut down all the trees, and burned them, out of spite or for firewood I know not. I stood in the blowing dust and sun, and I thought: *I am come two thousand years too late*.

"That was the sadness that haunted my happiness, you see. I did not despise the living Greeks, as so many of my countrymen did, and think them degenerate, and deserving their Turkish masters. No, I rejoiced in them, girls and boys, Albanians and Suliotes and Athenians. I loved Athens and the narrow squalid streets and the markets. I took exception to nothing. And yet . . . I wanted so much not to have *missed* it, and was so aware that I had. Homer's Greece; Pindar's; Sappho's. Yes, my young friend: you know soldiers and thieves with those names; I speak of others.

"I wintered in Athens. When summer came, I mounted an expedition into the Morea. I had with me my valet Fletcher, whom you know—still with me here; and my two Albanian servants, very fierce and greedy and loyal, drinking skinfuls of Zean wine at eight paras the oke every day. And there was my new Greek friend Nikos, who is your predecessor, Loukas, your *type* I might say, the original of all of you that I have loved; only the difference was, he loved me too.

"You know you can see the mountains into which we went from these windows, yes, on a clear cloudless day such as we have not seen now these many weeks; those mountains to the south across the bay, that look so bare and severe. The tops of them *are* bare, most of them; but down in the vales there are still bits of the ancient forests, and in the chasms where the underground rivers pour out. There are woods and pasture: yes, sheep and shepherds too in Arcady.

"That is Pan's country, you know—or perhaps you don't; sometimes I credit you Greeks with a knowledge that ought to have come down with your blood, but has not. Pan's country: where he was born, where he still lives. The old poets spoke of his hour as noon, when he sleeps upon the hills; when even if you did not see the god face-to-face—woe to you if you did—you could hear his voice, or the sound of his pipes: a sorrowful music, for he is a sad god at heart, and mourns for his lost love Echo."

The poet ceased to speak for a long moment. He remembered that music, heard in the blaze of the Arcadian sun, music not different from the hot nameless drone of noontide itself, compounded of insects, exhalation of the trees, the heated blood rushing in his head. Yet it was a song too, potent and vivifying—and sad, infinitely sad: that even a god could mistake the reflection of his own voice for love's.

There were other gods in those mountains besides great Pan, or had been once; the little party of travelers would pass through groves or near pools, where little stelae had been set up in another age, canted over now and pitted and mossy, or broken and worn away, but whose figures could sometimes still be read: crude nymphs, half-figures of squat horned bearded men with great phalluses, broken or whole. The Orthodox in their party crossed themselves passing these, the Mussulmen looked away or pointed and laughed.

"The little gods of woodland places," the poet said. "The gods of hunters and fishermen. It reminded me of my own home country of Scotland, and how the men and women still believe in pixies and kelpies, and leave food for them, or signs to placate them. It was very like that.

"And I doubt not those old Scotsmen have their reasons for acting as they do, as good reasons as the Greeks had. And have still—whereby hangs this tale."

He drank again (more than this cupful would be needed to get him through the night) and laid a careful hand on Loukas's dark curls. "It was in such a glen that one night we made our camp. So long did the Albanians dance and sing around the fire—'When we were thieves at Targa,' and I'm sure they were—and so sympathetic did I find the spot, that by noon next day we were still at ease there.

"Noon. Pan's song. But we became aware of other sounds as well, human sounds, a horn blown, thrashings and crashing in the glen beyond our camp. Then figures: villagers, armed with rakes and staves and one old man with a fowling-piece.

"A hunt of some sort was up, though what game could have been in these mountains large enough to attract such a crowd I could not imagine; it was hard to believe that many boar or deer could get a living here, and there was uproar enough among these villagers that they might have been after a tiger.

"We joined the chase for a time, trying to see what was afoot. A cry arose down where the forest was thickest, and for an instant I did see some beast ahead of the pack, crashing in the undergrowth, and heard an animal's cry—then no more. Nikos had no taste for pursuit in the heat of the day, and the hunt straggled on out of our ken.

"Toward evening we reached the village itself, over a mountain and a pass: a cluster of houses, a monastery on the scarp above where monks starved themselves, a *taberna* and a church. There was much excitement; men strutted with their weapons in the street. Apparently their hunt had been successful, but it was not easy to determine what they had caught. I spoke but little Romaic then; the Albanians knew none. Nikos, who could speak Italian and some English, held these mountain people in contempt, and soon grew bored with the work of translating. But gradually I conceived the idea that what they had hunted through the groves and glens was not an animal at all but a man—some poor madman, apparently, some wild man of the woods hunted down for sport. He was being kept caged outside the town, it seemed, awaiting the judgment of some village headman.

"I was well aware of the bigotries of people such as these villagers were; of Greeks in general, and of their Turkish masters too if it come to that. Whoever started their fear or incurred their displeasure, it would go hard with them. That winter in Athens I had interceded for a woman condemned to death by the Turkish authorities, she having been caught in illicit love. Not with me: with me she was not caught. Nonetheless I took it upon myself to rescue her, which with much bluster and a certain quantity of silver I accomplished. I thought perhaps I could help the poor wretch these people had taken. I cannot bear to see even a wild beast in a cage.

"No one welcomed my intervention. The village headman did not want to see me. The villagers fled from my Albanians, the loudest strutters fleeing first. When at last I found a priest I could get some sense from, he told me I was much mistaken and should not interfere. He was tremendously excited, and spoke of rape, not one but many, or the possibility of them anyway, now thank Christ avoided. But I could not credit what he seemed to say: that the captive was not a madman at all but a man of the woods, one who had never lived among men. Nikos translated what the priest said: 'He speaks, but no one understands him.'

"Now I was even more fascinated. I thought perhaps this might be one of the Wild Boys one hears of now and then, abandoned to die and raised by wolves; not a thing one normally credits, and yet . . . There was something in the air of the village, the wild distraction of the priest—compounded of fear and triumph—that kept me from inquiring further. I would bide my time.

"As darkness came on the people of the village seemed to be readying themselves for some further brutishness. Pine torches had been lit, leading the way to the dell where the captive was being held. It seemed possible that they planned to burn the fellow alive: any such idea as that of course I must prevent, and quickly.

"Like Machiavel, I chose a combination of force and suasion as best suited to accomplishing my purpose. I stood the men of the village to a quantity of drink at the *taberna,* and I posted my armed Albanians on the path out to the little dell where the captive was. Then I went in peace to see for myself.

"In the flare of the torches I could see the cage, green poles lashed together. I crept slowly to it, not wanting whoever was within to raise an alarm. I felt my heart beat fast, without knowing why it should. As I came close, a dark hand was put out, and took hold of a bar. Something in this hand's action—I cannot say what—was not the action of a man's hand, but of a beast's; what beast, though?

"What reached me next was the smell, a nose-filling rankness that I have never smelled again but would know in a moment. There was something of hurt and fear in it, the smell of an animal that has been wounded and soiled itself; but there was a life history in it too, a ferocious filthiness, something untrammeled and uncaring—well, it's quite impossible, the language has too few words for smells, potent though they be. Now I knew that what was in the cage was not a man; only a furbearer could retain so much odor. And yet: *He speaks,* the priest had said, *and no one understands him.*

"I looked within the cage. I could see nothing at first, though I could hear a labored breath, and felt a poised stillness, the tension of a creature waiting for attack. Then he blinked, and I saw his eyes turned on me.

"You know the eyes of your ancestors, Loukas, the eyes pictured on vases and on the ancientest of statues: those enormous almond-shaped eyes, outlined in black, black-pupiled too, and staring, overflowing with some life other than this world's. Those were his eyes, Greek eyes that no Greek ever had; white at the long corners, with great onyx centers.

"He blinked again, and moved within his cage—his captors had made it too small to stand in, and he must have suffered dreadfully in it—and drew up his legs. He struggled to get some ease, and one foot slid out between the bars below, and nearly touched my knee where I knelt in the dust. And I knew then why it was that he spoke but was not understood."

At first he had thought there must be more than one animal confined in the little cage, his mind unwilling to add together the reaching, twitching foot with its lean shin extended between the bars and the great-eyed hard-breathing personage inside. Cloven: that foot the Christians took from Pan and Pan's sons to give to their Devil. The poet had always taken his own clubbed foot as a sort of sign of his kinship with that race—which, however, along with the rest of modern mankind, he had still supposed to be merely fancies. They were not: not this one, stinking, breathing, waiting for words.

"Now I knew why my heart beat hard. I thought it astonishing but very likely that I alone, of all these Greeks about me here, I alone perhaps of all the mortals in Arcadia that night, knew the language this creature might know: for I had been made to study it, you see, forced with blows and implorings and bribes to learn it through many long years at Harrow. Was that fate? Had our father-god brought me here this night to do this child of his some good?

"I put my face close to the bars of the cage. I was afraid for a moment that all those thousands of lines learned by heart had fled from me. The only one I could think of was not so very appropriate. *Sing, Muse,* I said, *that man of many resources, who traveled far and wide . . .* and his eyes shone. I was right: he spoke the Greek of Homer, and not of these men of the iron age.

"Now what was I to say? He still lay quiet within the cage, but for the one hand gripping the bars, waiting for more. I realized he must be wounded—it seemed obvious that unless he were wounded he could not have been taken. I knew but one thing: I would not willingly be parted from him. I could have remained in his presence nightlong, forever. I sought his white almond eyes in the darkness and I thought: *I have not missed it after all: it awaited me here to find.*

"I would not have all night, though. My Albanians now discharged their weapons—the warning we'd agreed on—and I heard shouts; the men of the village, now suitably inflamed, were headed for this place. I took from my pocket a penknife—all I had—and set to work on the tough hemp of the cage's ropes.

"*Atrema,* I said, *atrema, atrema*—which I remembered was 'quietly, quietly.' He made no sound or movement as I cut, but when I took hold of a bar with my left hand to steady myself, he put out his long black-nailed hand and grasped my wrist. Not in anger, but not tenderly; strongly, purposefully. The hair rose on my neck. He did not release me until the ropes were cut and I tugged apart the bars.

"The moon had risen, and he came forth into its light. He was no taller than a boy of eight, and yet how he drew the night to him, as though it were a thing with a piece missing until he stepped out into it, and now was whole. I could see that indeed he had been hurt: stripes of blood ran round his bare chest where he had fallen or rolled down a steep declivity. I could see the ridged recurving horns that rose from the matted hair of his head; I could see his sex, big, held up against his belly by a fold of fur, like a dog's or a goat's. Alert, still breathing hard (his breast fluttering, as though the heart within him were huge) he glanced about himself, assessing which way were best to run.

"Now go, I said to him. *Live. Take care they do not come near you again. Hide from them when you must; despoil them when you can. Seize on their wives and daughters, piss in their vegetable gardens, tear down their fences, drive mad their sheep and goats. Teach them fear. Never never let them take you again.*

"I say I said this to him, but I confess I could not think of half the words; my Greek had fled me. No matter: he turned his great hot eyes on me as though he understood. What he said back to me I cannot tell you, though he spoke, and smiled; he spoke in a warm winey voice, but a few words, round and sweet. That was a surprise. Perhaps it was from Pan he had his music. I can tell you I have tried to bring those words up often from where I know they are lodged, in my heart of hearts; I think that it is really what I am about when I try to write poems. And now and again— yes, not often, but sometimes—I hear them again.

"He dropped to his hands, then, somewhat as an ape does; he turned and fled, and the tuft of his tail flashed once, like a hare's. At the end of the glen he turned—I could just see him at the edge of the trees—and looked at me. And that was all.

"I sat in the dust there, sweating in the night air. I remember thinking the striking thing about it was how *unpoetical* it had been. It was like no story about a meeting between a man and a god—or a godlet—that I had ever heard. No gift was given me, no promise made me. It was like freeing an otter from a fish trap. And that, most strangely, was what gave me joy in it. The difference, child, between the true gods and the imaginary ones is this: that the true gods are not less real than yourself."

It was deep midnight now in the villa; the tide was out, and rain had begun again to fall, spattering on the roof tiles, hissing in the fire.

It wasn't true, what he had told the boy: that he had been given no gift, made no promise. For it was only after Greece that he came to possess the quality for which, besides his knack for verse, he was chiefly famous: his gift (not always an easy one to live with) for attracting love from many different kinds and conditions of people. He had accepted the love that he attracted, and sought more, and had that too. *Satyr* he had been called, often enough. He thought, when he gave it any thought, that it had come to him through the grip of the horned one: a part of that being's own power of unrefusable ravishment.

Well, if that were so, then he had the gift no more: had used it up, spent it, worn it out. He was thirty-six, and looked and felt far older: sick and lame, his puffy features grey and haggard, his moustache white—foolish to think he could have been the object of Loukas's affection.

But without love, without its wild possibility, he could no longer defend himself against the void: against his black certainty that life mattered not a whit, was a brief compendium of folly and suffering, not worth the stakes. He would not take life on those terms; no, he would trade it for something more valuable . . . for Greece. Freedom. He would like to have given his life heroically, but even the ignoble death he seemed likely now to suffer here, in this mephitic swamp, even that was worth something: was owed, anyway, to the clime that made him a poet: to the blessing he had had.

"I have heard of no reports of such a creature in those mountains since that time," he said. "You know, I think the little gods are the oldest gods, older than the Olympians, older far than Jehovah. Pan forbid he should be dead, if he be the last of his kind . . ."

The firing of Suliote guns outside the villa woke him. He lifted his head painfully from the sweat-damp pillow. He put out his hand and thought for a moment his Newfoundland dog Lion lay at his feet. It was the boy Loukas: asleep.

He raised himself to his elbows. What had he dreamed? What story had he told?

NOTE: *Lord Byron died at Missolonghi, in Greece, April 19, 1824. He was thirty-six years old.*

Bears Discover Fire

Terry Bisson is the author of a number of critically acclaimed novels such as *Fire on the Mountain, Wyrldmaker,* the popular *Talking Man,* which was a finalist for the World Fantasy Award in 1986, and *Voyage to the Red Planet.* He is a frequent contributor to such markets as *Asimov's Science Fiction, Omni, Playboy,* and *The Magazine of Fantasy & Science Fiction,* and, in 1991, the famous story that follows, "Bears Discover Fire," won the Nebula Award, the Hugo Award, the Theodore Sturgeon Award, *and* the *Asimov's* Reader's Award, the only story ever to sweep them all. His most recent books are a collection, *Bears Discover Fire and Other Stories,* and a new novel, *Pirates of the Universe.* He lives with his family in Brooklyn, New York.

Here he offers us a gentle, wry, whimsical, and funny story—reminiscent to me of the best of early Lafferty and Bradbury—that's about exactly what it *says* that it's about . . .

I was driving with my brother, the preacher, and my nephew, the preacher's son, on I-65 just north of Bowling Green when we got a flat. It was Sunday night and we had been to visit Mother at the Home. We were in my car. The flat caused what you might call knowing groans since, as the old-fashioned one in my family (so they tell me), I fix my own tires, and my brother is always telling me to get radials and quit buying old tires.

But if you know how to mount and fix tires yourself, you can pick them up for almost nothing.

Since it was a left rear tire, I pulled over left, onto the median grass. The way my Caddy stumbled to a stop, I figured the tire was ruined. "I guess there's no need asking if you have any of that *FlatFix* in the trunk," said Wallace.

"Here, son, hold the light," I said to Wallace Jr. He's old enough to want to help and not old enough (yet) to think he knows it all. If I'd married and had kids, he's the kind I'd have wanted.

An old Caddy has a big trunk that tends to fill up like a shed. Mine's a '56. Wallace was wearing his Sunday shirt, so he didn't offer to help while I pulled magazines, fishing tackle, a wooden tool box, some old clothes, a comealong wrapped in a grass sack, and a tobacco sprayer out of the way, looking for my jack. The spare looked a little soft.

The light went out. "Shake it, son," I said.

It went back on. The bumper jack was long gone, but I carry a little 1/4-ton hydraulic. I finally found it under Mother's old *Southern Livings,* 1978–1986. I had been meaning to drop them at the dump. If Wallace hadn't been along, I'd have let Wallace Jr. position the jack under the axle, but I got on my knees and did it myself. There's nothing wrong with a boy learning to change a tire. Even if you're not going to fix and mount them, you're still going to have to change a few in this life. The light went off again before I had the wheel off the ground. I was surprised at how dark the night was already. It was late October and beginning to get cool. "Shake it again, son," I said.

It went back on but it was weak. Flickery.

"With radials you just don't *have* flats," Wallace explained in that voice he uses when he's talking to a number of people at once; in this case, Wallace Jr. and myself. "And even when you *do,* you just squirt them with this stuff called *FlatFix* and you just drive on. $3.95 the can."

"Uncle Bobby can fix a tire hisself," said Wallace Jr., out of loyalty I presume.

*"Him*self," I said from halfway under the car. If it was up to Wallace, the boy would talk like what Mother used to call "a helock from the gorges of the mountains." But drive on radials.

"Shake that light again," I said. It was about gone. I spun the lugs off into the hubcap and pulled the wheel. The tire had blown out along the sidewall. "Won't be fixing this one," I said. Not that I cared. I have a pile as tall as a man out by the barn.

The light went out again, then came back better than ever as I was fitting the spare over the lugs. "Much better," I said. There was a flood of dim orange flickery light. But when I turned to find the lug nuts, I was surprised to see that the flashlight the boy was holding was dead. The light was coming from two bears at the edge of the trees, holding torches. They were big, three-hundred pounders, standing about five feet tall. Wallace Jr. and his father had seen them and were standing perfectly still. It's best not to alarm bears.

I fished the lug nuts out of the hubcap and spun them on. I usually like to put a little oil on them, but this time I let it go. I reached under the car and let the jack down and pulled it out. I was relieved to see that the spare was high enough to drive on. I put the jack and the lug wrench and the flat into the trunk. Instead of replacing the hubcap, I put it in there too. All this time, the bears never made a move. They just held the torches up, whether out of curiosity or helpfulness, there was no way of knowing. It looked like there may have been more bears behind them, in the trees.

Opening three doors at once, we got into the car and drove off. Wallace was the first to speak. "Looks like bears have discovered fire," he said.

When we first took Mother to the Home, almost four years (forty-seven months) ago, she told Wallace and me she was ready to die. "Don't worry about me, boys," she whispered, pulling us both down so the nurse wouldn't hear. "I've drove a million miles and I'm ready to pass over to the other shore. I won't have long to linger here." She drove a consolidated school bus for thirty-nine years. Later, after Wallace left, she told me about her dream. A bunch of doctors were sitting around in a circle discussing her case. One said, "We've done all we can for her, boys, let's let her go." They all turned their hands up and smiled. When she didn't die that fall, she seemed disappointed, though as spring came she forgot about it, as old people will.

In addition to taking Wallace and Wallace Jr. to see Mother on Sunday nights, I go myself on Tuesdays and Thursdays. I usually find her sitting in front of the TV, even though she doesn't watch it. The nurses keep it on all the time. They say the old folks like the flickering. It soothes them down.

"What's this I hear about bears discovering fire?" she said on Tuesday. "It's true," I told her as I combed her long white hair with the shell comb Wallace had brought her from Florida. Monday there had been a story in the Louisville *Courier-Journal,* and Tuesday one on NBC or CBS Nightly News. People were seeing bears all over the state, and in Virginia as well. They had quit hibernating, and were apparently planning to spend the winter in the medians of the interstates. There have always been bears in the mountains of Virginia, but not here in western Kentucky, not for almost a hundred years. The last one was killed when Mother was a girl. The theory in the *Courier-Journal* was that they were following I-65 down from the forests of Michigan and Canada, but one old man from Allen County (interviewed on nationwide TV) said that there had always been a few bears left back in the hills, and they had come out to join the others now that they had discovered fire.

"They don't hibernate anymore," I said. "They make a fire and keep it going all winter."

"I declare," Mother said. "What'll they think of next!" The nurse came to take her tobacco away, which is the signal for bedtime.

Every October, Wallace Jr. stays with me while his parents go to camp. I realize how backward that sounds, but there it is. My brother is a minister (House of the Righteous Way, Reformed), but he makes two-thirds of his living in real estate. He and Elizabeth go to a Christian Success Retreat in South Carolina, where people from all over the country practice selling things to one another. I know what it's like not because they've ever bothered to tell me, but because I've seen the Revolving Equity Success Plan ads late at night on TV.

The school bus let Wallace Jr. off at my house on Wednesday, the day they left. The boy doesn't have to pack much of a bag when he stays with me. He has his own room here. As the eldest of our family, I hung onto the old home place near Smiths Grove. It's getting run down, but Wallace Jr. and I don't mind. He has his own room in Bowling Green, too, but since Wallace and Elizabeth move to a different house every three months (part of the Plan), he keeps his .22 and his comics, the stuff that's important to a boy his age, in his room here at the home place. It's the room his dad and I used to share.

Wallace Jr. is twelve. I found him sitting on the back porch that over-looks the interstate when I got home from work. I sell crop insurance.

After I changed clothes, I showed him how to break the bead on a tire two ways, with a hammer and by backing a car over it. Like making sorghum, fixing tires by hand is a dying art. The boy caught on fast, though. "Tomorrow I'll show you how to mount your tire with the hammer and a tire iron," I said.

"What I wish is I could see the bears," he said. He was looking across the field to I-65, where the northbound lanes cut off the corner of our field. From the house at night, sometimes the traffic sounds like a waterfall.

"Can't see their fire in the daytime," I said. "But wait till tonight." That night CBS or NBC (I forget which is which) did a special on the bears, which were becoming a story of nationwide interest. They were seen in Kentucky, West Virginia, Missouri, Illinois (southern), and, of course, Virginia. There have always been bears in Virginia. Some characters there were even talking about hunting them. A scientist said they were heading into the states where there is some snow but not too much, and where there is enough timber in the medians for firewood. He had gone in with a video camera, but his shots were just blurry figures sitting around a fire. Another scientist said the bears were attracted by the berries on a new bush that grew only in the medians of the interstates. He claimed this berry was the first new species in recent history, brought about by the mixing of seeds along the highway. He ate one on TV, making a face, and called it a "newberry." A climatic ecologist said that the warm winters (there was no snow last winter in Nashville, and only one flurry in Louisville) had changed the bears' hibernation cycle, and now they were able to remember things from year to year. "Bears may have discovered fire centuries ago," he said, "but forgot it." Another theory was that they had discovered (or remembered) fire when Yellowstone burned, several years ago.

The TV showed more guys talking about bears than it showed bears, and Wallace Jr. and I lost interest. After the supper dishes were done I took the boy out behind the house and down to our fence. Across the interstate and through the trees, we could see the light of the bears' fire. Wallace Jr. wanted to go back to the house and get his .22 and go shoot one, and I explained why that would be wrong. "Besides," I said, "a .22 wouldn't do much more to a bear than make it mad."

"Besides," I added, "It's illegal to hunt in the medians."

The only trick to mounting a tire by hand, once you have beaten or pried it onto the rim, is setting the bead. You do this by setting the tire upright, sitting on it, and bouncing it up and down between your legs while the air goes in. When the bead sets on the rim, it makes a satisfying "pop." On Thursday, I kept Wallace Jr. home from school and showed him how to do this until he got it right. Then we climbed our fence and crossed the field to get a look at the bears.

In northern Virginia, according to *Good Morning America,* the bears were keeping their fires going all day long. Here in western Kentucky, though, it was still warm for late October and they only stayed around the fires at night. Where they went and what they did in the daytime, I don't know. Maybe they were watching from the newberry bushes as Wallace Jr. and I climbed the government fence and crossed the northbound lanes. I carried an axe and Wallace Jr. brought his .22, not because he wanted to kill a bear but because a boy likes to carry some kind of a gun. The median was all tangled with brush and vines under the maples, oaks, and sycamores. Even though we were only a hundred yards from the house, I had never been there, and neither had anyone else that I knew of. It was like a created country. We found a path in the center and followed it down across a slow, short stream that flowed out of one grate and into another. The tracks in the gray mud were the first bear signs we saw. There was a musty but not really unpleasant smell. In a clearing under a big hollow beech, where the fire had been, we found nothing but ashes. Logs were drawn up in a rough circle and the smell was stronger. I stirred the ashes and found enough coals left to start a new flame, so I banked them back the way they had been left.

I cut a little firewood and stacked it to one side, just to be neighborly.

Maybe the bears were watching us from the bushes even then. There's no way to know. I tasted one of the newberries and spit it out. It was so sweet it as sour, just the sort of thing you would imagine a bear would like.

That evening after supper, I asked Wallace Jr. if he might want to go with me to visit Mother. I wasn't surprised when he said "yes." Kids have more consideration than folks give them credit for. We found her sitting on the concrete front porch of the Home, watching the cars go by on I-65. The nurse said she had been agitated all day. I wasn't surprised by that, either. Every fall as the leaves change, she gets restless, maybe the word is hopeful, again. I brought her into the dayroom and combed her long white hair. "Nothing but bears on TV anymore," the nurse complained, flipping the channels. Wallace Jr. picked up the remote after the nurse left, and we watched a CBS or NBC Special Report about some hunters in Virginia who had gotten their houses torched. The TV interviewed a hunter and his wife whose $117,500 Shenandoah Valley home had burned. She blamed the bears. He didn't blame the bears, but he was suing for compensation from the state since he had a valid hunting license. The state hunting commissioner came on and said that possession of a hunting license didn't prohibit (enjoin, I think, was the word he used) *the hunted* from striking back. I thought that was a pretty liberal view for a state commissioner. Of course, he had a vested interest in not paying off. I'm not a hunter myself.

"Don't bother coming on Sunday," Mother told Wallace Jr. with a wink. "I've drove a million miles and I've got one hand on the gate." I'm used to her saying stuff like that, especially in the fall, but I was afraid it would upset the boy. In fact, he looked worried after we left and I asked him what was wrong.

"How could she have drove a million miles?" he asked. She had told him 48 miles a day for 39 years, and he had worked it out on his calculator to be 336,960 miles.

"Have *driven*," I said. "And it's forty-eight in the morning and forty-eight in the afternoon. Plus there were the football trips. Plus, old folks exaggerate a little." Mother was the first woman school bus driver in the state. She did it every day and raised a family, too. Dad just farmed.

I usually get off the interstate at Smiths Grove, but that night I drove north all the way to Horse Cave and doubled back so Wallace Jr. and I could see the bears' fires. There were not as many as you would think from the TV—one every six or seven miles, hidden back in a clump of trees or under a rocky ledge. Probably they look for water as well as wood. Wallace Jr. wanted to stop, but it's against the law to stop on the interstate and I was afraid the state police would run us off.

There was a card from Wallace in the mailbox. He and Elizabeth were doing fine and having a wonderful time. Not a word about Wallace Jr., but the boy didn't seem to mind. Like most kids his age, he doesn't really enjoy going places with his parents.

On Saturday afternoon, the Home called my office (Burley Belt Drought & Hail) and left word that Mother was gone. I was on the road. I work Saturdays. It's the only day a lot of part-time farmers are home. My heart literally skipped a beat when I called in and got the message, but only a beat. I had long been prepared. "It's a blessing," I said when I got the nurse on the phone.

"You don't understand," the nurse said. "Not *passed* away, gone. *Ran* away, gone. Your mother has escaped." Mother had gone through the door at the end of the corridor when no one was looking, wedging the door with her comb and taking a bedspread which belonged to the Home. What about her tobacco? I asked. It was gone. That was a sure sign she was planning to stay away. I was in Franklin, and it took me less than an hour to get to the Home on I-65. The nurse told me that Mother had been acting more and more confused lately. Of course they are going to say that. We looked around the grounds, which is only an acre with no trees between the interstate and a soybean field. Then they had me leave a message at the Sheriff's office. I would have to keep paying for her care until she was officially listed as Missing, which would be Monday.

It was dark by the time I got back to the house, and Wallace Jr. was fixing supper. This just involves opening a few cans, already selected and grouped together with a rubber band. I told him his grandmother had gone, and he nodded, saying, "She told us she would be." I called Florida and left a message. There was nothing more to be done. I sat down and tried to watch TV, but there was nothing on. Then, I looked out the back door, and saw the firelight twinkling through the trees across the north-bound lane of I-65, and realized I just might know where she had gone to find her.

It was definitely getting colder, so I got my jacket. I told the boy to wait by the phone in case the Sheriff called, but when I looked back, halfway across the field, there he was behind me. He didn't have a jacket. I let him catch up. He was carrying his .22, and I made him leave it leaning against our fence. It was harder climbing the government fence in the dark, at my age, than it had been in the daylight. I am sixty-one. The highway was busy with cars heading south and trucks heading north.

Crossing the shoulder, I got my pants cuffs wet on the long grass, already wet with dew. It is actually bluegrass.

The first few feet into the trees it was pitch black and the boy grabbed my hand. Then it got lighter. At first I thought it was the moon, but it was the high beams shining like moonlight into the treetops, allowing Wallace Jr. and me to pick our way through the brush. We soon found the path and its familiar bear smell.

I was wary of approaching the bears at night. If we stayed on the path we might run into one in the dark, but if we went through the bushes we might be seen as intruders. I wondered if maybe we shouldn't have brought the gun.

We stayed on the path. The light seemed to drip down from the canopy of the woods like rain. The going was easy, especially if we didn't try to look at the path but let our feet find their own way.

Then through the trees I saw their fire.

The fire was mostly of sycamore and beech branches, the kind of fire that puts out very little heat or light and lots of smoke. The bears hadn't learned the ins and outs of wood yet. They did okay at tending it, though. A large cinnamon brown northern-looking bear was poking the fire with a stick, adding a branch now and then from a pile at his side. The others sat around in a loose circle on the logs. Most were smaller black or honey bears, one was a mother with cubs. Some were eating berries from a hub-cap. Not eating, but just watching the fire, my mother sat among them with the bedspread from the Home around her shoulders.

If the bears noticed us, they didn't let on. Mother patted a spot right next to her on the log and I sat down. A bear moved over to let Wallace Jr. sit on her other side.

The bear smell is rank but not unpleasant, once you get used to it. It's not like a barn smell, but wilder. I leaned over to whisper something to Mother and she shook her head. *It would be rude to whisper around these creatures that don't possess the power of speech,* she let me know without speaking. Wallace Jr. was silent too. Mother shared the bedspread with us and we sat for what seemed hours, looking into the fire.

The big bear tended the fire, breaking up the dry branches by holding one end and stepping on them, like people do. He was good at keeping it going at the same level. Another bear poked the fire from time to time, but the others left it alone. It looked like only a few of the bears knew how to use fire, and were carrying the others along. But isn't that how it is with everything? Every once in a while, a smaller bear walked into the circle of firelight with an armload of wood and dropped it onto the pile. Median wood has a silvery cast, like driftwood.

Wallace Jr. isn't fidgety like a lot of kids. I found it pleasant to sit and stare into the fire. I took a little piece of Mother's *Red Man,* though I don't generally chew. It was no different from visiting her at the Home, only more interesting, because of the bears. There were about eight or ten of them. Inside the fire itself, things weren't so dull, either: little dramas were being played out as fiery chambers were created and then destroyed in a crashing of sparks. My imagination ran wild. I looked around the circle at the bears and wondered what *they* saw. Some had their eyes closed. Though they were gathered together, their spirits still seemed solitary, as if each bear was sitting alone in front of its own fire.

The hubcap came around and we all took some newberries. I don't know about Mother, but I just pretended to eat mine. Wallace Jr. made a face and spit his out. When he went to sleep, I wrapped the bedspread around all three of us. It was getting colder and we were not provided, like the bears, with fur. I was ready to go home, but not Mother. She pointed up toward the canopy of trees, where a light was spreading, and then pointed to herself. Did she think it was angels approaching from on high? It was only the high beams of some southbound truck, but she seemed mighty pleased. Holding her hand, I felt it grow colder and colder in mine.

Wallace Jr. woke me up by tapping on my knee. It was past dawn, and his grandmother had died sitting on the log between us. The fire was banked up and the bears were gone and someone was crashing straight through the woods, ignoring the path. It was Wallace. Two state troopers were right behind him. He was wearing a white shirt, and I realized it was Sunday morning. Underneath his sadness on learning of Mother's death, he looked peeved.

The troopers were sniffing the air and nodding. The bear smell was still strong. Wallace and I wrapped Mother in the bedspread and started with her body back out to the highway. The troopers stayed behind and scattered the bears' fire ashes and flung their firewood away into the bushes. It seemed a petty thing to do. They were like bears themselves, each one solitary in his own uniform.

There was Wallace's Olds 98 on the median, with its radial tires looking squashed on the grass. In front of it there was a police car with a trooper standing beside it, and behind it a funeral home hearse, also an Olds 98.

"First report we've had of them bothering old folks," the trooper said to Wallace. "That's not hardly what happened at all," I said, but nobody asked me to explain. They have their own procedures. Two men in suits got out of the hearse and opened the rear door. That to me was the point at which Mother departed this life. After we put her in, I put my arms around the boy. He was shivering even though it wasn't that cold. Sometimes death will do that, especially at dawn, with the police around and the grass wet, even when it comes as a friend.

We stood for a minute watching the cars pass. "It's a blessing," Wallace said. It's surprising how much traffic there is at 6:22 A.M.

That afternoon, I went back to the median and cut a little firewood to replace what the troopers had flung away. I could see the fire through the trees that night.

I went back two nights later, after the funeral. The fire was going and it was the same bunch of bears, as far as I could tell. I sat around with them a while but it seemed to make them nervous, so I went home. I had taken a handful of newberries from the hubcap, and on Sunday I went with the boy and arranged them on Mother's grave. I tried again, but it's no use, you can't eat them.

Unless you're a bear.

Blunderbore

Esther M. Friesner's first sale was to *Isaac Asimov's Science Fiction Magazine* in 1982; she's subsequently become a regular contributor there, as well as selling frequently to markets such as *The Magazine of Fantasy & Science Fiction, Amazing, Pulphouse,* and elsewhere. In the years since 1982, she's also become one of the most prolific of modern fantasists, with thirteen novels in print, and has established herself as one of the funniest writers to enter the field in some while. Her many novels include *Mustapha and His Wise Dog, Elf Defense, Druid's Blood, Sphinxes Wild, Here Be Demons, Demon Blues, Hooray for Hellywood, Broadway Banshee, Ragnarok and Roll,* and *The Water King's Daughter.* She's reported to be at work on her first hard science fiction novel. She lives with her family in Madison, Connecticut.

Although Friesner's work can on occasion be somber and powerful, if not downright grim—as, for instance, in stories such as "All Vows" and "Death and the Librarian," which won her a Nebula Award in 1995—there can be little doubt that most of her reputation rests on her comic stuff. In fact, after the immensely popular Terry Prachett, she's probably one of the most successful comic writers in all of modern fantasy. Prachett rarely writes short fiction, nor do other comic fantasists such as Tom Holt or Christopher Stasheff—but fortunately for us, Friesner *does.* In fact, she's pleasingly prolific at short lengths.

In the hilarious story that follows, she takes us along on a very modern woman's very modern date in modern Manhattan with a very *old*-style bachelor . . .

"Jack? *That* pipsqueak? What do you *think* I did with the spunkless little blowhard?" Another dart flew from the huge hand, landed with surprising accuracy dead-center on the distant target. A long gob of spittle, no less precisely aimed, whizzed from between massive teeth gappy and yellow enough to pass for a jaundiced Stonehenge.

The lady shuddered as the giant's expectoration splatted *perfecto* right between her well-shined shoes. Not a driblet landed on their newly Vaselined black patent leather, but sometimes the *thought* is more than enough.

"I can't for the life of me imagine," she managed to reply. As a feeble jest she suggested, "Ground his bones to make your bread?"

The giant roared, a sound that might have been laughter or a bout with sinusitis. His nose was humped and sickled, red with many draughts of Guinness and lousy with pockmarks. Black hairs bristled angrily from the nostrils, hinting at hibernating porcupines.

"Grind his bones to make my bread? *There's* a good 'un!" He reached for another dart. The barkeep made haste to assure his client of a constant supply. "How'd the weensy manling live to juggle all them cowpats about killing me if I'd done *that,* eh?" The giant's lips pursed, the lower resembling a saddle of mutton, the upper two hams. "Oversight, that. I never thought he'd want it noised 'round how I used him. Writing it all up, though, telling it twisty, making out as he'd done for *me*—Well, I learned much of men from that, I did. Grind his bones. . . ." He grinned. "Not his bones. 'Tis nut bread I fancy."

The barkeep refilled the giant's mug and leaned across the counter to inquire softly, deferentially of the lady whether she would like another Bombay gin? She shook her head. Her lips were dry, her throat drier. The proper business suit that was her chrysalis of choice remained pressed, immaculate, entire, unsplit, though this was Saturday night and by rights she should be swinging by nyloned knees from the ceiling fixtures along about this hour.

The giant drained his measure and launched his dart. It split the first, just like Robin Hood's arrow always splintered those arrogant shafts of his unworthy rivals if they dared hog the bull's-eye before he shot. The legendary arrows were wood; the actual darts were steel. The metal let out a high, terrified shriek as it was so cavalierly violated from feathered wazoo to razored tip.

"But enough about me," said the giant. He shifted his weight on the bar. No stool would hold him, and he wasn't about to stand after a hard day's labor. The wood complained much, but only buckled a little. Bare feet with toes like hairy pattypan squashes swung back and forth, drumming the mahogany. "How'd a nice girl like *you* come to run a personal ad, then?"

The lady took a deep breath. Her left hand began to wrench at the rings on her right. "It was my roommate's idea," she began. The rush of red murder she sent bubbling over a vision of her roommate's face left her giddy. How could she speak coherently when every second sentence to come to mind was *the bitch dies?*

Carthago delenda esse.

Two hours ago she had been afflicted merely with the usual crawful of first-meeting jitters, the nausea and palpitations often prequel to lucky at love. Then the giant walked in. He knew her at once (his telephone voice gave no warning, its quaint accent, seductive pitch and timbre conspiring only to make her silly with lust, inspiring her to heights of self-descriptive facility that left her thoroughly, instantly identifiable among thousands). She could not evade him by pretending to be someone else, or via the more practical shrieks of the bar's other patrons as they fled wildly out of the place beneath the fuzzy arbors of his armpits.

She had tried, though. He caught her.

Trapped, she had spent the time since in imagining all the most agonizing, crippling, humiliating ways one might dispose of a roommate who gave bad advice and did not clean the kitchen sufficiently well to make up for it. She supposed she might turn her over to the giant. There *was* that. First, however, present survival.

"You see," she went on, "I've been involved with someone for a very long time. His name's Ian. We had a—an understanding. A completely open twoness based on mutual respect and noninterference. But he needed personal space, room for growth, emotional evolution."

"Oh, ar?" the giant commented politely.

She sighed. "Well, he's gone now, you see. To find himself. And I have to get on with maximizing my own life experience. That's why the ad. It's rather hard to go back to ordinary dating when a long-term relationship ends, don't you agree?"

The giant's brows slipped down into the trenches of his forehead. "Bashed his skull in, did they?" he asked.

"?" she answered. It was really the best she could do, and not too paltry, under the circumstances.

"Trolls. Else renegado knights. One tump of the mace upside your goodman's temple-bone, and you're left to dance the widow's bransle. Too bad, too bad. Likely they raped you after, it's only their way, but still—" His eyebrows now slumped back like eels amorously exhausted. "Did hope as you'd be a virgin. I likes virgins."

"Will you excuse me?" she said, slipping gracefully from the barstool. "I have to go powder my nose." As an out it was retro, and sexist, and shameful in the extreme, but all she asked was that it save her skin long enough for her to get some use out of her thirty-five session contract at the Tropitan Salon.

In the ladies' room was a stall, and in the stall was a toilet, and over the toilet was a window, and *out* the window she did go, as fast as ever she could slink. There were runs in her Dior pantyhose and wrinkles in her Anne Klein linen suit, raw scrapes striping the sides of her Maud Frizon patent heels (one of which landed in the toilet) and four scales gouged out of her genuine alligator belt, but she emerged alive enough to pitch headfirst into the alley outside. In the alley was a dumpster, and in the dumpster were a lot of empty liquor cartons and dud lottery tickets and some really ripe muddled fruit-leavings. This she added to her roommate's account of payments due as she huddled in the taxi, plucked lemon rinds from her hair, and cursed all the way home.

And cursed louder, with renewed gusto, when her roommate told her that *she* didn't have to sit there and listen to *this* crap. *She* hadn't told her to stick the fateful ad in the New York *Review*. *She* thought the *Village Voice* was quite good enough, thank you, and just see where pretensions can leave you, stuck in some downtown bar with a creature out of myth and Jungian archetype whose toenails want cleaning.

The roommate quit. She packed. She left and moved in with her boyfriend who played the saxophone and really *understood* the *ausgleibnicht Kunstfertseichnet* of Michael J. Fox movies.

The lady was left with vengeance placed on Hold eternal, and a full month's New York rent to pay in heart's blood.

There was also a message on her answering machine. It was from *him*. Why not?

She changed her telephone number. She changed the locks on her doors. She acquired a new roommate by means of utmost discretion. She made a serious commitment to oat bran and never, never more used the weather or the time of the month as excuses for neglecting her morning jog. She became a whole person, relentless mistress of a whole mind in a whole body. Giants never happened to holistic people. Could be it was attributable to all that fiber. Her wholeness was astonishingly complete, given the strain a middle-management position could put on one's full immersion in the universe. Nothing daunted, she immersed.

He was waiting for her one Friday evening as she came out of her office building on Third Avenue. The air smelled of April and perambulating hot dog wagons. He brought flowers and a dead sheep.

"Sorry I was I got too personal with asking you things," he said, tendering her the bouquet. She took it gingerly, only because if you counted the attaché case clutched tightly in her other hand, it left her no possibility of accepting the sheep.

Apparently he saw it that way, too, for he disposed of the beastie casually, in three bites, head first, fleece and all, just as if it were an afterthought instead of over a hundred pounds of mutton. Wiping lanolin from his chin, he said, "Find it in your heart, could you, to let me buy you a drink, and no hard feelings?"

What could she do? See if he'd take "Just Say No" for an answer? A poor gamble. Run away? Not with the lights and rush hour traffic against her. Scream for help? Her supervisor might be watching. He was everywhere, paranoia justified, like a February flu. He was always looking for excuses to shunt her career into corporate sandpits.

She smiled at the giant. "Why not?" she said. If only to discover how he'd found her. Magic? Sorcery? God's vengeance on her (so Mama would maintain) for the Pill?

No magic was at work, beyond the ordinary levels present in the city, nor any intervention even marginally divine. He reminded her that she herself had told him where she worked when first they'd spoken over the phone. It was a beginner's mistake. Give nothing away. She sipped her drink (*this* bar, too, had turned into a wasteland when they entered) and asked him to pass the bran-nuts.

When guided off the subject of giant-killers, he turned out to be a pleasant enough companion, or at any rate no worse than her mother's idea of a good catch. She wasn't getting any younger, *ipse dixit* Mama. Well, neither was *he*. Three hundred years old, and then some sum he chose not to mention. He had never felt better in his life. He ate right. He took responsibility for his place in the ecoverse. The American climate agreed with him. He loved New York.

She had had worse Friday evenings.

There was *CATS* on Saturday and a gallery opening Sunday morning after brunch at the Plaza. A hansom cab was waiting to convey her all the way home from the office on Monday afternoon. Her bedroom blazed lunatic with flowers. There were no more ovine incidents.

He supported Public Television. He preferred Ebert to Siskel, and had no use under God's great sky for Pauline Kael, unless his sourdough recipe needed an extra shot of calcium some time. He had season tickets to the opera, though he only went for Verdi and *Peter Grimes*. Wagner upset him. Fafnir and the frost giants, you know.

She sympathized. Prejudice was so *fifties*.

He didn't like zydeco, but for her sake he tried to understand it. While Springsteen left him cold, Steeleye Span was all right, and Clam Chower, and any old Joni Mitchell. He couldn't dance at *all*. He subscribed to *The New Yorker,* though only for the cartoons. Desconstructionist criticism gave him the quinsy. He couldn't find shoes that both fit him and made a fashion statement. He wore the poorly tanned skins of those few Central Park carriage horses in their declining years that he had been able to purchase. He had absolutely no taste in neckties.

He insisted that she pick all the restaurants they patronized, and relied on her judgment when it came to ordering the wine.

He was just *filthy* with money, all liquid assets, mostly gold and priceless gems that he had come by in the course of his European career. He didn't really get her joke about how he'd staged unfriendly takeovers of dragon-guarded hoards, but he laughed anyway. He offered to show her the skull of the last dragon he'd killed. That had been on Orkney, and the puny size of the Worm had been what decided him to move across the sea to a fresher, more vital world. A man likes a challenge. Things were better in the Catskills.

His voice in person slowly acquired the beguilement of that same voice over the phone. At her gentle prodding, Hoffritz provided the proper tools for him to trim toenails and nose bristles. He was never late for a date. He let her pay the tab on occasion, without turning it into a favor or patronage. Three hundred years and then some could give a man a certain high octane pickup rate in mastering the social graces, if he so wished. For her sake, he so wished, and he wasn't shy about letting her know as much. Vulnerability did not terrify him.

And she knew that he needed her.

The first time they made love, she had her qualms. She was haunted by the old chestnut about how the size of a man's nose may give the inquisitive some hint as to the relative proportion of an analogously shaped nether organ. The giant's *nose* was—well—gigantic, *voyons!* A sight too *much* so to leave the lady entirely comfortable in her mind.

Still, needs must. She wanted to. She felt a certain obligation, though through no deed or word of his. His few good-night kisses were not taken from her as if by right of conquest, or even secured as reparation for his having bought her dinner. He never treated her like a feedbag whore. All the marks of tenderness that passed between them were granted on her initiative alone. One kiss from him dewed fully half her face, left her skin atingle with moisture and mint residue from his hastily munched rolls of Breath-Savers. It was an unusual and exhilarating experience. Perverse curiosity needled her on to further experimental delvings.

Were she honest with herself, she would have admitted too that, since Ian, she was hornier than hell.

He was not so eager to accept her offer as she had imagined. "What's wrong?" she demanded. Angry gooseflesh rose beneath the peach satin of her lace-trimmed teddy. The dressing room at Victoria's Secret had been *much* warmer. Chills and rejection coupled together to nettle her deeply.

The giant's jowls drooped, laden with rue. "Ar, it's not *you,* dearie. Sweet as fresh plums you be, and welcome as spring. All as you've done for me up to this—" he fingered the charming regimental-stripe tie she'd had custom-made for him at Brooks Brothers "—that's been more'n I ever hoped for. I be content wi' that."

She crossed her arms, being unable to cross her legs. There was nothing in the room for her to sit on. Furniture had been displaced by futons, in deference to accommodating his needs. "You don't find me attractive!" she accused.

He tried to convince her otherwise, but she knew lies when she heard them. She'd lunched with enough salesfolk for that. By bullying and pouting and sniveling dangerously near the precipice of tears, she cudgeled out the truth.

"I ain't—I ain't so much—I don't got too big a—I has me lackings." He showed her proof.

Well, yes, he was right. What he said was *true*. If you were comparing him to other *giants*, that is.

She forced herself to look very solemn. She told him that size was not everything, but love conquers all. If he could lie, so could she.

They were very happy together.

Three weeks later, while she was at work, Ian called. "I've found myself," he told her. "I was right there, all along. I'm a better person now. I'm sensitive to a woman's needs. I can give you the support you want *and* the space you require. I'm ready to nurture. We can complete each other. I'm not afraid of commitment. Isn't that swell?"

"Drop dead," she said.

"But I *need* you."

Well, and what harm was there in meeting him for a drink after work, after all was said and done, after what they'd once meant to each other? She couldn't show herself to be afraid of seeing him again. They could talk about old times, catharsis over cocktails and a mouthwatering assortment of high-fiber, low-cholesterol veggies. She could handle that. She was strong. She was capable.

She was a fool for blonds with black eyebrows.

The giant's brows were black enough to satisfy, but as for *hair*, blond or otherwise, his pate gleamed smooth as a crystal goblet. Some things a woman doesn't miss until someone else points out that she does not have them. This holds as true for textured pantyhose as for men. In the bar with Ian, she found herself recalling how she used to run her fingers through his golden curls. Said fingers began to drum an antsy anthem on the sides of her lowball glass. Odd pulsings disturbed her body's chosen serenity. She really should be getting home.

"I like what you've done with the place," Ian said, kicking off his shoes, tossing his tie onto the futon. "So tell me about your new roommate."

"She minds her own business," she said. "She doesn't ask questions, she doesn't get ideas." She brought the drinks from the living room, even though he knew where everything was kept and had offered to do it. The giant's mug was in the liquor cabinet now. Ian might *not* mistake it for an oversized, spoutless martini pitcher. Few of those had BLUNDERBORE handpainted around their circumference, or an etched pattern of grinning skulls. *Damn* few.

Ian was essentially naked when she returned. A sheet counts for little in the strategies of such impromptu dalliances. He took his drink and raised it in her honor. "To your health," he said. He sipped while she stripped and slipped between the sheets beside him. He paused. A thought had touched him.

"Speaking of which. . . ." He made a pointed inquiry into her social life since last they'd shared bed linens.

Her eyes narrowed, her mouth screwed itself into a tight little macadamia nut of pique. "I've only seen one other man since you ran out. I'm still seeing him." She laced barbs to this last sentence but he remained unstung.

"And, uh, how well do you know him? I mean, what was he doing before he met *you*? Personal habits? Companions? Lifestyle of choice? *You* know."

"He killed dragons. He ground men's bones to make his bread. He never read any Garrison Keillor."

"Men's bones?" Ian's lovesome brows rose a moiety. "Um, did he ever give you any particular reason for, that is, in a manner of speaking, such exclusive tastes?"

"Put up," she told him, "or shut up. In fact, shut up whether you put up or no."

Ian steepled his fingers. "We are very hostile," he said, and *tsk'd* audibly.

"Blunderbore doesn't think so," she shot back. "Blunderbore isn't intimidated by a strong woman."

"Blunderbore?" Ian echoed. The steeple toppled. *"Blunderbore?"*

"It's a perfectly good name for a giant," she said, folding her arms.

Somewhere beyond the bedroom door—the apartment door, to be exact—a key jiggled in a lock.

"Your roommate?" Ian whispered.

"SURPRISE, ME DARLING!"

Oh, it was *very* sad, very sad indeed. A giant is like other men, only with a bigger heart to break. No vows had been uttered, and Blunderbore agreed in principle about mature adult persons in a modern relationship needing their own space, but *still*—

Temper, temper.

The bread was warm from the oven. "Have a piece, love. I'll butter it for you."

"I'm not that peckish now," said Blunderbore. He leaned his face on one hand and gazed morosely at the steaming slab, very white where it was not yellow with melting butter. "Like to clog me arteries sommat fierce, that be. Take it away."

"Tsk. You're just being difficult. You've eaten butter by the hogshead before this. And after all my trouble, following that silly old family recipe of yours. No appreciation. None whatsoever."

"Ar, all right, all right, cease yer cackling." The giant raised the slice to his lips and bit. He chewed. "Gritty," he said.

"You don't like my cooking." Ian pouted.

"Na, then, I never did say—It's *my* fault, 'tis, for not having a more careful eye at the handmill. I'll see to it as I grind 'em finer next time. Oh, it's as grand a baking as ever I've tasted, lad, and that's taking in some three hundred years. Don't take on so, there's me dearie. Come, sit you down on old Blunderbore's knee and tell us how them wicked, wicked futures traders has treated our Ian today."

Ian dimpled and dropped the sulks. Obediently he climbed the giant's knee.

Blunderbore smiled indulgently at his manling. Maybe this one would last. In a certain light, the lad looked just like Jack.

Maybe *this* one wouldn't kiss and tell.

Death and the Lady

One of the most popular and respected fantasists of the 1980s, Judith Tarr is also a medieval scholar with a Ph.D. in medieval studies from Yale University, which background has served her well in creating the richly detailed milieus of her critically acclaimed novels. She has published more than seventeen books, including the World Fantasy Award nominee *Lord of the Two Lands, The Isle of Glass, The Golden Horn, The Hounds of God, The Hall of the Mountain King, The Lady of Han-Gilen, A Fall of Princes, A Wind in Cairo, Ars Magica, Alamut,* and *The Dagger and the Cross: A Novel of the Crusades,* as well as historical novels such as *Throne of Isis, The Eagle's Daughter,* and *Pillar of Fire.* Born in Augusta, Maine, she now lives in Tucson, Arizona.

In the compelling, compassionate, and tough-minded story that follows, she takes us to a time when the Old World of Europe is dying and a New World is being painfully born from its ashes, and shows us how both Old World and New must of necessity deal with a still *older* World, the dark enchanted World that lies Beyond the Wood, and with the creatures who sometimes come *out* of it . . . and who sometimes want to go *back* . . .

The year after the Great Death, the harvest was the best that anyone could remember. The best, and the worst, because there were so few of us to get it in; and the men who had lived through the plague all gone, even to the fledgling boys, in the high ones' endless wars. The few that were left were the old and the lame and the witless, and the women. We made a joke of it that year, how the Angel of Death took his share of our men, and Sire and Comte the rest.

We did what we could, we in Sency-la-Forêt. I had lost a baby that summer, and almost myself, and I was weak a little still; even so I would have been reaping barley with my sisters, if Mère Adele had not caught me coming out with the scythe in my hand. She had a tongue on her, did Mère Adele, and Saint Benedict's black habit did nothing to curb it. She took the scythe and kilted up her habit and went to work down the long rows, and I went where she told me, to mind the children.

There were more maybe than some had, if travelers' tales told the truth. Every house had lost its share to the black sickness, and in the manor by the little river the dark angel had taken everyone but the few who had the wits to run. So we were a lordless demesne as well as a manless one, a city of women, one of the nuns from the priory called us; she read books, and not all of them were scripture.

If I looked from where I sat under the May tree, I could see her in the field, binding sheaves where the reapers passed. There were children with her; my own Celine, just big enough to work, had her own sheaf to gather and bind. I had the littlest ones, the babies in their pen like odd sheep, and the weanlings for the moment in my lap and in a circle round me, while I told them a story. It was a very old story; I hardly needed to pay attention to it, but let my tongue run on and watched the reapers, and decided that I was going to claim my scythe back. Let Mère Adele look after the babies. I was bigger than she, and stronger, too.

I was growing quite angry inside myself, while I smiled at the children and made them laugh. Even Francha, who never made a sound, nor had since her family died around her, had a glint of laughter in her eye, though she looked down quickly. I reached to draw her into my lap. She was stiff, all bones and tremblings like a wild thing, but she did not run away as she would have once. After a while she laid her head on my breast.

That quieted my temper. I finished the story I was telling. As I opened my mouth to begin another, Francha went rigid in my arms. I tried to soothe her with hands and voice. She clawed her way about, not to escape, but to see what came behind me.

Sency is Sency-la-Forêt not for that it was woodland once, though that is true enough; nor for that wood surrounds it, closing in on the road to Sency-les-Champs and away beyond it into Normandy; but because of the trees that are its westward wall. People pass through Sency from north to south and back again. Sometimes, from north or south, they go eastward into Maine or Anjou. West they never go. East and south and north is wood, in part the Sire de Sency's if the Death had left any to claim that title, in part common ground for hunting and woodcutting and pig-grazing. West is Wood. Cursed, the priest said before he took fright at the Death and fled to Avranches. Bewitched, said the old women by the fire in the evenings. Enchanted, the young men used to say before they went away. Sometimes a young man would swear that he would go hunting in the Wood, or a young woman would say that she meant to scry out a lover in the well by the broken chapel. If any of them ever did it, he never talked of it, nor she; nor did people ask. The Wood was best not spoken of.

I sat with Francha stiff as a stick in my arms, and stared where she was staring, into the green gloom that was the Wood. There was someone on the edge of it. It could almost have been a traveler from south or east, worked round westward by a turning of the road or by the lure of the trees. We were a formidable enough town by then, with the palisade that Messire Arnaud had built before he died, and no gate open but on the northward side.

Francha broke out of my arms. My Perrin, always the first to leap on anything that was new, bolted gleefully in Francha's wake. Half a breath more and they were all gone, the babies in their pen beginning to howl, and the reapers nearest pausing, some straightening to stare.

If I thought anything, I thought it later. That the Death was not so long gone. That the roads were full of wolves, two-legged nearly all of them, and deadly dangerous. That the Wood held things more deadly than any wolf, if even a tithe of the tales were true.

As I ran I thought of Perrin, and of Francha. I could have caught them easily, a season ago. Now the stitch caught me before I had run a furlong, doubled me up and made me curse. I ran in spite of it, but hobbling. I could see well enough. There was only one figure on the Wood's edge, standing very still before the onslaught of children. It was a woman. I did not know how I knew that. It was all in shapeless brown, hooded and faceless. It did not frighten our young at all. They had seen the Death. This was but a curiosity, a traveler on the road that no one traveled, a new thing to run after and shrill at and squabble over.

As the children parted like a flock of sheep and streamed around it, the figure bent. It straightened with one of the children in its arms. Francha, white and silent Francha who never spoke, who fled even from those she knew, clinging to this stranger as if she would never let go.

The reapers were leaving their reaping. Some moved slowly, weary or wary. Others came as fast as they were able. We trusted nothing in these days, but Sency had been quiet since the spring, when the Comte's man came to take our men away. Our woods protected us, and our prayers, too.

Still I was the first but for the children to come to the stranger. Her hood was deep but the light was on her. I saw a pale face, and big eyes in it, staring at me.

I said the first thing that came into my head. "Greetings to you, stranger, and God's blessing on you."

She made a sound that might have been laughter or a sob. But she said clearly enough, "Greetings and blessing, in God's name." She had a lady's voice, and a lady's accent, too, with a lilt in it that made me think of birds.

"Where are you from? Do you carry the sickness?"

The lady did not move at all. I was the one who started and spun about.

Mère Adele was noble born herself, though she never made much of it; she was as outspoken to the lord bishop as she was to any of us. She stood behind me now, hands on her ample hips, and fixed the stranger with a hard eye. "Well? Are you dumb, then?"

"Not mute," the lady said in her soft voice, "nor enemy either. I have no sickness in me."

"And how may we be sure of that?"

I sucked in a breath.

The lady spoke before I could, as sweetly as ever, and patient, with Francha's head buried in the hollow of her shoulder. I had been thinking that she might be a nun fled from her convent. If she was, I thought I knew why. No bride of the lord Christ would carry a man's child in her belly, swelling it under the coarse brown robe.

"You can never be certain," she said to Mère Adele, "not of a stranger; not in these times. I will take no more from you than a loaf, of your charity, and your blessing if you will give it."

"The loaf you may have," said Mère Adele. "The blessing I'll have to think on. If you fancy a bed for the night, there's straw in plenty to make one, and a reaper's dinner if you see fit to earn it."

"Even," the lady asked, "unblessed?"

Mère Adele was enjoying herself: I could see the glint in her eye. "Earn your dinner," she said, "and you'll get your blessing with it."

The lady bent her head, as gracious as a queen in a story. She murmured in Francha's ear. Francha's grip loosened on her neck. She set the child down in front of me—Francha all eyes and wordless reluctance—and followed Mère Adele through the field. None of the children went after her, even Perrin. They were meeker than I had ever seen them, and quieter; though they came to themselves soon enough, once I had them back under the May tree.

Her name, she said, was Lys. She offered no more than that, that night, sitting by the fire in the mown field, eating bread and cheese and drinking the ale that was all we had. In the day's heat she had taken off her hood and her outer robe and worked as the rest did, in a shift of fine linen that was almost new. She was bearing for a fact, two seasons gone, I judged, and looking the bigger for that she was so thin. She had bones like a bird's, and skin so white one could see the tracks of veins beneath, and hair as black as her skin was white, hacked off as short as a nun's.

She was not that, she said. Swore to it and signed herself, lowering the lids over the great grey eyes. Have I said that she was beautiful? Oh, she was, like a white lily, with her sweet low voice and her long fair hands. Francha held her lap against all comers, but Perrin was bewitched, and Celine, and the rest of the children whose mothers had not herded them home.

"No nun," she said, "and a great sinner, who does penance for her sins in this long wandering."

We nodded round the fire. Pilgrimages we understood; and pilgrims, even noble ones, alone and afoot and tonsured, treading out the leagues of their salvation. Guillemette, who was pretty and very silly, sighed and clasped her hands to her breast. "How sad," she said, "and how brave, to leave your lord and your castle—for castle you had, surely, you are much too beautiful to be a plain man's wife—and go out on the long road."

"My lord is dead," the lady said.

Guillemette blinked. Her eyes were full of easy tears. "Oh, how terrible! Was it the war?"

"It was the plague," said Lys. "And that was six months ago now, by his daughter in my belly, and you may weep as you choose, but I have no tears left."

She sounded it: dry and quiet. No anger in her, but no softness either. In the silence she stood up. "If there is a bed for me, I will take it. In the morning I will go."

"Where?" That was Mère Adele, abrupt as always, and cutting to the heart of things.

Lys stood still. She was tall; taller in the firelight. "My vow takes me west," she said.

"But there is nothing in the west," said Mère Adele.

"But," said Lys, "there is a whole kingdom, leagues of it, from these marches to the sea."

"Ah," said Mère Adele, sharp and short. "That's not west, that's Armorica. West is nothing that a human creature should meddle with. If it's Armorica that you're aiming for, you'd best go south first, and then west, on the king's road."

"We have another name for that kingdom," said Lys, "where I was born." She shook herself; she sighed. "In the morning I will go."

She slept in the house I had come to when I married Claudel, in my bed next to me with the children in a warm nest, Celine and Perrin and Francha, and the cats wherever they found room. That was Francha's doing, holding to her like grim death when she would have made her bed in the nun's barn, until my tongue spoke for me and offered her what I had.

I did not sleep overmuch. Nor, I thought, did she. She was still all the night long, coiled on her side with Francha in the hollow of her. The children made their night noises, the cats purred, Mamère Mondine snored in her bed by the fire. I listened to them, and to the lady's silence. Claudel's absence was an ache still. It was worse tonight, with this stranger in his place. My hand kept trying to creep toward the warmth and the sound of her breathing, as if a touch could change her, make her the one I wanted there. In the end I made a fist of it and pinned it under my head, and squeezed my eyes shut, and willed the dawn to come.

Dawn came and went, and another dawn, and Lys stayed. The sky that had been so clear was turning grey. We needed every hand we had, to get in the crops before the rain came. Even mine—Mère Adele scowled at me as I took my place, but I stared her down. Lys took the row beside me. No one said anything. We were all silent, that day and the next, racing the rain.

The last of the barley went in the barn as the first drops fell. We stood out in it, too tired and too shocked by the stopping of a race we had run for so long, to do more than stare. Then someone grinned. Then someone else. Then the whole lot of us. We had done it, we, the women and the children and the men too old or weak to fight. We had brought in the harvest in Sency-la-Forêt.

That night we had a feast. Mère Adele's cook slaughtered an ox, and the rest of us brought what we had or could gather. There was meat for everyone, and a cake with honey in it, and apples from the orchards, and even a little wine. We sat in the nuns' refectory and listened to the rain on the roof, and ate till we were sated. Lame Bertrand had his pipe and Raymonde her drum, and Guillemette had a voice like a linnet. Some of the younger ones got up to dance. I saw how Pierre Allard was looking at Guillemette, and he just old enough to tend his own sheep: too young and small as he had been in the spring for the Comte's men to take, but grown tall in the summer, and casting eyes at our pretty idiot as if he were a proper man.

I drank maybe more of the wine than was good for me. I danced, and people cheered: I had a neat foot even then, and Pierre Allard was light enough, and quick enough, to keep up with me.

It should have been Claudel dancing there. No great beauty, my Claudel, and not much taller than I, but he could dance like a leaf in the Wood; and sing, too, and laugh with me when I spun dizzy and breathless out of the dance. There was no one there to catch me and carry me away to a bed under the sky, or more likely on a night like this, in the barn among the cows, away from children and questions and eyes that pried.

I left soon after that, while the dancing was still in full whirl. The rain was steady, and not too cold. I was wet through soon enough, but it felt more pleasant than not. My feet knew the way in the black dark, along the path that followed the priory's wall, down to the river and then up again to a shadow in shadow and a scent of the midden that was mine and no one else's. There was light through a chink in the door: firelight, banked but not yet covered. Mamère Mondine nodded in front of it. She was blind and nearly deaf, but she smiled when I kissed her forehead. "Jeannette," she said. "Pretty Jeannette." And patted my hand that rested on her shoulder, and went back to her dreaming.

The children were abed, asleep. There was no larger figure with them. Francha's eyes gleamed at me in the light from the lamp. They were swollen and red; her cheeks were tracked with tears.

I started to speak. To say that Lys was coming, that she would be here soon, that she was still in the priory. But I could not find it in me to say it. She had eaten with us. She had been there when the children went out in a crowd, protesting loudly. When the dancing began, I had not seen her. I had thought, if I thought at all, that she had come here before me.

In the dark and the rain, a stranger could only too easily go astray. It was not far to the priory, a mile, maybe, but that was a good count of steps, and more than enough to be lost in.

What made me think of the Wood, I never knew. Her words to Mère Adele. My first sight of her on the Wood's edge. The simple strangeness of her, as I sat on the bed and tried to comfort Francha, and saw in the dimness the memory of her face. We had stories, we in Sency, of what lived in the Wood. Animals both familiar and strange, and shadows cast by no living thing, and paths that wound deep and deep, and yet ended where they began; and far within, behind a wall of mists and fear, a kingdom ruled by a deathless king.

I shook myself hard. What was it to me that a wayward stranger had come, brought in our harvest, and gone away again? To Francha it was too much, and that I would not forgive. Whatever in the world had made our poor mute child fall so perfectly in love with the lady, it had done Francha no good, and likely much harm. She would not let me touch her now, scrambled to the far corner of the bed when I lay down and tried to draw her in, and huddled there for all that I dared do without waking the others. In the end I gave it up and closed my eyes. I was on the bed's edge. Francha was pressed against the wall. She would have to climb over me to escape.

One moment, it seemed, I was fretting over Francha. The next, the red cock was crowing, and I was staggering up, stumbling to the morning's duties. There was no sign of Lys. She had had no more than the clothes on her back; those were gone. She might never have been there at all.

I unlidded the fire and poked it up, and fed it carefully. I filled the pot and hung it over the flames. I milked the cow, I found two eggs in the nest that the black hen had thought so well hidden. I fed the pigs and scratched the old sow's back and promised her a day in the wood, if I could persuade Bertrand to take her out with his own herd. I fed Mamère Mondine her bowl of porridge with a little honey dripped in it, and a little more for each of the children. Perrin and Celine gobbled theirs and wanted more. Francha would not eat. When I tried to feed her as I had when I first took her in, she slapped the spoon out of my hand. The other children were delighted. So were the cats, who set to at once, licking porridge from the wall and the table and the floor.

I sighed and retrieved the spoon. Francha's face was locked shut. There would be no reasoning with her today, or, I suspected, for days hereafter. Inside myself I cursed this woman who had come, enchanted a poor broken child, and gone away without a word. And if Francha sickened over it, if she pined and died—as she well could, as she almost had before I took her—

I dipped the porridge back into the pot. I wiped the children's faces and Francha's hands. I did what needed doing. And all the while my anger grew.

The rain had gone away with the night. The last of the clouds blew away eastward, and the sun came up, warming the wet earth, raising pillars and curtains of mist. The threshers would be at it soon, as should I.

But I stood in my kitchen garden and looked over the hedge, and saw the wall of grey and green that was the Wood. One of the cats wound about my ankles. I gathered her up. She purred. "I know where the lady went," I said. "She went west. She said she would. God protect her; nothing else will, where she was going."

The cat's purring stopped. She raked my hand with her claws and struggled free; hissed at me; and darted away round the midden.

I sucked my smarting hand. Celine ran out of the house, shrilling in the tone I was doing my best to slap out of her: "Francha's crying again, mama! Francha won't stop crying!"

What I was thinking of was quite mad. I should go inside, of course I should, and do what I could to comfort Francha, and gather the children together, and go to the threshing.

I knelt in the dirt between the poles of beans, and took Celine by the shoulders. She stopped her shrieking to stare at me. "Are you a big girl?" I asked her.

She drew herself up. "I'm grown up," she said. "You know that, mama."

"Can you look after Francha, then? And Perrin? And take them both to Mère Adele?"

She frowned. "Won't you come, too?"

Too clever by half, was my Celine. "I have to do something else," I said. "Can you do it, Celine? And tell Mère Adele that I'll be back as soon as I can?"

Celine thought about it. I held my breath. Finally she nodded. "I'll take Perrin and Francha to Mère Adele. And tell her you'll come back. Then can I go play with Jeannot?"

"No," I said. Then: "Yes. Play with Jeannot. Stay with him till I come back. Can you do that?"

She looked at me in perfect disgust. "Of course I can do that. I'm grown up."

I bit my lips to keep from laughing. I kissed her once on each cheek for each of the others, and once on the forehead for herself. "Go on," I said. "Be quick."

She went. I stood up. In a little while I heard them go, Perrin declaring loudly that he was going to eat honeycakes with Mère Adele. I went into the kitchen and filled a napkin with bread and cheese and apples, and put the knife in, too, wrapped close in the cloth, and tied it all in my kerchief. Mamère Mondine was asleep. She would be well enough till evening. If I was out longer, then Mère Adele would know to send someone. I kissed her and laid my cheek for a moment against her dry old one. She sighed but did not wake. I drew myself up and went back through the kitchen garden.

Our house is one of the last in the village. The garden wall is part of Messire Arnaud's palisade, though we train beans up over it, and I have a grapevine that almost prospers. Claudel had cut a door in it, which could have got us in trouble if Messire Arnaud had lived to find out about it; but milord was dead and his heirs far away, and our little postern was hidden well in vines within and brambles without.

I escaped with a scratch or six, but with most of my dignity intact. It was the last of the wine in me, I was sure, and anger for Francha's sake, and maybe a little honest worry, too. Lys had been a guest in my house. If any harm came to her, the guilt would fall on me.

And I had not gone outside the palisade, except to the fields, since Claudel went away. I wanted the sun on my face, no children tugging at my skirts, the memory of death far away. I was afraid of what I went to, of course I was; the Wood was a horror from my earliest memory. But it was hard to be properly terrified, walking the path under the first outriders of the trees, where the sun slanted down in long sheets, and the wind murmured in the leaves, and the birds sang sweet and unafraid. The path was thick with mould under my feet. The air was scented with green things, richer from the rain, with the deep earthy promise of mushrooms. I found a whole small field of them, and gathered as many as my apron would carry, but moving quickly through them and not lingering after.

By then Sency was well behind me and the trees were closing in. The path wound through them, neither broader nor narrower than before. I began to wonder if I should have gone to fetch the Allards' dog. I had company, it was true: the striped cat had followed me. She was more comfort than I might have expected.

The two of us went on. The scent of mushrooms was all around me like a charm to keep the devils out. I laughed at that. The sound fell soft amid the trees. Beeches turning gold with autumn. Oaks going bronze. Ash with its feathery leaves, thorn huddling in thickets. The birds were singing still, but the quiet was vast beneath.

The cat walked ahead of me now, tail up and elegantly curved. One would think that she had come this way before.

I had, longer ago than I liked to think. I had walked as I walked now, but without the warding of mushrooms, crossing myself, it seemed, at every turn of the path. I had taken that last, suddenly steep slope, and rounded the thicket–hedge, it might have been–of thorn, and come to the sunlit space. It had dazzled me then as it dazzled me now, so much light after the green gloom. I blinked to clear my eyes.

The chapel was as it had been when last I came to it. The two walls that stood; the one that was half fallen. The remnant of a porch, the arch of a gate, with the carving on it still, much blurred with age and weather. The upper arm of the cross had broken. The Lady who sat beneath it had lost her upraised hand, but the Child slept as ever in her lap, and her smile, even so worn, was sweet.

I crossed myself in front of her. No devils flapped shrieking through the broken roof. Nothing moved at all, except the cat, which picked its way delicately across the porch and vanished into the chapel.

My hands were cold. I shifted my grip on my bundle. I was hungry, suddenly, which made me want to laugh, or maybe to cry. My stomach lived in a time of its own; neither fear nor anger mattered in the least to it.

I would feed it soon enough. I gathered my courage and stepped under the arch, ducking my head though it was more than high enough: this was a holy place, though not, maybe, to the God I knew.

The pavement had been handsome once. It was dull and broken now. The altar was fallen. The font was whole, but blurred as was the carving on the gate. A spring bubbled into it and bubbled out again through channels in the wall. It was itself an odd thing, the stump of a great tree–oak, the stories said–lined with lead long stripped of its gilding, and carved with crosses. Here the roof was almost intact, giving shelter from the rain; or the ancient wood would long ago have crumbled into dust.

She was kneeling on the edge of the font, her dark head bent over it, her white hands clenched on its rim. I could not see the water. I did not want to see it. I could hear her, but she spoke no language I knew. Her tone was troubling enough: pure throttled desperation, pleading so strong that I lurched forward, hand outstretched. I stopped myself before I could touch her. If she was scrying her lover, then she was calling him up from the dead.

I shuddered. I made no sound, but she started and wheeled. Her face was white as death. Her eyes–

She lidded them. Her body eased by degrees. She did not seem surprised or angered, or anything but tired. "Jeannette," she said.

"You left," I said. "Francha cried all night."

Her face tightened. "I had to go."

"Here?"

She looked about. She might have laughed, maybe, if she had had the strength. "It was to be here first," she said. "Now it seems that it will be here last, and always. And never."

I looked at her.

She shook her head. "You don't understand. How can you?"

"I can try," I said. "I'm no lady, I grant you that, but I've wits enough for a peasant's brat."

"Of course you have." She seemed surprised. As if I had been doing the doubting, and not she. "Very well. I'll tell you. He won't let me back."

"He?"

"He," said Lys, pointing at the font. There was nothing in it but water. No face. No image of a lover that would be. "My lord of the Wood. The cold king."

I shivered. "We don't name him here."

"Wise," said Lys.

"He won't let you pass?" I asked. "Then go around. Go south, as Mère Adele told you. It's a long way, but it's safe, and it takes you west eventually."

"I don't want to go around," said Lys. "I want to go in."

"You're mad," I said.

"Yes," she said. "He won't let me in. I walked, you see. I passed this place. I went where the trees are old, old, and where the sun seldom comes, even at high noon. Little by little they closed in front of me. Then at last I could go no farther. *Go back,* the trees said to me. *Go back and let us be.*"

"You were wise to do it," I said.

"Mad," she said, "and wise." Her smile was crooked. "Oh, yes. So I came back to this place, which is the gate and the guard. And he spoke to me in the water. *Go back,* he said, as the trees had. I laughed at him. Had he no better word to offer me? *Only this,* he said. *The way is shut. If you would open it, if you can—then you may. It is not mine to do.*"

I looked at her. She was thinner than ever, the weight of her belly dragging her down. "Why?" I asked. "Why do you want to get in? It's madness there. Every story says so."

"So it is," Lys said. "That was why I left."

There was a silence. It rang.

"You don't look like a devil," I said. "Or a devil's minion."

She laughed. It was a sweet, awful sound. "But, my good woman, I am. I am everything that is black and terrible."

"You are about to drop where you stand." I got my arm around her before she did it, and sat her down on the font's rim. I could not help a glance at the water. It was still only water.

"We are going to rest," I said, "because I need it. And eat, because I'm hungry. Then we're going back to Sency."

"Not I," said Lys.

I paid her no mind. I untied my kerchief and spread out what I had, and put in a fistful of mushrooms, too; promising myself that I would stop when I went back, and fill my apron again. There was nothing to drink but water, but it would do. Lys would not drink from the font, but from the spring above it. I did as she did, to keep the peace. The cat came to share the cheese and a nibble or two of the bread. She turned up her nose at the mushrooms. "All the more for us," I said to her. She filliped her tail and went in search of better prey.

We ate without speaking. Lys was hungry: she ate as delicately and fiercely as a cat. A cat was what I thought of when I looked at her, a white she-cat who would not meet my eyes.

When we were done I gathered the crumbs in my skirt and went out to the porch and scattered them for the birds. I slanted an eye at the sun. A bit past noon. I had thought it would be later.

Lys came up behind me. Her step was soundless but her shadow fell cool across me, making me shiver.

"There is another reason," she said, "why I should stay and you should leave. My lord who is dead: he had a brother. That one lives, and hunts me."

I turned to face her.

"He wants me for what I am," she said, "and for what he thinks I can give him. For myself, too, maybe. A little. I tricked him in Rouen: cut my hair and put on a nun's habit and walked out peacefully in the abbess's train. He will have learned of that long since, and begun his tracking of me."

I shrugged. "What's one man in the whole of Normandy—or one woman, for the matter of that? Chance is he'll never find you."

"He'll find me," Lys said with quelling certainty.

"So let him." I shook my skirts one last time and stepped down off the porch.

I was not at all sure that she would follow. But when I came to the trees, she was behind me. "You don't know who he is. He'll come armed, Jeannette, and with his men at his back."

That gave me pause, but I was not about to let her see that. "We have walls," I said. "If he comes. Better he find you there than in a broken chapel, beating on a door that stays fast shut."

"Walls can break," said Lys.

"And doors?"

She did not answer that. Neither did she leave me.

After a while she asked it. "Why?"

"You're my guest," I said.

"Not once I left you."

"What does that have to do with it?"

She started to speak. Stopped. Started again. One word. "Francha."

"Francha." I let some of the anger show. "God knows why, God knows how, but she has decided that she belongs to you. You went off and left her. Her mother is dead, her father died on top of her; we found her so, mute as she is now, and he had begun to rot." I could not see her, to know if she flinched. I hoped that she did. "I took her in. I coaxed her to eat, to face the world, to live. Then you came. She fixed the whole of herself on you. And you left her."

"I had no choice."

"Of course you did," I said. "You had to have known that the way was shut. He exiled you, didn't he? your cold king."

"I exiled myself."

Her voice was stiff with pride. I snorted at it. "I believe you, you know. That you're one of Them. No one but a soulless thing would do what you did to Francha."

"Would a soulless thing go back? Would it admit that it had erred?"

"Have you done either?"

She seized my sleeve and spun me about. She was strong; her fingers were cruel, digging into my arm. She glared into my face.

I glared back. I was not afraid, not at all. Even when I saw her true. Cat, had I thought, back in the chapel? Cat, yes, and cat-eyed, and nothing human in her at all.

Except the voice, raw and roughened with anger. "Now you see. Now you know."

I crossed myself, to be safe. She did not go up in a cloud of smoke. I had not honestly expected her to. That was a cross she wore at her throat, glimmering under the robe. "So they're true," I said. "The stories."

"Some of them." She let me go. "He wants that, my lord Giscard. He wants the child I carry, that he thinks will be the making of his house."

"Then maybe you should face him," I said, "and call the lightnings down on him."

She looked as shocked as if I had done as much myself. "That is the Sin! How can you speak so lightly of it?"

"Sin?" I asked. "Among the soulless ones of the Wood?"

"We are as Christian as you," she said.

That was so improbable that it could only be true. I turned my back on her—not without a pricking in my nape—and went on down the path. In a little while she followed me.

II

When the threshing was done and the granaries full, the apples in and the windfalls pressed for cider, my lone proud grapevine harvested and its fruit dried in the sun, and all of Sency made fast against a winter that had not yet come, a company of men rode up to our gate. We had been expecting them, Lys and I and Mère Adele, since the leaves began to fall. We kept a boy by the gate, most days, and shut and barred it at night. Weapons we had none of, except our scythes and our pruning hooks, and an ancient, rusted sword that the smith's widow had unearthed from the forge.

Pierre Allard was at the gate the day milord Giscard came, and Celine tagging after him as she too often did. It was she who came running to find me.

I was nearly there already. All that day Lys had been as twitchy as a cat. Suddenly in the middle of mending Francha's shirt, she sprang up and bolted. I nearly ran her down just past the well, where she stood rigid and staring, the needle still in one hand, and the shirt dangling from the other. I shook her hard.

She came to herself, a little. "If he sees me," she said, "if he knows I'm here . . ."

"So," I said. "You're a coward, then."

"No!" She glared at me, all Lys again, and touchy-proud as ever she could be. "I'm a coward for your sake. He'll burn the village about your ears, for harboring me."

"Not," I said, "if we have anything to say about it."

I tucked up my skirt and climbed the gate. Pierre was up there, and Mère Adele come from who knew where; it was a good long run from the priory, and she was barely breathing hard. She had her best wimple on, I noticed, and her jeweled cross. The sun struck dazzles on the stones, white and red and one as green as new grass. She greeted me with a grunt and Lys with a nod, but kept her eyes on the men below.

They were a pretty company. Much like the one that had taken Claudel away: men in grey mail with bright surcoats, and one with a banner—red, this, like blood, with something gold on it.

"Lion rampant," said Lys. She was still on the stair below the parapet. She could hardly have seen the banner. But she would know what it was. "Arms of Montsalvat."

The lord was in mail like his men. There was a mule behind him, with what I supposed was his armor on it. He rode a tall red horse, and he was tall himself, as far as I could tell. I was not so much above him, standing on the gate. He turned his face up to me. It was a surprising face, after all that I had heard. Younger, much, than I had expected, and shaven clean. Not that he would have much beard, I thought. His hair was barley-fair.

He smiled at me. His teeth were white and almost even. His eyes were pure guileless blue. "Now here's a handsome guardsman!" he said laughing, sweeping a bow in his high saddle. "Fair lady, will you have mercy on poor travelers, and let us into your bower?"

Mère Adele snorted. "I'd sooner let a bull in with the cows. Are you here to take what's left of our men? Or will you believe that we're drained dry?"

"That," said Lys behind, still on the stair, "was hardly wise."

"Let me judge that," said Mère Adele without turning. She folded her arms on the parapet and leaned over, for all the world like a good wife at her window. "That's not a device from hereabouts," she said, cocking her head at the banner. "What interest has Montsalvat in poor Sency?"

"Why, none," said milord, still smiling. "Nor in your men, indeed, reverend lady. We're looking for one of our own who was lost to us. Maybe you've seen her? She would seem to be on pilgrimage."

"We see a pilgrim now and then," said Mère Adele. "This would be an old woman, then? With a boy to look after her, and a little dog, and a fat white mule?"

I struggled not to laugh. My lord Giscard—for that he was, no doubt of it—blinked his wide blue eyes and looked a perfect fool. "Why, no, madam, nothing so memorable. She is young, our cousin, and alone." He lowered his voice. "And not . . . not quite, if you understand me. She was my brother's mistress, you see. He died, and she went mad with grief, and ran away."

"Poor thing," said Mère Adele. Her tone lacked somewhat of sympathy.

"Oh," he said, and if he did not shed a tear, he wept quite adequately with his voice. "Oh, poor Alys! She was full of terrible fancies. We had to bind her lest she harm herself; but that only made her worse. Hardly had we let her go when she escaped."

"Commendable of you," said Mère Adele, "to care so much for a brother's kept woman that you'll cross the width of Normandy to find her. Unless she took somewhat of the family jewels with her?"

Lys hissed behind me. Mère Adele took no notice. Milord Giscard shook his head. "No. No, of course not! Her wits were all we lost, and those were hers to begin with."

"So," said Mère Adele. "Why do you want to find her?"

His eyes narrowed. He did not look so pretty now, or so much the fool. "She's here, then?"

"Yes, I am here." Lys came up beside me. She had lost a little of her thinness, living with us. The weight of the child did nothing to hamper her grace. Her hands cradled it, I noticed, below the parapet where he could not see. She looked down into his face. For a moment I thought that she would spit. "Where were you? I looked for you at Michaelmas, and here it's nigh All Hallows."

He looked somewhat disconcerted, but he answered readily enough. "There was trouble on the road," he said: "English, and Normans riding with them."

"You won," she said. It was not a question.

"We talked our way out of it." He studied her. "You look well."

"I am well," she said.

"The baby?"

"Well."

I saw the hunger in him then, a dark, yearning thing, so much at odds with his face that I shut my eyes against it. When I opened them again, it was gone. He was smiling. "Good news, my lady. Good news, indeed."

"She is not for you," said Lys, hard and cold and still.

"If it is a son, it is an heir to Montsalvat."

"It is a daughter," said Lys. "You know how I know it."

He did not move, but his men crossed themselves. "Even so," he said. "I loved my brother, too. Won't you share what is left of him?"

"You have his bones," said Lys, "and his tomb in Montsalvat."

"I think," said Mère Adele, cutting across this gentle, deadly colloquy, "that this were best discussed in walls. And not," she added as hope leaped in milord's face, "Sency's. St. Agnes's priory can house a noble guest. Let you go there, and we will follow."

He bowed and obeyed. We went down from the gate. But Mère Adele did not go at once to St. Agnes's. People had come to see what we were about. She sent them off on errands that she had given them long since: shoring up the walls, bringing in such of the animals as were still without, shutting Sency against, if need be, a siege.

"Not that I expect a fight," she said, "but with these gentry you never know." She turned to me. "You come." She did not need to turn to Lys. The lady would go whether she was bidden or no: it was written in every line of her.

It was also written in Francha, who was never far from her side. But she took the child's face in her long white hands, and said, "Go and wait for me. I'll come back."

One would hardly expect Francha to trust her, and yet the child did. She nodded gravely, not a flicker of resistance. Only acceptance, and adoration.

Not so Celine. In the end I bribed her with Pierre, and him with the promise of a raisin tart if he took her home and kept her there.

Mère Adele set a brisk pace to the priory, one which gave me no time to think about my frayed kerchief and my skirt with the stains around the hem and my bare feet. Of course milord would come when I had been setting out to clean the pigsty.

Lys stopped us at the priory's gate, came round to face us. The men had gone inside; we could hear them, horses clattering and snorting, deep voices muted in the cloister court. Lys spoke above it, softly, but with the edge which she had shown Messire Giscard. "Why?"

Mère Adele raised her brows.

Lys looked ready to shake her. "Why do you do so much for me?"

"You're our guest," said Mère Adele.

Lys threw back her head. I thought that she would laugh, or cry out. She did neither. She said, "This goes beyond plain hospitality. To chance a war for me."

"There will be no war," said Mère Adele. "Unless you're fool enough to start one." She set her hand on the lady's arm and set her tidily aside, and nodded to Sister Portress, who looked near to bursting with the excitement of it all, and went inside.

Messire Giscard had time for all the proper things, food and rest and washing if he wanted it. He took all three, while we waited, and I wished more than ever that I had stopped to change my dress. I brushed at the one I had, and one of the sisters lent me a clean kerchief. When they brought him in at last, I was as presentable as I could be.

Mère Adele's receiving room was an imposing place, long and wide with a vaulted ceiling, carved and painted and gilded, and a great stone hearth at the end of it. It was not her favored place to work in; that was the closet by her cell, bare and plain and foreign to pretension as the prioress herself. This was for overaweing strangers; and friends, too, for the matter of that. I hardly knew what to do with the chair she set me in, so big as it was, and carved everywhere, and with a cushion that must have been real silk—it was impossibly soft, like a kitten's ear. It let me tuck up my feet at least, though I was sorry for that when the servant let milord in, and I had to untangle myself and stand and try to bow and not fall over. Lys and Mère Adele sat as soon as milord did, which meant that I could sit, too: stiffly upright this time.

He was at his ease, of course. He knew about chairs, and gilded ceilings. He smiled at me—there was no mistaking it: I was somewhat to the side, so that he had to turn a little. I felt my cheeks grow hot.

"This lady I know," he said, turning his eyes away from me and fixing them on Lys. "And you, reverend prioress? And this charming demoiselle?"

Well, I thought. That cured my blush. Charming I was not, whatever else I was.

"I am Mère Adele," said Mère Adele, "and this is Jeannette Laclos of

Sency. You are Giscard de Montsalvat from the other side of Normandy, and you say you have a claim on our guest?"

That took him properly aback. He was not used to such directness, maybe, in the courts that he had come from. But he had a quick wit, and a smooth tongue to go with it. "My claim is no more than I have said. She was my brother's lover. She carries his child. He wished to acknowledge it; he bound me before he died, to do all that I could on its behalf."

"For bastard seed?" asked Mère Adele. "I should think you'd be glad to see the last of her. Wasn't your brother the elder? And wouldn't her baby be his heir, if it were male, and she a wife?"

"She would never marry him," said Messire Giscard. "She was noble enough, she said, but exiled, and no dowry to her name."

"Then all the more cause for you to let her go. Why do you hunt her down? She's no thief, you say. What does she have that you want?"

He looked at his feet in their fine soft shoes. He was out of his reckoning, maybe. My stomach drew tight as I watched him. Men like that—big beautiful animals who had never known a moment's thirst or hunger except what they themselves chose, in war or in the chase; who had never been crossed, nor knew what to do when they were—such men were dangerous. One of them had met me in the wood before I married Claudel; and so Celine was a fair child, like the Norman who had sired her. A Norman very like this one, only not so pretty to look at. He had been gentle in his way. But he wanted me, and what he wanted, he took. He never asked my name. I never asked his.

This one had asked. It softened me—more than I liked to admit. Of course he did not care. He wanted to know his adversaries, that was all. If it had been the two of us under the trees and the blood rising in him, names would not have mattered.

Lys spoke, making me start; I was deep in myself. "He wants me," she said. "Somewhat for my beauty. More for what he thinks that I will give."

Messire Giscard smiled his easy smile. "So then, you tempt me. I'd hardly sin so far as to lust after my brother's woman. That is incest, and forbidden by holy Church." He crossed himself devoutly. "No, Mère Adele; beautiful she may be, but I swore a vow to my brother."

"You promised to let me go," said Lys.

"Poor lady," he said. "You were beside yourself with grief. What could I do but say yes to anything you said? I beg your pardon for the falsehood; I reckoned, truly, that it was needful. I never meant to cast you out."

"You never meant to set me free."

"Do you hate him that much?" asked Mère Adele.

Lys looked at her, and then at him. He was still smiling. Pretty, oh, so pretty, with the sun aslant on his bright hair, and his white teeth gleaming.

"Aymeric was never so fair," said Lys. "That was all given to his brother. He was a little frog-mouthed bandy-legged man, as swarthy as a Saracen, bad eyes and bad teeth and nothing about him that was beautiful. Except," she said, "he was. He would come into a room, and one would think, 'What an ugly little man!' Then he would smile, and nothing in the world would matter, except that he was happy. Everyone loved him. Even his enemies—they hated him with sincere respect, and admired him profoundly. I was his enemy, in the beginning. I was a hard proud cruel thing, exile by free choice from my own country, sworn to make my way in the world, myself alone and with no other. He—he wanted to protect me. 'You are a woman,' he said. As if that was all the reason he needed.

"I hate him for that. He was so certain, and so insufferable, mere mortal man before all that I was and had been. But he would not yield for aught that I could do, and in the end, like all the rest, I fell under his spell."

"Or he under yours," said Messire Giscard. "From the moment he saw you, he was bewitched."

"That was my face," said Lys, "and no more. The rest grew as I resisted him. He loved a fight, did Aymeric. We never surrendered, either of us. To the day he died he was determined to protect me, as was I to resist him."

Messire Giscard smiled, triumphant. "You see!" he said to Mère Adele. "Still she resists. And yet, am I not her sole kinsman in this world? Did not my brother entrust her to me? Shall I not carry out my promise that I made as he was dying?"

"She doesn't want you to," said Mère Adele.

"Ah," said Messire Giscard. "Bearing women—you know how they are. She's distraught; she grieves. As in truth she should. But she should be thinking too of the baby, and of her lover's wishes. He would never have allowed her to tramp on foot across the width of Normandy, looking for God knew what."

"Looking for my kin," said Lys. "I do have them, Giscard. One of them even is a king."

"What, the fairy king?" Giscard shook his head. "Mère Adele, if you'll believe it, she says that she's the elf-king's child."

"I am," said Lys, "his brother's daughter." And she looked it, just then, with her white wild face. "You can't shock them with that, Giscard, or hope to prove me mad. They know. They live on the edge of his Wood."

He leaned forward in his chair. All the brightness was gone, all the sweet false seeming. He was as hard and cold and cruel as she. "So," he said. "So, Alys. Tell them the rest. Tell them what you did that made my brother love you so."

"What, that I was his whore?"

I looked at her and shivered. No, he could not be so hard, or so cold, or so cruel. He was a human man. She . . .

She laughed. "That should be obvious to a blind man. Which these," she said, "are not. Neither blind, nor men, nor fools."

"Do they know what else you are?" He was almost standing over her. "Do they know that?"

"They could hardly avoid it," she said, "knowing whose kin I am."

"If they believe you. If they don't just humor the madwoman."

"We believe her," said Mère Adele. "Is that what you want? To burn her for a witch?"

He crossed himself. "Sweet saints, no!"

"No," said Lys. "He wants to use me. For what he thinks I am. For what he believes I can do."

"For what you *can* do," he said. "I saw you. Up on the hill at night, with stars in your hair. Dancing; and the moon came down and danced at your side. And he watched, and clapped his hands like a child." His face twisted. "*I* would never have been so simple. I would have wielded you like a sword."

Lys was beyond speech. Mère Adele spoke dryly in her silence. "I can see," she said, "why she might be reluctant to consent to it. Women are cursed enough by nature, weak and frail as all the wise men say they are; and made, it's said, for men's use and little else. Sometimes they don't take kindly to it. It's a flaw in them, I'm sure."

"But a flaw that can be mended," said Messire Giscard. "A firm hand, a touch of the spur—but some gentleness, too. That's what such a woman needs."

"It works for mares," said Mère Adele. She stood up. I had never seen her look as she did then, both smaller and larger than she was. Smaller, because he was so big. Larger, because she managed, one way and another, to tower over him. "We'll think on what you've said. You're welcome meanwhile to the hospitality of our priory. We do ask you, of your courtesy, to refrain from visiting the town. There's been sickness in it; it's not quite past."

He agreed readily: so readily that I was hard put not to laugh. He did not need to know that it was an autumn fever, a fret among the children, and nothing to endanger any but the weakest. Sickness, that year, spoke too clearly of the Death.

"That will hold him for a while," said Mère Adele when we were back in safety again: inside Sency's walls, under my new-thatched roof. People walking by could lift a corner of it and look in, but I was not afraid of that. Most were in their own houses, eating their dinner, or down in the tavern drinking it.

We had finished our own, made rich with a joint from a priory sheep.

Perrin's face was shiny with the grease. Even Francha had eaten enough for once to keep a bird alive. She curled in her lady's lap, thumb in mouth, and drowsed, while we considered what to do.

"He won't go where there's sickness," Mère Adele said, "but I doubt he'll go away. He wants you badly."

Lys's mouth twisted. "He wants my witchcraft. No more and no less. If my body came with it—he'd not mind. But it's my power he wants; or what he fancies is my power."

"Why?" I asked. "To make himself lord of Normandy?"

"Oh, no," said Lys. "He'd never aim so high. Just to be a better lord in Montsalvat. Just that. If later it should be more—if his good angel should call him to greater glory—why then, would he be wise to refuse?"

"He'd burn for it," said Mère Adele. "And you with him. They're not gentle now with witches."

"Were they ever?" Lys combed Francha's hair with her fingers, smoothing out the tangles. "It's worse in the south, in Provence, where the Inquisition hunts the heretics still. But the north is hardly more hospitable to such as I."

"We're northerners," I said.

She glanced at me: a touch like a knife's edge. "You live on the edge of the Wood. That changes you."

I shrugged. "I don't feel different. Is the story true? That your king was a mortal king once, in the western kingdom?"

"He was never mortal," she said. "He was king of mortal men, yes, for a hundred years and more. But in the end he left. It was no mercy for his people, to be ruled by one who could never age nor die."

"No mercy for him, either," said Mère Adele, "to see them grow old and die." And when Lys looked at her with wide startled eyes: "No, I'm no wiser than I ought to be. I read a book, that's all. I wanted to know what the stories were. He swore a vow, they said, that he would go under the trees and never come out; not in this age of the world."

"Nor will he," Lys said, bitter. "Nor any who went in with him, nor any who was born thereafter. It's a wider realm than you can conceive of, and this world is but a corner of it; and yet it is a prison. I wanted this air, this sun, this earth. His vow—sworn before ever I was born—forbade me even to think of it."

"So of course you thought of it," Mère Adele sighed. "Young things never change."

"That is what he said," said Lys, so tight with anger that I could barely hear her. "That is exactly what he said."

"He let you go."

"How could he stop me? He knew what would happen. That the walls would close, once I'd opened them. That there'd be no going back."

"Did you want to?"

"Then," said Lys, "no. Now . . ." Her fingers knotted in Francha's curls. Carefully she unclenched them. "This is no world for the likes of me. It hates me, or fears me, or both together; it sees me as a thing, to use or to burn. Even you who took me in, who dare to be fond of me—you know how you could suffer for it. You will, you're as brave as that. But in the end you'd come to loathe me."

"Probably," said Mère Adele. "Possibly not. I doubt you'll be here long enough for that."

"I will not go back to Montsalvat," said Lys, each word shaped and cut in stone.

"You might not have a choice," Mère Adele said. "Unless you can think of a way to get rid of milord. We can hold him off for a while, but he has armed men, and horses. We have neither."

Lys lowered her head. "I know," she said. "Oh, I know."

"You know too much," I said. I was angry, suddenly; sick of all this talk. "Why don't you stop knowing and do? There are twenty men out there, and a man in front of them who wants a witch for a pet. Either give in to him now, before he kills somebody, or find a way to get him out. You can call down the moon, he said. Why not the lightning, too?"

"I can't kill," said Lys, so appalled that I knew it for truth. "I *can't* kill."

"You said that before," I said. "Is that all your witching is worth, then? To throw up your hands and surrender, and thank God you won't use what He gave you?"

"If He gave it," she said, "and not the Other."

"That's heresy," said Mère Adele, but not as if she cared about it. "I think you had better do some thinking. Playing the good Christian woman brought you where you are. He'll take you, child. Be sure of it. And make us pay for keeping you."

Lys stood up with Francha in her arms, sound asleep. She laid the child in the bed and covered her carefully, and kissed her. Then she turned. "Very well," she said. "I'll give myself up. I'll let him take me back to Montsalvat."

Mère Adele was up so fast, and moved so sudden, that I did not know what she had done till I heard the slap.

Lys stood with her hand to her cheek. I could see the red weal growing on the white skin. She looked perfectly, blankly shocked.

"Is that all you can do?" Mère Adele snapped at her. "Hide and cower and whine, and make great noises about fighting back, and give in at the drop of a threat?"

"What else can I do?" Lys snapped back.

"Think," said Mère Adele. And walked out.

It was a very quiet night. I surprised myself: I slept. I was even more surprised to wake and find Lys still there. She had been sitting by the fire when I went to sleep. She was sitting there still, but the cover was on the fire, and her knees were up as far as they would go with her belly so big, and she was rocking, back and forth, back and forth.

She came to herself quickly enough once I reached past her to lift the firelid; did the morning duties she had taken for her own, seemed no different than she ever had. But I had seen the tracks of tears on her face, that first moment, before she got up to fetch the pot.

When she straightened herself with her hands in the small of her back like any bearing woman since Mother Eve, I was ready to hear her say it. "I'm going to the priory."

I went with her. It was a grey morning, turning cold; there was a bite in the air. This time I had on my good dress and my best kerchief, and Claudel's woolen cloak. They were armor of a sort. Lys had her beauty and my blue mantle that I had woven for my wedding. She had a way of seeming almost ordinary—of looking less than she was. A glamour, Mère Adele called it. It was not on her this morning. She looked no more human than an angel on an altar.

Messire Giscard met us a little distance from the priory, up on his big horse with a handful of his men behind him. He smiled down at us. "A fair morning to you, fair ladies," he said.

We did not smile back. Lys kept on walking as if he had not been there. I was warier, and that was foolish: he saw me looking at him, and turned the full measure of his smile on me. "Will you ride with me, Jeannette Laclos? It's not far, I know, but Flambard would be glad to carry you."

I fixed my eyes on Lys and walked faster. The red horse walked beside me. I did not look up, though my nape crawled. In a moment—in just a moment—he would seize me and throw me across his saddle.

"Oh, come," he said in his light, princely voice. "I'm not as wicked a devil as that. If I do fancy you, and you are well worth a man's fancy— what can I do you but good? Wouldn't you like to live in a fine house and dress in silk?"

"And bear your bastards?" I asked him, still not looking at him. "Thank you, no. I gave that up six years ago Lent."

He laughed. "Pretty, and a sharp wit, too! You're a jewel in this midden."

I stopped short. "Sency is no man's dungheap!"

I was angry enough to dare a glance. He was not angry at all. He was grinning. "I like a woman with spirit," he said.

His horse, just then, snaked its head and tried to bite. I hit it as hard as I could. It veered off, shying, and its master cursing. I let myself laugh, once, before I greeted Sister Portress.

*   *   *

"I will go back with you," said Lys.

We were in Mère Adele's receiving room again, the four of us. This time he had his sergeant with him, whether to guard him or bear witness for him I did not know. The man stood behind his lord's chair and watched us, and said nothing, but what he thought of us was clear enough. We were mere weak women. We would never stand against his lord.

Lys sat with her hands in what was left of her lap, knotting and unknotting them. "I've done my thinking," she said. "I can do no more. I'll give you what you ask. I'll go back to Montsalvat."

I opened my mouth. But this was not my place to speak. Messire Giscard was openly delighted. Mère Adele had no expression at all. "You do mean this?" she asked.

"Yes," said Lys.

Messire Giscard showed her his warmest, sweetest face. "I'll see that you don't regret it," he said.

Lys raised her eyes to him. Her real eyes, not the ones people wanted to see. I heard the hiss of his breath. His sergeant made the sign of the horns, and quickly after, that of the cross.

She smiled. "That will do you no good, Raimbaut."

The sergeant flushed darkly. Lys turned the force of her eyes upon Giscard. "Yes, I will go back with you," she said. "I will be your witch. Your mistress, too, maybe, when my daughter is born; if you will have me. I am an exile, after all, and poor, and I have no kin in this world."

His joy was fading fast. Mine was not rising, not yet. But Lys had not surrendered. I saw it in her face; in the fierceness of her smile.

"But before I go," she said, "or you accept me, you should know what it is that you take."

"I know," he said a little sharply. "You are a witch. You won't grow old, or lose your beauty. Fire is your servant. The stars come down when you call."

"Men, too," she said, "if I wish."

For a moment I saw the naked greed. He covered it as children learn to do. "You can see what will be. Aymeric told me that."

"Did he?" Lys arched a brow. "He promised me he wouldn't."

"I coaxed it out of him," said Messire Giscard. "I'd guessed already, from things he said."

"He was never good at hiding anything," said Lys. "Yes, I have that gift."

"A very great one," he said, "and very terrible."

"You have the wits to understand that," said Lys. "Or you imagine that you do." She rose. The sergeant flinched. Messire Giscard sat still, but his eyes had narrowed. Lys came to stand in front of him. Her hand was on the swell of her belly, as if to protect it. "Let us make a bargain, my lord. I have agreed to yield to your will. But before you take me away, let me read your fate for you. Then if you are certain still that I am the making of your fortune, you may have me, and do with me as you will."

He saw the trap in it. So could I; and I was no lord's child. "A fine bargain," he said, "when all you need do is foretell my death, and so be rid of me."

"No," she said. "It's not your death I see. I'll tell you the truth, Giscard. My word on it."

"On the cross," he said.

She laid her hand on Mère Adele's cross and swore to it. Mère Adele did not say anything. She was waiting, as I was, to see what Lys would do.

She crossed herself; her lips moved in what could only be a prayer. Then she knelt in front of Giscard and took his hands in hers. I saw how he stiffened for a moment, as if to pull away. She held. He eased. She met his eyes. Again he made as if to resist; but she would not let him go.

My hands were fists. My heart was beating. There were no bolts of lightning, no clouds of brimstone. Only the slender big-bellied figure in my blue mantle, and the soft low voice.

She read his future for him. How he would ride out from Sency, and she behind. How they would go back to Rouen. How the war was raging there, and how it would rage for years out of count. How the Death would come back, and come back again. How he would fight in the war, and outlive the Death, and have great glory, with her at his side: ever young, ever beautiful, ever watchful for his advantage. "Always," she said. "Always I shall be with you, awake and asleep, in war and at peace, in your heart as in your mind, soul of your soul, indissolubly a part of you. Every breath you draw, every thought you think, every sight your eye lights upon—all these shall be mine. You will be chaste, Giscard, except for me; sinless, but that you love me. For nothing that you do shall go unknown to me. So we were, Aymeric and I, perfect in love as in amity. So shall we two be."

For a long while after she stopped speaking, none of us moved. Messire Giscard's lips were parted. Gaping, I would have said, in a man less good to look at.

Lys smiled with awful tenderness. "Will you have me, Giscard? Will you have the glory that I can give you?"

He wrenched free. The sweep of his arm sent her sprawling.

I leaped for him, veered, dropped beside her. She was doubled up, knotted round her center.

Laughing. Laughing like a mad thing. Laughing till she wept.

By the time she stopped, he was gone. She lay exhausted in my arms. My dress was soaked with her tears.

"Could you really have done it?" I asked her.

She nodded. She struggled to sit up. I helped her; gave her my kerchief to wipe her face.

"I can do it to you, too," she said. Her voice was raw. "I can hear every-thing, see it, feel it–every thought in every head. Every hope, dream, love, hate, fear, folly–everything." She clutched her head. *"Everything!"*

I held her and rocked her. I did not know why I was not afraid. Too far past it, I supposed. And she had lived with us since Michaelmas; if there was anything left to hide from her, then it was hidden deeper than I could hope to find.

She was crying again, deep racking sobs. "I was the best, my father said. Of all that are in the Wood, the strongest to shield, the clearest to see both how the walls were raised, and how to bring them down. None of us was better fit to walk among human folk. So I defied them all, brought down the ban, walked out of the Wood. And I could do it. I *could* live as the hu-mans lived. But I could–not–die as they died. I could not." Her voice rose to a wail. "I wanted to die with Aymeric. And I could not even take sick!"

"Oh, hush." Mère Adele stood over us, hands on hips. She had gone out when Giscard took flight; now she was back, not an eyelash out of place, and no awe at all for the woman of the Wood. "If you had really wanted to cast yourself in your lover's grave, you would have found a way to do it. There's no more *can't* in killing yourself than in killing some-one else. It's all *won't,* and a good fat measure of *pity-me.*"

Lys could have killed her then. Oh, easily. But I was glad for whatever it was that stopped her, *can't* or *won't* or plain astonishment.

She got to her feet with the first failing of grace that I had ever seen in her. Even her beauty was pinched and pale, too thin and too sharp and too odd.

Mère Adele regarded her with utter lack of sympathy. "You got rid of his lordship," she said, "and handily, too. He'll see the back of hell before he comes by Sency again. You do know, I suppose, that he could have sworn to bring the Inquisition down on us, and burn us all for what you did to him."

"No," said Lys. "He would not. I made sure of that."

"You–made–sure?"

Even Lys could wither in the face of Mère Adele's wrath. She raised her hands to her face, let them fall. "I made him do nothing but what he was best minded to do."

"You made him."

"Would you rather he came back with fire and sword?"

For a moment they faced one another, like fire and sword themselves. Mère Adele shook her head and sighed. "It's done. I can't say I want it undone. That's a wanting I'll pay dearly for in penance. You–maybe you've paid already. You never should have left your Wood."

"No," said Lys. "I don't think that. But that I've stayed too long–yes." Mère Adele started a little. Lys smiled a thin cold smile. "No, I'm not in your mind. It's written in your face. You want me gone."

"Not gone," said Mère Adele. "Gone home."

Lys closed her eyes. "Sweet saints, to be home—to live within those walls again—to be what I am, all that I am, where my own people are—" Her breath shuddered as she drew it in. "Don't you think I've tried? That's why I came here. To find the door. To break it down. To go back."

"You didn't try hard enough," said Mère Adele. *"Won't* again. Always *won't."*

"Not my *won't,"* said Lys. "My king's."

"Yours," said Mère Adele, immovable. "I can read faces, too. Are they all as stubborn as you, where you come from?"

"No," said Lys. Her eyes opened. She drew herself up. "Some are worse."

"I doubt that," said Mère Adele. "You're welcome here. Don't ever doubt it. But this isn't your world. We aren't your kind. You said it yourself. You love us, and we die on you."

"You can't help it," said Lys.

Mère Adele laughed, which made Lys stare. "Go on, child. Go home. We're no better for you than you are for us."

Lys was mortally insulted. She was older than Mère Adele, maybe, and higher born. But she held her tongue. She bent her head in honest reverence. If not precisely in acceptance.

III

The Wood was cold in the grey light of evening. No bird sang. No wind stirred the branches of the trees.

Lys had tried to slip away alone. She should have known better. This time it was not my fault, not entirely: I had followed Francha. So we stood on the porch of the ruined chapel, Francha with both arms about her waist, I simply facing her.

"If the walls can open at all," Lys said, careful and cold, "your mortal presence will assure that they stay shut."

I heard her, but I was not listening. "Are you going to leave Francha again?"

Lys frowned and looked down at the child who clung to her. "She can't go, even if I can get in."

"Why not?"

"She's human."

"She can't live in this world," I said. "She was barely doing it when you came. When you go, she'll die."

"We are forbidden—"

"You were forbidden to leave. But you did it."

Lys had her arms around Francha, almost as if she could not help it. She gathered the child up and held her. "Oh, God! If I could only be the hard cold creature that I pretend to be!"

"You're cold enough," I said, "and as heartless as a cat. But even a cat has its weaknesses."

Lys looked at me. "You should have been one of us."

I shivered. "Thank God He spared me that." I glanced at the sky. "You'd best do it if you're going to. Before it's dark."

Lys might have argued, but even she could not keep the sun from setting.

She did not go into the chapel as I had thought she would. She stood outside of it, facing the Wood, still holding Francha. It was already dark under the trees; a grey mist wound up, twining through the branches.

Lys's eyes opened wide. "It's open," she said. "The walls are down. But—"

"Stop talking," I said. My throat hurt. "Just go."

She stayed where she was. "It's a trap. Or a deception. The ban is clever; it knows what it is for."

Francha struggled in her arms. She let the child go. Francha slid down the curve of her, keeping a grip on her hand. Pulling her toward the Wood.

She looked into wide eyes as human as hers were not. "No, Francha. It's a trap."

Francha set her chin and leaned, putting all her weight into it. It was as loud as a shout. *Come!*

"Go," I said. "How will you know it's a trap till you've tried it? Go!"

Lys glared at me. "How can humans know—"

I said a word that shocked her into silence. While she wavered I pushed, and Francha pulled. Dragging her toward the thing she wanted most in the world.

Later it would hurt. Now I only wanted her gone. Before I gave in. Before I let her stay.

She was walking by herself now, if slowly. The trees were close. I could smell the mist, dank and cold, like the breath of the dead.

"No!" cried Lys, flinging up her hand.

Light flew from it. The mist withered and fled. The trees towered higher than any mortal trees, great pillars upholding a roof of gold.

The light shrank. The trees were trees again, but their leaves were golden still, pale in the evening. There was a path among them, glimmering faintly as it wound into the gloom. It would not be there long, I knew in my bones. I braced myself to drag her down it. What would happen if it closed while I was on it, I refused to think.

She set foot on it of her own will. Walked a step, two, three.

Turned.

Held out her hand. She was going. I had won that much. Now she offered me what I had made her take. The bright country. The people who knew no age nor sickness nor death. Escape. Freedom.

From what? I asked her inside myself. I would grow old no matter where I was.

"Let Francha have it," I said. "Maybe you can heal her; maybe she'll find a voice again. Maybe she'll learn to sing."

Lys did not lower her hand. She knew, damn her. How easily, how happily, I could take it.

My fists knotted in my skirt. "I was born on this earth. I will die on it."

Francha let go Lys's hand. She ran to me, hugged me tight. But not to hold. Not to stay. Her choice was made. Had been made at harvest time, on another edge of this Wood.

Lys looked as if she would speak. I willed her not to. She heard me, maybe; or she simply understood, as humans did, from the look on my face. She said nothing. Only looked, long and long.

The path was fading fast. She turned suddenly, swept Francha up, began to run. Down into the glimmering dark; down to a light that I could almost see. There were people there. Pale princes, pale queens. Pale king who was not cold at all. Almost–almost–I could see his grey eyes; how they smiled, not only at the prodigal come home, but at me, mere mortal flesh, alone beside a broken shrine.

I laughed painfully. She had my wedding cloak. What Claudel would say when he came back–

If he came back.

When, said a whisper in the Wood. A gift. A promise.

I turned my back on the shadow and the trees, and turned my face toward home: warmth and light, and my children's voices, and Mamère Mondine asleep by the fire. Above me as I walked, like a guard and a guide, rose a lone white star.

Michael Swanwick

The Changeling's Tale

Michael Swanwick made his debut in 1980, and has gone on to become one of the most popular and respected of all that decade's new writers. He has several times been a finalist for the Nebula Award, as well as for the World Fantasy Award and for the John W. Campbell Award, and has won the Theodore Sturgeon Award and the *Asimov's* Readers Award poll. In 1991, his novel *Stations of the Tide* won him a Nebula Award as well. His other books include his first novel, *In the Drift,* which was published in 1985, a novella-length book, *Griffin's Egg,* and 1987's popular novel *Vacuum Flowers*. His critically acclaimed short fiction has been assembled in *Gravity's Angels* and in a collection of his collaborative short work with other writers, *Slow Dancing through Time*. His most recent book is a new novel, *The Iron Dragon's Daughter,* which was a finalist for the World Fantasy Award and the Arthur C. Clarke Award. Swanwick lives in Philadelphia with his wife, Marianne Porter, and their son Sean.

Although Swanwick has made his reputation as a writer of pyrotechnic and innovative "hard science fiction," and even has been claimed as a "cyberpunk" by some, his *first* love is fantasy, and he has begun to explore that territory in recent years. His unique, bizarre, and highly imaginative novel *The Iron Dragon's Daughter* may be one of the most brilliant fantasies of the 1990s to date, and is so far the most substantial representative of a nascent subgenre Swanwick himself has named "Hard Fantasy"— sort of a mix between the Dickensian sensibilities of "steampunk," high-tech science fiction, and traditional Tolkienenesque fantasy. He's also explored similar territory in such genre-mixing stories as "The Dragon Line," "Cold Iron," "Golden Apples of the Sun," "The Man Who Met Picasso," and "The Edge of the World."

The dazzling story that follows is an odd sort of homage to the work of J. R. R. Tolkien, one of Swanwick's major influences, inspired by a market report for the then-upcoming Tolkien tribute anthology *After the King*. It turned out that by the time Swanwick actually finished *writing* this story, that anthology was not only completed but already on sale in bookstores, and so Swanwick had to sell the story elsewhere. In it, he takes us to a world of intense beauty, horrifying cruelty, and incandescent strangeness, for a classic study of how you Can't Go Home Again . . . or *can* you? And would you *want* to, if you could?

Fill the pipe again. If I'm to tell this story properly, I'll need its help. That's good. No, the fire doesn't need a new log. Let it die. There are worse things than darkness.

How the tavern creaks and groans in its sleep! 'Tis naught but the settling of its bones and stones, and yet never a wraith made so lonesome a sound. It's late, the door is bolted, and the gates to either end of the Bridge are closed. The fire burns low. In all the world only you and I are awake. This is no fit tale for such young ears as yours, but—oh, don't scowl so! You'll make me laugh, and that's no fit beginning to so sad a tale as mine. All right, then.

Let us pull our stools closer to the embers and I'll tell you all.

I must begin twenty years ago, on a day in early summer. The Ogre was dead. Our armies had returned, much shrunken, from their desperate adventures in the south and the survivors were once again plying their trades. The land was at peace at last, and trade was good. The tavern was often full.

The elves began crossing Long Bridge at dawn.

I was awakened by the sound of their wagons, the wheels rumbling, the silver bells singing from atop the high poles where they had been set to catch the wind. All in a frenzy I dressed and tumbled down from the chimney loft and out the door. The wagons were painted with bright sigils and sinuous overlapping runes, potent with magic I could neither decipher nor hope to understand. The white oxen that pulled them spoke gently in their own language, one to the other. Music floated over the march, drums and cymbals mingling with the mournful call of the long curling horn named Serpentine. But the elves themselves, tall and proud, were silent behind their white masks.

One warrior turned to look at me as he passed, his eyes cold and unfriendly as a spearpoint. I shivered, and the warrior was gone.

But I had *known* him. I was sure of it. His name was . . .

A hand clasped my shoulder. It was my uncle. "A stirring sight, innit? Those are the very last, the final elven tribe. When they are passed over Long Bridge, there will be none of their kind left anywhere south of the Awen."

He spoke with an awful, alien sadness. In all the years Black Gabe had been my master—and being newborn when my father had marched away to the Defeat of Blackwater, I had known no other—I had never seen him in such a mood before. Thinking back, I see that it was at that instant I first realized in a way so sure I could feel it in my gut that he would some-day die and be forgotten, and after him me. Then, though, I was content simply to stand motionless with the man, sharing this strangely com-panionable sense of loss.

"How can they tell each other apart?" I asked, marveling at how sim-ilar were their richly-decorated robes and plain, unfeatured masks.

"They—"

A fire-drake curled in the air, the morning rocket set off to mark the instant when the sun's disk cleared the horizon, and my eyes traveled up to watch it explode. When they came down again, my uncle was gone. I never saw him again.

Eh? Forgive me. I was lost in thought. Black Gabe was a good master, though I didn't think so then, who didn't beat me half so often as I de-served. You want to know about my scars? There is nothing special about them—they are such markings as all the *am'rta skandayaksa* have. Some are for deeds of particular merit. Others indicate allegiance. The triple slashes across my cheeks mean that I was sworn to the Lord Cakaravartin, a war leader whose name means "great wheel-turning king." That is a name of significance, though I have forgotten exactly what, much as I have for-gotten the manner and appearance of the great wheel-turner himself, though there was a time when I would happily have died for him. The squiggle across my forehead means I slew a dragon.

Yes, of course you would. What youth your age would not? And it's a tale I'd far more gladly tell you than this sorry life of mine. But I can-not. That I did kill a dragon I remember clearly—the hot gush of blood, its bleak scream of despair—but beyond that nothing. The events leading to and from that instant of horror and—strangely—guilt are gone from me entirely, like so much else that happened since I left the Bridge, lost in mist and forgetfulness.

Look at our shadows, like giants, nodding their heads in sympathy.

What then? I remember scrambling across the steep slate rooftops, leap-ing and slipping in a way that seems quite mad to me now. Corwin the glover's boy and I were stringing the feast-day banners across the street to honor the procession below. The canvases smelled of mildew. They were stored in the Dragon Gate in that little room above the portcullis, the one with the murder hole in the floor. Jon and Corwin and I used to crouch over it betimes and take turns spitting, vying to be the first to hit the head of an unsuspecting merchant.

Winds gusted over the roofs, cold and invigorating. Jumping the gaps between buildings, I fancied myself to be dancing with the clouds. I crouched to lash a rope through an iron ring set into the wall just beneath the eaves. Cor had gone back to the gateroom for more banners. I looked up to see if he were in place yet and realized that I could see right into Becky's garret chamber.

There was nothing in the room but a pallet and a chest, a small table and a washbasin. Becky stood with her back to the window, brushing her hair.

I was put in mind of those stories we boys told each other of wanton women similarly observed. Who, somehow sensing their audience, would put on a lewd show, using first their fingers and then their hairbrushes. We had none of us ever encountered such sirens, but our faith in them was boundless. Somewhere, we knew, were women depraved enough to mate with apes, donkeys, mountain trolls—and possibly even the likes of us.

Becky, of course, did nothing of the sort. She stood in a chaste woolen nightgown, head raised slightly, stroking her long, coppery tresses in time to the faint elven music that rose from the street. A slant of sunlight touched her hair and struck fire.

All this in an instant. Then Cor came bounding over her roof making a clatter like ten goats. He shifted the bundle of banners 'neath one arm and extended the other. "Ho, Will!" he bellowed. "Stop daydreaming and toss me that rope end!"

Becky whirled and saw me gawking. With a most unloving shriek of outrage, she slammed the shutters.

All the way back to the tavern, my mind was filled with thoughts of Becky and her hairbrush. As I entered, my littlest cousin, Thistle, danced past me, chanting, "elves-elves-elves," spinning and twirling as if she need never stop. She loved elves and old stories with talking animals and all things bright and magical. They tell me she died of the whitepox not six years later. But in my mind's eye she still laughs and spins, evergreen, immortal.

The common room was empty of boarders and the table planks had been taken down. Aunt Kate, Dolly, and my eldest sister Eleanor were cleaning up. Kate swept the breakfast trash toward the trap. "It comes of keeping bad company," she said grimly. "That Corwin Glover and his merry band of rowdies. Ale does not brew overnight—he's been building toward this outrage for a long time."

I froze in the doorway vestibule, sure that Becky's people had reported my Tom-Peepery. And how could I protest my innocence? I'd've done as much and worse long ago, had I known such was possible.

A breeze leapt into the room when Eleanor opened the trap, ruffling her hair and making the dust dance. "They gather by the smokehouse every sennight to drink themselves sick and plot mischief," Dolly observed. "May Chandler's Anne saw one atop the wall there, making water into the river, not three nights ago."

"Oh, fie!" The trash went tumbling toward the river and Eleanor slammed the trap. Some involuntary motion on my part alerted them to my presence then. They turned and confronted me.

A strange delusion came over me then, and I imagined that these three gossips were part of a single mechanism, a twittering machine going through predetermined motions, as if an unseen hand turned a crank that made them sweep and clean and talk.

Karl Whitesmith's boy has broken his indenture, I thought.

"Karl Whitesmith's boy has broken his indenture," Dolly said.

He's run off to sea.

"He's run off to sea," Kate added accusingly.

"What?" I felt my mouth move, heard the words come out independent of me. "Jon, you mean? Not Jon!"

How many 'prentices does Karl have? Of course Jon.

"How many 'prentices does Karl have? Of course Jon."

"Karl spoiled him," Kate said (and her words were echoed in my head before she spoke them). "A lad his age is like a walnut tree which suffers not but rather benefits from thrashings." She shook her besom at me. "Something the likes of you would do well to keep in mind."

Gram Birch amazed us all then by emerging from the back kitchen.

Delicate as a twig, she bent to put a plate by the hearth. It held two re-fried fish, leftovers from the night before, and a clutch of pickled roe. She was slimmer than your little finger and her hair was white as an aged dandelion's. This was the first time I'd seen her out of bed in weeks; the passage of the elves, or perhaps some livening property of their music, had brought fresh life to her. But her eye was as flinty as ever. "Leave the boy alone," she said.

My delusion went away, like a mist in the morning breeze from the Awen.

"You don't understand!"

"We were only—"

"This saucy lad—"

"The kitchen tub is empty," Gram Birch told me. She drew a schooner of ale and set it down by the plate. Her voice was warm with sympathy, for I was always her favorite, and there was a kindly tilt to her chin. "Go and check your trots. The head will have subsided by the time you're back."

Head in a whirl, I ran upbridge to the narrow stairway that gryed down the interior of Tinker's Leg. It filled me with wonder that Jon—gentle, laughing Jon—had shipped away. We all of us claimed to be off to sea someday; it was the second or third most common topic on our night-time eeling trips upriver. But that it should be Jon, and that he should leave without word of farewell!

A horrible thing happened to me then: With the sureness of prophecy I knew that Jon would not come back. That he would die in the western isles. That he would be slain and eaten by a creature out of the sea such as none on the Bridge had ever imagined.

I came out at the narrow dock at the high-water mark. Thoughts else-where, I pulled in my lines and threw back a bass for being shorter than my forearm. Its less fortunate comrades I slung over my shoulder.

But as I was standing there on the dark and slippery stones, I saw some-thing immense and silent move beneath the water. I thought it a monstrous tortoise at first, such as that which had taken ten strong men with ropes and grappling hooks to pull from the bay at Mermaid Head. But as it ap-proached I could see it was too large for that. I did not move. I could not breathe. I stared down at the approaching creature.

The surface of the river exploded. A head emerged, shedding water. Each of its nostrils was large enough for a man to crawl into. Its hair and beard were dark, like the bushes and small trees that line the banks up-river and drown in every spring flood. Its eyes were larger than cartwheels and lustreless, like stone.

The giant fixed his gaze upon me, and he spoke.

What did he say, you ask? I wonder that myself. In this regard, I am like the victim of brigands who finds himself lying by the wayside, and then scrabbles in the dust for such small coppers as they may have left behind. What little I possess, I will share with you, and you may guess from it how much I have lost. One moment I stood before the giant and the next I found myself tumbled into the river. It was late afternoon and I was splashing naked with the knackery boys.

I had spent most of that day mucking out the stables in the Approach, part of an arrangement Black Gabe had made whereby the Pike and Bar-rel got a half a penny for each guest who quartered a horse there. I was as sweaty and filthy as any of the horses by the time I was done, and had gladly fallen in with the butcher's apprentices who would cleanse them-selves of the blood and gore their own labors had besmirched them with.

This was on the south side of the river, below the Ogre Gate. I was scrubbing off the last traces of ordure when I saw the elven lady staring down at me from the esplanade.

She was small with distance, her mask a white oval. In one hand she carried a wicker cage of finches. I found her steady gaze both discon-certing and arousing. It went through me like a spear. My manhood began of its own accord to lift.

That was my first sight of Ratanavivicta.

It lasted only an instant, that vision. The light of her eyes filled and blinded me. And then one of my fellow bathers—Hodge the tanner's son it was, who we in our innocence considered quite the wildling—leaped upon my back, forcing me under the water. By the time I emerged, choking and sputtering, the elf-woman was gone.

I shoved Hodge away, and turned my gaze over the river. I squinted at the rafts floating downstream, sweepsmen standing with their oars up, and the carracks making harbor from their voyages across the sea. On the far bank, pier crowded upon shack and shanty upon warehouse. Stone buildings rose up behind, rank after rank fading blue into the distance, with here and there a spire or tower rising up from the general ruck.

Long snakelike necks burst from the water, two river lizards fighting over a salmon. A strange elation filled me then and I laughed with joy at the sight.

At sunset the elf-host was still crossing the Bridge. Their numbers were that great. All through the night they marched, lighting their way with lanterns carried on poles. I sat in the high window of a room we had not let that evening, watching their procession, as changing-unchanging as the Awen itself. They were going to the mountains of the uttermost north, people said, through lands no living man had seen. I sat yearning, yearning after them, until my heart could take no more.

Heavily I started down the stairs to bed.

To my astonishment the common room was filled with elves. A little wicker cage hung from a ceiling hook. In it were five yellow finches. I looked down from it to the eyes of a white-masked woman. She crooked a finger beckoningly, then touched the bench to her left. I sat beside her.

An elven lord whose manner and voice are gone from me, a pillar of shadow, Cakaravartin himself, stood by the fireplace with one fingertip lazily tracing the shells and coiled serpents embedded in the stone. "I remember," he said in a dreamy voice, "when there was no ford across the Awenasamaga and these stones were part of Great Asura, the city of the giants."

"But how could you—?" I blurted. Masked faces turned to look at me. I bit my tongue in embarrassment.

"I was here when this bridge was built," the speaker continued unheedingly. "To expiate their sins, the last of the giants were compelled to dismantle their capital and with its stones build to the benefit of men. They were a noble race once, and I have paused here in our quest for *parikasaya* because I would see them once more."

Dolly swept in, yawning, with a platter of raw salmon and another holding a stacked pyramid of ten mugs of ale. "Who's to pay?" she asked.

Then, seeing me, she frowned. "Will. You have chores in the morning. Ought not you be abed?"

Reddening, I said, "I'm old enough to bide my own judgment."

An elf proferred a gold coin which, had it been silver, would have paid for the service ten times over, and asked, "Is this enough?"

Dolly smiled and nodded. Starting to my feet, I said, "I'll wake the coin-merchant and break change for you." Ignoring the exasperation that swept aside my sister's look of avaricious innocence.

But the elf-woman at my side stilled me with a touch. "Stay. The coin is not important, and there is much I would have you learn."

As the coin touched Dolly's hand she changed, for the merest instant, growing old and fat. I gawked and then she was herself again. With a flip of her skirts she disappeared with the coin so completely I was not to see her for another twenty years. One of the elves turned to the wall, lifting her mask for a quick sip of ale, restoring it with nothing exposed.

The finch-bearer brought out a leather wallet and opened it, revealing dried herbs within. Someone took a long-stemmed clay tavern pipe from the fireplace rack and gave her it. As Ratanavivicta filled the bowl, she said, "This is *margakasaya,* which in your language means 'the path to extinction.' It is rare beyond your knowing, for it grows nowhere in the world now that we have given up our gardens in the south. Chewed, it is a mild soporific. Worked into a balm it can heal minor wounds. Smoked, it forms a bridge through the years, so that one's thoughts may walk in past times or future, at will."

"How can that be?" I asked. "The past is gone, and the future—who is to say what will happen? Our every action changes it, else our deeds were for naught."

She did not answer, but instead passed the pipe to me. With a pair of tongs she lifted a coal from the fire to light it. I put the stem to my lips, exhaled nervously, inhaled. I drew the smoke deep into my lungs, and a whirring and buzzing sensation rose up from my chest to fill my head, first blinding me and then opening my eyes:

It was night, and Cakaravartin's raiders were crying out in anger and despair, for the enemy had stolen a march on us and we were caught by the edge of the marshes, lightly armed and afoot.

Screaming, crazy, we danced ourselves into a frenzy. At a sign from Cakaravartin, we loosed the bundles from our backs and unfolded a dozen horsehides. We pulled our knives and slashed ourselves across arms and chests. Where the blood fell across the hides, the black loam filled them, lending them form, billowing upward to become steeds of earth, forelegs flailing, nostrils wild, eyes cold and unblinking stars.

Then we were leaping onto our mounts, drawing our swords, galloping toward the east. Where hoof touched sod, fresh earth flowed up into the necromantic beasts, and down again through the rearmost leg.

"Tirathika!"

On hearing my adoptive name, I turned to see Krodasparasa riding maskless alongside me, his markings shining silver on his face. His eyes were gleeful and fey. Krodasparasa gestured, and I tore free of my own mask. I felt my cock stiffen with excitement.

Krodasparasa saw and laughed. Our rivalry, our hatred of each other was as nothing compared to this comradeship. Riding side by side, we traded fierce grins compounded of mockery and understanding, and urged our steeds to greater efforts.

"It's a good day to die," Krodasparasa cried. "Are you ready to die, little brother?" He shifted his sword to his far side so we could clasp hands briefly at full gallop, and then swung it around in a short, fast chop that took all of my skill to evade.

I exhaled.

The common room wrapped itself about me again. I found myself staring up at the aurochs horns nailed as a trophy to the west wall, at the fat-bellied withy baskets hanging from the whale-rib rafters. Overhead, a carved and painted wooden mermaid with elk's antlers sweeping back from her head to hold candles turned with excruciating slowness.

The elf-woman took the pipe from my nerveless fingers. She slid the long stem under her mask so skillfully that not a fingertip's worth of her face showed. Slowly, she inhaled. The coal burned brighter, a wee orange bonfire that sucked in all the light in the room. "That was not what I wished to see," she murmured. She drew in a second time and then handed the pipe on.

Slowly the pipe passed around the room again, coming last of all to me. Clumsily, I accepted it and put the end, now hot, to my lips. I drew the magic in:

I stood on an empty plain, the silk tents of the encampment to my back. Frost rimed the ground in crisscross starbursts. My blood was pounding.

It was a festival night, and we had cut the center-poles for our conical tents twice as high as usual. Small lanterns hung from their tips like stars. All was still. For the *am'rta skandayaksa,* venturing out on a festival night was a great impiety.

Tortured with indecision I turned away and then back again, away and back. I could be killed for what I intended, but that bothered me less than the possibility that I had misread the signs, that I was not wanted. I stood before one particular tent, glaring at it until it glowed like the sun. Finally I ducked within.

Ratanavivicta was waiting for me.

Throwing aside my mask, I knelt before her. Slowly, lingeringly, I slid my fingers beneath her mask and drew it off. Her face was scarred, like the moon, and like the moon it was beautiful and cold. My hand was black

on her breast. A pale nipple peeked between my fingers like the first star
of twilight.

"Ahhh," she sighed voicelessly, and the pipe passed to the next hand.

Everything had changed.

You cannot imagine how it felt, after twenty years of wandering, to return at last to Long Bridge. My heart was so bitter I could taste it in my
mouth. Two decades of my life were gone, turned to nothing. My memory of those years was but mists and phantoms, stolen away by those I
had trusted most. The Dragon Gate was smaller than I remembered it
being, and nowhere near so grand. The stone buildings whose spires had
combed the passing clouds were a mere three and four stories high. The
roadway between them was scarce wide enough to let two carts pass.

My face felt tight and dry. I slid a finger under my mask to scratch at
the scar tissue where it touched one corner of my mouth.

Even the air smelled different. The smoky haze of my boyhood, oak
and cedar from the chimneys of the rich, driftwood and dried dung from
the roofholes of the poor, was changed utterly, compounded now of charcoal and quarry-dug coal with always a sharp tang of sulfur pinching at
the nose. Wondrous odors still spilled from the cookshop where old Hal
Baldpate was always ready with a scowl and a sugar bun, but the pep-
pery admixture of hams curing next door was missing, and the smokehouse itself converted to a lens-grinder's shop.

The narrow gap between the two buildings remained, though—do you
young ones still call it the Gullet?—and through it rose a light breeze from
the Awen. I halted and leaned on my spear. It was exactly here one long-
ago evening that Becky had showed me her freckled breasts and then
fleered at me for being shocked. Here Jon and I would kneel to divvy up
the eggs we'd stolen from the cotes of Bankside which, being off the
Bridge, was considered fair game by all good river-brats—I see you smiling! Here I crouched in ambush for a weaver's 'prentice whose name and
face and sin are gone from me now, though that folly cost me a broken
arm and all of Becky's hard-won sympathy.

Somebody bumped into me, cursed, and was gone before I could turn
and crave pardon. I squeezed into the Gullet so others could pass, and
stared out over the sun-dazzled river.

Down the Awen, a pyroscaph struggled toward the bay, smoke billowing from its stack, paddles flashing in unison, as if it were a water beetle
enchanted beyond natural size. The merchanters entering and leaving the
harbor were larger than I remembered, and the cut of their sails was unfamiliar. Along the banks the city's chimneys had multiplied, pillaring
smoke into the darkened heavens. It was a changed world, and one that
held no place for such as me.

The ghosts of my youth thronged so thickly about me then that I could not distinguish past from present, memory from desire. It was as if I had turned away for an instant and on turning back discovered myself two decades older.

Fill the bowl again. One last time I would hear the dawn-music of my youth, the sound of lodgers clumping sleepily down the stairs, the clink and rattle of plates and pewter in the kitchen. The quick step of Eleanor returning from the cookshop with her arms full of fresh-smelling bread. The background grumbles of Black Gabe standing just out of sight, finding fault with my work.

What a cruel contrast to this morning! When I turned away from the Awen, the Bridge was thick with scurrying city folk, shopkeepers and craftsmen in fussy, lace-trimmed clothes. The air was full of the clicking of their heels. Men and women alike, their faces were set and grim. For an instant my spirit quailed at the thought of rejoining human company. I had spent too many years in the company of owls and wolves, alone in the solitudes of the north, to be comfortable here. But I squared my shoulders and went on.

The old Pike and Barrel stood where it has always stood, midway down the Bridge. From a distance it seemed unbearably small and insignificant, though every stone and timber of it was burned forever into my heart. The tavern placard swung lazily on its rod. That same laughing fish leaped from that same barrel that a wandering scholar had executed in trade for a night's stay when Aunt Kate was young. I know, for she spoke of him often.

Below the sign a crowd had formed, an angry eddy in the flow of passersby. A hogshead had been upended by the door and atop it a stout man with a sheriff's feather in his cap was reading from a parchment scroll. By him stood a scarecrow underling with a handbell and behind him a dozen bravos with oaken staves, all in a row.

It was an eviction.

Kate was there, crying with rage and miraculously unchanged. I stared, disbelieving, and then, with a pain like a blow to the heart, realized my mistake. This worn, heavy woman must be my sister Dolly, turned horribly, horribly old. The sight of her made me want to turn away. The painted pike mocked me with its silent laughter. But I mastered my unease and bulled my way through the crowd.

Without meaning to, I caused a sensation. Murmuring, the bystanders made way. The sheriff stopped reading. His bravos stirred unhappily, and the scrawny bellman cringed. The center of all eyes, I realized that there must be some faint touch of the elven glamour that clung to me yet.

"What is happening here?" My voice was deep, unfamiliar, and the words came hesitantly from my mouth, like water from a pump grown stiff with disuse.

The sheriff blusteringly shook his parchment at me. "Don't interfere! This is a legal turning-out, and I've the stavesmen to back me up."

"You're a coward, Tom Huddle, and an evil man indeed to do this to folk who were once your friends!" Dolly shouted. "You're the rich man's lickspittle now! A hireling to miscreants and usurers, and naught more!"

A mutter of agreement went up from the crowd.

The sheriff ducked his massive head and without turning to meet her eye, grumbled, "By damn, Dolly, I'm only doing my—"

"I'll pay," I said.

Tom Huddle gaped. "Eh? What's that?"

I shrugged off my backsack, of thick dwarven cloth embroidered with silk orchids in a woods-elf stitch, and handed my spear to a gangly youth, who almost dropped it in astonishment. That was you, wasn't it? I thought so. The haft is ebony, and heavier than might be thought.

Lashed to the frame, alongside my quiver and the broken shards of what had once been my father's sword, was a leather purse. After such long commerce with elves I no longer clearly knew the value of one coin over another. But there would be enough, that much I knew. The elvenkind are generous enough with things that do not matter. I handed it to my sister, saying, "Take as much as you need."

Dolly stood with the purse in her outstretched hand, making no move to open it. "Who are you?" she asked fearfully. "What manner of man hides his features behind a mask?"

My hand rose involuntarily—I'd forgotten the mask was there. Now, since it no longer served a purpose, I took it off. Fresh air touched my face. I felt dizzy almost to sickness, standing exposed before so many people.

Dolly stared at me.

"Will?" she said at last. "Is it really you?"

When the money had been counted over thrice and the sprig of broom the sheriff had nailed over the doorsill had been torn down and trampled underfoot, the house and neighbors all crowded about me and bore me into the Pike and Barrel's common room and gave me the honored place by the fire. The air was close and stuffy—I could not think. But nobody noticed. They tumbled question upon question so that I had but little chance to answer, and vied to reintroduce themselves, crying, "Here's one you're not expecting!" and "Did you ever guess little Sam would turn out such a garish big gossoon?" and roaring with laughter. Somebody put a child on my knee, a boy, they said his name was Pip. Somebody else brought down the lute from its peg by the loft and struck up a song.

Suddenly the room was awhirl with dancers. Unmoved, I watched them, these dark people, these strangers, all sweaty and imperfect flesh.

After my years with the pale folk, they all seemed heavy and earthbound. Heat radiated from their bodies like steam.

A woman with wrinkles at the corners of her eyes and mischief within them drew me up from the stool, and suddenly I was dancing too. The fire cast an ogreish shadow upon the wall behind me and it danced as well, mocking my clumsy steps.

Everything felt so familiar and yet so alien, all the faces of my youth made strange by age, and yet dear to me in an odd, aching way, as if both tavern and Bridge were but clever simulacra of the real thing, lacking the power to convince and yet still able to rend the heart. My childhood was preternaturally clear, as close to me now as the room in which I sat. It was as if I had never left. All the years between seemed a dream.

"You don't know who I am, do you?" my dancing partner said.

"Of course I do," I lied.

"Who, then?" She released me and stood back, hands on hips.

Challenged, I actually *looked* at her for the first time. She moved loosely within her blouse, a plump woman with big brown freckles on her face and forearms. She crossed her arms in a way that caused her breasts to balloon upward, and laughed when I flushed in embarrassment.

Her laughter struck me like the clapper of a great bell.

"Becky!" I cried. "By the Seven, it's you! I never expected–"

"You never expected I'd grow so fat, eh?"

"No, no!" I protested. "It's not–"

"You're a fool, Will Taverner. But that's not totally unbecoming in a man." She drew me into the shadow of the stairway where there was privacy, and a small bench as well. We talked for a long time. And at the end of that conversation I thought she looked dissatisfied. Nor could I account for it until she reached between my legs to feel what was there. My cod, though, was a wiser man than I and stood up to greet her. "Well," she said, "that's a beginning. Cold dishes aren't brought back to a boil in a minute."

She left me.

You look unhappy. Becky's your mam, isn't she? Now that I come to think of it, there's that glint in your eye and a hint at that same *diabolus* that hides at the edge of her mouth. Well, she's a widow now, which means she can do as she pleases. But I will horrify you with no more details of what we said.

Where's my pipe? What happened to that pouch of weed? Thank you. I'd be long asleep by now if not for its aid. This is the last trace of the *margakasaya* left in all the world. With me will die even the memory of it, for there are no elves abroad in the realms of men anymore. They have found *parikayasa,* "final extinction" you would say, or perhaps "the end of all." Did you know that *am'rta skandayaksa* means "deathless elf-group"? There's irony there, knew we only how to decipher it.

Maybe I was wrong to kill the dragon.

Maybe he was all that kept them from oblivion.

When we had all shared Cakaravartin's vision of Great Asura and of the giants at labor, their faces stolid and accepting of both their guilt and their punishment, and spoken with Boramohanagarahant, their king, it was almost dawn. Cakaravartin passed around the pipe one more time. "I see that you are determined to come with us," he said to me, "and that is your decision to make. But first you should know the consequences."

Ratanavivicta's mask tilted in a way that I would later learn indicated displeasure. But Cakaravartin drew in deeply and passed the pipe around again. I was trembling when it came to me. The mouthpiece was slick with elf-spit. I put it between my lips.

I inhaled.

At first I thought nothing had happened. The common room was exactly as before, the fire dying low in the hearth, the elkmaid slowly quartering out the air as ever she had done. Then I looked around me. The elves were gone. I was alone, save for one slim youth of about my own age, whom I did not recognize.

That youth was you.

Do I frighten you? I frighten myself far more, for I have reached that moment when I see all with doubled sight and apprehend with divided heart. Pray such possession never seizes you. This—now—is what I was shown all these many years ago, and this is the only chance I will ever have to voice my anger and regret to that younger self, who I know will not listen. How could he? A raggedy taverner's boy with small prospects and a head stuffed full of half-shaped ambitions. What could I say to make him understand how much he is giving up?

By rights, you should have been my child. There's the bitter nub of the thing, that Becky, who had all but pledged her heart to me, had her get by someone else. A good man, perhaps—they say half the Bridge turned out to launch his fireboat when he was taken by the dropsy—but not me.

I have lost more than years. I have lost the life I was meant to have, children on my knee and a goodwife growing old and fat with me as we sank into our dotage. Someone to carry my memory a few paces beyond the emptiness of the grave, and grandchildren to see sights I will not. These were my birthright, and I have them not. In his callowness and ignorance, my younger self has undone me.

I can see him, even now, running madly after the elves, as he will in the shadowy hour before dawn. Heart pounding with fear that he will not catch up, lungs agonized with effort. Furious to be a hero, to see strange lands, to know the love of a lady of the *am'rta skandayaksa*.

They are fickle and cruel, are the elves. Ratanavivicta snatched me from my life on a whim, as casually as she might pick up a bright pebble from the roadside. She cast me aside as easily as she would a gemstone of which she had wearied. There is no faith in her kind.

Ah, it is a dreadful night! The winds prowl the rooftops like cats, bringing in the winter. There'll be frost by morning, and no mistake.

Is the story over, you ask? Have you not been listening? There is no story. Or else it all—your life and mine and Krodasparasa's alike—is one story and that story always ending and never coming to a conclusion. But my telling ends now, with my younger self starting from his dream of age and defeat and finding himself abandoned, the sole mortal awake on all the Bridge, with the last of the elf horde gone into the sleeping streets of the city beyond the Dragon Gate.

He will leap to his feet and snatch up his father's sword from its place over the hearth—there, where my spear hangs now. He will grab a blanket for a cloak and a handful of jerked meat to eat along the road, and nothing more, so great will be his dread of being left behind.

I would not stop him if I could. Run, lad, run! What do you care what becomes of me? Twenty years of glory lie at your feet. The dream is already fading from your head. You feel the breeze from the river as you burst out the door.

Your heart *sings*.

The moment is past. I have been left behind.

Only now can I admit this. Through all this telling, I have been haunted by a ghost and the name of that ghost was Hope. So long as I had not passed beyond that ancient vision, there was yet the chance that I was not my older self at all, but he who was destined to shake off his doubts and leap out that door. In the innermost reaches of my head, I was still young. The dragon was not slain, the road untravelled, the elves alive, the adventures ahead, the magic not yet passed out of the world.

And now, well. I'm home.

Peter S. Beagle

Professor Gottesman and the Indian Rhinoceros

Peter S. Beagle was born in New York City in 1939. Although not prolific by genre standards, he has published four well-received fantasy novels, and his first such, *A Fine and Private Place,* was widely influential. In fact, Beagle may be the most successful writer of lyrical and evocative modern fantasy since Bradbury, something he proves once again in the gentle, wry, wise, and whimsical story that follows, in which a reclusive professor reluctantly takes on a *very* unusual roommate . . .

Beagle's other books include the novels *The Last Unicorn, The Folk of the Air,* and, most recently, the critically acclaimed *The Innkeeper's Song,* which certainly must be in the running for the title of most successful fantasy novel of the 1990s to date. His short fiction has appeared in such varied places as *Seventeen* and *Ladies Home Journal* as well as in fantasy anthologies such as *New Worlds of Fantasy* and *After the King,* and has been collected in *The Fantasy Worlds of Peter S. Beagle.* His film work includes screenplays for Ralph Bakshi's animated film *The Lord of the Rings, The Last Unicorn, Dove,* and an episode of *Star Trek: The Next Generation.* He has also written a stage adaptation of *The Last Unicorn,* the libretto of an opera, *The Midnight Angel,* and a popular autobiographical travel book, *I See By My Outfit.* His most recent book is the fantasy anthology *Peter S. Beagle's Immortal Unicorn,* edited in collaboration with Janet Berliner. Beagle lives in Davis, California, with his wife, the Indian writer Padma Hejmadi.

Professor Gustave Gottesman went to a zoo for the first time when he was thirty-four years old. There is an excellent zoo in Zurich, which was Professor Gottesman's birthplace, and where his sister still lived, but Professor Gottesman had never been there. From an early age he had determined on the study of philosophy as his life's work; and for any true philosopher this world is zoo enough, complete with cages, feeding times, breeding programs, and earnest docents, of which he was wise enough to know that he was one. Thus, the first zoo he ever saw was the one in the middle-sized Midwestern American city where he worked at a middle-sized university, teaching Comparative Philosophy in comparative contentment. He was tall and rather thin, with a round, undistinguished face, a snub nose, a random assortment of sandyish hair, and a pair of very intense and very distinguished brown eyes that always seemed to be looking a little deeper than they meant to, embarrassing the face around them no end. His students and colleagues were quite fond of him, in an indulgent sort of way.

And how did the good Professor Gottesman happen at last to visit a zoo? It came about in this way: his older sister Edith came from Zurich to stay with him for several weeks, and she brought her daughter, his niece Nathalie, along with her. Nathalie was seven, both in years, and in the number of her that there sometimes seemed to be, for the Professor had never been used to children even when he was one. She was a generally pleasant little girl, though, as far as he could tell; so when his sister besought him to spend one of his free afternoons with Nathalie while she went to lunch and a gallery opening with an old friend, the Professor graciously consented. And Nathalie wanted very much to go to the zoo and see tigers.

"So you shall," her uncle announced gallantly. "Just as soon as I find out exactly where the zoo is." He consulted with his best friend, a fat, cheerful, harmonica-playing professor of medieval Italian poetry named Sally Lowry, who had known him long and well enough (she was the only person in the world who called him Gus) to draw an elaborate two-colored map of the route, write out very precise directions beneath it, and make several copies of this document, in case of accidents. Thus equipped, and accompanied by Charles, Nathalie's stuffed bedtime tiger, whom she desired to introduce to his grand cousins, they set off together for the zoo on a gray, cool spring afternoon. Professor Gottesman quoted Thomas Hardy to Nathalie, improvising a German translation for her benefit as he went along.

> *This is the weather the cuckoo likes,*
> *And so do I;*
> *When showers betumble the chestnut spikes,*
> *And nestlings fly.*

"Charles likes it too," Nathalie said. "It makes his fur feel all sweet."

They reached the zoo without incident, thanks to Professor Lowry's excellent map, and Professor Gottesman bought Nathalie a bag of something sticky, unhealthy, and forbidden, and took her straight off to see the tigers. Their hot, meaty smell and their lightning-colored eyes were a bit too much for him, and so he sat on a bench nearby and watched

Nathalie perform the introductions for Charles. When she came back to Professor Gottesman, she told him that Charles had been very well-behaved, as had all the tigers but one, who was rudely indifferent. "He was probably just visiting," she said. "A tourist or something."

The Professor was still marvelling at the amount of contempt one small girl could infuse into the word *tourist,* when he heard a voice, sounding almost at his shoulder, say, "Why, Professor Gottesman—how nice to see you at last." It was a low voice, a bit hoarse, with excellent diction, speaking good Zurich German with a very slight, unplaceable accent.

Professor Gottesman turned quickly, half-expecting to see some old acquaintance from home, whose name he would inevitably have forgotten. Such embarrassments were altogether too common in his gently preoccupied life. His friend Sally Lowry once observed, "We see each other just about every day, Gus, and I'm still not sure you really recognize me. If I wanted to hide from you, I'd just change my hairstyle."

There was no one at all behind him. The only thing he saw was the rutted, muddy rhinoceros yard, for some reason placed directly across from the big cats' cages. The one rhinoceros in residence was standing by the fence, torpidly mumbling a mouthful of moldy-looking hay. It was an Indian rhinoceros, according to the placard on the gate: as big as the Professor's compact car, and the approximate color of old cement. The creaking slabs of its skin smelled of stale urine, and it had only one horn, caked with sticky mud. Flies buzzed around its small, heavy-lidded eyes, which regarded Professor Gottesman with immense, ancient unconcern. But there was no other person in the vicinity who might have addressed him.

Professor Gottesman shook his head, scratched it, shook it again, and turned back to the tigers. But the voice came again. "Professor, it was indeed I who spoke. Come and talk to me, if you please."

No need, surely, to go into Professor Gottesman's reaction: to describe in detail how he gasped, turned pale, and looked wildly around for any corroborative witness. It is worth mentioning, however, that at no time did he bother to splutter the requisite splutter in such cases: "My God, I'm either dreaming, drunk, or crazy." If he was indeed just as classically absentminded and impractical as everyone who knew him agreed, he was also more of a realist than many of them. This is generally true of philosophers, who tend, as a group, to be on terms of mutual respect with the impossible. Therefore, Professor Gottesman did the only proper thing under the circumstances. He introduced his niece Nathalie to the rhinoceros.

Nathalie, for all her virtues, was not a philosopher, and could not hear the rhinoceros's gracious greeting. She was, however, seven years old, and a well-brought-up seven-year-old has no difficulty with the notion that a rhinoceros—or a goldfish, or a coffee table—might be able to talk; nor in accepting that some people can hear coffee-table speech and some people cannot. She said a polite hello to the rhinoceros, and then became involved in her own conversation with stuffed Charles, who apparently had a good deal to say himself about tigers.

"A mannerly child," the rhinoceros commented. "One sees so few here. Most of them throw things."

His mouth dry, and his voice shaky but contained, Professor Gottesman asked carefully, "Tell me, if you will—can all rhinoceri speak, or only the Indian species?" He wished furiously that he had thought to bring along his notebook.

"I have no idea," the rhinoceros answered him candidly. "I myself, as it happens, am a unicorn."

Professor Gottesman wiped his balding forehead. "Please," he said earnestly. "Please. A rhinoceros, even a rhinoceros that speaks, is as real a creature as I. A unicorn, on the other hand, is a being of pure fantasy, like mermaids, or dragons, or the chimera. I consider very little in this universe as absolutely, indisputably certain, but I would feel so much better if you could see your way to being merely a talking rhinoceros. For my sake, if not your own."

It seemed to the Professor that the rhinoceros chuckled slightly, but it might only have been a ruminant's rumbling stomach. "My Latin designation is *Rhinoceros unicornis*," the great animal remarked. "You may have noticed it on the sign."

Professor Gottesman dismissed the statement as brusquely as he would have if the rhinoceros had delivered it in class. "Yes, yes, yes, and the manatee, which suckles its young erect in the water and so gave rise to the myth of the mermaid, is assigned to the order *sirenia*. Classification is not proof."

"And proof," came the musing response, "is not necessarily truth. You look at me and see a rhinoceros, because I am not white, not graceful, far from beautiful, and my horn is no elegant spiral but a bludgeon of matted hair. But suppose that you had grown up expecting a unicorn to look and behave and smell exactly as I do—would not the rhinoceros then be the legend? Suppose that everything you believed about unicorns—everything except the way they look—were true of me? Consider the possibilities, Professor, while you push the remains of that bun under the gate."

Professor Gottesman found a stick and poked the grimy bit of pastry—about the same shade as the rhinoceros, it was—where the creature could wrap a prehensile upper lip around it. He said, somewhat tentatively, "Very well. The unicorn's horn was supposed to be an infallible guide to detecting poisons."

"The most popular poisons of the Middle Ages and Renaissance," replied the rhinoceros, "were alkaloids. Pour one of those into a goblet made of compressed hair, and see what happens." It belched resoundingly, and Nathalie giggled.

Professor Gottesman, who was always invigorated by a good argument with anyone, whether colleague, student, or rhinoceros, announced, "Isidore of Seville wrote in the seventh century that the unicorn was a cruel beast, that it would seek out elephants and lions to fight with them. Rhinoceri are equally known for their fierce, aggressive nature, which often leads them to attack anything that moves in their shortsighted vision. What have you to say to that?"

"Isidore of Seville," said the rhinoceros thoughtfully, "was a most learned man, much like your estimable self, who never saw a rhinoceros in his life, or an elephant either, being mainly preoccupied with church history and canon law. I believe he did see a lion at some point. If your charming niece is quite done with her snack?"

"She is not," Professor Gottesman answered, "and do not change the subject. If you are indeed a unicorn, what are you doing scavenging dirty buns and candy in this public establishment? It is an article of faith that a unicorn can only be taken by a virgin, in whose innocent embrace the ferocious creature becomes meek and docile. Are you prepared to tell me that you were captured under such circumstances?"

The rhinoceros was silent for some little while before it spoke again. "I cannot," it said judiciously, "vouch for the sexual history of the gentleman in the baseball cap who fired a tranquilizer dart into my left shoulder. I would, however, like to point out that the young of our species on occasion become trapped in vines and slender branches which entangle their horns—and that the Latin for such branches is *virge*. What Isidore of Seville made of all this . . ." It shrugged, which is difficult for a rhinoceros, and a remarkable thing to see.

"Sophistry," said the Professor, sounding unpleasantly beleaguered even in his own ears. "Casuistry. Semantics. Chop-logic. The fact remains, a rhinoceros is and a unicorn isn't." This last sounds much more impressive in German. "You will excuse me," he went on, "but we have other specimens to visit, do we not, Nathalie?"

"No," Nathalie said. "Charles and I just wanted to see the tigers."

"Well, we have seen the tigers," Professor Gottesman said through his teeth. "And I believe it is beginning to rain, so we will go home now." He took Nathalie's hand firmly and stood up, as that obliging child snuggled Charles firmly under her arm and bobbed a demure European curtsy to the rhinoceros. It bent its head to her, the mud-thick horn almost brushing the ground. Professor Gottesman, mildest of men, snatched her away.

"Good-bye, Professor," came the hoarse, placid voice behind him. "I look forward to our next meeting." The words were somewhat muffled, because Nathalie had tossed the remainder of her sticky snack into the yard as her uncle hustled her off. Professor Gottesman did not turn his head.

Driving home through the rain—which had indeed begun to fall, though very lightly—the Professor began to have an indefinably uneasy feeling that caused him to spend more time peering at the rearview mirror than in looking properly ahead. Finally he asked Nathalie, "Please, would you and—ah—you and Charles climb into the backseat and see whether we are being followed?"

Nathalie was thrilled. "Like in the spy movies?" She jumped to obey, but reported after a few minutes of crouching on the seat that she could detect nothing out of the ordinary. "I saw a helicopiter," she told him, attempting the English word. "Charles thinks they might be following us that way, but I don't know. Who is spying on us, Uncle Gustave?"

"No one, no one," Professor Gottesman answered. "Never mind, child, I am getting silly in America. It happens, never mind." But a few moments later the curious apprehension was with him again, and Nathalie was happily occupied for the rest of the trip home in scanning the traffic behind them through an imaginary periscope, yipping "It's that one!" from time to time, and being invariably disappointed when another prime suspect turned off down a side street. When they reached Professor Gottesman's house, she sprang out of the car immediately, ignoring her mother's welcome until she had checked under all four fenders for possible homing devices. "Bugs," she explained importantly to the two adults. "That was Charles's idea. Charles would make a good spy, I think."

She ran inside, leaving Edith to raise her fine eyebrows at her brother. Professor Gottesman said heavily, "We had a nice time. Don't ask." And Edith, being a wise older sister, left it at that.

The rest of the visit was enjoyably uneventful. The Professor went to work according to his regular routine, while his sister and his niece explored the city, practiced their English together, and cooked Swiss-German specialties to surprise him when he came home. Nathalie never asked to go to the zoo again—stuffed Charles having lately shown an interest in international intrigue—nor did she ever mention that her uncle had formally introduced her to a rhinoceros and spent part of an afternoon sitting on a bench arguing with it. Professor Gottesman was genuinely sorry when she and Edith left for Zurich, which rather surprised him. He hardly ever missed people, or thought much about anyone who was not actually present.

It rained again on the evening that they went to the airport. Returning alone, the Professor was startled, and a bit disquieted, to see large muddy footprints on his walkway and his front steps. They were, as nearly as he could make out, the marks of a three-toed foot, having a distinct resemblance to the ace of clubs in a deck of cards. The door was locked and bolted, as he had left it, and there was no indication of any attempt to force an entry. Professor Gottesman hesitated, looked quickly around him, and went inside.

The rhinoceros was in the living room, lying peacefully on its side before the artificial fireplace—which was lit—like a very large dog. It opened one eye as he entered and greeted him politely. "Welcome home, Professor. You will excuse me, I hope, if I do not rise?"

Professor Gottesman's legs grew weak under him. He groped blindly for a chair, found it, fell into it, his face white and freezing cold. He managed to ask, "How—how did you get in here?" in a small, faraway voice.

"The same way I got out of the zoo," the rhinoceros answered him. "I would have come sooner, but with your sister and your niece already here, I thought my presence might make things perhaps a little too crowded for you. I do hope their departure went well." It yawned widely and contentedly, showing blunt, fist-sized teeth and a gray-pink tongue like a fish fillet.

"I must telephone the zoo," Professor Gottesman whispered. "Yes, of course, I will call the zoo." But he did not move from the chair.

The rhinoceros shook its head as well as it could in a prone position. "Oh, I wouldn't bother with that, truly. It will only distress them if anyone learns that they have mislaid a creature as large as I am. And they will never believe that I am in your house. Take my word for it, there will be no mention of my having left their custody. I have some experience in these matters." It yawned again and closed its eyes. "Excellent fireplace you have," it murmured drowsily. "I think I shall lie exactly here every night. Yes, I do think so."

And it was asleep, snoring with the rhythmic roar and fading whistle of a fast freight crossing a railroad bridge. Professor Gottesman sat staring in his chair for a long time before he managed to stagger to the telephone in the kitchen.

Sally Lowry came over early the next morning, as she had promised several times before the Professor would let her off the phone. She took one quick look at him as she entered and said briskly, "Well, whatever came to dinner, you look as though it got the bed and you slept on the living room floor."

"I did not sleep at all," Professor Gottesman informed her grimly. "Come with me, please, Sally, and you shall see why."

But the rhinoceros was not in front of the fireplace, where it had still been lying when the Professor came downstairs. He looked around for it increasingly frantic, saying over and over, "It was just here, it has been here all night. Wait, wait, Sally, I will show you. Wait only a moment."

For he had suddenly heard the unmistakable gurgle of water in the pipes overhead. He rushed up the narrow hairpin stairs (his house was, as the real-estate agent had put it, "an old charmer") and burst into his bathroom, blinking through clouds of steam to find the rhinoceros lolling blissfully in the tub, its nose barely above water and its hind legs awkwardly sticking straight up in the air. There were puddles all over the floor.

"Good morning," the rhinoceros greeted Professor Gottesman. "I could wish your facilities a bit larger, but the hot water is splendid, pure luxury. We never had hot baths at the zoo."

"Get out of my tub!" the Professor gabbled, coughing and wiping his face. "You will get out of my tub this instant!"

The rhinoceros remained unruffled. "I am not sure I can. Not just like that. It's rather a complicated affair."

"Get out exactly the way you got in!" shouted Professor Gottesman. "How did you get up here at all? I never heard you on the stairs."

"I tried not to disturb you," the rhinoceros said meekly. "Unicorns can move very quietly when we need to."

"Out!" the Professor thundered. He had never thundered before, and it made his throat hurt. "Out of my bathtub, out of my house! And clean up that floor before you go!"

He stormed back down the stairs to meet a slightly anxious Sally Lowry waiting at the bottom. "What was all that yelling about?" she wanted to know. "You're absolutely pink—it's sort of sweet, actually. Are you all right?"

"Come up with me," Professor Gottesman demanded. "Come right now." He seized his friend by the wrist and practically dragged her into his bathroom, where there was no sign of the rhinoceros. The tub was empty and dry, the floor was spotlessly clean; the air smelled faintly of tile cleaner. Professor Gottesman stood gaping in the doorway, muttering over and over, "But it was here. It was in the tub."

"What was in the tub?" Sally asked. The Professor took a long, deep breath and turned to face her.

"A rhinoceros," he said. "It says it's a unicorn, but it is nothing but an Indian rhinoceros." Sally's mouth opened, but no sound came out. Professor Gottesman said, "It followed me home."

Fortunately, Sally Lowry was no more concerned with the usual splutters of denial and disbelief than was the Professor himself. She closed her mouth, caught her own breath, and said, "Well, any rhinoceros that could handle those stairs, wedge itself into that skinny tub of yours, and tidy up afterwards would have to be a unicorn. Obvious. Gus, I don't care what time it is, I think you need a drink."

Professor Gottesman recounted his visit to the zoo with Nathalie, and all that had happened thereafter, while Sally rummaged through his minimally stocked liquor cabinet and mixed what she called a "Lowry Land Mine." It calmed the Professor only somewhat, but it did at least restore his coherency. He said earnestly, "Sally, I don't know how it talks. I do not know how it escaped from the zoo, or found its way here, or how it got into my house and my bathtub, and I am afraid to imagine where it is now. But the creature is an Indian rhinoceros, the sign said so. It is simply not possible—not possible—that it could be a unicorn."

"Sounds like *Harvey,*" Sally mused. Professor Gottesman stared at her.

"You know, the play about the guy who's buddies with an invisible white rabbit. A big white rabbit."

"But this one is not invisible!" the Professor cried. "People at the zoo, they saw it—Nathalie saw it. It bowed to her, quite courteously."

"Um," Sally said. "Well, I haven't seen it yet, but I live in hope. Meanwhile, you've got a class, and I've got office hours. Want me to make you another Land Mine?"

Professor Gottesman shuddered slightly. "I think not. We are discussing today how Fichte and von Schelling's work leads us to Hegel, and I need my wits about me. Thank you for coming to my house, Sally. You are a good friend. Perhaps I really am suffering from delusions, after all. I think I would almost prefer it so."

"Not me," Sally said. "I'm getting a unicorn out of this, if it's the last thing I do." She patted his arm. "You're more fun than a barrel of MFA candidates, Gus, and you're also the only gentleman I've ever met. I don't know what I'd do for company around here without you."

Professor Gottesman arrived early for his seminar on "The Heirs of Kant." There was no one in the classroom when he entered, except for the rhinoceros. It had plainly already attempted to sit on one of the chairs, which lay in splinters on the floor. Now it was warily eyeing a ragged hassock near the coffee machine.

"What are you doing here?" Professor Gottesman fairly screamed at it.

"Only auditing," the rhinoceros answered. "I thought it might be rewarding to see you at work. I promise not to say a word."

Professor Gottesman pointed to the door. He had opened his mouth to order the rhinoceros, once and for all, out of his life, when two of his students walked into the room. The Professor closed his mouth, gulped, greeted his students, and ostentatiously began to examine his lecture notes, mumbling professorial mumbles to himself, while the rhinoceros, unnoticed, negotiated a kind of armed truce with the hassock. True to its word, it listened in attentive silence all through the seminar, though Professor Gottesman had an uneasy moment when it seemed about to be drawn into a heated debate over the precise nature of von Schelling's intellectual debt to the von Schlegel brothers. He was so desperately careful not to let the rhinoceros catch his eye that he never noticed until the last student had left that the beast was gone, too. None of the class had even once commented on its presence; except for the shattered chair, there was no indication that it had ever been there.

Professor Gottesman drove slowly home in a disorderly state of mind. On the one hand, he wished devoutly never to see the rhinoceros again; on the other, he could not help wondering exactly when it had left the classroom. "Was it displeased with my summation of the *Ideas for a Philosophy of Nature*?" he said aloud in the car. "Or perhaps it was something

I said during the argument about *Die Weltalter*. Granted, I have never been entirely comfortable with that book, but I do not recall saying anything exceptionable." Hearing himself justifying his interpretations to a rhinoceros, he slapped his own cheek very hard and drove the rest of the way with the car radio tuned to the loudest, ugliest music he could find.

The rhinoceros was dozing before the fireplace as before, but lumbered clumsily to a sitting position as soon as he entered the living room. "Bravo, Professor!" it cried in plainly genuine enthusiasm. "You were absolutely splendid. It was an honor to be present at your seminar."

The Professor was furious to realize that he was blushing; yet it was impossible to respond to such praise with an eviction notice. There was nothing for him to do but reply, a trifle stiffly, "Thank you, most gratifying." But the rhinoceros was clearly waiting for something more, and Professor Gottesman was, as his friend Sally had said, a gentleman. He went on, "You are welcome to audit the class again, if you like. We will be considering Rousseau next week, and then proceed through the romantic philosophers to Nietzsche and Schopenhauer."

"With a little time to spare for the American Transcendentalists, I should hope," suggested the rhinoceros. Professor Gottesman, being some distance past surprise, nodded. The rhinoceros said reflectively, "I think I should prefer to hear you on Comte and John Stuart Mill. The Romantics always struck me as fundamentally unsound."

This position agreed so much with the Professor's own opinion that he found himself, despite himself, gradually warming toward the rhinoceros. Still formal, he asked, "May I perhaps offer you a drink? Some coffee or tea?"

"Tea would be very nice," the rhinoceros answered, "if you should happen to have a bucket." Professor Gottesman did not, and the rhinoceros told him not to worry about it. It settled back down before the fire, and the Professor drew up a rocking chair. The rhinoceros said, "I must admit, I do wish I could hear you speak on the scholastic philosophers. That's really my period, after all."

"I will be giving such a course next year," the Professor said, a little shyly. "It is to be a series of lectures on medieval Christian thought, beginning with St. Augustine and the Neoplatonists and ending with William of Occam. Possibly you could attend some of those talks."

The rhinoceros's obvious pleasure at the invitation touched Professor Gottesman surprisingly deeply. Even Sally Lowry, who often dropped in on his classes unannounced, did so, as he knew, out of affection for him, and not from any serious interest in epistemology or the Milesian School. He was beginning to wonder whether there might be a way to permit the rhinoceros to sample the cream sherry he kept aside for company, when the creature added, with a wheezy chuckle, "Of course, Augustine and the rest never did quite come to terms with such pagan survivals as unicorns. The best they could do was to associate us with the Virgin Mary, and to suggest that our horns somehow represented the unity of Christ and his church. Bernard of Trèves even went so far as to identify Christ directly with the unicorn, but it was never a comfortable union. Spiral peg in square hole, so to speak."

Professor Gottesman was no more at ease with the issue than St. Augustine had been. But he was an honest person—only among philosophers is this considered part of the job description—and so he felt it his duty to say, "While I respect your intelligence and your obvious intellectual curiosity, none of this yet persuades me that you are in fact a unicorn. I still must regard you as an exceedingly learned and well-mannered Indian rhinoceros."

The rhinoceros took this in good part, saying, "Well, well, we will agree to disagree on that point for the time being. Although I certainly hope that you will let me know if you should need your drinking water purified." As before, and as so often thereafter, Professor Gottesman could not be completely sure that the rhinoceros was joking. Dismissing the subject, it went on to ask, "But about the Scholastics—do you plan to discuss the later Thomist reformers at all? Saint Cajetan rather dominates the movement, to my mind; if he had any real equals, I'm afraid I can't recall them."

"Ah," said the Professor. They were up until five in the morning, and it was the rhinoceros who dozed off first.

The question of the rhinoceros's leaving Professor Gottesman's house never came up again. It continued to sleep in the living room, for the most part, though on warm summer nights it had a fondness for the young willow tree that had been a Christmas present from Sally. Professor Gottesman never learned whether it was male or female, nor how it nourished its massive, noisy body, nor how it managed for toilet facilities—a reticent man himself, he respected reticence in others. As a houseguest, the rhinoceros's only serious fault was a continuing predilection for hot baths (with Epsom salts, when it could get them.) But it always cleaned up after itself, and was extremely conscientious about not tracking mud into the house; and it can be safely said that none of the Professor's visitors—even the rare ones who spent a night or two under his roof—ever remotely suspected that they were sharing living quarters with a rhinoceros. All in all, it proved to be a most discreet and modest beast.

The Professor had few friends, apart from Sally, and none whom he would have called on in a moment of bewildering crisis, as he had called her. He avoided whatever social or academic gatherings he could reasonably avoid; as a consequence his evenings had generally been lonely ones, though he might not have called them so. Even if he had admitted the term, he would surely have insisted that there was nothing necessarily wrong with loneliness, in and of itself. *"I think,"* he would have said—

did often say, in fact, to Sally Lowry. "There are people, you know, for whom thinking is company, thinking is entertainment, parties, dancing even. The others, other people, they absolutely will not believe this."

"You're right," Sally said. "One thing about you, Gus, when you're right you're really right."

Now, however, the Professor could hardly wait for the time of day when, after a cursory dinner (he was an indifferent, impatient eater, and truly tasted little difference between a frozen dish and one that had taken half a day to prepare), he would pour himself a glass of wine and sit down in the living room to debate philosophy with a huge mortar-colored beast that always smelled vaguely incontinent, no matter how many baths it had taken that afternoon. Looking eagerly forward all day to anything was a new experience for him. It appeared to be the same for the rhinoceros.

As the animal had foretold, there was never the slightest suggestion in the papers or on television that the local zoo was missing one of its larger odd-toed ungulates. The Professor went there once or twice in great trepidation, convinced that he would be recognized and accused immediately of conspiracy in the rhinoceros's escape. But nothing of the sort happened. The yard where the rhinoceros had been kept was now occupied by a pair of despondent-looking African elephants; when Professor Gottesman made a timid inquiry of a guard, he was curtly informed that the zoo had never possessed a rhinoceros of any species. "Endangered species," the guard told him. "Too much red tape you have to go through to get one these days. Just not worth the trouble, mean as they are."

Professor Gottesman grew placidly old with the rhinoceros—that is to say, the Professor grew old, while the rhinoceros never changed in any way that he could observe. Granted, he was not the most observant of men, nor the most sensitive to change, except when threatened by it. Nor was he in the least ambitious: promotions and pay raises happened, when they happened, somewhere in the same cloudily benign middle distance as did those departmental meetings that he actually had to sit through. The companionship of the rhinoceros, while increasingly his truest delight, also became as much of a cozily reassuring habit as his classes, his office hours, the occasional dinner and movie or museum excursion with Sally Lowry, and the books on French and German philosophy that he occasionally published through the university press over the years. They were indifferently reviewed, and sold poorly.

"Which is undoubtedly as it should be," Professor Gottesman frequently told Sally when dropping her off at her house, well across town from his own. "I think I am a good teacher—that, yes—but I am decidedly not an original thinker, and I was never much of a writer even in German. It does no harm to say that I am not an exceptional man, Sally. It does not hurt me."

"I don't know what exceptional means to you or anyone else," Sally would answer stubbornly. "To me it means being unique, one of a kind, and that's definitely you, old Gus. I never thought you belonged in this town, or this university, or probably this century. But I'm surely glad you've been here."

Once in a while she might ask him casually how his unicorn was getting on these days. The Professor, who had long since accepted the fact that no one ever saw the rhinoceros unless it chose to be seen, invariably rose to the bait, saying, "It is no more a unicorn than it ever was, Sally, you know that." He would sip his latté in mild indignation, and eventually add, "Well, we will clearly never see eye to eye on the Vienna Circle, or the logical positivists in general—it is a very conservative creature, in some ways. But we did come to a tentative agreement about Bergson, last Thursday it was, so I would have to say that we are going along quite amiably."

Sally rarely pressed him further. Sharp-tongued, solitary, and profoundly irreverent, only with Professor Gottesman did she bother to know when to leave things alone. Most often, she would take out her battered harmonica and play one or another of his favorite tunes—"Sweet Georgia Brown" or "Hurry On Down." He never sang along, but he always hummed and grunted and thumped his bony knees. Once he mentioned diffidently that the rhinoceros appeared to have a peculiar fondness for "Slow Boat to China." Sally pretended not to hear him.

In the appointed fullness of time, the university retired Professor Gottesman in a formal ceremony, attended by, among others, Sally Lowry, his sister Edith, all the way from Zurich, and the rhinoceros—the latter having spent all that day in the bathtub, in anxious preparation. Each of them assured him that he looked immensely distinguished as he was invested with the rank of *emeritus,* which allowed him to lecture as many as four times a year, and to be available to counsel promising graduate students when he chose. In addition, a special chair with his name on it was reserved exclusively for his use at the Faculty Club. He was quite proud of never once having sat in it.

"Strange, I am like a movie star now," he said to the rhinoceros. "You should see. Now I walk across the campus and the students line up, they line up to watch me totter past. I can hear their whispers—'Here he comes!' 'There he goes!' Exactly the same ones they are who used to cut my classes because I bored them so. Completely absurd."

"Enjoy it as your due," the rhinoceros proposed. "You were entitled to their respect then—take pleasure in it now, however misplaced it may seem to you." But the Professor shook his head, smiling wryly.

"Do you know what kind of star I am really like?" he asked. "I am like the old, old star that died so long ago, so far away, that its last light is only reaching our eyes today. They fall in on themselves, you know, those dead stars, they go cold and invisible, even though we think we are seeing them in the night sky. That is just how I would be, if not for you. And for Sally, of course."

In fact, Professor Gottesman found little difficulty in making his peace with age and retirement. His needs were simple, his pension and savings adequate to meet them, and his health as sturdy as generations of Swiss peasant ancestors could make it. For the most part he continued to live as he always had, the one difference being that he now had more time for study, and could stay up as late as he chose arguing about structuralism with the rhinoceros, or listening to Sally Lowry reading her new translation of Cavalcanti or Frescobaldi. At first he attended every conference of philosophers to which he was invited, feeling a certain vague obligation to keep abreast of new thought in his field. This compulsion passed quickly, however, leaving him perfectly satisfied to have as little as possible to do with academic life, except when he needed to use the library. Sally once met him there for lunch to find him feverishly rifling the ten Loeb Classic volumes of Philo Judaeus. "We were debating the concept of the logos last night," he explained to her, "and then the impossible beast rampaged off on a tangent involving Philo's locating the roots of Greek philosophy in the Torah. Forgive me, Sally, but I may be here for awhile." Sally lunched alone that day.

The Professor's sister Edith died younger than she should have. He grieved for her, and took much comfort in the fact that Nathalie never failed to visit him when she came to America. The last few times, she had brought a husband and two children with her—the youngest hugging a ragged but indomitable tiger named Charles under his arm. They most often swept him off for the evening; and it was on one such occasion, just after they had brought him home and said their good-byes, and their rented car had rounded the corner, that the mugging occurred.

Professor Gottesman was never quite sure himself about what actually took place. He remembered a light scuffle of footfalls, remembered a savage blow on the side of his head, then another impact as his cheek and forehead hit the ground. There were hands clawing through his pockets, low voices so distorted by obscene viciousness that he lost English completely, becoming for the first time in fifty years a terrified immigrant, once more unable to cry out for help in this new and dreadful country. A faceless figure billowed over him, grabbing his collar, pulling him close, mouthing words he could not understand. It was brandishing something menacingly in its free hand.

Then it vanished abruptly, as though blasted away by the sidewalk-shaking bellow of rage that was Professor Gottesman's last clear memory until he woke in a strange bed, with Sally Lowry, Nathalie, and several policemen bending over him. The next day's newspapers ran the marvelous story of a retired philosophy professor, properly frail and elderly, not only fighting off a pair of brutal muggers but beating them so badly that they had to be hospitalized themselves before they could be arraigned. Sally impishly kept the incident on the front pages for some days by confiding to reporters that Professor Gottesman was a practitioner of a long-forgotten martial-arts discipline, practiced only in ancient Sumer and Babylonia. "Plain childishness," she said apologetically, after the fuss had died down. "Pure self-indulgence. I'm sorry, Gus."

"Do not be," the Professor replied. "If we were to tell them the truth, I would immediately be placed in an institution." He looked sideways at his friend, who smiled and said, "What, about the rhinoceros rescuing you? I'll never tell, I swear. They could pull out my fingernails."

Professor Gottesman said, "Sally, those boys had been *trampled,* practically stamped flat. One of them had been *gored,* I saw him. Do you really think I could have done all that?"

"Remember, I've seen you in your wrath," Sally answered lightly and untruthfully. What she had in fact seen was one of the ace-of-clubs footprints she remembered in crusted mud on the Professor's front steps long ago. She said, "Gus. How old am I?"

The Professor's response was off by a number of years, as it always was. Sally said, "You've frozen me at a certain age, because you don't want me getting any older. Fine, I happen to be the same way about that rhinoceros of yours. There are one or two things I just don't want to know about that damn rhinoceros, Gus. If that's all right with you."

"Yes, Sally," Professor Gottesman answered. "That is all right."

The rhinoceros itself had very little to say about the whole incident. "I chanced to be awake, watching a lecture about Bulgarian icons on the Learning Channel. I heard the noise outside." Beyond that, it sidestepped all questions, pointedly concerning itself only with the Professor's recuperation from his injuries and shock. In fact, he recovered much faster than might reasonably have been expected from a gentleman of his years. The doctor commented on it.

The occurrence made Professor Gottesman even more of an icon himself on campus; as a direct consequence, he spent even less time there than before, except when the rhinoceros requested a particular book. Nathalie, writing from Zurich, never stopped urging him to take in a housemate, for company and safety, but she would have been utterly dumbfounded if he had accepted her suggestion. "Something looks out for him," she said to her husband. "I always knew that, I couldn't tell you why. Uncle Gustave is *somebody's* dear stuffed Charles."

Sally Lowry did grow old, despite Professor Gottesman's best efforts. The university gave her a retirement ceremony too, but she never showed up for it. "Too damn depressing," she told Professor Gottesman, as he helped her into her coat for their regular Wednesday walk. "It's all right for you, Gus, you'll be around forever. Me, I drink, I still smoke, I still eat all kinds of stuff they tell me not to eat—I don't even floss, for God's sake. My circulation works like the post office, and even my cholesterol has arthritis. Only reason I've lasted this long is I had this stupid job teaching beautiful, useless stuff to idiots. Now that's it. Now I'm a goner."

"Nonsense, nonsense, Sally," Professor Gottesman assured her vigorously. "You have always told me you are too mean and spiteful to die. I am holding you to this."

"Pickled in vinegar only lasts just so long," Sally said. "One cheery note, anyway—it'll be the heart that goes. Always is, in my family. That's good, I couldn't hack cancer. I'd be a shameless, screaming disgrace, absolutely no dignity at all. I'm really grateful it'll be the heart."

The Professor was very quiet while they walked all the way down to the little local park, and back again. They had reached the apartment complex where she lived, when he suddenly gripped her by the arms, looked straight into her face, and said loudly, "That is the best heart I ever knew, yours. I will not *let* anything happen to that heart."

"Go home, Gus," Sally told him harshly. "Get out of here, go home. Christ, the only sentimental Switzer in the whole world, and I get him. Wouldn't you just know?"

Professor Gottesman actually awoke just before the telephone call came, as sometimes happens. He had dozed off in his favorite chair during a minor intellectual skirmish with the rhinoceros over Spinoza's ethics. The rhinoceros itself was sprawled in its accustomed spot, snoring authoritatively, and the kitchen clock was still striking three when the phone rang. He picked it up slowly. Sally's barely audible voice whispered, "Gus. The heart. Told you." He heard the receiver fall from her hand.

Professor Gottesman had no memory of stumbling coatless out of the house, let alone finding his car parked on the street—he was just suddenly standing by it, his hands trembling so badly as he tried to unlock the door that he dropped his keys into the gutter. How long his frantic fumbling in the darkness went on, he could never say; but at some point he became aware of a deeper darkness over him, and looked up on hands and knees to see the rhinoceros.

"On my back," it said, and no more. The Professor had barely scrambled up its warty, unyielding flanks and heaved himself precariously over the spine his legs could not straddle when there came a surge like the sea under him as the great beast leaped forward. He cried out in terror.

He would have expected, had he had wit enough at the moment to expect anything, that the rhinoceros would move at a ponderous trot, farting and rumbling, gradually building up a certain clumsy momentum. Instead, he felt himself flying, truly flying, as children know flying, flowing with the night sky, melting into the jeweled wind. If the rhinoceros's huge, flat, three-toed feet touched the ground, he never felt it: nothing existed, or ever had existed, but the sky that he was and the bodiless power that he had become—he himself, the once and foolish old Professor Gustave Gottesman, his eyes full of the light of lost stars. He even forgot Sally Lowry, only for a moment, only for the least little time.

Then he was standing in the courtyard before her house, shouting and banging maniacally on the door, pressing every button under his hand. The rhinoceros was nowhere to be seen. The building door finally buzzed open, and the Professor leaped up the stairs like a young man, calling Sally's name. Her own door was unlocked; she often left it so absent-mindedly, no matter how much he scolded her about it. She was in her bedroom, half-wedged between the side of the bed and the night table, with the telephone receiver dangling by her head. Professor Gottesman touched her cheek and felt the fading warmth.

"Ah, Sally," he said. "Sally, my dear." She was very heavy, but somehow it was easy for him to lift her back onto the bed and make a place for her among the books and papers that littered the quilt, as always. He found her harmonica on the floor, and closed her fingers around it. When there was nothing more for him to do, he sat beside her, still holding her hand, until the room began to grow light. At last he said aloud, "No, the sentimental Switzer will not cry, my dear Sally," and picked up the telephone.

The rhinoceros did not return for many days after Sally Lowry's death. Professor Gottesman missed it greatly when he thought about it at all, but it was a strange, confused time. He stayed at home, hardly eating, sleeping on his feet, opening books and closing them. He never answered the telephone, and he never changed his clothes. Sometimes he wandered endlessly upstairs and down through every room in his house; sometimes he stood in one place for an hour or more at a time, staring at nothing. Occasionally the doorbell rang, and worried voices outside called his name. It was late autumn, and then winter, and the house grew cold at night, because he had forgotten to turn on the furnace. Professor Gottesman was perfectly aware of this, and other things, somewhere.

One evening, or perhaps it was early one morning, he heard the sound of water running in the bathtub upstairs. He remembered the sound, and presently he moved to his living room chair to listen to it better. For the first time in some while, he fell asleep, and woke only when he felt the rhinoceros standing over him. In the darkness he saw it only as a huge, still shadow, but it smelled unmistakably like a rhinoceros that has just had a bath. The Professor said quietly, "I wondered where you had gone."

"We unicorns mourn alone," the rhinoceros replied. "I thought it might be the same for you."

"Ah," Professor Gottesman said. "Yes, most considerate. Thank you."

He said nothing further, but sat staring into the shadow until it appeared to fold gently around him. The rhinoceros said, "We were speaking of Spinoza."

Professor Gottesman did not answer. The rhinoceros went on, "I was very interested in the comparison you drew between Spinoza and Thomas Hobbes. I would enjoy continuing our discussion."

"I do not think I can," the Professor said at last. "I do not think I want to talk anymore."

It seemed to him that the rhinoceros's eyes had become larger and brighter in its own shadow, and its horn a trifle less hulking. But its stomach rumbled as majestically as ever as it said, "In that case, perhaps we should be on our way."

"Where are we going?" Professor Gottesman asked. He was feeling oddly peaceful and disinclined to leave his chair. The rhinoceros moved closer, and for the first time that the Professor could remember its huge, hairy muzzle touched his shoulder, light as a butterfly.

"I have lived in your house for a long time," it said. "We have talked together, days and nights on end, about ways of being in this world, ways of considering it, ways of imagining it as a part of some greater imagining. Now has come the time for silence. Now I think you should come and live with me."

They were outside, on the sidewalk, in the night. Professor Gottesman had forgotten to take his coat, but he was not at all cold. He turned to look back at his house, watching it recede, its lights still burning, like a ship leaving him at his destination. He said to the rhinoceros, "What is your house like?"

"Comfortable," the rhinoceros answered. "In honesty, I would not call the hot water as superbly lavish as yours, but there is rather more room to maneuver. Especially on the stairs."

"You are walking a bit too rapidly for me," said the Professor. "May I climb on your back once more?"

The rhinoceros halted immediately, saying, "By all means, please do excuse me." Professor Gottesman found it notably easier to mount this time, the massive sides having plainly grown somewhat trimmer and smoother during the rhinoceros's absence, and easier to grip with his legs. It started on briskly when he was properly settled, though not at the rapturous pace that had once married the Professor to the night wind. For some while he could hear the clopping of cloven hooves far below him, but then they seemed to fade away. He leaned forward and said into the rhinoceros's pointed silken ear, "I should tell you that I have long since come to the conclusion that you are not after all an Indian rhinoceros, but a hitherto unknown species, somehow misclassified. I hope this will not make a difference in our relationship."

"No difference, good Professor," came the gently laughing answer all around him. "No difference in the world."

Suzy McKee Charnas

Beauty and the Opéra or the Phantom Beast

Born in Manhattan, Suzy McKee Charnas spent some time with the Peace Corps in Nigeria, and now resides in New Mexico with her family. She first made her reputation with the well-known SF novel *Walk to the End of the World* and its sequel *Motherlines.* Her fantasy novel/collection *The Vampire Tapestry* (one of the first "revisionist" looks at the vampire legend, and still one of the best) was one of the most popular and critically acclaimed fantasies of the early 1980s; a novella from it, "Unicorn Tapestry," won her a Nebula Award in 1980. She won a Hugo in 1989 for her controversial coming-of-age horror story, "Boobs." Her other books include the novels *Dorothea Dreams, The Bronze King, The Silver Glove,* and *The Golden Thread,* and a chapbook collection, *Moonstone and Tiger Eye,* as well as the recent novel *The Furies.*

In the unforgettable story that follows, she takes us deep into the catacombs beneath the Paris Opera House for a rich, erotic, passionate, and gorgeously colored new look at an old fantasy story, breathing new life into that old story in such a vivid and compelling way that you'll find you're never able to look at it in quite the same way again . . .

For the first few months, it was very hard to take my meals with him. I kept my gaze schooled to my own plate while he hummed phrases of music and dribbled crumbs down his waistcoat. His mouth, permanently twisted and swollen on one side, held food poorly. Unused to dining in company, he barely noticed.

But to write of such things, I must first set the stage. No more need be known, I think, than anyone might learn from M. Gaston Leroux's novel, *The Phantom of the Opéra,* which that gentleman wrote using certain details he had from me in the winter of 1907 (he was a very persuasive and convivial man, and I spoke far too freely to him); or even from this "moving picture" they have made now from his book.

M. Leroux tells (as best he can in mere words) of a homicidal musical genius who wears a mask to hide the congenital deformity of his face. This monstrous prodigy lives secretly under the Paris Opéra, tyrannizing the staff as the mysterious "Phantom" of the title. He falls in love with a foolish young soprano whose voice he trains and whose career he advances by fair means and foul.

She, thinking him the ghost of her dead father or else an angel of celestial inspiration, is dominated by him until *she* falls in love—with a rich young aristocrat, the Vicomte Raoul de Chagny (the name I shall use here also). The jealous Phantom courts her for himself, with small hope of success however, since he sleeps in a coffin and has cold, bony hands that "smell of death."

Our soprano, although pliant and credulous, is not a complete dolt: not surprisingly, she chooses the Vicomte. Enraged, the Phantom kidnaps her—

It was the night of my debut as Marguerite in *Faust*. The Opéra's Prima Donna was indisposed, due perhaps to the terrible accident that had interrupted the previous evening's performance: one of the counterweights of the great chandelier had unaccountably fallen, killing a member of the audience.

Superstitious people (which in a theatre means everyone) whispered that this catastrophe was the doing of the legendary Phantom of the Opéra, whom someone must have displeased. If so, that someone, I knew, was me. Raoul de Chagny and I had just become secretly engaged. My eccentric and mysterious teacher, whom I was certain was the person known as the Phantom, surely had other plans for me than marriage to a young man of Society.

Nervously, I anticipated confronting my tutor over the matter of the fatal counterweight when next he appeared in my dressing room to give me a singing lesson. I was sure that he would come when the evening's performance was over, as was his habit.

But just as I finished my first number in Act Three, darkness flooded the theatre. Gripped in mid-breath by powerful arms, I dropped, a prisoner, through a trap in the stage.

I was mortified at being snatched away with my performance barely begun, but knowing that I had not sung well I also felt rather relieved. It is possible, too, that some drug was used to calm me. At any rate I did not scream, struggle, or swoon as my abductor carried me down the cellar passages at an odd, crabwise run that was nonetheless very quick. I knew it was the Phantom, for I had felt the cool smoothness of his mask against my cheek.

No word passed between us until I found myself sitting in a little boat lit by a lantern at the bow. Opposite me sat my mentor, rowing us with practiced ease across the lake that lies in the fifth cellar down, beneath the opera house.

"I am sorry if I frightened you, Christine," he said, his voice echoing hollowly in that watery vault, "but 'Il était un Roi de Thule' was a disgrace, wobbling all over the place, and you ended a full quarter tone flat! You see the result of your distracting flirtation with a shallow boy of dubious quality, titled though he may be. I could not bear to hear what you would have made of the Jewel Song, let alone the duet!"

"My voice was not sufficiently warmed up," I murmured, for indeed Marguerite does not truly begin to sing until the third act. "I might have improved, had I been given time."

"No excuses!" he snapped. "You were not concentrating."

I ought to have challenged him about the lethal counterweight, to which my concentration had in fact fallen victim; but alone with him on that black, subterranean water, I did not dare.

"It was nerves," I said, cravenly. "I never meant to disappoint you, Maestro."

We completed the crossing in silence. In some way that I could not quite see he made the far wall open and admit us to his secret home, which I later learned was hidden between the thick barriers retaining the waters of the lake.

In an ordinary draped and carpeted drawing room, amid a profusion of fresh-cut flowers and myriad gleaming brass candlesticks and lamps, my teacher swore that he loved me and would love me always (despite the inadequate performance I had just attempted in *Faust*). He knelt before me and asked me to live with him in the city above as his wife.

Now I was but a girl, and even down on his knee he was an imposing figure. He always wore formal dress, which flatters any tall man; carried himself with studied grace and dignity; and had (till tonight) behaved impeccably toward me. I imagined the features behind the white, half-face mask he always wore as being sad and noble, concealed for a vow of love or honor, or both.

But he had always seemed much older than I was and, acting as the Opéra's demonic spirit, must live at best a highly irregular life. I had simply never imagined him as a suitor.

In fact, I had named him from the first my "Angel of Music," not because I thought he was some sort of Heavenly visitor—I was a singer, not a convent-school girl—but to both state and remind him of a standard of conduct that I wished him to uphold in his dealings with me (it had not escaped my notice that he asked no payment for my lessons).

Taken aback by his proposal—and with Raoul's ring hanging hidden on a chain round my neck!—I temporized: "I am flattered, Monsieur. As my father is dead, you must speak with my guardian. But, forgive me, I do not even know your name, or who you are."

The side of his mouth that I could see curved in a smile. "Your guardian is both deaf and senile; it is no use talking to him. As for me, I am the

Opéra Ghost, as you surmise. My name is Erik." He paused, breathed deeply, and added, "There, I have told you who I am; now I shall show you!"

With a sudden, extravagant gesture, he swept off his mask and with it all of his thick, dark hair—a wig! I gasped, hardly believing my eyes as he displayed to me the full measure, the positively baroque detail and extraordinary extent, of his phenomenal ugliness.

Large and broad, with bruise-colored patches staining the pallid skin, his head resembled nothing so much as an overripe melon. The fully-revealed face was a nightmare. One eye was sunk in a crooked socket, the nose was half-formed and cavernous, and his cheek resembled a welter of ornamental plaster work, all lumps and hollows and odd tags of skin. His mouth spread and twisted on that same side into a shocking blur of pink flesh, moist and shining. Only his ears were fine, curled tightly to the sides of his freckled crown with its scanty dusting of pale, lank hair. In short, he was a stomach-turning sight.

Abject and defiant at once this monster gazed up at me, clearly apprehending how I recoiled but bearing it in silence while he awaited my answer.

In that blood-freezing instant all my childish fancies and conceits—that with his teaching I would become a great singer, that he and my dear Raoul would gladly join forces to that end—were swept away. Words from the interrupted third act of *Faust* came unbidden to my mind: "Oh, let me, let me, gaze upon your face!" I nearly burst into shrieks of hysterical laughter.

I managed to say, "I think you must be mad, Monsieur, to ask me to accept you!"

"Mad? Certainly not!" He sprang to his feet and glared down at me. "But I am every bit as dangerous as Opéra gossip makes me out to be. Do you remember the stagehand Joseph Buquet, who supposedly hanged himself last Christmas? He died at my hands to stop his chattering about me. You may look to me also in the death caused by the fallen counterweight. I was *very* displeased with your behavior on the roof of my theatre the other evening with the importunate young man whose ring you wear secretly even now; and I made my protest.

"Also that crash, with certain communications from me, is what persuaded Madame Carlotta to step aside tonight and give you your chance to sing Marguerite, of which you made so little. I tell you these things so that you will believe me when I say that your Vicomte's life depends upon your answer, and other lives also."

My heart dropped. "You haven't hurt Raoul! Where is he?"

"Why, he is here, unharmed. Only his fine feathers are somewhat ruffled." He drew a heavy curtain, revealing a window into an adjoining room.

There sat the Vicomte de Chagny, struggling wildly in a chair to which he was lashed by a crisscrossing of thin, bright chains. His clothes were all awry from his wrenchings to get loose, his opera cape was rucked up on the floor at his feet, and his top hat lay on its side in a corner.

Seeing me, Raoul began shouting mightily, his face so reddened that I feared apoplexy. The Phantom touched some switch in the wall and Raoul's voice became audible, bawling out my name: "Christine! Christine, has he touched you, has he insulted you? Charlatan! Scoundrel! Let me go! You ugly devil, I will break you in pieces, I will—"

The curtain fell again. Raoul's yells subsided into frustrated grunting as he renewed his attempts to free himself.

I was horrified. I loved Raoul for his (normally) ebullient and affectionate nature and I dreaded to see him hurt. Of course he was as artistically sensitive as a large veal calf, but we cannot all serve the muses; nor is it a capital offense to be a Philistine.

I sank onto a velvet-seated chair, trying to collect myself. The Opéra Ghost stepped close and said darkly, "His life is in your hands, Christine."

Now I understood his meaning, and I was aghast; yet my heart rose up in exhilaration at the grant of such power. That love of justice found mainly in children burned in my breast. Feeling at fault for the death of the counterweight victim at least, I longed to do right. The Phantom's words seemed to mean that right lay within my grasp—if I had the courage to seize it.

Gripping the arms of my chair, I looked up into his awful face with what I hoped would seem a fearless gaze. "Monsieur Erik, I see in you a man of violence and cruelty. You wish to hurt Raoul because he loves me, and from what you say you plan some wider gesture of destruction as well if I refuse to be your wife."

A vindictive gleam in his eyes confirmed this. I trembled for myself, and for Raoul who groaned and struggled in the next room. Clearly he could not rescue me; I must rescue *him,* and, with him, apparently, others unknown to me but equally at risk.

In fact, this great goblin in evening dress who called himself Erik, whom I had rashly taken for a friend and mentor, offered me a role grander than any I had yet sung on stage (this was the spring of 1881; *Tosca* had not yet been written), a challenge of breathtaking proportions. Still costumed as honest Marguerite and bursting with her unsung music, I determined to meet the test. I was very young.

"Here is my answer," I said. "If you let Raoul go and swear, moreover, to commit no further violence so long as you live, I will stay with you—for five years."

One does not survive in the arts without learning to bargain.

"Five years!" exclaimed the Ghost. "Why, I have lived with *her* for ten, and there have been no complaints!" He indicated with a wave the major oddity of his décor, a fashion mannequin seated at the piano wearing my costume as Susanna in *The Marriage of Figaro*.

"Monsieur Erik," I replied, "I mean what I say: I offer my talent, such as it is, for you to shape and train as you choose, as well as my acceptance of your love—" my throat nearly closed on these words, and I was afraid I might vomit "—on the terms I have stated, for five years."

I chose the number out of the air; five years was the length of time I had been at the Paris Opéra.

How well prepared I was for that moment I understood only upon later reflection. A French music professor had seen my father and me performing in our native Sweden, and, thinking my father a rustic genius on the violin, had brought us both to France. But my father—more at ease, perhaps, as an exhibitor of my talents than as someone else's prize exhibit—had gone into a steep decline.

Extremity makes a monster of any dying man to those who must answer his incessant, heart-wringing, and ultimately vain demands for help and comfort. I did not begrudge the duty I had owed, and paid; but I had learned in those long months the price of yielding to another person unbounded power over my days and nights. In life as in art, limitation is all.

The Phantom frowned, plainly perplexed by a response he had not foreseen. I added hurriedly, "And we must live here below, not out in the everyday world. The strain of pretending to be just like other people would be more than I could bear. That is my offer. Will you take it?"

He showed wolfish teeth. "Remember where you are. I can take what I want and keep what I like, for as long as I wish."

"But, my dear Angel," I quavered, "you may not like to have me with you even as long as five years. You are accustomed to your own ways, untrammeled by considerations of the wants of a living companion." I glanced aside at the undemanding mannequin to make my meaning clear. "And we will not be honing my talents for public performance, but only for our own satisfaction, which may lessen the pleasure of my constant company."

"What do you mean?" he demanded. "I have promised from the first to make a famous diva of you!"

"Maestro," I said, "please understand: you have allowed your passions to drive you too far. I doubt that the Opéra managers would accept your direction of my career now on any terms. You have just said that you killed a stagehand and loosed the counterweight on the head of a helpless old woman. In the world above, you are not a great music-master but a callous murderer."

"In the world above—" he repeated intently. "But not here below? Then you forgive me?"

"I do not presume to forgive crimes committed against others," said I, with the lofty severity of youth. "But neither can anything you or I might do bring back your victims alive and well, so what use is blame and condemnation? You have treated me—for the most part—with consideration and respect, and I mean to respond in kind. But I can accept no more advancement of my career by your efforts. I must reject a success made for me by the heartless criminality of the Opéra Ghost."

He wrung his hands, a poignant gesture when coupled with his ghastly head and threatening demeanor. "But what have I to offer you, except my knowledge of music and my influence here at the Opéra?"

"That we must discover," I replied more gently, for his question had touched me. As the answer was "nothing," I dared to hope that I might induce him to acknowledge the futility of his plans and release Raoul and me. "But making a career for me is out of the question now. Please put that possibility from your mind."

Drawing a square of cambric from his pocket and patting his lips dry with it, he stared gloomily at the floor. No apology, no instant grant of liberty was forthcoming. I saw that he would not reconsider, and it was too late for me to do so.

"So," I finished dejectedly, "my choice is to join you in exile and obscurity, not fame and glory. All crimes have their costs, it seems, with or without forgiveness."

"Then you won't sing in my opera, when it is staged?" he said, sounding near to tears himself. "But I composed it for you!"

He had previously told me that he had been working on this opus for twenty years and that it was too advanced for me in any case; but I judged his emotion honest enough.

"And I will sing it for you if you wish," I said quickly, "here in your home. Won't that suffice? Can it be, my angel and teacher, that you do not want *me* at all, just my voice for your opera? Is it only my talent, put to use for your own recognition, that you love? I am sorry, but you must give that up. Guiltless as I am of your crimes, if I let you raise me up with hands tainted by murder I shall be as bloodstained as you are yourself."

He blinked at me in pained bafflement. "How is it, Christine, that I love you to the depths of my soul, but I do not understand you at all? You are scarcely more than a child, yet you speak like a jurist. What do you want of me? What must I do?"

Taking a deep breath of the warm, flower-scented air I repeated my terms: "You must release the Vicomte, unharmed. You must swear to do no more violence to him or to anyone. And five years from now, you must let me go, too."

He flung away from me and began to pace the carpeted floor, raising puffs of dust with every step (for he had no servants, and, like many artistic people, he was an indifferent housekeeper). Freed from his oppressive hovering, I arose from my chair and surreptitiously breathed in the calming way that he had taught me.

"I have said that I love you," he said sulkily over his shoulder, "And I mean love that lasts and informs a lifetime—not the trifling fancy of an Opéra dandy whose true loves are the gaming tables and the racetrack!"

This jeer, spoken with deliberate loudness, provoked renewed sounds of struggle in the next room, which I resolutely ignored.

"I am young yet, Maestro," I said meekly. "Five years is a very long time to me." He sighed, crossed his arms on his breast, and bowed his dreadful head. "But I can school myself to spend that time with you so long as I know there is an end to it; and if you will promise to sing for me, often, in your splendid voice that I have never heard equaled."

"With songs or without them, I can keep you here forever if I choose," he muttered.

"As a prisoner filled with hatred for you, yes," I dared to reply, for I sensed that he was losing heart. "But prisoners are the chains of their jailers, and they often pine and die. If I were to perish here, my poor dead body would stink and rot like any other. You would be worse off than you are now with your poupette, there, that you have dressed in my costume. I offer more than that, dear Angel; for five years, no less and no more."

I think that no one had argued with Erik, face-to-face, for a very long time. He certainly had not expected reasoned opposition from me. I was sure that he was on the verge of giving way.

Raoul chose this moment to issue a challenge at the top of his lungs from next door: "Fight me like a man, if you *are* a man, you filthy freak! Choose your weapons and fight for her!"

The Phantom's head came sharply up and he rounded on me so fiercely that I could not keep from flinching.

"Liar!" he shouted. "It's a trick! You maneuver to save your little Vicomte, that is all! Do you think he would wait for you? Do you think he would *want* you, after I have had you by me for even your paltry five years? You would be sadly disappointed, Ma'amselle. Or do you mean to coax and befool me, and then escape in a month or two when my back is turned and run to your Raoul? I will kill him first. You lying vixen, I will kill you both!"

"I am not a liar!" I cried, my eyes brimming over at last.

"Prove it!" he screamed, in a very ecstasy of grief and rage. "Liar! Little liar! Prove it!"

I stepped forward, caught him round the neck, and kissed him. I shut my eyes, I could not help that, but I pressed my mouth full on his bloated, glistening lips and leant my breast on his. My trembling hands fitted themselves to the back of his nearly naked head, holding his face tight to mine;

and he was not cold and toad-like to the touch as I had anticipated, but vigorous and warm.

How can I describe that kiss? It was like putting my mouth to an open wound, as intimate an act as if I had somehow slipped my hand in among his entrails.

After a blind and breathless moment, I stepped away again, much shaken. He had not moved but had gone utterly rigid from head to foot in my embrace. We looked one another in the eyes in shocked silence.

"So be it," he said at last in a hoarse voice. "The boy goes free, and I will submit my hatreds to your authority." His eyes narrowed. "But you must marry me, Christine. I will have no shadow cast upon your name or character on my account; and there must be no misunderstanding between us as to the duties owed whilst you live with me."

"I accept," I whispered, though I quailed inwardly at the mention of those "duties."

He left me. There came some muffled, unsettling sounds from the next room, during which I had time to wonder wretchedly how my Raoul had fallen into the hands of this monster.

But according to Opéra gossip the Phantom was supremely clever, while I had reluctantly noticed in Raoul flashes (if that is the word) of the obdurate, uncomprehending stupidity of the privileged. I was familiar with this quality from my childhood days of entertaining, with my father, the wealthy farmers and burghers who hired us to make music for them. Apparently the addition of noble blood only exacerbated the condition.

In a few moments, Erik reappeared holding his rival's limp body in his arms like that of a sleeping child. Raoul had recently begun growing a beard, and he looked very downy and dear. The sight of him all but undid me.

"He is not hurt," said the Phantom gruffly. "Bid him good-bye, Christine. You shall not see him again in my domain."

I longed to press a parting kiss to Raoul's flushed and slack-jawed face, for he looked like Heaven itself to me. But my kisses were pledged now, every one. I must wait, in an agony of mingled terror and queasy anticipation, for their claimed redemption—not by Raoul, but by the Opéra Ghost.

I slipped off the chain with Raoul's ring on it, wound it round his hand, and stood back helplessly as Erik bore him away.

Left alone, I rushed about the underground house like a bird trapped in a mine shaft. Fear drove me this way and that and would not let me rest. I was locked in, for Erik quite correctly mistrusted me; had I found a way out, I would have taken it.

The rooms of his house, modest and snug, were warm, with lamps and candles burning everywhere. The furniture, apart from a pair of pretty Empire chairs in the drawing room, consisted of heavy, dark, provincial pieces. A few murky landscape paintings hung on the walls. There were shelves of books and of ornamental oddments—a little glass shoe full of centime pieces, some carved jade scent bottles, a display of delicate porcelain flowers—which I dared not touch lest I doom myself forever, like Persephone eating the pomegranate seeds in Hades.

In my distraction, I intruded into my captor's bedroom, which was hung with tapestries of hunting scenes and pale green bed-curtains dappled in gold, like a vision from the life of the young Siegfried. The sylvan effect was diminished by the presence of a number of gilded, elaborate clocks showing not only the hour but whether it was day or night. I did not own a clock, being unable to afford one; clearly I was not in the home of a poor man.

There was no mirror in which to see my frightened face (nor even a windowpane, for behind the drapes lay blank walls). The only sound was the ticking of the clocks.

At last, I sank onto a divan in the drawing room and gave way to sobs of misery and bitter self-reproach. I could scarcely believe myself caught in such a desperate coil. Yet here I was, a foreigner, a poor orphan with no family but my fellow workers at the Opéra. I had made friends among the ballet rats, but no one listens to an alarm raised by fifteen-year-old girls. The professor, my guardian, was only intermittently aware of my existence these days. Who would miss me, who would search?

Raoul was my one hope. I had met him years before, during a summer I had spent with my father at Chagny. Grown to be a handsome, lively man of fashion, the young Vicomte had turned up lately in Paris as the proud new owner of a box at the Opéra. I had been flattered that he even remembered me.

His proposal of marriage was typical of his impetuous and optimistic nature. In my more realistic moments I had not really believed that his family would ever permit such a joining. Now I had not even his ring to remember him by.

But he would save me, surely! I told myself that Raoul loved me, that he would lead an attack on the underground house and never give up until he had me back again.

How he might overcome the obstacle of my having spent—however long it was to be—unchaperoned in the home of another man, I could not imagine. Raoul's people were not Bohemians. His brother the Comte had already expressed displeasure over the warm relations between Raoul and me, and that was without a kidnapping.

Still, my cheerful and enthusiastic Vicomte would not allow me to languish in captivity (I tried to blot out the image of him, red-faced, roaring, and chained to a chair). I had only to stand fast and keep my head and he would rescue me.

Erik, returning at long last, showed me to a very pretty little bedroom with my meager selection of clothing already hanging in the wardrobe and my toiletries laid out on the table.

He behaved from this point as a gracious host, always polite, faultlessly turned out, and considerately masked. This surface normality was all that enabled me to keep my own composure. At night I slept undisturbed (when I did sleep), although there was no lock on my door. Daytimes, the Phantom spent absorbed in composition, humming pitches and runs under his breath, pausing to play a phrase on the piano or to stab his pen into a brass inkwell in the shape of a spaniel's head.

I continued my own work as best I could. Each morning he listened to me vocalize, but he made no comment. When I ventured to ask him for a lesson, trying to restore our relationship to some semblance of its old footing, he said, "No, Christine. You must see how you get along without the aid of your Angel of Music."

So I saw that my initial rejection still rankled, and that he was inclined to hold a grudge.

The third morning after *Faust,* I burst into tears over breakfast: "You said you would free Raoul! He would come back for me if he were alive! You monster, you have killed him!"

Erik tapped his fingers impatiently upon the smooth white cheek of his mask. "Why should I do such a thing? He is an absurd young popinjay with no understanding of music, but I do not hate him; after all, you are here with me, not run off with him."

I flung down my napkin, knocking over my water glass. "You murdered poor Joseph Buquet for gossiping about you. I daresay you did not *hate* him, but you killed him all the same!"

Erik moved his knee to avoid the dripping water. "Oh, Buquet! One deals differently with aristocrats. I assure you, the boy is alive and well. His brother has taken him home to Chagny. Now eat your omelette, Christine. Cold eggs are bad for the throat."

That evening he brought a ledger from the Opéra offices and set before me a page showing that the Vicomte de Chagny had given up his box two days after the night of *Faust.* Raoul had signed personally for his refund of the remainder of the season's fee. There was no doubt; I recognized his writing.

So in his own way Erik *had* chosen his weapons, had fought for me—and won. At least no blood had been shed. I ceased accusing him and resigned myself to making the best of my situation.

I spent two weeks as his guest, solicitously and formally attended by him in my daily wants. He even took me on a tour of the lake in the little boat, and showed me the subterranean passage from the Opéra cellars to the Rue Scribe through which he obtained provisions from the outside world.

Then, during the wedding procession in a performance of *Lohengrin,* the Opéra Ghost and I exchanged vows beneath the stage. He placed upon my finger a ring that had been his mother's, or so he supposed since he had found it in a bureau of hers (most of his furniture he had inherited from his mother, he told me; and that was all the mention he ever made of her).

He solemnly wrote out and presented to me a very handsome and official-looking civil certificate, and he said that having had his first kiss already he would not trouble me for another yet, since he was so ugly and must be gotten used to.

Thus began my marriage to the Phantom of the Opéra.

In M. Leroux's story the Phantom's heart is melted by the compassion of the young singer. He releases the lovers and dies soon after, presumably of a morbid enlargement of the organ of renunciation. The soprano and her Vicomte take a train northward and are never heard of again.

But that is not what happened.

When he said "first kiss," Erik may have spoken literally. Like any man in funds he could buy sexual favors, and had certainly done so in the past. But with what wincing, perfunctory haste those services must have been rendered! And he was proud and in his own way gallant, or at any rate he wished to be both proud and gallant. I thought then and think still that although more than twice my age at least, he was very inexperienced with women.

For my part, I was virginal but not completely naïve. Traveling with my father I had observed much of life in its cruder aspects, in particular that ubiquitous army of worn-out, perpetually gravid country girls through whose lives we had briefly passed. My own mother, whom I scarcely recalled, had died bearing a stillborn son when I was two years old.

I regarded sexual matters as I did the stinks and wallowings of the pigsty. Before Raoul's reappearance, I had determined to remain celibate, reserving all my energies for my art. Even my dalliance with him had been chaste, barring a kiss or two. In any case, I had no idea what to expect from a monster.

No expectation could have prepared me for what followed.

For two nights Erik came and sat silently in a chair by my bed. I sensed him listening in the dark to my breathing and to the small rustlings I made as I shifted and turned, unable to sleep. I felt observed by some nocturnal beast of prey that might claw me to pieces at any moment.

On the third night he brought a candle. I saw that he was masked and wore a long red silken robe. His feet, which like his hands were strong and well-shaped, gleamed palely on the dark Turkish carpet.

He set the candle on the little table by my bed and said in a hushed tone, "Christine, you are my wife. Take off your gown."

In those days decent women did not show their nakedness to anyone, not even their own husbands. But I had stepped beyond the pale; no convention or nicety protected me in Grendel's lair.

He turned away, and when I had done as he said and lain down again in a trembling sweat of fear he leaned over me and folded back the sheet, exposing the length of my body to the warm air of the room. Then he sat in his chair and looked at me. I stared at the ceiling, tears of shame and terror running from the corners of my eyes into my hair, until I fell into an exhausted sleep.

Next morning, I lay a long time in bed wondering how much more I could bear of his stifled desire. I thought he meant to be considerate, gentling me to his presence as a rider gentles an unbroken horse, little by little.

Instead, he was crushing me slowly to death.

The following night he came again and set the candle down. "Christine, take off your gown."

I answered, "Erik, you are my husband. Take off your mask."

A moment passed during which I dared not breathe. Then he snatched off the mask, in his agitation dropping it on the floor. He managed not to grab after it but stood immobile under my scrutiny, his face turned away only a little.

When I could gaze on that grotesque visage without my gorge rising, I knew I was as ready as I could ever be. I shrugged out of my nightdress, and taking his hand I drew him toward me. He reached quickly to pinch out the candle.

"No," I said, "let it burn," and I turned down the sheet.

After that, he always came to my bed unmasked. He would lie so that I looked straight into his terrible face while his hands touched me, rousing and warming the places where his mouth would soon follow, that hideous mouth that devoured without destruction all the juices, heats, and swellings of passion.

He proved a barely banked fire, scorched and scorching with a lifetime of need. And I—I went up like summer grass, I flamed like pitch, clasped to his straining breast. As beginners, everything that we did was unbearably disgusting to us both, and so frantically exciting that we could not stop nor hold back anything. My God, how we burned!

Knowing himself to be only a poor, rough sketch of a man, he had few expectations and never thought to blame me for his own shortcomings (or, for that matter, for mine). He was at first too swift for my satisfaction, but he set himself to master the gratifications of lust as he might a demanding musical score. Some very rare books appeared on his shelves.

He studied languor, lightness of touch, and the uses of raw energy. I learned to lure him from his work, to meet his advances with revulsion and open arms at once, and to invite to my shrinking cheek his crooked kisses that came all intermixed with moans and whisperings and that seemed to liquefy my heart.

I learned to twine my legs round his, guiding him home to that secret part of myself, the odorous, the blood-seeping, the unsightly, puckered mouth of my sex. To whom else could I have exposed that humid breach in my body's defenses, all sleek with avidity? With what other person could I have shared my sweat, my spit, my rising deliriums of need and release filled with animal cries and groans?

Initially I suffered the utmost, soul-wringing terror and shame. But then came an intoxication that I can only compare to the trance of song, and this was the lyric of that song: my monster adored the monstrous in me.

Oh, he enjoyed my pretty face, my good figure, and my long, thick hair, all the simple, human handsomeness denied him in his own right. But what he craved was the gorgon under my skirts. His deepest pleasure depended on the glaring difference between my comely outward looks and the seeming deformity of my hidden female part. He loved to love me with his twisted mouth, monster to monster, gross and shapeless flesh to its like, slippery heat to slippery heat, and cry to convulsion.

We awoke new voices in one another. To the slow coiling of our entangled limbs we crooned like doves. His climax wrung from him half-strangled, exultant cries like those of a soul tearing free from its earthly roots. In turn, I sang for him the throaty songs of a body drowning rapturously in its own depths.

I commanded, praised, begged, and reviled him, calling him my loathsome demon, my leprous ape, my ruined, rutting angel, never stooping to the pretense that he was other than awful to look at. I felt that if I treated his appearance as normal, he would be grateful; but in time he would come to hate and despise me for accepting what he hated and despised in himself. A man who feels this way beats the woman who shares his life, whether he is a handsome man or an ugly one.

Erik did strike me once.

It was quite early in our life together. We were studying Antonia's trio with her mother and Dr. Miracle from *The Tales of Hoffmann,* which Erik had heard at its Opéra Comique premiere some three months earlier. From memory, he played Dr. Miracle's music on the piano; and he sang the dead mother's part, transposed downward, with an otherworldly tenderness and nobility that greatly moved and distracted me.

I struggled vainly with Antonia's music (which he had written out for me), until Erik's largely unsolicited advice spurred me to observe rather tartly that he was very arrogant in his opinions, for an ugly man who lived in a cellar singing songs and writing music that no one would ever hear.

He leaped to his feet and sharp as a whip he slapped me. I stood my ground, my cheek hot and stinging, and said, "Erik, stop! By the terms of our bargain, you are not to be that sort of monster."

"Am I not?" he snapped, glaring hatefully at me. "You go tripping out onstage in your finery and you open your mouth and everyone throws flowers and shouts the house down. I have twice the voice of any singer in Paris, but as you so kindly remind me, no audience will ever hear me and beg me for an encore! If you write a little song that is not too terrible, they will say what a clever creature you are to be able to sing songs and make them too. But they will never be brought to tears by my music. So what sort of monster will *you* allow *me* to be, Christine?"

"I am sorry for what I said," I replied. I could not help but see how his lips gleamed with the saliva sprayed out during this tirade; repelled, I thrust my handkerchief toward him.

He snatched it from me and blotted his mouth, snarling, "Oh, spare me your so-called apologies! Why should you care for the feelings of a miserable freak?"

"I have said I am sorry for my words," I said, more angrily than I had meant to. "I have not heard you say that you are you sorry for your action. Do you understand that the next time you strike me, whatever the provocation, I will leave you and I will never, ever come back? You will have to kill me to stop me; and then I will be revenged in the pain it will cost you if I die in your house, at your hands, that are beautiful and strong and that wish only to love me."

He stared down at the handkerchief clenched in his fingers, and I knew by the droop of his shoulders that the perilous moment was past. Still I forged recklessly onward, for my heart was in a turmoil of confused and painful emotion. "If you must hit something go and beat the poupette, which you have dressed in my old costume, until your rage is spent. But never raise your hand to me again!"

In low tones he began, "Christine, I–"

"It is all your fault!" I burst out. "You should not have sung her music, the dead mother's music!"

"Ah," he said. "The dead mother's music."

I stiffened, dreading that I had exposed a weakness to him that he would surely exploit. But he only raised his head and sang once more, unaccompanied and more gloriously than before, that same lofty music of the ghostly mother urging her daughter to sing.

"Now," he said afterward, "if you are moved to say cutting things to me, say them. I will endure it quietly."

My eyes stung, for the music had again affected me deeply. So had the realization that he of all men knew why it did so, for surely his own mother had been dead to him from the day she first saw his terrible face. In his way, he was offering a very handsome apology indeed.

I shook my head, not trusting my voice.

He nodded gravely. "Very good, your restraint is commendable. After all, Christine, it is our task to master the music, not to let the music master us. Now, let us begin again."

We began again.

Other crises arose, of course. His habitual cruelty and malice inclined him toward outrageous gestures of annoyance, as when I found him preparing to burn alive a chorus girl's little poodle that he had lured away for the purpose. The animal's backstage yapping had disturbed an otherwise unusually good *Abduction from the Seraglio*.

I seized the matches from his unresisting hands. With the shawl from the costumed mannequin I blotted as much lamp oil as I could from the dog's coat. Then I carried the terrified creature to the appropriate dressing area and left it there, its muzzle still tied shut with Erik's handkerchief (the dog was not seen, or heard, at the Opéra again).

Returning, I found Erik in an agony of penitence, offering to drink lamp oil himself or to wear a tightly tied gag for as long as I chose, to redeem his transgression. He showed no remorse for the agonies he had meant to inflict on the dog and its owner, but he was deeply agitated at having nearly failed his promise again, and in such a spectacular fashion.

I approved the gag as a fitting punishment. That night the Opéra Ghost cried like a cat into the layered thicknesses of cloth crushing his lips, while on my knees I ignited our own sweet-burning immolation.

Don't misunderstand: in music he was my master and would be my master still if he stood here now. His talent and learning were broad, discriminating, and seemingly inexhaustible. It was he who led me to the study that became my absorbing delight, of the sorts of chromatic and key shifts that irresistibly evoke certain powerful emotions in the hearer.

But his violence was mine to rule, so long as I had the strength and the wit to command it, by the submission I had won from him with that first kiss.

Between us we sustained a steep pitch of passion despite the muting effects of familiarity, I think because of the time limit I had set. Never repeat even the prettiest melody more than thrice at a go, my father used to say. Knowing it must end enhances its beauty and prevents boredom in its hearers.

Domestic chores gave Erik's life a sense of normality; he yielded them only reluctantly to me. Nor did I wish to become his drudge. However, his standards of housekeeping and cooking (two areas in which he had no talents whatsoever) were far below mine; and I did not expect him to wait on me as he had when I was his guest. I had chosen a life (albeit a truncated one), not an escapade.

We wrangled cautiously over household duties and came to a rough arrangement, with many exceptions and renegotiations as circumstances required. When his compositional impulse flagged, if he could not relieve his frustration by prowling the opera house I did not hesitate to assign him extra chores. More than once I sent him out of the house with a dusty carpet, a beater, and instructions to vigorously apply the latter to the former.

Having had none of the normal social experience that matures ordinary people, he could behave very childishly. This lent him an air of perennial youthfulness at once attractive and extremely trying. His emotions, when tapped, poured from him like lava, and he had great difficulty mastering the molten flow once it began. Physical work, like the demands of operatic singing, helped to bleed off at least some of his ungovernable energy.

In our leisure time I asked about his past. I had thought him an aristocrat, but his arrogance was that of talent, not of blood. He was the son of a master mason in Rouen. When he was still a child his parents had either given or sold him (he did not know which) to a traveling fair.

As a young man, he had ranged far and wide, living by his wits and his abilities as an artificer of ingenious structures and devices. He regaled me with tales of his exotic travels before he had settled in Paris, where, commanding some Turkish laborers (whose language he spoke) at work on Garnier's great opera house, he had secretly constructed his home in its bowels. He had always worn a kerchief over his nose and mouth "for the dust," but his workmen had been less interested in his face than in the extra wages he paid for their clandestine labor.

Given my knowledge of his character I guessed that he omitted much repellent detail from these lively narratives. Though troubled, I never pressed him, reasoning that such matters lay between him, the souls of those he had harmed, and God.

In my turn I read aloud to him from the biographies and travel books that he favored, or repeated anecdotes of café life and gossip (no matter how stale) about composers and performers whose names he knew. I taught him some Swedish, a language of interest to him because of its strong tonal element, and he enjoyed hearing songs and legends of the northern lands, which he had never visited. As a child, I had absorbed many tales from folk tradition and from books, which now stood me in good stead. People raised in countries with long winters treasure stories and tell them well.

Outside of music, Erik was not so widely read as I had supposed. Many of his books had only a few of their pages cut. He hungered for books but was impatient with their contents once he had them. In the first place, he was sure that he knew more about everything than anyone else did because he was a prodigy and well-traveled in the world.

And then, he spent far more time roaming "his" opera house and working on the various small, mechanical contrivances he was always inventing and refining than he did reading. Indeed, he was in a continual ferment of activity of one kind or another, from the orbit of which I sometimes had to withdraw simply to rest myself.

I came to regard him as a flood of notes and markings falling in a tempestuous jumble upon the blank page of his life. He had instinctively tried to create order in himself through composing, with limited success: a well-orchestrated life is not typified by ferocious obsessions and quixotic crimes. I believe he submitted to my scoring, as it were, in order to experience his own melody, in place of a ceaseless chaos of all but random noise.

Weeks and months passed, bringing our scheduled parting closer by increments almost too small to notice, and never spoken of. Even inadvertent allusions to my future departure sent Erik storming off to work on the darkest of his music, with its plunging, wheeling figures of mockery and despair.

It hurt me, that music. I think it hurt him. I never tried to sing any of it, nor, despite his previously stated intentions, did he ask me to.

In his opera, *Don Juan Triumphant,* Don Juan seduces an Archangel who helps him to master the Devil in Hell. From this position of power, the Don decrees a regime of true justice on Earth that wins over Heaven also to his side; whereupon God, dethroned, pulls down Creation in a mighty cataclysm in which all are swallowed up. A moral tale, then (as operas tend to be), the music and lyrics of which combined wild extremes of fury, yearning, and savage satire.

Of its quality, I will say this: Erik's music was magnificent but too radical to have been accepted, let alone admired, in its time (as he often said himself). Some days, his raw, raging chords drove me out to walk beside the lake in blessed quiet. Some days I sat weak with weeping for the extraordinary beauty and poignance of what I heard. His music offered nothing familiar, comforting, or merely pretty. Parisian audiences would not have stood it.

Nonetheless, he spent hours planning the premiere of his opera, which he projected for the turn of the century. All the great men of the world would be invited, and all would come (or else). The experience would change their lives. The course of history itself would be altered for the better by Erik's music.

My lessons resumed soon after the night of *Lohengrin.* Erik taught me the rudiments of composition, which I spent many hours refining in practice. In particular, he had me sing and play my own alternate versions of musical figures from the works of the masters, by comparison with which I learned the measure of true genius (as well as the best directions of my own modest talents). This, he said, was how he had taught himself.

He was critical of men like Bizet, Wagner, Verdi, and Gounod, and fiercely jealous of their fame. Yet he worked long and hard with me on their music, for he did not deny greatness when he heard it. At leisure, he would play Bach on the piano with a stiff but sure touch; and then his eyes often glittered with tears—of gratitude, I think, for the sublime *order* of that music.

It was a terror and a joy to sing for him. I have never known anyone to whom music was so all-absorbing, so demanding, and so painfully essential.

His vocal instruction was founded on carefully designed drill and on breathing techniques that he had learned in the Orient. Freed from constriction, my voice began to show its natural qualities. I saw that I might move from the bright but relatively empty soubrette repertoire to the lower-lying, richer, lyric roles.

"Your voice will darken as it ages," he said, "but you have the vocal capacity for some of the great lyric roles already, I can hear it. And the emotional capacity, too; you are not the child you were, Christine. Your Marguerite is much improved, and you will soon be ready to attempt Violetta."

Under his tutelage my range expanded downward with minimal loss of agility above, and I gained a certain sumptuosity of tone overall. I would hear myself produce a beautifully floated pianissimo and wonder how on earth I had done it.

Of course, the next day it was unattainable—these achievements torment singers by their evanescence. Erik would not permit me to overwork my voice, striving to retake such heights. "Wait," he said. "Rest. It will come." About such things he was almost always right.

I bitterly missed performing in public with my improved skills. But in my heart I knew this sacrifice to be well-suited to my collusion (however innocent) in Erik's most recent crimes.

There was much that I was incapable of learning from him, for he was gifted with a degree of musicality that I simply did not possess. I came to prefer hearing him sing for me (as he did often, true to his promise) to producing the finest singing of which I myself was capable. One's most glorious tones are inevitably distorted out of true inside one's own head.

Also, I came to realize that I had a very good voice but not a great one. He said otherwise; but he was in love. And I think he was well content—knowingly or unknowingly—to train up a good voice that was still not quite as fine as his own.

For he sang like a god, with a beauty that cannot be imagined by those who never heard him. He had a tenor voice of remarkable power, flexibility, and range, which because of his superb musicianship was never merely, monotonously, perfect. I was reminded of descriptions I had read of the singing of the great castrati of the previous century.

Without apparent effort, Erik produced long, flowing lines of thrilling richness, like molten gold pouring improbably from the mouth of a stony basilisk. Joyous, meditative, amorous, wild or sad, his singing enraptured me; I could not hear enough of it. As we worked together, he increased the bolder, rougher, more dramatic capabilities of his own voice, producing song expressive enough to pierce a heart of steel.

Or to calm a heart in panic. I had been prey to night terrors from an early age; when I cried out in my sleep Erik would come with a candle to remind me that I lived with a veritable walking nightmare of flesh, so how could I allow mere dreams to trouble me? Then he would sit by my bed and sing. Often he chose "Cielo e Mar," from *Gioconda,* which he rendered with a soothing sweetness that soon sent me drifting off again.

How his moisture-spraying travesty of a mouth could produce song of such precision, versatility, and lustre I never understood. He ought not even to have sung tenor; tall men are almost always baritones. But he was anomalous in so many respects that I gave up trying to account for him. Every time I heard him sing I reminded myself that from the first I had named him an angel.

Sometimes he talked of traveling together like gypsies, singing for our supper as each of us had in youth. He was fascinated by the resemblances in our respective upbringings, I as a child-performer accompanying my peripatetic father, he as a circus freak astonishing audiences with feats of legerdemain and song, and of course with his shocking appearance.

But I saw the differences, which were stark.

My father was a country fiddler with no education, a hard drinker and a fanatical gambler. He had not hesitated to exploit my pretty face and voice at the fairs, fine homes, and festivals where we performed. He played, I sang. Ours was not a sentimental relationship. Yet while he lived I never went hungry or found myself thrown naked upon the spiny mercies of the world.

Erik, expelled from his home like a leper, had ranged the earth in the isolation to which his repulsive face condemned him. Leaving the circus, he had worked for despots who half the time would have murdered him instead of paying him had he not outwitted them, like some branded Odysseus. He had taken the name "Erik," he said, because he liked its bold, Viking sound.

Occasionally, wondering how I had come to this strange new life, I fantasized that he and I were magical siblings, the ugly one and the pretty one, the "bad" one and the "good" one, joined at the soul by music. Parted early through mischance, we were now drawn close again—voluptuously, unlawfully close—by that indissoluble bond.

I did not share such fancies with Erik. He was stubbornly conventional about some things, family among them. But I was mated to a monster: what better occasion for my most perverse imaginings?

Erik's own imaginings were far more dangerous.

One day when I called him to our noon meal, he sprang up from his writing desk and made me come sit down in his place. Pressing a pen into my hand and closing my fingers hard upon it, he tried to force me to shape letters on the blank page before me.

"Write," he said tightly in my ear. "Surely there is some message you wish to send? Write to Raoul, at Chagny. You let him kiss you that night on the roof. Don't you think about those expert kisses of his? Of course you do—you think of them when my clumsy mouth kisses you. Write and tell him, make him glad!"

The wildness of his accusations, the painful grip of his fingers on mine, and the palpable heat of jealous rage pouring off him all combined to scare me half out of my wits.

"Let me go!" I cried. I managed to lift my hand a little and fling the pen away. My arm knocked down the inkwell, which fortunately was nearly empty and which did not break.

Erik stooped to retrieve it, muttering furiously, "Now see what you have done!"

"See what *you* have done," I answered. "You have raised your hand."

"Coward!" he spat. "I barely touched you!"

"Your words are blows, just as you intend them to be," I said. "I have told you what I will do if you abuse me."

"Go or stay, it is all the same!" he shouted. "Your promise is a sham! Do you think me such a fool? You lie in my arms and dream of your pretty Vicomte, and in your heart you mock me!"

His face was dark with hatred—hatred of *me,* for my power to cause him pain. It meant nothing that I intended him no ill and in truth had no such power, save what he himself assigned to me. I saw that I was lost, for his fury was fed not by any actions of mine but by his own inner demons, which only he could master.

Terror closed my throat. Injustice drove me to speak.

"Now you have clenched your fist," I choked out. "Very well. Hit hard, Erik, punish the fraud you wrongly say I am. But strike to kill, for living or dead I shall be lost to you for good."

In his rage he may not have heard my words; but he heard their music (for it welled from the same dark sources as his own) and he could not help but stop and listen.

"Why do you prevent me?" He struck his fist had upon his thigh. "It is the pretext you long for, the blow that will free you! Why do you thwart me? Why?"

Even as he spoke I saw the obvious answer dawn upon him (as it dawned upon me at the same moment): that I did not wish to be freed, but to live out my commitment to the end.

The frenzied glare died from his face, leaving him pale and haggard. "Oh, Christine," he said. "Sometimes I imagine horrible things, and now I have nearly made them come true."

"Do you think you have not?" I said, savage in my turn. "I warned you!"

I did not truly mean to leave him, now that his fury was in retreat. But I did mean to hurt him, and I succeeded. He stared at me with a stricken look.

Then he cast himself down before me, stretched prone upon the floor in a posture of such limitless submission that in the West it is only ever displayed before God. At one stroke he transformed himself from a cultured, willful man of my own world (albeit outcast in it) into a faceless beggar groveling before some barbarian overlord or the lawless caprice of Fate.

It was a vertiginous moment, appalling, piteous, and thrilling. I longed to stoop at once, all merciful forgiveness, and lift him up again; or else to grind my heel into the nape of his neck until he writhed, gasping, at my feet. Paralyzed, I stared down at him, scarcely breathing.

In a hollow voice he begged my pardon. I stammered that I would pardon him when I could, for he had wronged me very deeply. He accepted this, rising without a word.

He would not look me in the face or touch even the sleeve of my dress afterward. Two dismal days passed. Then I bade him to my bed, where we fell desperately upon one another as if deprived for two years, not two nights.

Resting beside him while our hearts' tumult slowed again, I said, "You were thinking of someone just now, Erik; who?"

"I thought of you," he whispered. "There is no other."

With the lightest touch I cupped my hand to his twisted cheek, encompassing as much as I could of what his mask normally concealed. "It is just the same for me. If you can believe me when I say so, then you are forgiven."

He groaned and pressed his face blindly into my palm, wetting my fingers with his tears.

Raoul's name was never spoken between us again.

Otherwise (and apart from his run-of-the-mill sulks and fits of spleen) Erik continued to show me the most constant and ardent regard. This was not as pleasant as it sounds. Worship from afar is flattering, but to be loved with consuming intensity by a person who lives cheek by jowl with all one's frailties and failings is not only exhilarating but tremendously exhausting.

For my part, I continually reminded him what a triumph of character it was (his character as well as mine, since he managed for the most part to fulfill his side of our agreement) for me to keep my word and stay with him. Even when his deformity had acquired a strange beauty of its own in my eyes, I still called upon him (while we fervidly plundered each other's bodies) as my disgusting incubus, my foul and greedy gargoyle, my lecherous ogre.

I must have been a wise child. I knew that love worthy of the name gives not what the beloved needs, but what the beloved wants.

What Erik needed was recognition of his full humanity, in spite of his repulsive looks and criminal behavior, from another human being who addressed him as an equal. What he *wanted* was to worship a woman exalted by both quality and attainment who could be repeatedly persuaded to descend to the level of his own base and hideous physicality, thus demonstrating again and again her exceptional love for him.

As for me, I exulted in each leap from my pedestal. What lesser achievement could be worth such a plunge into the bestial, ecstatic depths?

Well, we were opera folk. Only extremes would do.

So I continued to merit his devotion and my own self-respect, despite and because of the fact that I lived for that shudder of delicious horror when he laid his hand on me, and the exquisite creeping of my skin into tiny peaks at the touch of his wet, misshapen lips. In my eager body, he took his revenge many times over on all the well-made men in the world. I suppose I had my vengeance too, although I do not know upon whom.

Perhaps I harp on this "distasteful" subject. Perhaps I should refer more circumspectly to the craving of my ghastly Caliban for the delights of the flesh. Or is Caliban's craving acceptable but not his gratification? And what of *my* desires and delights? I can guess what Raoul de Chagny would have said had I begged of him those kisses thought in his world to be proper only between men and their whores.

Between the Opéra Ghost and myself, nothing was "proper" or "improper." "Morality" meant my dictum that he must not express his critical judgment by murdering people who annoyed him.

For the rest, we consumed each other with willful abandon, two starvelings at a feast.

After an early phase of keeping me close (I had expected this and endured it patiently), he began to open his world to me. He showed me the trapdoors and passages he used to get quietly about the Opéra. The Phantom patrolled "his" theatre often, restless, watchful, and intensely critical of all that occurred there. He seemed pleased that I found my own uses for his private pathways.

He routinely helped himself to fresh clothes from the costume racks, altering garments to fit and returning them to be cleaned with the rest (the wardrobe mistress, grown weary of constantly undoing his tailoring, now left a selection of clothing at the very back of the racks to be worn only by the Opéra Ghost).

Taking a leaf from his book, I filched the more tattered costumes of the chorus and ballet rats, mended them in my leisure time (for I had been taught that idleness is both wasteful and a sin), and stealthily returned them again.

The Opéra girls, struggling along in their difficult and demanding world, took to leaving chocolates for their "good fairy" as well as the occasional pretty ribbon or fresh-cut bloom. If they guessed my secret, they kept it. I pitied their passions and their pains. They had no potent Angel of Music to inspire and encourage them. There was only one of those, and he devoted himself to me alone.

In time, Erik ventured outside with me. I always wore a veil and he went masked and covered in cloak and wide-brimmed hat. Some evenings he would hire a carriage and take me driving in the Bois de Boulogne to listen to gypsy music played in the restaurants there. Or we would take a night train out of town for a country walk. An enthusiastic amateur astronomer, he taught me to recognize not only the constellations but many stars by name.

In the city, we spent fine evenings strolling the grandes boulevardes. We even attended, anonymous in costume, the lavish masquerade balls given at the Opéra itself, although for us these were not precisely *social* occasions.

We always came late, and left early to avoid the midnight supper after the gala. As we danced (he was a correct but uninspired dancer) or looked on from some quieter vantage point, Erik would murmur in my ear a stream of comments on the flirtations, machinations, and vendettas that he claimed to observe transpiring around us. These vitriolic, often scurrilous remarks always made me laugh, despite my resolve not to encourage the exercise of his more malevolent humor.

On our first anniversary he gave me my own key to the iron gate of the passage to the Rue Scribe. I made frequent use of it, for living as we did we needed time out of each other's company. Most of the daily marketing he did himself, being very pleased with his skill at passing unremarked (as he imagined) among ordinary folk. Closely muffled even in warm weather, he was not, I am sure, so inconspicuous as he thought. But he was both proud and jealous of his self-sufficiency, and I took care not to intrude upon it. He often bought gifts for me—a book of poetry, a pair of gloves, a pretty bit of Meissen, or fresh flowers.

For my part, I brought back reports of the day and what occurred in it, and perhaps a colorful poster to replace one of the dreary pictures on his walls, a book for him from the stalls along the Seine, or a box of the little sweet meringues that he loved.

I took upon myself the task of posting the mail. I wrote to no one, but Erik was an enthusiastic, if menacing, correspondent to whomever caught his attention in the world of music. We attended most Opéra performances, seated in a sort of blind he had built in the shelter of a large, carved nymph on the wall (I always noticed with a pang the strangers seated in Raoul's old box). Afterward, Erik often addressed pages of venomous criticism to the managers, the newspapers, and to composers and artists as well.

Many of these missives I intercepted. But sometimes he mailed a letter himself while he was out, for there were occasional replies to be picked up addressed to "Erik Rouen," Poste Restante. He did not share their contents with me.

We were always buying candles and lamp oil; it took great quantities of fuel to heat and light Erik's home. He could well afford it: we lived on the spoils of years of extortion from the Opéra managers. In fact, by means of threats enforced by ingenious acts of sabotage Erik had accumulated a small fortune.

He exhibited a lordly carelessness about money, mislaying sizable sums with evident unconcern; but in the normal course of things he spent modestly on books, wine, and other minor luxuries. It was apparent that he had extracted large payments from the Opéra managers primarily to demonstrate his power over them. I was always free to draw what cash I needed for my errands abroad.

Herbs and medicines were staples on my shopping list. Erik was prey to fevers, and to other ailments stemming perhaps from distortion of his internal organs. He had learned, of necessity, to doctor himself.

A deformity of the pelvic bones affected his carriage and his gait. His sinewy body was prodigiously strong, but the strain of holding himself straight and moving with a fluidity not natural to him caused him severe muscular tension and cramping; for the easing of which I brought home one day an almond-scented rubbing oil.

But I had hardly begun gliding my oiled palms down the long muscles on either side of his spine when he began to tremble, then to shake with dreadful, racking sobs. I was bewildered that I could have hurt him so. My touch was light, and in any case he was normally stoical, being accustomed to chronic aches and pains.

Now he gasped, "No, don't!" and twisted violently away. He sat rocking and crying, his clasped hands wedged tight between his knees as if to prevent even his own touch on his body.

This was not pain. It was grief.

I saw that while in my bed sheer lust carried him triumphant on its tide, the everyday intimacy of casual contact was more than he could bear. Even as an infant he must have been rarely *touched* by anyone, let alone touched kindly. The undemanding pressure of my hands had wakened in him the vast, deep-rooted anguish of that irremediable loss.

I could no more withstand this upwelling of sorrow—a child's sorrow ravaging a man's body—than he could. All childhoods leave scars. Old hurts of my own throbbed in bitter sympathy with his. I fled to walk by the lake, filled with impotent rage against the common cruelty and indifference of humankind. And I cursed my own deficiency in that same cruelty and indifference; placed as I was, how much pity could *I* afford?

But I could not let the matter rest. The next day, with great difficulty, I persuaded him to let me try again on the understanding that he must stop me when his emotions threatened to overpower him. He did so, saying in a strained whisper, "Thank you, Christine!" Persevering in this fashion we extended his endurance to well over an hour at a time. Rubbing him down became a routine for which I searched out fine oils and salves on my forays above ground.

It was strange, how the slow, wordless process of kneading the knots and torsions out of his muscles wove a spell of peace over us both. In those placid hours of mute, almost animal tranquility nothing was to be heard but our breathing, mine effortful and deliberate, his marked by the occasional painful gasp or deep, surrendering sigh.

I had no great experience at massage, and, as I discovered, no healing gift. I could soothe and sweeten, but I could not mend. Yet he came to openly look forward to these sessions, which he clearly valued and benefited by.

So did I. In the attentive handling of his gnarled and canted body I could express my tenderer feelings without putting myself at his mercy, which quality I knew to be in short supply and that unreliable at best.

For his more intractable pains I bought laudanum, which he hated because it clouded his mind but accepted from me when all else failed.

Abroad alone in the noisy streets, I looked at the tradesmen bustling about their business, the ladies with their parasols or their muffs, the swaggering gentlemen swinging their canes, the very sparrows pecking the pavements; and I considered escape. Once or twice I thought I saw Raoul, but this was only fancy. Nor did I need his help, nor anyone's.

At any time, I might have betrayed Erik to the authorities. Or I might have silently slipped away with enough of his money to buy my passage back to Sweden, or to anywhere.

But what could it mean, to wander freely in the wide, inhospitable world, when the dark angel whose life I shared owned all Paris at night? How could social chatter or the giggling gossip of friends rival the joy of spinning melody out of empty air, with Erik standing rapt like some lightning-struck Titan or else raising his awful head to embrace my song and lift it with his own supple and ravishing voice?

Whenever I seriously contemplated flight, I had only to remind myself that beyond the Rue Scribe gate I was just another woman going about her domestic business. In the house under the Opéra, I was someone potent enough to raise fallen Lucifer into the splendor of Heaven, again and again. Underground, we soared.

And I had given my word.

I cannot pretend to know all that he felt. My absences seemed to increase his attachment to me. Perhaps the risk brought him to the sharpened edge of life, reminding him of his younger, more adventuresome years. I do know that he dreaded that one day I would fly for good, lured by some stranger's wholesome beauty. It need not be Raoul. Any man was handsomer than Erik.

Often he followed me clandestinely through the streets. I made no objection. I had observed how the lovers of pretty singers imagined treachery where there was none. So long as Erik could see for himself how I comported myself when I was abroad "alone," he would be better able to hold his fear and suspicion in check.

I always knew he had been tracking me when he questioned me upon my return: whom had I seen or spoken to, by what route had I gone to the stationer's? At my answers (which he knew by his own furtive observation to be true) he exuded such a vibrancy of relief and joy that my own heart was invariably lightened.

But I wondered sometimes whether it was right and good to make him happy, for by any sane standard he was a wicked man.

I could not deny that it pleased me to dissolve his rages, griefs, and anxieties into something approaching, and sometimes far exceeding, contentment. Doing so made life with him pleasanter, of course; but beyond that, such ease as I could grant him seemed all the sweeter in the giving for being completely gratuitous.

Was I, then, wicked too? I went into a church one damp afternoon and prayed for guidance on this point. As usual in my experience none was forthcoming, so I used the time to assess my spiritual situation, and, insofar as it was perceptible to me, his.

All that I had been taught told me that in due course God must condemn Erik to the torments of Hell. To pardon him would be outrageous: what of Joseph Buquet, whose murder cried out to Heaven? Or the woman crushed beneath the counterweight, which Erik had thrown down in a fit of pique? "Thou shalt not kill"; having made that law, God must surely punish a murderer.

Not being God, however, I could do otherwise, like disobedient Eve. I already had: I had comforted the wicked, and gladly.

As I saw it, I could repent of my error and henceforth grudgingly yield up only the bare minimum of my promise. Or I could willfully continue to offer to Erik, for whom life in this world was already Hell and always had been, such solace as I had power to confer.

This latter course, for good or ill, was the one I chose. How could I not? It might be all the mercy there is.

That evening he sat behind me brushing my hair as I read aloud from the *Revue Musicale* about a new production of *Tristan and Isolde*. He interrupted to remark how my long tresses glowed in the lamplight. Had I taken off my hat and veil to let the sun shine on my hair, chancing recognition and exposure?

"It was raining," I said. "I spent much of the day sheltering in a church, and of course I kept my hat on. But the softened air is doubtless healthy for the hair even so."

With a sigh he pressed his naked face to the back of my neck. My blood leaped. He stroked my skin, following with his fingertips the beat of that thick pulse which shook me softly from root to crown. "How can you give up the freedom of the day and come back to this dim grave where neither sunlight nor rain ever falls?"

What could I answer that he did not already know? Wordless, I leaned my throat into his hand, the warm, muscular, bloodstained hand of the Minotaur of the Opéra labyrinth.

"But I forget," he added in low and husky tones, "you are a northern girl and used to darkness from your childhood. Turn and kiss your darkness, Christine; he loves and misses you."

The sun's finest glories—its corona and its great, flaring prominences—only show when the moon eclipses it completely; he had told me that. I meant to remind him of it as he bent close over me, shrouding my face in his shadow. But I had already given up my mouth and my breath, and later, I forgot.

Another time, having been delayed an hour past when I had said I would be back, I found unlocked the door to the gunpowder room (which he had planned to blow up, obliterating himself along with the Opéra and everyone in it, if I had refused him). While I was gone he must have paced among the neatly stacked little barrels of death, goading the sleeping demon of his fury to make sure it was still alive and purposeful in case I failed to reappear.

I did not become pregnant. God cannot admire brainlessness in his creatures, to whom he has gone to the trouble to give very good brains indeed. In all likelihood Erik was sterile, like most sports of Nature. Still, I regularly used certain preparations to subdue my fertility as best I might. Erik agreed wholeheartedly with this practice. He said he had no wish to perpetuate the horrors of his own childhood (nor, I believe, to share my attention with a helpless and demanding infant).

We did quarrel sometimes, as couples do. The newspapers were a constant provocation, for Erik's political views were barbaric.

I maintained that the world would benefit from rather more kindness and mutual care than from less, as he himself had reason to know. He espoused brutal notions of social order, supporting his position with blood-curdling accounts of punishments and tortures he had seen in his travels. As men are both wicked and foolish, he said, they must have priests to keep them penitent and kings to keep them obedient, and the harsher the better.

Sometimes he mocked my "naïveté" and "tenderheartedness" so piti-lessly that I left the room in tears. It always ended in his kissing my hands and begging a penance for having upset me; but his Draconian ideas never changed.

He deplored the new freedom of the press from government censor-ship, but devoured news of sensational crimes, which excited his most wrathful responses: "Listen to this, Christine! A water carrier in Mont-martre has beaten his infant daughter to death, having first burnt her in the kitchen fire. He threw her body into a bucket of slops and went to sleep in his bed. The French working man is the only brute beast in the world with the vote!"

Looking up from my sewing I replied as steadily as I could, "Then what a good thing that now, by law, his surviving children must go to school, where they can learn to be less brutal than their father and to use their votes intelligently."

"You cannot teach an ass to sing," he said scathingly, casting the news-paper down at his feet. "Republicanism is no more than government by brutes representing brutes."

I could not resist answering. "Yet some say that poor people are better off now, and that your 'brutes' do no worse than all the monarchs and dictators France has had in this century."

"Precisely the problem!" he said triumphantly. "There has been no po-litical stability since the Terror, and there never will be so long as the mob is encouraged in rebellion. Without public order no nation can prosper, but your common man hates nothing so much as the rule of law."

I said, "Can *you* speak of the 'rule of law'?"

Bending upon me a very knowing and ironic glance he said, "Why, I think I know a little about it."

I saw that he referred to the rule of *my* law that he had accepted over his own conduct; and I had no ready answer.

He nodded approvingly. "Good, you had best not argue further. You are a fine student of music, but careless and ill-informed when it comes to other matters."

"I do the best I can," I retorted, "having little education myself except in music."

"Weak," he said, "a very weak answer, Christine. But you are of the weaker sex, so I suppose I must allow it; which is how your weakness weakens me." He held up his hand to check my objection. "This is im-plicit in our bargain, by which you secured the right to wind me round your little finger. I make no complaint. But do not imagine your author-ity to be absolute, however compliantly I may bend to your will; I am an ugly man, not a stupid one."

"Erik," I said, "the last word I would ever apply to you is 'stupid.' Will you tell me plainly what you mean?"

"No more than I have said," he replied, and with that he got up and returned, humming to himself, to a project that he had recently begun behind locked doors.

A few days after this exchange, he invited me to accompany him to the public execution of a convicted murderer outside La Roquette Prison. I accepted. I had never witnessed such a degrading spectacle but felt that I was sworn to share Erik's life as fully as I might. And I did not like him saying that I was weak.

As we joined the crowd of spectators (which was dismayingly large for such a happening, and on such a cold dawn), a man hissed sharply, "Look, Death mask is here!" They drew aside before us. Erik strode the path thus made for him with princely hauteur, and I saw people reach furtively to touch his cloak as he passed. We ended much nearer to the guillotine than I wished to be.

Of what followed, the less said the better. The curious can still see such things for themselves.

My companion offered no comfort. Erik's scorn for the doomed criminal, the presiding officials and the watching crowd was boundless, his approval of the execution itself unclouded by any hint of empathy or horror. He clearly did not imagine himself pinned beneath the roaring blade, for all that he was guilty of extortion, two murders at least, and, I was sure, much else.

On the way home, profoundly disturbed by what we had witnessed, I said accusingly that the people had seemed to know him there, as if by his repeated presence.

"Yes, the habitués see me often," he replied, his mask gleaming pale as a skull in the dimness of our carriage. "But they do not know me. No one knows me but you, Christine."

"Yet I do *not* know," I said, "why you join the mob you profess to despise in this depraved and disgusting diversion!"

"To see done such justice as is to be had in this world," he said, "and to remind myself what death is. Also I like to think that my presence lends some distinction to the proceedings. They miss me when I am absent, and sometimes call upon the executioners to wait a little in case I am only delayed."

I never discovered whether he was joking about this. He was fully capable of it.

After that, I always went with him to La Roquette. I never grew used to it. Yet I went. The satisfaction he took in these gruesome displays forced me to acknowledge that subjection of his crueler impulses to my ban was not the same thing as change in his own character. It is very tempting to overestimate one's influence upon another.

It must also be said that, disdaining everyone equally, Erik did not share the common prejudices of the time. He did not hate the English or the

Germans more than other nations, and he taught me to recognize the ingrained anti-Semitism and xenophobia of the French (which I had taken for granted) for the spiteful, willful ignorance that it was and is.

But he was no champion of the downtrodden; his sympathies were reserved entirely for himself. He frequently worked up a fine passion of resentment over the availability to others of advantages that he had never enjoyed. There was nothing to do but wait out these moods of bitter self-pity.

Nor could I persuade him away from the vengefulness his life had taught him. Given the nature of that life, it was perhaps arrogant of me to have tried.

As for the secret project conducted behind locked doors, it proved to be his gift to me that Christmas. I gave him a dressing gown sewn of velvet patches I had cut from discarded costumes. He gave me a replica in miniature of the Taj Mahal that he had carved and painted in wood. He had once visited that monument to tragic love to examine and memorize every detail, an adventure in itself that he recounted zestfully to me over our holiday meal.

Indeed, a whole lifetime of hitherto unshared incident was lavished upon me during my years with him, like fine wine poured eagerly for my delectation and delight.

Had I been older and more experienced, I might have tried to reply in kind. This would have been an error. He did not need a *past* from me, having a rather over-rich one of his own. It was my *present* that he desired, all the immediate hours and days that I had promised him. And these I gave with open hands.

No doubt some would rather hear that we fought incessantly, that I tired of him or he of me, that we failed each other and parted in mutual hatred and disillusion. Had we lived in some suburb or narrow street of Paris, or worse yet on some grand boulevard, we might have come to that. Many marriages are stoven and sunk on the rocks of Parisian life.

Now and again, he reminded me that he had intended for us to vacate the Opéra cellars and lead a "normal" life like everybody else. I was always quick to point out that he was not in the least like everybody else, and for that matter, on the evidence at hand, neither was I; and eventually these objections ceased.

As the end of our time together drew near, he became markedly morose and irritable. I saw that he was already grieving.

I walked through the streets and squares in chilly rain and fitful sun that last winter, chafing unbearably for my freedom now that it loomed so close. More than once I nearly flung the key to the Rue Scribe gate into the Seine. I longed to be borne quietly away on some gliding riverbarge, empty-handed and friendless perhaps but bound by no pledge or promise.

At the same time I struggled to find some way to extend my time with Erik. I could not imagine a life without him. Restless and distraught, I thought of every possibility a hundred times over and rejected them all as many times.

It seemed to me that any meddling with the deadline I had set would undercut and cheapen all that we had achieved together, making a liar of me and a fool of him. Sooner or later our hard-won mastery of ourselves must surely decline into a wretched and debasing struggle for mastery of each other. I had first pledged myself to him in ignorance; now I knew the enormity of the task, and the thoughtless self-confidence of my youth was gone. How much longer could I trust myself to be bold enough, quick enough, steady enough, my instincts true enough, for both of us?

Whole lifetimes spun out in my mind as I searched for a different conclusion. But I could find nothing acceptable other than to keep to the terms of our bargain. It is when Faust tries to fix the transient moment beyond its natural term, saying "Stay, thou art fair!" that he is lost.

I wandered miserably through Erik's rooms, touching papers and furniture and books when what I ached to do was to touch him, to press him close with feverish possessiveness. I often felt his gaze upon me, scalding with similar, unspoken agony.

He now suffered odd spells of lassitude, sitting for long periods with the newspaper yet scarcely turning a page, his face white as marble and his forehead moistly gleaming. My questions about the nature of this unwonted fatigue were met with withering rebuffs. But when I came upon him mixing up a dose of laudanum for himself, I demanded an explanation. He admitted that for some time he had been experiencing severe pains in his teeth.

The condition must have begun years before. Still, I blamed myself. If I had not got in the habit of bringing down the dainties left me by the dancers and chorus girls, he might not have indulged so immoderately his taste for sweets.

Now abscesses had developed, this much I could determine; and I was very worried. But Erik flatly refused to go to a dentist, who must of necessity see his face. So these sieges of toothache came and went, borne by him with his customary fortitude.

We continued our studies, although I was in poor voice, being easily brought to tears by emotional music (and there is no other kind in opera). The last piece that he sang through for me was "Why do you wake me," from *Werther* (we had been discussing the French insistence upon verbal articulation at the expense of beauty of tone).

At the end, he rose from the piano and sharply shut its lid. The spell of Werther's plaint was broken as if Erik had snapped the neck of a living thing between his hands.

"When you know that I am dead," he said, "–and I will make sure you learn of it, Christine–I beg you to come back here to bury me. I hope you will continue to wear my ring until that time, when I ask that you be good enough to return it to me with your prayers before you cover me over."

He meant his mother's ring, a wreath of tiny flowers in pale gold that I had worn since the night of *Lohengrin*. I turned the ring on my finger, trying to take comfort from the fact that he spoke as if he meant to go on living in my absence. But living in what manner? I could no longer avoid that question, which had been burning in my thoughts:

"When I have gone, will you keep to your promise to be good?"

"Why should I?" he growled, shooting me an evil look. Then he quoted the monster of Mary Shelley's *Frankenstein* (a book he *had* read, many times over by the look of its pages), " 'Misery made me a fiend. Make me happy and I shall again be virtuous.' "

My heart pounded. Suddenly we stood at the edge of a precipice. "Erik, you gave your word!"

"I am not some titled nobleman," he sneered. "I have no honor to preserve."

I said, "You wrong yourself to say so. You have held to our agreement as only an honorable man would."

He turned away without replying, dabbing at his mouth with his handkerchief, and fell to moodily rearranging the porcelain flowers on their shelf. I heard every tiny tick and brush of sound of these small actions, for I was listening harder than I ever had in my life. In my mind a cowardly voice said, *Fool, have you forgotten that he is a monster? Look at him! He will never let you go! You should have fled when you had the chance!*

"So you think I have behaved honorably?" he said at last. "Well, if I have, I am sorry for it."

Stung out of my fearful reverie, I answered with some heat, "You have no right to be! You have been happier these past years than most men are in a lifetime. Deny it if you can!"

"I do not deny it!" He turned to me with inflamed eyes, his hands clenched at his sides. "For pity's sake, Christine, must I beg? *Don't leave.* I love you. I need you. Stay with me!"

I had been braced for sarcasm and threats; this naked entreaty pierced me through. I shook my head, unable to speak.

"Set new terms, make any rules you like," he urged. "I will keep to them, you know I can!"

"No," I said, "no, Erik. It is time for you to see how you get along without your Angel of Conscience. I want my freedom, which I have won fairly."

He stared at me with those burning eyes. The walls of his house pressed in upon me like dungeon walls, and I felt a fierce passion for my liberty, sparked by the dread of losing it again before ever regaining it. In my fear, I hated him.

He said, "What if I say you must return to live with me for six months of every year? It is a nice, classical solution."

I answered angrily, "It is no solution at all!"

"I don't care." His voice rose toward the loss of control that I—and perhaps he, too—dreaded. "I want *more!*"

"Erik," I said, my mouth as dry as ashes, "you are above all a musician, and musicians know better than anyone that at some point there is no *more*—no more beats to the measure, no more notes to the phrase, no more loudness or softness or purity or vibrato—or else music becomes mere noise, incoherent, ugly, and valueless. You know this to be true."

Of course he knew it. On this principle was based all his instruction and all our achievement together. I wished that he had been wearing his mask, for it was torture to watch his face.

At length he said bitterly, "You have had too good a teacher." He shielded his eyes with his hand, as he did when he wished to listen closely to my singing without visual distraction. "Have you been happy here, Christine?"

"I have been happy," I said. "I am not happy at this moment, but I *have* been happy."

"Good," he said; and that was all.

We spent those last nights stroking and kissing one another between fitful sleeps, pressed together to the point of pain and past it. He stayed till morning in my bed. I would have held him back had he tried to go, but once he slept I quickly put the candle out. I dared not look long at his face, open and unguarded in sleep (his utmost, cleverest plea and offering), for fear that my resolve would crumble to nothing.

He was a wise child too, but I was wiser. I knew how to defend us from each other and protect us from ourselves.

A week before I was to leave, I came in from a long, troubled walk and saw him slumped at his writing desk. When I spoke to him, he answered faintly in a language that I did not know. Alarmed, I hurried to him and caught hold of his arm to bring him to himself again. My hand flew back: his whole body quaked with massive, deep-seated shudders. At my touch he collapsed, seized by such violent chills that I thought he was having convulsions.

I held him tightly to keep him from injuring himself and to warm him as best I could; and because I had to do something and could think of nothing else. When the shaking subsided, I helped him to his bed. I saw that the infection in his jaws had attacked again with terrifying virulence:

his face was swollen, his skin was searingly hot, and it was evident that he did not know me.

In his first lucid moment, I implored him to let me bring a doctor. He was adamant against it, made me swear to bring no one, and would not be persuaded otherwise by anything I said.

He had committed no crimes since my taking up residence with him, of that I am certain; but he still had old deaths to answer for, and he was absolutely unwilling to risk exposure to the claims of the law. Perhaps now he could imagine his own goblin head under the blade at La Roquette, before the greedy eyes of the crowd.

I imagined it; and I could not bear the thought.

So I nursed him as best I could, with drugs, folk remedies, and treatments that I found described in the medical texts on his shelves. It was not enough.

He had no pain, the nerves in his teeth being destroyed by then, but fever devoured him before my eyes. He ate nothing and kept down little of the medicines I prepared for him. At last he sank into a heavy sleep from which he rarely roused.

Late one afternoon he said, "I am so thirsty, Christine; the Devil is coming for me, and his fires are very hot!"

"No," I said, "God is coming to apologize to you for your afflictions. It is His burning remorse that you feel."

"What angel shall I send to comfort and befriend you when I am gone?" he asked. "The Angel of Death?"

"Don't talk, it only tires you." I poured him some water, spilling more than went into the cup.

"Never mind," he muttered when he had taken a few dribbling sips, "that angry angel has not done my bidding for some time now. But I should curse you somehow before I die."

"Curse me?" I cried. "Oh, Erik, why?"

His febrile gaze fastened hungrily upon my face. "Because you will be alive and abroad in the world, and I will be dead, down here. Your hair will glow like polished chestnuts in the sunlight when you throw off your hat and veil. If I had had such hair, I would have ventured onto the stage despite everything. With really good makeup, would it have been so bad?"

"I hate my hair!" I said. "I'll cut it off."

"It will grow back," he answered dreamily. "As many times as you cut it, it will grow back more beautiful than ever, for the delight of other men."

"Well, go on and curse me, then!" I said fiercely, but other words echoed in my thoughts: *I will not let thee go, unless thou bless me.* Fresh, amazing tears flooded my eyes; I had thought myself drained dry as the Gobi by then.

"Oh, don't cry," Erik said with feeble exasperation. "What have you to cry about? Now I cannot fail my promise. Look, I will make you another: should this 'honor' you have required of me win me a few hours' respite from Hell, I will spend them singing for you. Listen sometimes and you may hear me." Then he exclaimed, "My opera! Where is my *Don Juan?*"

He struggled to sit up, gazing around the candlelit room with that huge-pupiled stare that I remembered from my father's deathbed. It is an unmistakable look, and seeing it again all but drove the heart right out of me.

"Your work is safe," I said. "I will get it published—"

"No, no," he broke in, with some force. "Leave it. I have told you, that music is not for this epoch. You will not let them come picking and clucking over my miserable carcass, will you? Be as kind toward my music. Bury it with me; bury it all."

He caught my hand and pressed it to his malformed cheek, and only when I agreed to do as he asked did he release me. Then he sank back, white-faced and panting, on his pillows. I saw that his time was near, and that he knew it.

"Let me at least fetch you a priest," I said, for I knew he had been born into a Catholic household.

He said, "What for? I would only frighten him to death, adding to my burden of sins. You be my priest, Christine."

So I lay down in his bed and he breathed horrific details of his past into my ear. I told him that if he truly repented of the evil he had done he must be forgiven. He said, "Just *listen*, Christine." So I did; though I dozed through much of this grim catalog, being very tired by then.

The chiming fugue of his clocks all striking woke me. It was eight at night. I opened my eyes to find him quietly watching me, his face—that freakish face that was now better known to me than my own—just inches from mine. His lips were crusted from the fever and his poisoned breath fouled the air between us.

"Good, you are awake in time to see a wonder," he whispered. "This ugly monster, the Phantom of the Opéra, will make himself vanish before your very eyes; and before the eyes of everyone else there will appear, as if out of nowhere, a beautiful young woman of passion, talent, and valiant character."

I said something, "Oh, don't," or "Please." It makes no difference what I said.

His eyelids drooped and the shallow rasping of his breathing grew more regular. Unable to keep my own aching eyes open, I slept. At some later point, I heard him remark in a surprised and drowsy tone, "Do you hear birds singing, Christine? Imagine, songbirds, in a cellar! Open a door, let them out."

That night he died.

Left alone with the cooling remains of the singular creature with whom I had spent a lifetime's passion in a handful of incandescent years, I thought I would die myself. I wished that I might, stretched out beside his corpse in that damp and fetid bed with its curtains of fresh forest green.

In a while I rose, and found that I could scarcely bear to look at him. Absent the faintest animation, his face was a repulsive parody of a human face in a state of ruin and decay. I closed his eyes and set his mask in place to hide the worst.

I said no prayers then; I was too angry and too weary and could barely drive myself to do what needed doing. I washed him and dressed him in the formal attire that he had always favored and put the ring of little flowers on his finger.

My choice would have been to turn him adrift on the lake in his boat, a hundred candles flaming on the thwarts; or to build him a pyre on the bank, like Shelley's pyre. But by then I was exhausted from tending to him, from grief, and from the not inconsiderable labor of preparing his lifeless body for its last rest.

So, with strength drawn from I know not where, I disposed him decently on my own clean bed, with his musical manuscripts piled round him as he had wished. I covered him with his opera cloak and used the patchwork robe that I had given him to cushion his head. Against his lunar skin the velvet folds glowed rich and deep, like a sumptuous setting for some pale, exotic jewel.

Seeing his face so remote and stony on that makeshift pillow, I understood that we touched no longer, he and I. We sped on invisible, divergent trajectories, driven farther apart by every passing instant. Nothing remained to keep me there.

In a trance of exhaustion I packed a few belongings and keepsakes, left the house, and tripped the concealed triggers he had shown me. A long, deep thundering sound followed, and I tasted stone-dust in the air.

Panic seized me: how like him it would be, to contrive beforehand to bring the whole Paris Opéra crashing down in ruins upon his grave!

But all was as he had told me, according to his design: stone blocks placed within the walls rumbled into their chiseled beds, sealing off every entrance and air shaft of the Phantom's home. Erik slept in a tomb more secure than Pharaoh's pyramid.

I paced beside the underground lake, spent and weeping. Now I prayed. I was afraid for him. Apart from everything else, if he had somehow willed himself to die then that was the sin of suicide, which grows from the sin of despair.

Yet this possibility is part of every strong union. Someone departs first, and the one left behind decides whether to die, or to stay on awhile, chewing the dusty flavor of words like "desolate" and "bereft."

In the end, fearing that somebody might have heard the noise or felt the reverberations and might come to investigate, I roused myself to the final task of sinking the little boat in the lake. Then I let myself out by the Rue Scribe gate for the last time, five years and eleven days from the night of my debut in *Faust*.

Rain had fallen overnight; puddles gleamed. A draggled white cat sheltering in a doorway watched me go.

Of my life since there is little to tell. My aged guardian having died, I was able to make arrangements to live quietly in Paris under my own name. Hardly anyone remembered the Phantom of the Opéra and the deeds attributed to him, for great cities thrive on novelty and their citizens' memories are short (that is why M. Leroux felt free to publish his nonsense later on).

I tried to avoid knowledgeable or inquisitive people. To those who knew me I said that I had been driven away by the family of a noble admirer and had been singing since in opera houses in distant lands (Raoul, I learned, had emigrated to America in the spring of 1881, shortly after my own disappearance).

While reestablishing myself, I found I could live well enough. During my years underground I had published some vocal pieces using my father's name. I continued to sell my compositions, and drew investment income as well from the remains of Erik's fortune.

But singing on the stage again disappointed me. My own voice seemed dull, and audiences—no matter how they applauded—even duller. Without an edge of fear and a need for approval, no singer can bring an audience, or a performance, to life. Having resumed my career with some success, I retired early and advertised for students. I found that I loved teaching and did it well.

Rejoicing daily in my freedom, I was nevertheless lonelier than I could bear all by myself. I took comfort where I could; there are good men from that time of whom I still think fondly. But none ever came to me trailing the clouds of sinister and turbulent glory in which the Opéra Ghost had enfolded me.

During the Great War I volunteered as a nurse. Not surprisingly, I dealt calmly with the most frightful facial wounds. Erik's awful countenance would not have been out of place on those wards, just as his music would suit perfectly the emerging character of the new century. Perhaps he was a true phantom after all, as well, as a brilliant, cruel, afflicted man: a phantom of this brilliant, cruel, afflicted future.

My hospital work brought me to the admiring attention of a doctor several years my junior, and I married late in life for the first time, or so it seemed. The marriage was good, being founded in the shared trials and mutual respect of wartime service.

To the day he died, René never knew the truth of my life before. If God holds that deception against me, I stand ready to answer for it along with everything else.

Nowadays I coach voice at the Opéra, although my own instrument has of course decayed with time. A gratifying number of well-known singers have trained with me over the years. My students are like my children, and I help them as I can, awarding to the needier ones small stipends out of Erik's money. He would not approve.

Does it seem incredible, to have gone from such a bizarre, outlaw existence to a placid one indistinguishable from millions of others? Yet many people walk through the world hiding shocking memories. I glance sometimes at a man or a woman in a shop or café, at a friend or a student sitting over a coffee with me, and I wonder what towering joys and howling depths lie concealed behind the mask of ordinary life that each one wears.

Even extraordinary lives are not entirely as they seem. Recently I discovered that the base of Erik's spaniel inkwell (into which I have just now dipped my pen) contains a secret drawer. Inside I found a sheaf of receipts all dated early in April, 1881, made out to "Erik Rouen" for large cash payments from him to various men, in settlement of the formidable debts of a third party: Raoul de Chagny.

Underneath lay a pile of bank drafts running from that time until June, 1885, four or five of them per year, for considerable amounts of money. Each had been signed by Erik in Paris, and cashed by Raoul de Chagny in the city of New Orleans.

Finally, my shaking fingers drew out an envelope, posted from New Orleans and addressed to Erik. It contained a yellowed news clipping in English, dated July 17, 1885, announcing the marriage of Raoul de Chagny, a rising young dealer in cotton, and Juliet Ravenal, daughter of a prominent local broker and businessman. With this notice was enclosed a final bank draft (for yet another of those large sums that Erik had been in the inexplicable habit of mislaying) returned to him uncashed. There was no letter.

The message was clear enough: Raoul did not come back for me because Erik paid him not to. My Vicomte had gone to America as a Remittance Man! At least he had had the decency (or pride or whatever it was) to refuse further bribes from his rival once established in his new country.

I wept over those papers and all that they implied. But I smiled, too, at the resourcefulness, the cunning, and the sheer determination of my incomparable monster, who had thus firmly secured his victory without breaking his promise to me.

Age robs me of easy sleep, and many nights I lie awake remembering the little glass shoe full of centimes; and the shivering poodle stinking of lamp-oil; and the brush being drawn through my heavy hair by a man who sits behind me, where I cannot see his face until I turn. In the dark, I listen for some echo of the radiant voice of my teacher, my brother, my lover and accomplished master of my body's joys, that dire, disfigured angel with whom I wrestled for over a thousand days and nights in all the youthful vigor of my hunger and my pride.

My hair is short now, in the modern style. It has turned quite white.

The Comte de Chagny (Raoul's title since his elder brother's death) arrived this month from America to see to his French holdings. He came to the Opéra asking after me. I avoided him, and he has gone away again.

Awaiting my own exit, I live my days in this brash and cynical present as other people do. But I nourish my soul on the sweet pangs of looking back, more than forty years now, to the time when the Opéra Ghost and I lived together underground, in a candlelit world of passion and music.

I have thought of writing an opera about it, but time seems short and I know my limitations. Someone else will write it, someday. They will get the story wrong, of course; but perhaps, all the same, the music will be right.

RECOMMENDED READING

NOVELS AND COLLECTIONS

Modern fantasy is much too large and various a genre for it to really be possible to assemble a definitive list of novels and collections, without such a list itself being nearly book-length. For starters, I recommend that you read the novels and collections of the authors who are included in this anthology, the titles of which can be found in the story notes. Contemporary authors (more or less), who, for one reason or another, were *not* included in this anthology, but who have done or are doing good work in fantasy, include Pat Murphy, Lisa Goldstein, Charles de Lint, Orson Scott Card, Patricia A. McKillip, Ian R. MacLeod, Robin McKinley, Jack Dann, Emma Bull, Susan Casper, Tim Powers, Stephen R. Donaldson, Terry Pratchett, Tom Holt, Andre Norton, Karen Joy Fowler, Joanna Russ, Lisa Mason, S. P. Somtow, Tim Sullivan, Pat Cadigan, Susan Shwartz, Mike Resnick, Kristine Kathryn Rusch, Mary Rosenblum, Maureen F. McHugh, Harlan Ellison, Gwyneth Jones, Mary Gentle, Robert Holdstock, R. Garcia y Robertson, Rebecca Ore, Marina Fitch, Neal Barrett, Jr., Michael Armstrong, Dave Smeds, Edward Bryant, William Sanders, Michael Bishop, Delia Sherman, Eliot Fintushel, Walter Jon Williams, Sage Walker, Brian Stableford, Kathleen Ann Goonan, Judith Berman, Gregory Frost, Eleanor Arnason, John Brunner, Jonathan Carroll, Sterling E. Lanier, M. John Harrison, Kandis Elliot, Nicola Griffith, Elizabeth Hand, Ian McDonald, Nina Kiriki Hoffman, Nancy Kress, Tony Daniel, Megan Lindholm, Connie Willis, George R. R. Martin, Ellen Kushner, William Browning Spencer, Don Webb, and many others; in the multi-dimensional, infinitely expansible version of this anthology, I would have included work by all of those people, and more besides, because the above list is by no means exhaustive—in fact, no doubt I'll read it later and realize how woefully far it *is* from exhaustive, as the names of a half a dozen authors I *should* have included as well spring immediately to mind.

FANTASY MAGAZINES

Your most reliable source for intelligent adult short fantasy probably remains *The Magazine of Fantasy & Science Fiction,* although *Asimov's Science Fiction* magazine, in spite of its title, also publishes a surprising amount of good fantasy every year. *Realms of Fantasy* is a promising new professional slick large-format fantasy magazine, and *Century* a promising new semi-professional magazine, less genre-oriented, although it does print good fantasy along with the less-classifiable stuff. *Worlds of Fantasy and Horror* leans a bit more toward horror than fantasy, but it's fairly mild horror by today's standards, and they have published good fantasy work by people like Tanith Lee, Keith Roberts, and Ian R. MacLeod. *Marion Zimmer Bradley's Fantasy Magazine* is not, generally speaking, to my taste, but it is a professional fantasy magazine, and, at eight years and counting, one of the more reliably published ones. Subscription information for these magazines follows:

The Magazine of Fantasy & Science Fiction, Mercury Press, Inc., 143 Cream Hill Road, West Cornwall, CT, 06796, annual subscription–$29.90 in U.S.

Asimov's Science Fiction, Dell Magazines, P.O. Box 5130, Harlan, IA, 51593-5130, annual subscription–$33.97.

Realms of Fantasy, P.O. Box 736, Mt. Morris, IL 61054–yearly subscription in U.S., $16.95.

Worlds of Fantasy and Horror, Terminus Publishing Company, 123 Crooked Lane, King of Prussia, PA 19406-2570–$16.00 for 4 issues in U.S.

Century, P.O. Box 259270, Madison, WI 53715-0270–$27 for a one-year subscription.

Marion Zimmer Bradley's Fantasy Magazine, P.O. Box 249, Berkeley, CA 94701–$16 for 4 issues in U.S.

FANTASY ANTHOLOGIES

(Again, this is by no means an exhaustive list. There have been a lot of fantasy anthologies, and there are likely to be a lot more in the future. Listings are alphabetical by the name of the editor.)

Tales of the Great Turtle, ed. by Piers Anthony and Richard Gilliam (Tor).
The Camelot Chronicles, ed. by Mike Ashley (Carroll & Graf).
The Merlin Chronicles, ed. by Mike Ashley (Carroll & Graf).
Peter S. Beagle's Immortal Unicorn, ed. by Peter S. Beagle and Janet Berliner (HarperPrism).
The Unknown, ed. by D. R. Bensen (Pyramid).

The Unknown Five, ed. by D. R. Bensen (Pyramid).
Light Years and Dark, ed. by Michael Bishop (Berkley).
The Best from The Magazine of Fantasy & Science Fiction, Volumes 1–8, ed. by
  Anthony Boucher (Ace).
Dragons of Light, ed. by Orson Scott Card (Ace).
Dragons of Darkness, ed. by Orson Scott Card (Ace).
A Treasury of Modern Fantasy, ed. by Terry Carr and Martin H. Greenberg
  (Avon).
New Worlds of Fantasy, ed. by Terry Carr (Ace).
New Worlds of Fantasy #2, ed. by Terry Carr (Ace).
The Year's Finest Fantasy, ed. by Terry Carr (Berkley).
The Year's Finest Fantasy, Vol. 2, ed. by Terry Carr (Berkley).
Fantasy Annual III, ed. by Terry Carr (Pocket Books).
Fantasy Annual IV, ed. by Terry Carr (Pocket Books).
Fantasy Annual V, ed. by Terry Carr (Pocket Books).
The Others, ed. by Terry Carr (Fawcett).
The Year's Best Fantasy Stories, Volumes 1–6, ed. by Lin Carter (DAW).
The Young Magicians, ed. by Lin Carter (Ballantine).
Flashing Swords, Volumes 1–4, ed. by Lin Carter (Dell).
Unicorns!, ed. by Jack Dann and Gardner Dozois (Ace).
Magicats!, ed. by Jack Dann and Gardner Dozois (Ace).
Bestiary!, ed. by Jack Dann and Gardner Dozois (Ace).
Sorcerers!, ed. by Jack Dann and Gardner Dozois (Ace).
Seaserpents!, ed. by Jack Dann and Gardner Dozois (Ace).
Little People!, ed. by Jack Dann and Gardner Dozois (Ace).
Dragons!, ed. by Jack Dann and Gardner Dozois (Ace).
Horses!, ed. by Jack Dann and Gardner Dozois (Ace).
Angels!, ed. by Jack Dann and Gardner Dozois (Ace).
Unicorns II, ed. by Jack Dann and Gardner Dozois (Ace).
Magicats II, ed. by Jack Dann and Gardner Dozois (Ace).
The Year's Best Fantasy and Horror, Volumes One through Nine, ed. by Ellen Dat-
  low and Terri Windling (St. Martin's Press).
Snow White, Blood Red, ed. by Ellen Datlow and Terri Windling (AvoNova
  Morrow).
Black Thorn, White Rose, ed. by Ellen Datlow and Terri Windling (AvoNova
  Morrow).
Ruby Slippers, Golden Tears, ed. by Ellen Datlow and Terri Windling
  (AvoNova Morrow).
The Best from The Magazine of Fantasy & Science Fiction, Volumes 12–14, ed. by
  Avram Davidson (Ace).
Magic For Sale, ed. by Avram Davidson (Ace).
Swords and Sorcery, ed. by L. Sprague de Camp (Pyramid).
The Spell of Seven, ed. by L. Sprague de Camp (Pyramid).
The Fantastic Swordsmen, ed. by L. Sprague de Camp (Pyramid).

Isaac Asimov's Ghosts, ed. by Gardner Dozois and Sheila Williams (Ace).

Isaac Asimov's Vampires, ed. by Gardner Dozois and Sheila Williams (Ace).

Isaac Asimov's Camelot, ed. by Gardner Dozois and Sheila Williams (Ace).

Other Edens, Volumes 1–3, ed. by Christopher Evans and Robert Holdstock (Unwin).

The Best Fantasy Stories from The Magazine of Fantasy & Science Fiction, ed. by Edward L. Ferman (Octopus Books).

The Magazine of Fantasy & Science Fiction, a 30-Year Retrospective, ed. by Edward L. Ferman (Doubleday).

The Best from The Magazine of Fantasy & Science Fiction, a 45th Anniversary Anthology, ed. by Edward L. Ferman and Kristine Kathryn Rusch (St. Martin's Press).

The Best from The Magazine of Fantasy & Science Fiction, Volumes 15–23, ed. by Edward L. Ferman (Ace).

Grails: Quests, Visitations, and Other Occurrences, ed. by Richard Gilliam, Ed Kramer, and Martin H. Greenberg (Unnameable Press).

After the King: Stories in Honor of J. R. R. Tolkien, ed. by Martin H. Greenberg (Tor).

Masterpieces of Fantasy and Enchantment, ed. by David G. Hartwell (St. Martin's Press).

Masterpieces of Fantasy and Wonder, ed. by David G. Hartwell (St. Martin's Press).

The Dark Side, ed. by Damon Knight (Doubleday).

A Shocking Thing, ed. by Damon Knight (Pocket Books).

Basilisk, ed. by Ellen Kushner (Ace).

Alchemy & Academe, ed. by Anne McCaffrey (Del Rey).

Isaac Asimov's Fantasy, ed. by Shawna McCarthy (Dial Press).

Imaginary Lands, ed. by Robin McKinley (Ace).

Off the Beaten Orbit, ed. by Judith Merril (Pyramid).

The Best from The Magazine of Fantasy & Science Fiction, Volumes 9–11, ed. by Robert P. Mills (Ace).

The Year's Best Fantasy Stories, Volumes 7–13, ed. by Art Saha (DAW).

Unknown, ed. by Stanley Schmidt (Baen).

The Oxford Book of Fantasy, ed. by Tom Shippey (Oxford University Press).

The Fantasy Hall of Fame, ed. by Robert Silverberg and Martin H. Greenberg (Arbor House).

The Penguin Book of Modern Fantasy by Women, ed. by Susan Williams and Richard Glyn Jones (Viking).

Elsewhere, Volumes 1–3, ed. by Terri Windling and Mark Alan Arnold (Ace).

Faery!, ed. by Terri Windling (Ace).

The Armless Maiden and Other Tales for Childhood's Survivors, ed. by Terri Windling (Tor).

Xanadu, Volumes 1–3, ed. by Jane Yolen (Tor).

Wheel of Fortune, ed. by Roger Zelazny (AvoNova).
Warriors of Blood and Dream, ed. by Roger Zelazny (AvoNova).

CRITICAL ARTICLES

"In the Tradition . . . ," by Michael Swanwick—first published in *Asimov's Science Fiction,* November 1994; reprinted in *The Year's Best Fantasy and Horror: Eighth Annual Collection,* edited by Ellen Datlow and Terri Windling (St. Martin's Press).

"A Farewell to Fantasy," by Michael Swanwick—first published in *Asimov's Science Fiction,* September 1993.